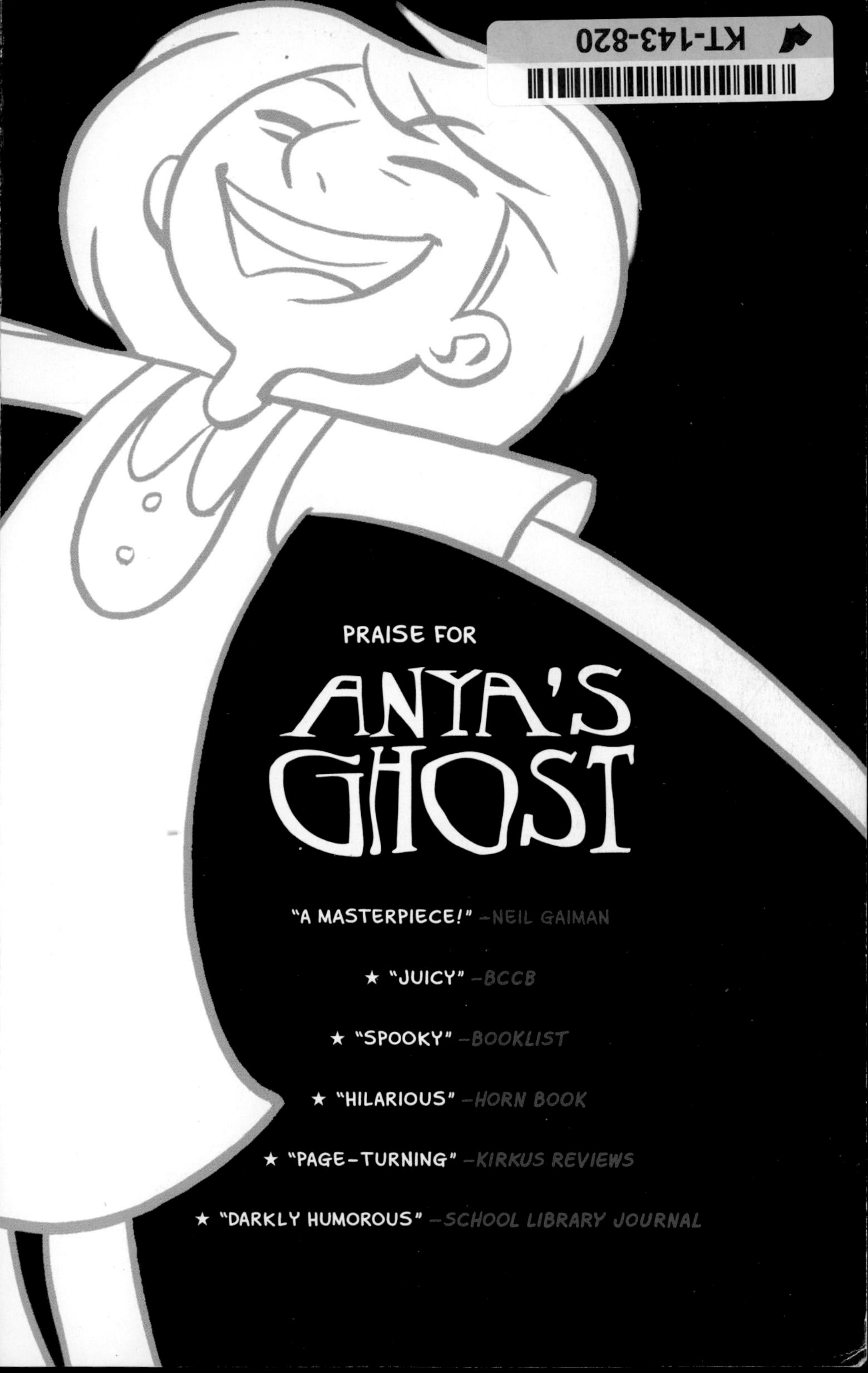

PRAISE FOR

ANYA'S GHOST

"A MASTERPIECE!" –NEIL GAIMAN

★ "JUICY" –*BCCB*

★ "SPOOKY" –*BOOKLIST*

★ "HILARIOUS" –*HORN BOOK*

★ "PAGE-TURNING" –*KIRKUS REVIEWS*

★ "DARKLY HUMOROUS" –*SCHOOL LIBRARY JOURNAL*

AN EISNER AWARD WINNER FOR BEST GRAPHIC NOVEL FOR TEENS

A CYBIL AWARD WINNER

A YALSA POPULAR PAPERBACK FOR YOUNG ADULTS

AN ALSC NOTABLE BOOK

A YALSA QUICK PICK FOR RELUCTANT READERS

A YALSA GREAT GRAPHIC NOVEL FOR TEENS – TOP TEN

A JEZEBEL.COM BEST FEMALE CREATOR OF THE YEAR

A *BCCB* BEST BOOK OF THE YEAR

A *HORN BOOK* FANFARE TITLE

A *KIRKUS* BEST TEEN BOOK

A GRAPHIC NOVEL REPORTER BEST OF THE YEAR

AN *SLJ* BEST BOOK OF THE YEAR

A *BOOKLIST* EDITORS' CHOICE TITLE

A LIBRARY MEDIA CONNECTION BEST OF THE BEST

A *BOOKLIST* TOP TEN FIRST NOVELS FOR YOUTH

AN AMAZON BEST OF THE YEAR

"IT'S BOTH SERIOUSLY CREEPY AND . . . REALLY KINDA SWEET. FROM THE VERY FIRST PAGE, BROSGOL'S ARTWORK CHARMS."
—NPR

"IF YOU'RE TRYING TO COMPILE A SUMMER BOOK LIST, THIS IS DEFINITELY WORTH ADDING."
—SEVENTEEN.COM

"A DAMN GOOD GRAPHIC NOVEL."
—*REALMS OF FANTASY*

"REMARKABLE . . . A SMART, FUNNY, AND COMPASSIONATE PORTRAIT."
—*THE NEW YORK TIMES*

"INSTANT APPEAL FOR ANYONE WHO FEELS LIKE AN OUTSIDER."
—*THE LOS ANGELES TIMES*

"*ANYA'S GHOST* IS FUNNY, CREEPY, AND A DELIGHTFUL PAGE-TURNER."
—*USA TODAY*

"REALLY SWEET, REALLY FUNNY, AND REALLY SCARY."
—BOINGBOING.NET

"VERA BROSGOL IS THE KIND OF CARTOONIST I WANT TO BE WHEN I GROW UP."
—SCOTT MCCLOUD

ANYA'S GHOST

VERA BROSGOL

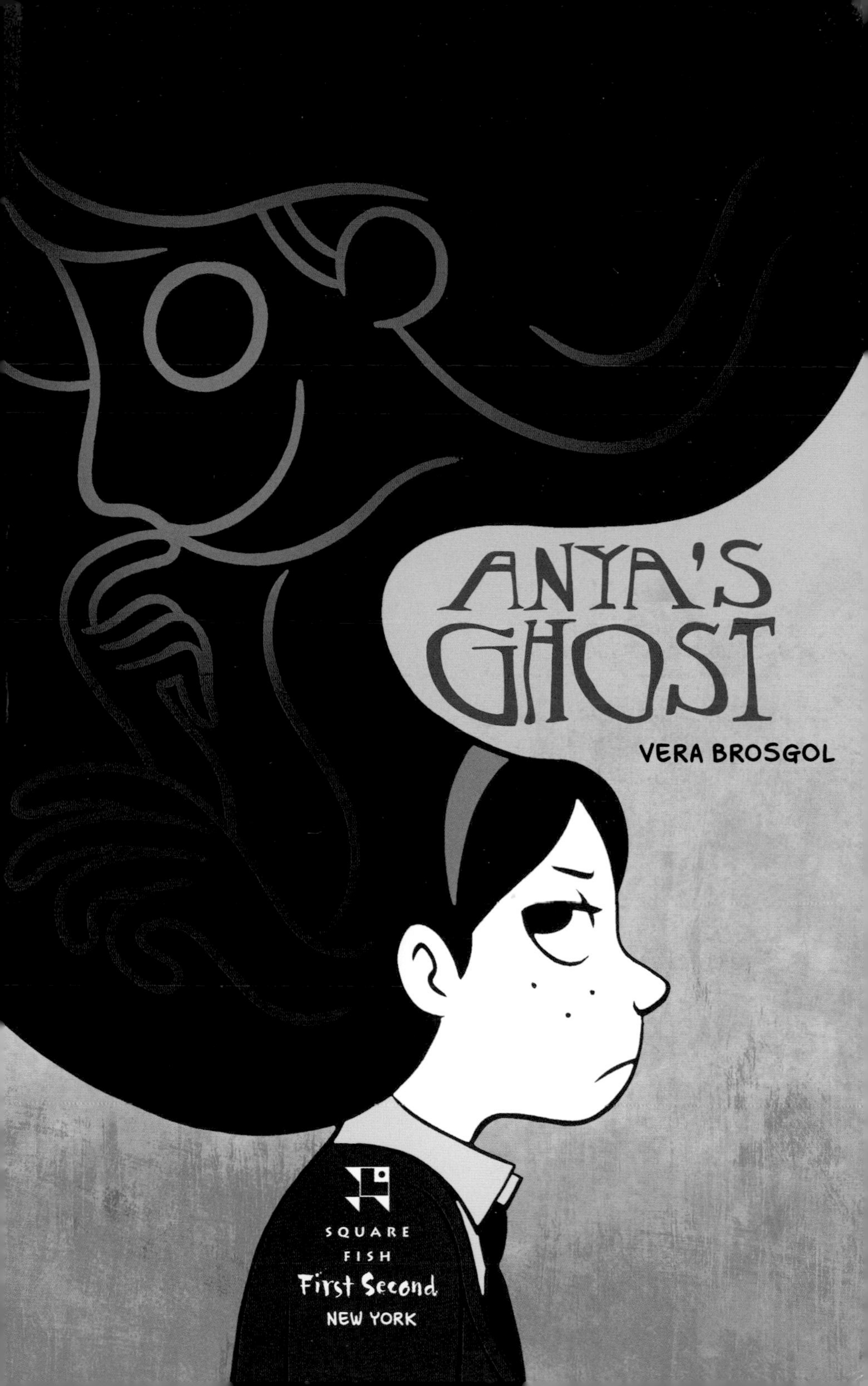
ANYA'S GHOST
VERA BROSGOL
SQUARE FISH
First Second
NEW YORK

SQUARE FISH

AN IMPRINT OF MACMILLAN
175 FIFTH AVENUE
NEW YORK, NY 10010
MACTEENBOOKS.COM

 PRINTED IN CHINA BY RR DONNELLEY ASIA PRINTING SOLUTIONS LTD., DONGGUAN CITY, GUANGDONG PROVINCE.

SQUARE FISH BOOKS MAY BE PURCHASED FOR BUSINESS OR PROMOTIONAL USE. FOR INFORMATION ON BULK PURCHASES, PLEASE CONTACT THE MACMILLAN CORPORATE AND PREMIUM SALES DEPARTMENT AT (800) 221-7945 X 5442 OR BY E-MAIL AT SPECIALMARKETS@MACMILLAN.COM.

CATALOGING-IN-PUBLICATION DATA IS ON FILE AT THE LIBRARY OF CONGRESS
ISBN 978-1-250-04001-5 (SQUARE FISH PAPERBACK)
ISBN 978-1-4668-0558-3 (E-BOOK)

ORIGINALLY PUBLISHED IN THE UNITED STATES BY FIRST SECOND
FIRST SQUARE FISH EDITION: 2014
DESIGN BY COLLEEN AF VENABLE
TYPE SET IN "HELVERICA," DESIGNED BY JOHN MARTZ
SQUARE FISH LOGO DESIGNED BY FILOMENA TUOSTO

10 9 8 7 6 5 4

AR: 2.3 / LEXILE: AD560L

THANKS TO:

JUDY HANSEN, JEN WANG, GRAHAM ANNABLE, RAINA TELGEMEIER,
HOPE LARSON, AMY KIM AND KAZU KIBUISHI, NEIL BABRA,
SCOTT MCCLOUD, JEREMY SPAKE,
THE LOVELY FOLKS AT :01,
AND MY MOM.

ANYA'S GHOST

VERA BROSGOL

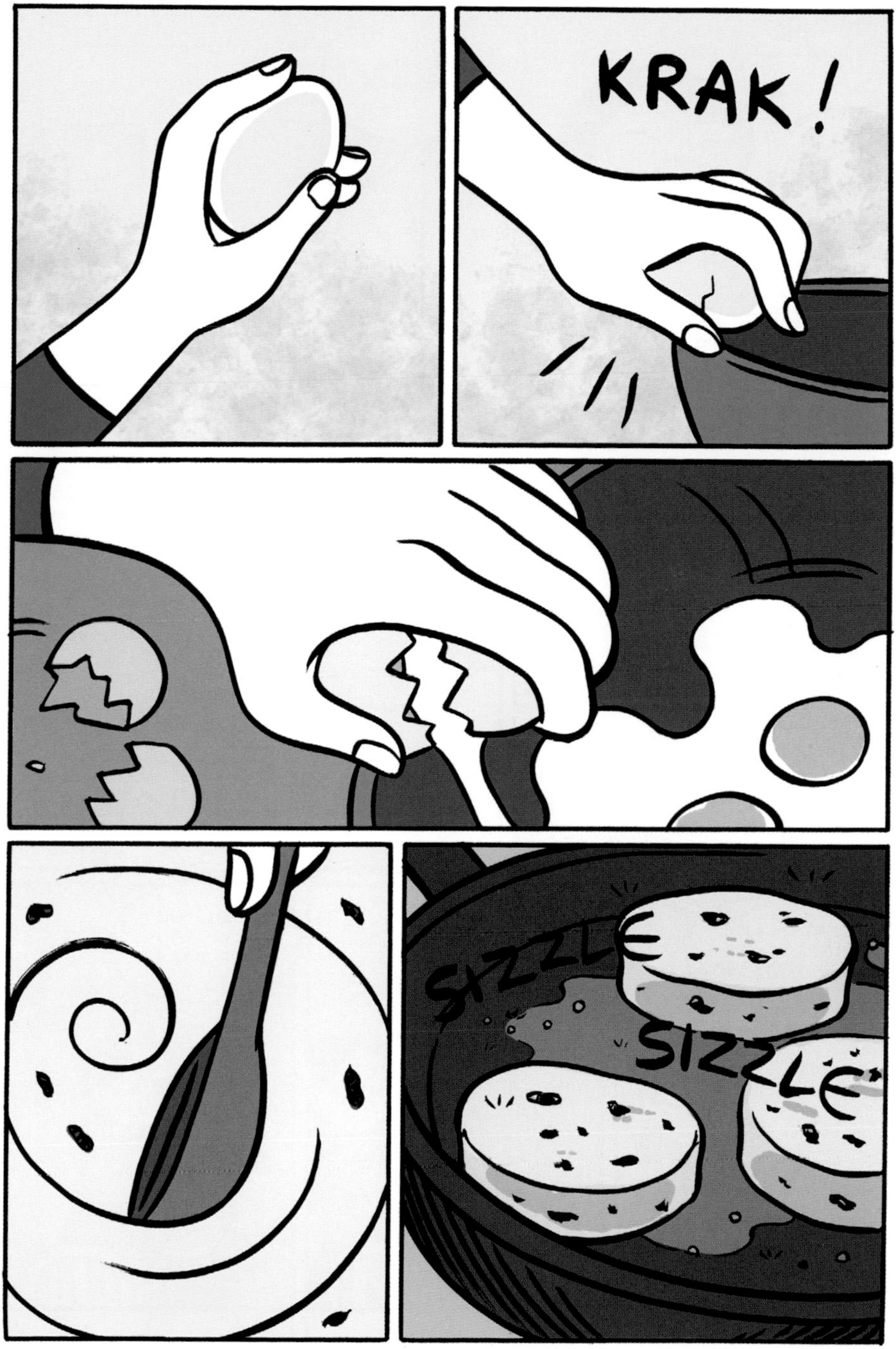
KRAK!
SIZZLE
SIZZLE

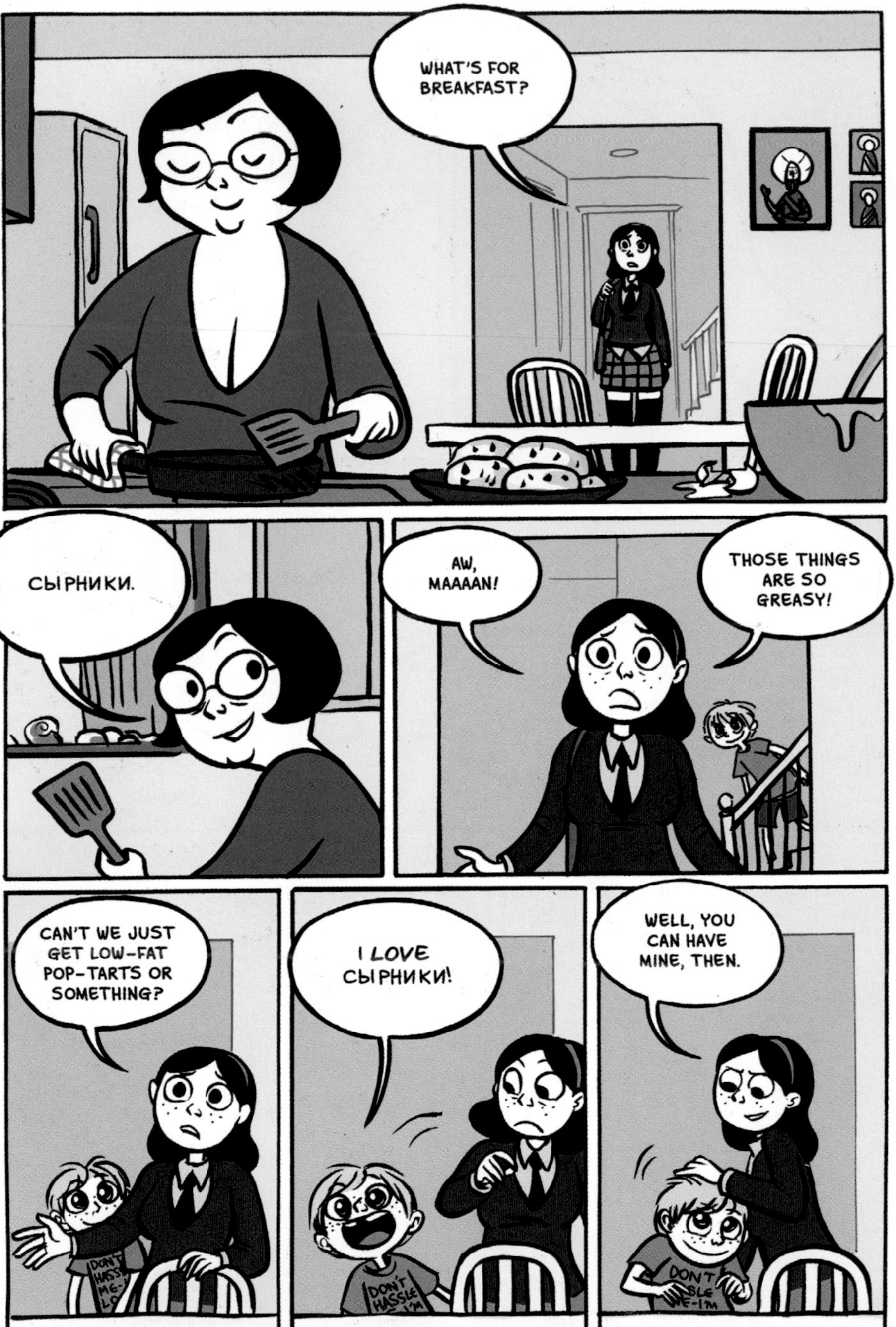
WHAT'S FOR BREAKFAST?
СЫРНИКИ.
AW, MAAAAN!
THOSE THINGS ARE SO GREASY!
CAN'T WE JUST GET LOW-FAT POP-TARTS OR SOMETHING?
I LOVE СЫРНИКИ!
WELL, YOU CAN HAVE MINE, THEN.

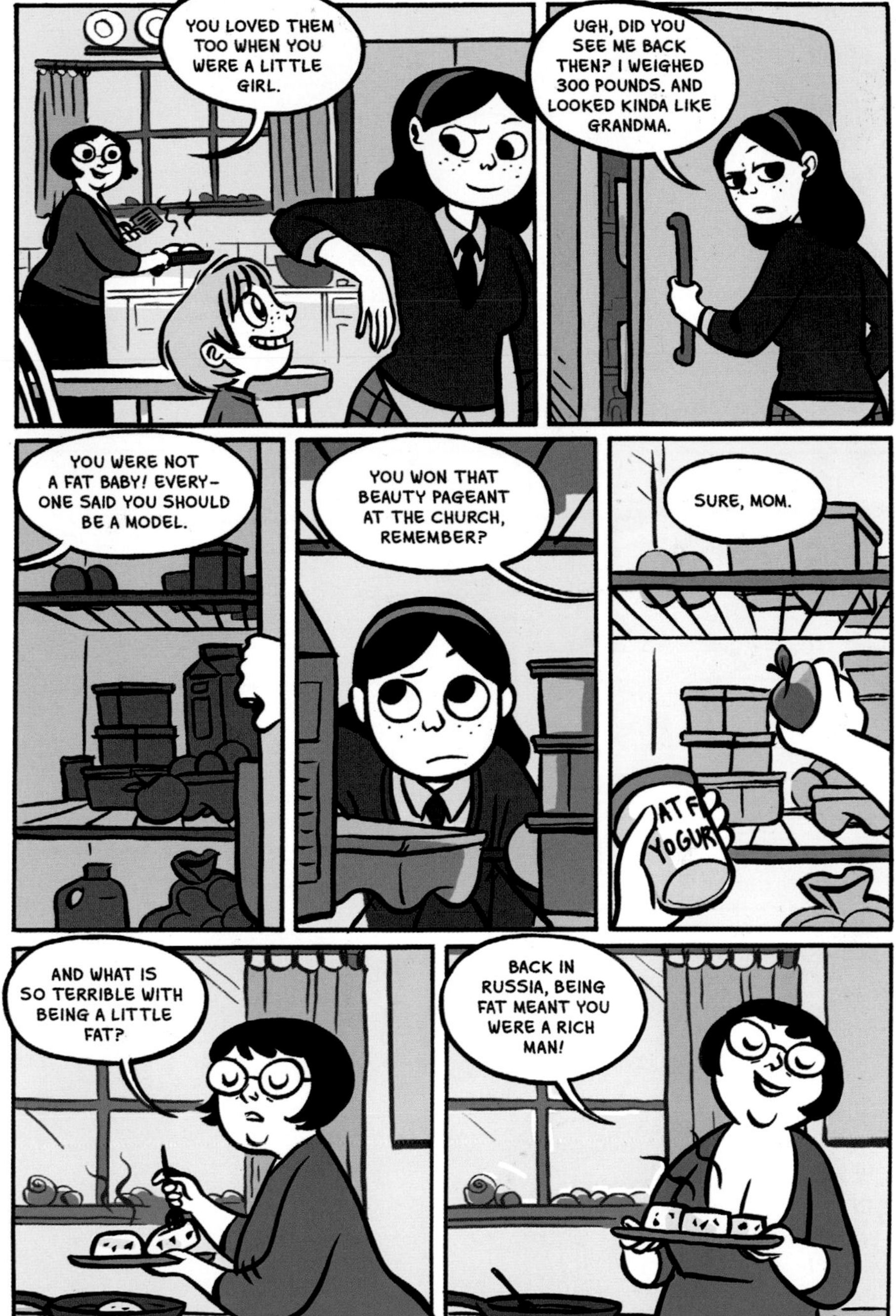
YOU LOVED THEM TOO WHEN YOU WERE A LITTLE GIRL.
UGH, DID YOU SEE ME BACK THEN? I WEIGHED 300 POUNDS. AND LOOKED KINDA LIKE GRANDMA.
YOU WERE NOT A FAT BABY! EVERY-ONE SAID YOU SHOULD BE A MODEL.
YOU WON THAT BEAUTY PAGEANT AT THE CHURCH, REMEMBER?
SURE, MOM.
AND WHAT IS SO TERRIBLE WITH BEING A LITTLE FAT?
BACK IN RUSSIA, BEING FAT MEANT YOU WERE A RICH MAN!

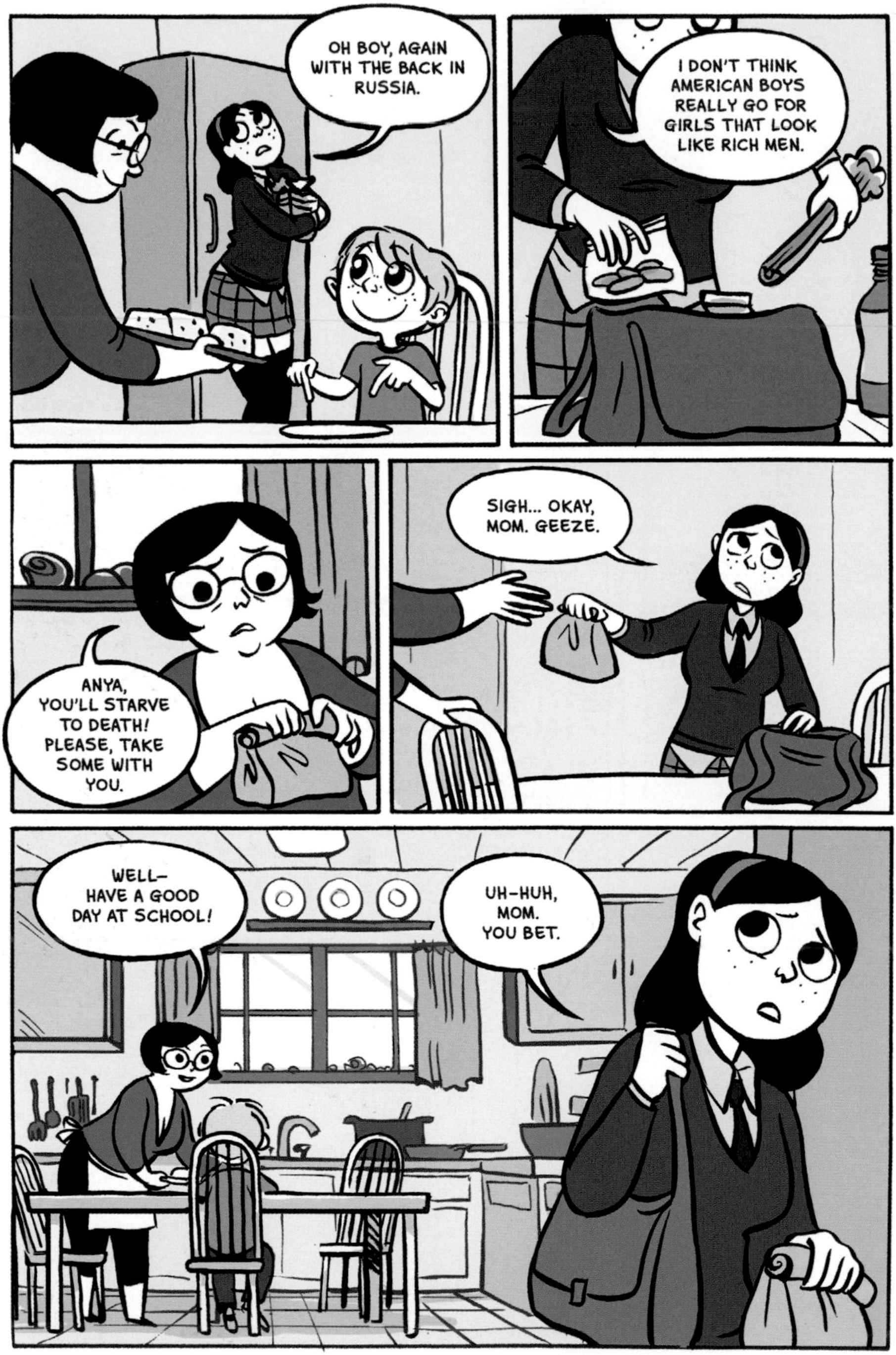

OH BOY, AGAIN WITH THE BACK IN RUSSIA.
I DON'T THINK AMERICAN BOYS REALLY GO FOR GIRLS THAT LOOK LIKE RICH MEN.
ANYA, YOU'LL STARVE TO DEATH! PLEASE, TAKE SOME WITH YOU.
SIGH... OKAY, MOM. GEEZE.
WELL— HAVE A GOOD DAY AT SCHOOL!
UH-HUH, MOM. YOU BET.

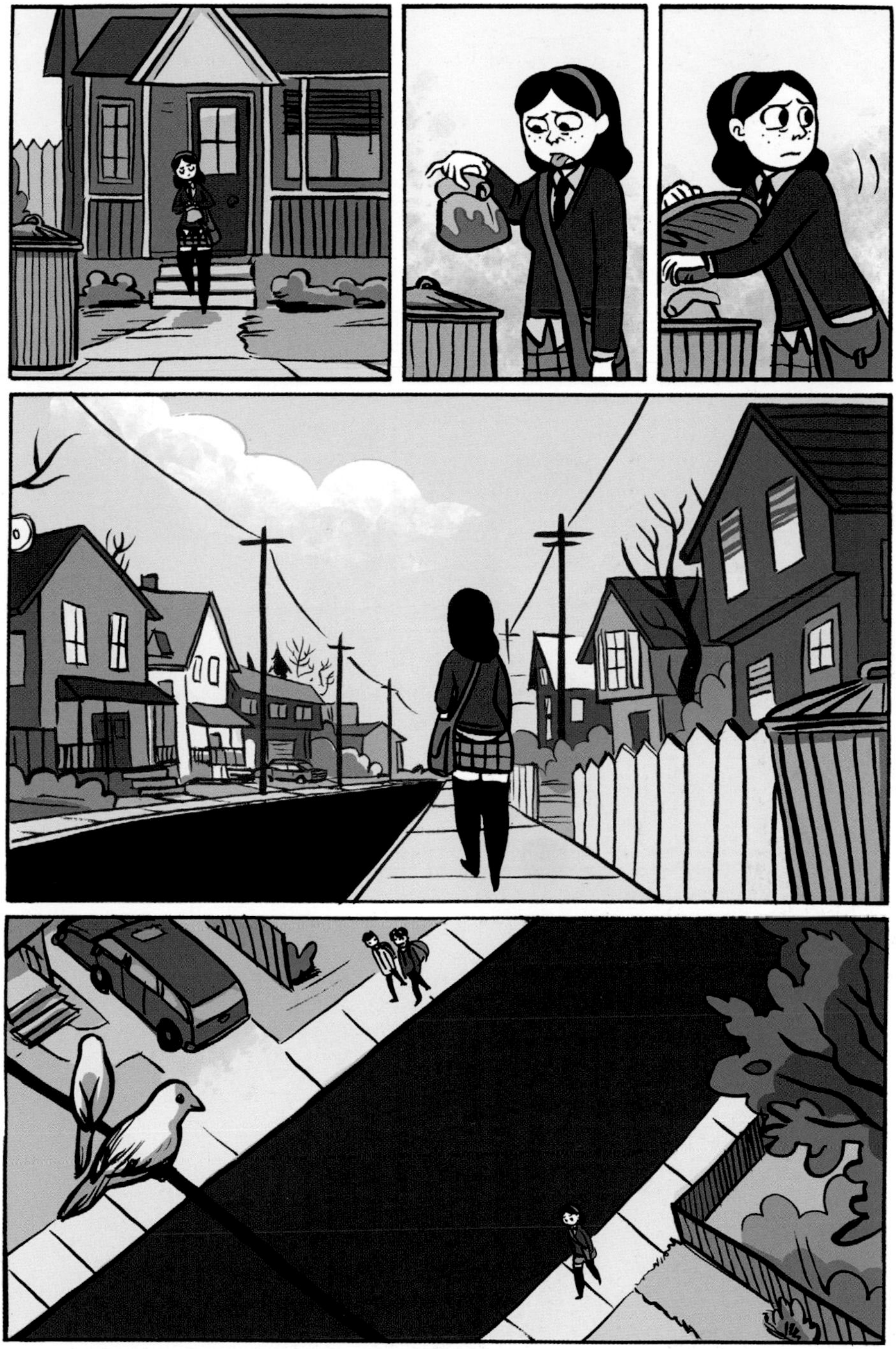

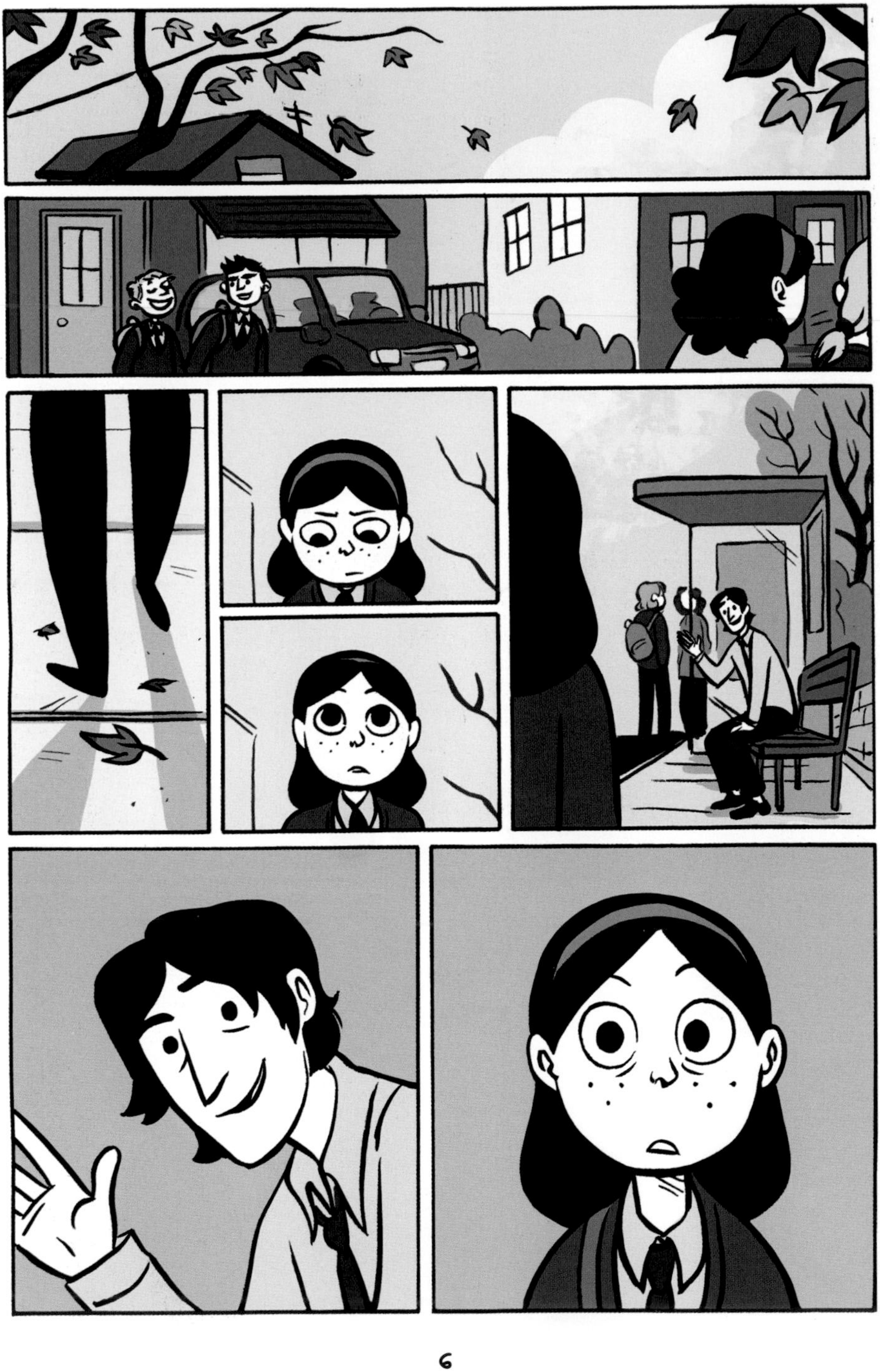

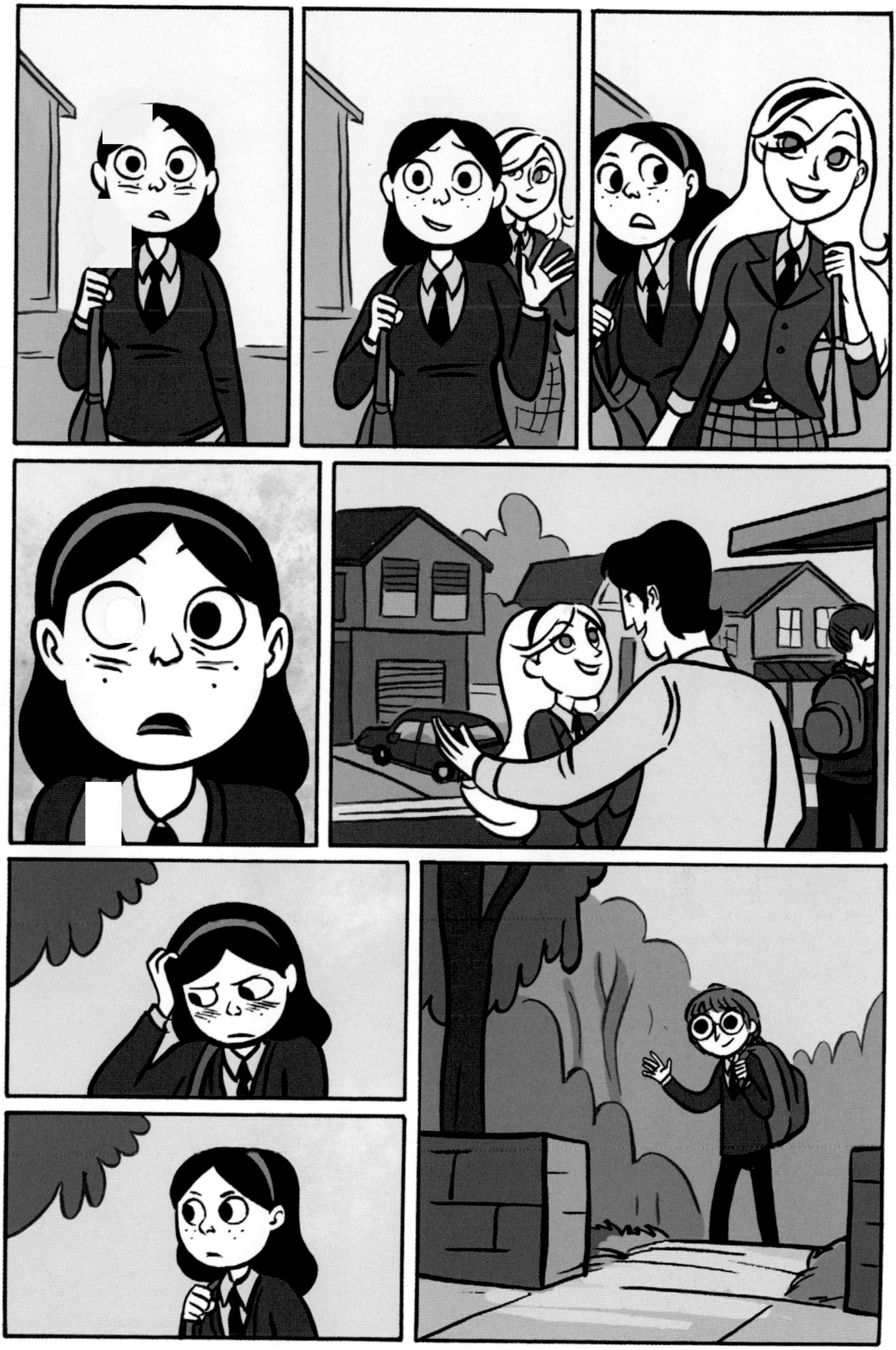

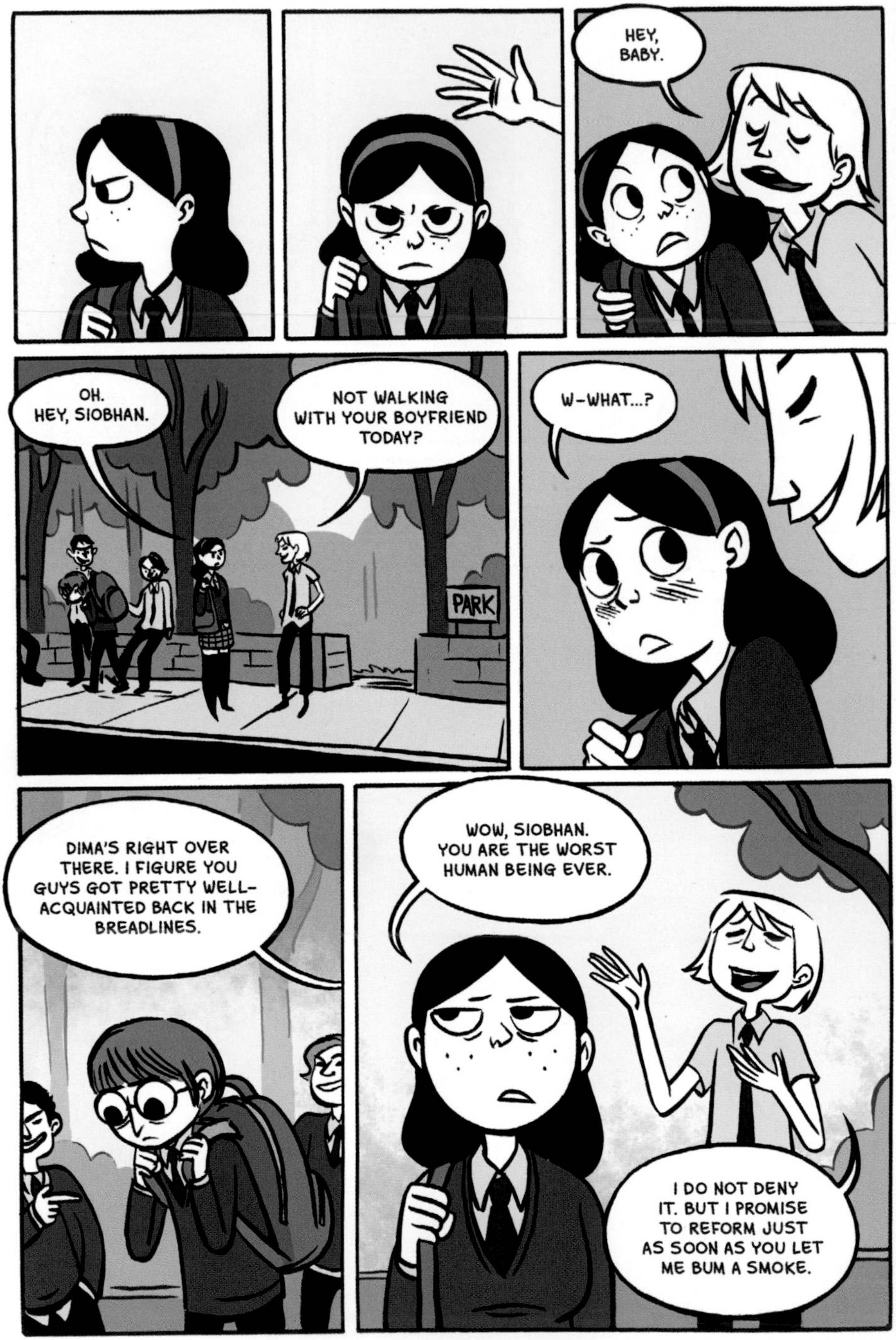
HEY, BABY.
OH. HEY, SIOBHAN.
NOT WALKING WITH YOUR BOYFRIEND TODAY?
PARK
W-WHAT...?
DIMA'S RIGHT OVER THERE. I FIGURE YOU GUYS GOT PRETTY WELL-ACQUAINTED BACK IN THE BREADLINES.
WOW, SIOBHAN. YOU ARE THE WORST HUMAN BEING EVER.
I DO NOT DENY IT. BUT I PROMISE TO REFORM JUST AS SOON AS YOU LET ME BUM A SMOKE.

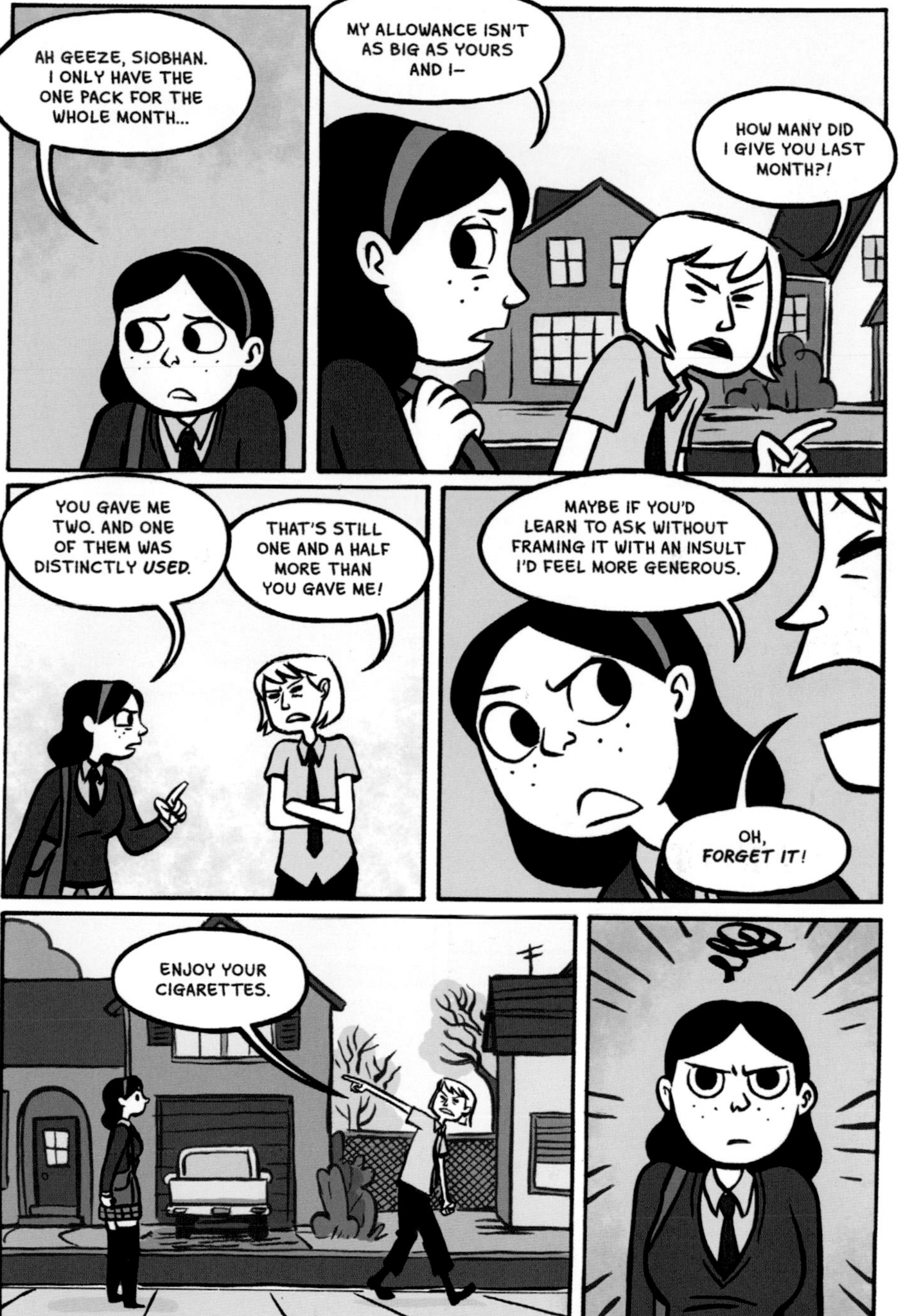
AH GEEZE, SIOBHAN. I ONLY HAVE THE ONE PACK FOR THE WHOLE MONTH...
MY ALLOWANCE ISN'T AS BIG AS YOURS AND I–
HOW MANY DID I GIVE YOU LAST MONTH?!
YOU GAVE ME TWO. AND ONE OF THEM WAS DISTINCTLY *USED*.
THAT'S STILL ONE AND A HALF MORE THAN YOU GAVE ME!
MAYBE IF YOU'D LEARN TO ASK WITHOUT FRAMING IT WITH AN INSULT I'D FEEL MORE GENEROUS.
OH, **FORGET IT!**
ENJOY YOUR CIGARETTES.

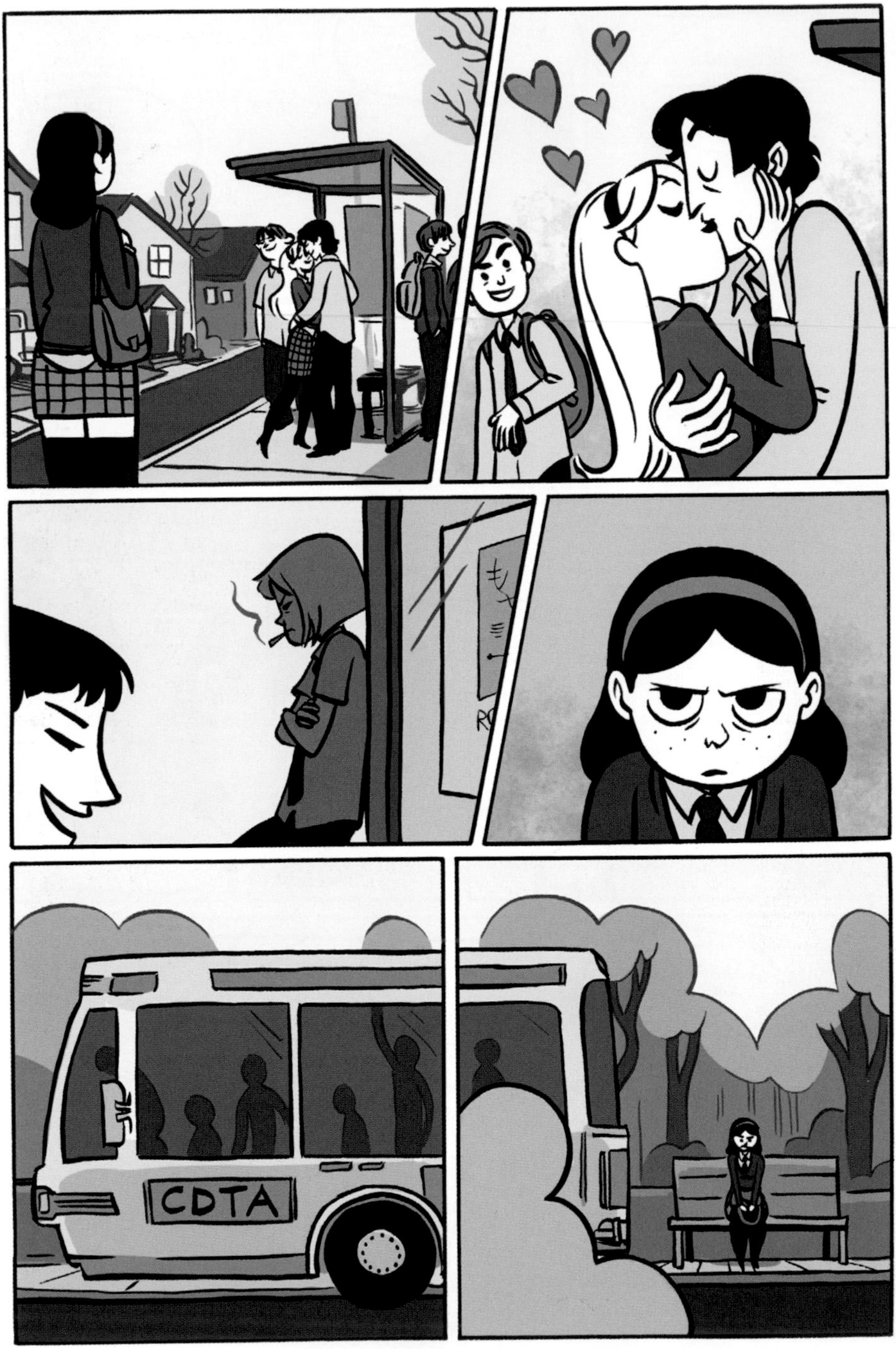
CDTA

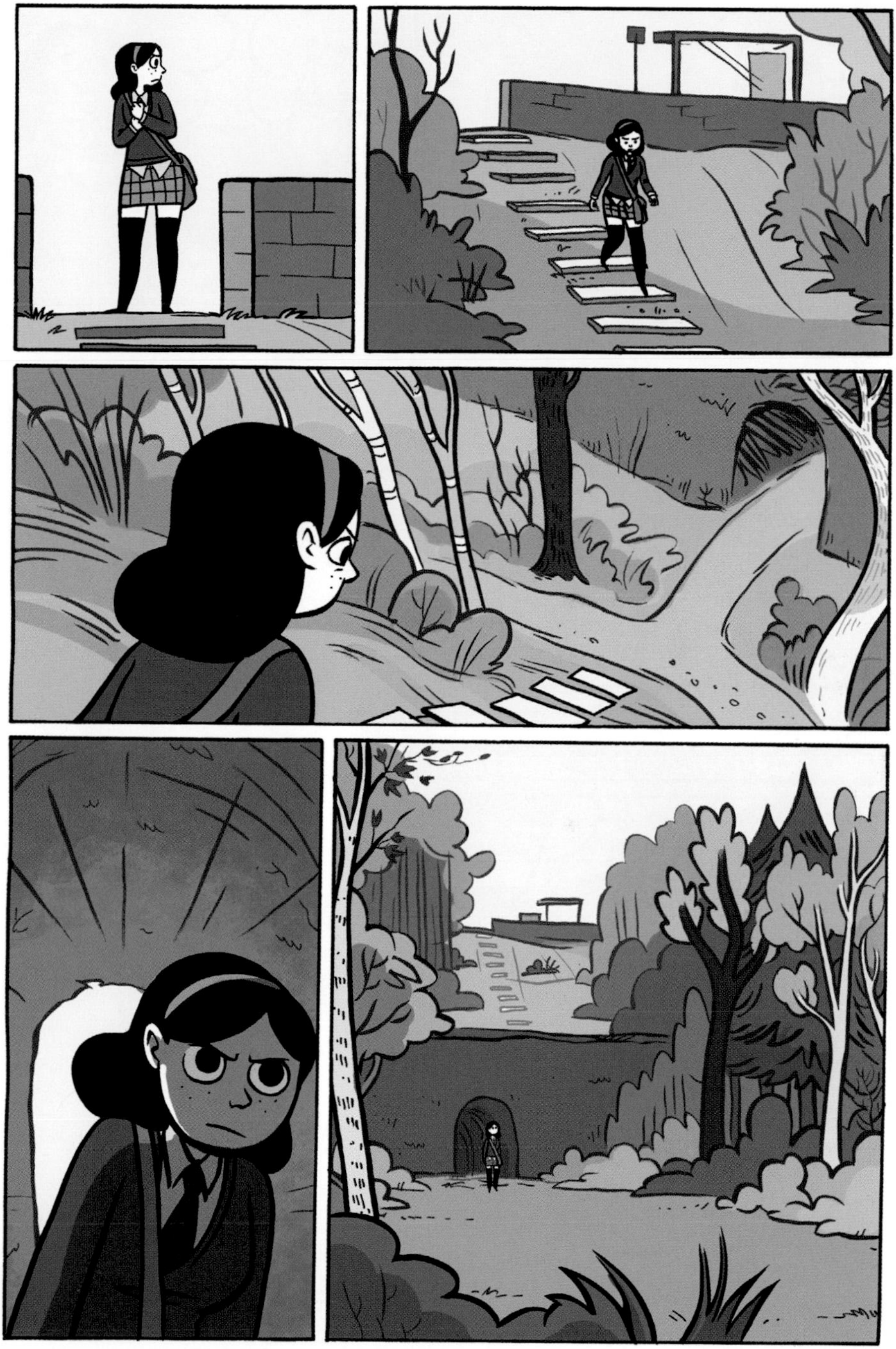

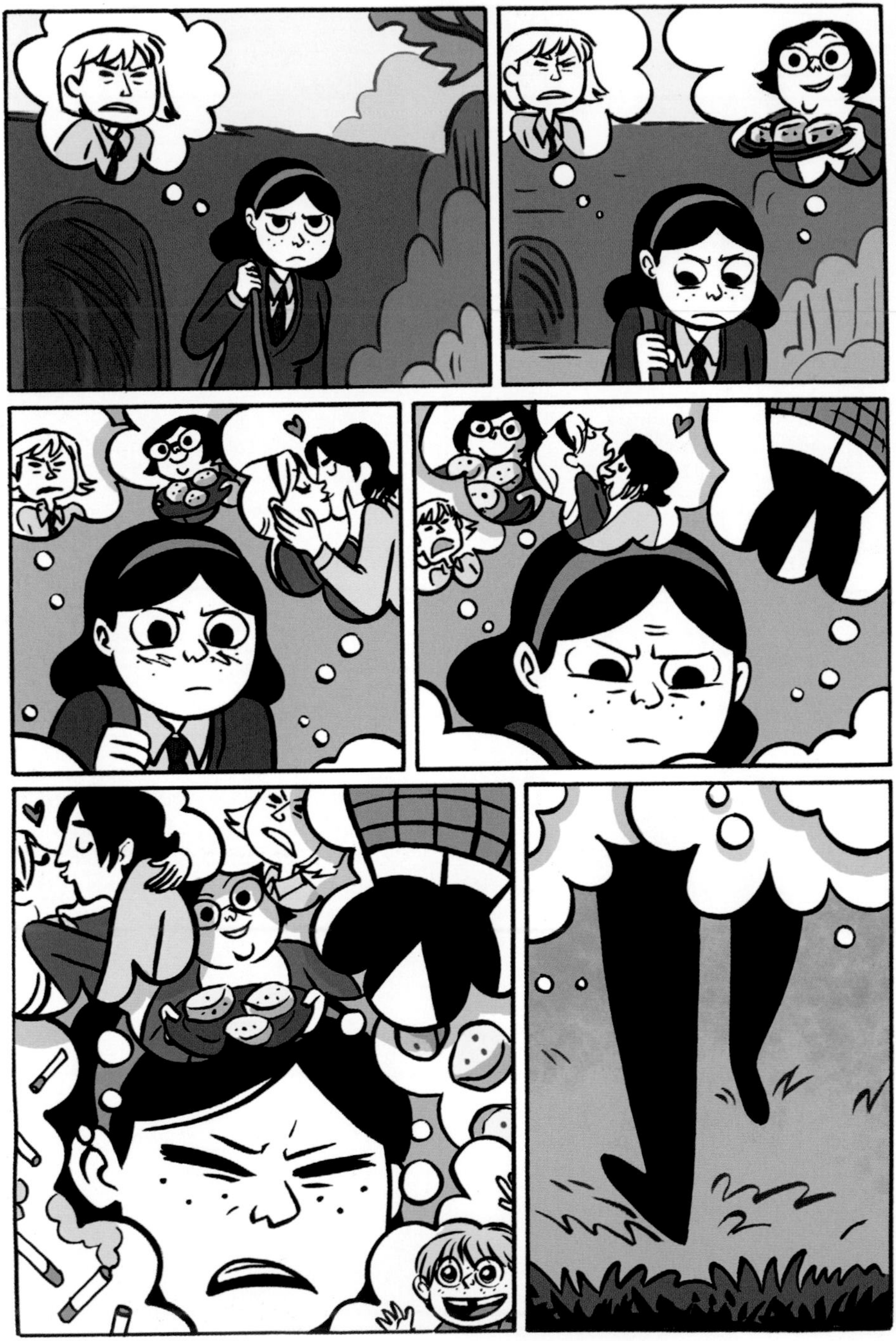

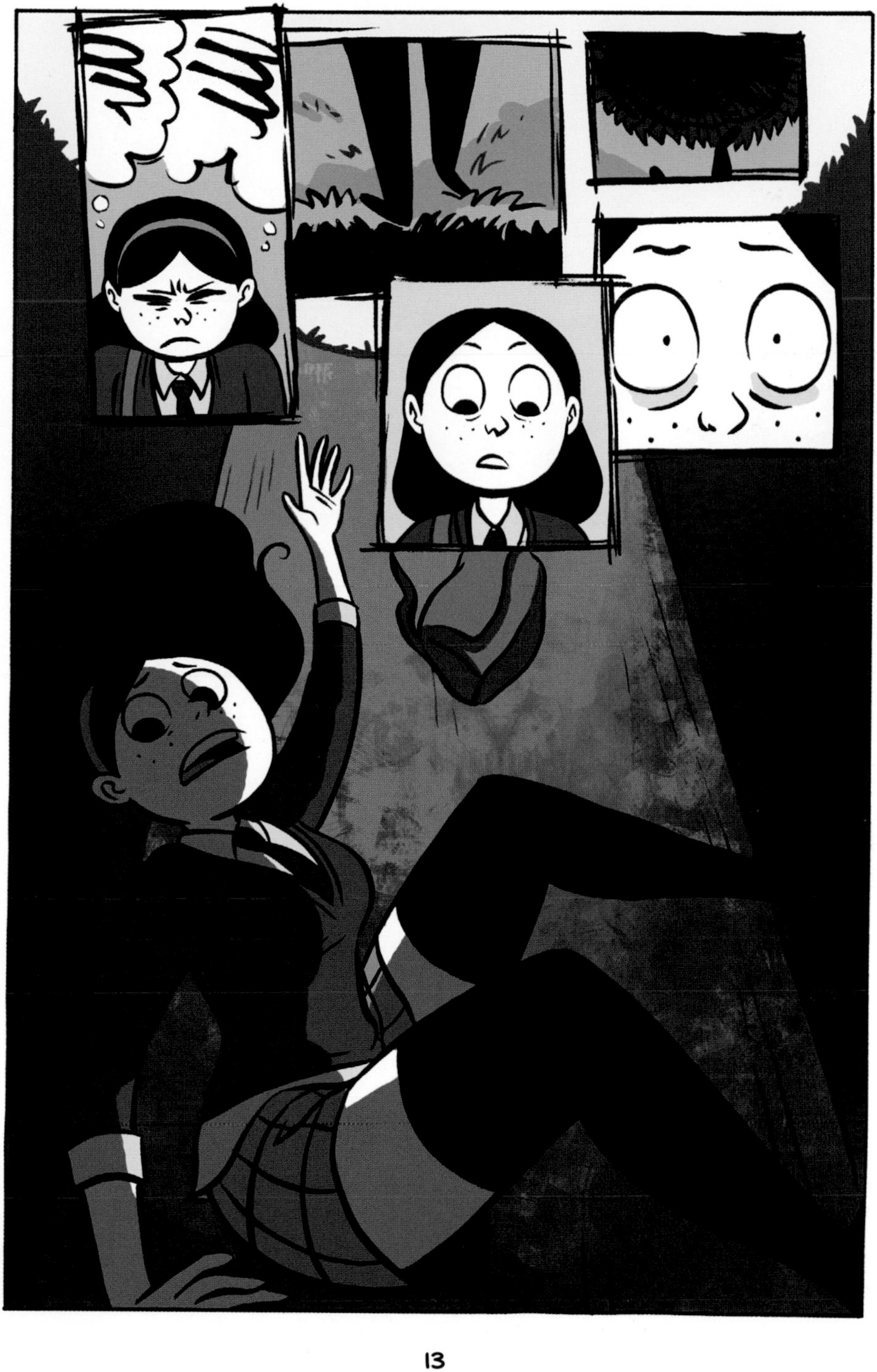

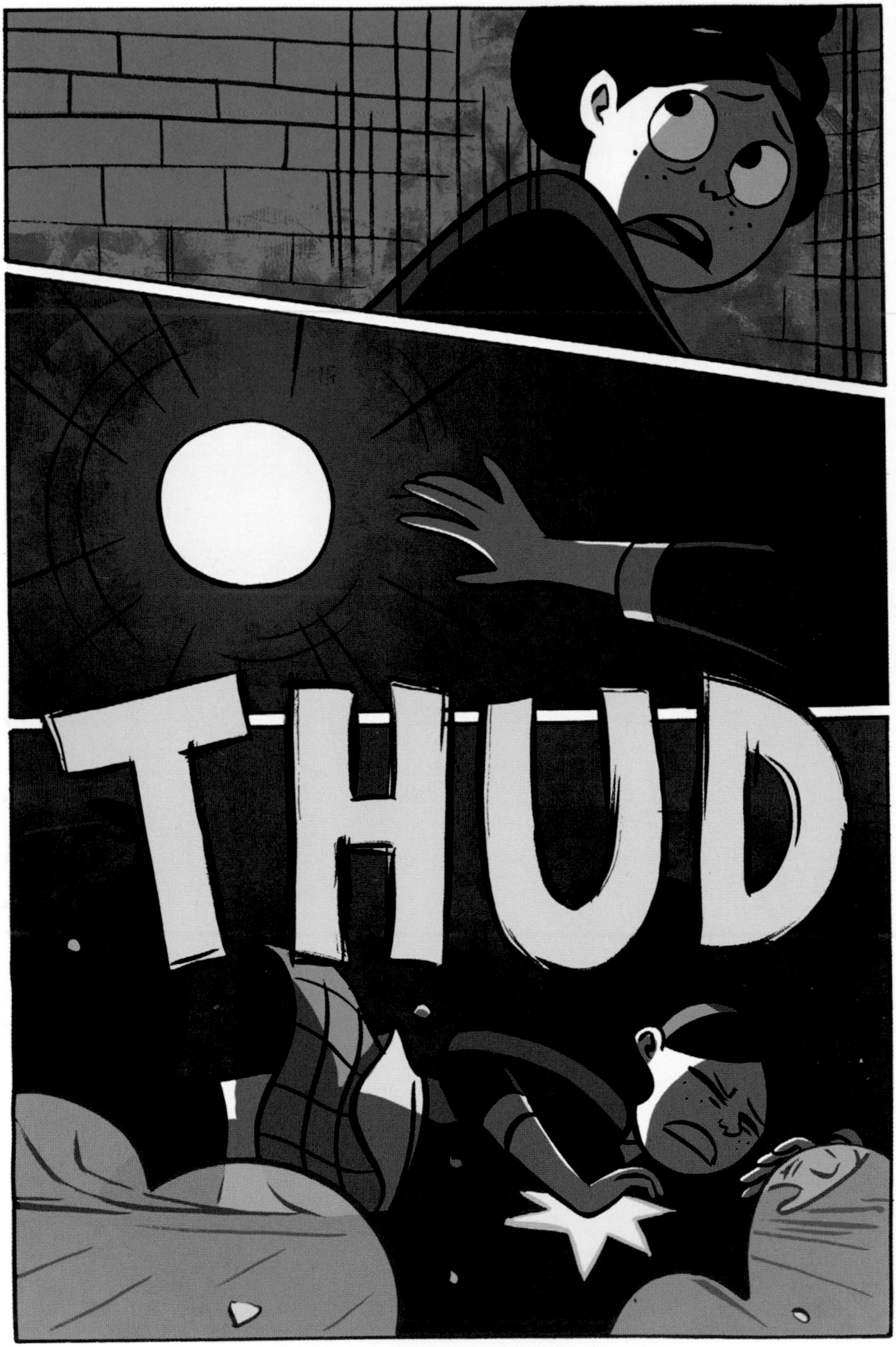
THUD

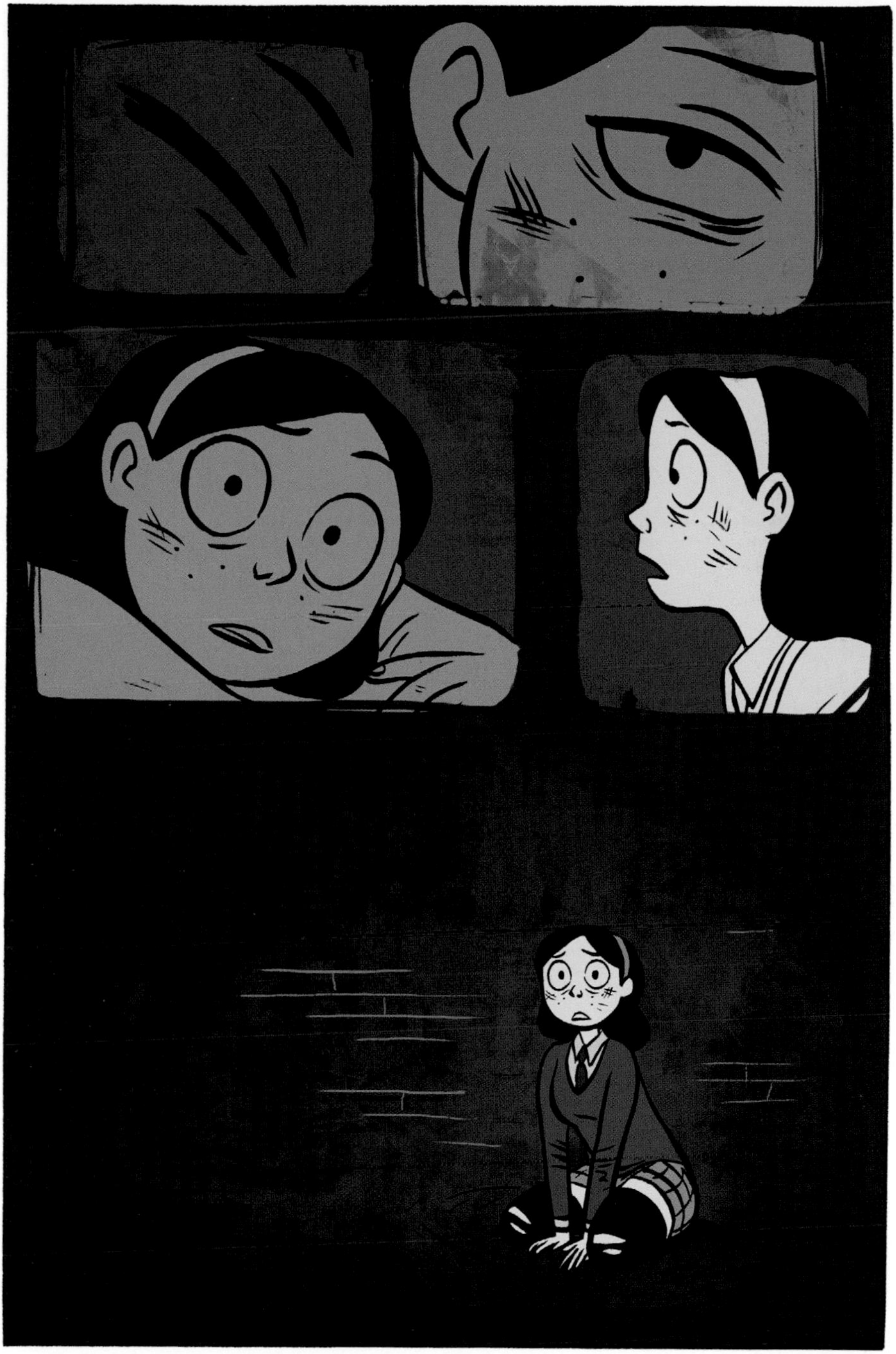

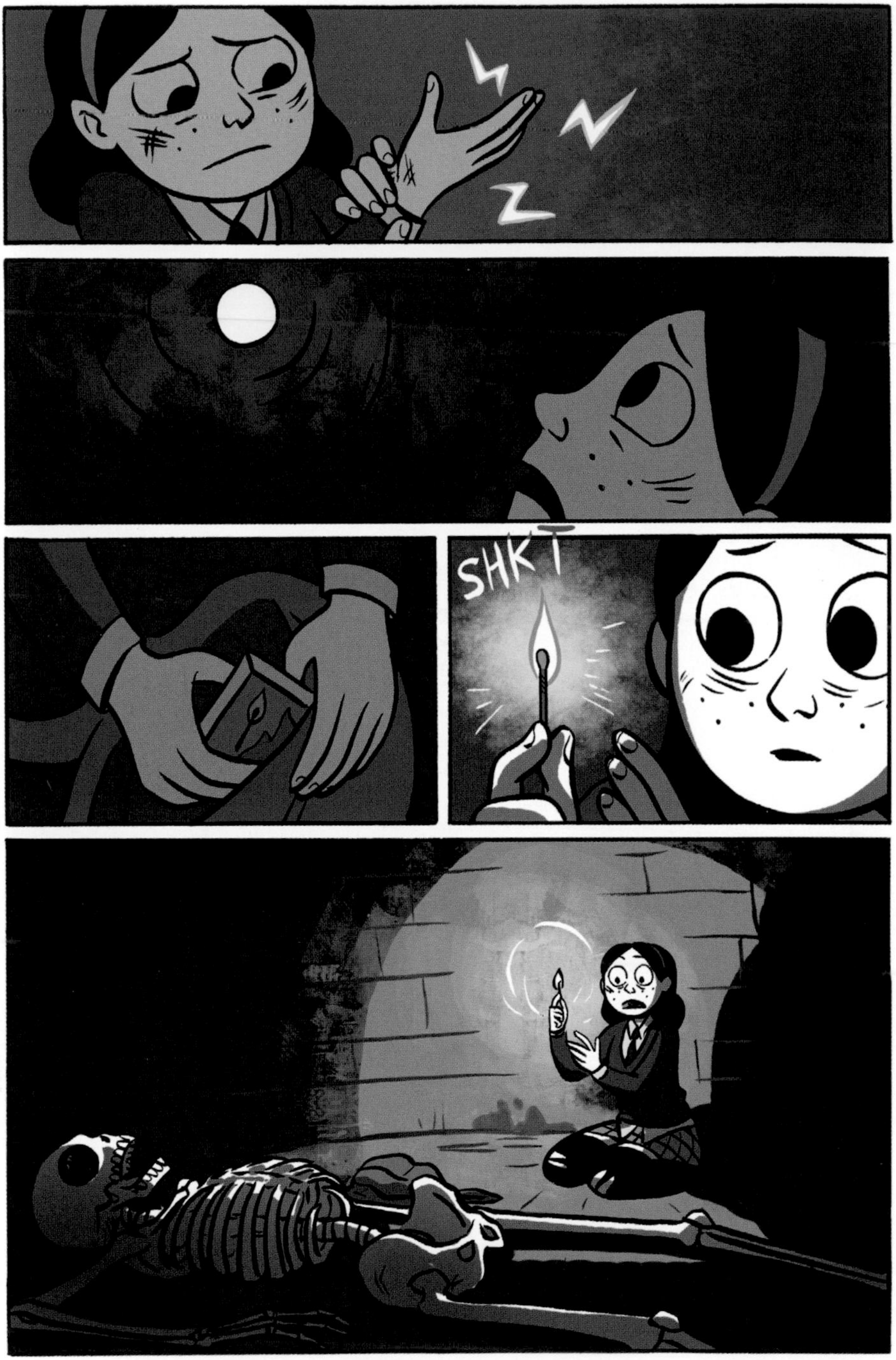
SHKT

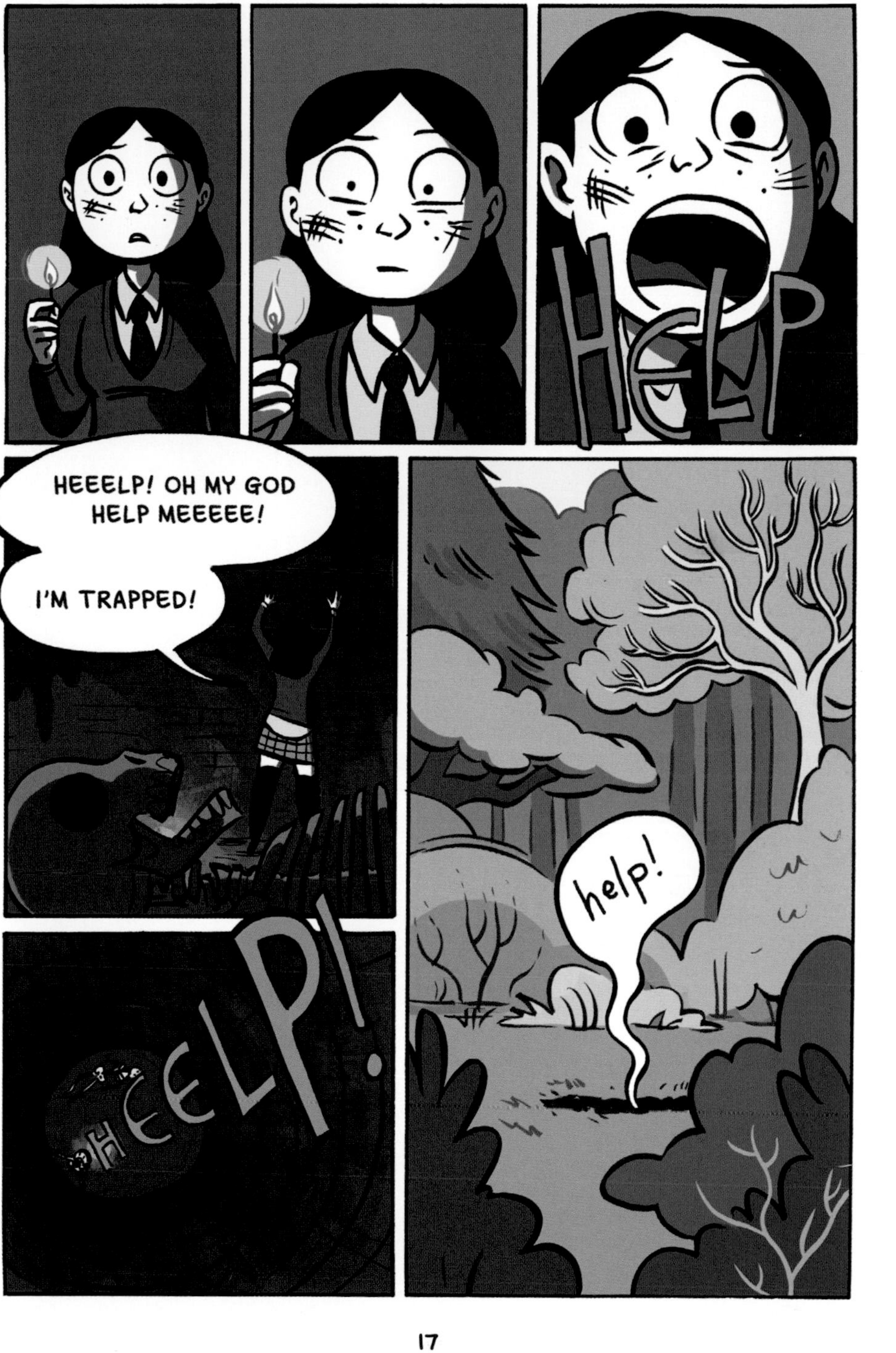
HELP
HEEELP! OH MY GOD HELP MEEEEE!
I'M TRAPPED!
HEELP!
help!

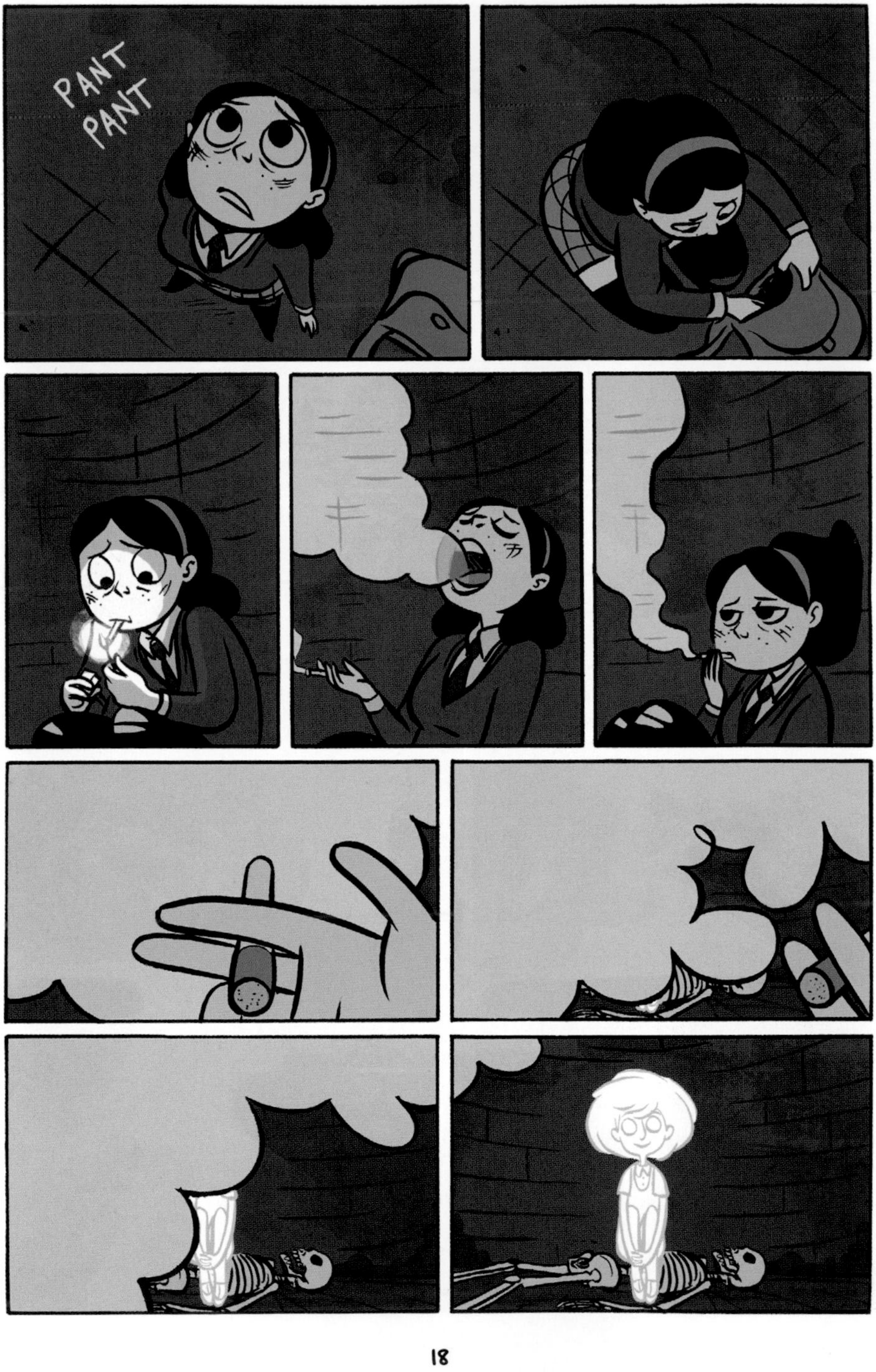
PANT
PANT

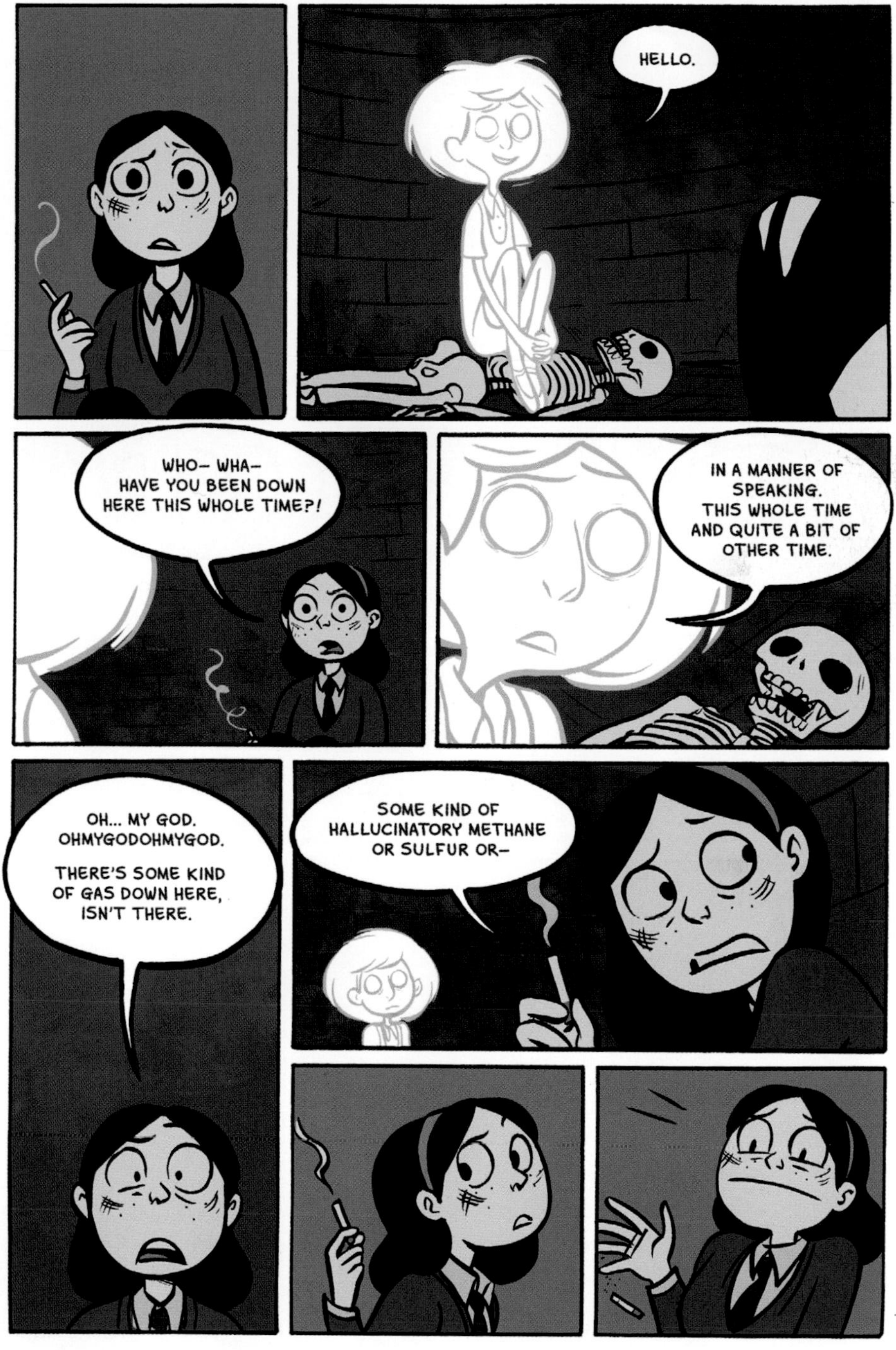
HELLO.
WHO– WHA– HAVE YOU BEEN DOWN HERE THIS WHOLE TIME?!
IN A MANNER OF SPEAKING. THIS WHOLE TIME AND QUITE A BIT OF OTHER TIME.
OH... MY GOD. OHMYGODOHMYGOD.
THERE'S SOME KIND OF GAS DOWN HERE, ISN'T THERE.
SOME KIND OF HALLUCINATORY METHANE OR SULFUR OR–

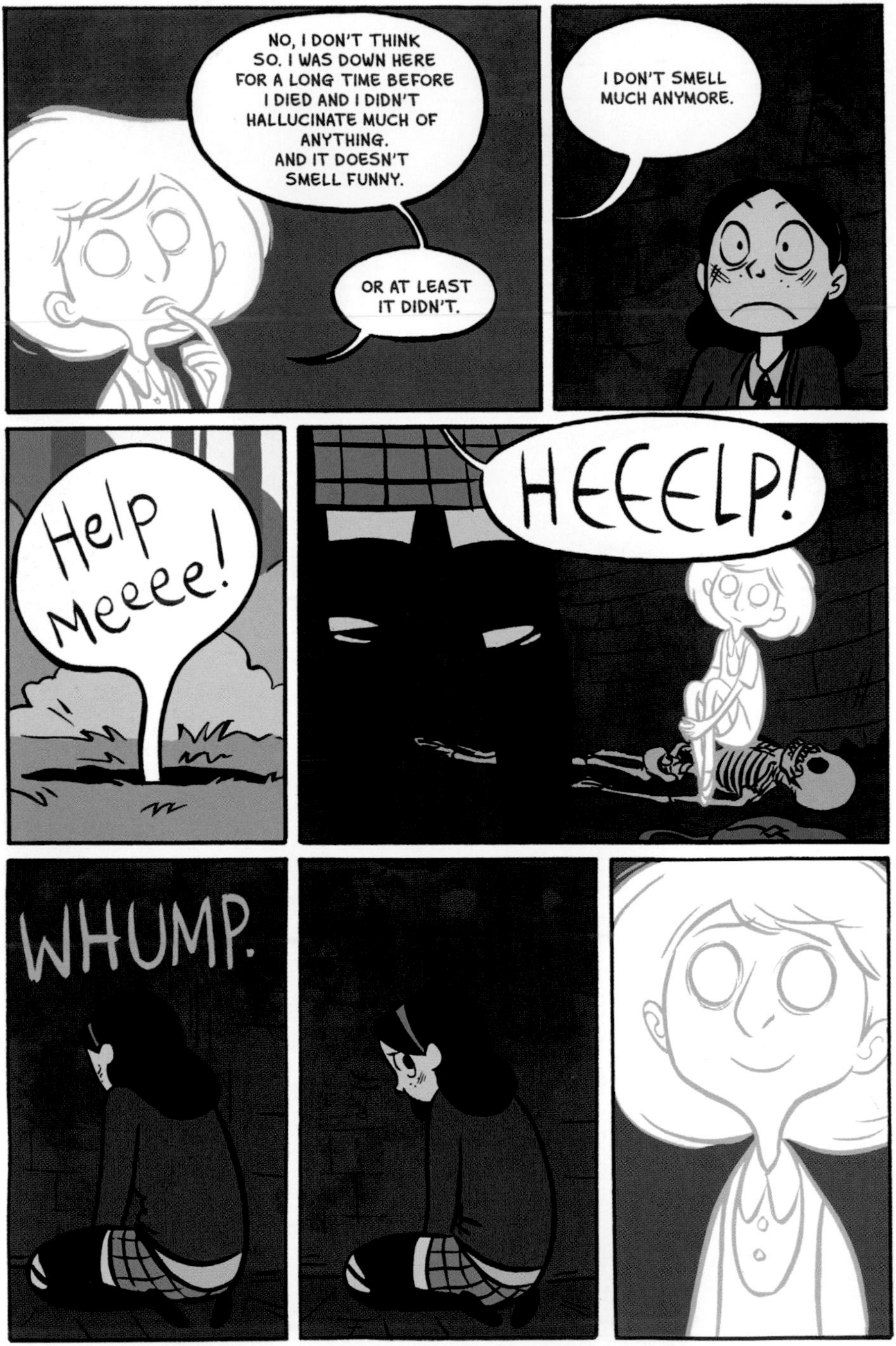
NO, I DON'T THINK SO. I WAS DOWN HERE FOR A LONG TIME BEFORE I DIED AND I DIDN'T HALLUCINATE MUCH OF ANYTHING. AND IT DOESN'T SMELL FUNNY.
OR AT LEAST IT DIDN'T.
I DON'T SMELL MUCH ANYMORE.
Help Meeee!
HEEELP!
WHUMP.

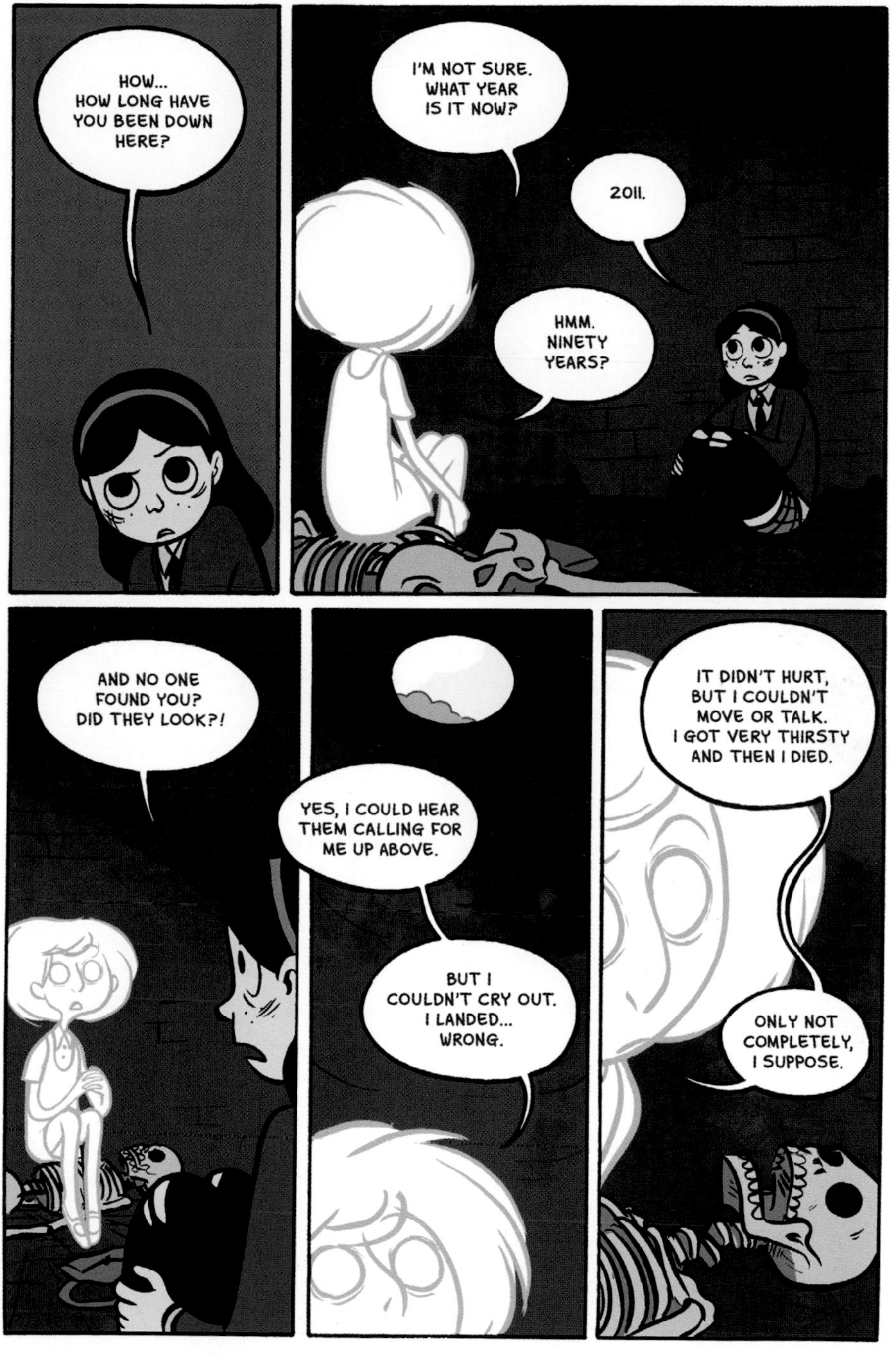
HOW...
HOW LONG HAVE YOU BEEN DOWN HERE?
I'M NOT SURE. WHAT YEAR IS IT NOW?
2011.
HMM. NINETY YEARS?
AND NO ONE FOUND YOU? DID THEY LOOK?!
YES, I COULD HEAR THEM CALLING FOR ME UP ABOVE.
BUT I COULDN'T CRY OUT. I LANDED... WRONG.
IT DIDN'T HURT, BUT I COULDN'T MOVE OR TALK. I GOT VERY THIRSTY AND THEN I DIED.
ONLY NOT COMPLETELY, I SUPPOSE.

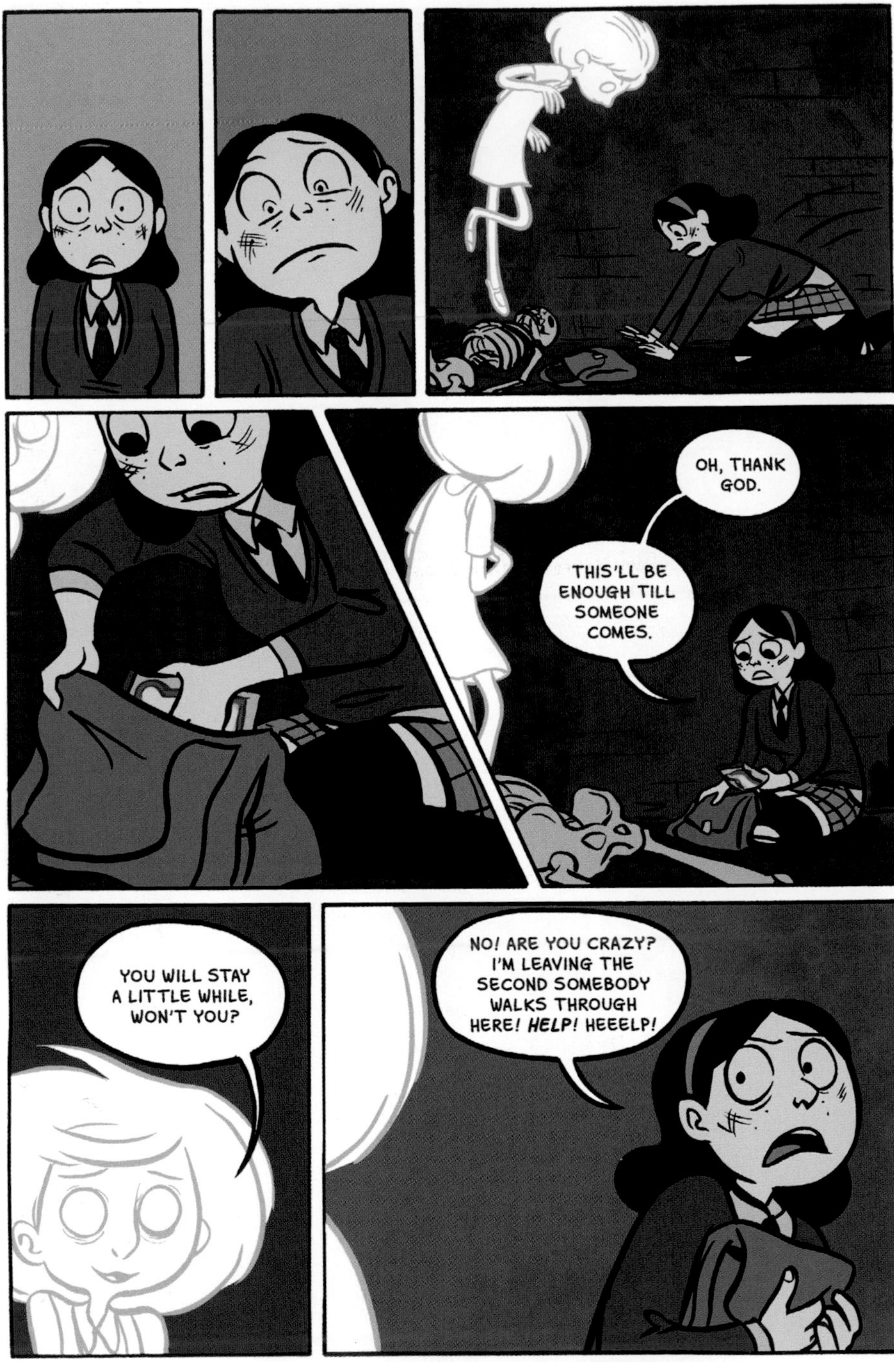
OH, THANK GOD.
THIS'LL BE ENOUGH TILL SOMEONE COMES.
YOU WILL STAY A LITTLE WHILE, WON'T YOU?
NO! ARE YOU CRAZY? I'M LEAVING THE SECOND SOMEBODY WALKS THROUGH HERE! **HELP**! HEEELP!

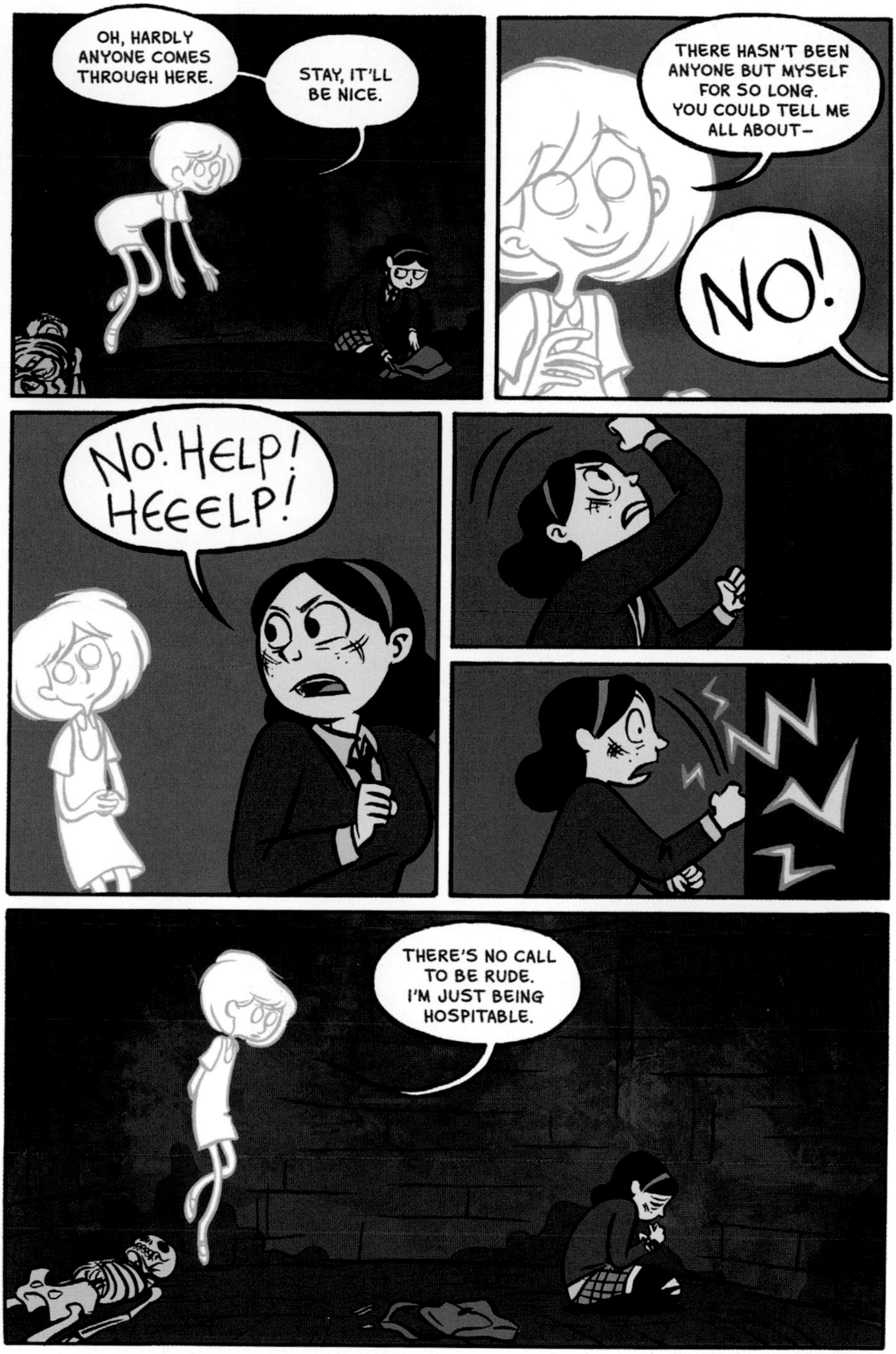
OH, HARDLY ANYONE COMES THROUGH HERE.
STAY, IT'LL BE NICE.
THERE HASN'T BEEN ANYONE BUT MYSELF FOR SO LONG. YOU COULD TELL ME ALL ABOUT—
NO!
NO! HELP! HEEELP!
THERE'S NO CALL TO BE RUDE. I'M JUST BEING HOSPITABLE.

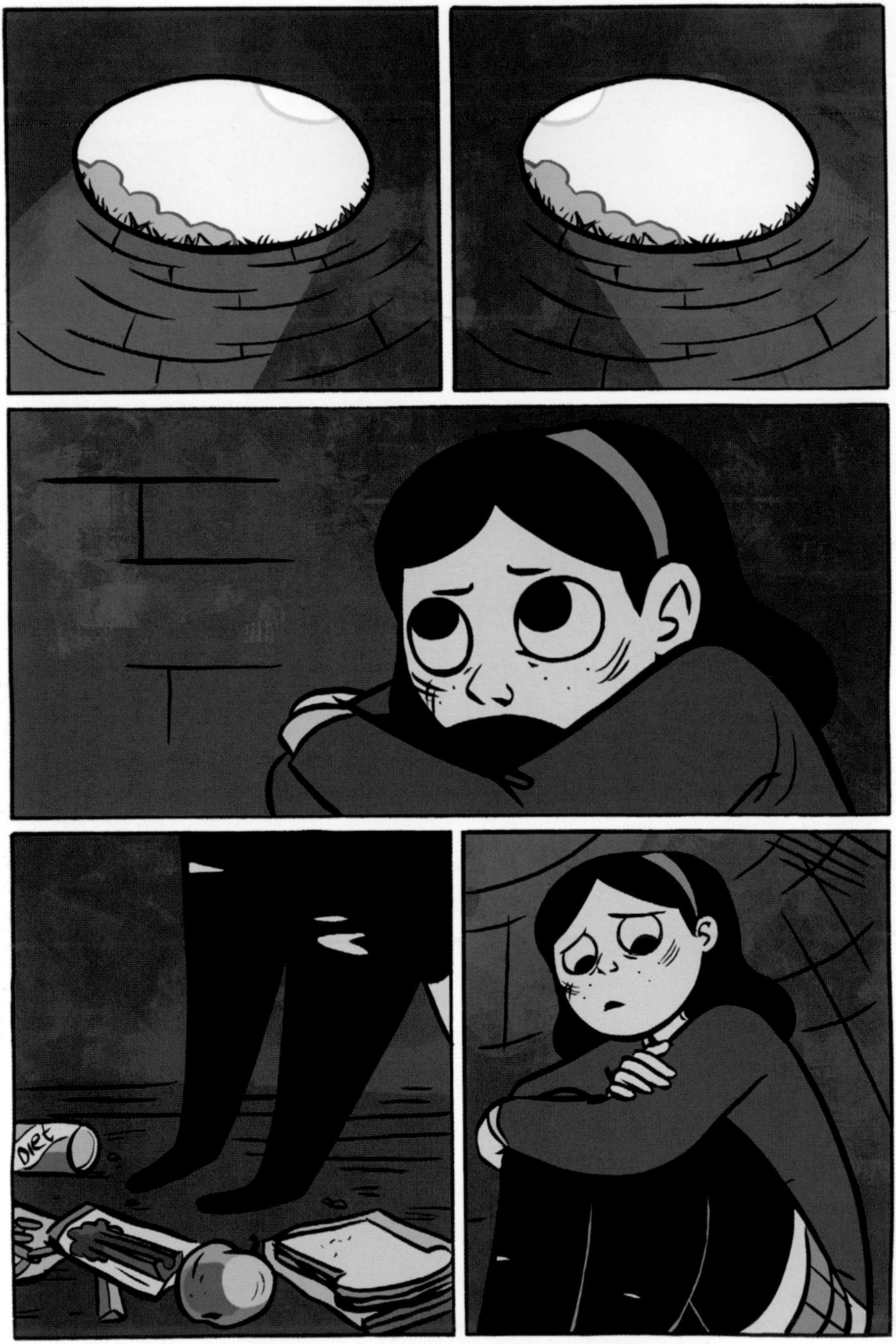
DIET

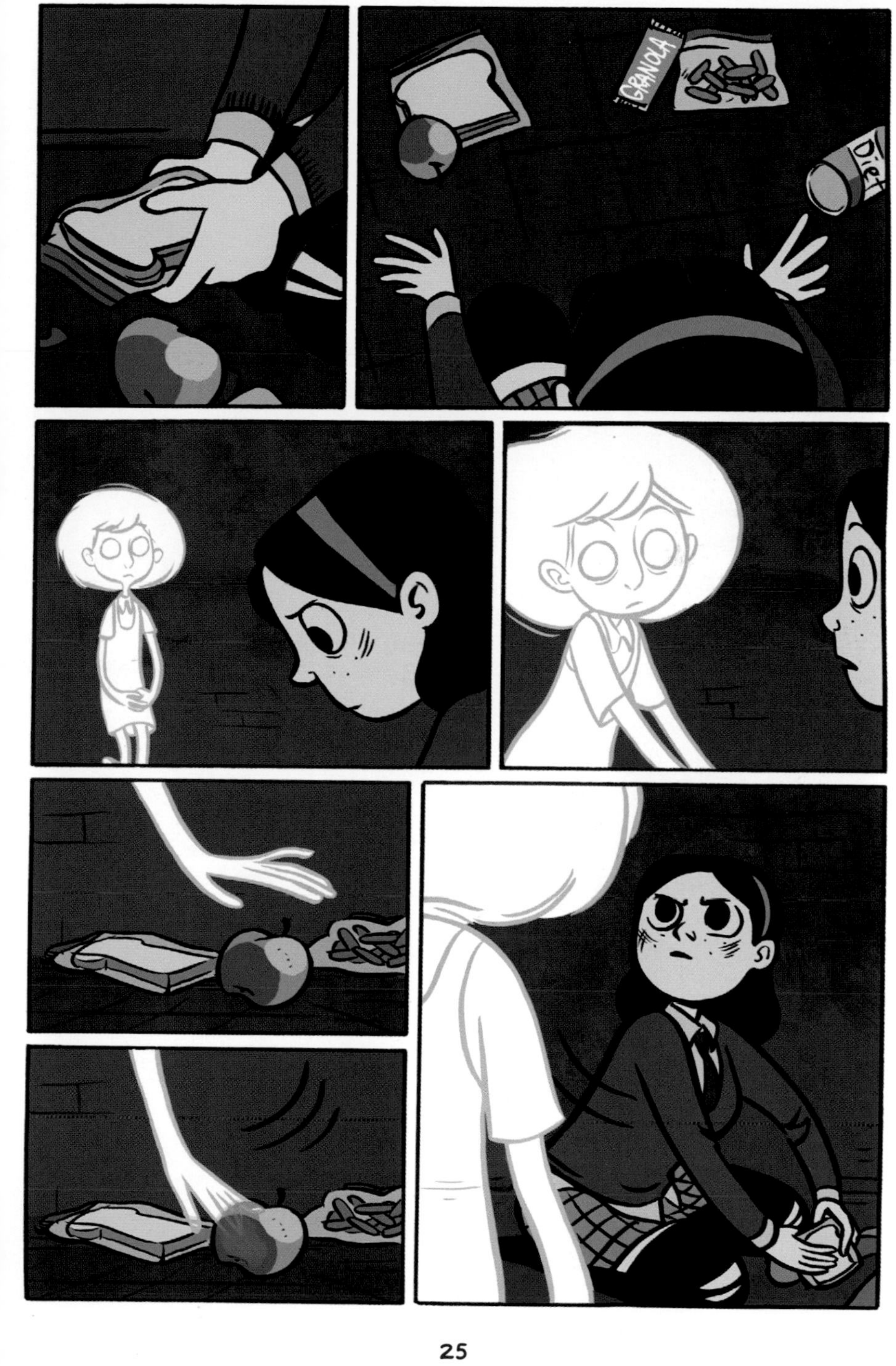
GRANOLA
Diet

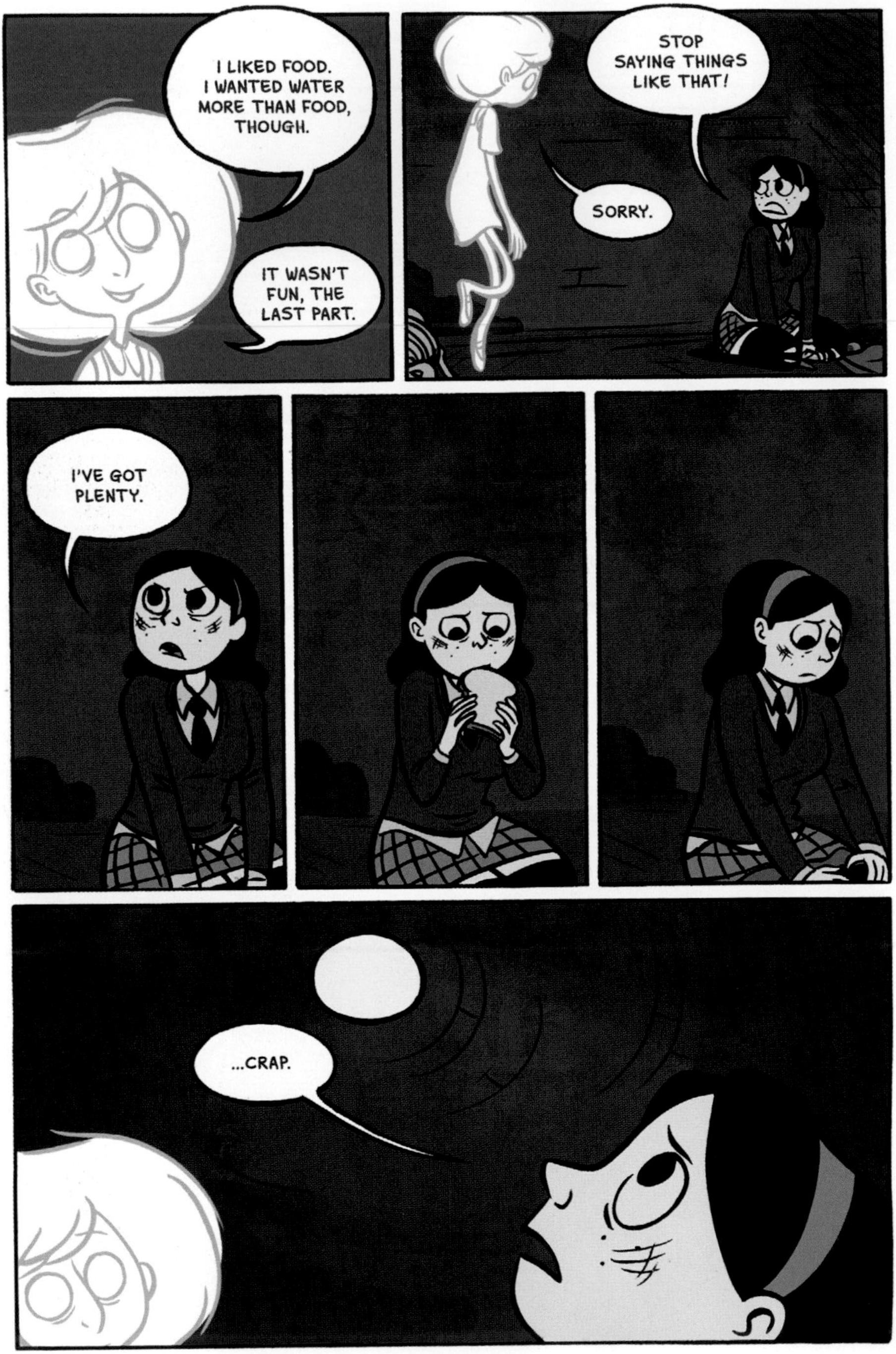
I LIKED FOOD. I WANTED WATER MORE THAN FOOD, THOUGH.
IT WASN'T FUN, THE LAST PART.
STOP SAYING THINGS LIKE THAT!
SORRY.
I'VE GOT PLENTY.
...CRAP.

DOES EVERYONE DRESS LIKE THAT NOW? IT DOESN'T LOOK VERY WARM.

YES. EVERYONE DRESSES LIKE THIS.

IT'S A GREAT OUTFIT FOR FALLING DOWN GIANT HOLES IN.

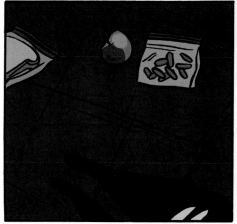

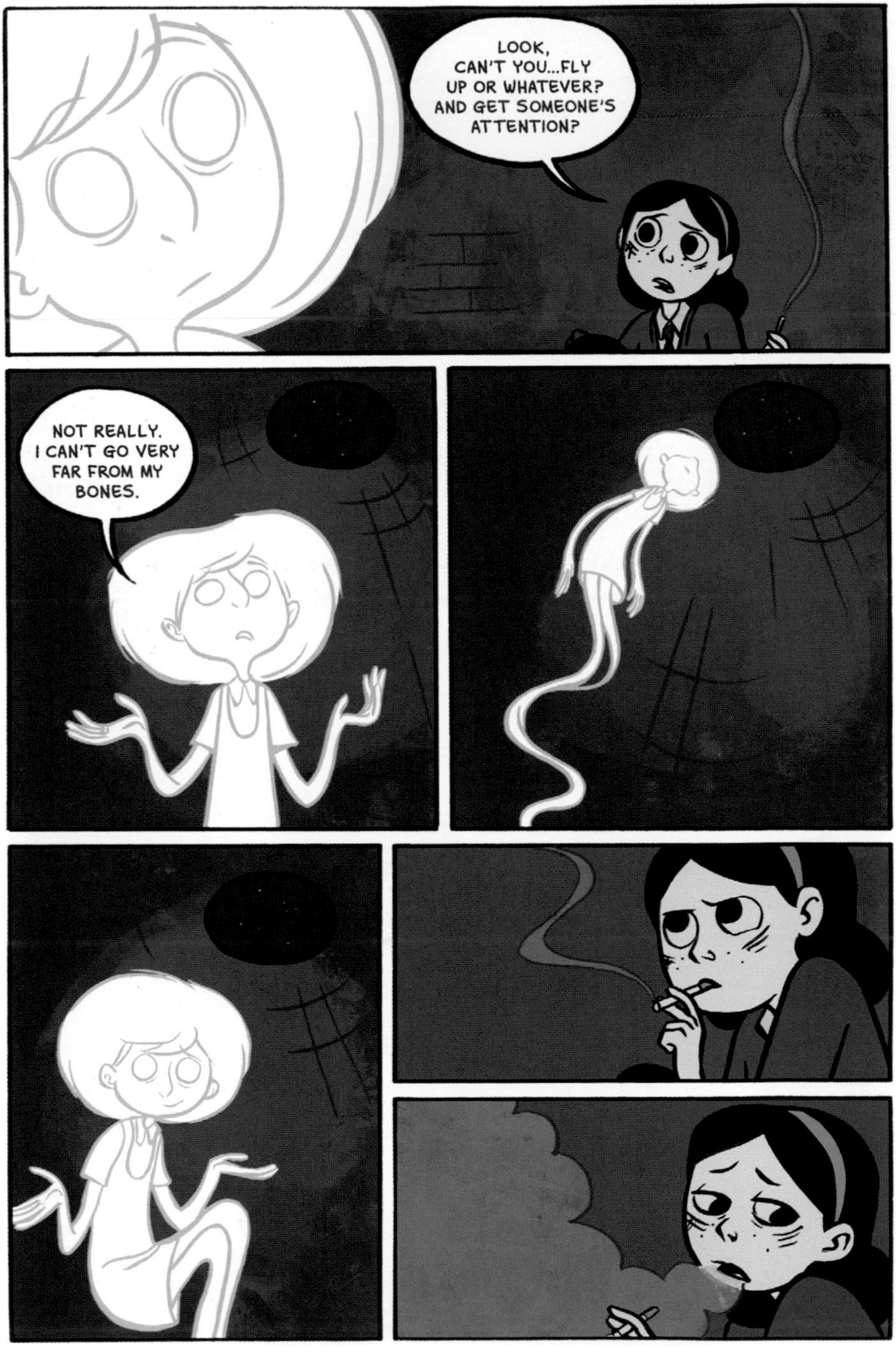
LOOK, CAN'T YOU...FLY UP OR WHATEVER? AND GET SOMEONE'S ATTENTION?
NOT REALLY. I CAN'T GO VERY FAR FROM MY BONES.

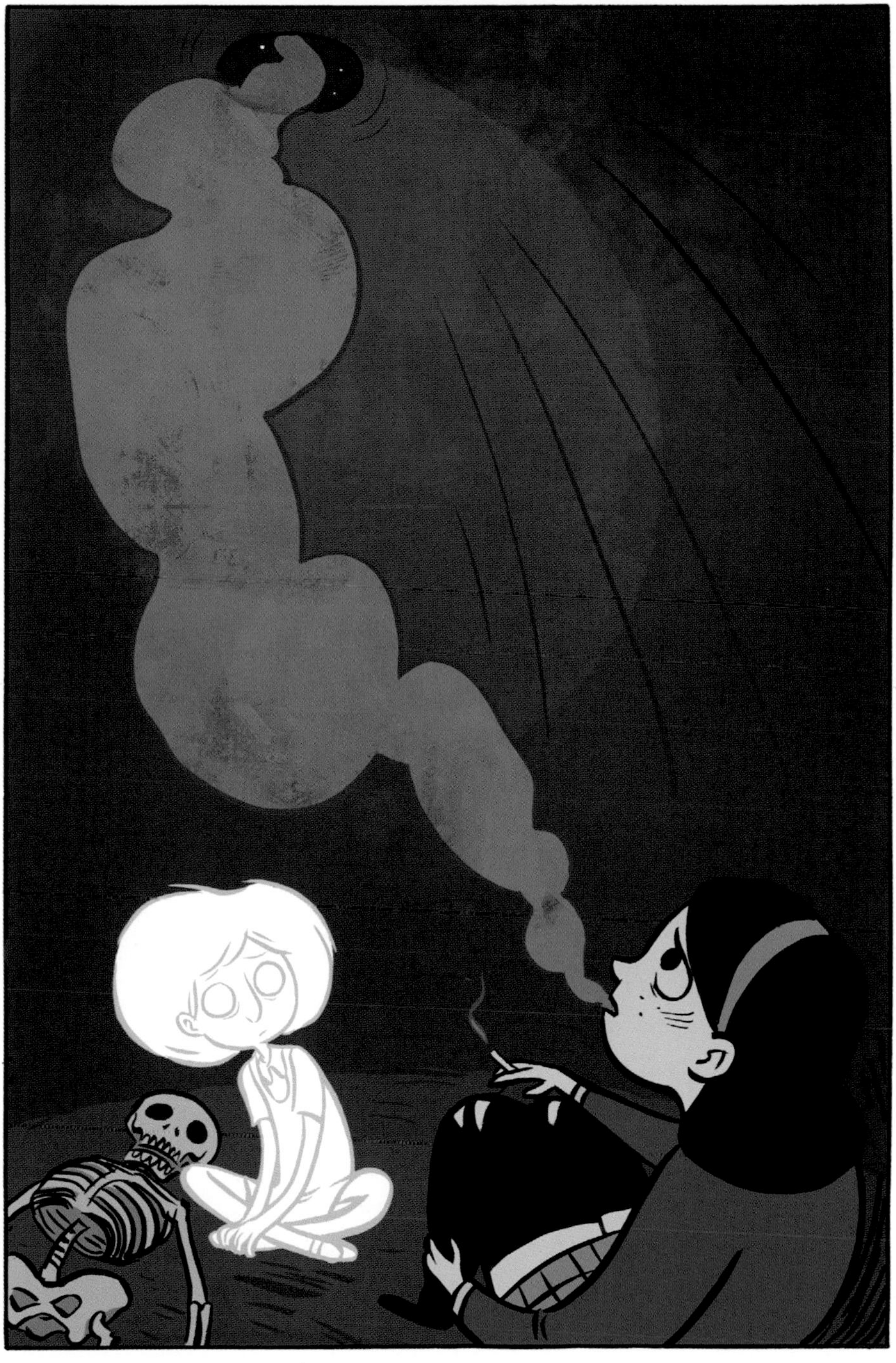

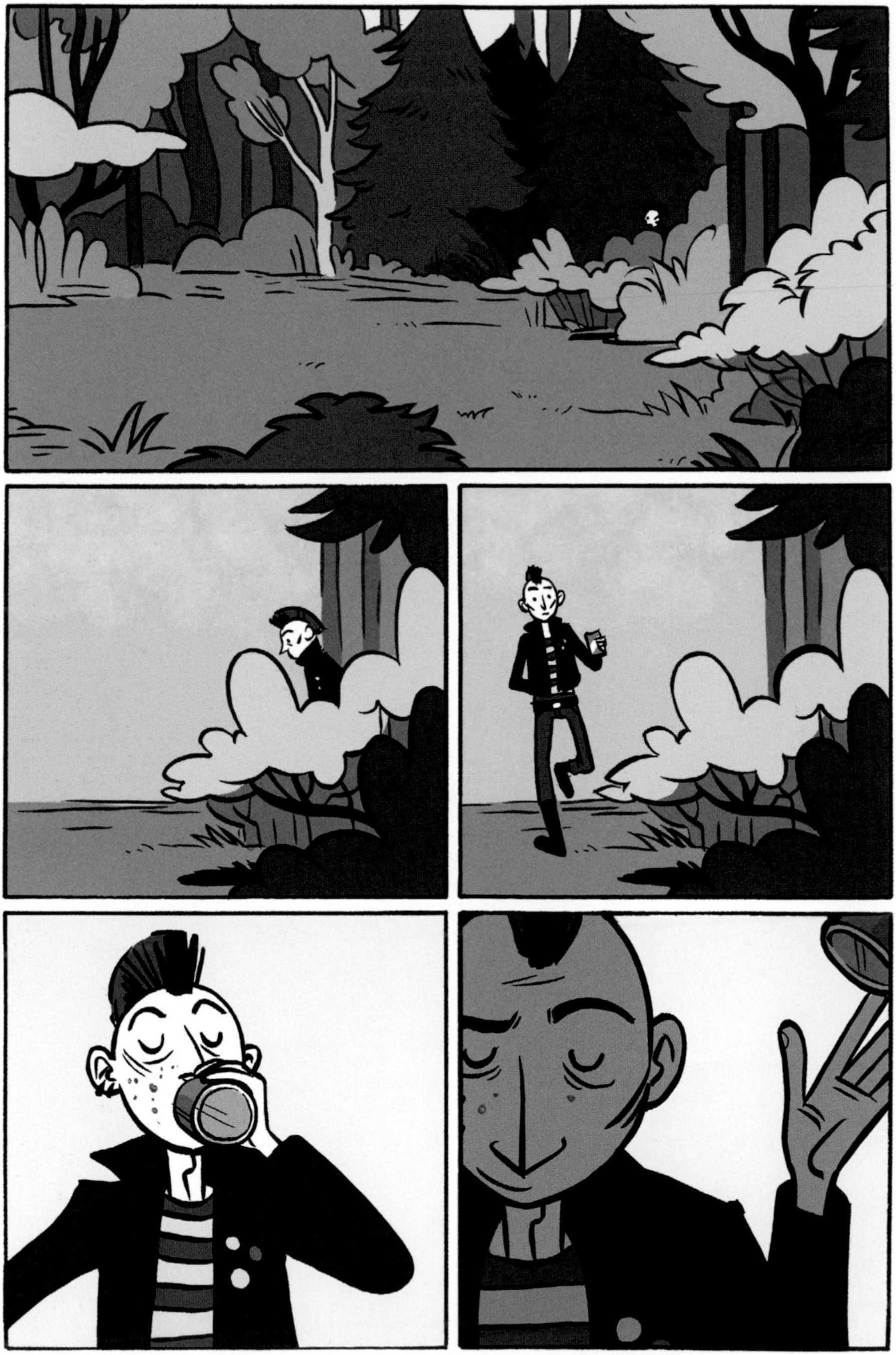

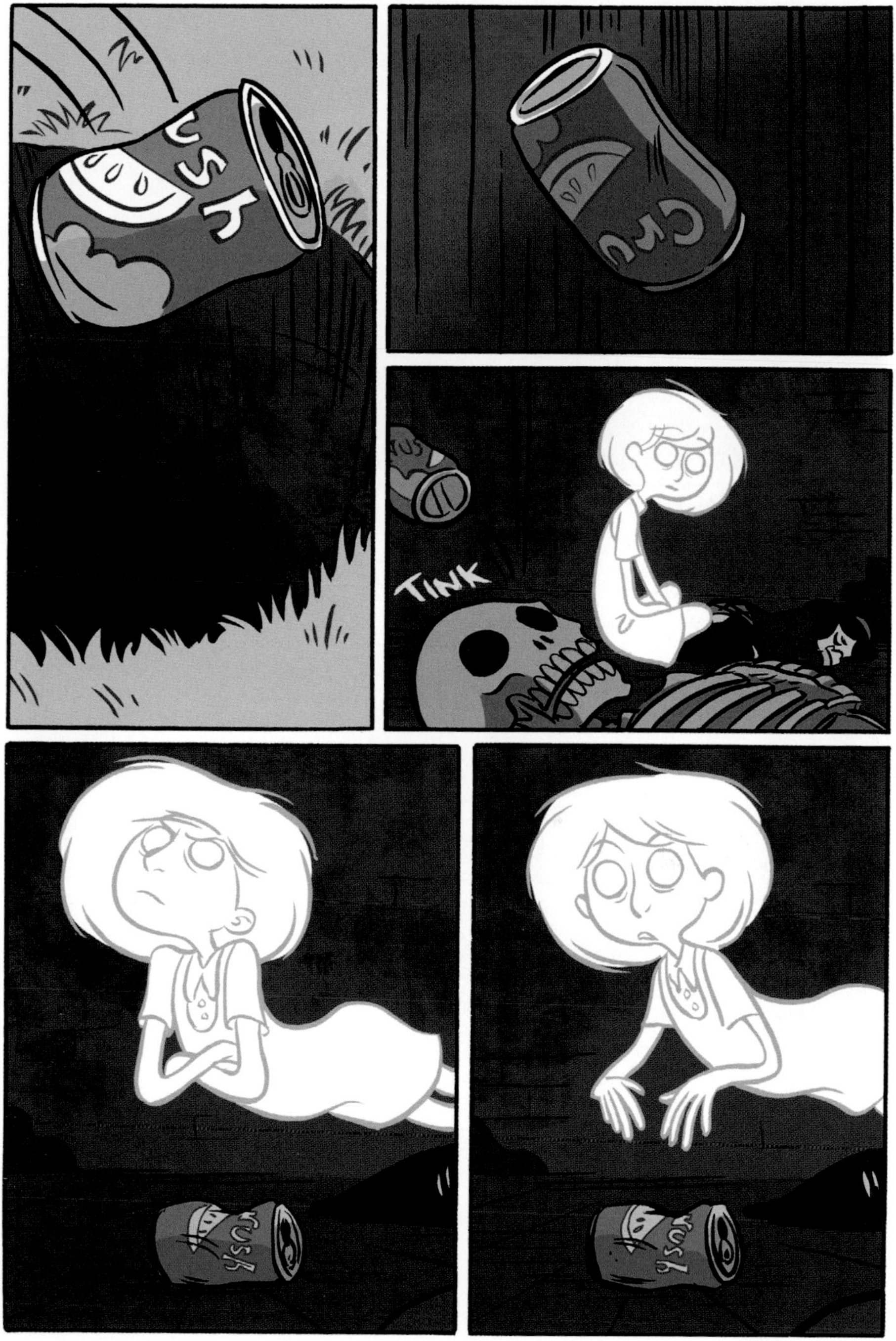
TINK

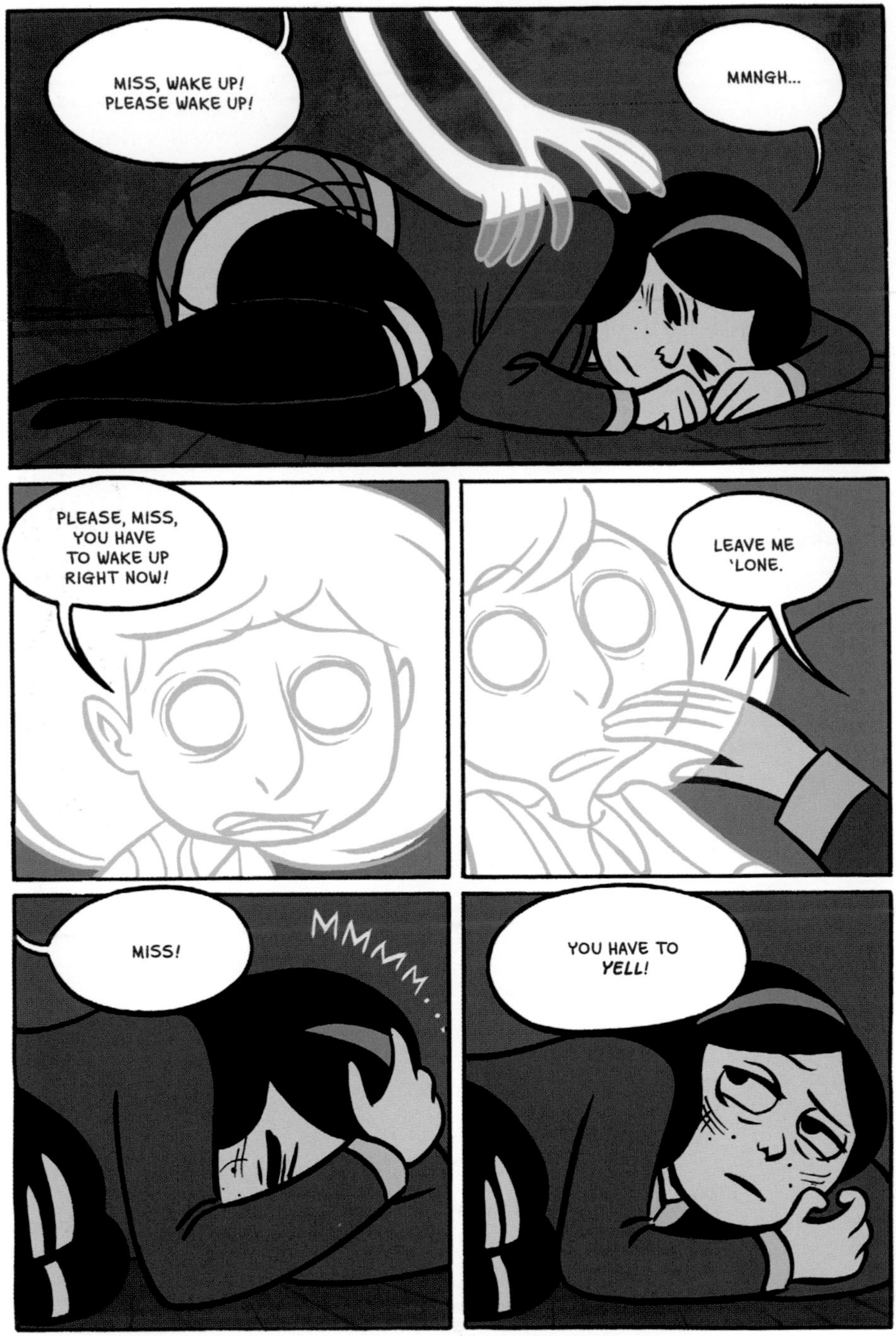
MISS, WAKE UP!
PLEASE WAKE UP!
MMNGH...
PLEASE, MISS, YOU HAVE TO WAKE UP RIGHT NOW!
LEAVE ME 'LONE.
MISS!
MMMM...
YOU HAVE TO *YELL!*

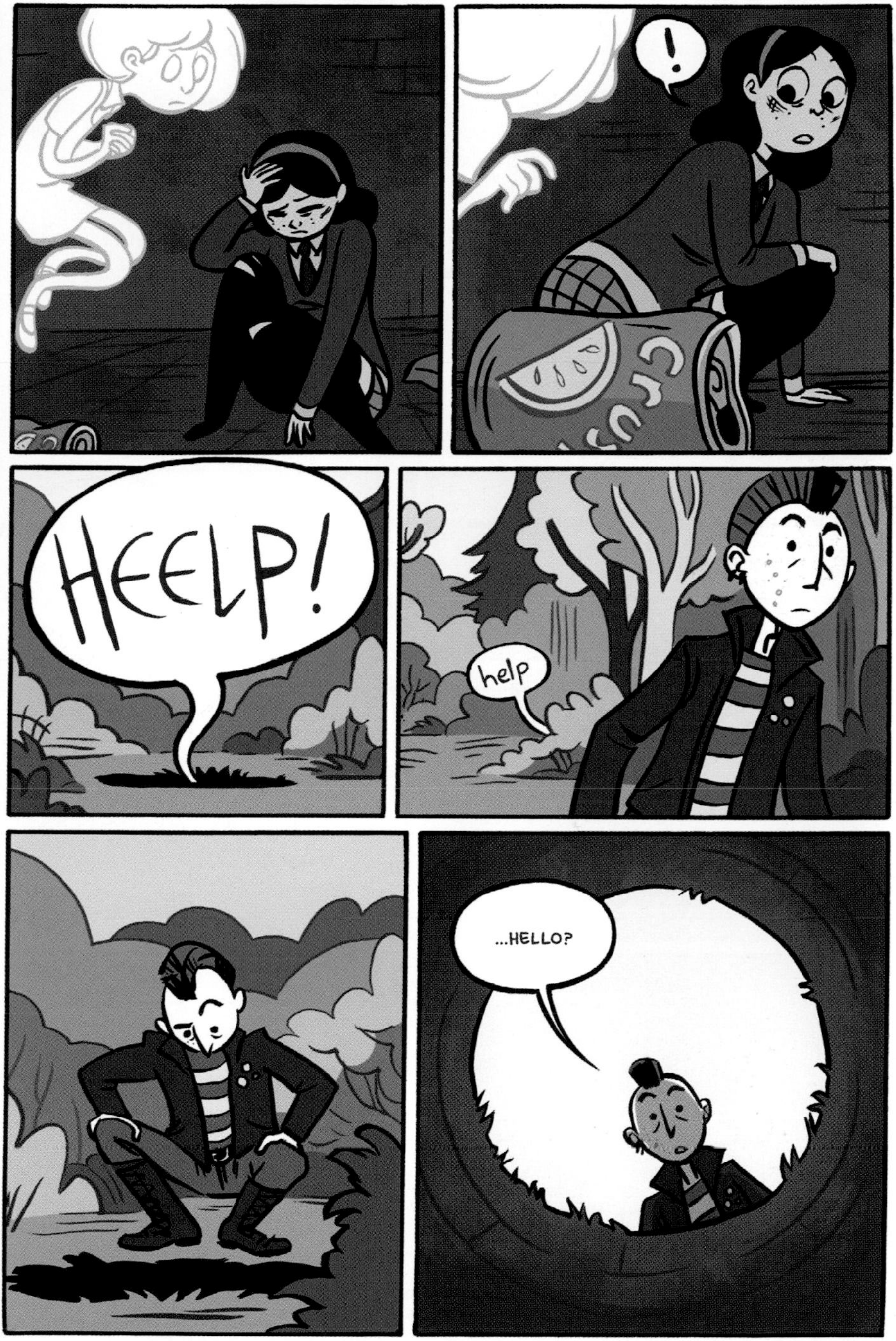
!
CRUSH
HEELP!
help
...HELLO?

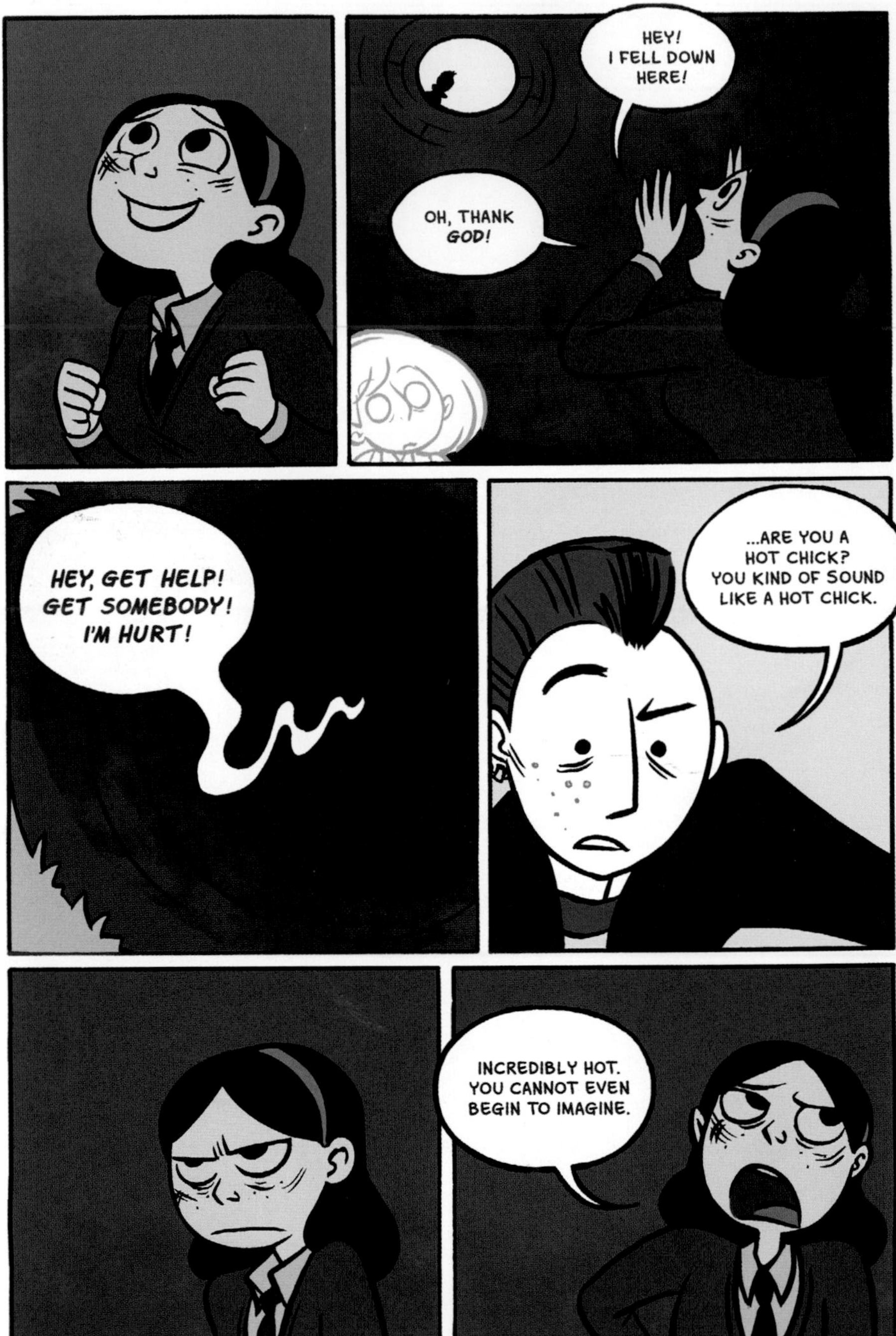
HEY! I FELL DOWN HERE!
OH, THANK GOD!
HEY, GET HELP! GET SOMEBODY! I'M HURT!
...ARE YOU A HOT CHICK? YOU KIND OF SOUND LIKE A HOT CHICK.
INCREDIBLY HOT. YOU CANNOT EVEN BEGIN TO IMAGINE.

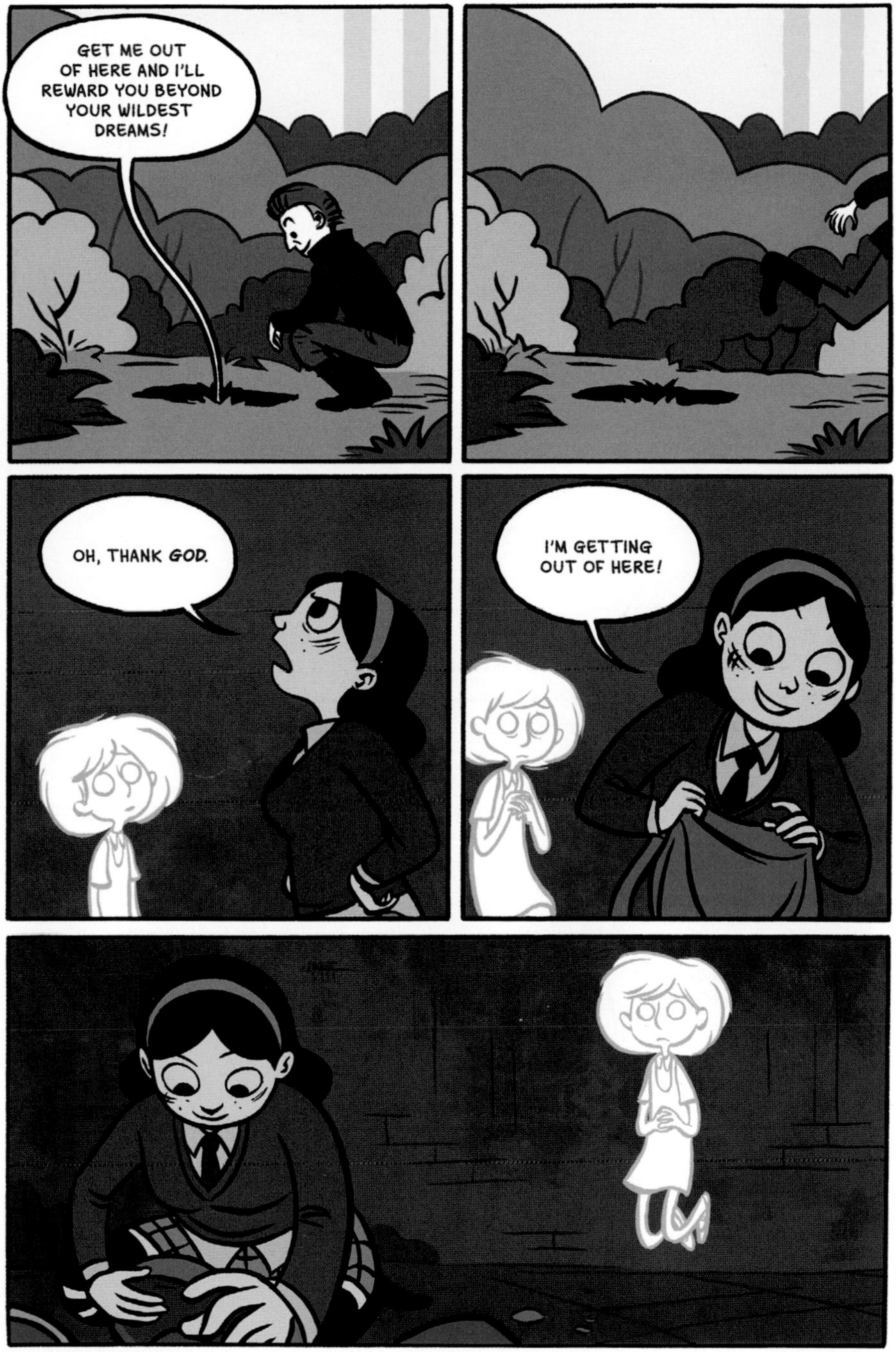
GET ME OUT OF HERE AND I'LL REWARD YOU BEYOND YOUR WILDEST DREAMS!
OH, THANK *GOD.*
I'M GETTING OUT OF HERE!

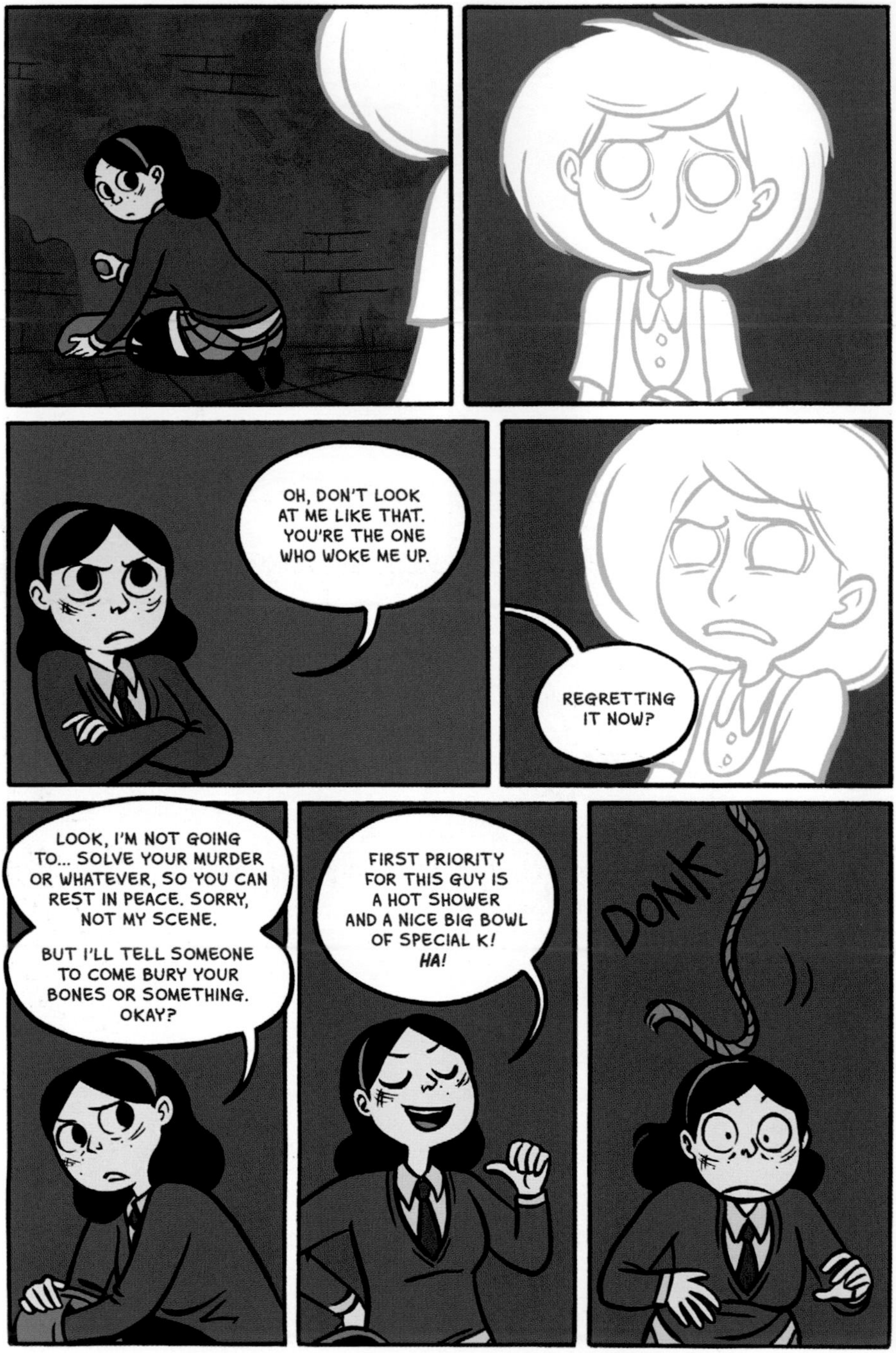
OH, DON'T LOOK AT ME LIKE THAT. YOU'RE THE ONE WHO WOKE ME UP.
REGRETTING IT NOW?
LOOK, I'M NOT GOING TO... SOLVE YOUR MURDER OR WHATEVER, SO YOU CAN REST IN PEACE. SORRY, NOT MY SCENE.
BUT I'LL TELL SOMEONE TO COME BURY YOUR BONES OR SOMETHING. OKAY?
FIRST PRIORITY FOR THIS GUY IS A HOT SHOWER AND A NICE BIG BOWL OF SPECIAL K! *HA!*
DONK

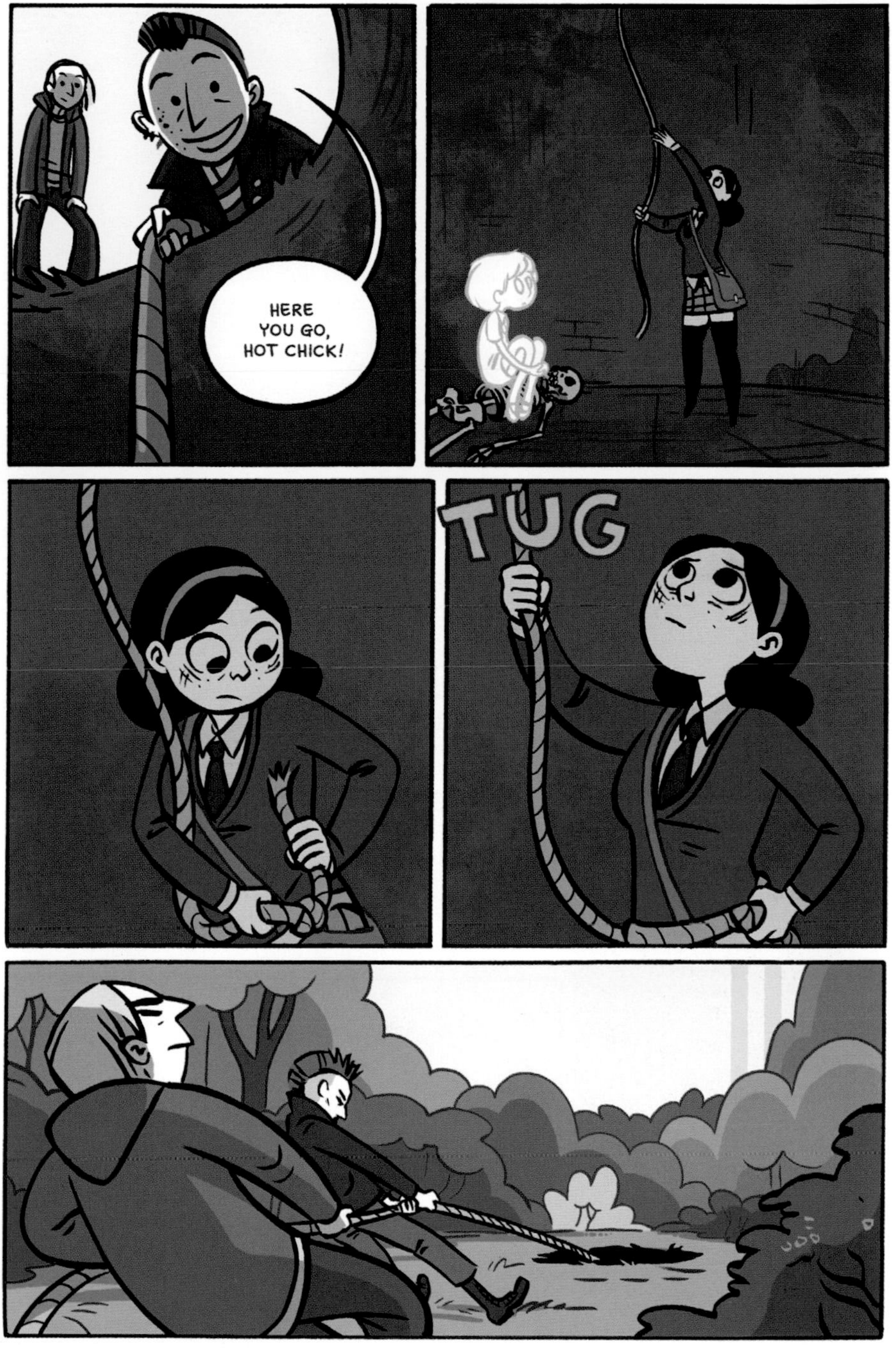
HERE YOU GO, HOT CHICK!
TUG

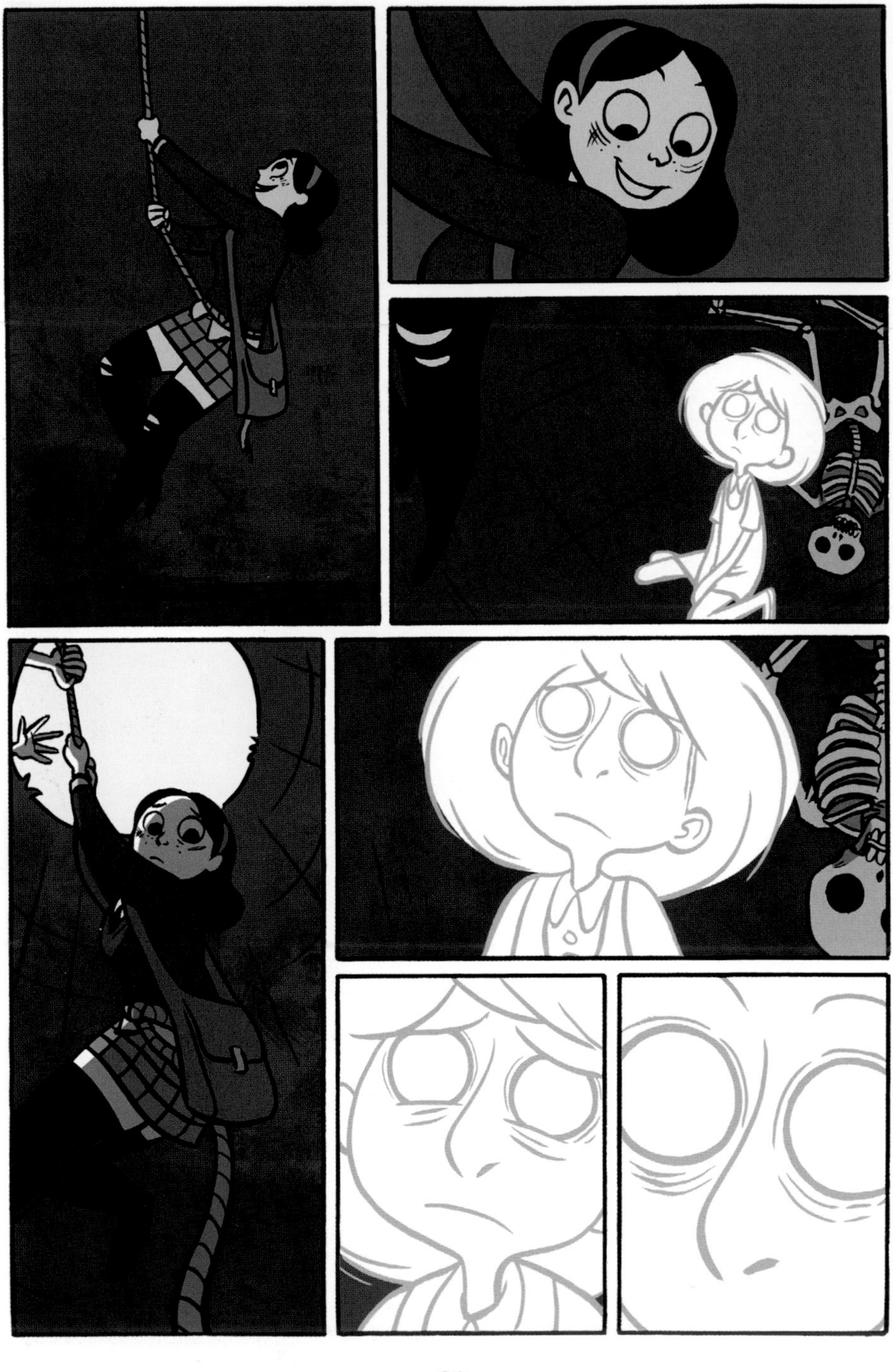

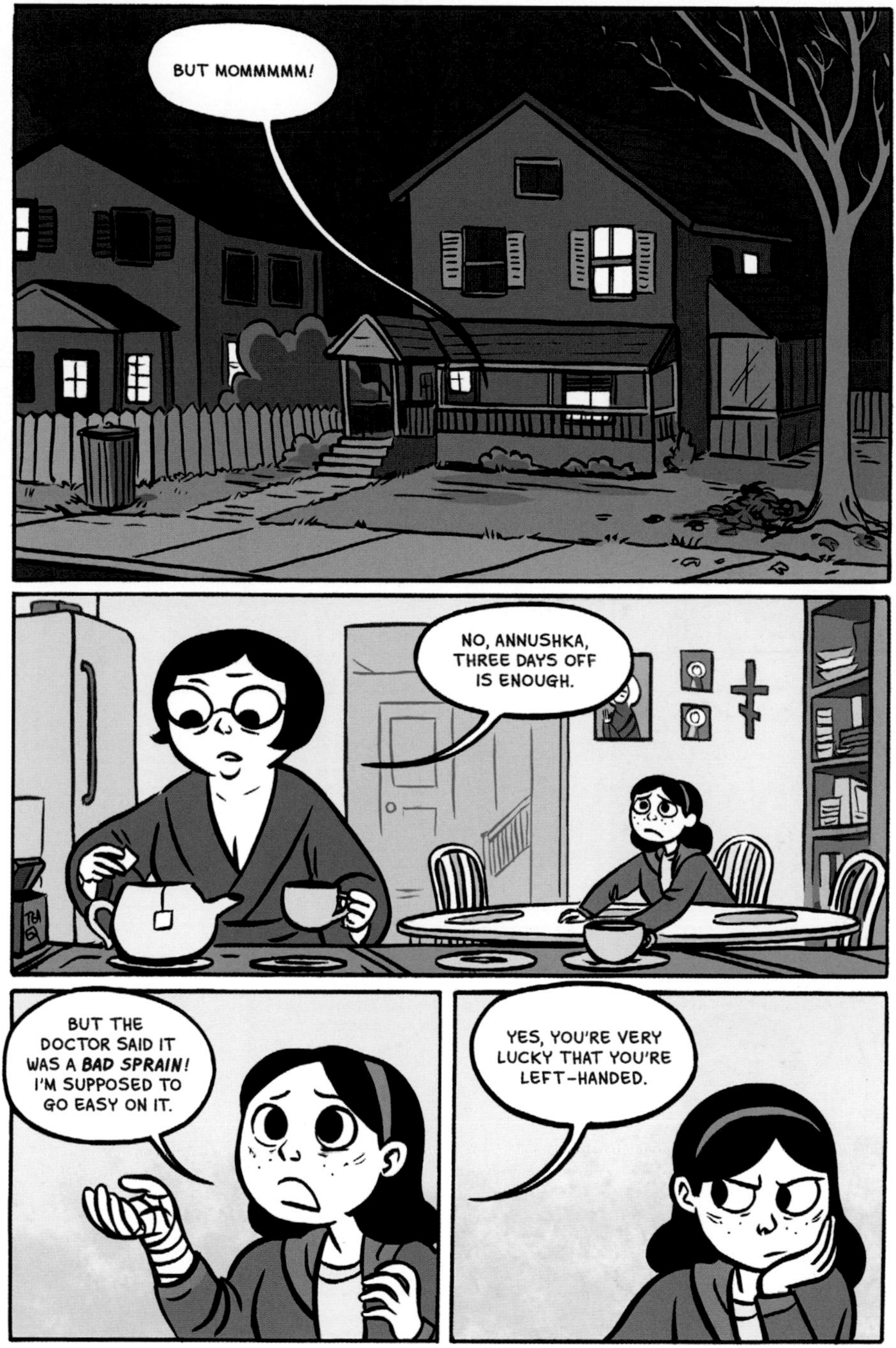
BUT MOMMMMM!
NO, ANNUSHKA, THREE DAYS OFF IS ENOUGH.
TEA
BUT THE DOCTOR SAID IT WAS A ***BAD SPRAIN***! I'M SUPPOSED TO GO EASY ON IT.
YES, YOU'RE VERY LUCKY THAT YOU'RE LEFT-HANDED.

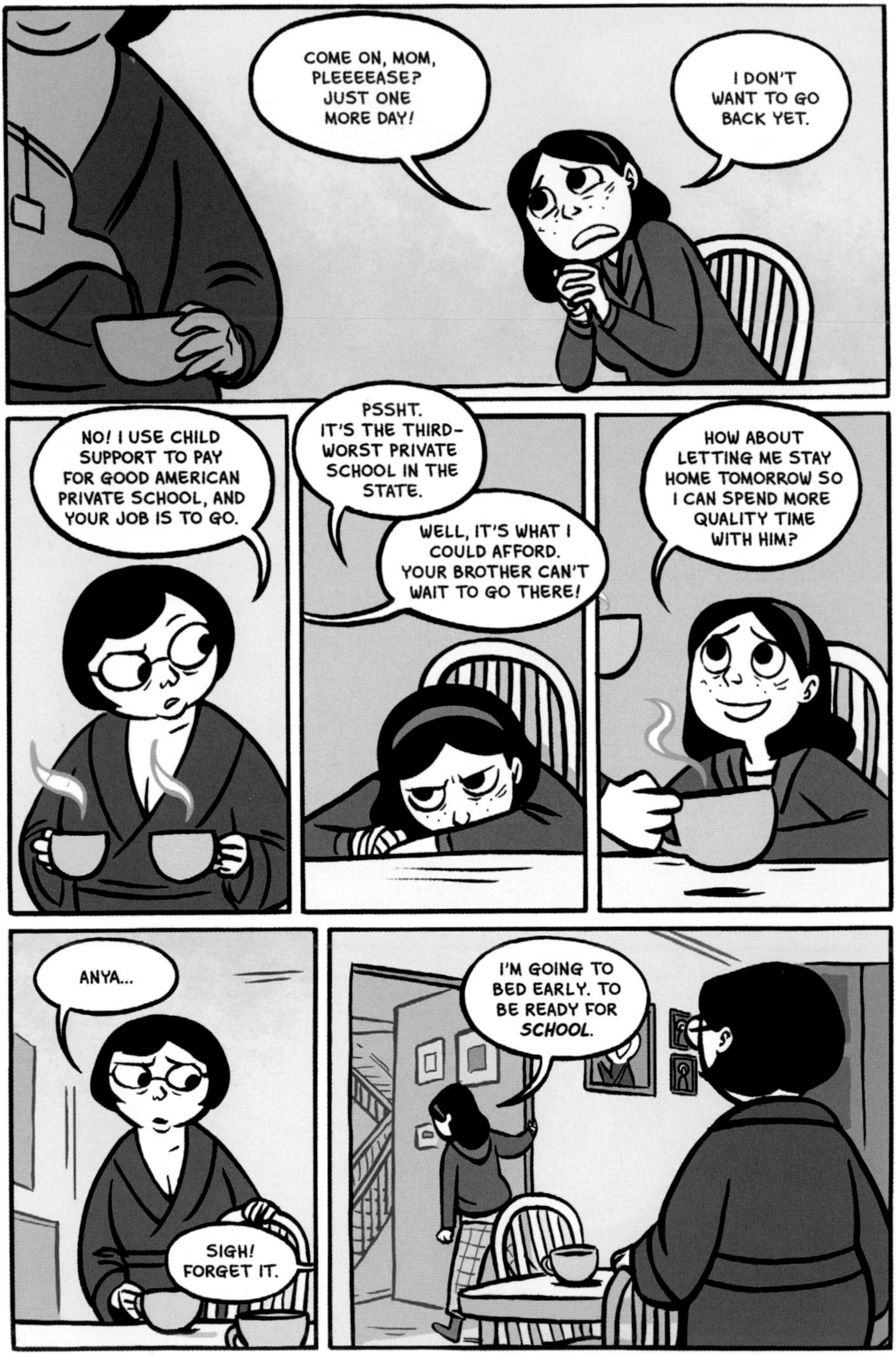
COME ON, MOM, PLEEEEASE? JUST ONE MORE DAY!
I DON'T WANT TO GO BACK YET.
NO! I USE CHILD SUPPORT TO PAY FOR GOOD AMERICAN PRIVATE SCHOOL, AND YOUR JOB IS TO GO.
PSSHT. IT'S THE THIRD-WORST PRIVATE SCHOOL IN THE STATE.
WELL, IT'S WHAT I COULD AFFORD. YOUR BROTHER CAN'T WAIT TO GO THERE!
HOW ABOUT LETTING ME STAY HOME TOMORROW SO I CAN SPEND MORE QUALITY TIME WITH HIM?
ANYA...
SIGH! FORGET IT.
I'M GOING TO BED EARLY. TO BE READY FOR *SCHOOL*.

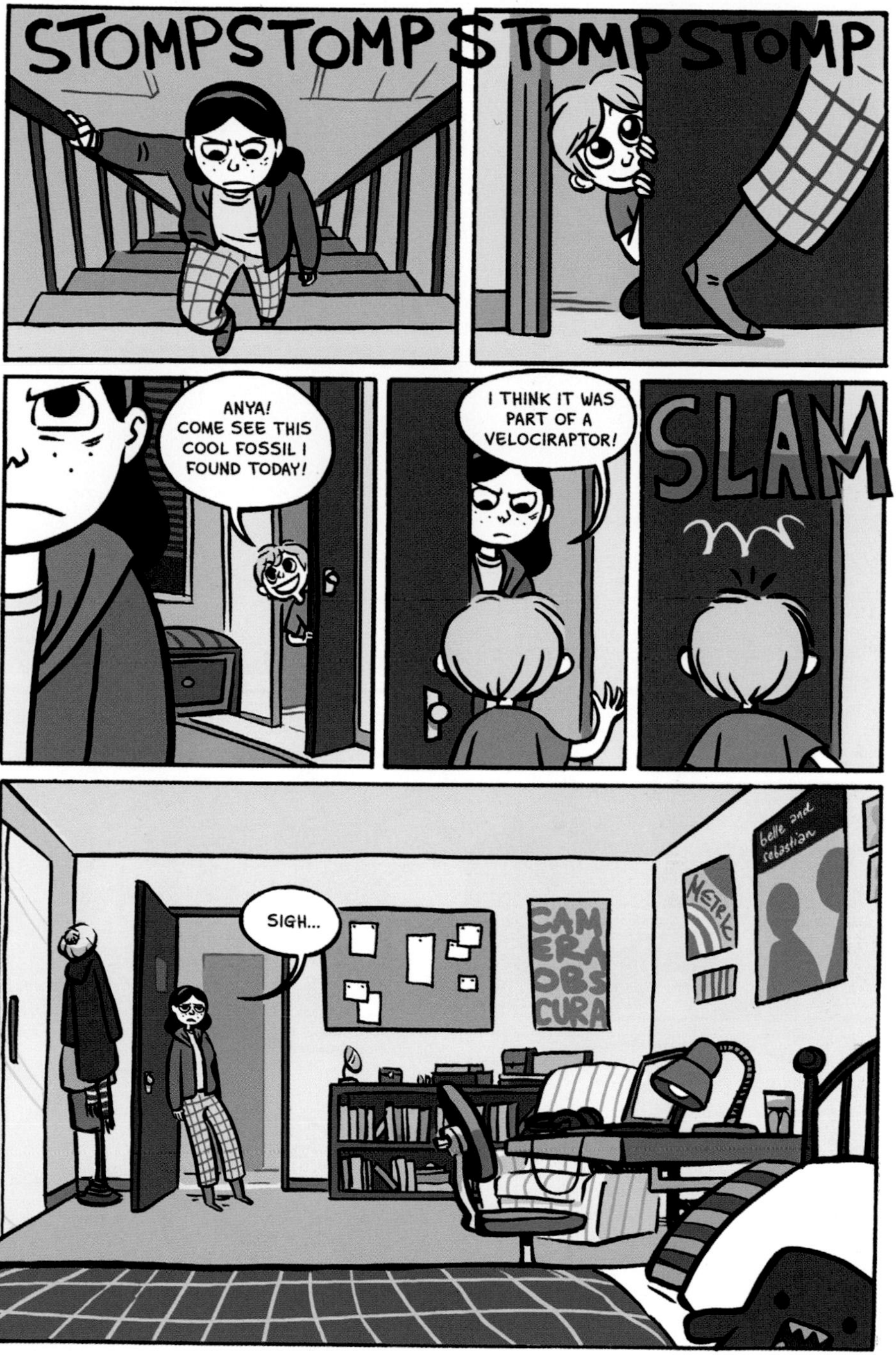
STOMPSTOMP
STOMPSTOMP
ANYA! COME SEE THIS COOL FOSSIL I FOUND TODAY!
I THINK IT WAS PART OF A VELOCIRAPTOR!
SLAM
SIGH...
CAMERA OBSCURA
METRIC
belle and sebastian

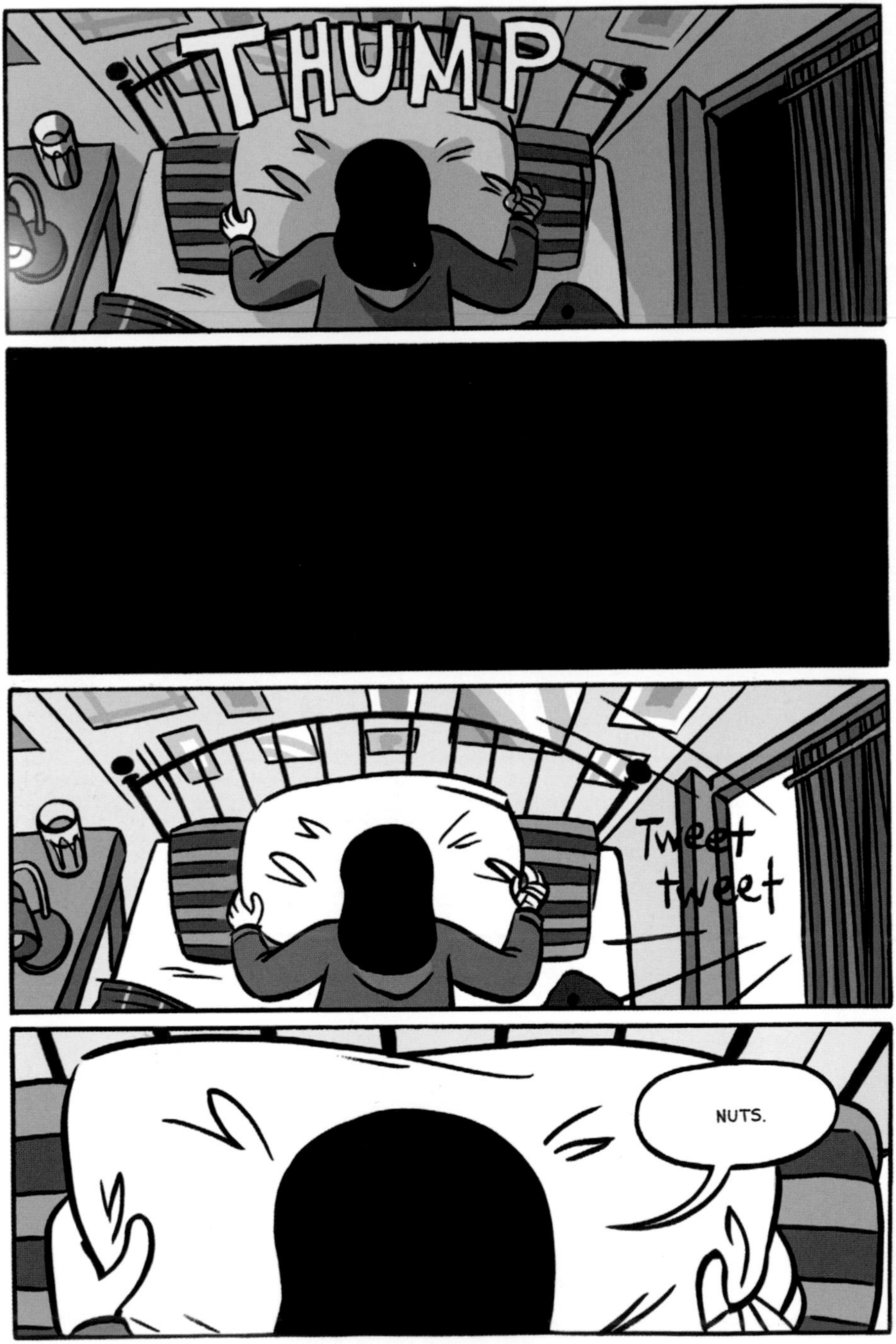
THUMP
Tweet tweet
NUTS.

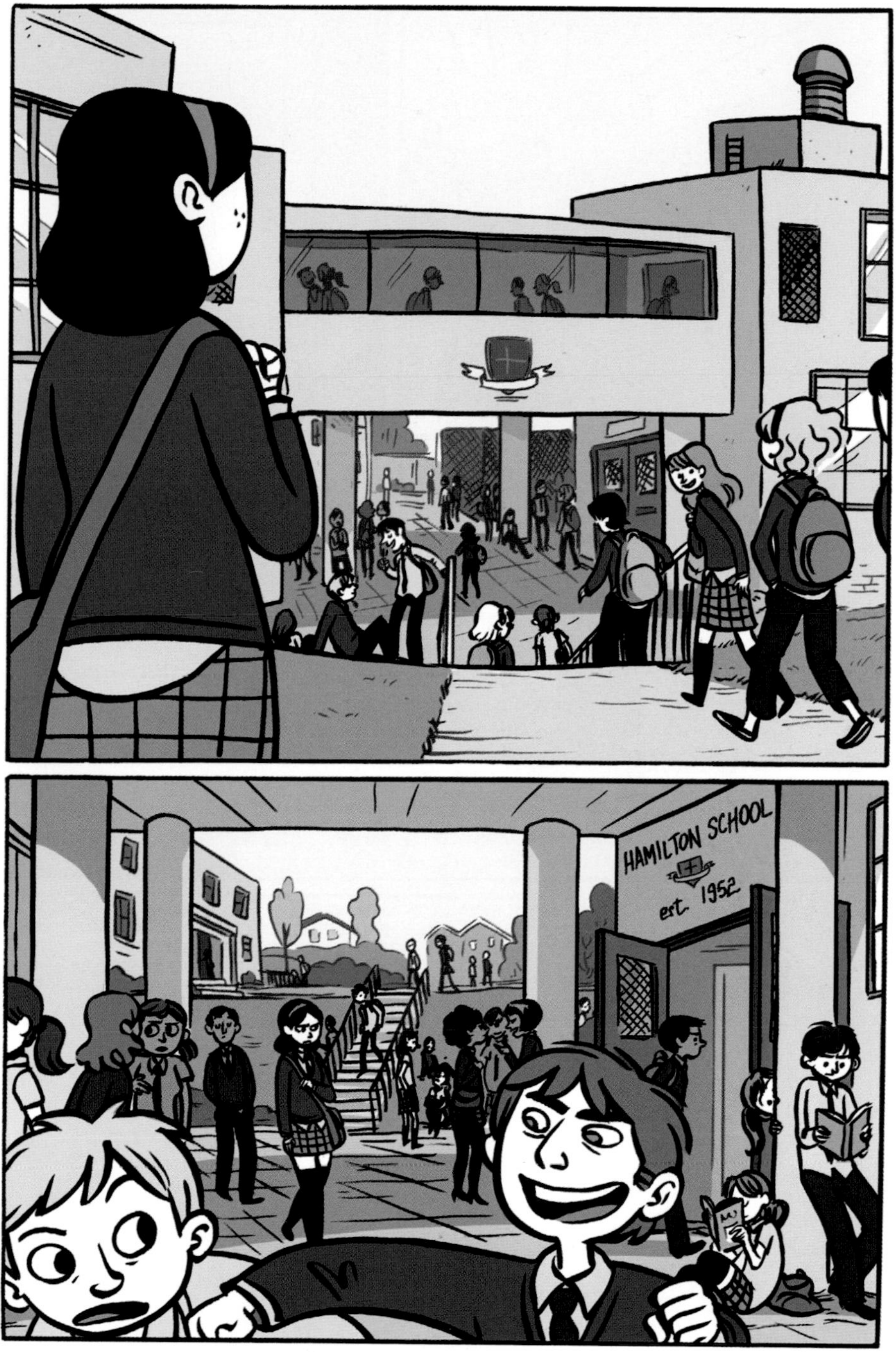
HAMILTON SCHOOL
est. 1952

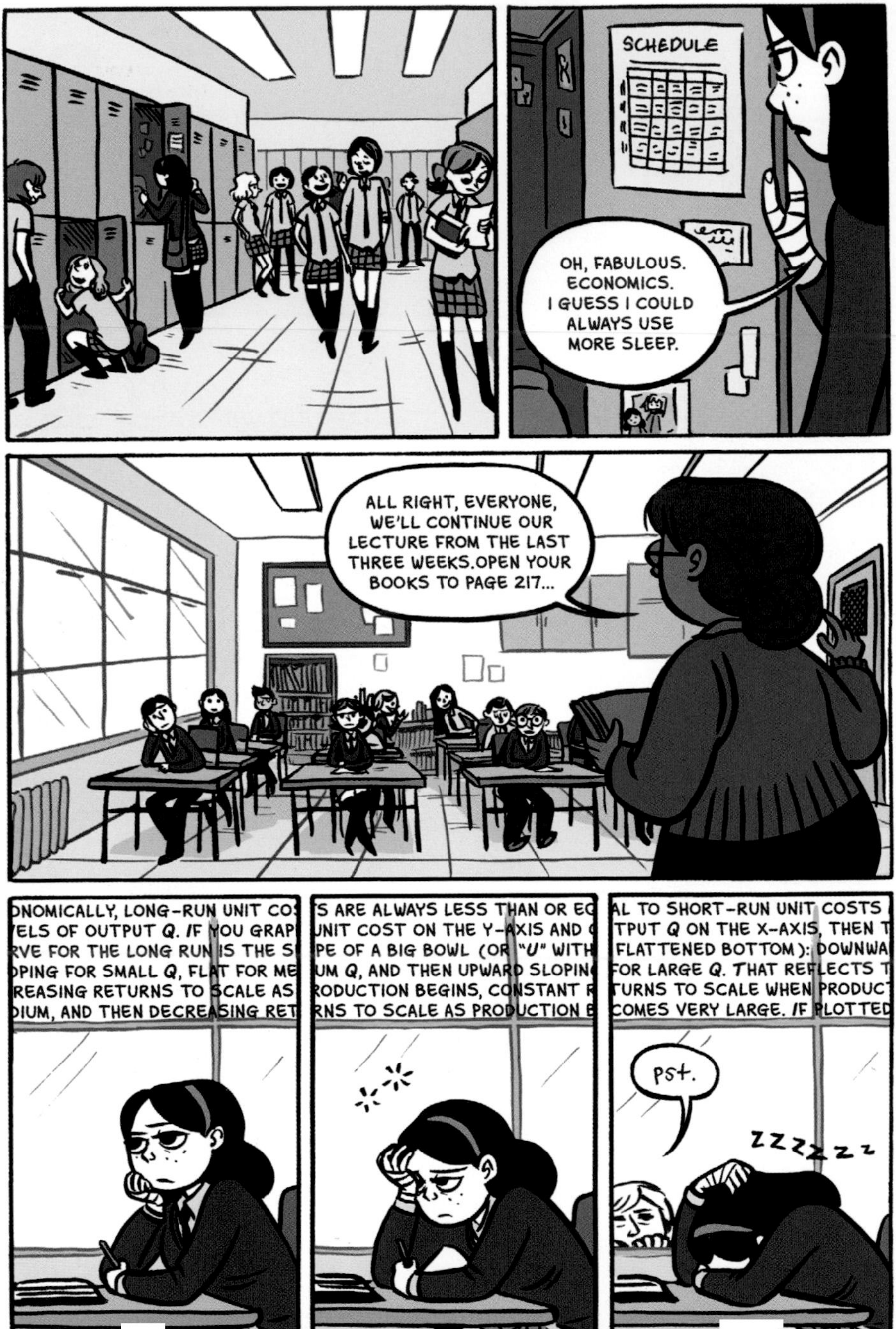
SCHEDULE
OH, FABULOUS. ECONOMICS. I GUESS I COULD ALWAYS USE MORE SLEEP.
ALL RIGHT, EVERYONE, WE'LL CONTINUE OUR LECTURE FROM THE LAST THREE WEEKS.OPEN YOUR BOOKS TO PAGE 217...
ONOMICALLY, LONG-RUN UNIT CO
VELS OF OUTPUT Q. IF YOU GRAP
RVE FOR THE LONG RUN IS THE S
OPING FOR SMALL Q, FLAT FOR ME
REASING RETURNS TO SCALE AS
DIUM, AND THEN DECREASING RET
S ARE ALWAYS LESS THAN OR EQ
UNIT COST ON THE Y-AXIS AND
PE OF A BIG BOWL (OR "U" WITH
UM Q, AND THEN UPWARD SLOPIN
RODUCTION BEGINS, CONSTANT R
RNS TO SCALE AS PRODUCTION B
AL TO SHORT-RUN UNIT COSTS
TPUT Q ON THE X-AXIS, THEN T
FLATTENED BOTTOM): DOWNWA
FOR LARGE Q. THAT REFLECTS T
TURNS TO SCALE WHEN PRODUCT
COMES VERY LARGE. IF PLOTTED
pst.
ZZZZZZ

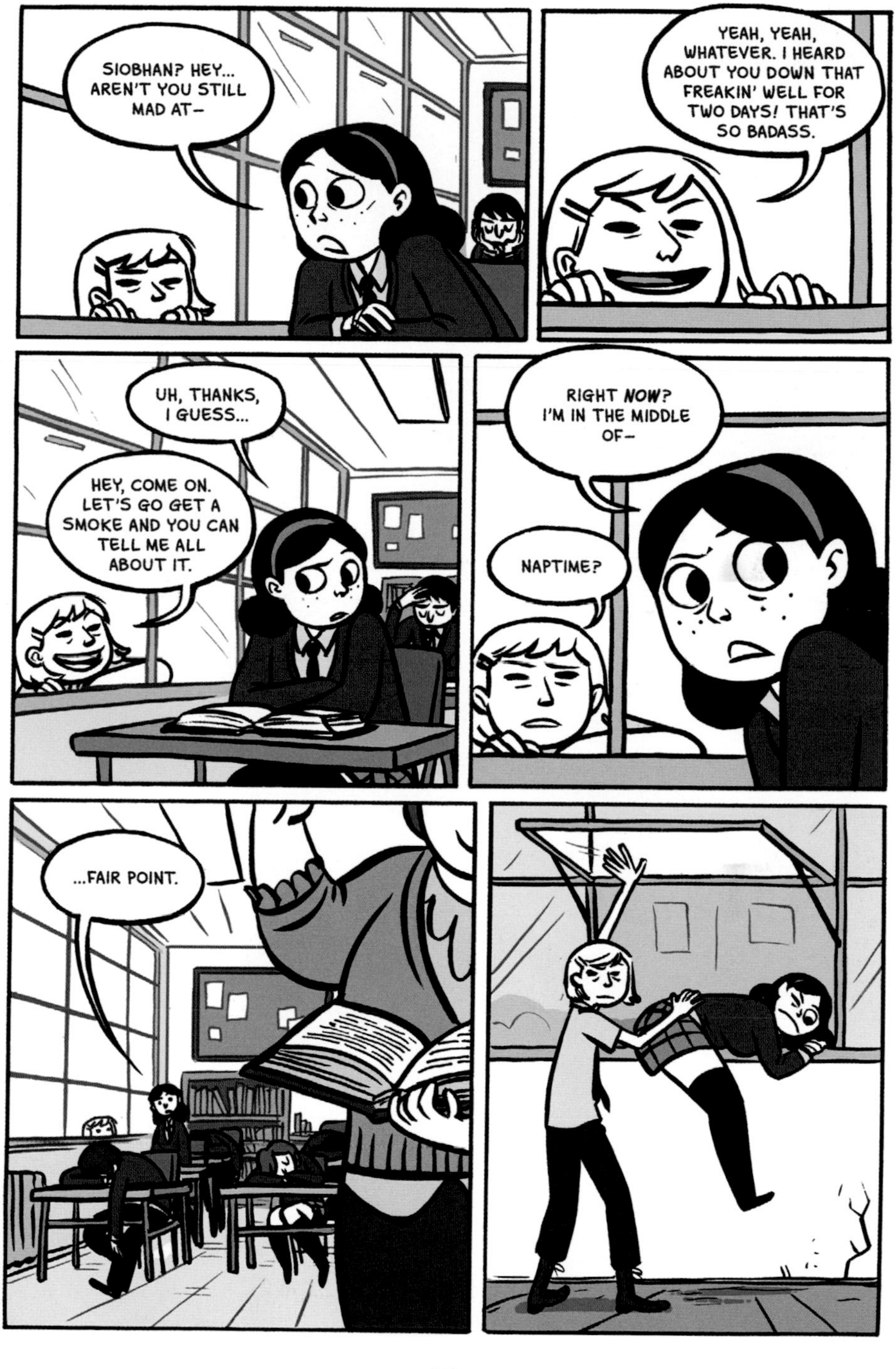
SIOBHAN? HEY... AREN'T YOU STILL MAD AT–
YEAH, YEAH, WHATEVER. I HEARD ABOUT YOU DOWN THAT FREAKIN' WELL FOR TWO DAYS! THAT'S SO BADASS.
UH, THANKS, I GUESS...
HEY, COME ON. LET'S GO GET A SMOKE AND YOU CAN TELL ME ALL ABOUT IT.
RIGHT *NOW*? I'M IN THE MIDDLE OF–
NAPTIME?
...FAIR POINT.

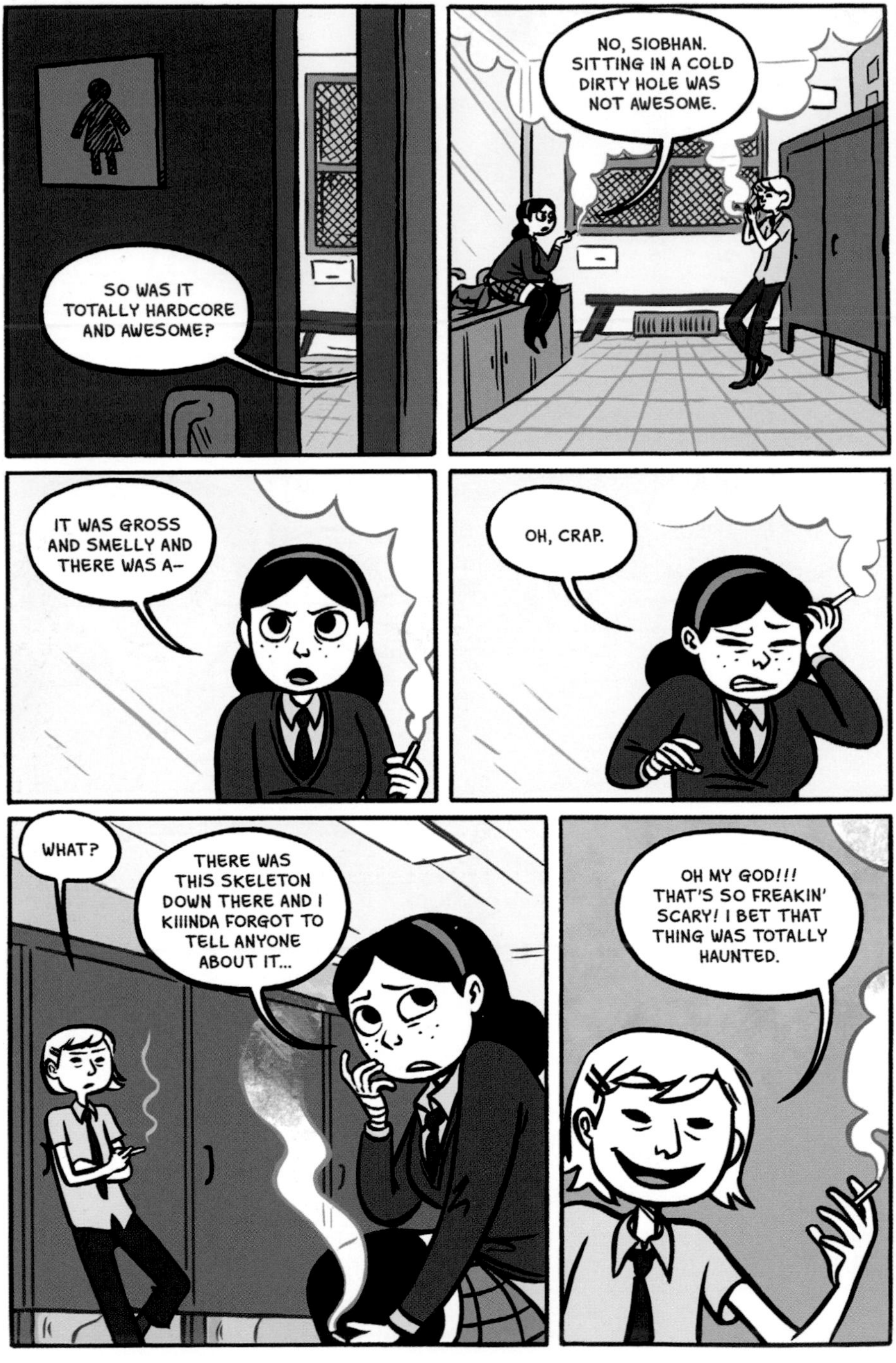
SO WAS IT TOTALLY HARDCORE AND AWESOME?
NO, SIOBHAN. SITTING IN A COLD DIRTY HOLE WAS NOT AWESOME.
IT WAS GROSS AND SMELLY AND THERE WAS A--
OH, CRAP.
WHAT?
THERE WAS THIS SKELETON DOWN THERE AND I KIIINDA FORGOT TO TELL ANYONE ABOUT IT...
OH MY GOD!!! THAT'S SO FREAKIN' SCARY! I BET THAT THING WAS TOTALLY HAUNTED.

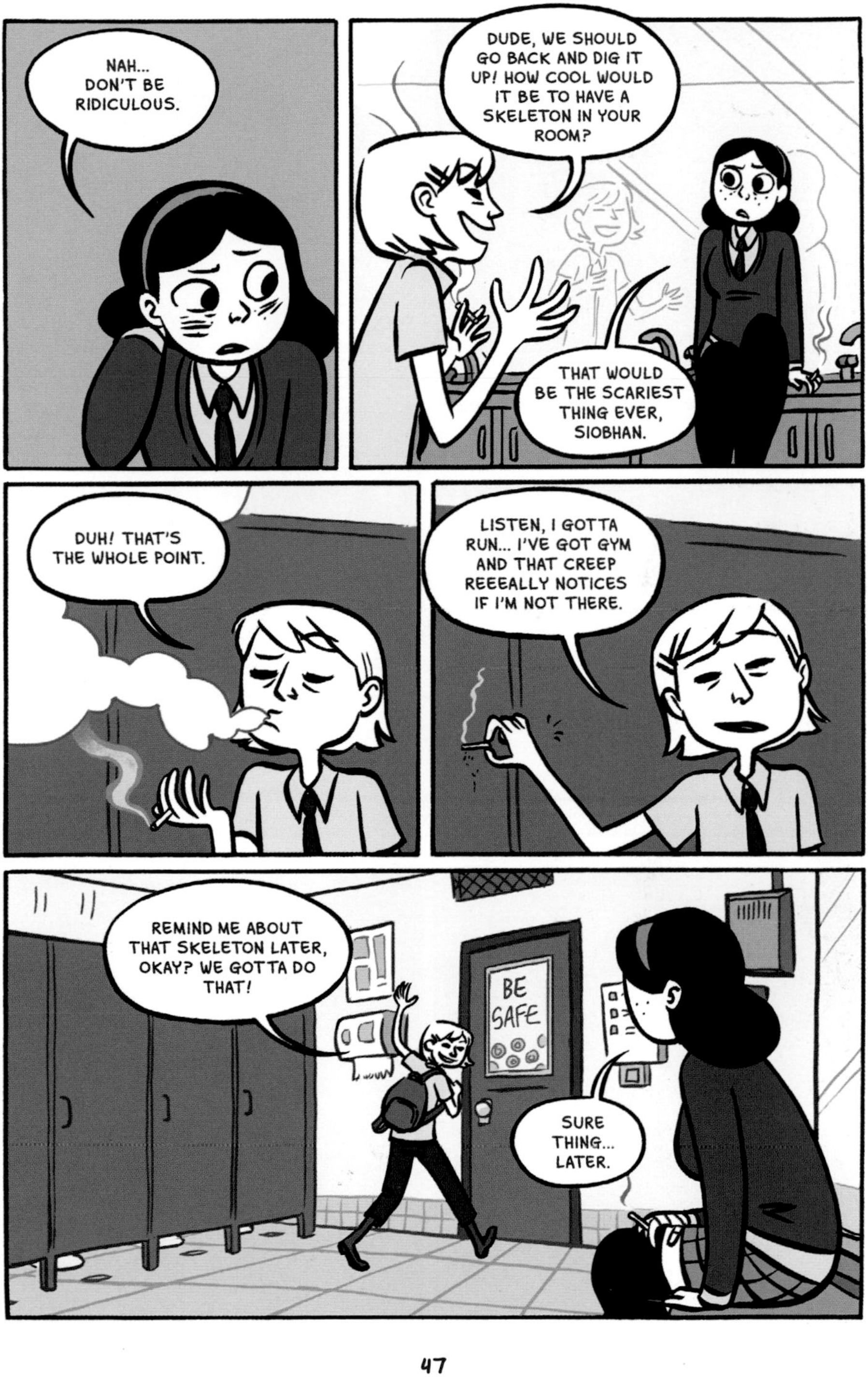
NAH... DON'T BE RIDICULOUS.
DUDE, WE SHOULD GO BACK AND DIG IT UP! HOW COOL WOULD IT BE TO HAVE A SKELETON IN YOUR ROOM?
THAT WOULD BE THE SCARIEST THING EVER, SIOBHAN.
DUH! THAT'S THE WHOLE POINT.
LISTEN, I GOTTA RUN... I'VE GOT GYM AND THAT CREEP REEEALLY NOTICES IF I'M NOT THERE.
REMIND ME ABOUT THAT SKELETON LATER, OKAY? WE GOTTA DO THAT!
BE SAFE
SURE THING... LATER.

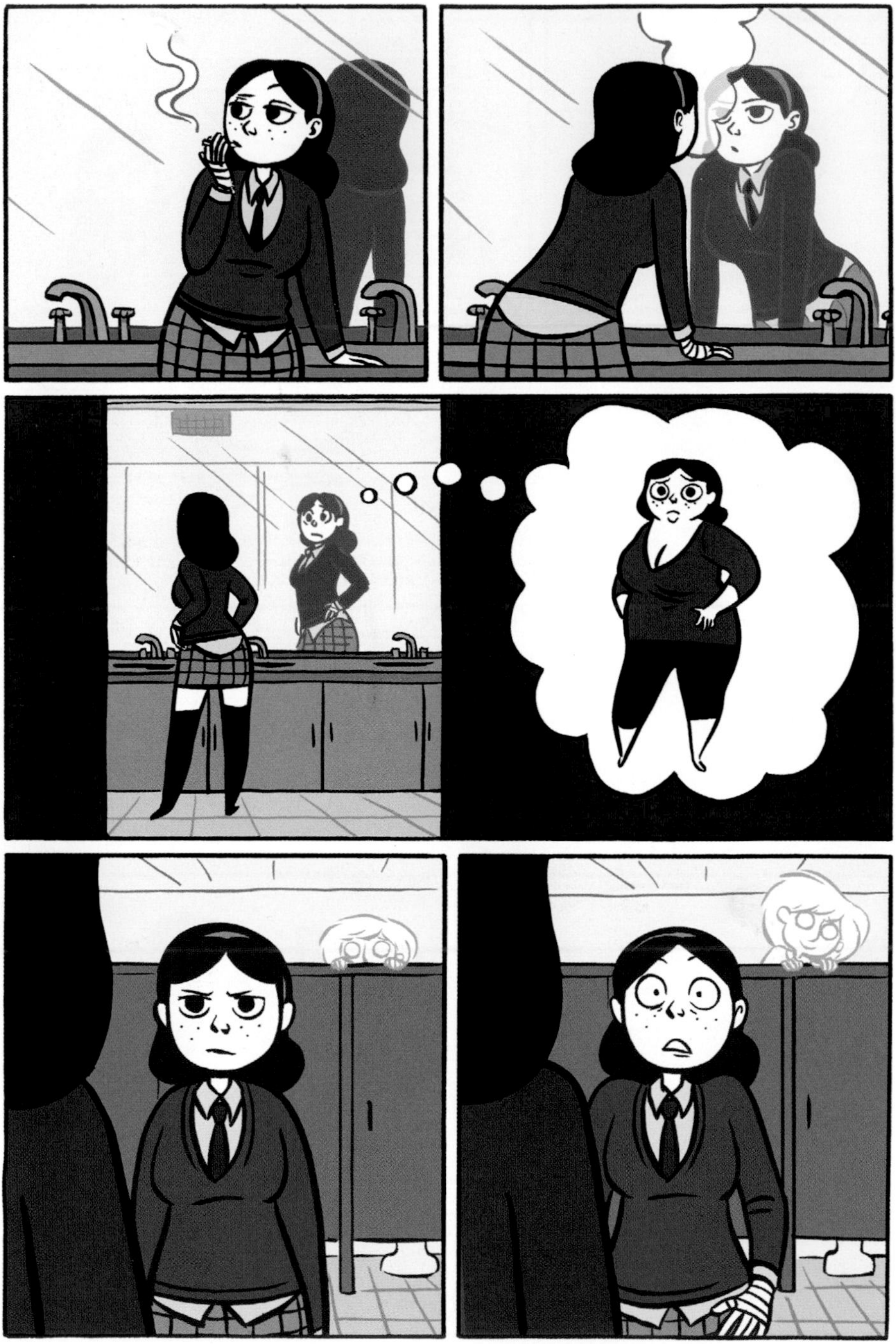

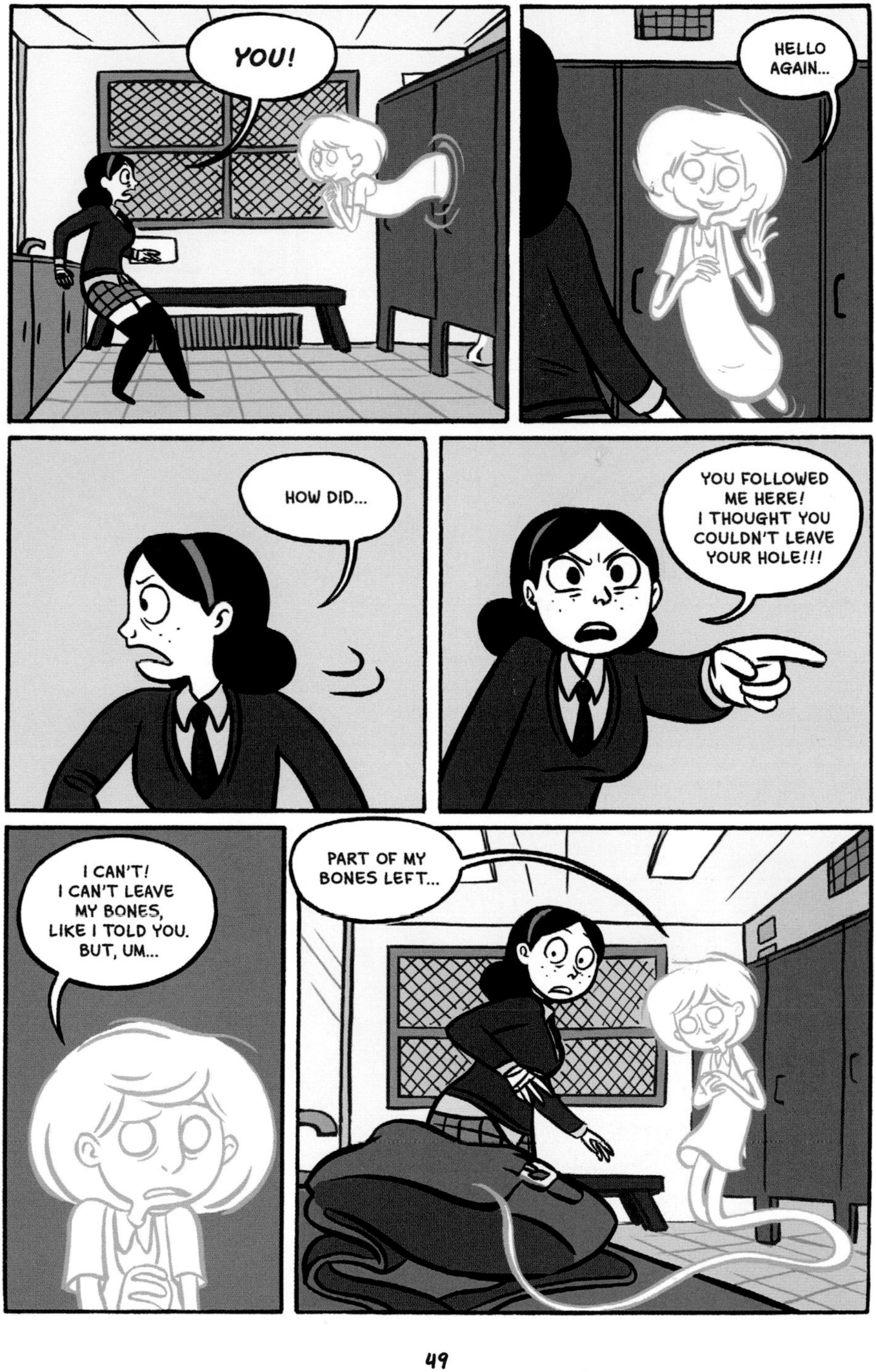
YOU!
HELLO AGAIN...
HOW DID...
YOU FOLLOWED ME HERE! I THOUGHT YOU COULDN'T LEAVE YOUR HOLE!!!
I CAN'T! I CAN'T LEAVE MY BONES, LIKE I TOLD YOU. BUT, UM...
PART OF MY BONES LEFT...

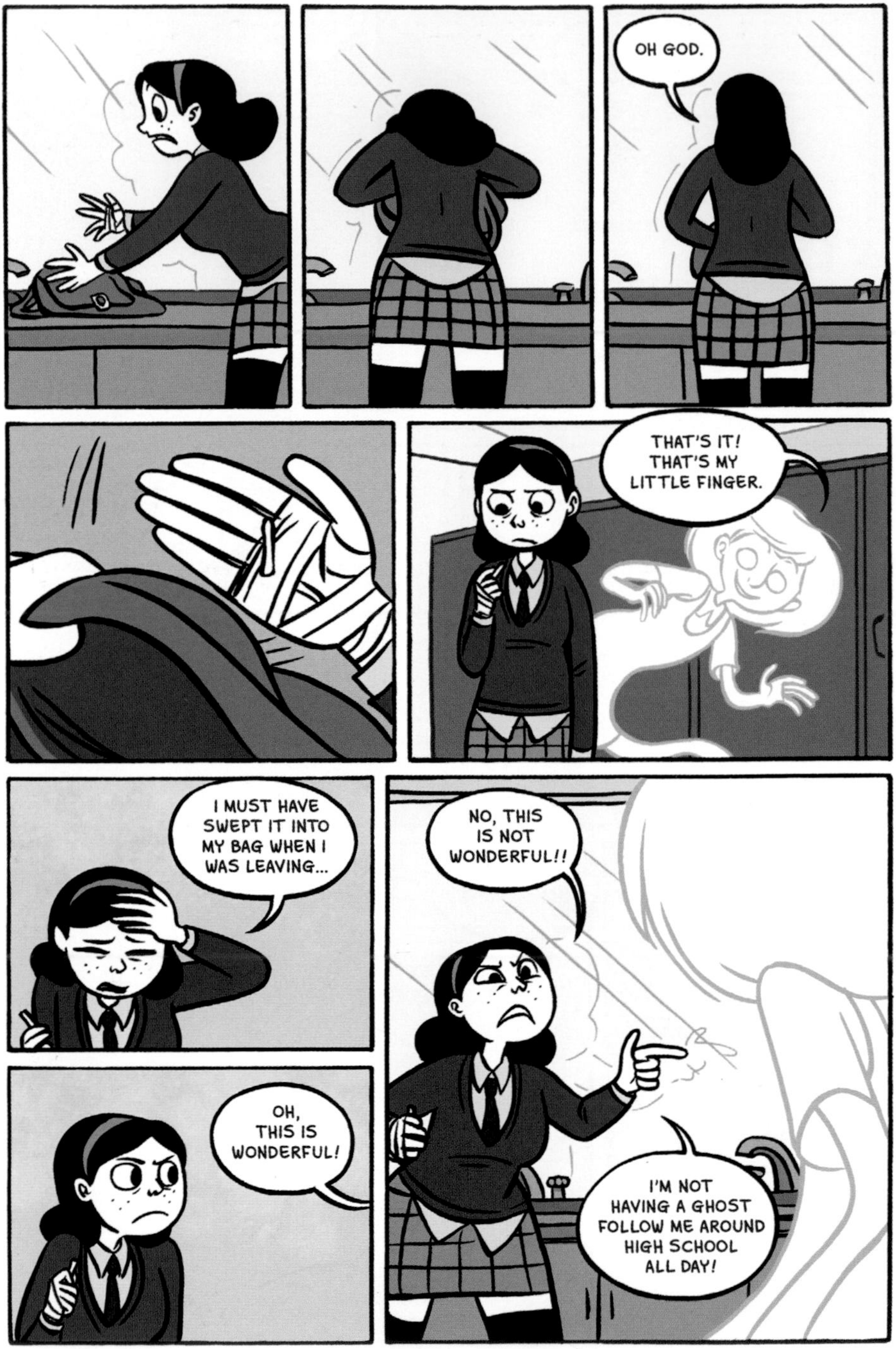
OH GOD.
THAT'S IT! THAT'S MY LITTLE FINGER.
I MUST HAVE SWEPT IT INTO MY BAG WHEN I WAS LEAVING...
OH, THIS IS WONDERFUL!
NO, THIS IS NOT WONDERFUL!!
I'M NOT HAVING A GHOST FOLLOW ME AROUND HIGH SCHOOL ALL DAY!

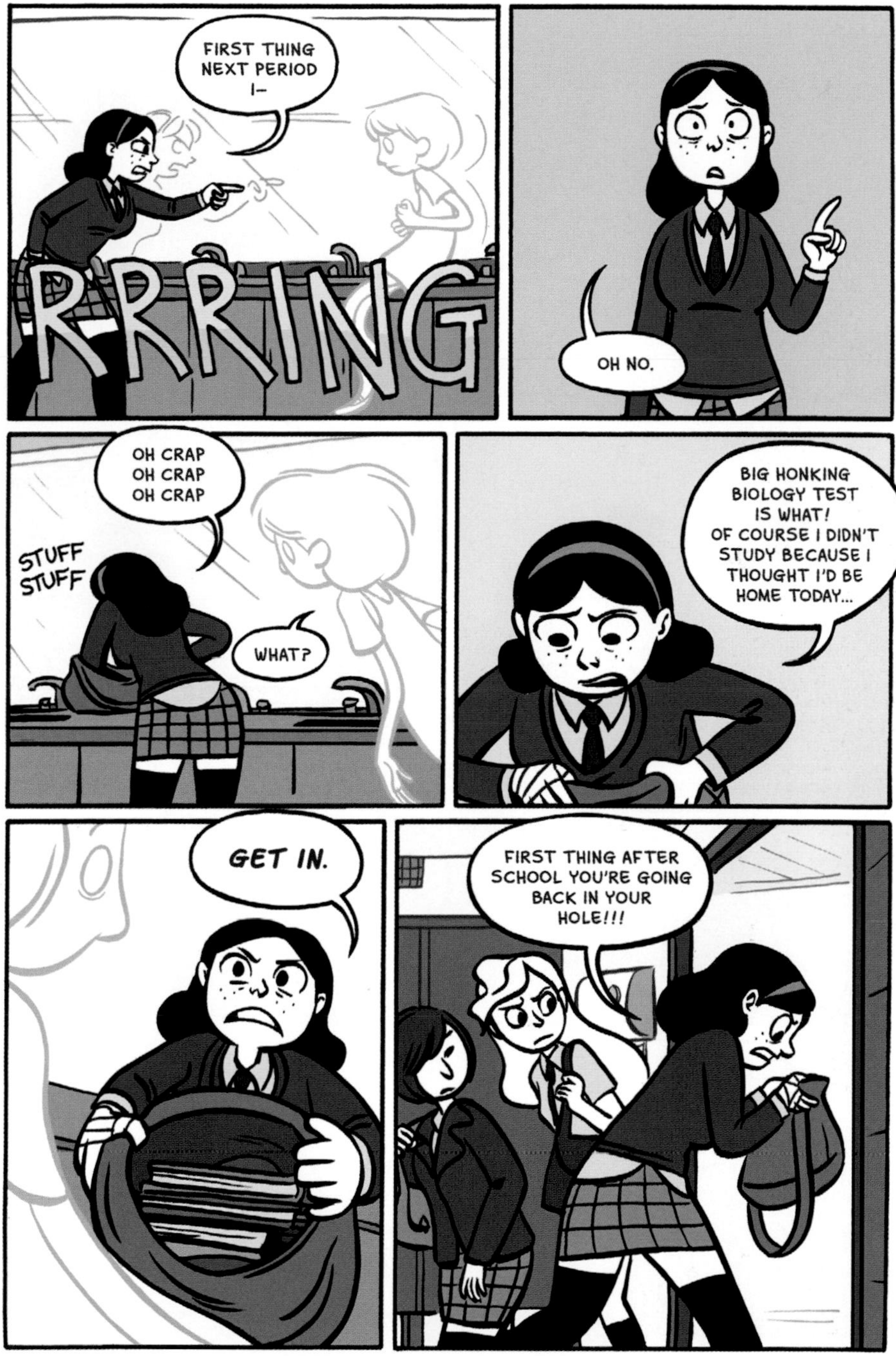
FIRST THING NEXT PERIOD I–
RRRING
OH NO.
OH CRAP OH CRAP OH CRAP
STUFF STUFF
WHAT?
BIG HONKING BIOLOGY TEST IS WHAT! OF COURSE I DIDN'T STUDY BECAUSE I THOUGHT I'D BE HOME TODAY...
GET IN.
FIRST THING AFTER SCHOOL YOU'RE GOING BACK IN YOUR HOLE!!!

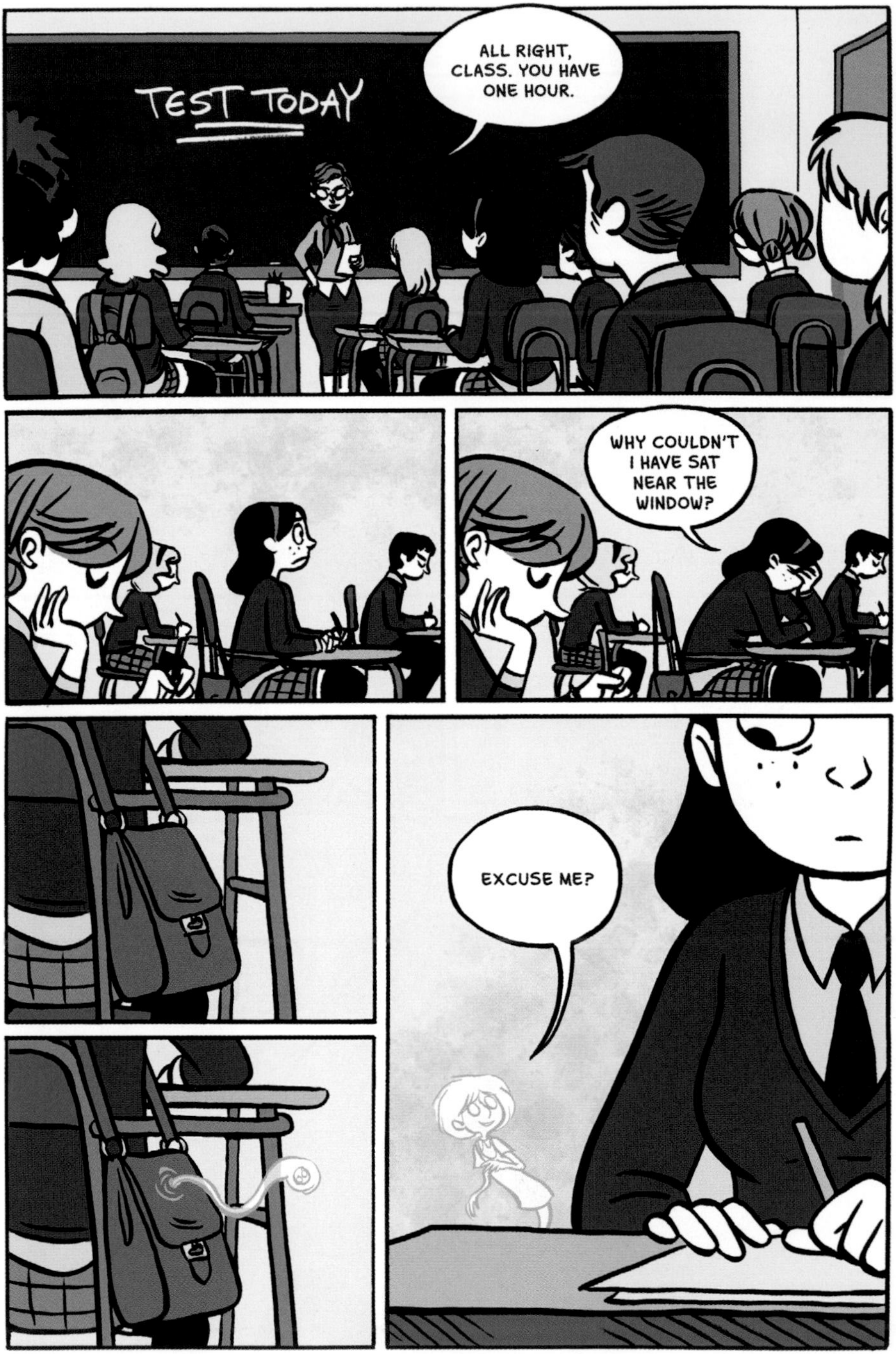
TEST TODAY
ALL RIGHT, CLASS. YOU HAVE ONE HOUR.
WHY COULDN'T I HAVE SAT NEAR THE WINDOW?
EXCUSE ME?

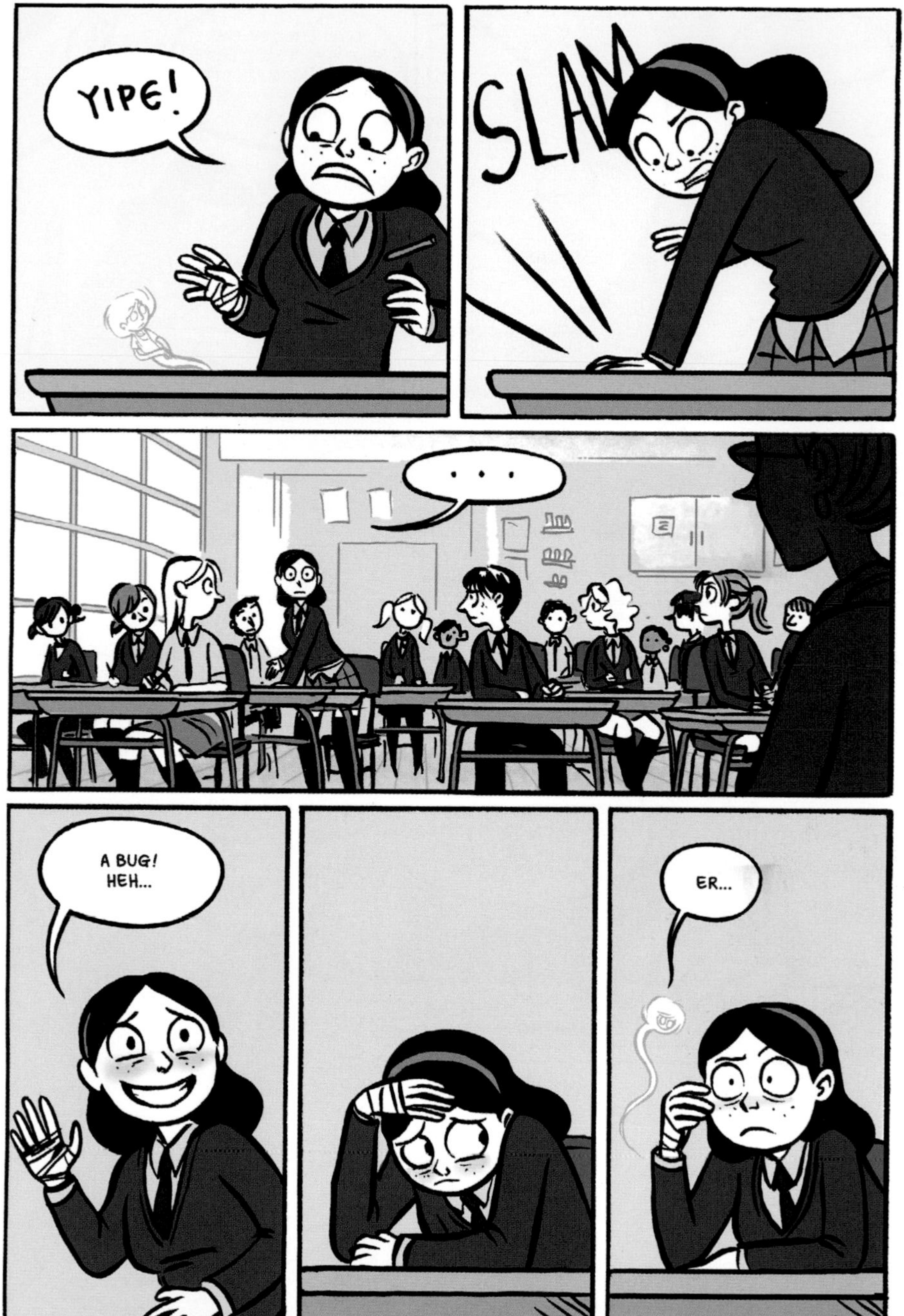
YIPE!
SLAM
...
A BUG! HEH...
ER...

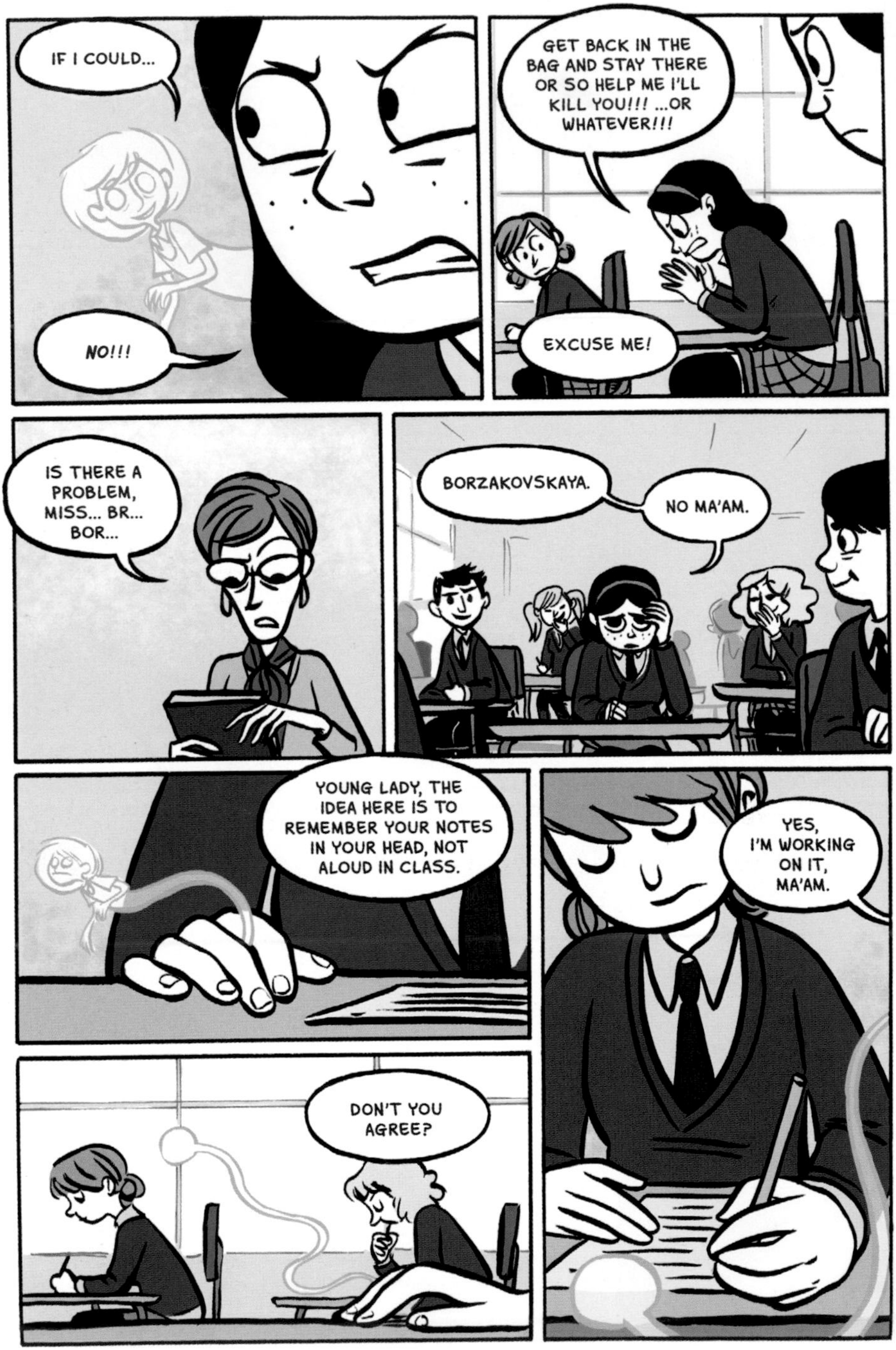
IF I COULD...
NO!!!
GET BACK IN THE BAG AND STAY THERE OR SO HELP ME I'LL KILL YOU!!! ...OR WHATEVER!!!
EXCUSE ME!
IS THERE A PROBLEM, MISS... BR... BOR...
BORZAKOVSKAYA.
NO MA'AM.
YOUNG LADY, THE IDEA HERE IS TO REMEMBER YOUR NOTES IN YOUR HEAD, NOT ALOUD IN CLASS.
YES, I'M WORKING ON IT, MA'AM.
DON'T YOU AGREE?

I'M DEAD.

C.

WHAT?

THAT'S THE ANSWER TO THE FIRST QUESTION. I HOPE YOU DON'T MIND, BUT I CHECKED WHAT SOME OF THE OTHER STUDENTS MARKED.

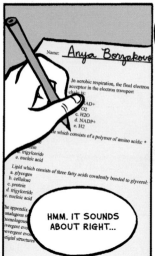

Name: Anya Boryakova

In aerobic respiration, the final electron acceptor in the electron transport chain is:
a. NAD+
b. CO2
c. H2O
d. NADP+
e. H2

...e which consists of a polymer of amino acids: *
...tein
d. triglyceride
e. nucleic acid

Lipid which consists of three fatty acids covalently bonded to glycerol:
a. glycogen
b. cellulose
c. protein
d. triglyceride
e. nucleic acid

...e appendix
analagous s...
homologous...
...vergent evo...
...vergent evo...
...digial structures

HMM. IT SOUNDS ABOUT RIGHT...

I CAN HELP YOU WITH THE REST OF IT IF YOU LIKE...

UH, SURE! OKAY!

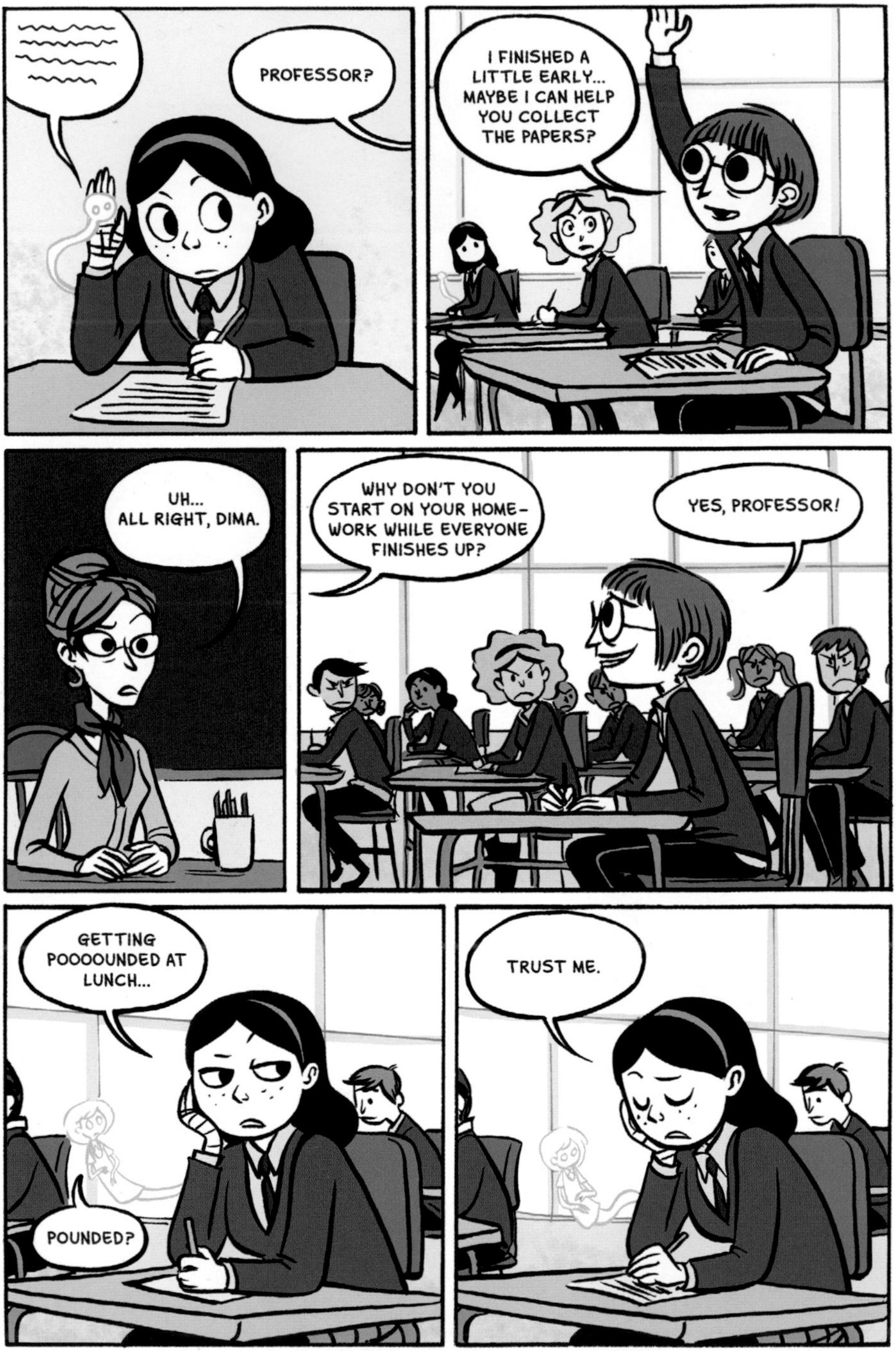
PROFESSOR?
I FINISHED A LITTLE EARLY... MAYBE I CAN HELP YOU COLLECT THE PAPERS?
UH... ALL RIGHT, DIMA.
WHY DON'T YOU START ON YOUR HOME-WORK WHILE EVERYONE FINISHES UP?
YES, PROFESSOR!
GETTING POOOOUNDED AT LUNCH...
POUNDED?
TRUST ME.

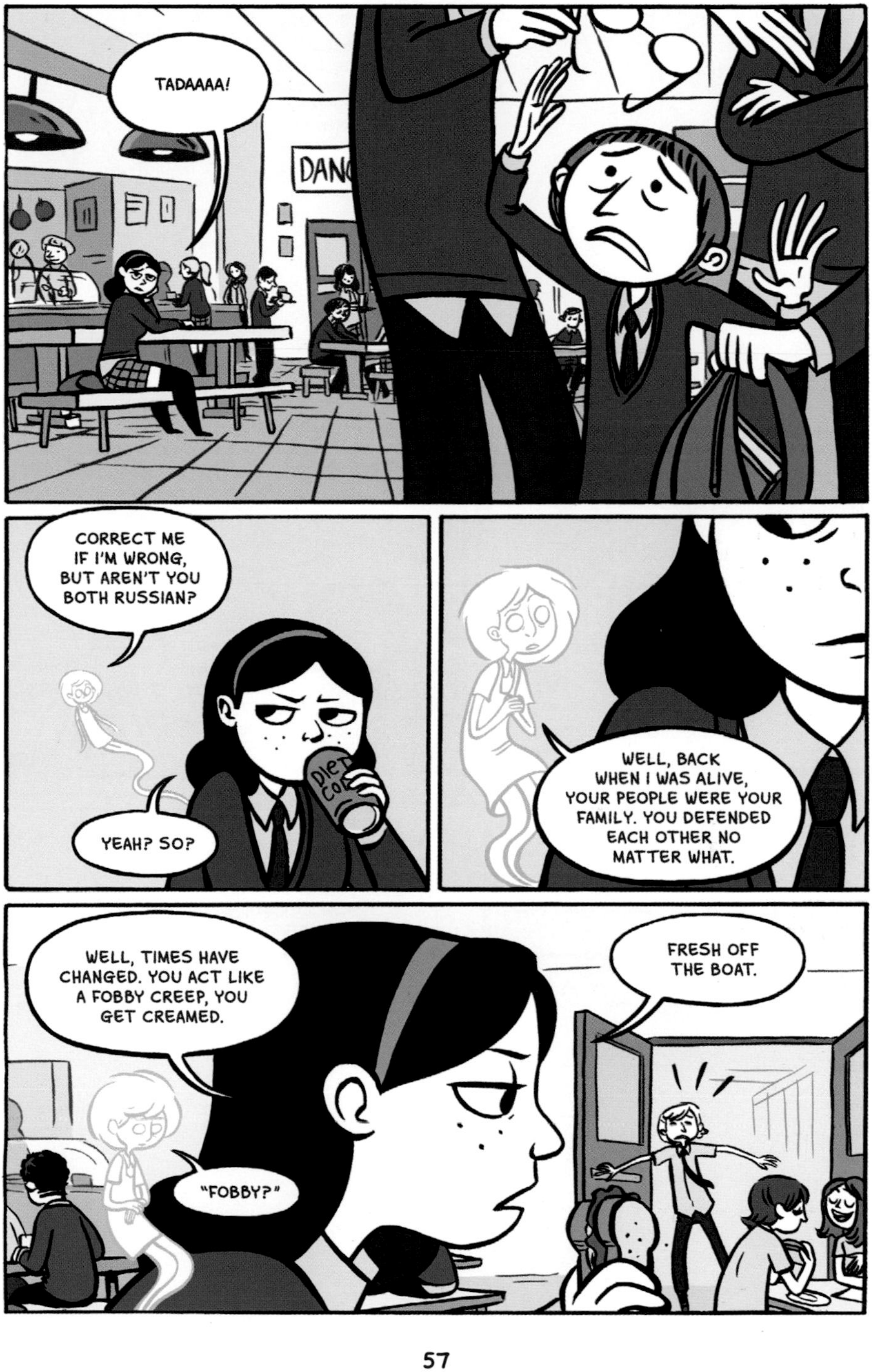
TADAAAA!
DANG
CORRECT ME IF I'M WRONG, BUT AREN'T YOU BOTH RUSSIAN?
YEAH? SO?
DIET COKE
WELL, BACK WHEN I WAS ALIVE, YOUR PEOPLE WERE YOUR FAMILY. YOU DEFENDED EACH OTHER NO MATTER WHAT.
WELL, TIMES HAVE CHANGED. YOU ACT LIKE A FOBBY CREEP, YOU GET CREAMED.
"FOBBY?"
FRESH OFF THE BOAT.

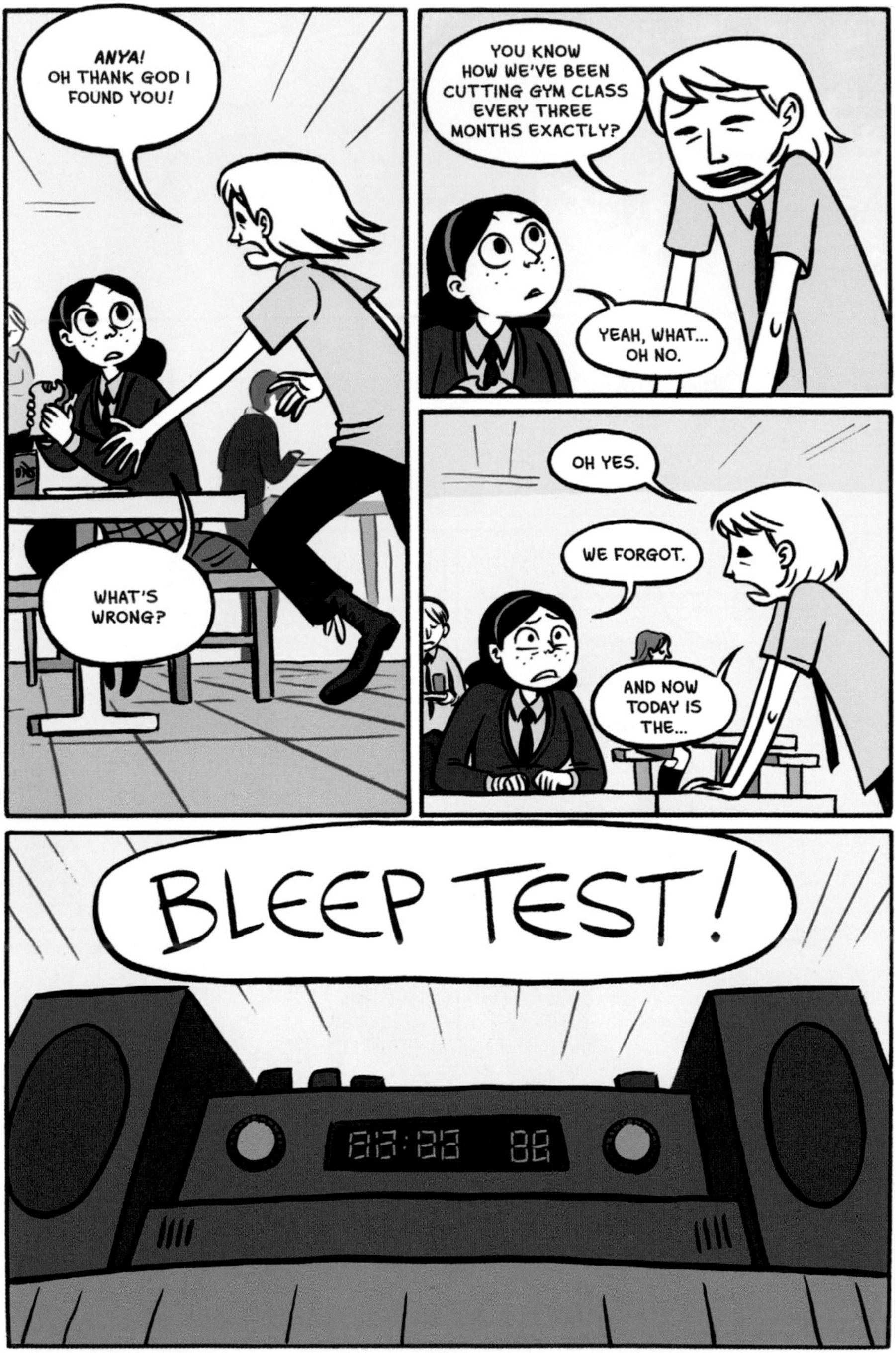
ANYA! OH THANK GOD I FOUND YOU!
WHAT'S WRONG?
YOU KNOW HOW WE'VE BEEN CUTTING GYM CLASS EVERY THREE MONTHS EXACTLY?
YEAH, WHAT... OH NO.
OH YES.
WE FORGOT.
AND NOW TODAY IS THE...
BLEEP TEST!

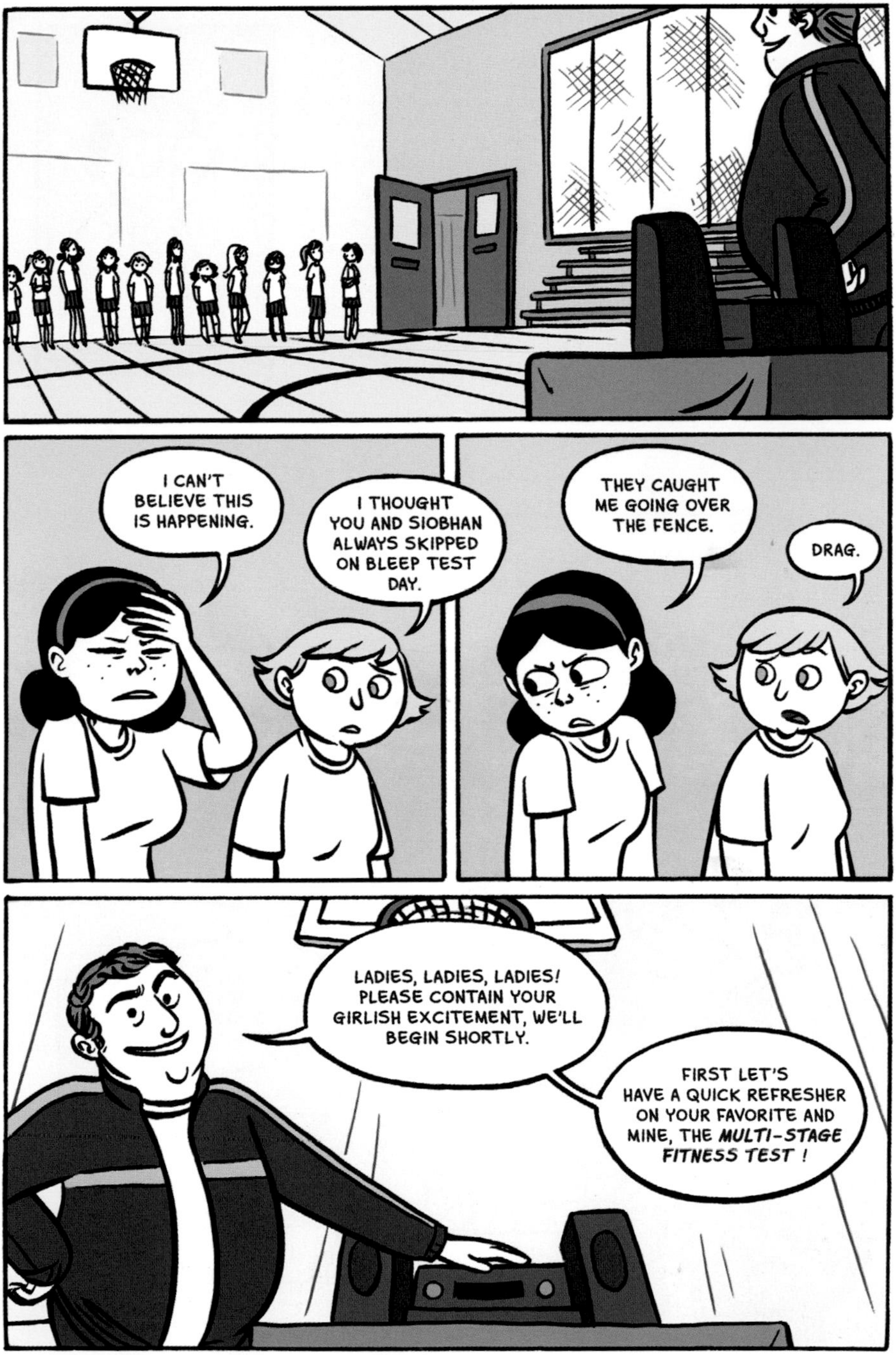
I CAN'T BELIEVE THIS IS HAPPENING.
I THOUGHT YOU AND SIOBHAN ALWAYS SKIPPED ON BLEEP TEST DAY.
THEY CAUGHT ME GOING OVER THE FENCE.
DRAG.
LADIES, LADIES, LADIES! PLEASE CONTAIN YOUR GIRLISH EXCITEMENT, WE'LL BEGIN SHORTLY.
FIRST LET'S HAVE A QUICK REFRESHER ON YOUR FAVORITE AND MINE, THE *MULTI-STAGE FITNESS TEST* !

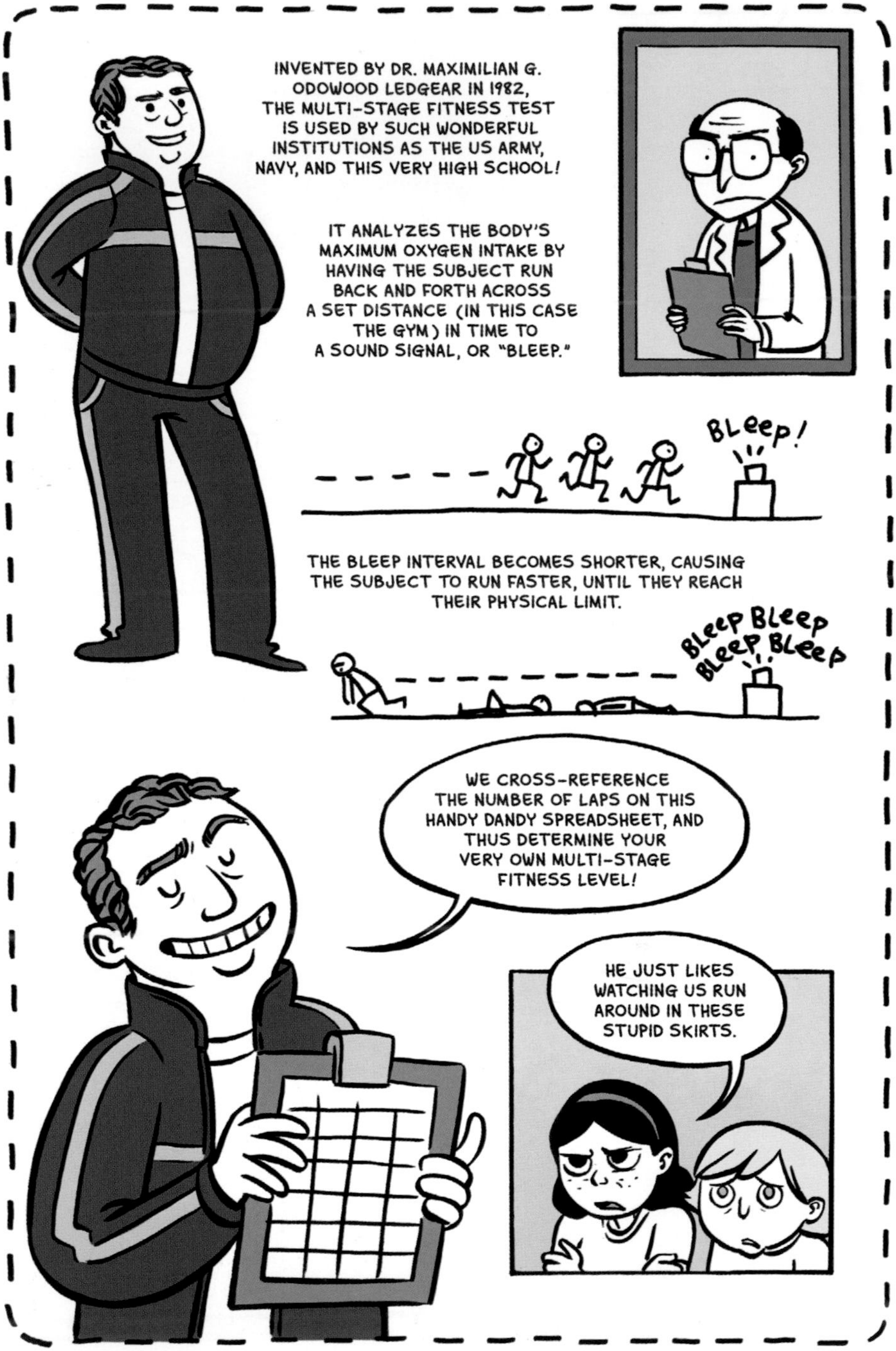
INVENTED BY DR. MAXIMILIAN G. ODOWOOD LEDGEAR IN 1982, THE MULTI-STAGE FITNESS TEST IS USED BY SUCH WONDERFUL INSTITUTIONS AS THE US ARMY, NAVY, AND THIS VERY HIGH SCHOOL!
IT ANALYZES THE BODY'S MAXIMUM OXYGEN INTAKE BY HAVING THE SUBJECT RUN BACK AND FORTH ACROSS A SET DISTANCE (IN THIS CASE THE GYM) IN TIME TO A SOUND SIGNAL, OR "BLEEP."
BLeep!
THE BLEEP INTERVAL BECOMES SHORTER, CAUSING THE SUBJECT TO RUN FASTER, UNTIL THEY REACH THEIR PHYSICAL LIMIT.
Bleep Bleep Bleep Bleep
WE CROSS-REFERENCE THE NUMBER OF LAPS ON THIS HANDY DANDY SPREADSHEET, AND THUS DETERMINE YOUR VERY OWN MULTI-STAGE FITNESS LEVEL!
HE JUST LIKES WATCHING US RUN AROUND IN THESE STUPID SKIRTS.

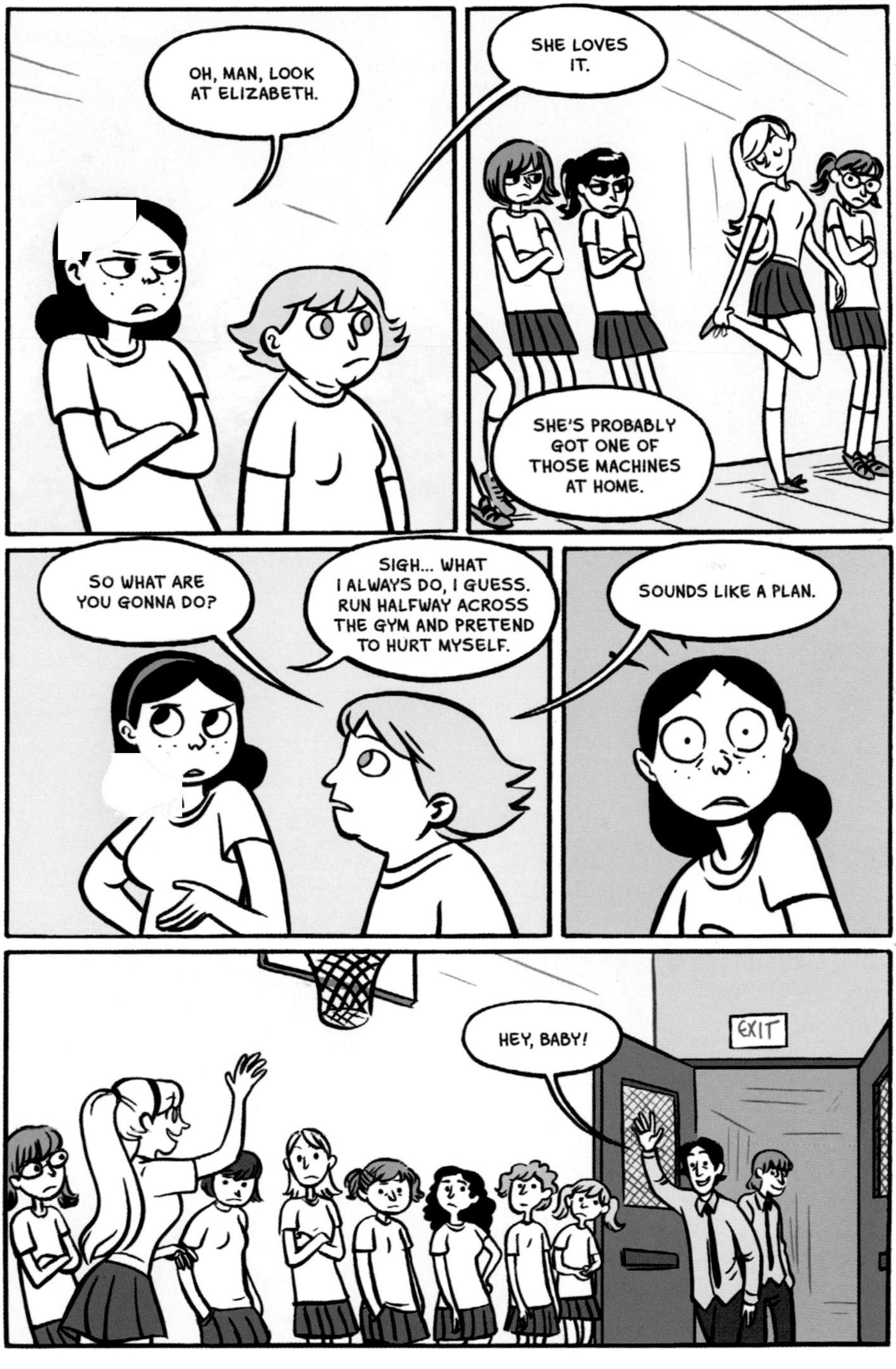
OH, MAN, LOOK AT ELIZABETH.
SHE LOVES IT.
SHE'S PROBABLY GOT ONE OF THOSE MACHINES AT HOME.
SO WHAT ARE YOU GONNA DO?
SIGH... WHAT I ALWAYS DO, I GUESS. RUN HALFWAY ACROSS THE GYM AND PRETEND TO HURT MYSELF.
SOUNDS LIKE A PLAN.
HEY, BABY!
EXIT

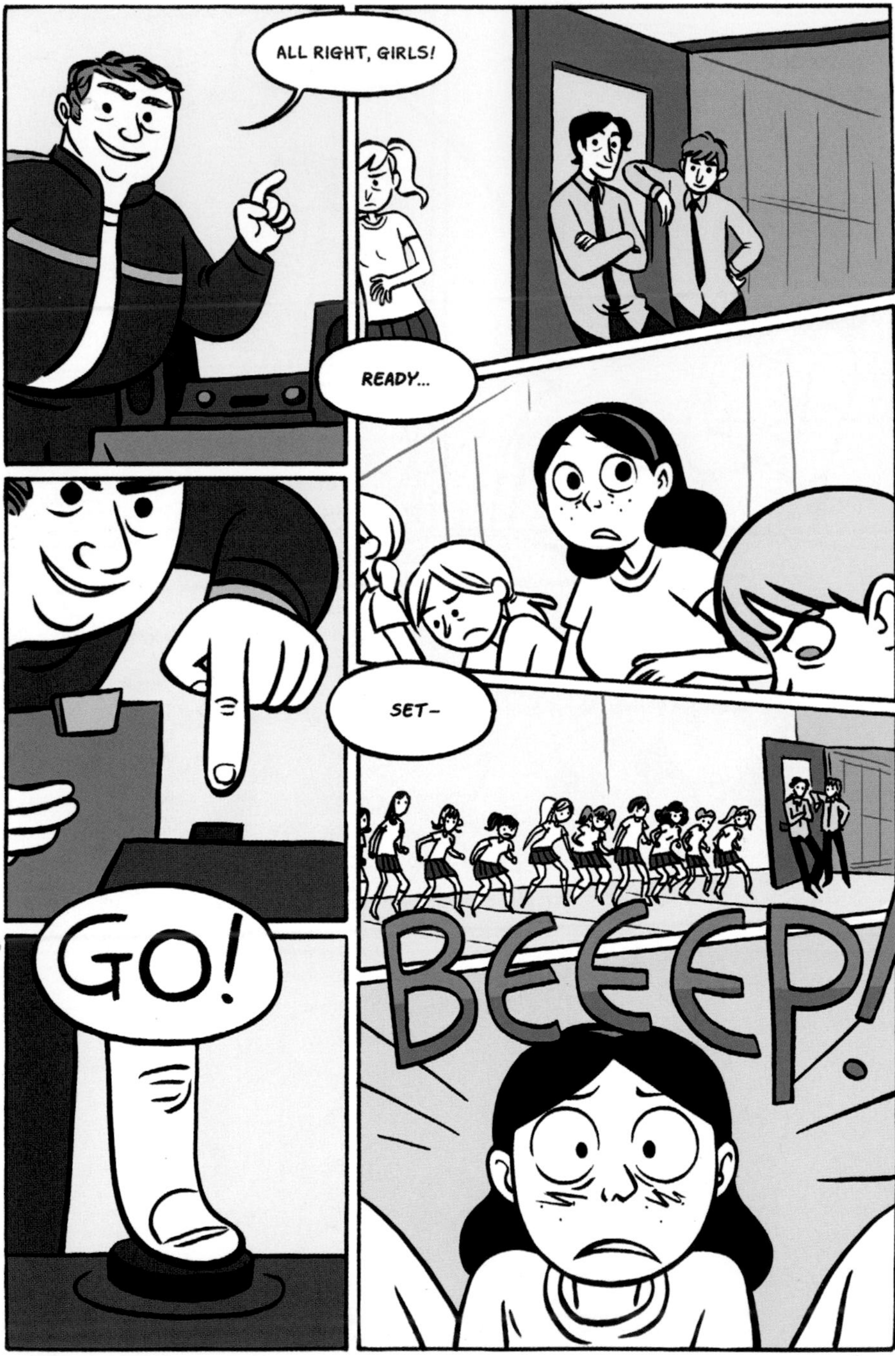
ALL RIGHT, GIRLS!
READY...
SET-
GO!
BEEEP!

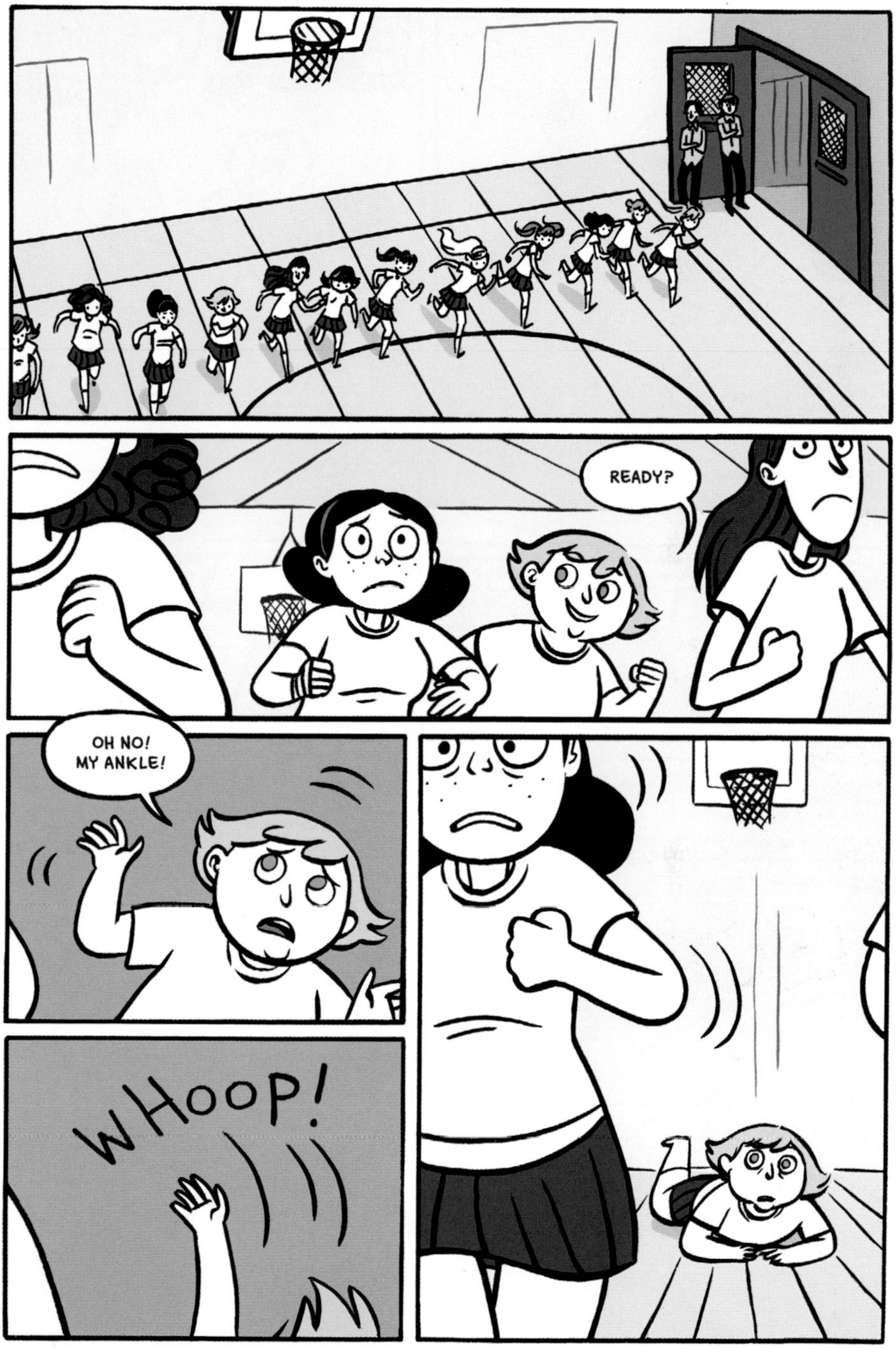
READY?
OH NO! MY ANKLE!
WHOOP!

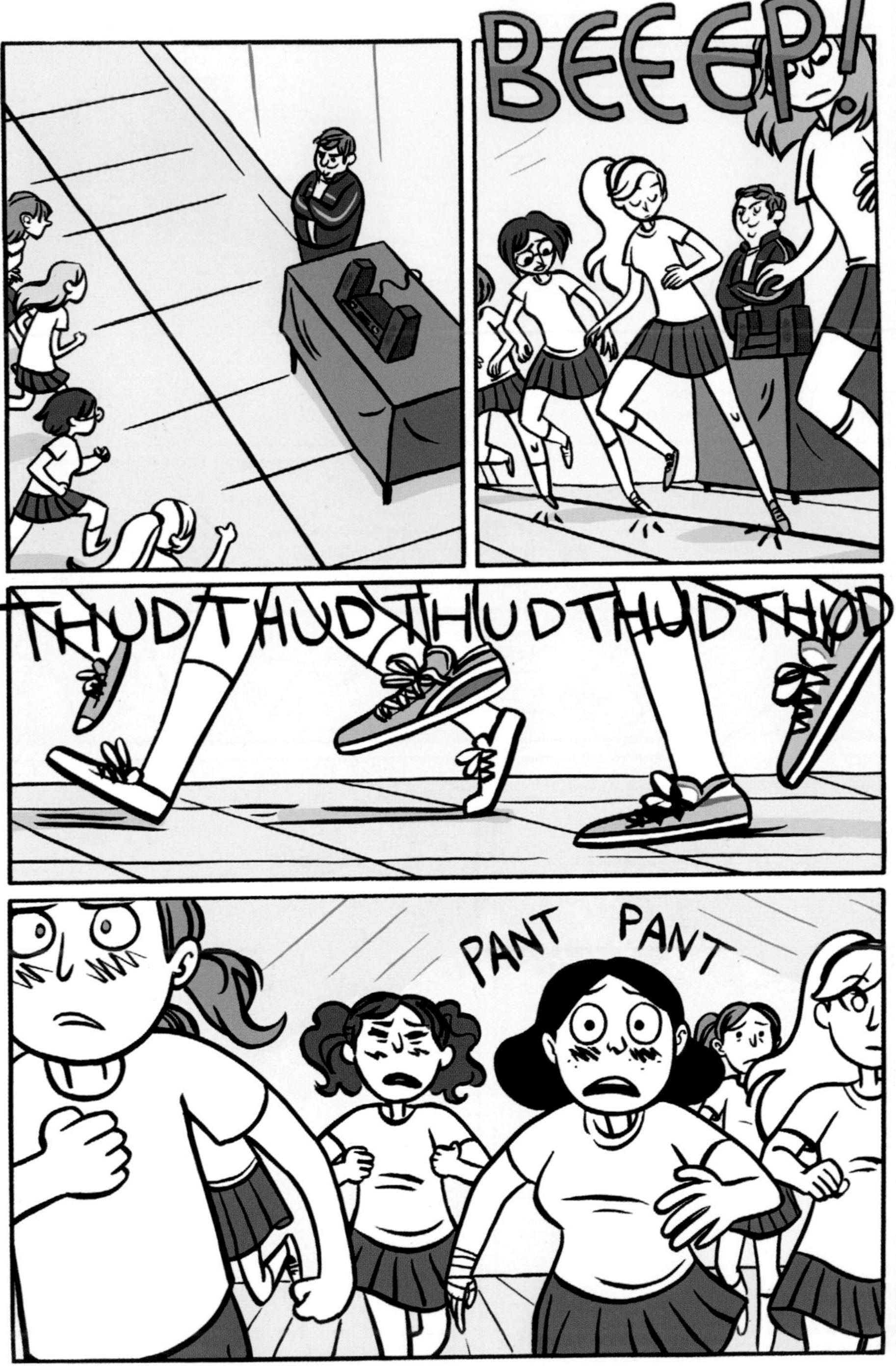
BEEEP!
THUD THUD THUD THUD THUD
PANT PANT

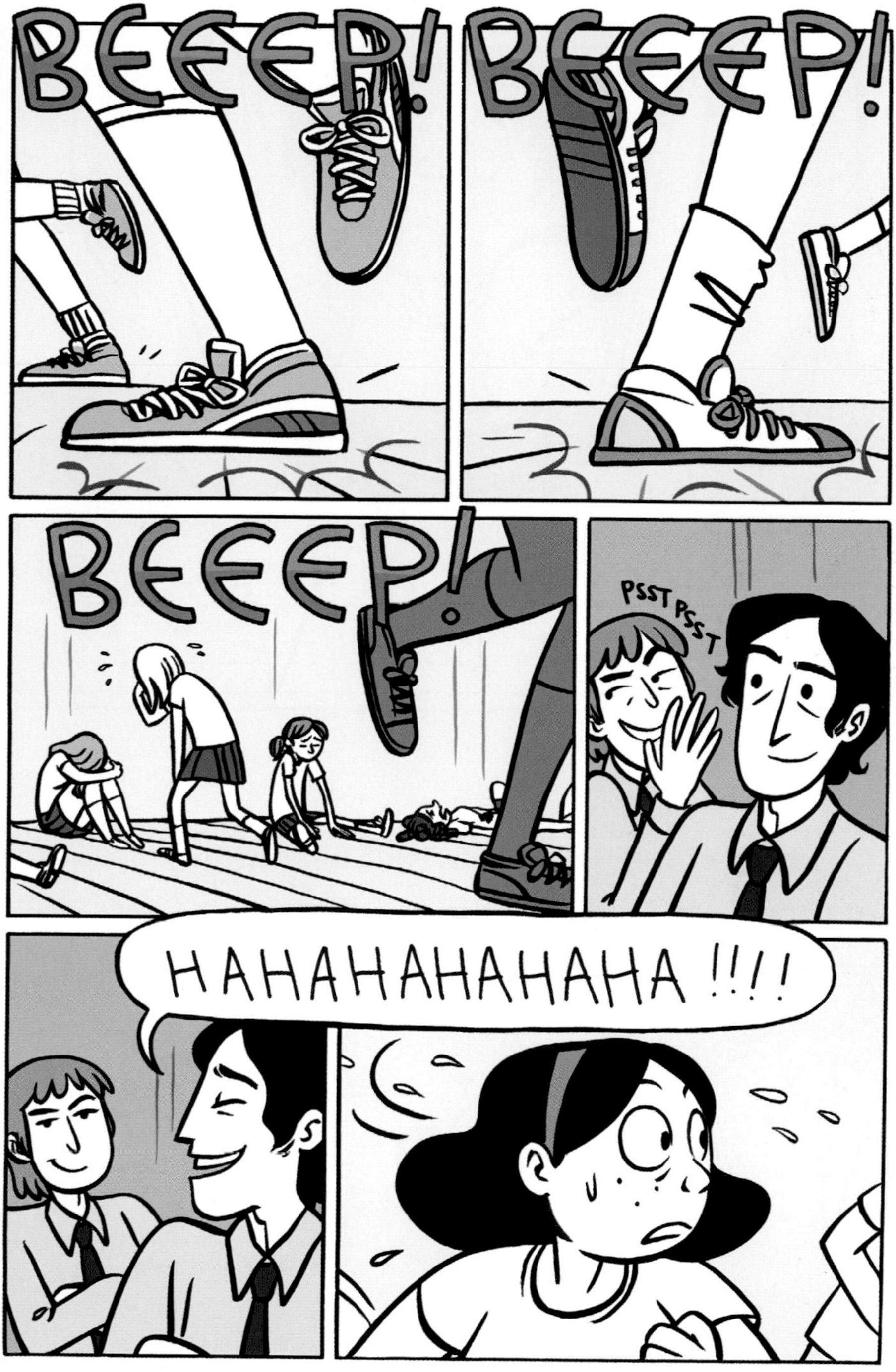
BEEEP!
BEEEEP!
BEEEP!
PSST PSSST
HAHAHAHAHAHA !!!!

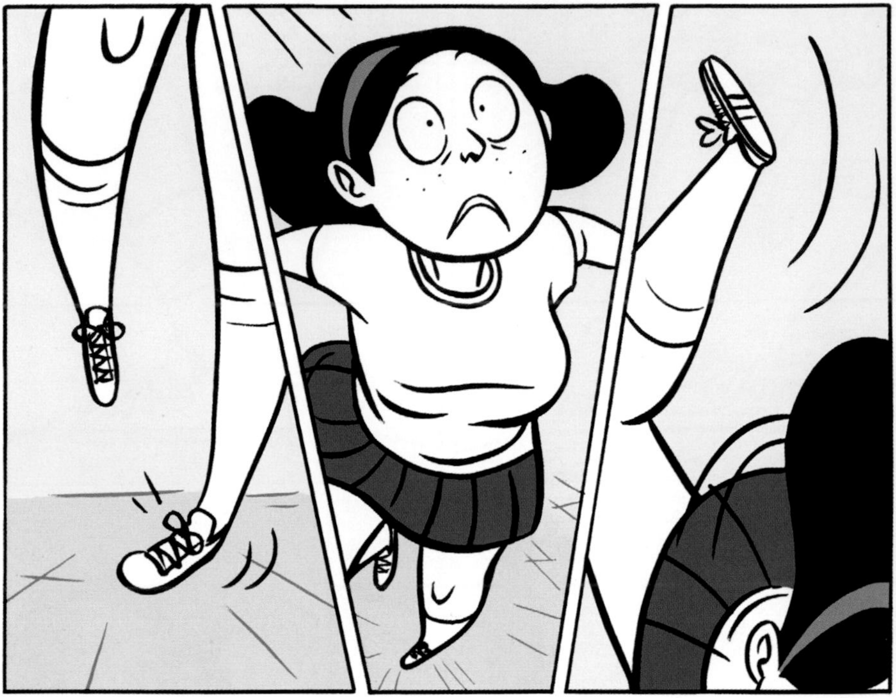

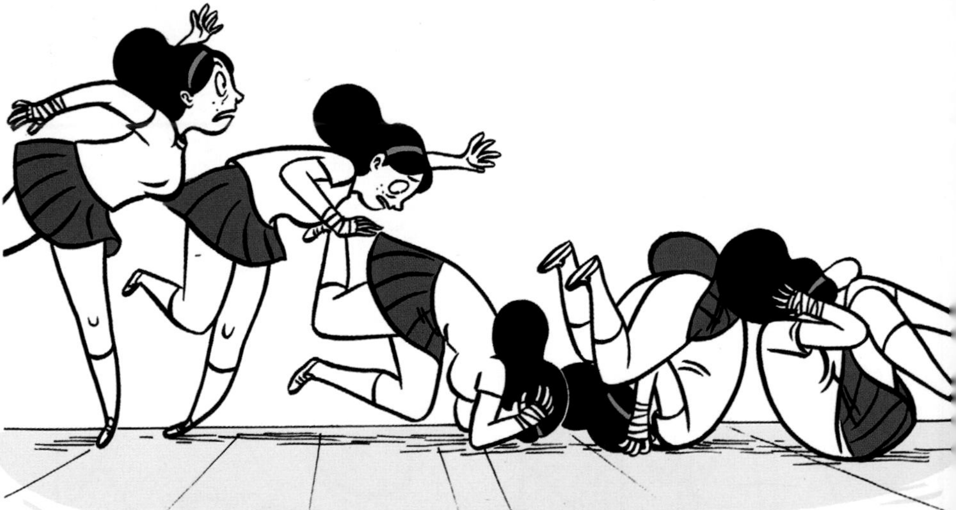

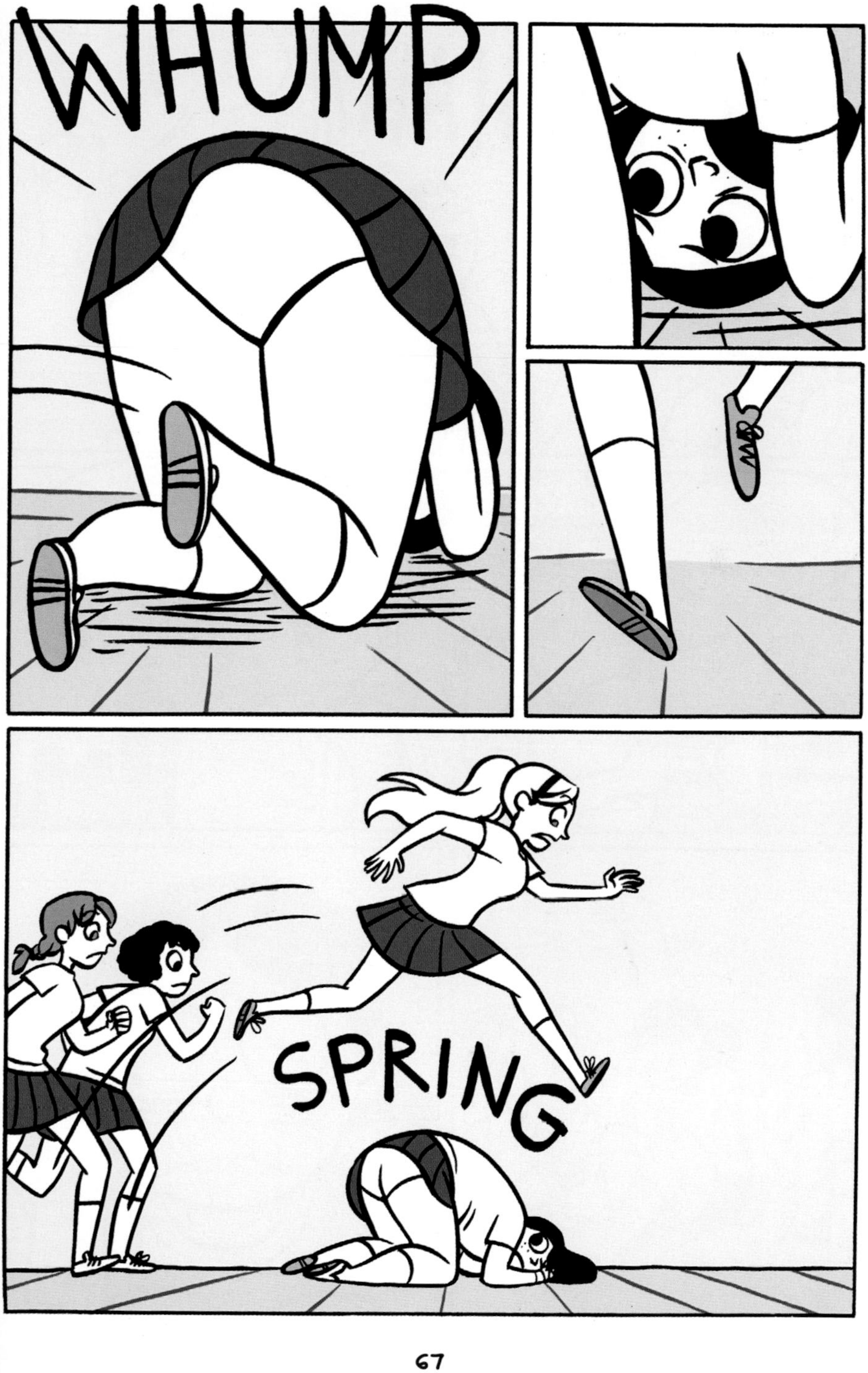
WHUMP
SPRING

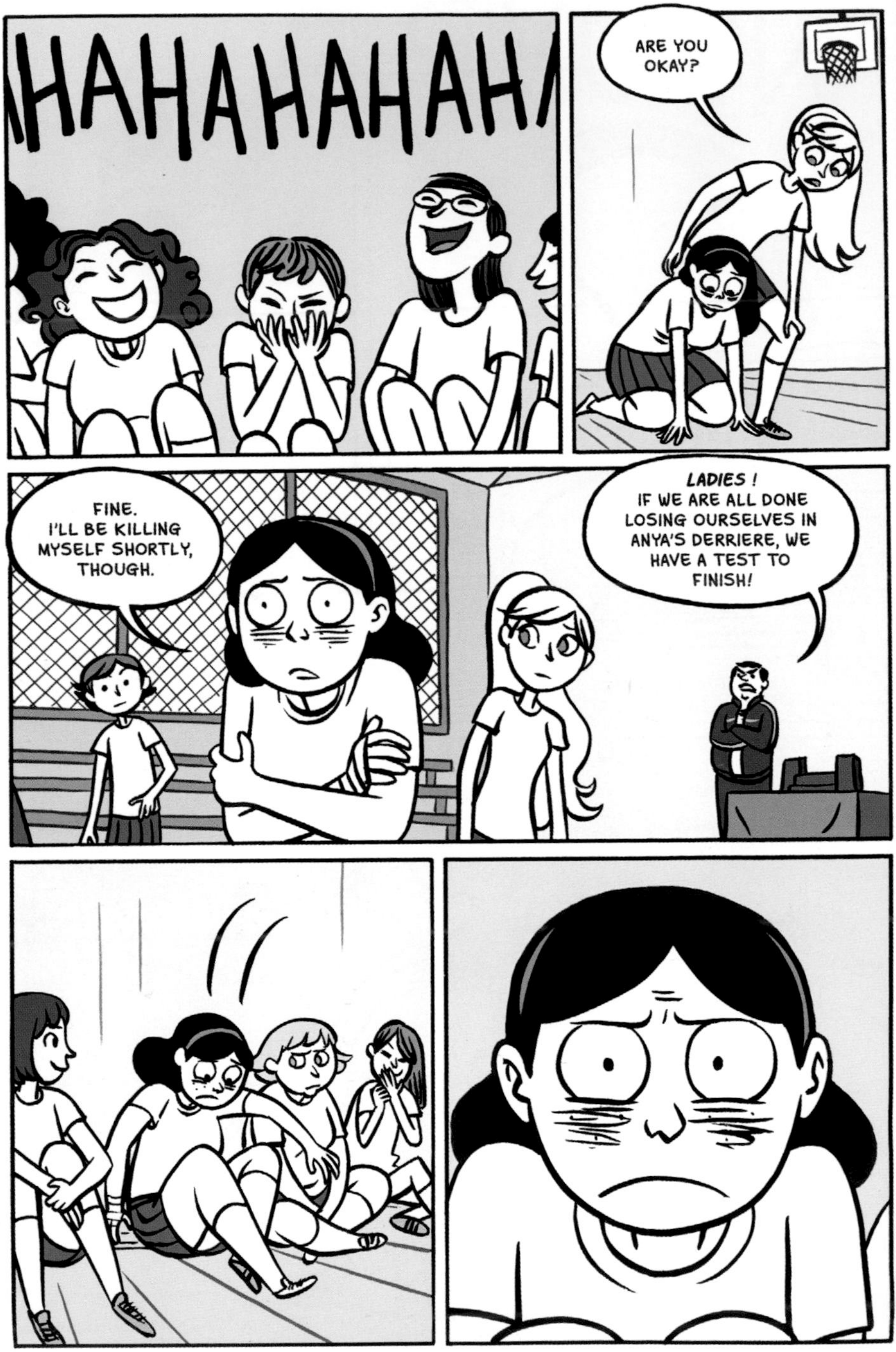
HAHAHAHAHAHAH
ARE YOU OKAY?
FINE. I'LL BE KILLING MYSELF SHORTLY, THOUGH.
LADIES ! IF WE ARE ALL DONE LOSING OURSELVES IN ANYA'S DERRIERE, WE HAVE A TEST TO FINISH!

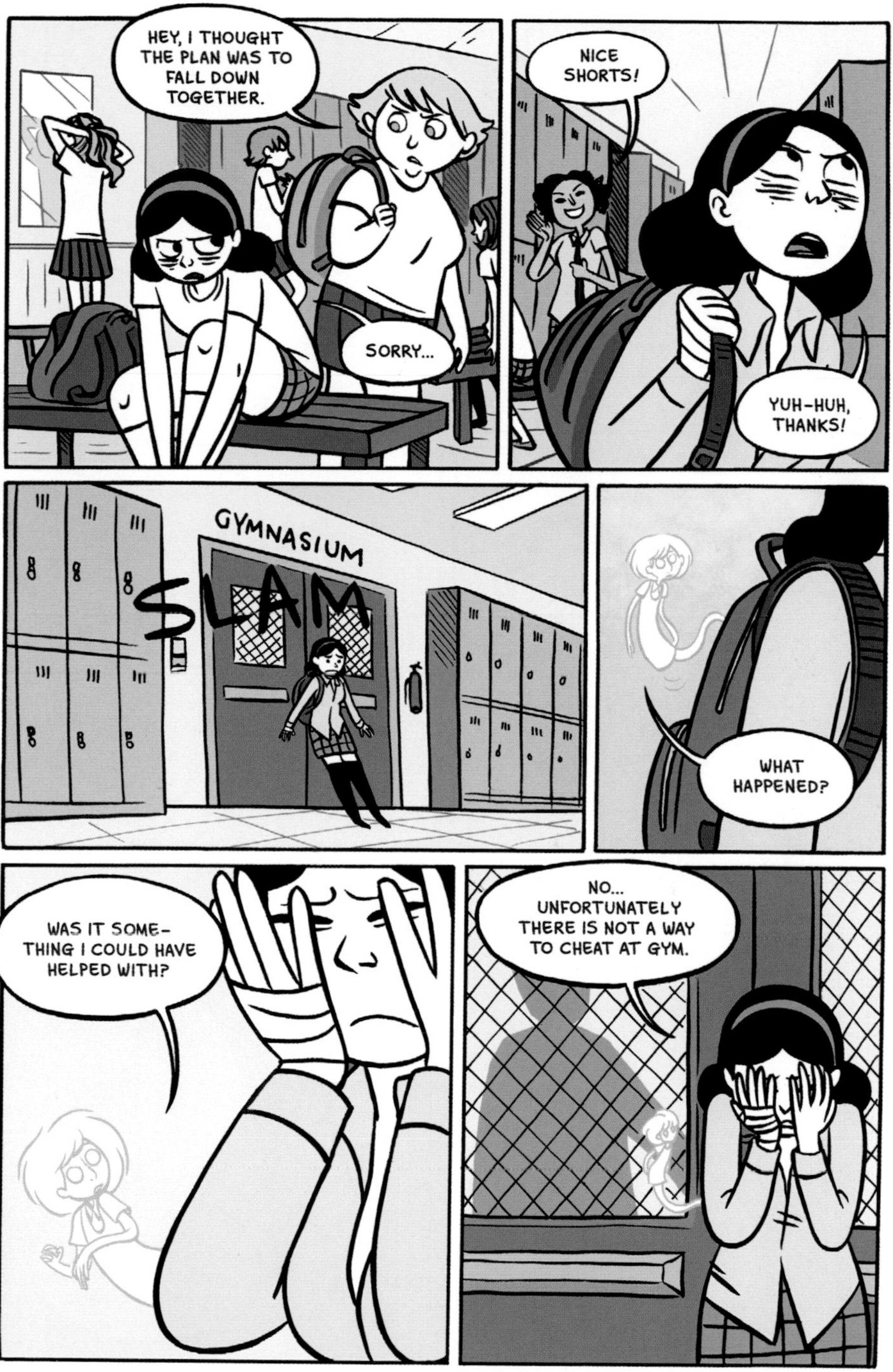
HEY, I THOUGHT THE PLAN WAS TO FALL DOWN TOGETHER.
SORRY...
NICE SHORTS!
YUH-HUH, THANKS!
GYMNASIUM
SLAM
WHAT HAPPENED?
WAS IT SOMETHING I COULD HAVE HELPED WITH?
NO... UNFORTUNATELY THERE IS NOT A WAY TO CHEAT AT GYM.

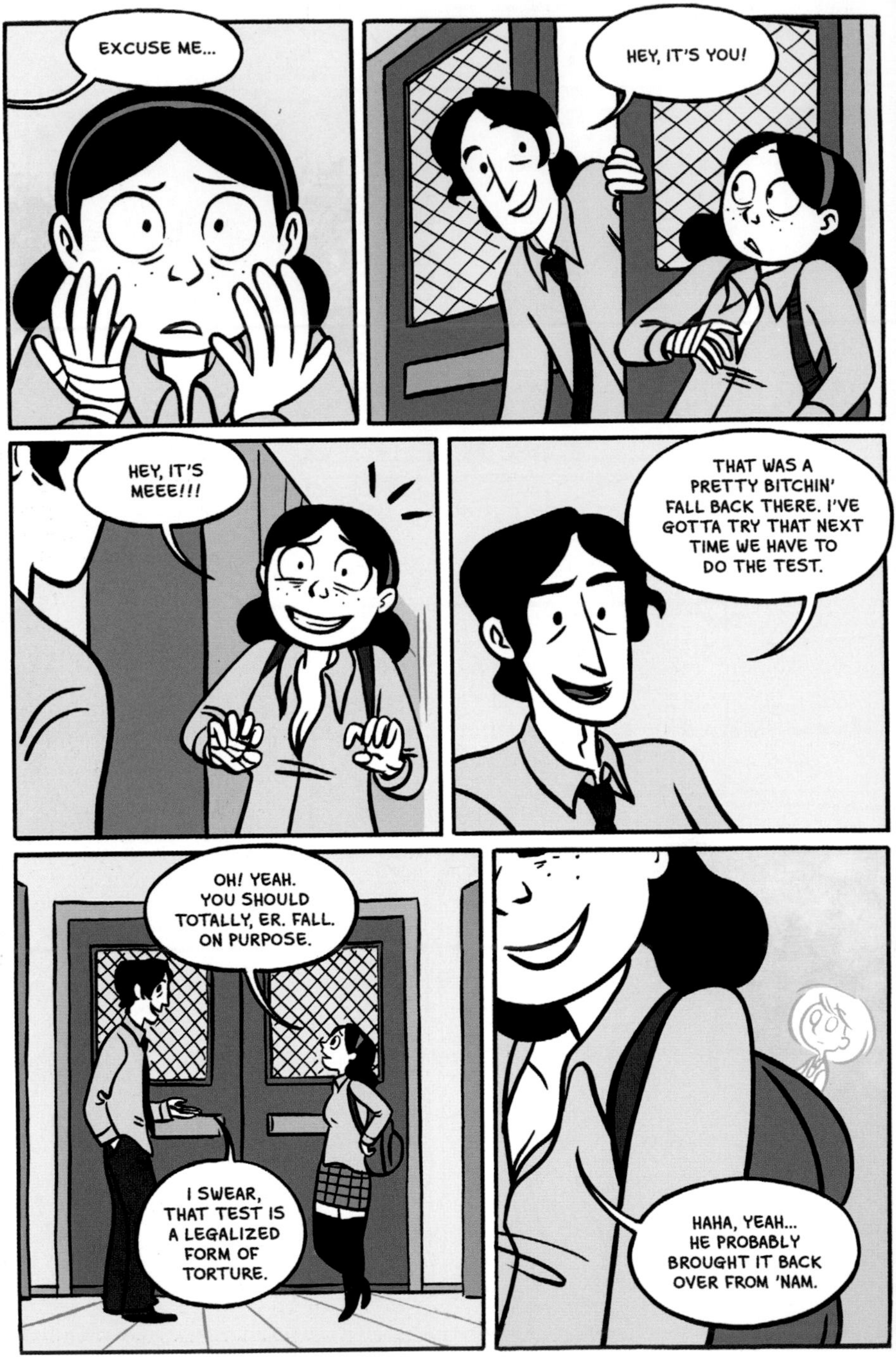

EXCUSE ME...
HEY, IT'S YOU!
HEY, IT'S MEEE!!!
THAT WAS A PRETTY BITCHIN' FALL BACK THERE. I'VE GOTTA TRY THAT NEXT TIME WE HAVE TO DO THE TEST.
OH! YEAH. YOU SHOULD TOTALLY, ER. FALL. ON PURPOSE.
I SWEAR, THAT TEST IS A LEGALIZED FORM OF TORTURE.
HAHA, YEAH... HE PROBABLY BROUGHT IT BACK OVER FROM 'NAM.

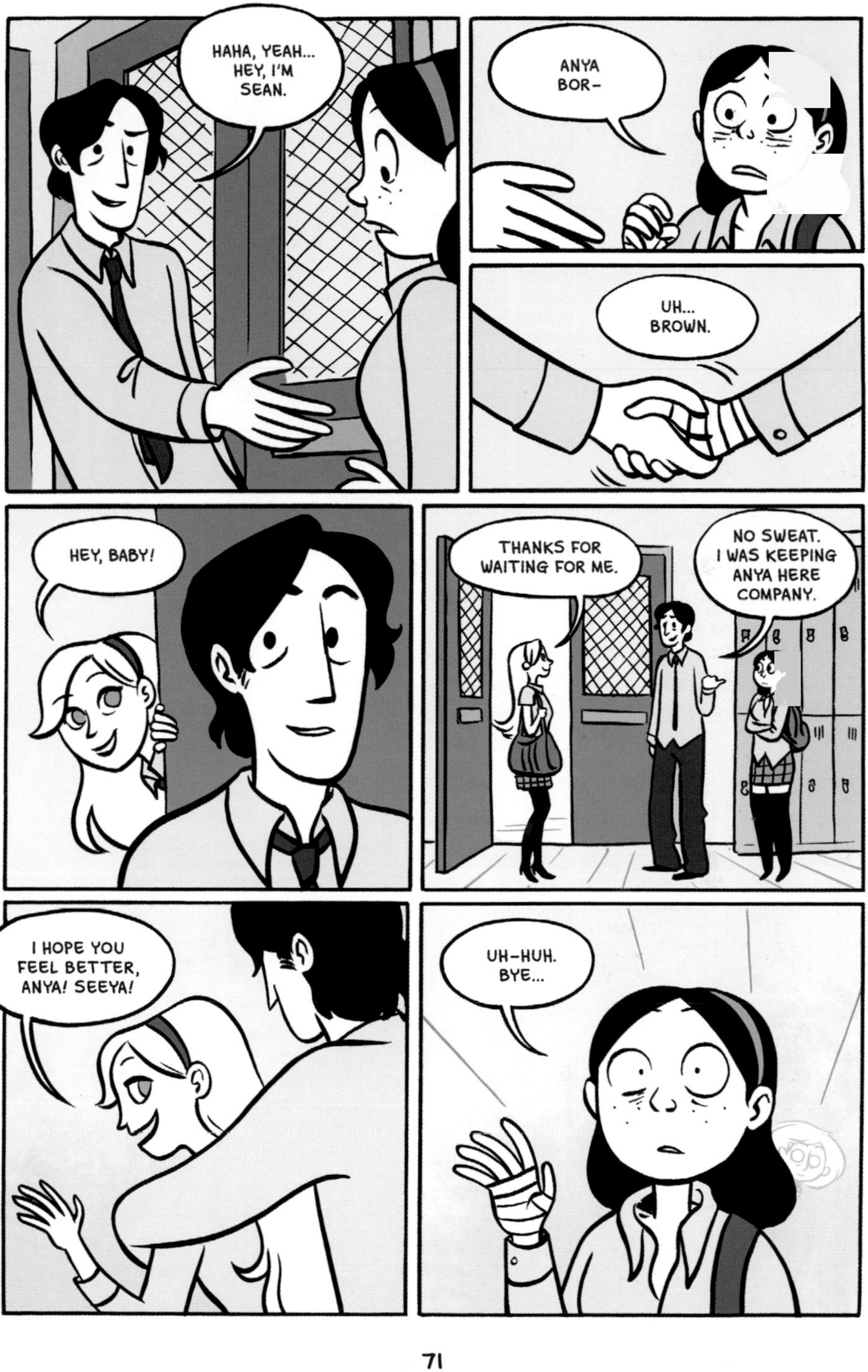
HAHA, YEAH... HEY, I'M SEAN.
ANYA BOR-
UH... BROWN.
HEY, BABY!
THANKS FOR WAITING FOR ME.
NO SWEAT. I WAS KEEPING ANYA HERE COMPANY.
I HOPE YOU FEEL BETTER, ANYA! SEEYA!
UH-HUH. BYE...

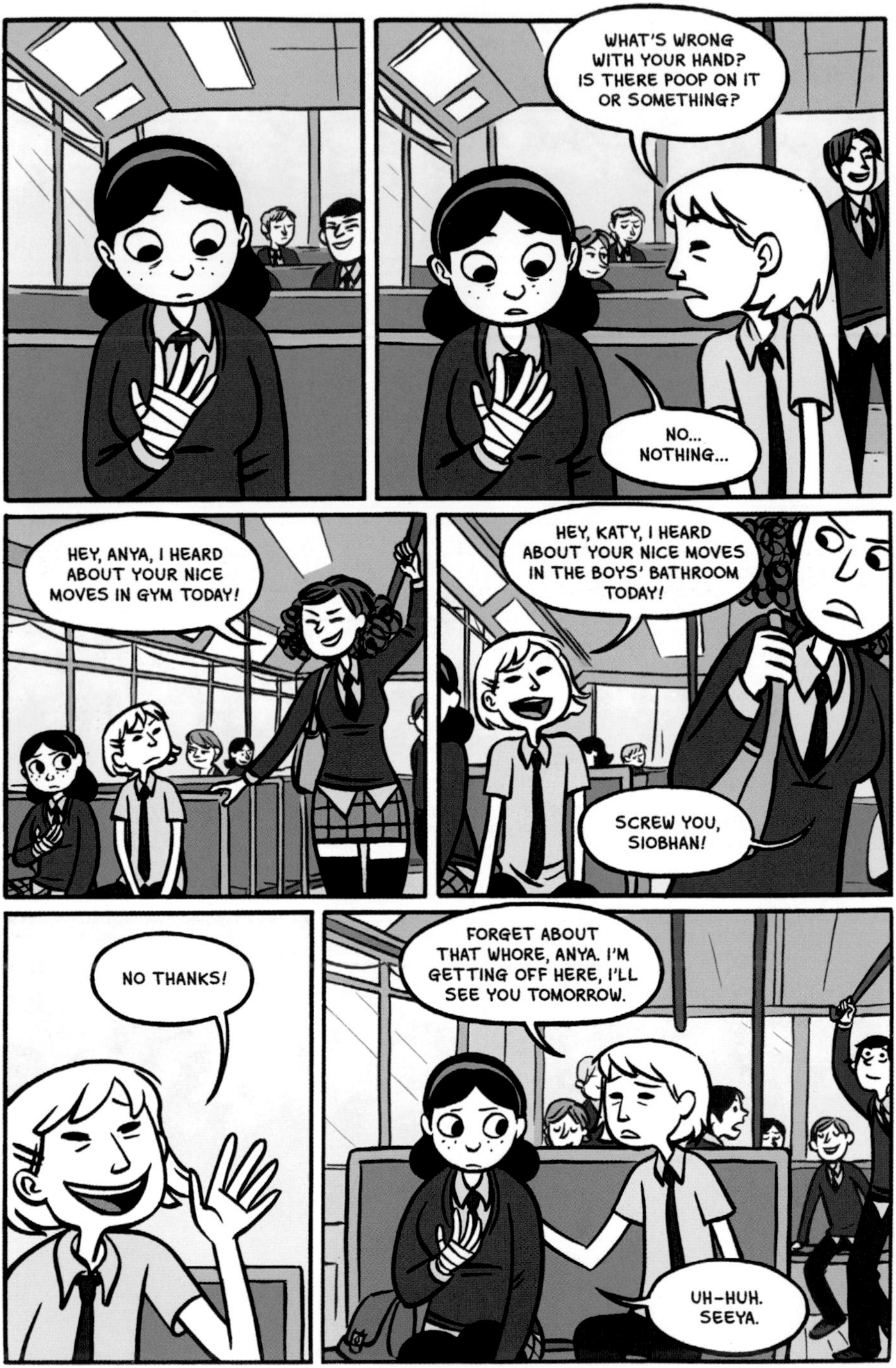
WHAT'S WRONG WITH YOUR HAND? IS THERE POOP ON IT OR SOMETHING?
NO... NOTHING...
HEY, ANYA, I HEARD ABOUT YOUR NICE MOVES IN GYM TODAY!
HEY, KATY, I HEARD ABOUT YOUR NICE MOVES IN THE BOYS' BATHROOM TODAY!
SCREW YOU, SIOBHAN!
NO THANKS!
FORGET ABOUT THAT WHORE, ANYA. I'M GETTING OFF HERE, I'LL SEE YOU TOMORROW.
UH-HUH. SEEYA.

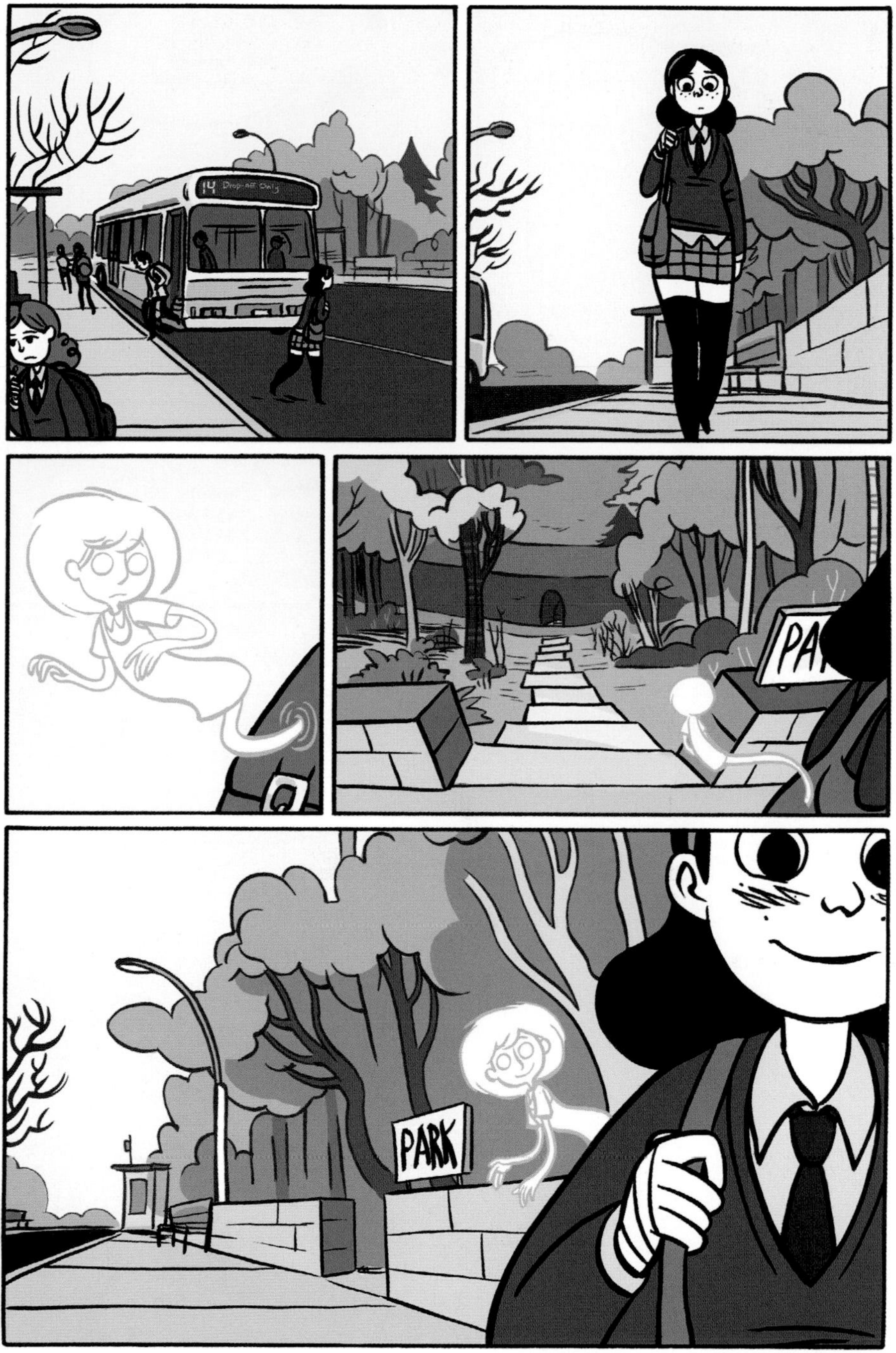
14 Drop-off Only
PARK

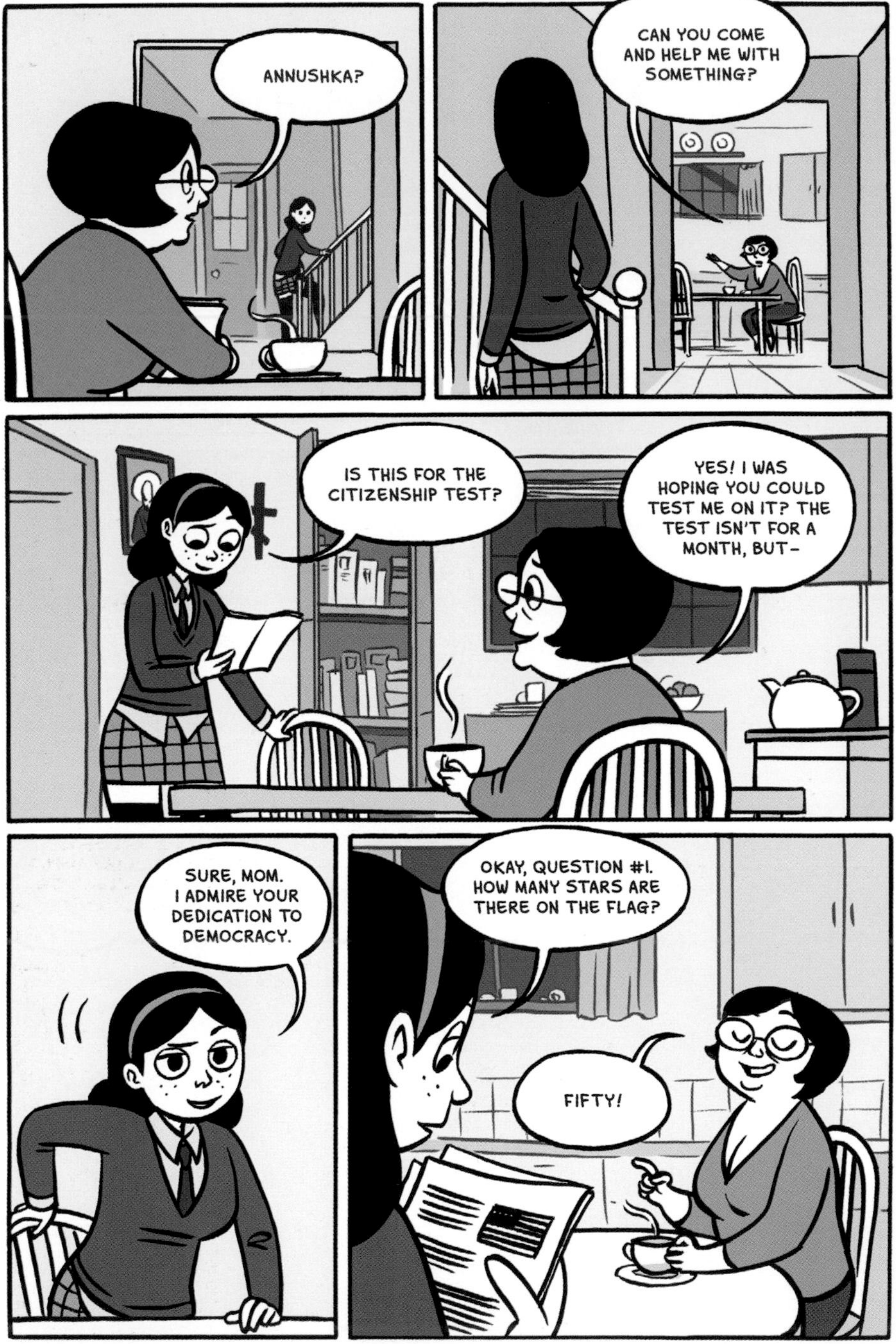
ANNUSHKA?
CAN YOU COME AND HELP ME WITH SOMETHING?
IS THIS FOR THE CITIZENSHIP TEST?
YES! I WAS HOPING YOU COULD TEST ME ON IT? THE TEST ISN'T FOR A MONTH, BUT-
SURE, MOM. I ADMIRE YOUR DEDICATION TO DEMOCRACY.
OKAY, QUESTION #1. HOW MANY STARS ARE THERE ON THE FLAG?
FIFTY!

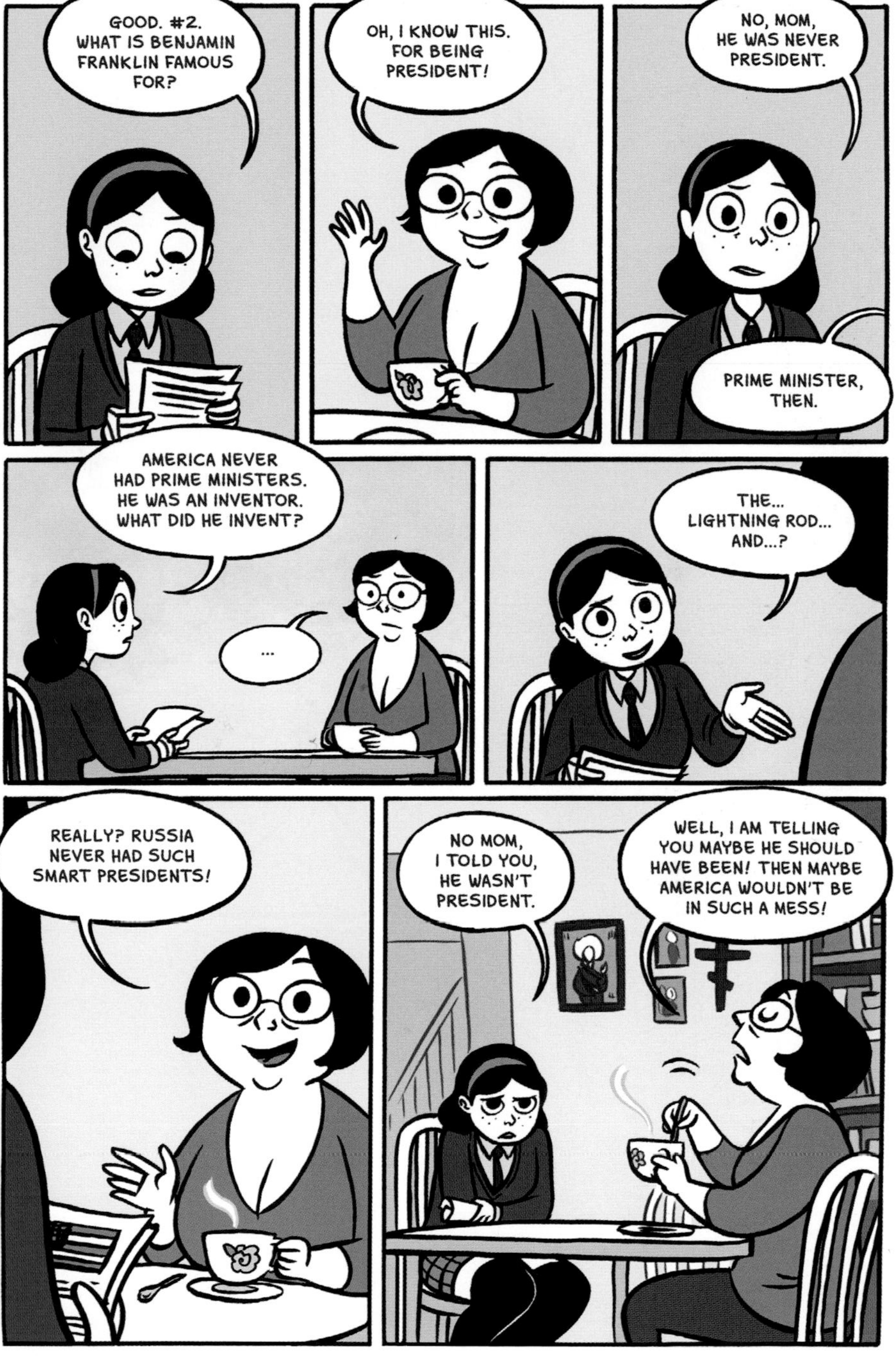
GOOD. #2. WHAT IS BENJAMIN FRANKLIN FAMOUS FOR?
OH, I KNOW THIS. FOR BEING PRESIDENT!
NO, MOM, HE WAS NEVER PRESIDENT.
PRIME MINISTER, THEN.
AMERICA NEVER HAD PRIME MINISTERS. HE WAS AN INVENTOR. WHAT DID HE INVENT?
...
THE... LIGHTNING ROD... AND...?
REALLY? RUSSIA NEVER HAD SUCH SMART PRESIDENTS!
NO MOM, I TOLD YOU, HE WASN'T PRESIDENT.
WELL, I AM TELLING YOU MAYBE HE SHOULD HAVE BEEN! THEN MAYBE AMERICA WOULDN'T BE IN SUCH A MESS!

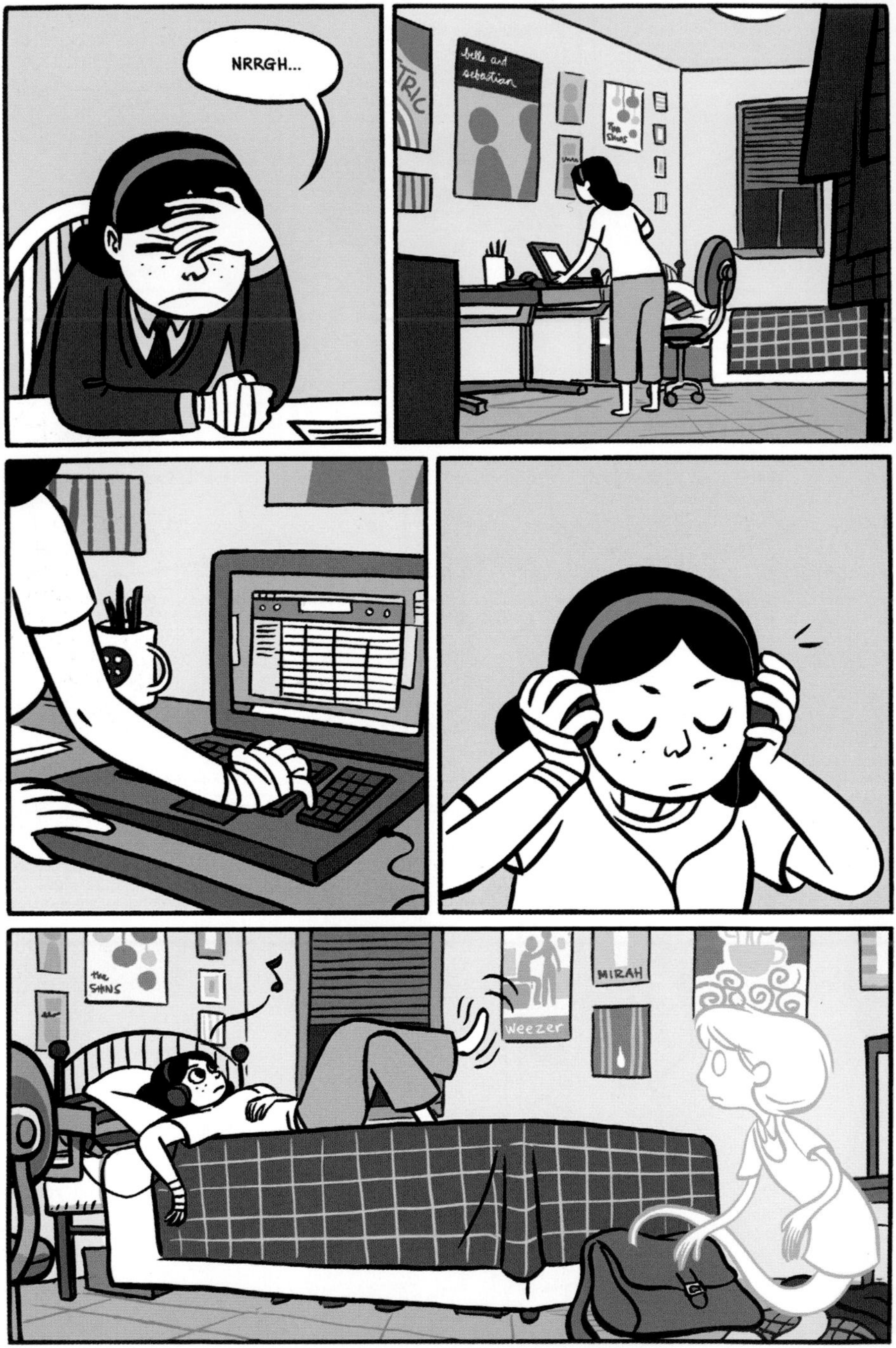
NRRGH...
the SHINS
MIRAH
weezer

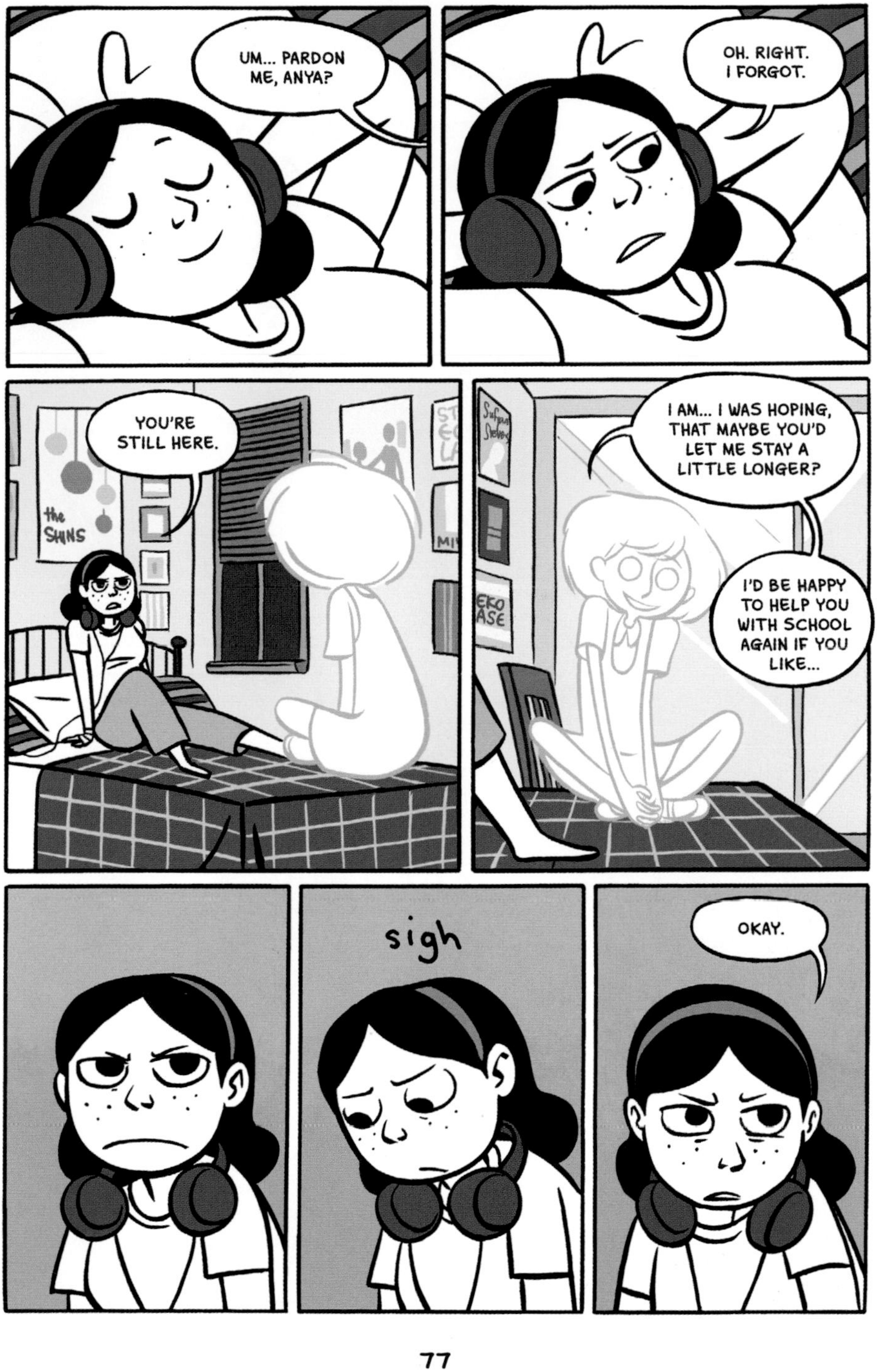
UM... PARDON ME, ANYA?
OH. RIGHT. I FORGOT.
YOU'RE STILL HERE.
the SHINS
I AM... I WAS HOPING, THAT MAYBE YOU'D LET ME STAY A LITTLE LONGER?
I'D BE HAPPY TO HELP YOU WITH SCHOOL AGAIN IF YOU LIKE...
sigh
OKAY.

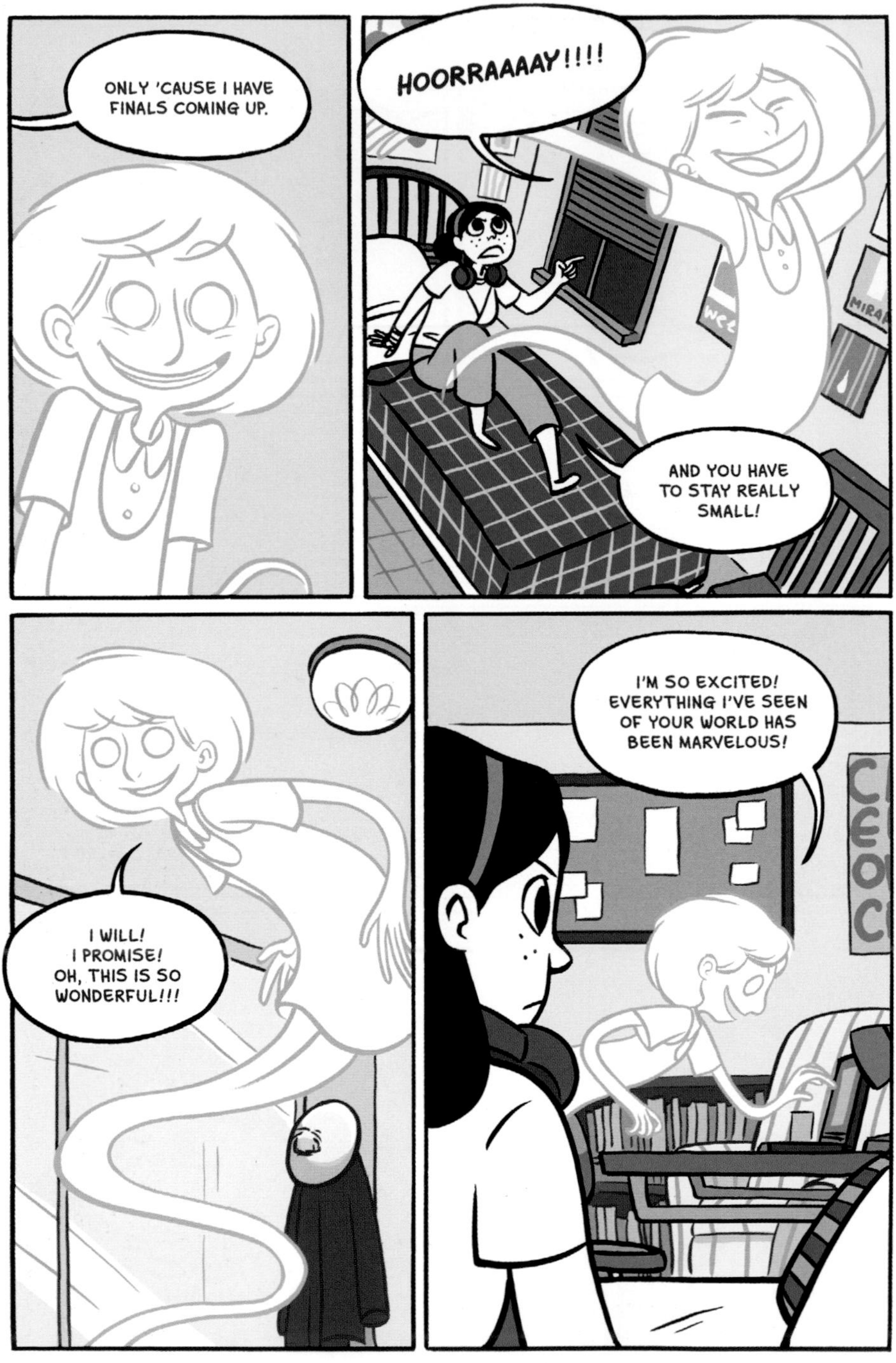
ONLY 'CAUSE I HAVE FINALS COMING UP.
HOORRAAAAY!!!!
AND YOU HAVE TO STAY REALLY SMALL!
I WILL! I PROMISE! OH, THIS IS SO WONDERFUL!!!
I'M SO EXCITED! EVERYTHING I'VE SEEN OF YOUR WORLD HAS BEEN MARVELOUS!

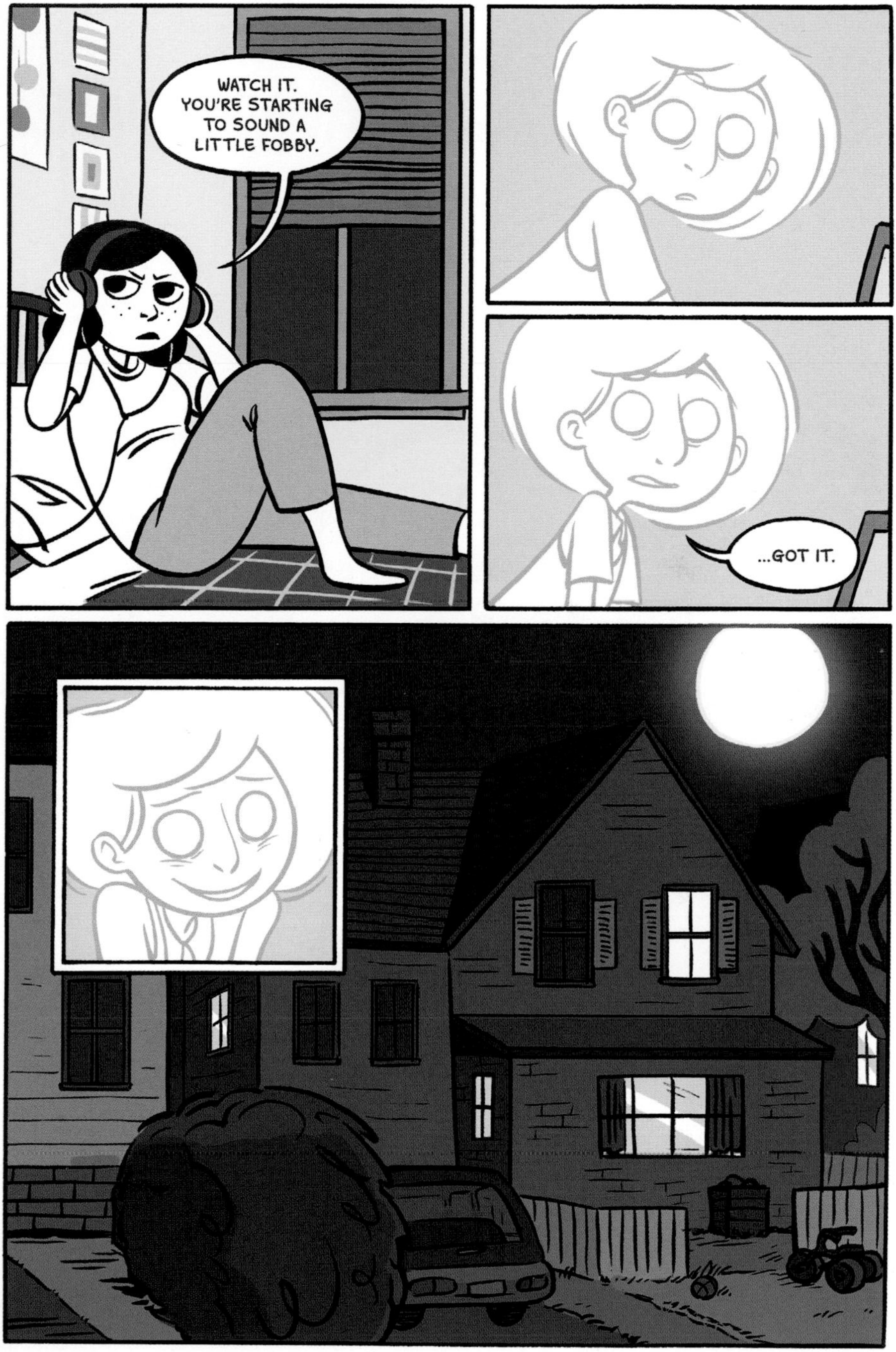
WATCH IT. YOU'RE STARTING TO SOUND A LITTLE FOBBY.
...GOT IT.

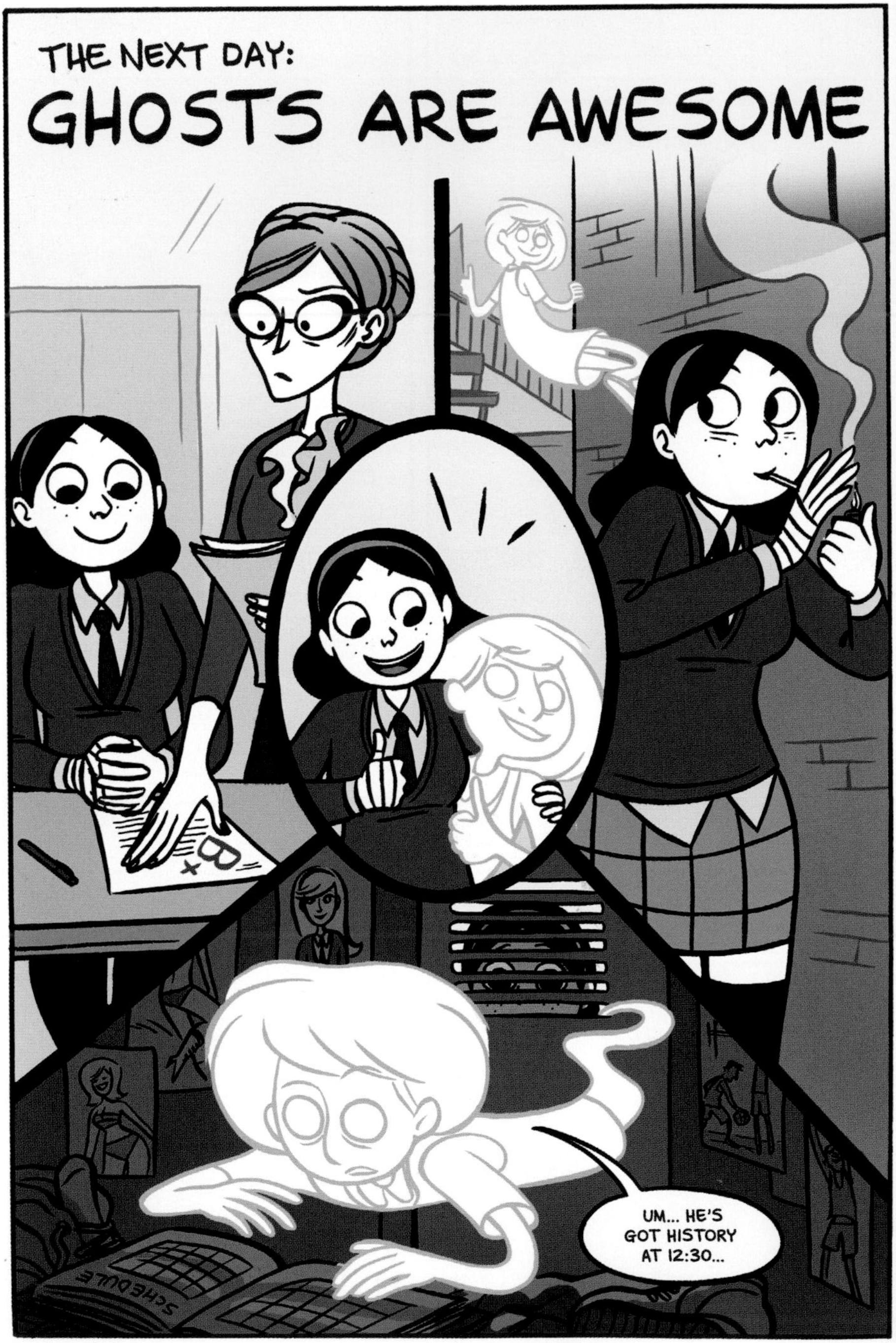
THE NEXT DAY:
GHOSTS ARE AWESOME
UM... HE'S GOT HISTORY AT 12:30...
SCHEDULE

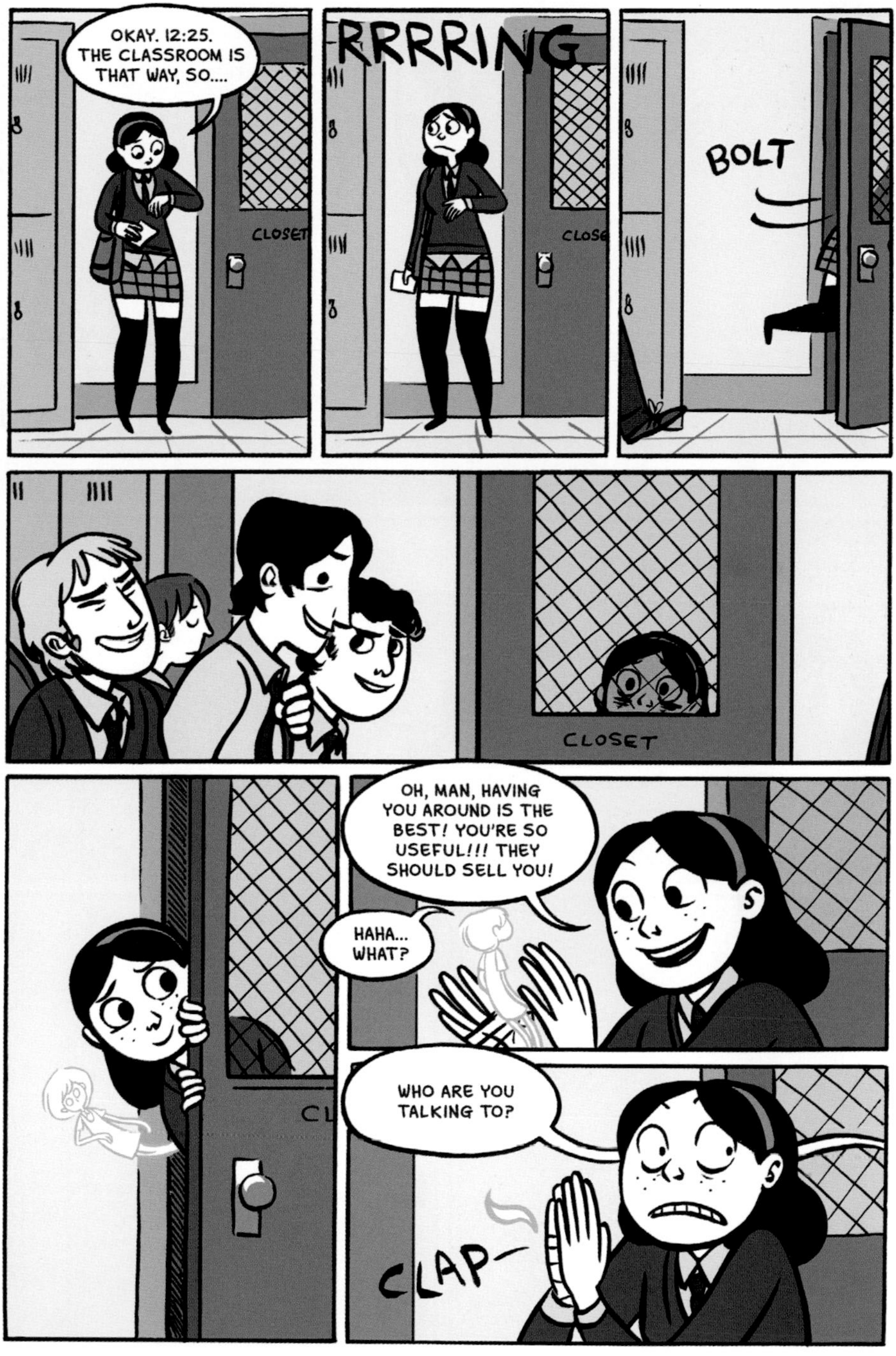
OKAY. 12:25. THE CLASSROOM IS THAT WAY, SO....
CLOSET
RRRRING
CLOSE
BOLT
CLOSET
OH, MAN, HAVING YOU AROUND IS THE BEST! YOU'RE SO USEFUL!!! THEY SHOULD SELL YOU!
HAHA... WHAT?
WHO ARE YOU TALKING TO?
CLAP-

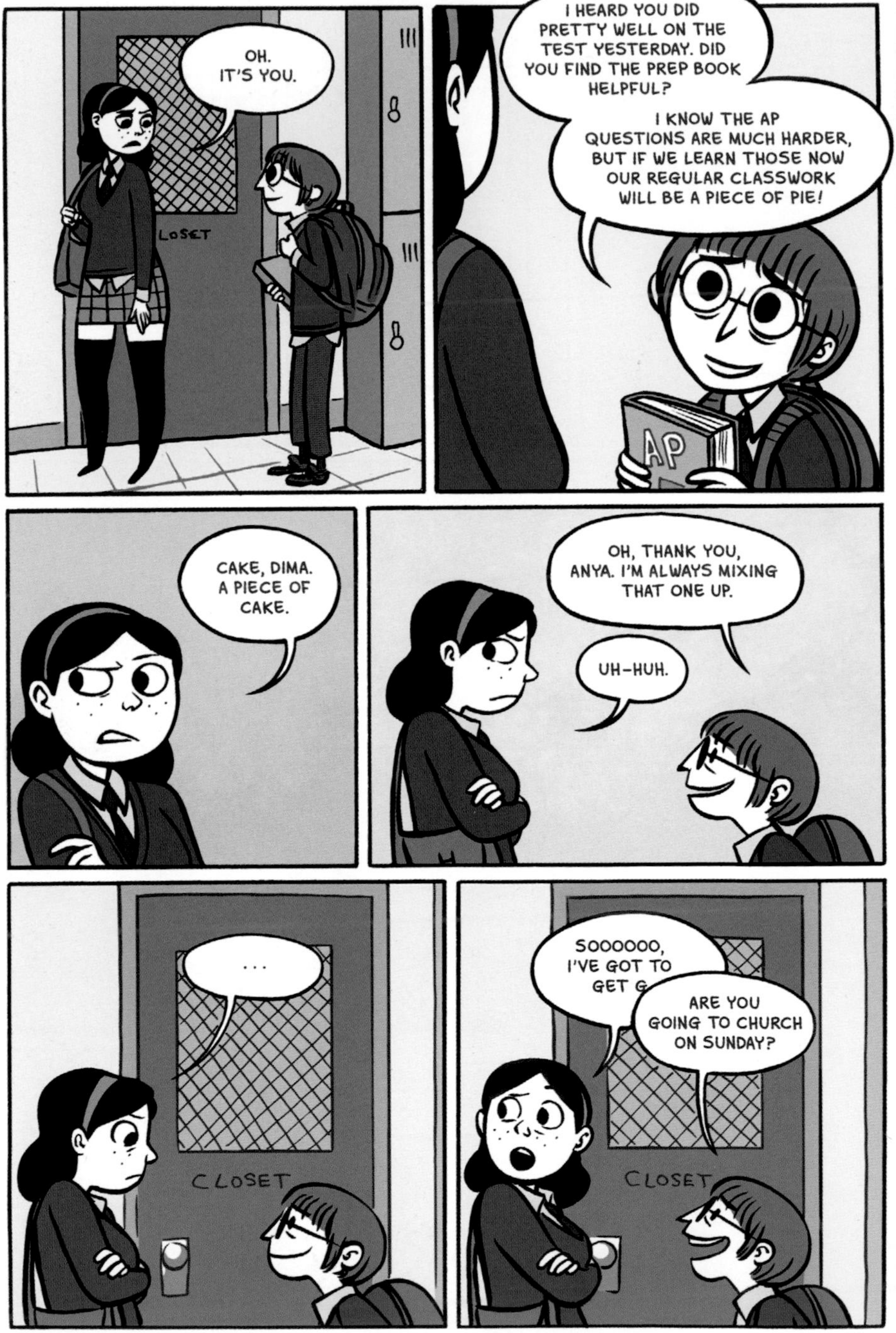
LOSET
OH. IT'S YOU.
I HEARD YOU DID PRETTY WELL ON THE TEST YESTERDAY. DID YOU FIND THE PREP BOOK HELPFUL?
I KNOW THE AP QUESTIONS ARE MUCH HARDER, BUT IF WE LEARN THOSE NOW OUR REGULAR CLASSWORK WILL BE A PIECE OF PIE!
AP
CAKE, DIMA. A PIECE OF CAKE.
OH, THANK YOU, ANYA. I'M ALWAYS MIXING THAT ONE UP.
UH-HUH.
...
CLOSET
SOOOOOO, I'VE GOT TO GET G
ARE YOU GOING TO CHURCH ON SUNDAY?
CLOSET

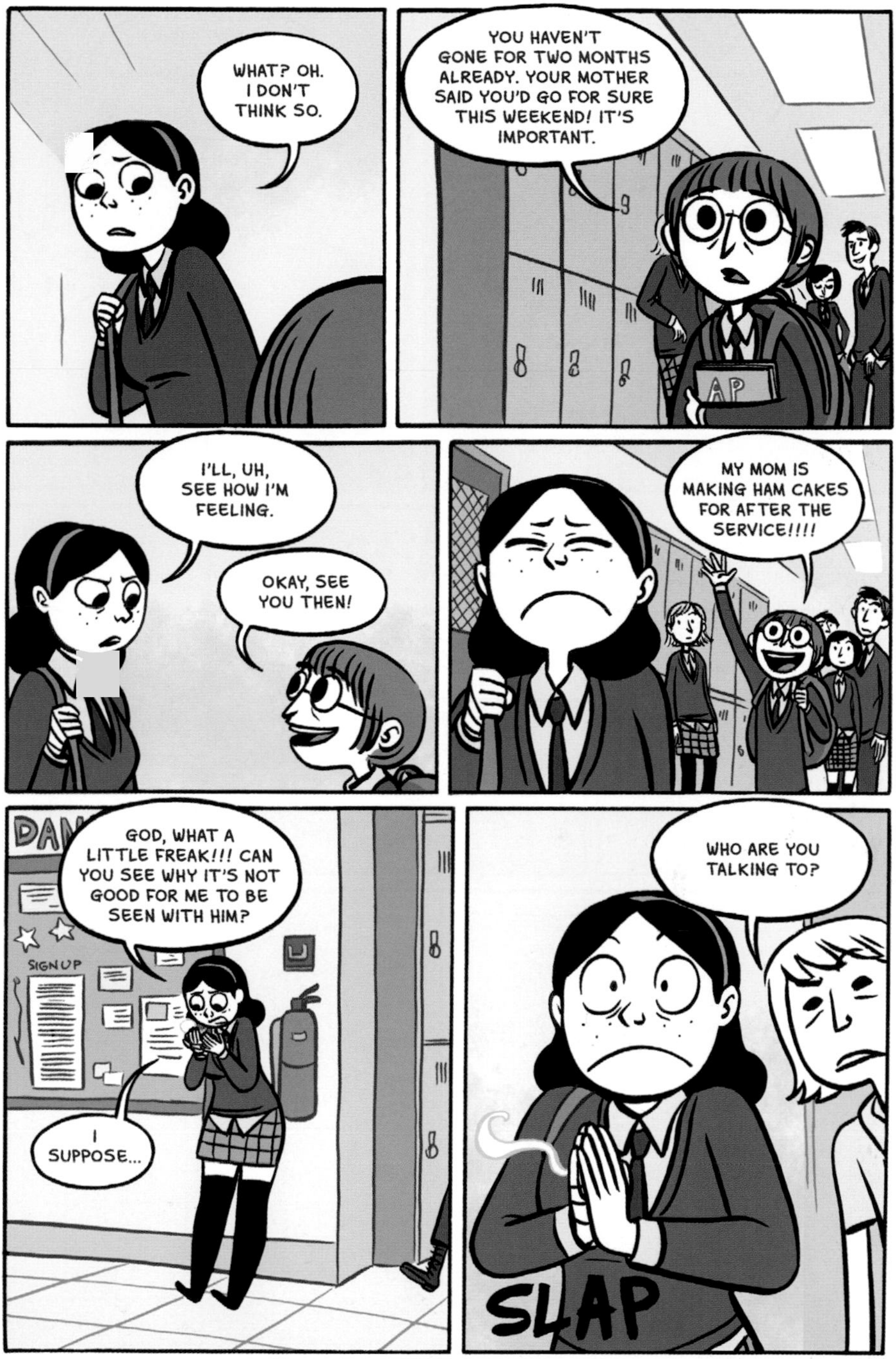
WHAT? OH. I DON'T THINK SO.
YOU HAVEN'T GONE FOR TWO MONTHS ALREADY. YOUR MOTHER SAID YOU'D GO FOR SURE THIS WEEKEND! IT'S IMPORTANT.
AP
I'LL, UH, SEE HOW I'M FEELING.
OKAY, SEE YOU THEN!
MY MOM IS MAKING HAM CAKES FOR AFTER THE SERVICE!!!!
GOD, WHAT A LITTLE FREAK!!! CAN YOU SEE WHY IT'S NOT GOOD FOR ME TO BE SEEN WITH HIM?
SIGNUP
I SUPPOSE...
WHO ARE YOU TALKING TO?
SLAP

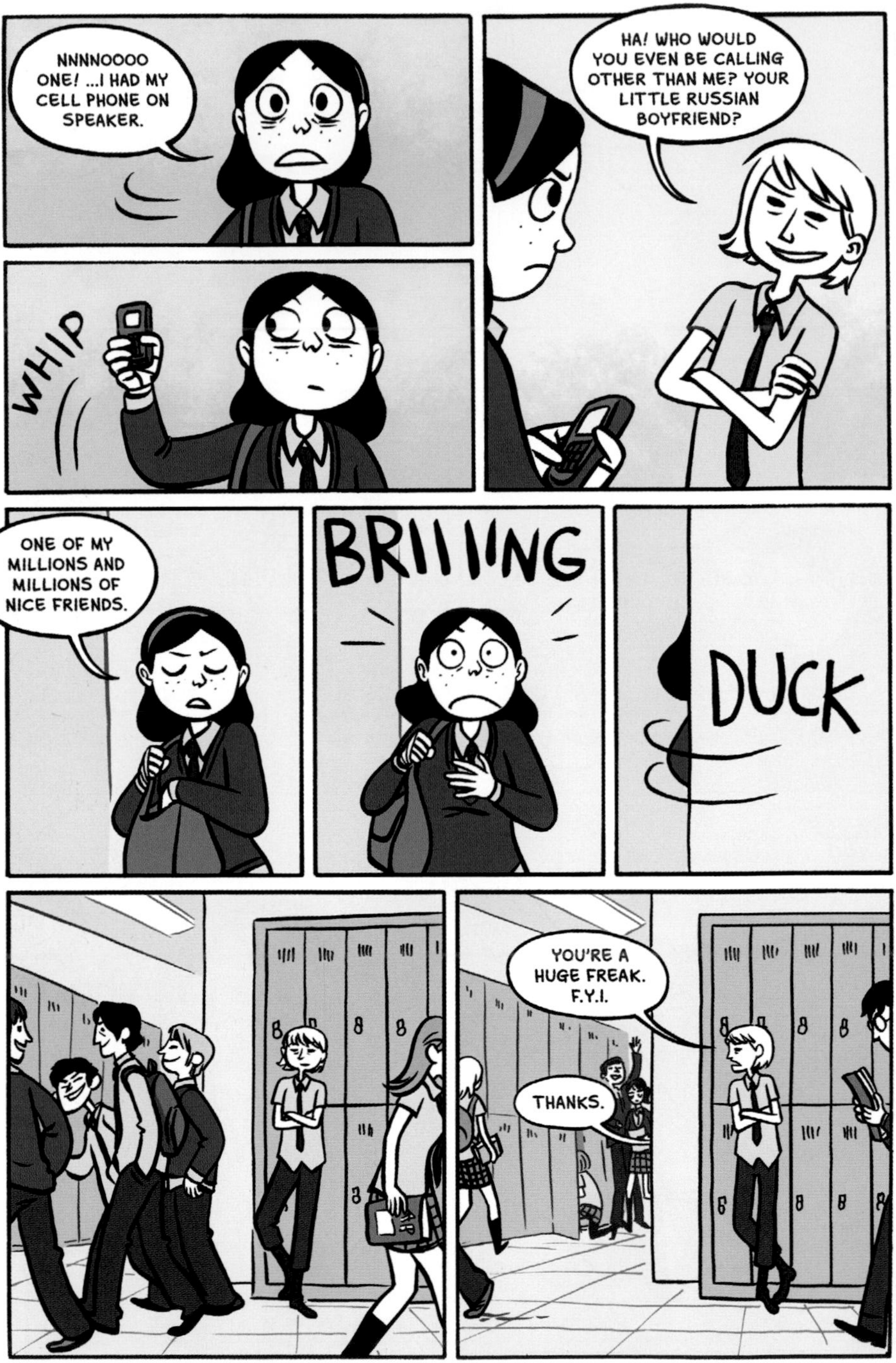
NNNNOOOO ONE! ...I HAD MY CELL PHONE ON SPEAKER.
HA! WHO WOULD YOU EVEN BE CALLING OTHER THAN ME? YOUR LITTLE RUSSIAN BOYFRIEND?
WHIP
ONE OF MY MILLIONS AND MILLIONS OF NICE FRIENDS.
BRIIIING
DUCK
YOU'RE A HUGE FREAK. F.Y.I.
THANKS.

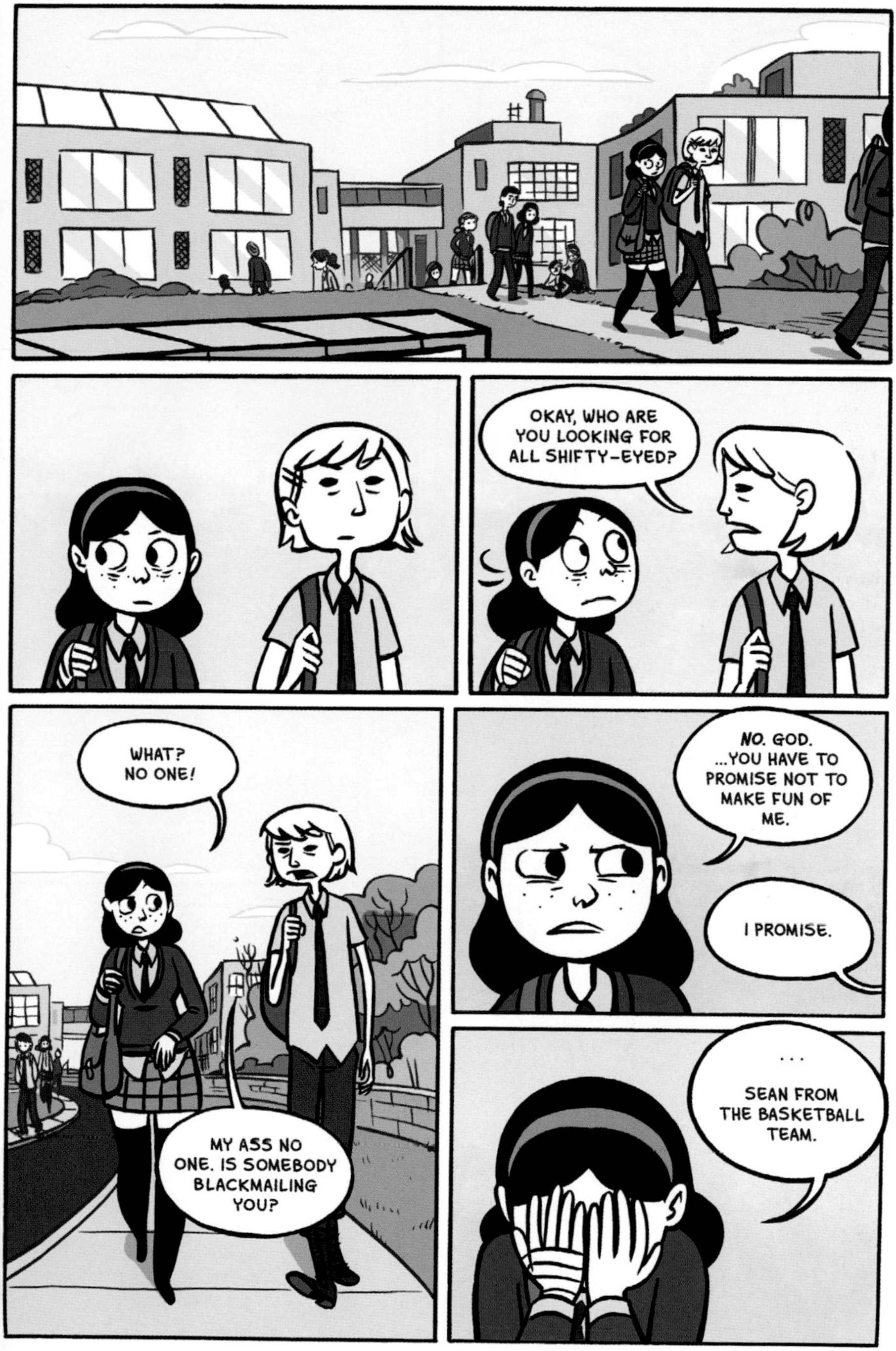
OKAY, WHO ARE YOU LOOKING FOR ALL SHIFTY-EYED?
WHAT? NO ONE!
MY ASS NO ONE. IS SOMEBODY BLACKMAILING YOU?
NO. GOD. ...YOU HAVE TO PROMISE NOT TO MAKE FUN OF ME.
I PROMISE.
. . .
SEAN FROM THE BASKETBALL TEAM.

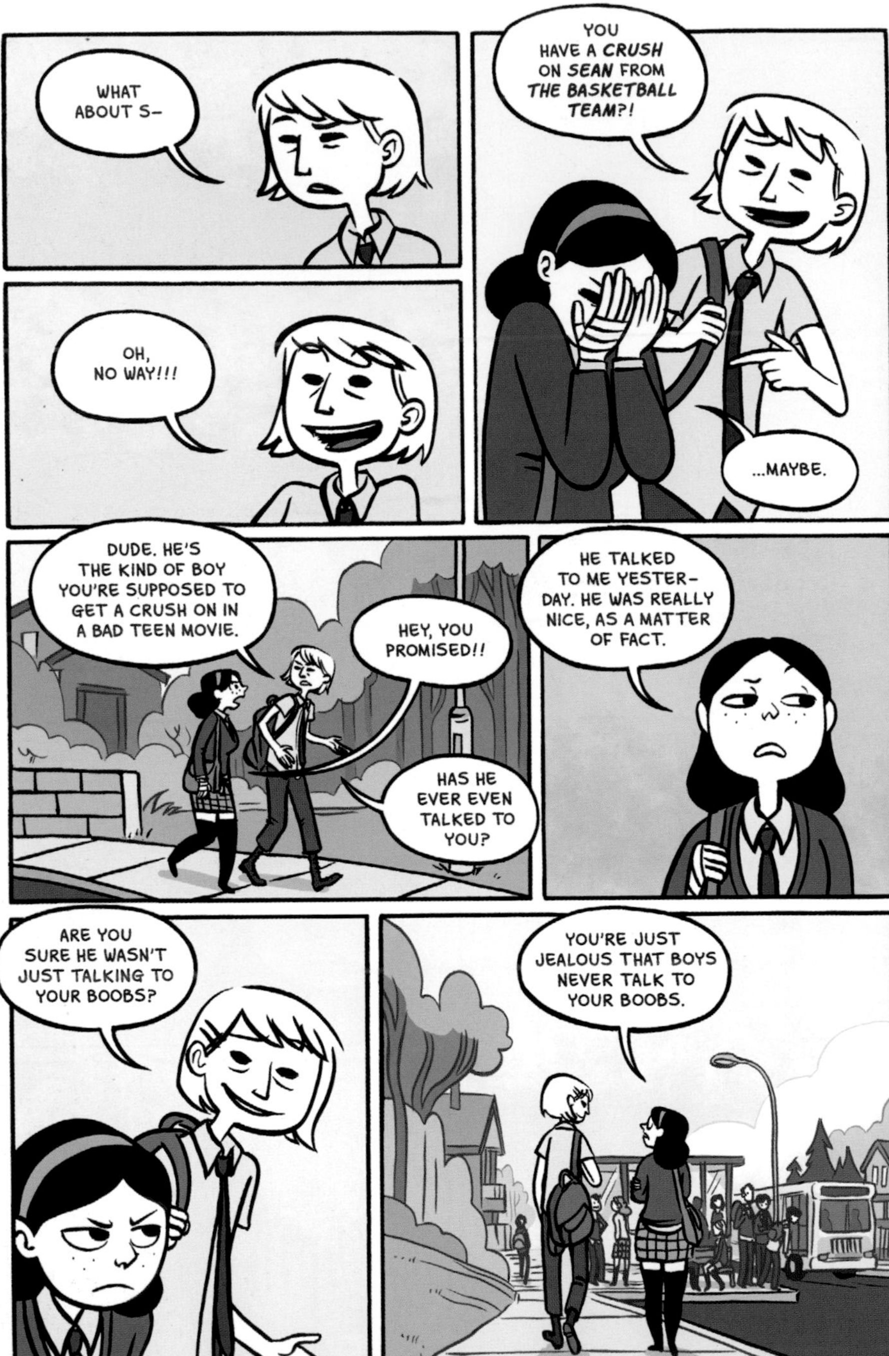
WHAT ABOUT S–
OH, NO WAY!!!
YOU HAVE A *CRUSH* ON *SEAN* FROM *THE BASKETBALL TEAM*?!
...MAYBE.
DUDE. HE'S THE KIND OF BOY YOU'RE SUPPOSED TO GET A CRUSH ON IN A BAD TEEN MOVIE.
HEY, YOU PROMISED!!
HAS HE EVER EVEN TALKED TO YOU?
HE TALKED TO ME YESTER-DAY. HE WAS REALLY NICE, AS A MATTER OF FACT.
ARE YOU SURE HE WASN'T JUST TALKING TO YOUR BOOBS?
YOU'RE JUST JEALOUS THAT BOYS NEVER TALK TO YOUR BOOBS.

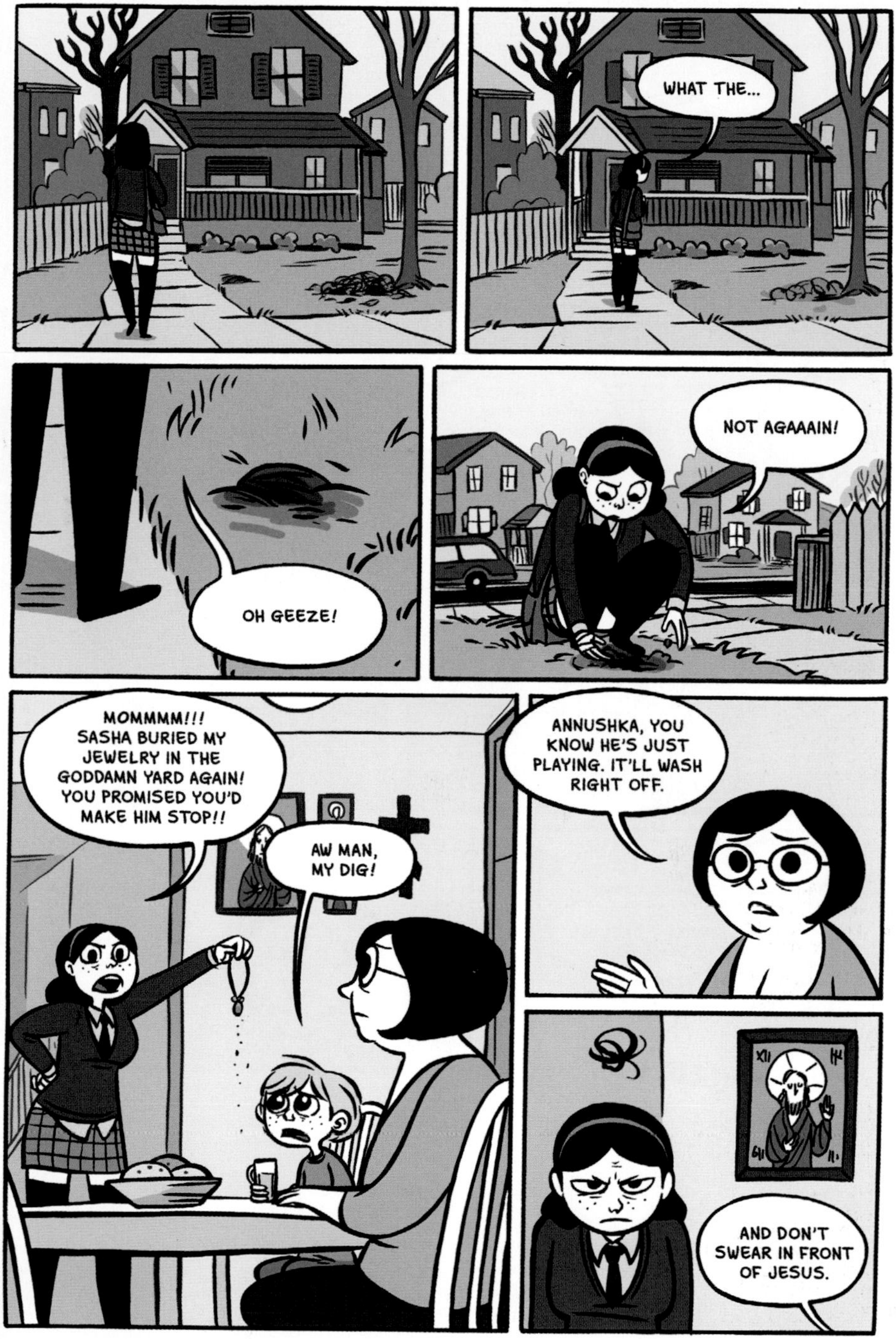
WHAT THE...
OH GEEZE!
NOT AGAAAIN!
MOMMMM!!! SASHA BURIED MY JEWELRY IN THE GODDAMN YARD AGAIN! YOU PROMISED YOU'D MAKE HIM STOP!!
AW MAN, MY DIG!
ANNUSHKA, YOU KNOW HE'S JUST PLAYING. IT'LL WASH RIGHT OFF.
AND DON'T SWEAR IN FRONT OF JESUS.

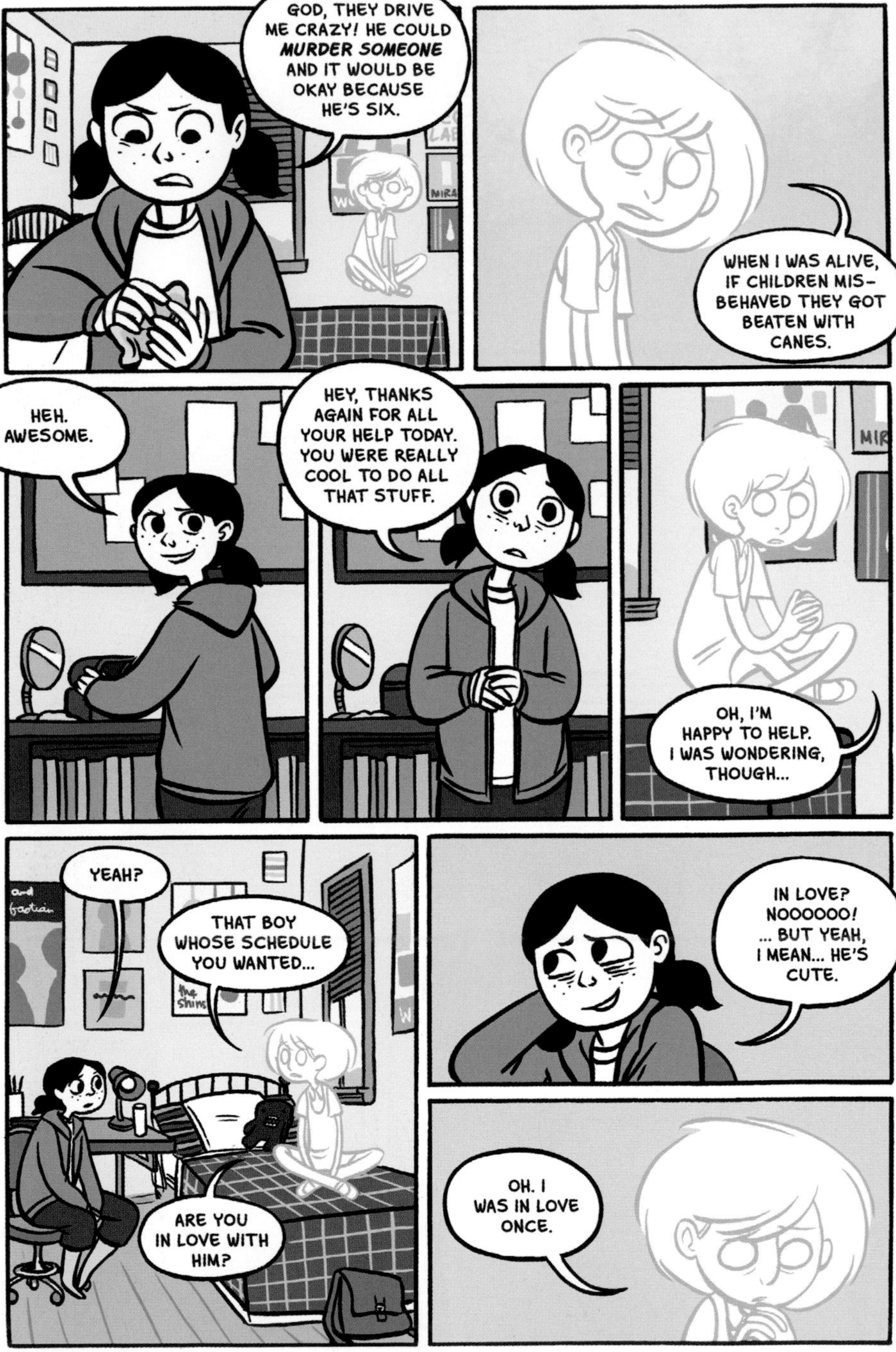
GOD, THEY DRIVE ME CRAZY! HE COULD *MURDER SOMEONE* AND IT WOULD BE OKAY BECAUSE HE'S SIX.
WHEN I WAS ALIVE, IF CHILDREN MIS-BEHAVED THEY GOT BEATEN WITH CANES.
HEH. AWESOME.
HEY, THANKS AGAIN FOR ALL YOUR HELP TODAY. YOU WERE REALLY COOL TO DO ALL THAT STUFF.
OH, I'M HAPPY TO HELP. I WAS WONDERING, THOUGH...
YEAH?
THAT BOY WHOSE SCHEDULE YOU WANTED...
ARE YOU IN LOVE WITH HIM?
IN LOVE? NOOOOOO! ... BUT YEAH, I MEAN... HE'S CUTE.
OH. I WAS IN LOVE ONCE.

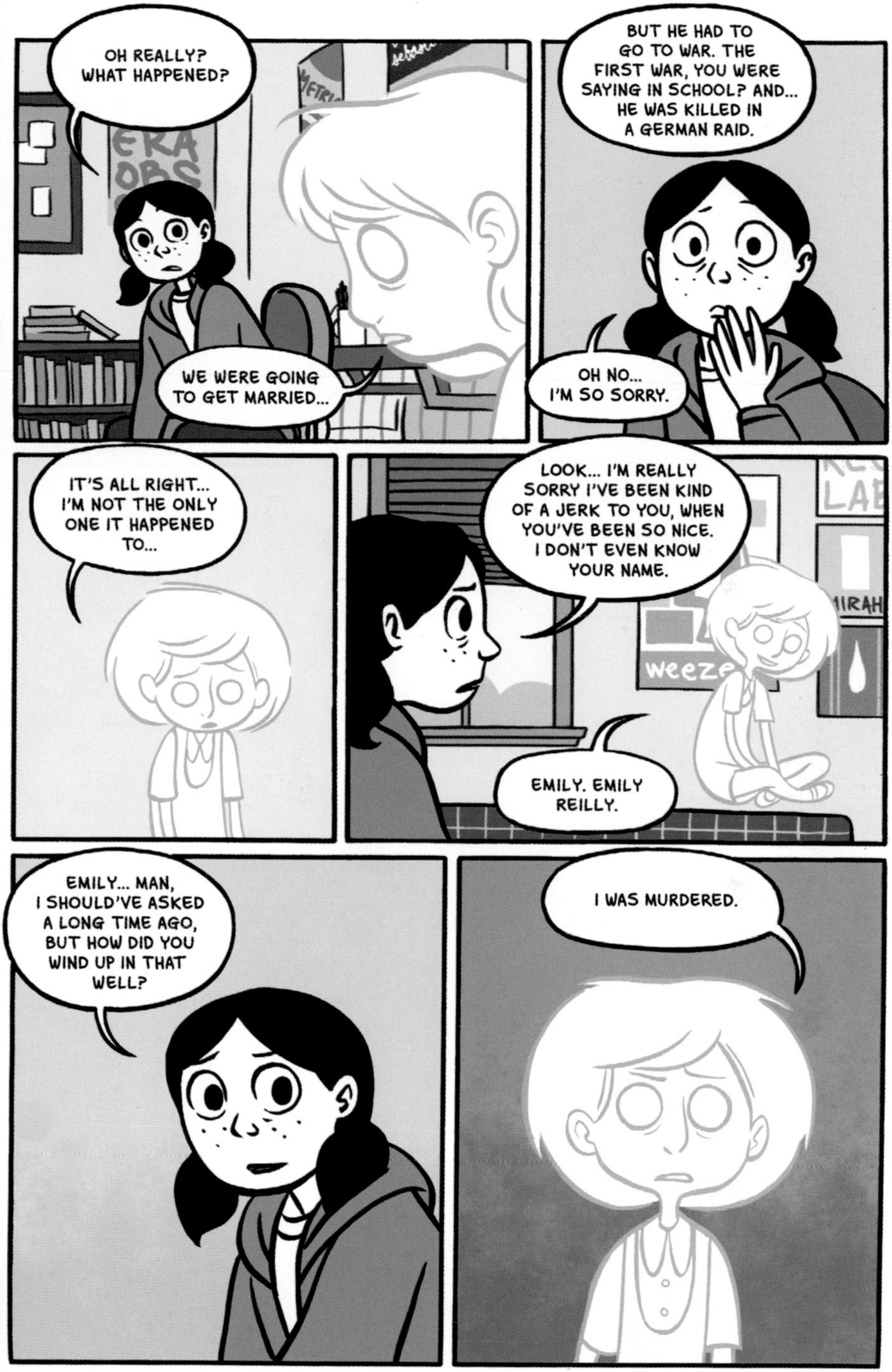
OH REALLY? WHAT HAPPENED?
WE WERE GOING TO GET MARRIED...
BUT HE HAD TO GO TO WAR. THE FIRST WAR, YOU WERE SAYING IN SCHOOL? AND... HE WAS KILLED IN A GERMAN RAID.
OH NO... I'M SO SORRY.
IT'S ALL RIGHT... I'M NOT THE ONLY ONE IT HAPPENED TO...
LOOK... I'M REALLY SORRY I'VE BEEN KIND OF A JERK TO YOU, WHEN YOU'VE BEEN SO NICE. I DON'T EVEN KNOW YOUR NAME.
EMILY. EMILY REILLY.
EMILY... MAN, I SHOULD'VE ASKED A LONG TIME AGO, BUT HOW DID YOU WIND UP IN THAT WELL?
I WAS MURDERED.

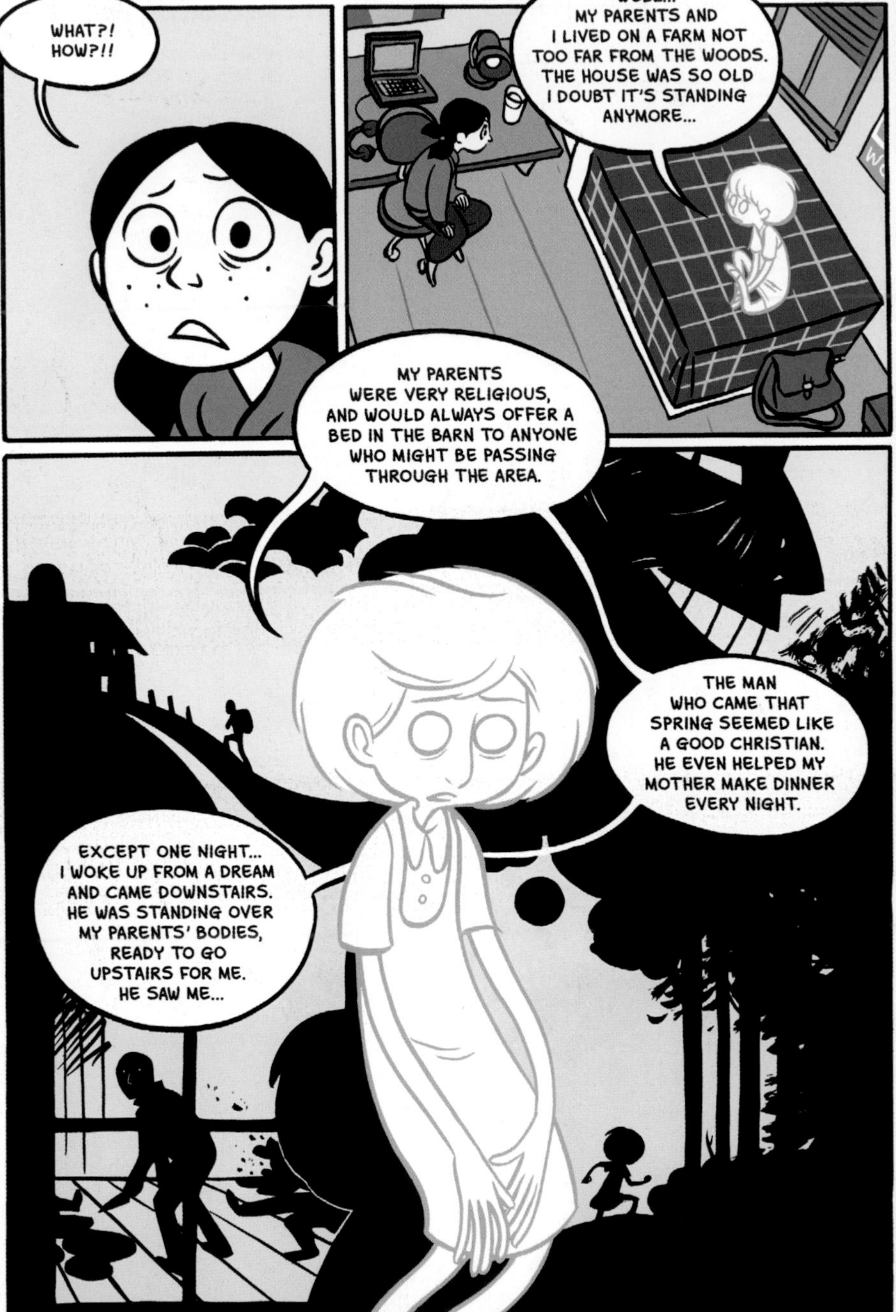
WHAT?! HOW?!!
WELL... MY PARENTS AND I LIVED ON A FARM NOT TOO FAR FROM THE WOODS. THE HOUSE WAS SO OLD I DOUBT IT'S STANDING ANYMORE...
MY PARENTS WERE VERY RELIGIOUS, AND WOULD ALWAYS OFFER A BED IN THE BARN TO ANYONE WHO MIGHT BE PASSING THROUGH THE AREA.
THE MAN WHO CAME THAT SPRING SEEMED LIKE A GOOD CHRISTIAN. HE EVEN HELPED MY MOTHER MAKE DINNER EVERY NIGHT.
EXCEPT ONE NIGHT... I WOKE UP FROM A DREAM AND CAME DOWNSTAIRS. HE WAS STANDING OVER MY PARENTS' BODIES, READY TO GO UPSTAIRS FOR ME. HE SAW ME...

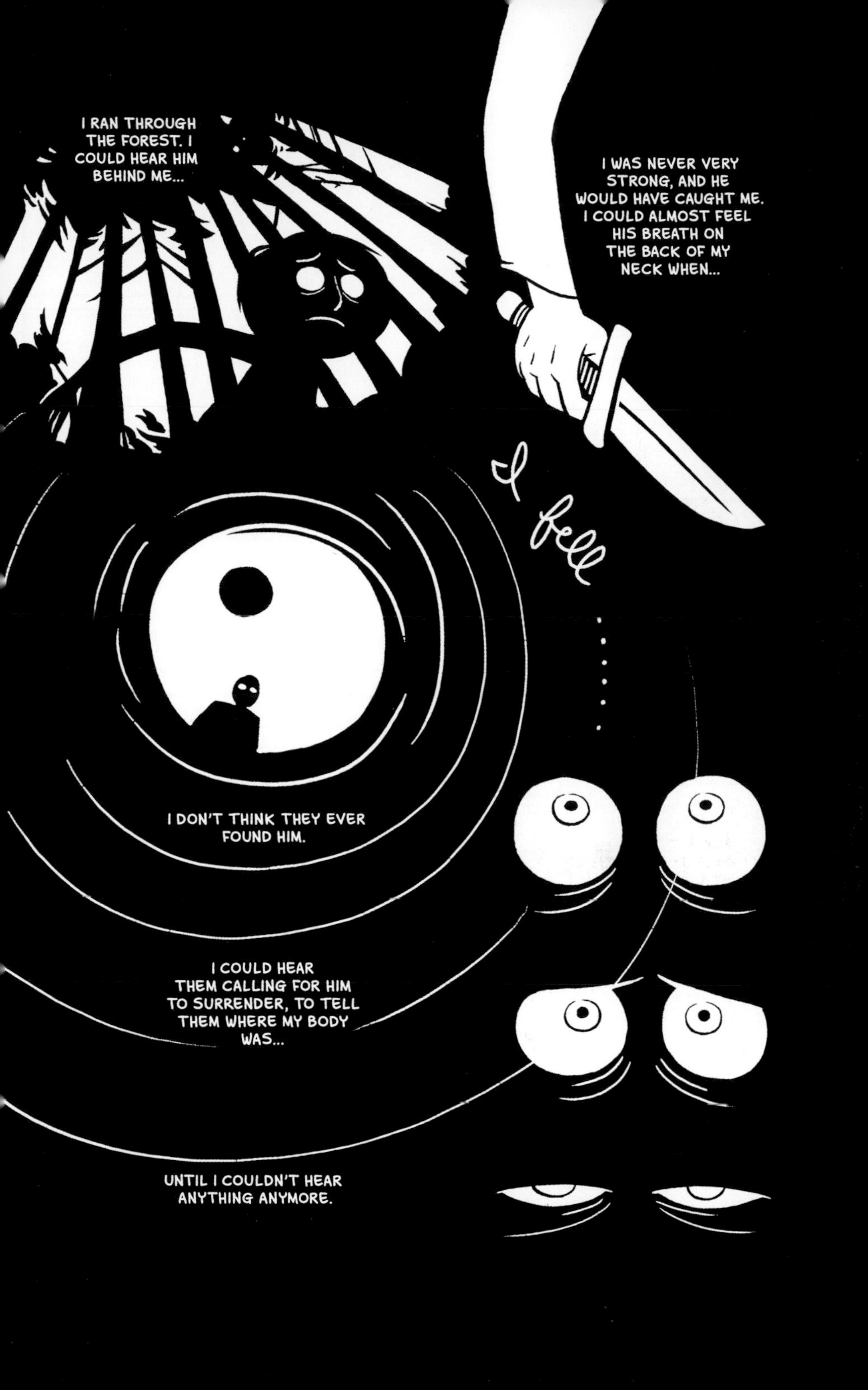
I RAN THROUGH THE FOREST. I COULD HEAR HIM BEHIND ME...
I WAS NEVER VERY STRONG, AND HE WOULD HAVE CAUGHT ME. I COULD ALMOST FEEL HIS BREATH ON THE BACK OF MY NECK WHEN...
I fell
....
I DON'T THINK THEY EVER FOUND HIM.
I COULD HEAR THEM CALLING FOR HIM TO SURRENDER, TO TELL THEM WHERE MY BODY WAS...
UNTIL I COULDN'T HEAR ANYTHING ANYMORE.

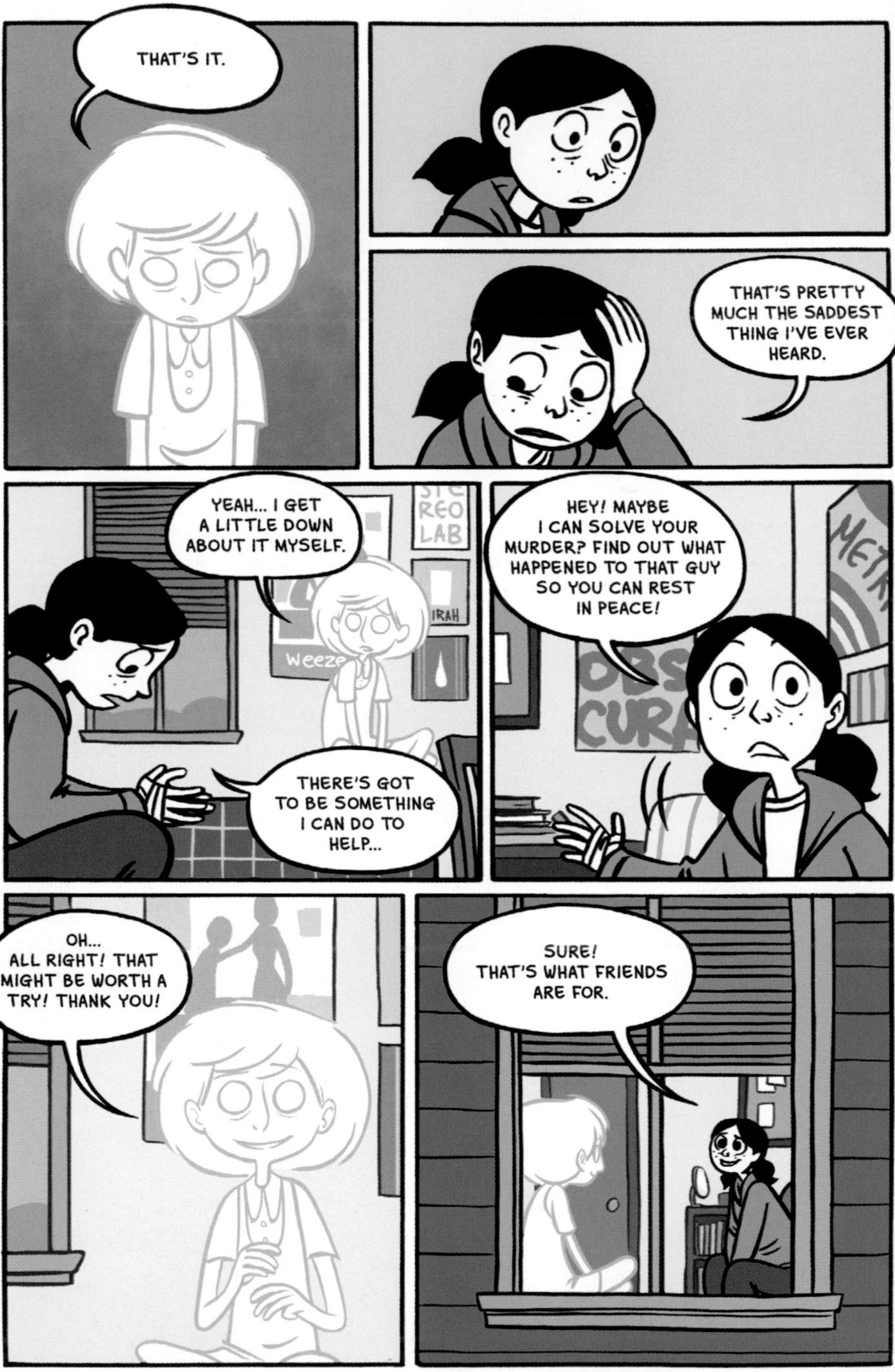
THAT'S IT.
THAT'S PRETTY MUCH THE SADDEST THING I'VE EVER HEARD.
YEAH... I GET A LITTLE DOWN ABOUT IT MYSELF.
STE REO LAB
WEEZE
THERE'S GOT TO BE SOMETHING I CAN DO TO HELP...
HEY! MAYBE I CAN SOLVE YOUR MURDER? FIND OUT WHAT HAPPENED TO THAT GUY SO YOU CAN REST IN PEACE!
OBS CURA
OH... ALL RIGHT! THAT MIGHT BE WORTH A TRY! THANK YOU!
SURE! THAT'S WHAT FRIENDS ARE FOR.

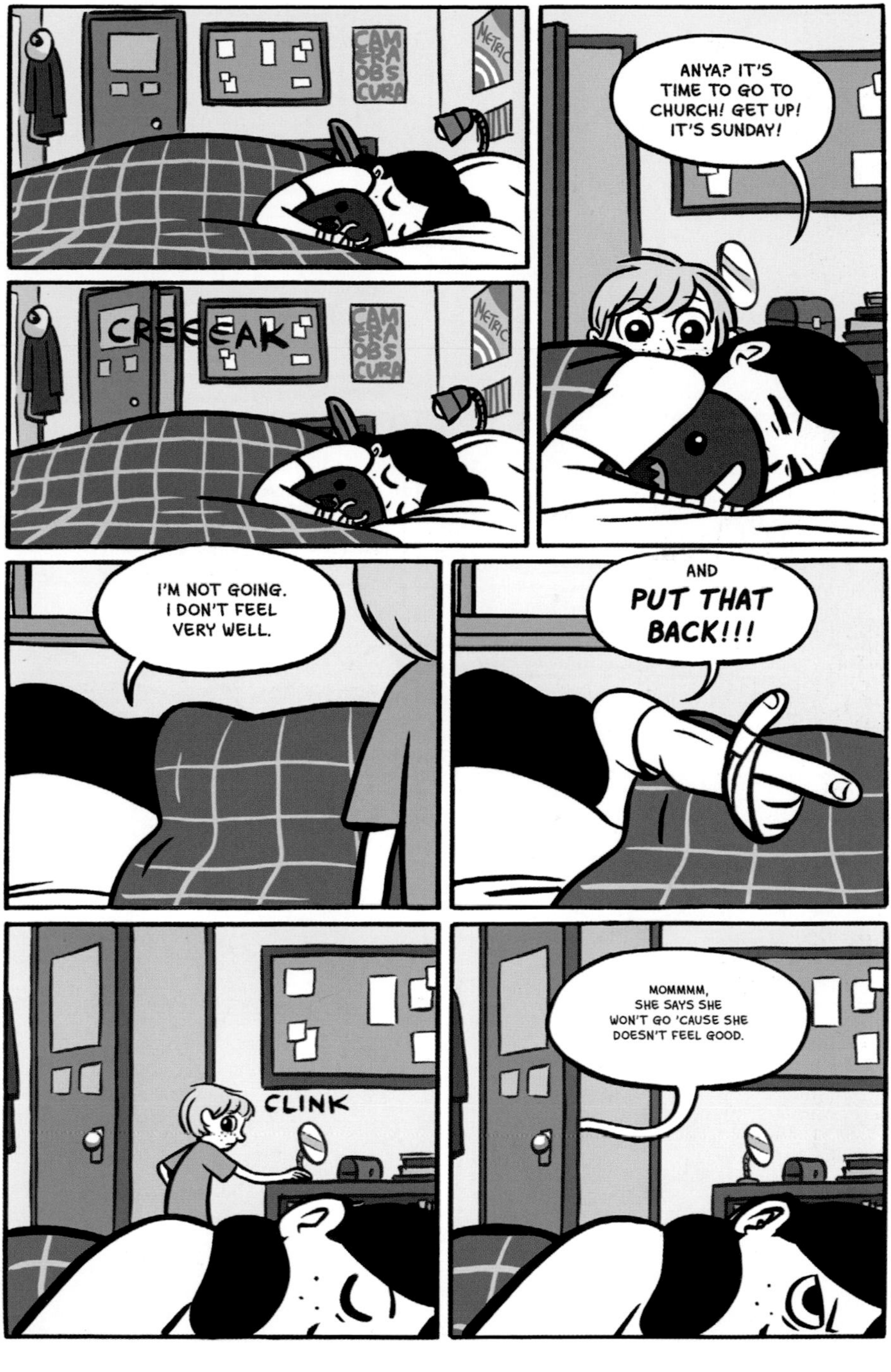
CAMERA OBSCURA
METRIC
CREEEAK
ANYA? IT'S TIME TO GO TO CHURCH! GET UP! IT'S SUNDAY!
I'M NOT GOING. I DON'T FEEL VERY WELL.
AND PUT THAT BACK!!!
CLINK
MOMMMM, SHE SAYS SHE WON'T GO 'CAUSE SHE DOESN'T FEEL GOOD.

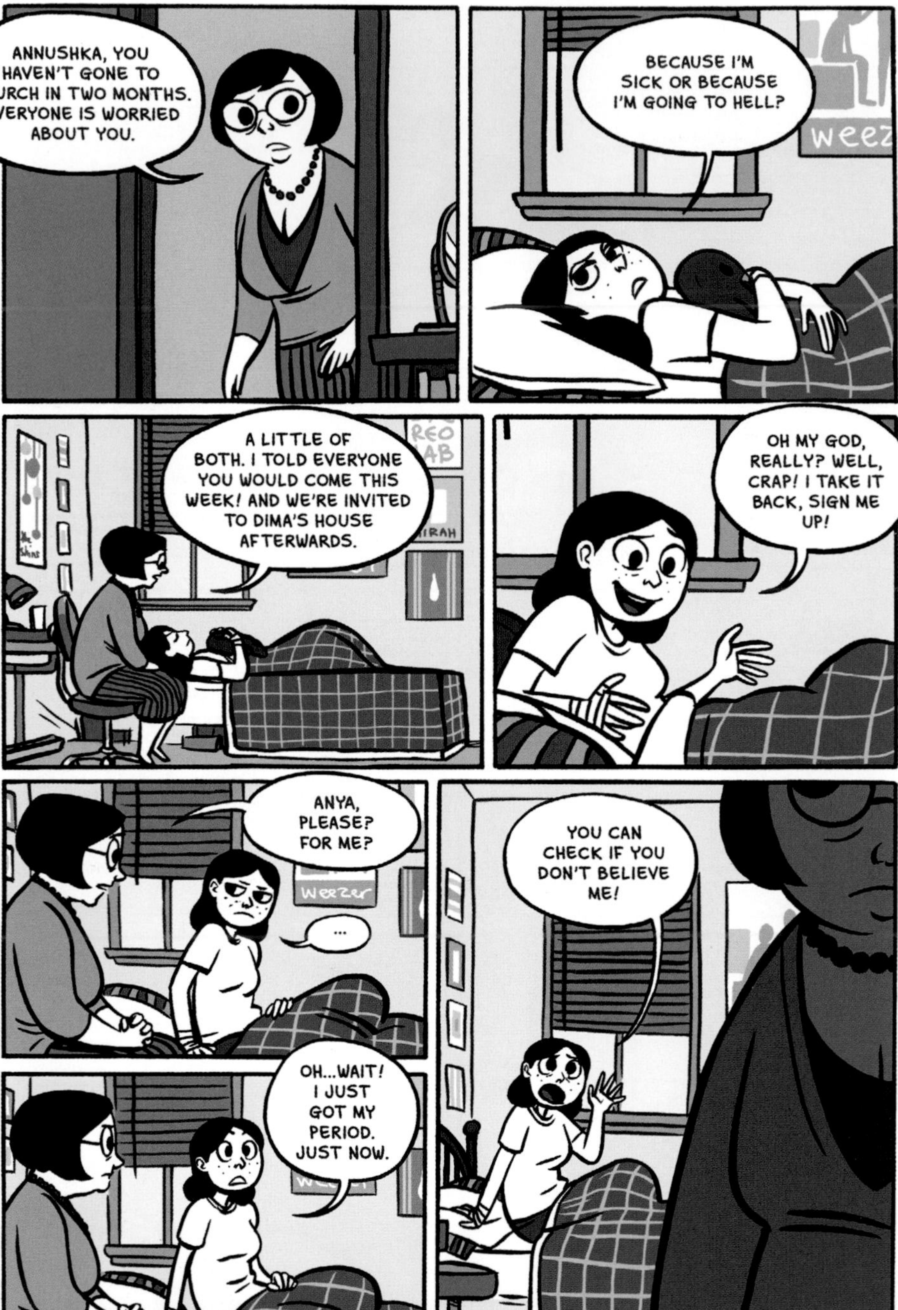
ANNUSHKA, YOU HAVEN'T GONE TO CHURCH IN TWO MONTHS. EVERYONE IS WORRIED ABOUT YOU.
BECAUSE I'M SICK OR BECAUSE I'M GOING TO HELL?
weez
A LITTLE OF BOTH. I TOLD EVERYONE YOU WOULD COME THIS WEEK! AND WE'RE INVITED TO DIMA'S HOUSE AFTERWARDS.
OH MY GOD, REALLY? WELL, CRAP! I TAKE IT BACK, SIGN ME UP!
ANYA, PLEASE? FOR ME?
weezer
...
OH...WAIT! I JUST GOT MY PERIOD. JUST NOW.
YOU CAN CHECK IF YOU DON'T BELIEVE ME!

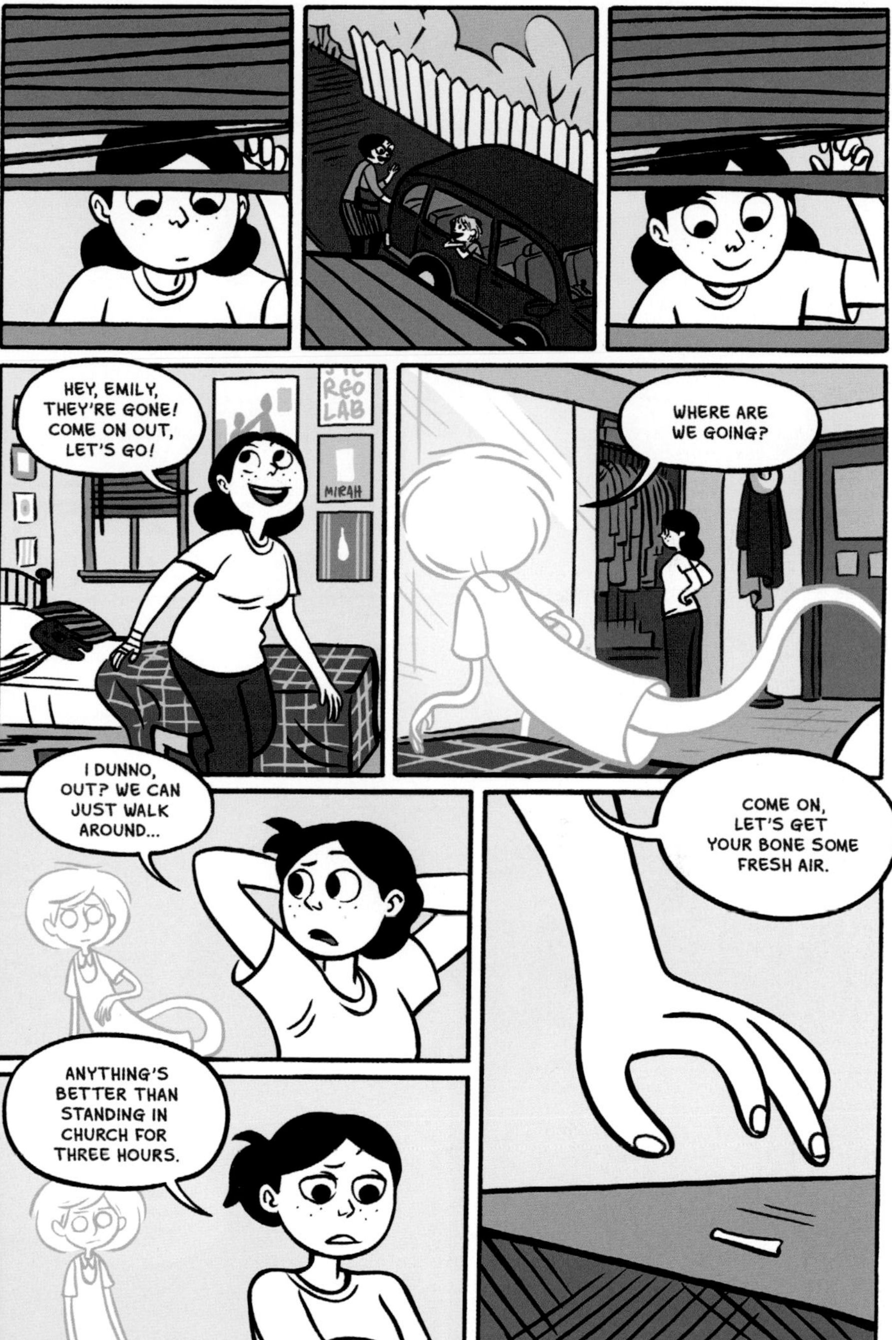

HEY, EMILY, THEY'RE GONE! COME ON OUT, LET'S GO!
STEREOLAB
MIRAH
WHERE ARE WE GOING?
I DUNNO, OUT? WE CAN JUST WALK AROUND...
COME ON, LET'S GET YOUR BONE SOME FRESH AIR.
ANYTHING'S BETTER THAN STANDING IN CHURCH FOR THREE HOURS.

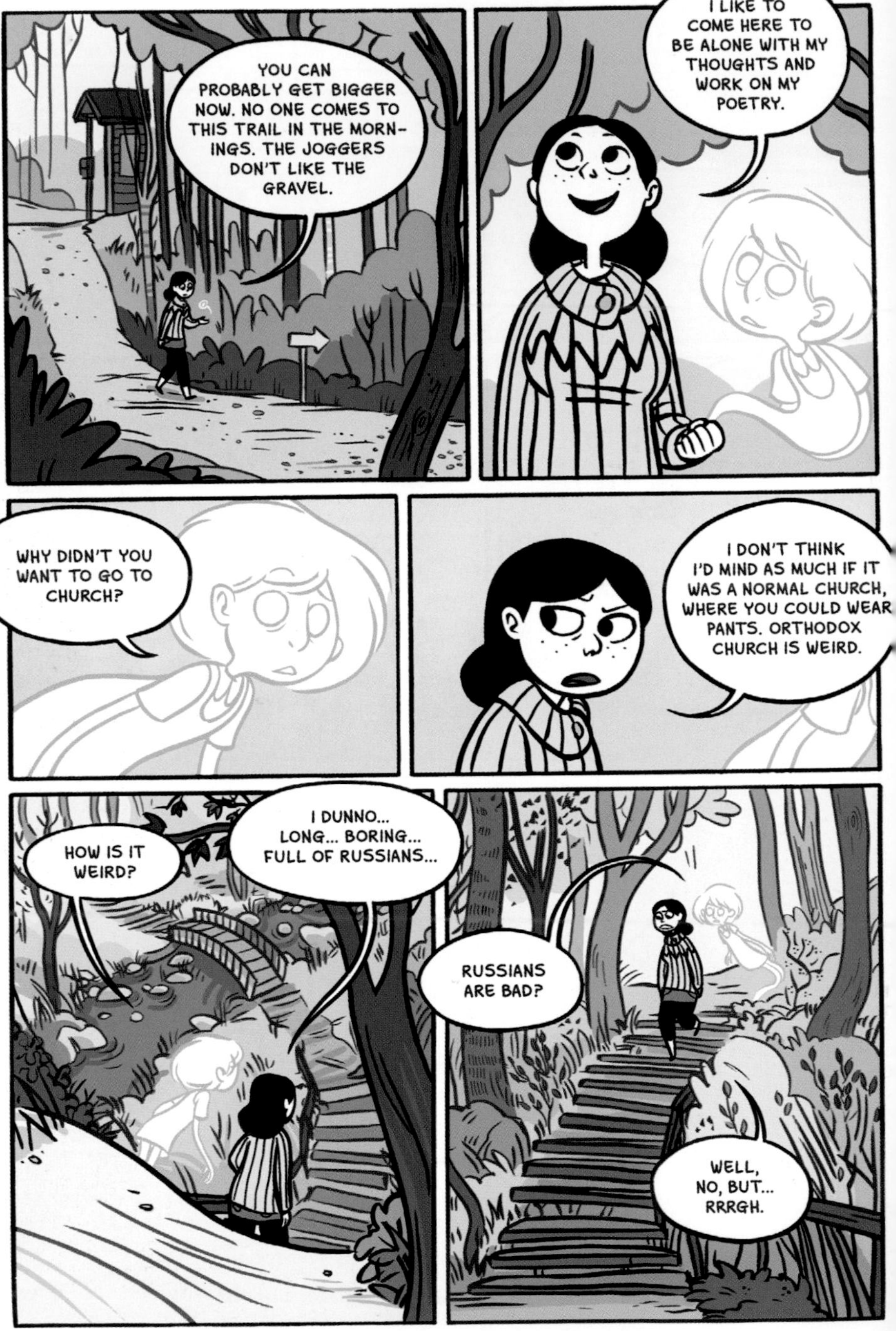
YOU CAN PROBABLY GET BIGGER NOW. NO ONE COMES TO THIS TRAIL IN THE MORNINGS. THE JOGGERS DON'T LIKE THE GRAVEL.
I LIKE TO COME HERE TO BE ALONE WITH MY THOUGHTS AND WORK ON MY POETRY.
WHY DIDN'T YOU WANT TO GO TO CHURCH?
I DON'T THINK I'D MIND AS MUCH IF IT WAS A NORMAL CHURCH, WHERE YOU COULD WEAR PANTS. ORTHODOX CHURCH IS WEIRD.
HOW IS IT WEIRD?
I DUNNO... LONG... BORING... FULL OF RUSSIANS...
RUSSIANS ARE BAD?
WELL, NO, BUT... RRRGH.

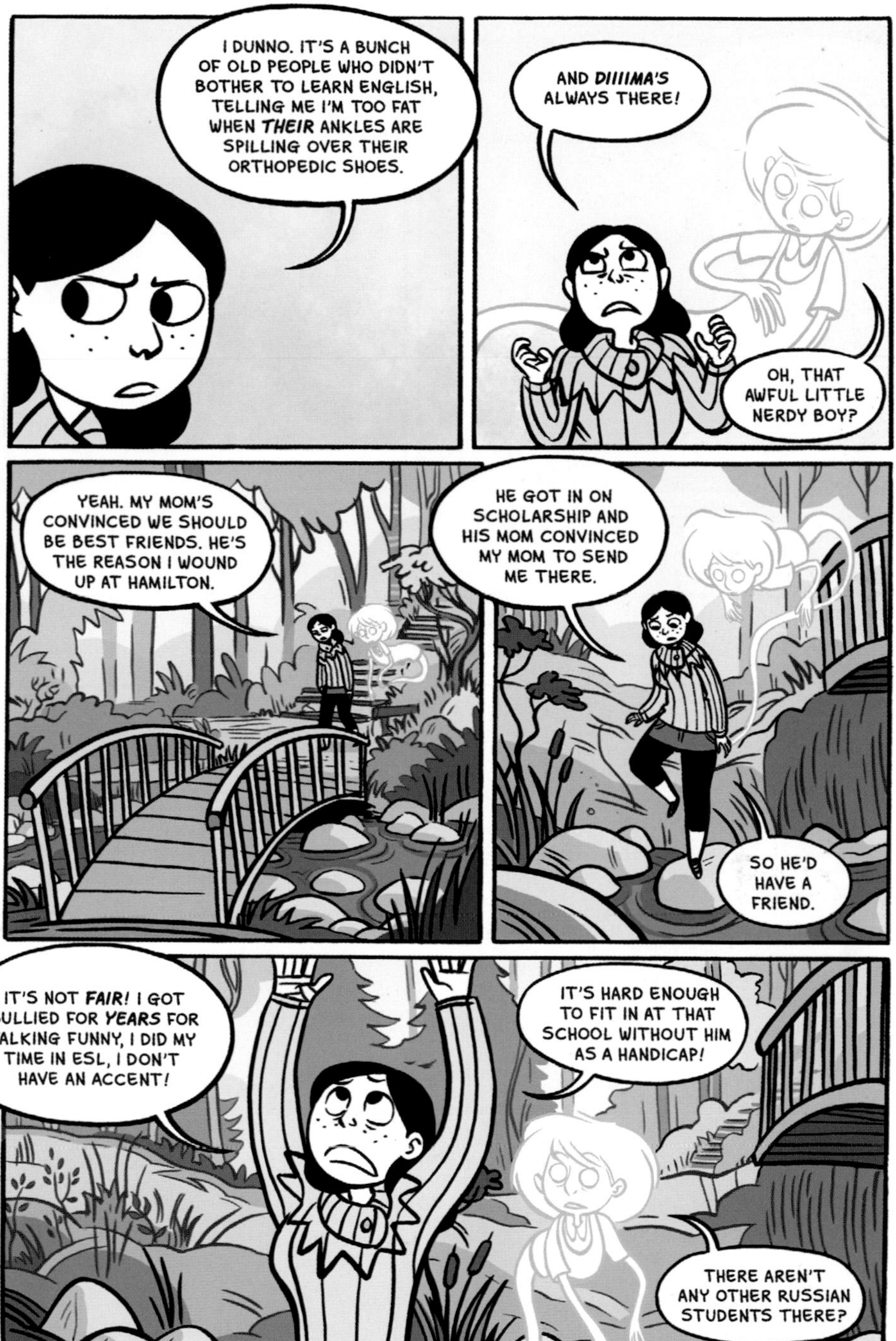
I DUNNO. IT'S A BUNCH OF OLD PEOPLE WHO DIDN'T BOTHER TO LEARN ENGLISH, TELLING ME I'M TOO FAT WHEN *THEIR* ANKLES ARE SPILLING OVER THEIR ORTHOPEDIC SHOES.
AND *DIIIIMA'S* ALWAYS THERE!
OH, THAT AWFUL LITTLE NERDY BOY?
YEAH. MY MOM'S CONVINCED WE SHOULD BE BEST FRIENDS. HE'S THE REASON I WOUND UP AT HAMILTON.
HE GOT IN ON SCHOLARSHIP AND HIS MOM CONVINCED MY MOM TO SEND ME THERE.
SO HE'D HAVE A FRIEND.
IT'S NOT *FAIR*! I GOT BULLIED FOR *YEARS* FOR TALKING FUNNY, I DID MY TIME IN ESL, I DON'T HAVE AN ACCENT!
IT'S HARD ENOUGH TO FIT IN AT THAT SCHOOL WITHOUT HIM AS A HANDICAP!
THERE AREN'T ANY OTHER RUSSIAN STUDENTS THERE?

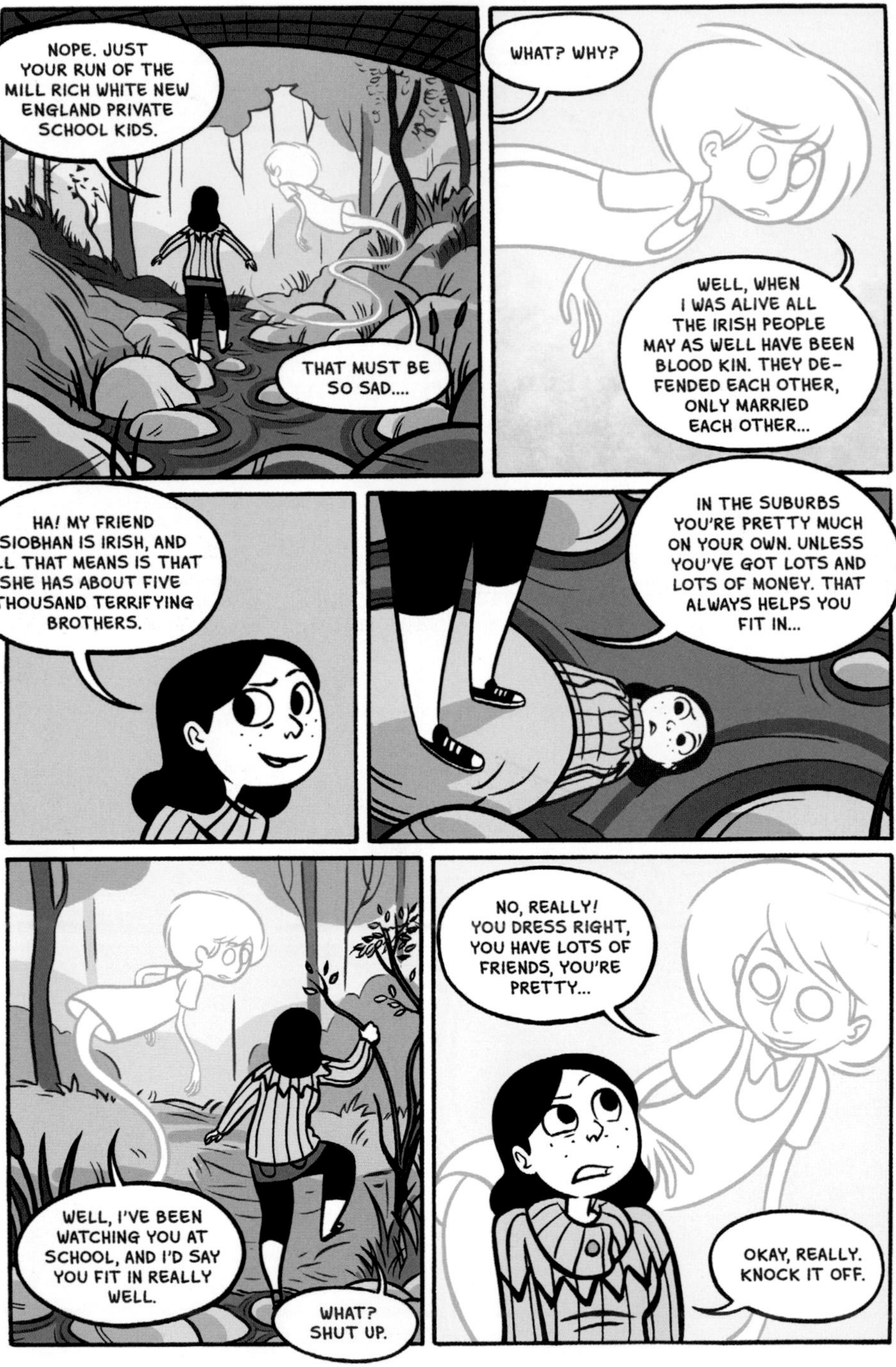
NOPE. JUST YOUR RUN OF THE MILL RICH WHITE NEW ENGLAND PRIVATE SCHOOL KIDS.
THAT MUST BE SO SAD....
WHAT? WHY?
WELL, WHEN I WAS ALIVE ALL THE IRISH PEOPLE MAY AS WELL HAVE BEEN BLOOD KIN. THEY DE-FENDED EACH OTHER, ONLY MARRIED EACH OTHER...
HA! MY FRIEND SIOBHAN IS IRISH, AND ALL THAT MEANS IS THAT SHE HAS ABOUT FIVE THOUSAND TERRIFYING BROTHERS.
IN THE SUBURBS YOU'RE PRETTY MUCH ON YOUR OWN. UNLESS YOU'VE GOT LOTS AND LOTS OF MONEY. THAT ALWAYS HELPS YOU FIT IN...
WELL, I'VE BEEN WATCHING YOU AT SCHOOL, AND I'D SAY YOU FIT IN REALLY WELL.
WHAT? SHUT UP.
NO, REALLY! YOU DRESS RIGHT, YOU HAVE LOTS OF FRIENDS, YOU'RE PRETTY...
OKAY, REALLY. KNOCK IT OFF.

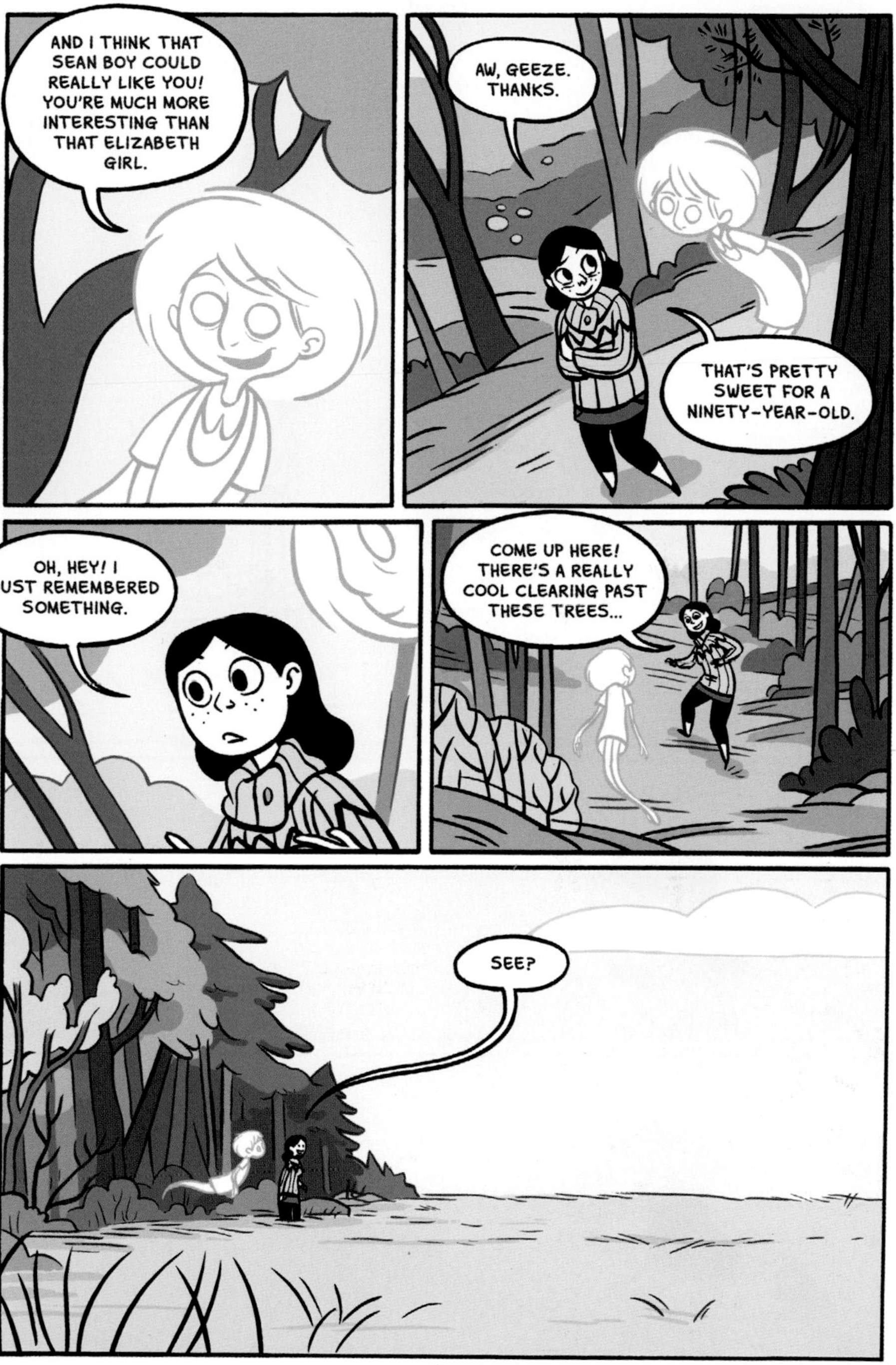
AND I THINK THAT SEAN BOY COULD REALLY LIKE YOU! YOU'RE MUCH MORE INTERESTING THAN THAT ELIZABETH GIRL.
AW, GEEZE. THANKS.
THAT'S PRETTY SWEET FOR A NINETY-YEAR-OLD.
OH, HEY! I JUST REMEMBERED SOMETHING.
COME UP HERE! THERE'S A REALLY COOL CLEARING PAST THESE TREES...
SEE?

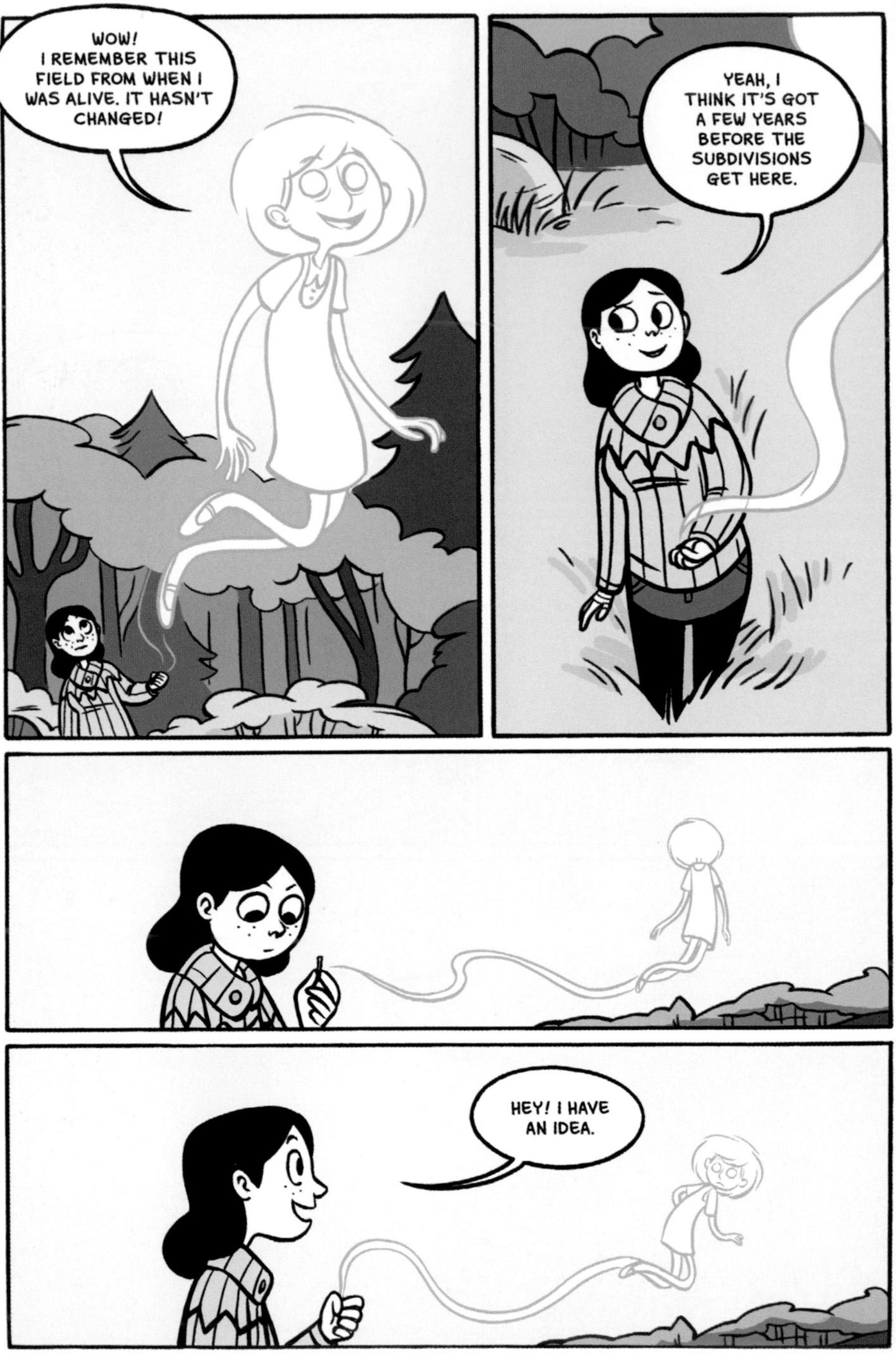
WOW!
I REMEMBER THIS FIELD FROM WHEN I WAS ALIVE. IT HASN'T CHANGED!
YEAH, I THINK IT'S GOT A FEW YEARS BEFORE THE SUBDIVISIONS GET HERE.
HEY! I HAVE AN IDEA.

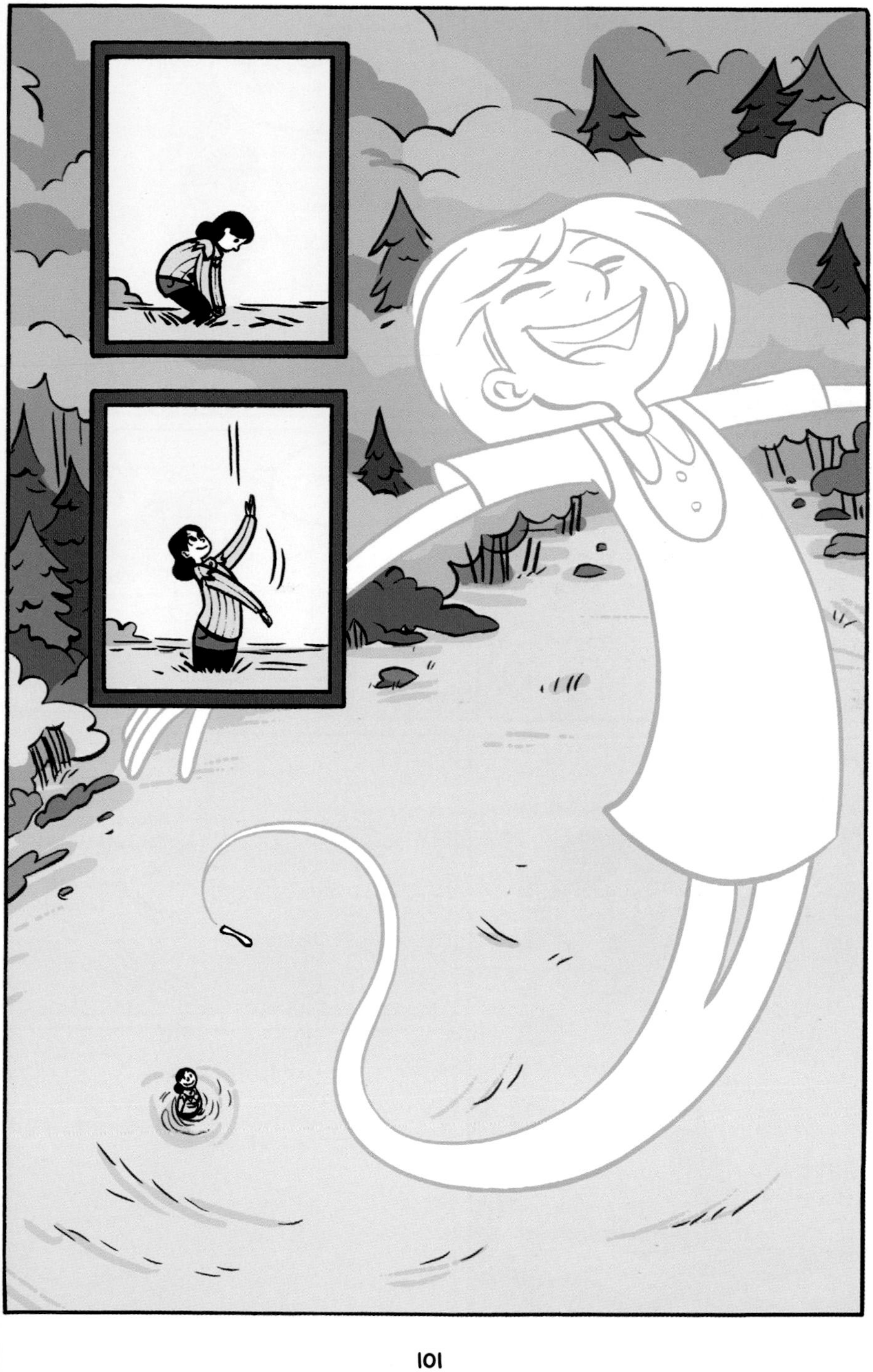

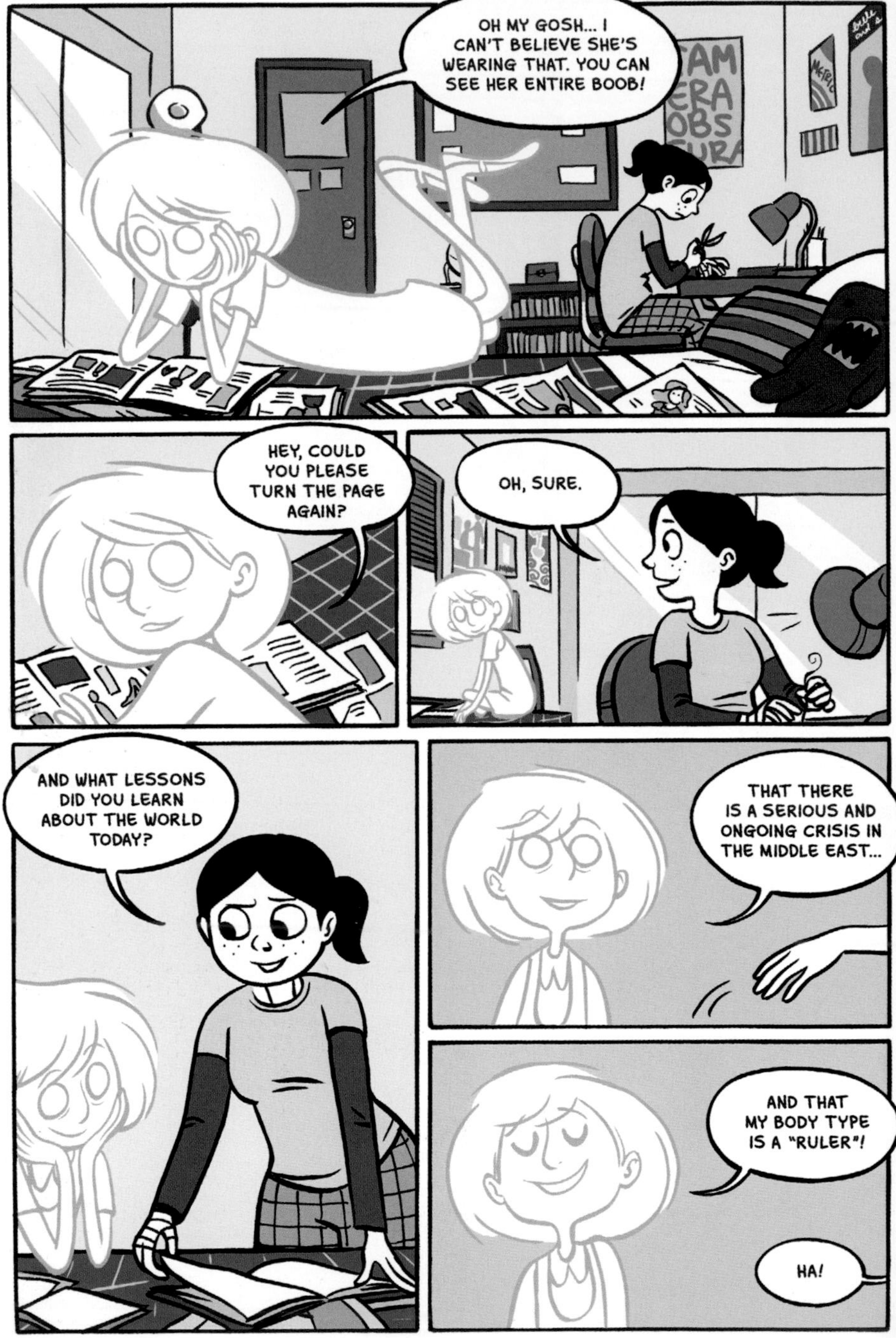
OH MY GOSH... I CAN'T BELIEVE SHE'S WEARING THAT. YOU CAN SEE HER ENTIRE BOOB!
HEY, COULD YOU PLEASE TURN THE PAGE AGAIN?
OH, SURE.
AND WHAT LESSONS DID YOU LEARN ABOUT THE WORLD TODAY?
THAT THERE IS A SERIOUS AND ONGOING CRISIS IN THE MIDDLE EAST...
AND THAT MY BODY TYPE IS A "RULER"!
HA!

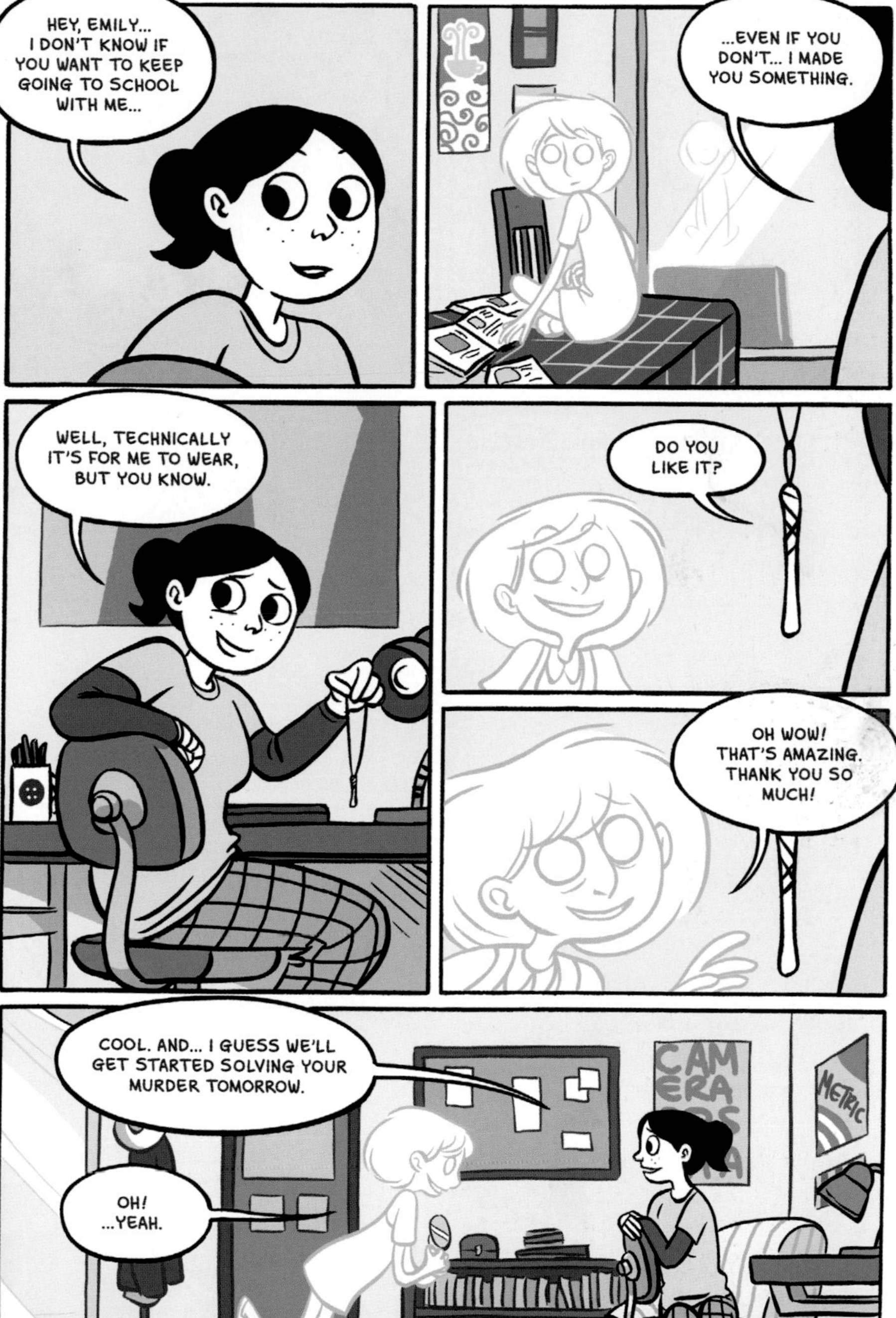
HEY, EMILY... I DON'T KNOW IF YOU WANT TO KEEP GOING TO SCHOOL WITH ME...
...EVEN IF YOU DON'T... I MADE YOU SOMETHING.
WELL, TECHNICALLY IT'S FOR ME TO WEAR, BUT YOU KNOW.
DO YOU LIKE IT?
OH WOW! THAT'S AMAZING. THANK YOU SO MUCH!
COOL. AND... I GUESS WE'LL GET STARTED SOLVING YOUR MURDER TOMORROW.
OH! ...YEAH.
METRIC

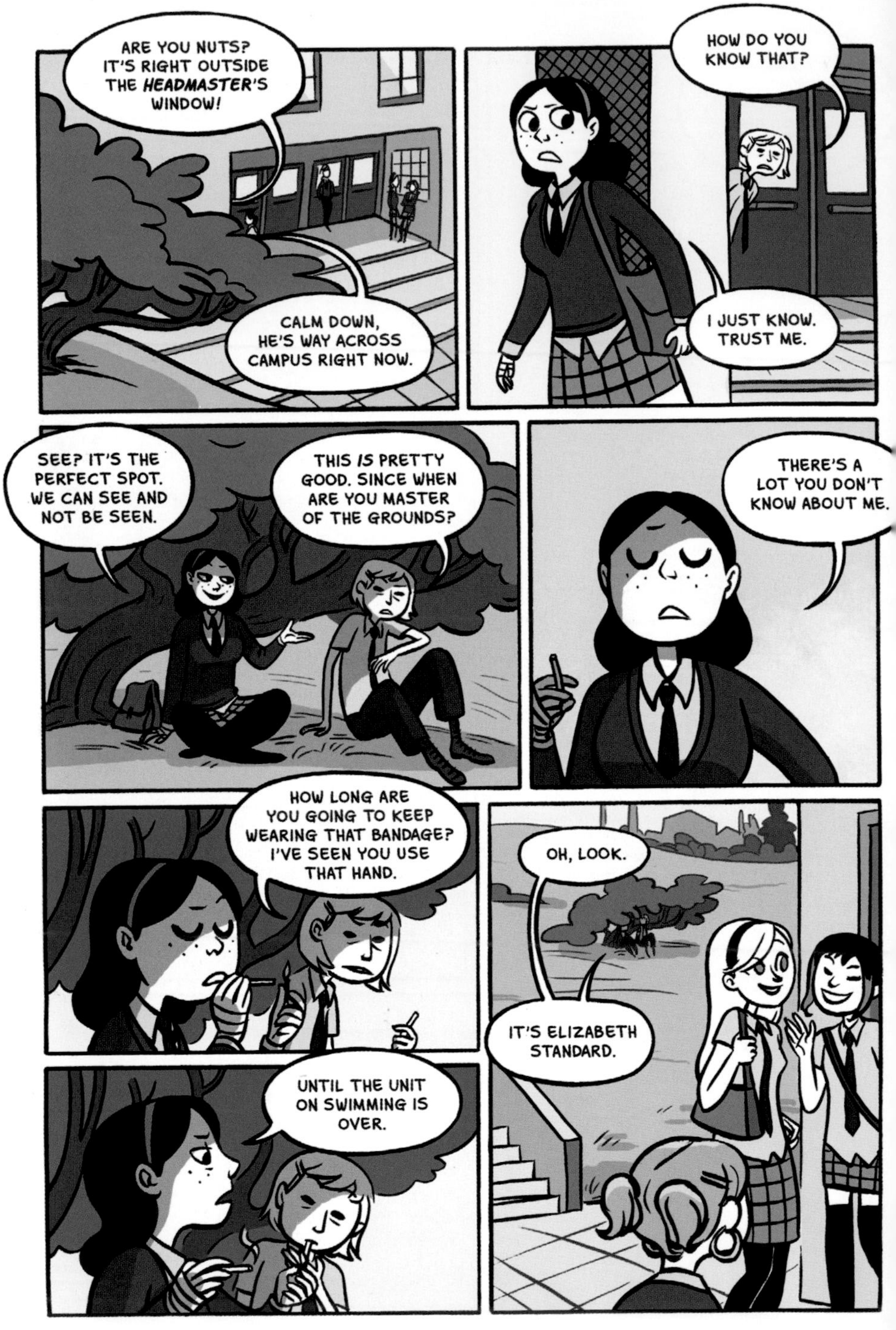
ARE YOU NUTS? IT'S RIGHT OUTSIDE THE *HEADMASTER*'S WINDOW!
CALM DOWN, HE'S WAY ACROSS CAMPUS RIGHT NOW.
HOW DO YOU KNOW THAT?
I JUST KNOW. TRUST ME.
SEE? IT'S THE PERFECT SPOT. WE CAN SEE AND NOT BE SEEN.
THIS *IS* PRETTY GOOD. SINCE WHEN ARE YOU MASTER OF THE GROUNDS?
THERE'S A LOT YOU DON'T KNOW ABOUT ME.
HOW LONG ARE YOU GOING TO KEEP WEARING THAT BANDAGE? I'VE SEEN YOU USE THAT HAND.
UNTIL THE UNIT ON SWIMMING IS OVER.
OH, LOOK.
IT'S ELIZABETH STANDARD.

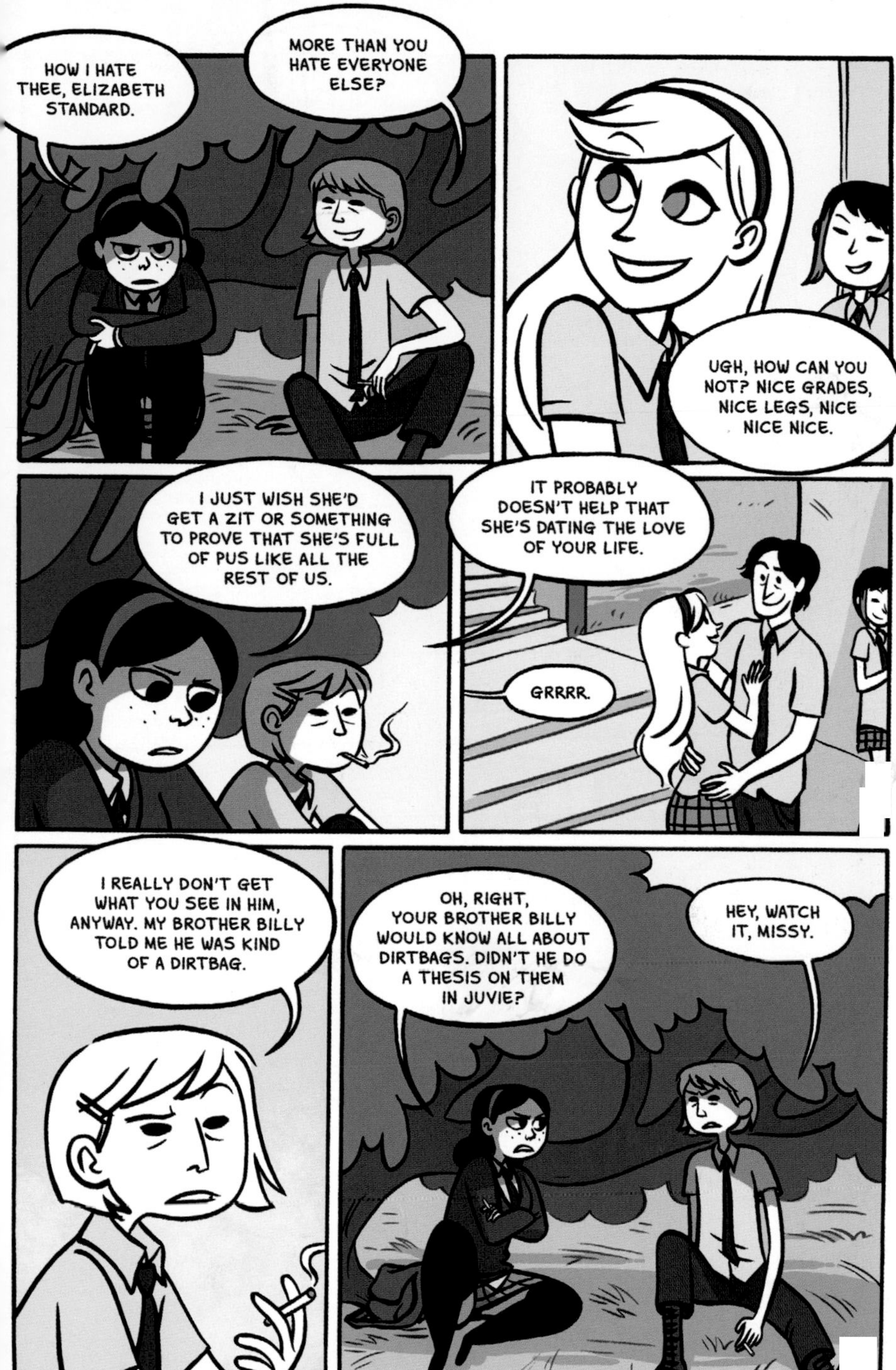
HOW I HATE THEE, ELIZABETH STANDARD.
MORE THAN YOU HATE EVERYONE ELSE?
UGH, HOW CAN YOU NOT? NICE GRADES, NICE LEGS, NICE NICE NICE.
I JUST WISH SHE'D GET A ZIT OR SOMETHING TO PROVE THAT SHE'S FULL OF PUS LIKE ALL THE REST OF US.
IT PROBABLY DOESN'T HELP THAT SHE'S DATING THE LOVE OF YOUR LIFE.
GRRRR.
I REALLY DON'T GET WHAT YOU SEE IN HIM, ANYWAY. MY BROTHER BILLY TOLD ME HE WAS KIND OF A DIRTBAG.
OH, RIGHT, YOUR BROTHER BILLY WOULD KNOW ALL ABOUT DIRTBAGS. DIDN'T HE DO A THESIS ON THEM IN JUVIE?
HEY, WATCH IT, MISSY.

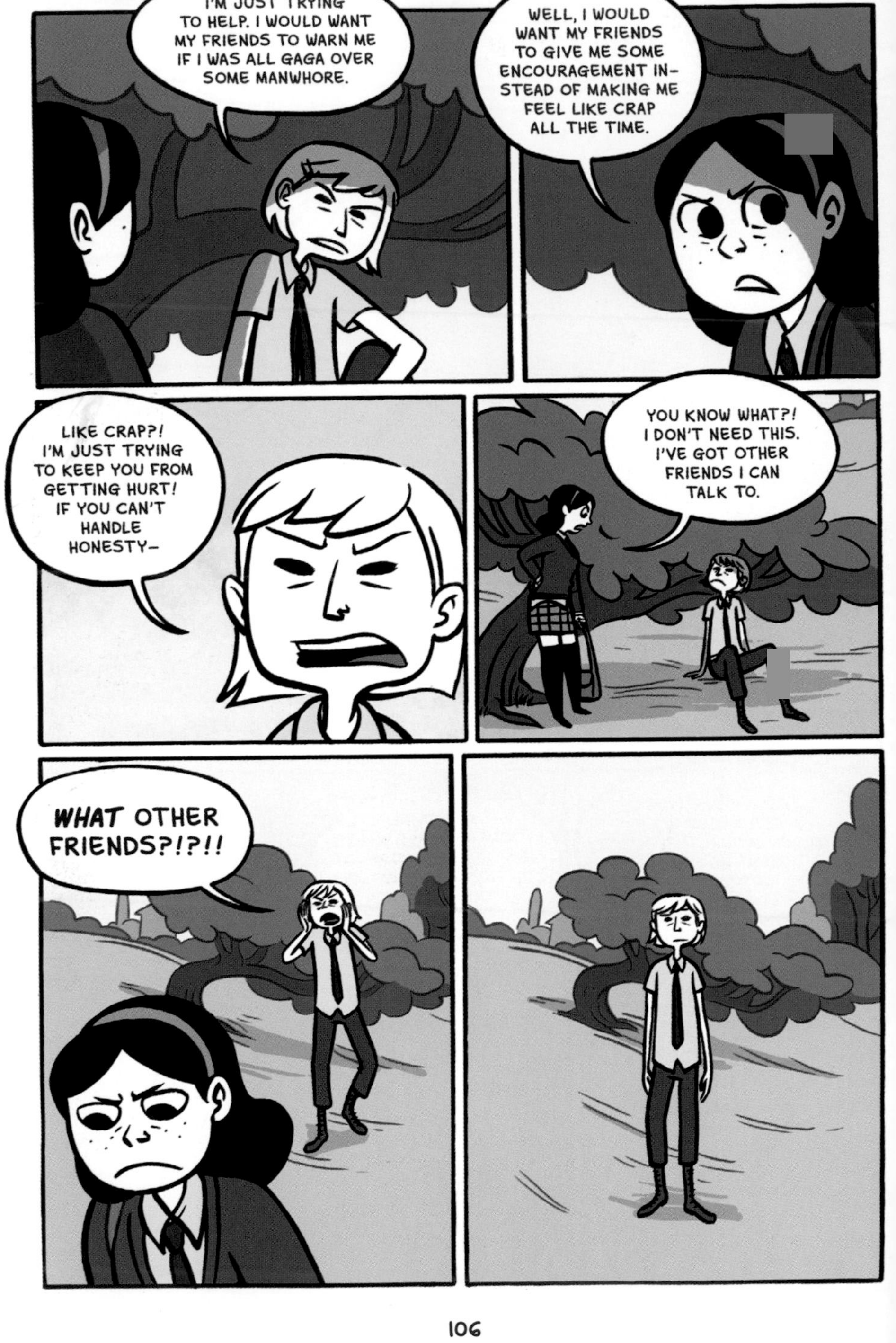
I'M JUST TRYING TO HELP. I WOULD WANT MY FRIENDS TO WARN ME IF I WAS ALL GAGA OVER SOME MANWHORE.
WELL, I WOULD WANT MY FRIENDS TO GIVE ME SOME ENCOURAGEMENT INSTEAD OF MAKING ME FEEL LIKE CRAP ALL THE TIME.
LIKE CRAP?! I'M JUST TRYING TO KEEP YOU FROM GETTING HURT! IF YOU CAN'T HANDLE HONESTY—
YOU KNOW WHAT?! I DON'T NEED THIS. I'VE GOT OTHER FRIENDS I CAN TALK TO.
WHAT OTHER FRIENDS?!?!!

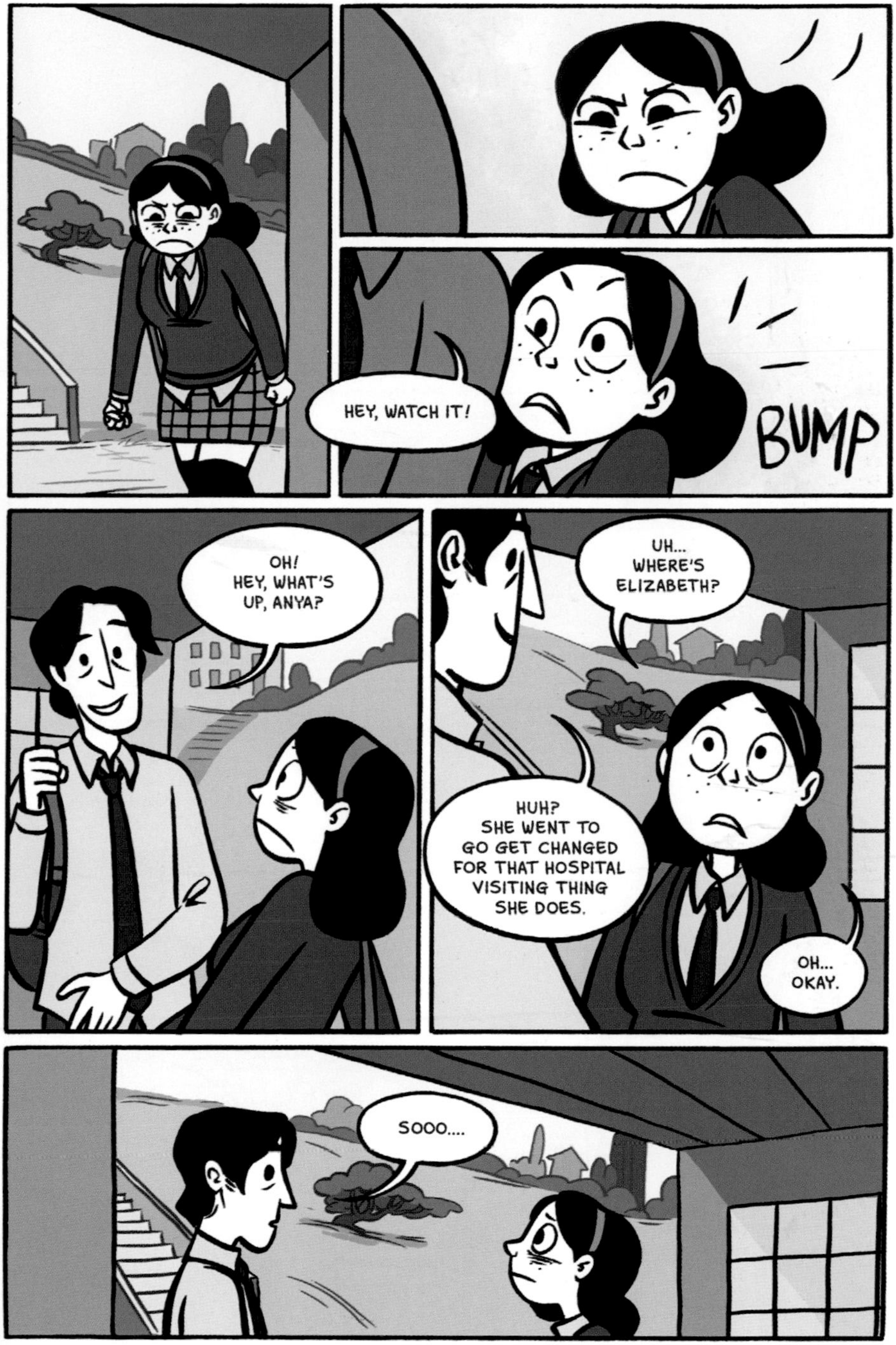
HEY, WATCH IT!
BUMP
OH! HEY, WHAT'S UP, ANYA?
UH... WHERE'S ELIZABETH?
HUH? SHE WENT TO GO GET CHANGED FOR THAT HOSPITAL VISITING THING SHE DOES.
OH... OKAY.
SOOO....

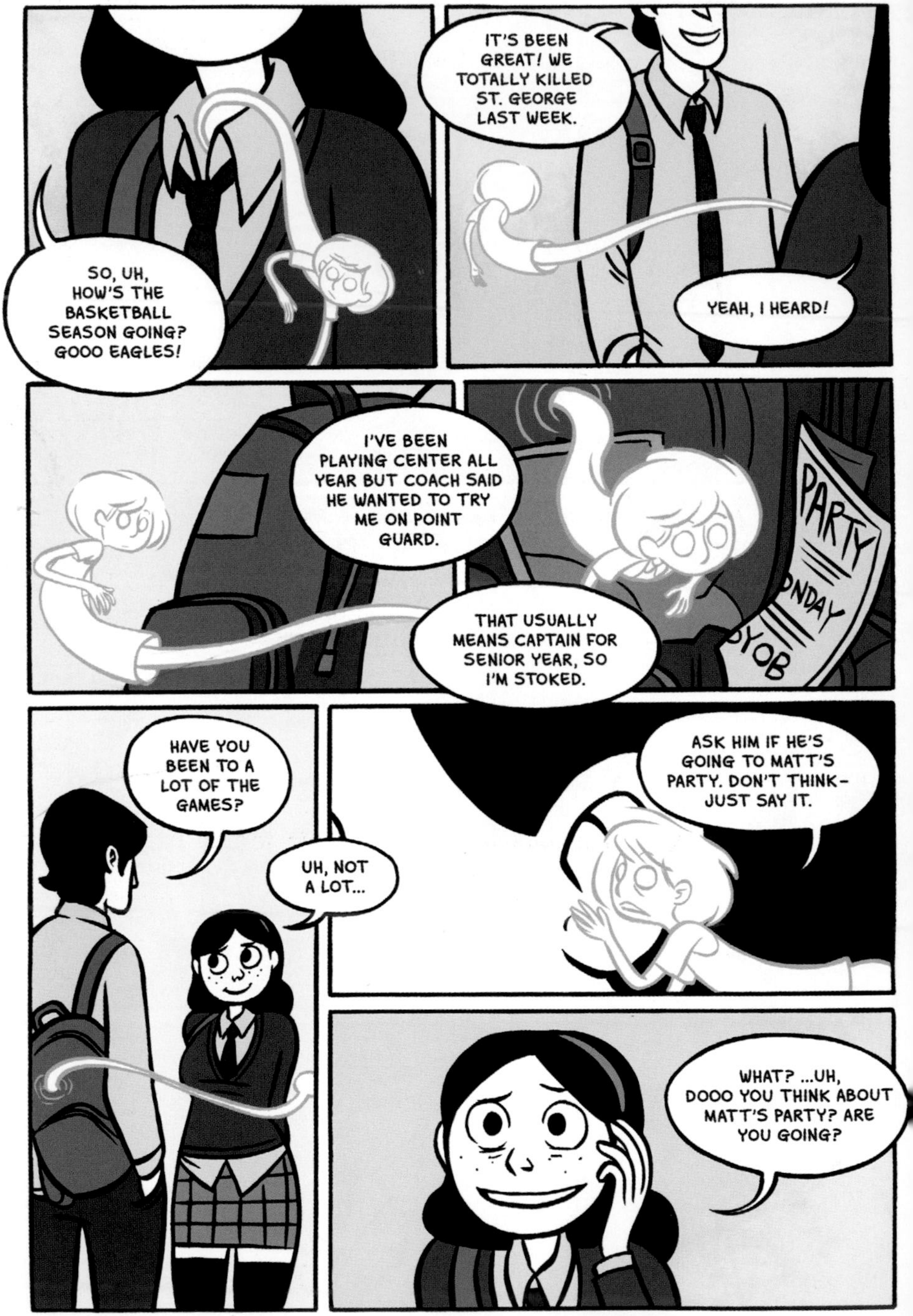
SO, UH, HOW'S THE BASKETBALL SEASON GOING? GOOO EAGLES!
IT'S BEEN GREAT! WE TOTALLY KILLED ST. GEORGE LAST WEEK.
YEAH, I HEARD!
I'VE BEEN PLAYING CENTER ALL YEAR BUT COACH SAID HE WANTED TO TRY ME ON POINT GUARD.
PARTY
NDAY
YOB
THAT USUALLY MEANS CAPTAIN FOR SENIOR YEAR, SO I'M STOKED.
HAVE YOU BEEN TO A LOT OF THE GAMES?
UH, NOT A LOT...
ASK HIM IF HE'S GOING TO MATT'S PARTY. DON'T THINK-JUST SAY IT.
WHAT? ...UH, DOOO YOU THINK ABOUT MATT'S PARTY? ARE YOU GOING?

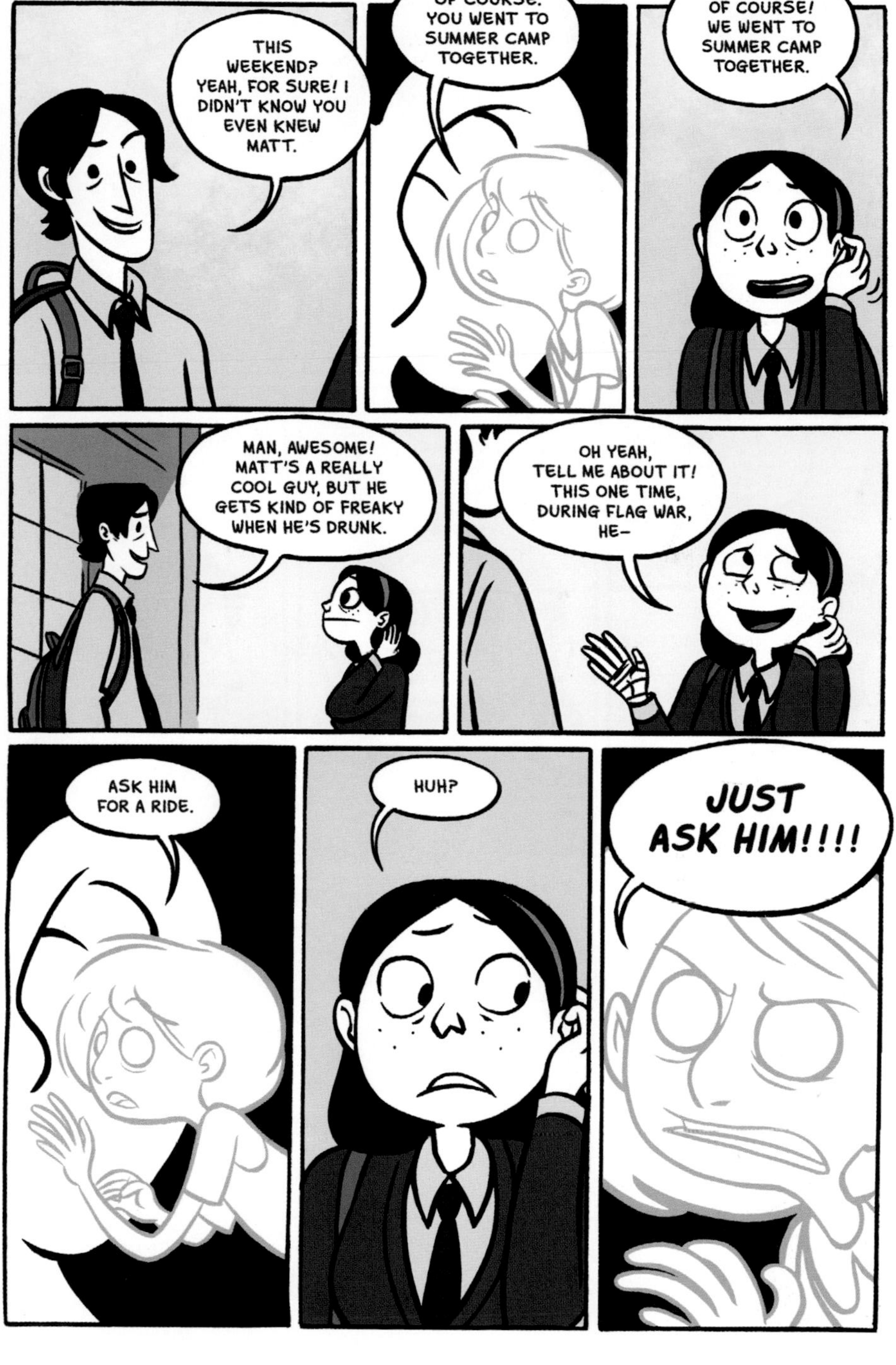
THIS WEEKEND? YEAH, FOR SURE! I DIDN'T KNOW YOU EVEN KNEW MATT.
OF COURSE. YOU WENT TO SUMMER CAMP TOGETHER.
OF COURSE! WE WENT TO SUMMER CAMP TOGETHER.
MAN, AWESOME! MATT'S A REALLY COOL GUY, BUT HE GETS KIND OF FREAKY WHEN HE'S DRUNK.
OH YEAH, TELL ME ABOUT IT! THIS ONE TIME, DURING FLAG WAR, HE–
ASK HIM FOR A RIDE.
HUH?
JUST ASK HIM!!!!

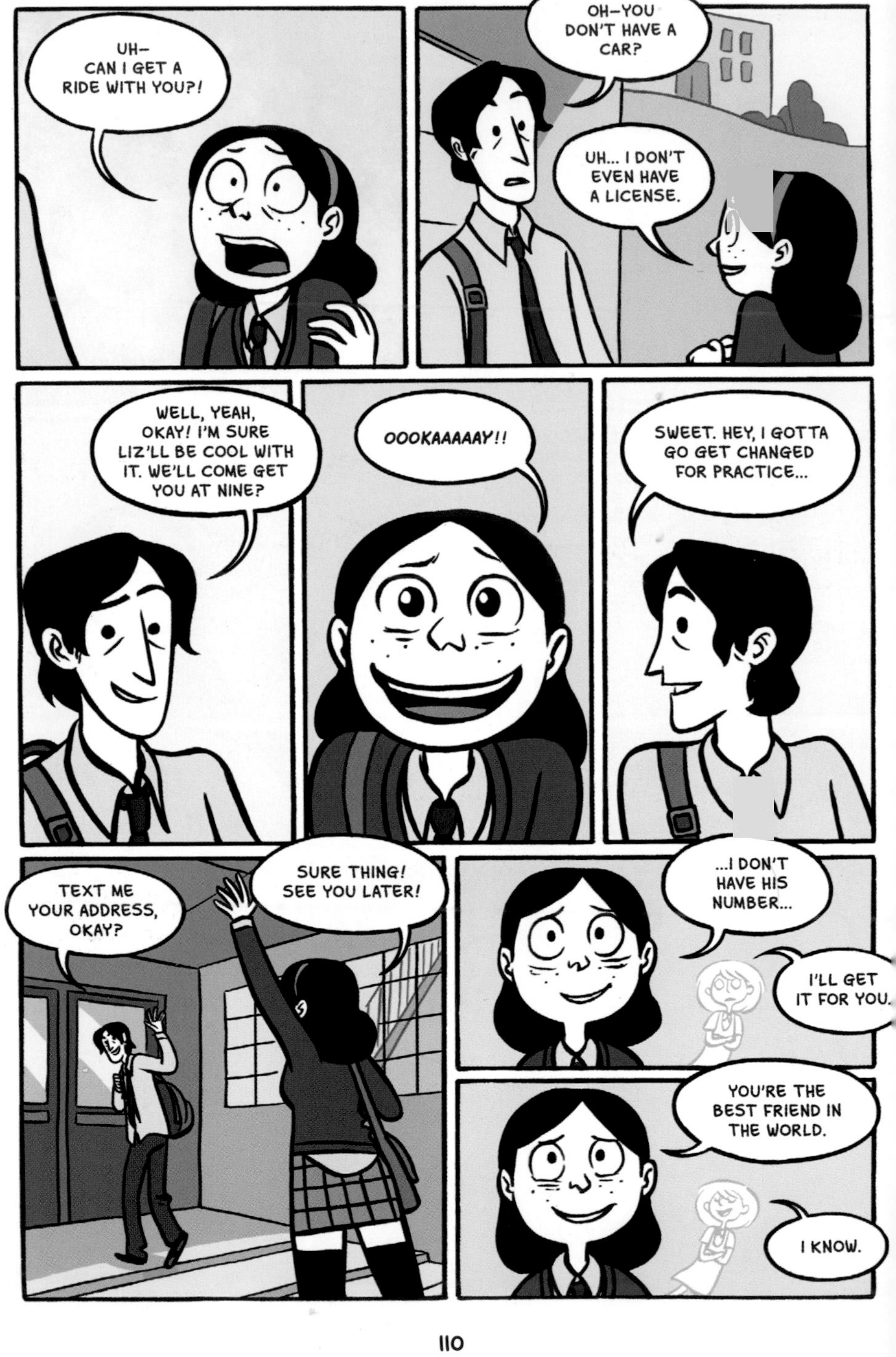

UH— CAN I GET A RIDE WITH YOU?!
OH—YOU DON'T HAVE A CAR?
UH... I DON'T EVEN HAVE A LICENSE.
WELL, YEAH, OKAY! I'M SURE LIZ'LL BE COOL WITH IT. WE'LL COME GET YOU AT NINE?
OOOKAAAAAY!!
SWEET. HEY, I GOTTA GO GET CHANGED FOR PRACTICE...
TEXT ME YOUR ADDRESS, OKAY?
SURE THING! SEE YOU LATER!
...I DON'T HAVE HIS NUMBER...
I'LL GET IT FOR YOU.
YOU'RE THE BEST FRIEND IN THE WORLD.
I KNOW.

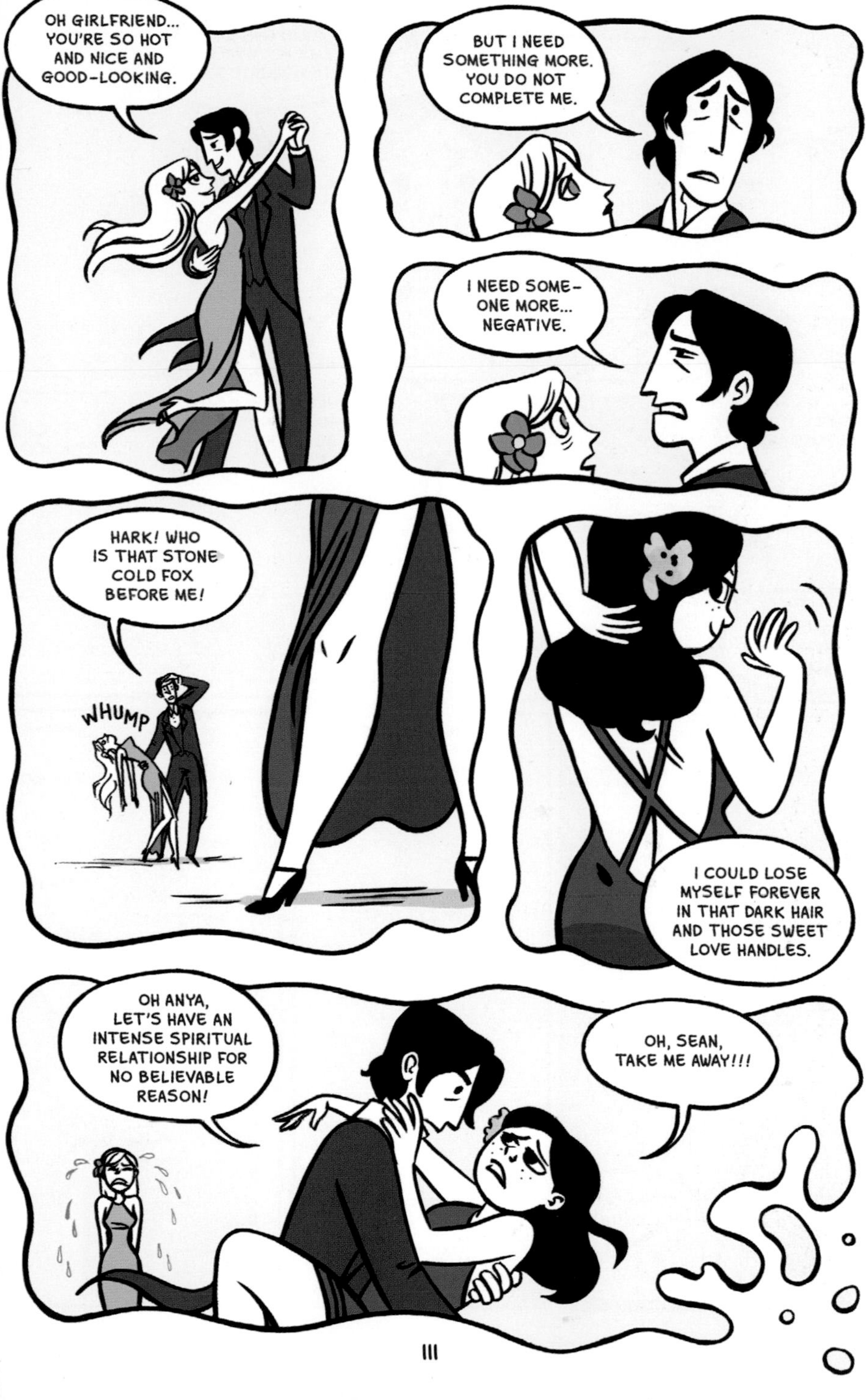
OH GIRLFRIEND... YOU'RE SO HOT AND NICE AND GOOD-LOOKING.
BUT I NEED SOMETHING MORE. YOU DO NOT COMPLETE ME.
I NEED SOME-ONE MORE... NEGATIVE.
HARK! WHO IS THAT STONE COLD FOX BEFORE ME!
WHUMP
I COULD LOSE MYSELF FOREVER IN THAT DARK HAIR AND THOSE SWEET LOVE HANDLES.
OH ANYA, LET'S HAVE AN INTENSE SPIRITUAL RELATIONSHIP FOR NO BELIEVABLE REASON!
OH, SEAN, TAKE ME AWAY!!!

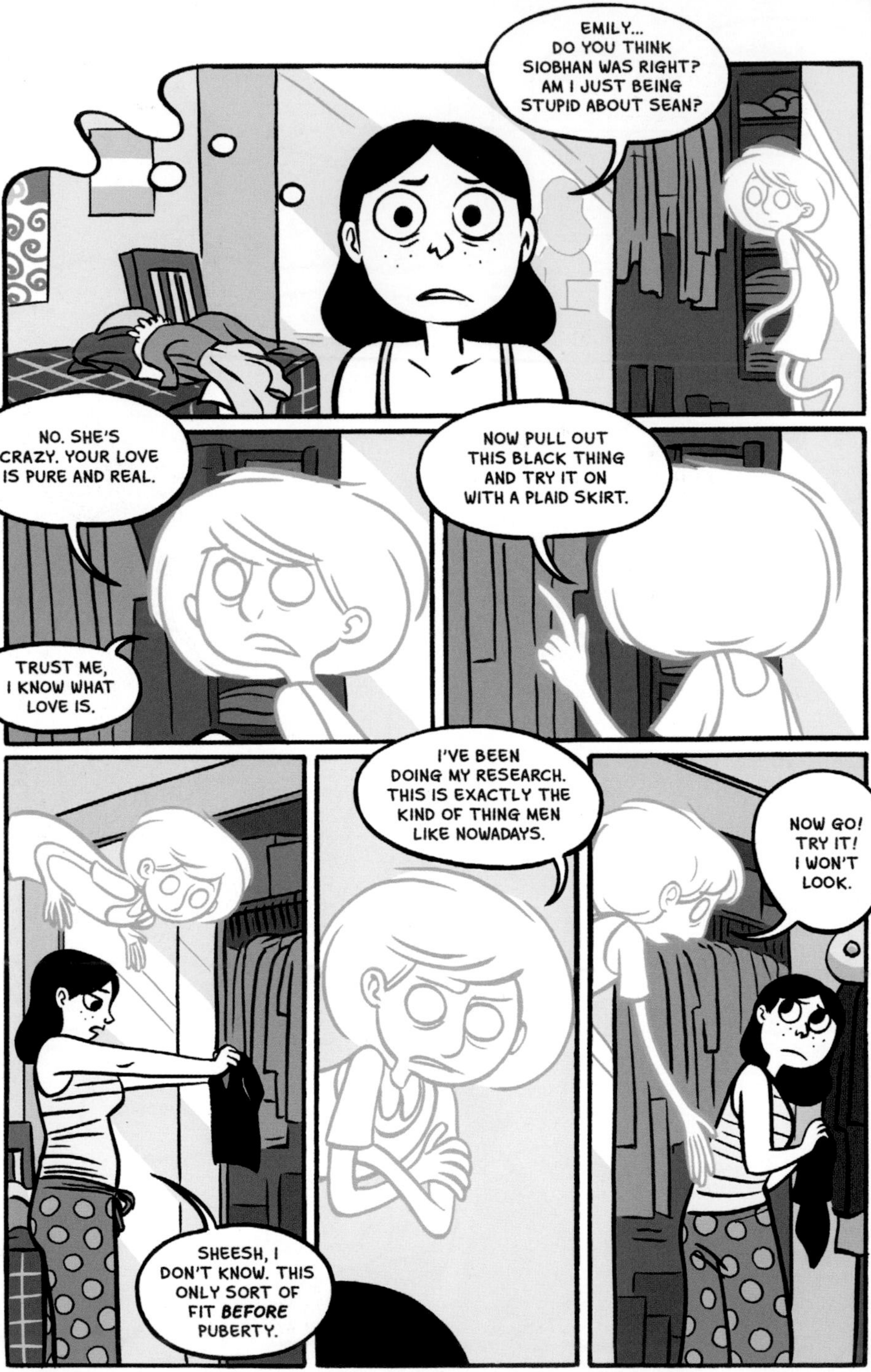
EMILY... DO YOU THINK SIOBHAN WAS RIGHT? AM I JUST BEING STUPID ABOUT SEAN?
NO. SHE'S CRAZY. YOUR LOVE IS PURE AND REAL.
TRUST ME, I KNOW WHAT LOVE IS.
NOW PULL OUT THIS BLACK THING AND TRY IT ON WITH A PLAID SKIRT.
SHEESH, I DON'T KNOW. THIS ONLY SORT OF FIT *BEFORE* PUBERTY.
I'VE BEEN DOING MY RESEARCH. THIS IS EXACTLY THE KIND OF THING MEN LIKE NOWADAYS.
NOW GO! TRY IT! I WON'T LOOK.

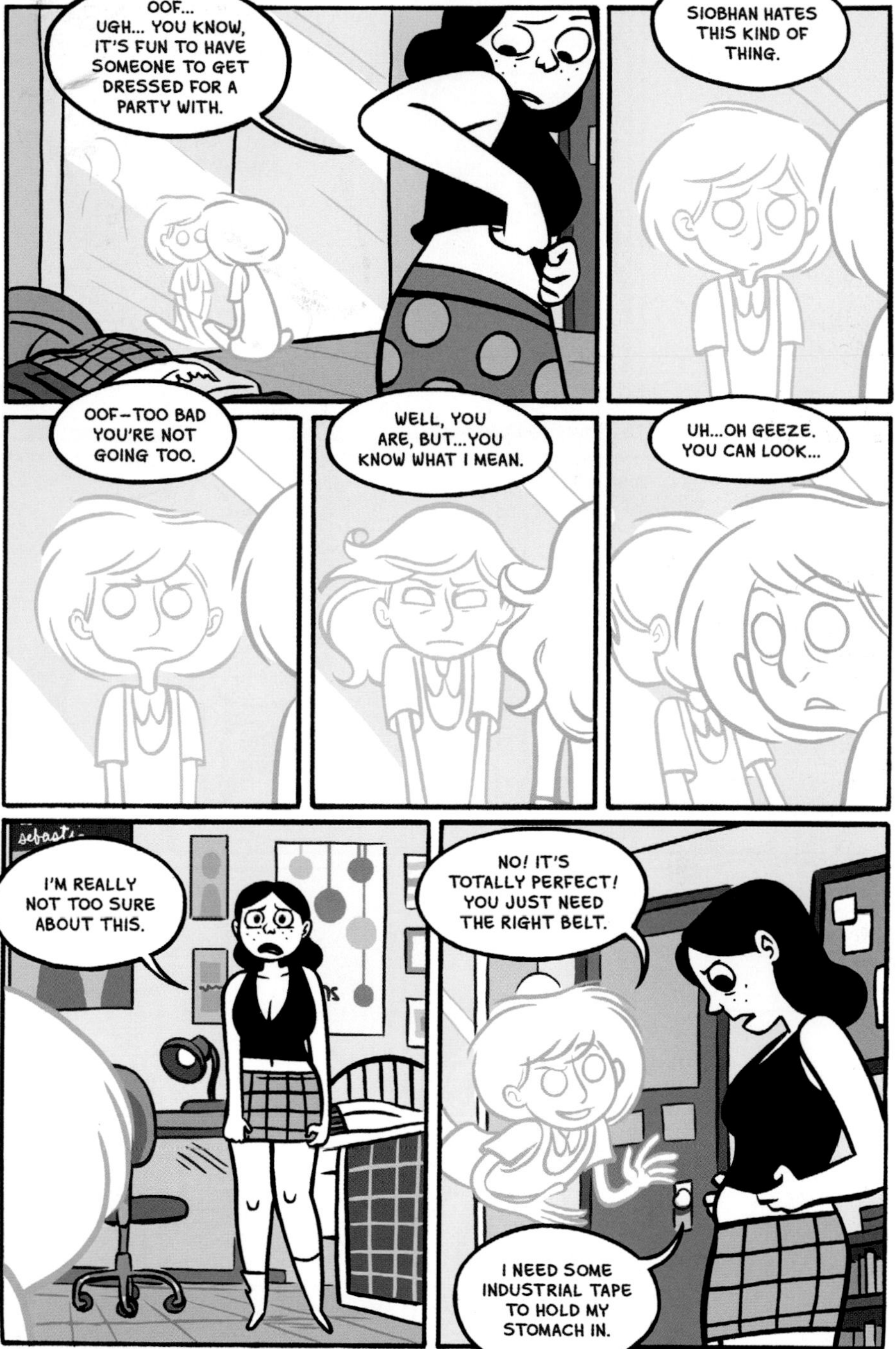
OOF...
UGH... YOU KNOW, IT'S FUN TO HAVE SOMEONE TO GET DRESSED FOR A PARTY WITH.
SIOBHAN HATES THIS KIND OF THING.
OOF—TOO BAD YOU'RE NOT GOING TOO.
WELL, YOU ARE, BUT...YOU KNOW WHAT I MEAN.
UH...OH GEEZE. YOU CAN LOOK...
I'M REALLY NOT TOO SURE ABOUT THIS.
NO! IT'S TOTALLY PERFECT! YOU JUST NEED THE RIGHT BELT.
I NEED SOME INDUSTRIAL TAPE TO HOLD MY STOMACH IN.

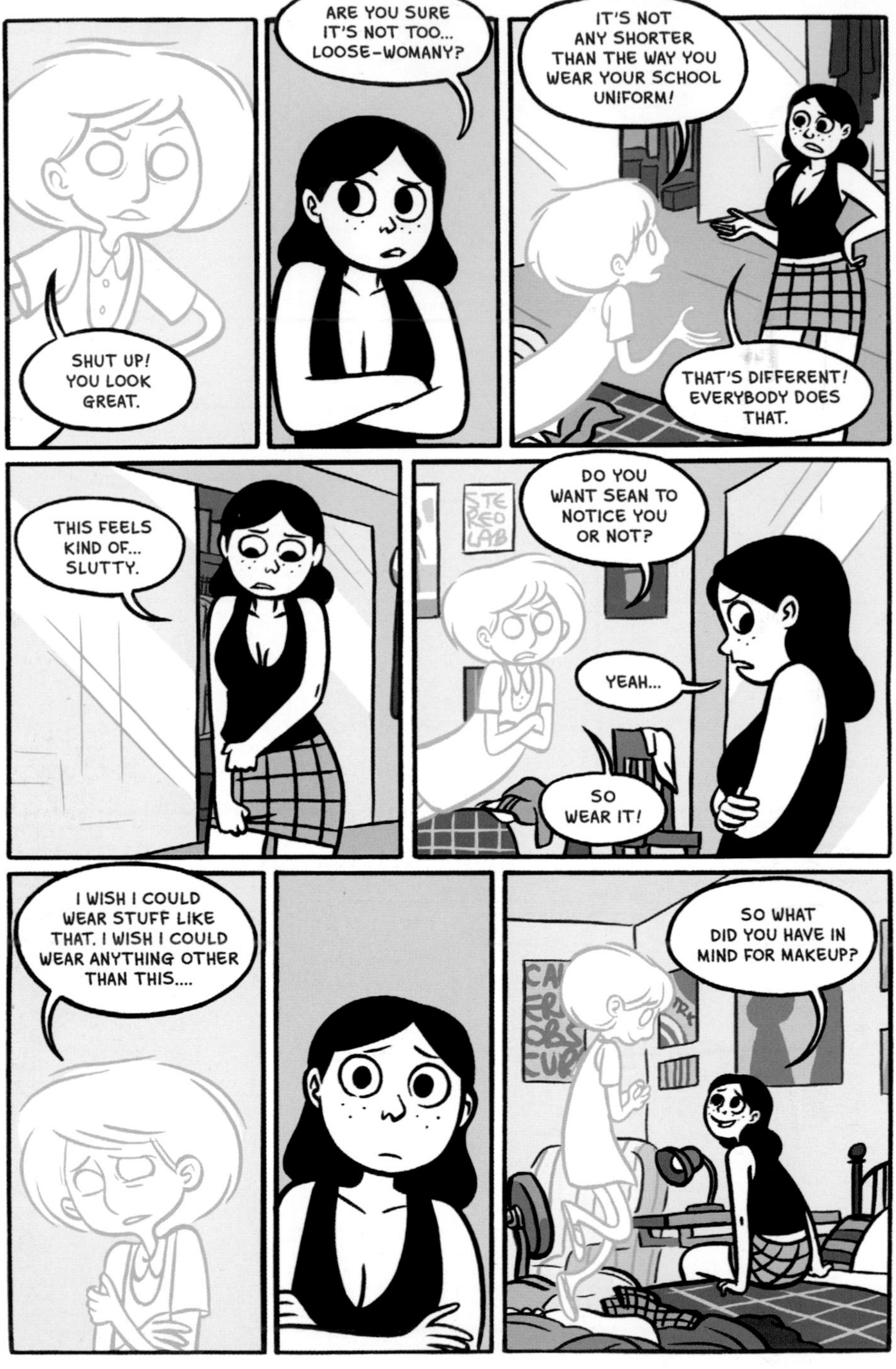

SHUT UP! YOU LOOK GREAT.
ARE YOU SURE IT'S NOT TOO... LOOSE-WOMANY?
IT'S NOT ANY SHORTER THAN THE WAY YOU WEAR YOUR SCHOOL UNIFORM!
THAT'S DIFFERENT! EVERYBODY DOES THAT.
THIS FEELS KIND OF... SLUTTY.
STEREOLAB
DO YOU WANT SEAN TO NOTICE YOU OR NOT?
YEAH...
SO WEAR IT!
I WISH I COULD WEAR STUFF LIKE THAT. I WISH I COULD WEAR ANYTHING OTHER THAN THIS....
SO WHAT DID YOU HAVE IN MIND FOR MAKEUP?

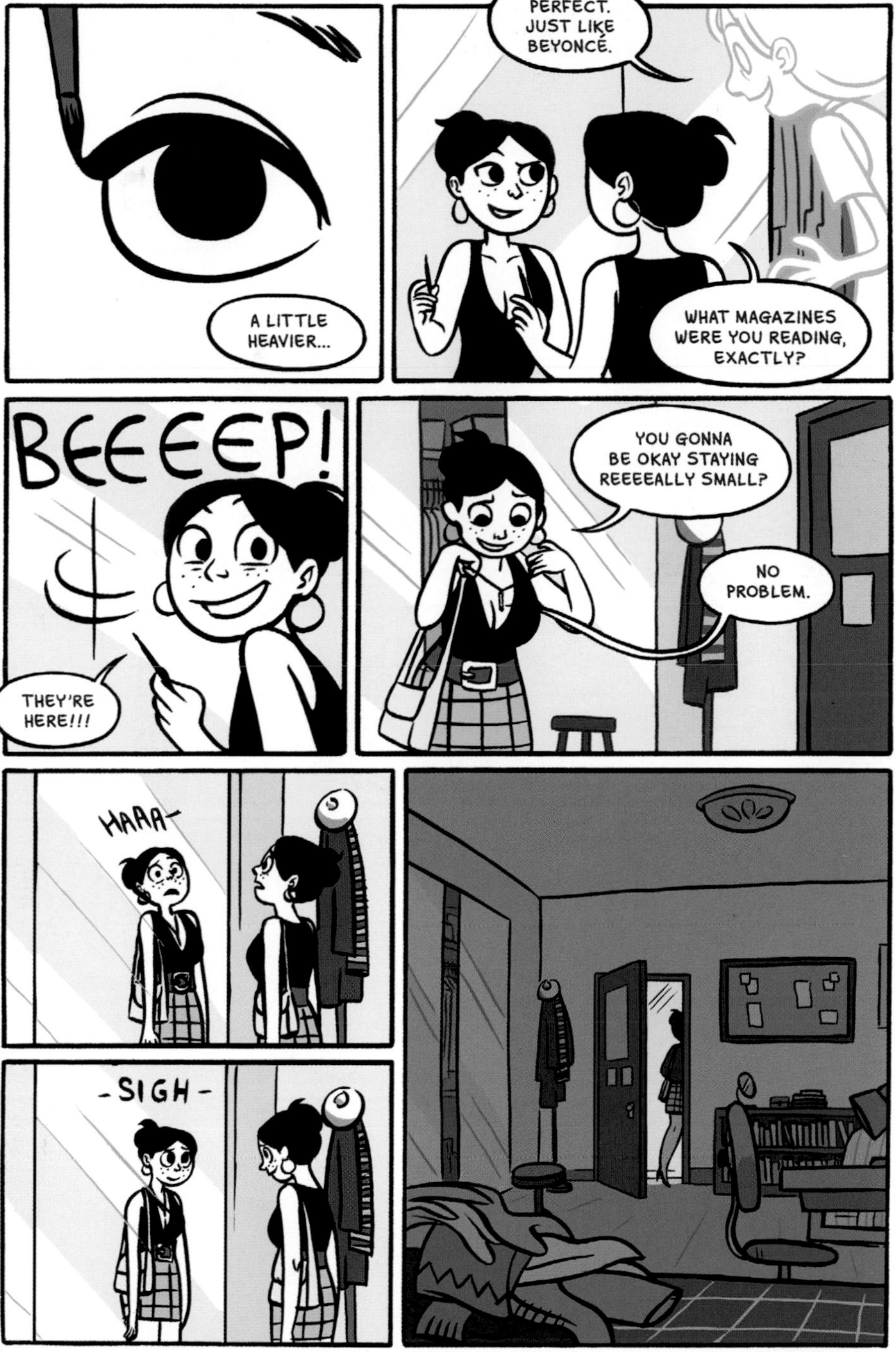
A LITTLE HEAVIER...
PERFECT. JUST LIKE BEYONCÉ.
WHAT MAGAZINES WERE YOU READING, EXACTLY?
BEEEEP!
THEY'RE HERE!!!
YOU GONNA BE OKAY STAYING REEEEALLY SMALL?
NO PROBLEM.
HAAA-
-SIGH-

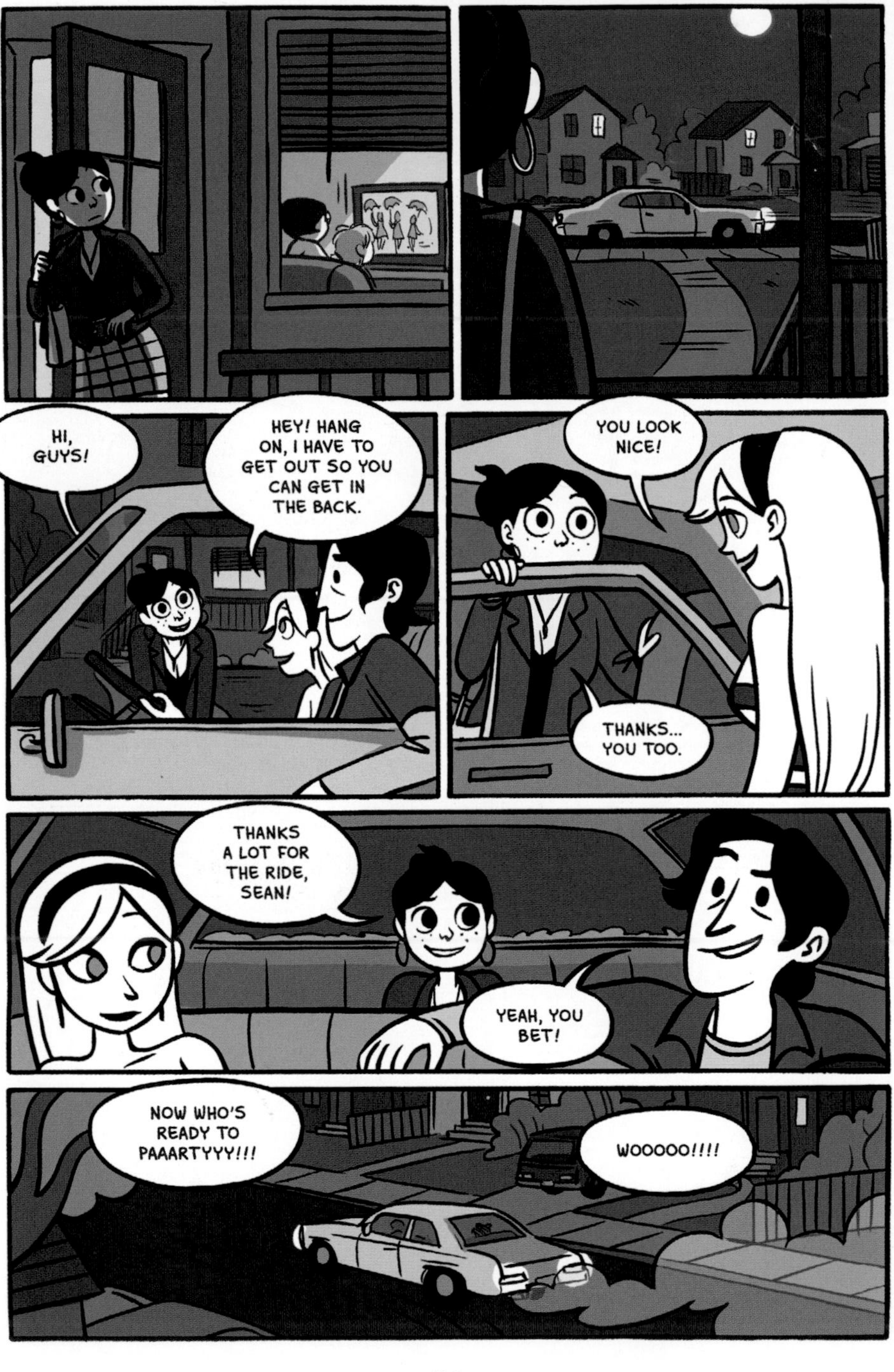
HI, GUYS!
HEY! HANG ON, I HAVE TO GET OUT SO YOU CAN GET IN THE BACK.
YOU LOOK NICE!
THANKS... YOU TOO.
THANKS A LOT FOR THE RIDE, SEAN!
YEAH, YOU BET!
NOW WHO'S READY TO PAAARTYYY!!!
WOOOOO!!!!

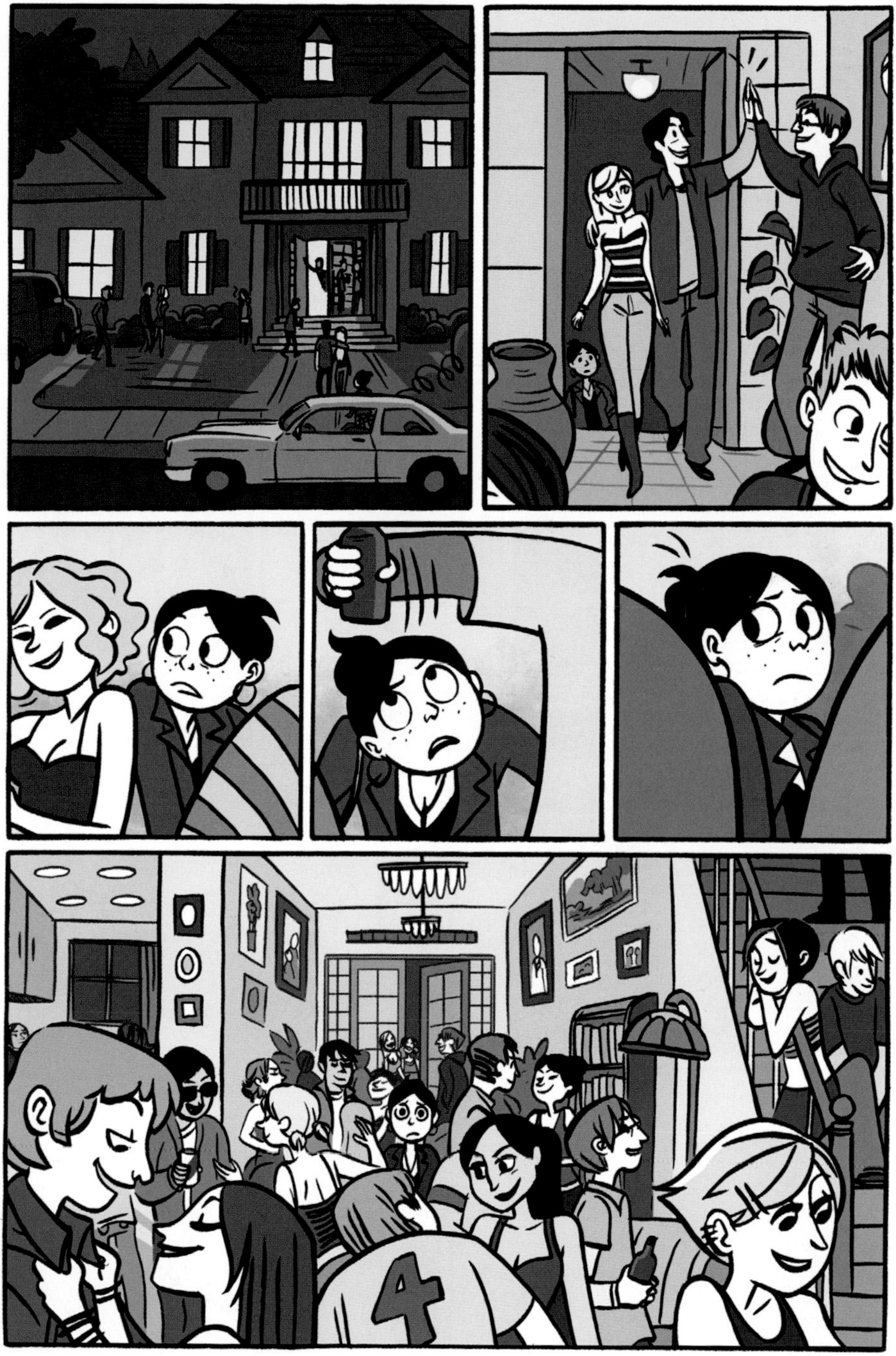
4

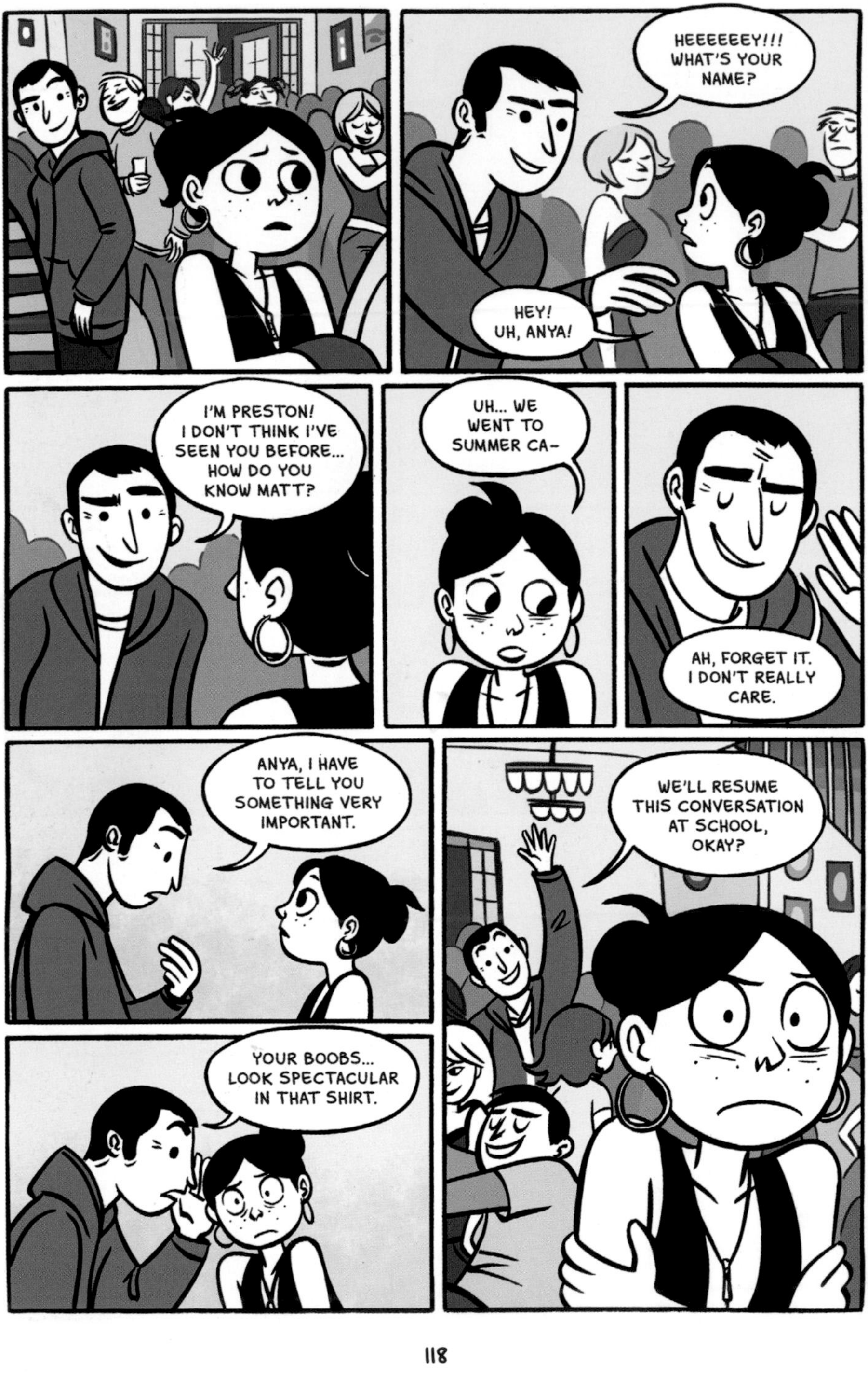
HEEEEEEY!!! WHAT'S YOUR NAME?
HEY! UH, ANYA!
I'M PRESTON! I DON'T THINK I'VE SEEN YOU BEFORE... HOW DO YOU KNOW MATT?
UH... WE WENT TO SUMMER CA-
AH, FORGET IT. I DON'T REALLY CARE.
ANYA, I HAVE TO TELL YOU SOMETHING VERY IMPORTANT.
YOUR BOOBS... LOOK SPECTACULAR IN THAT SHIRT.
WE'LL RESUME THIS CONVERSATION AT SCHOOL, OKAY?

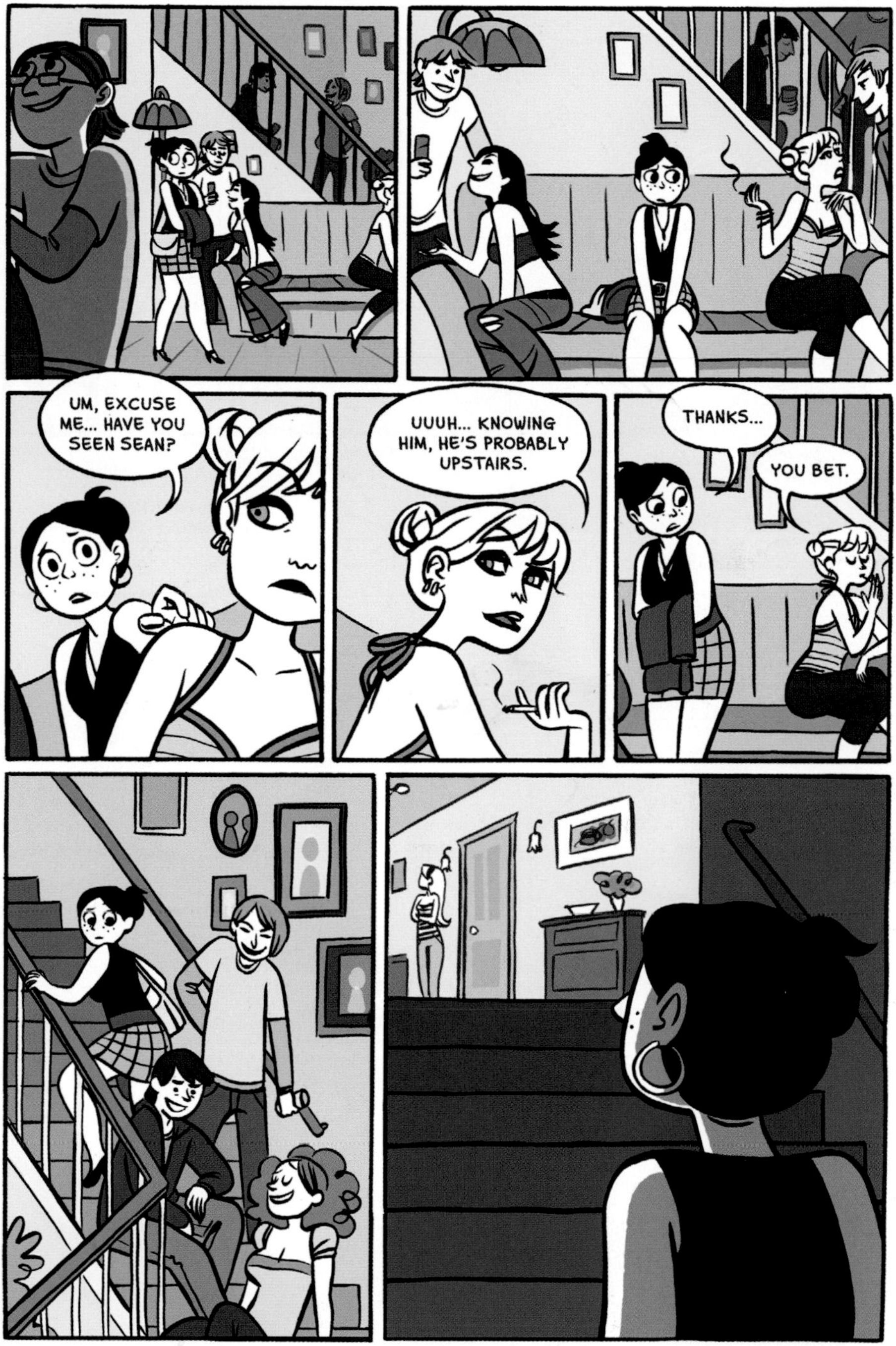
UM, EXCUSE ME... HAVE YOU SEEN SEAN?
UUUH... KNOWING HIM, HE'S PROBABLY UPSTAIRS.
THANKS...
YOU BET.

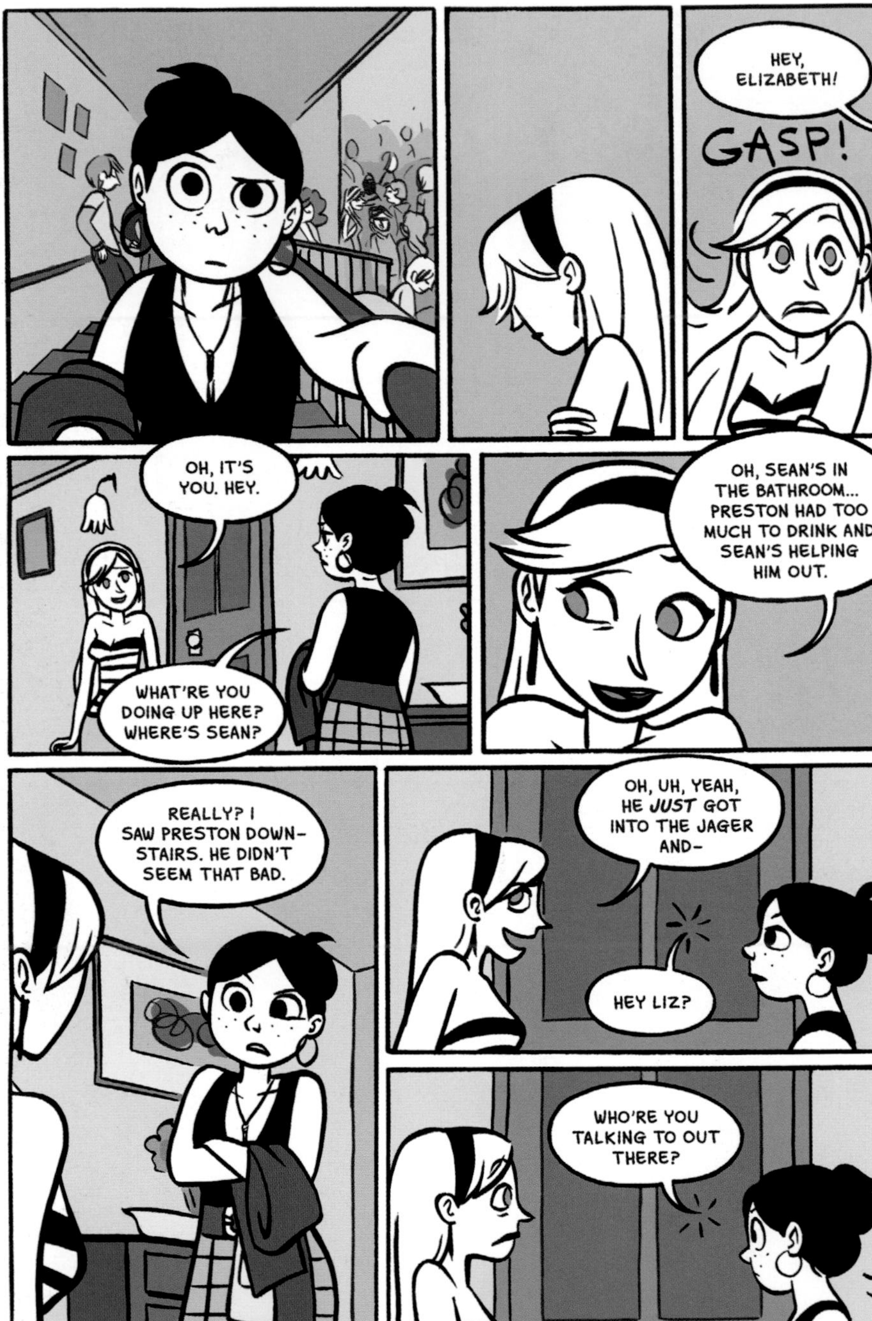
HEY, ELIZABETH!
GASP!
OH, IT'S YOU. HEY.
WHAT'RE YOU DOING UP HERE? WHERE'S SEAN?
OH, SEAN'S IN THE BATHROOM... PRESTON HAD TOO MUCH TO DRINK AND SEAN'S HELPING HIM OUT.
REALLY? I SAW PRESTON DOWN-STAIRS. HE DIDN'T SEEM THAT BAD.
OH, UH, YEAH, HE *JUST* GOT INTO THE JAGER AND-
HEY LIZ?
WHO'RE YOU TALKING TO OUT THERE?

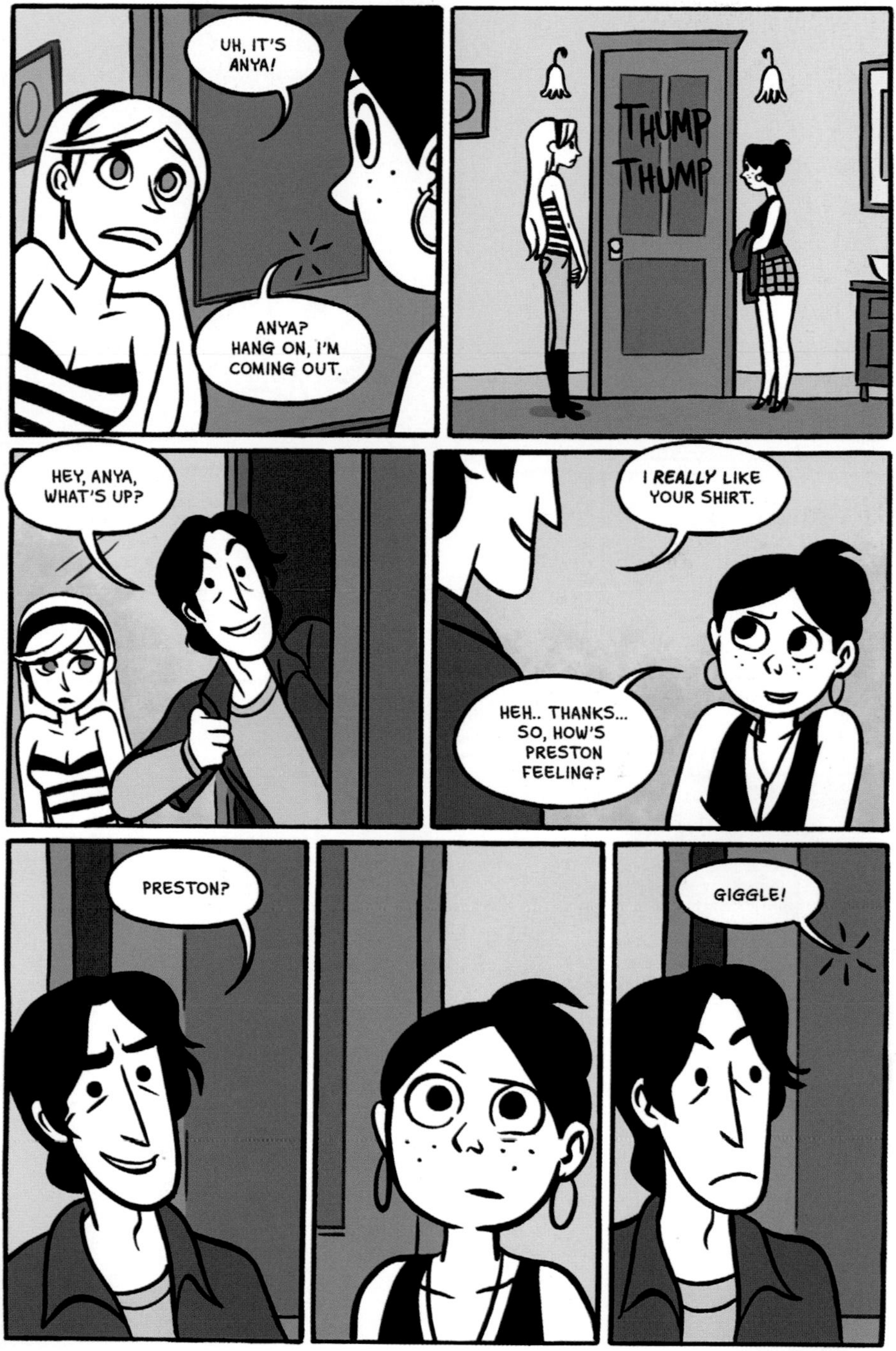
UH, IT'S ANYA!
ANYA? HANG ON, I'M COMING OUT.
THUMP THUMP
HEY, ANYA, WHAT'S UP?
I REALLY LIKE YOUR SHIRT.
HEH.. THANKS... SO, HOW'S PRESTON FEELING?
PRESTON?
GIGGLE!

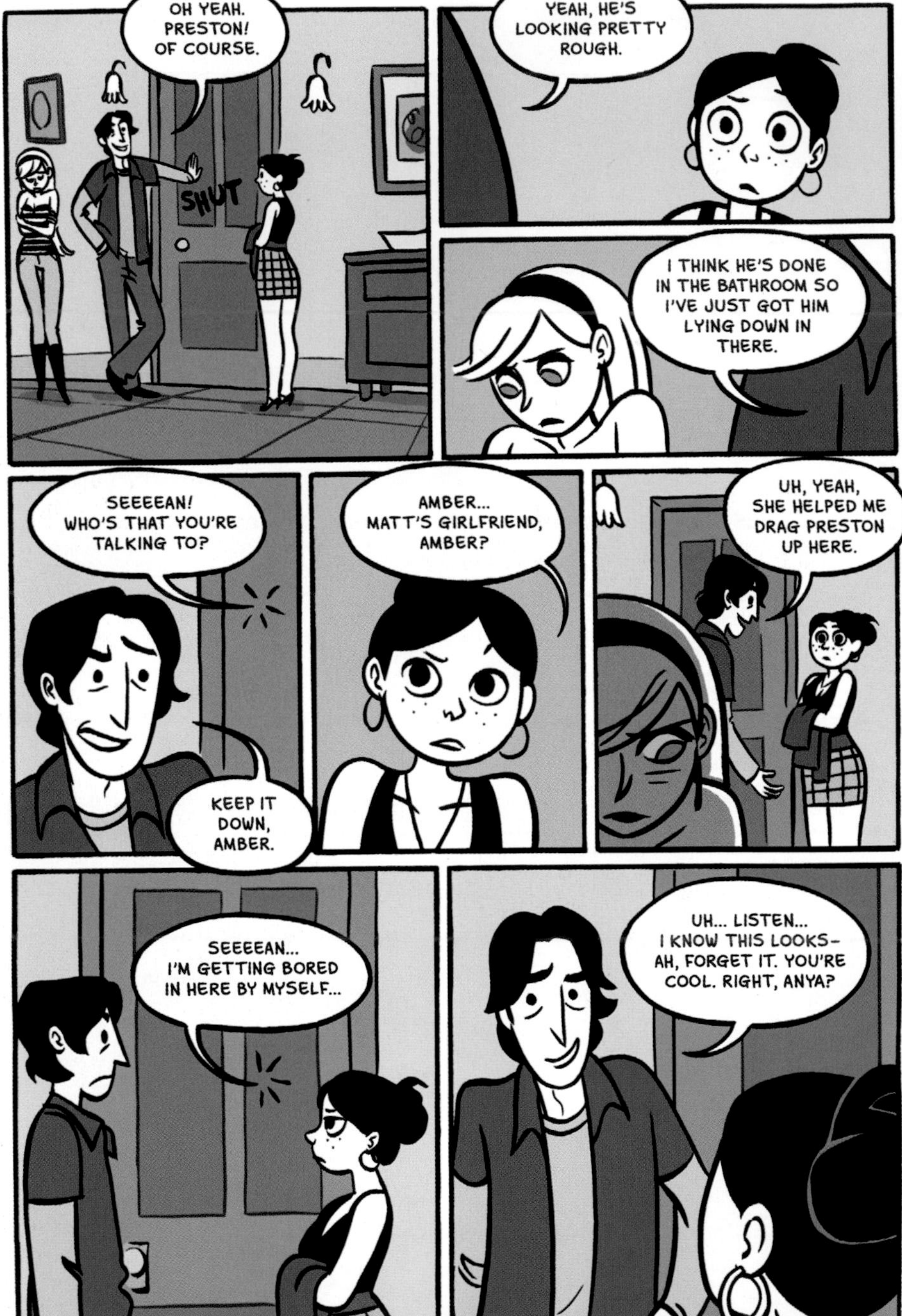
OH YEAH. PRESTON! OF COURSE.
SHUT
YEAH, HE'S LOOKING PRETTY ROUGH.
I THINK HE'S DONE IN THE BATHROOM SO I'VE JUST GOT HIM LYING DOWN IN THERE.
SEEEEAN! WHO'S THAT YOU'RE TALKING TO?
KEEP IT DOWN, AMBER.
AMBER... MATT'S GIRLFRIEND, AMBER?
UH, YEAH, SHE HELPED ME DRAG PRESTON UP HERE.
SEEEEAN... I'M GETTING BORED IN HERE BY MYSELF...
UH... LISTEN... I KNOW THIS LOOKS- AH, FORGET IT. YOU'RE COOL. RIGHT, ANYA?

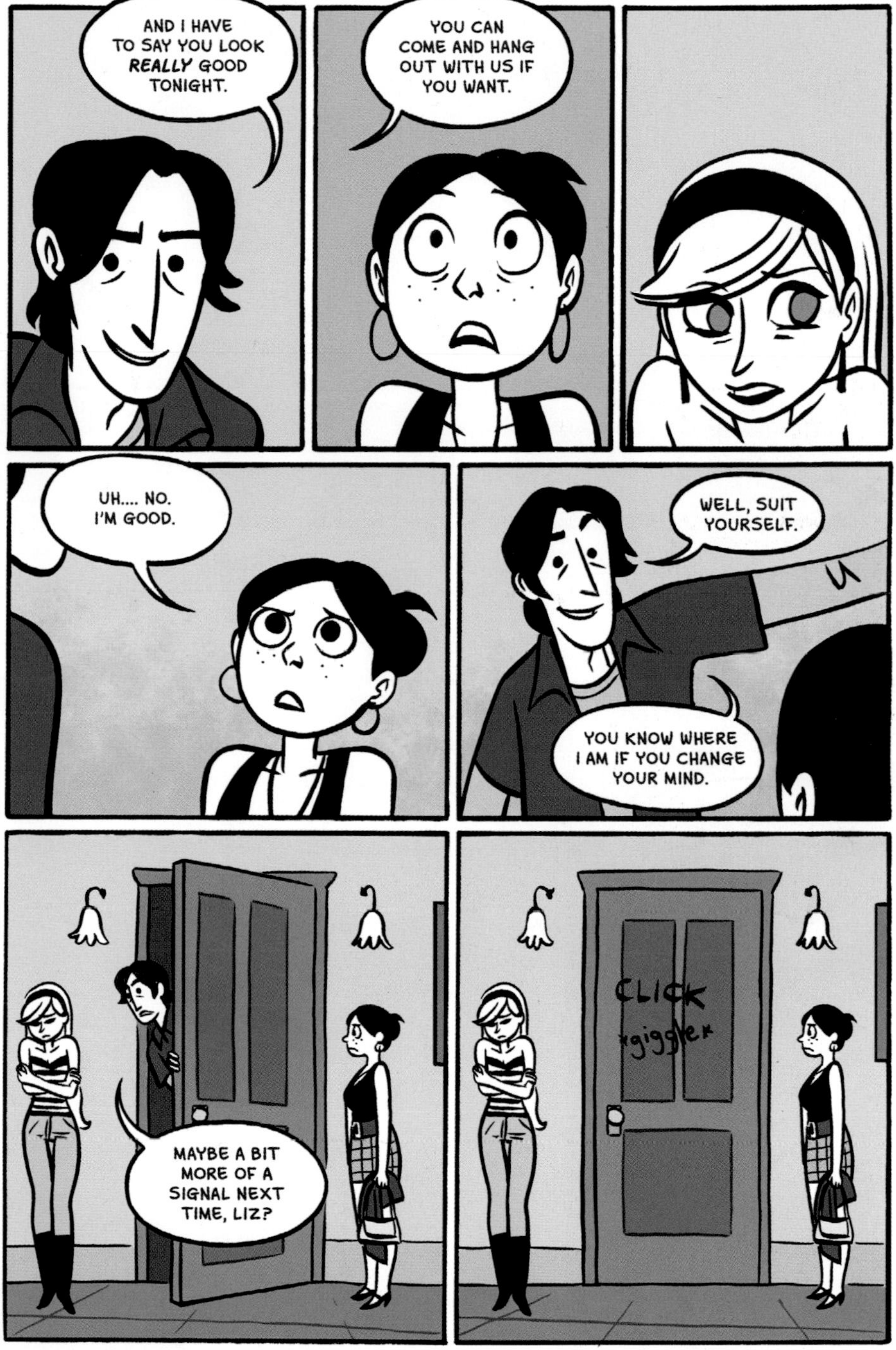
AND I HAVE TO SAY YOU LOOK REALLY GOOD TONIGHT.
YOU CAN COME AND HANG OUT WITH US IF YOU WANT.
UH.... NO. I'M GOOD.
WELL, SUIT YOURSELF.
YOU KNOW WHERE I AM IF YOU CHANGE YOUR MIND.
MAYBE A BIT MORE OF A SIGNAL NEXT TIME, LIZ?
CLICK
giggle

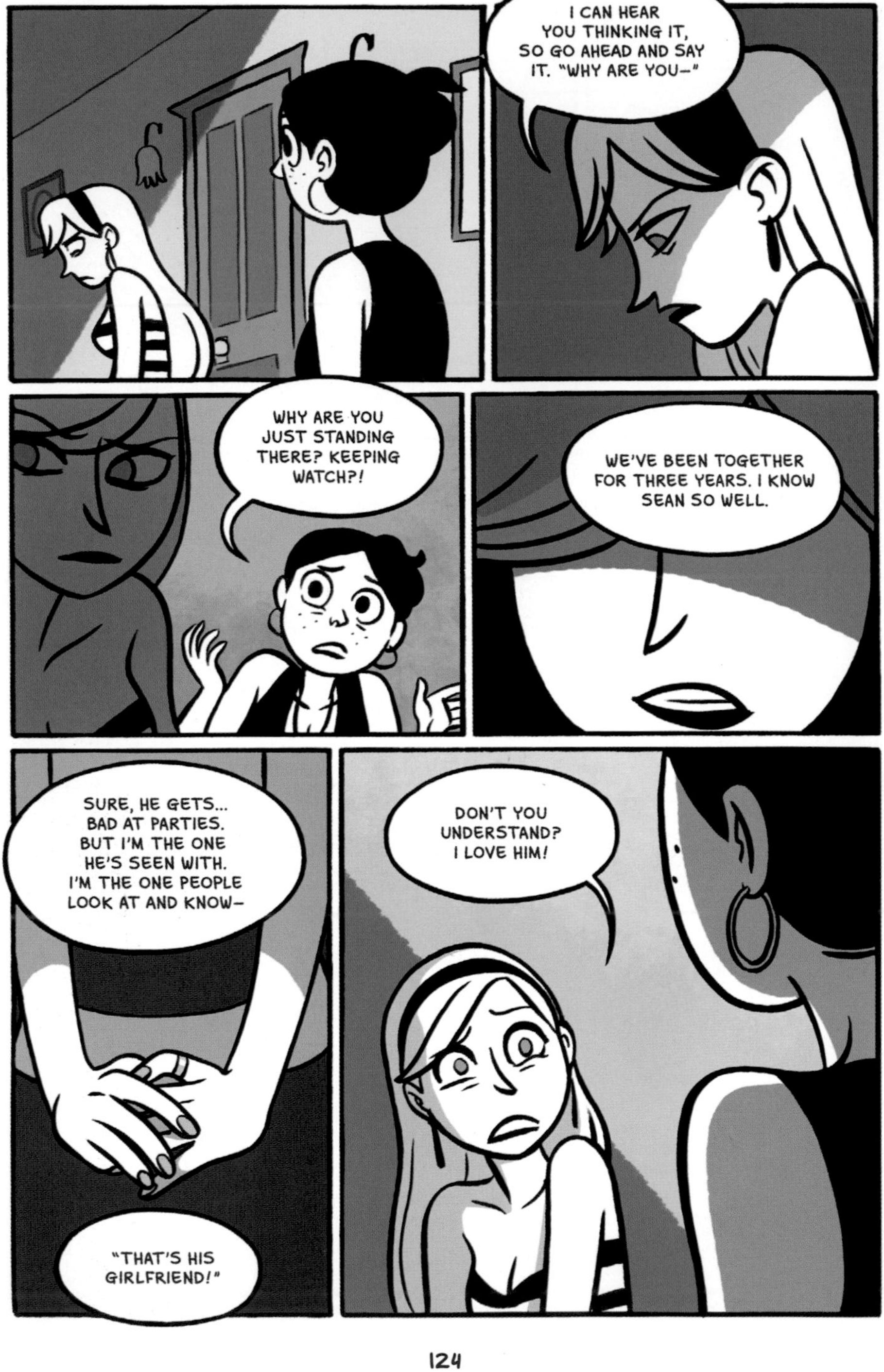
I CAN HEAR YOU THINKING IT, SO GO AHEAD AND SAY IT. "WHY ARE YOU—"
WHY ARE YOU JUST STANDING THERE? KEEPING WATCH?!
WE'VE BEEN TOGETHER FOR THREE YEARS. I KNOW SEAN SO WELL.
SURE, HE GETS... BAD AT PARTIES. BUT I'M THE ONE HE'S SEEN WITH. I'M THE ONE PEOPLE LOOK AT AND KNOW—
"THAT'S HIS GIRLFRIEND!"
DON'T YOU UNDERSTAND? I LOVE HIM!

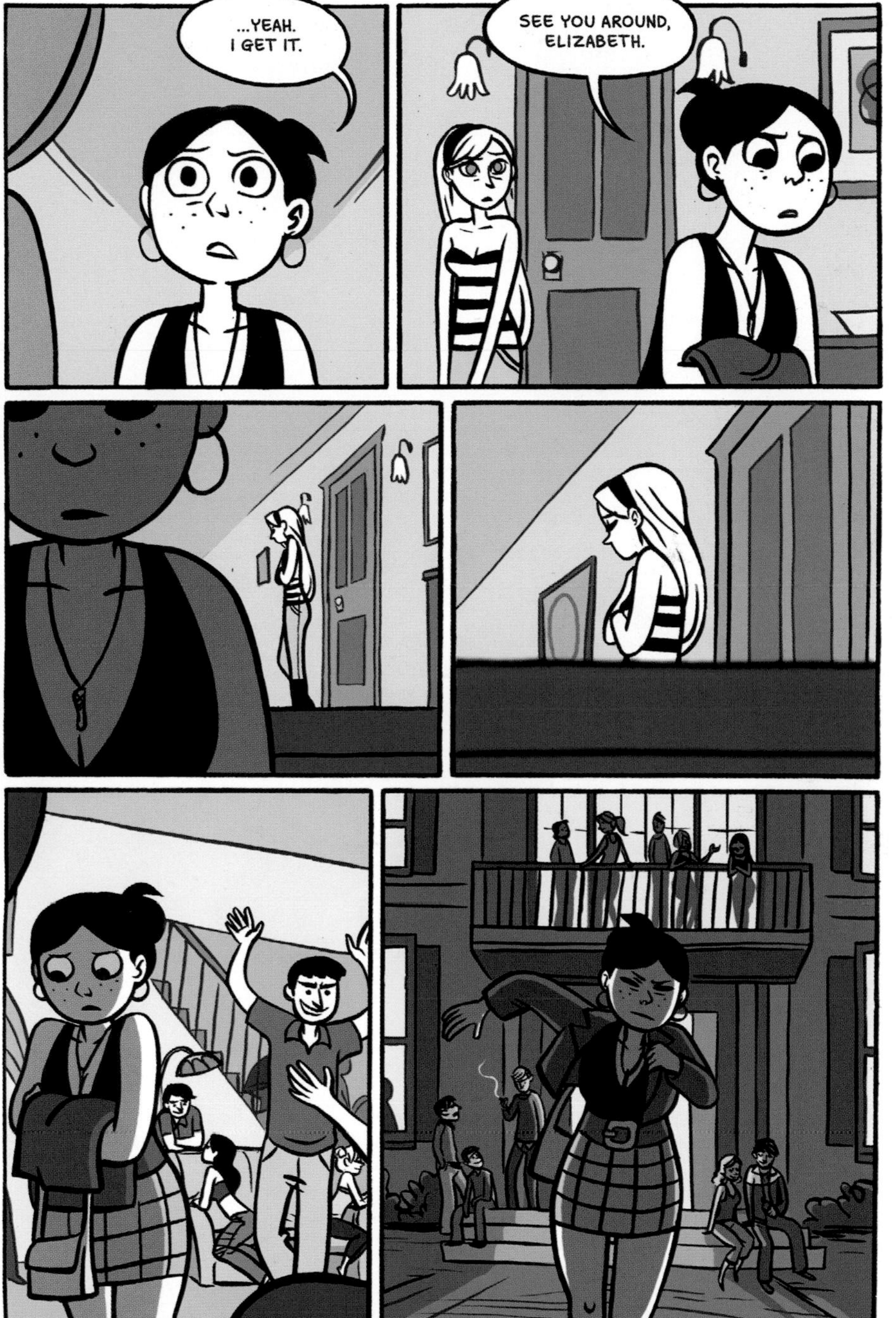
...YEAH.
I GET IT.
SEE YOU AROUND,
ELIZABETH.

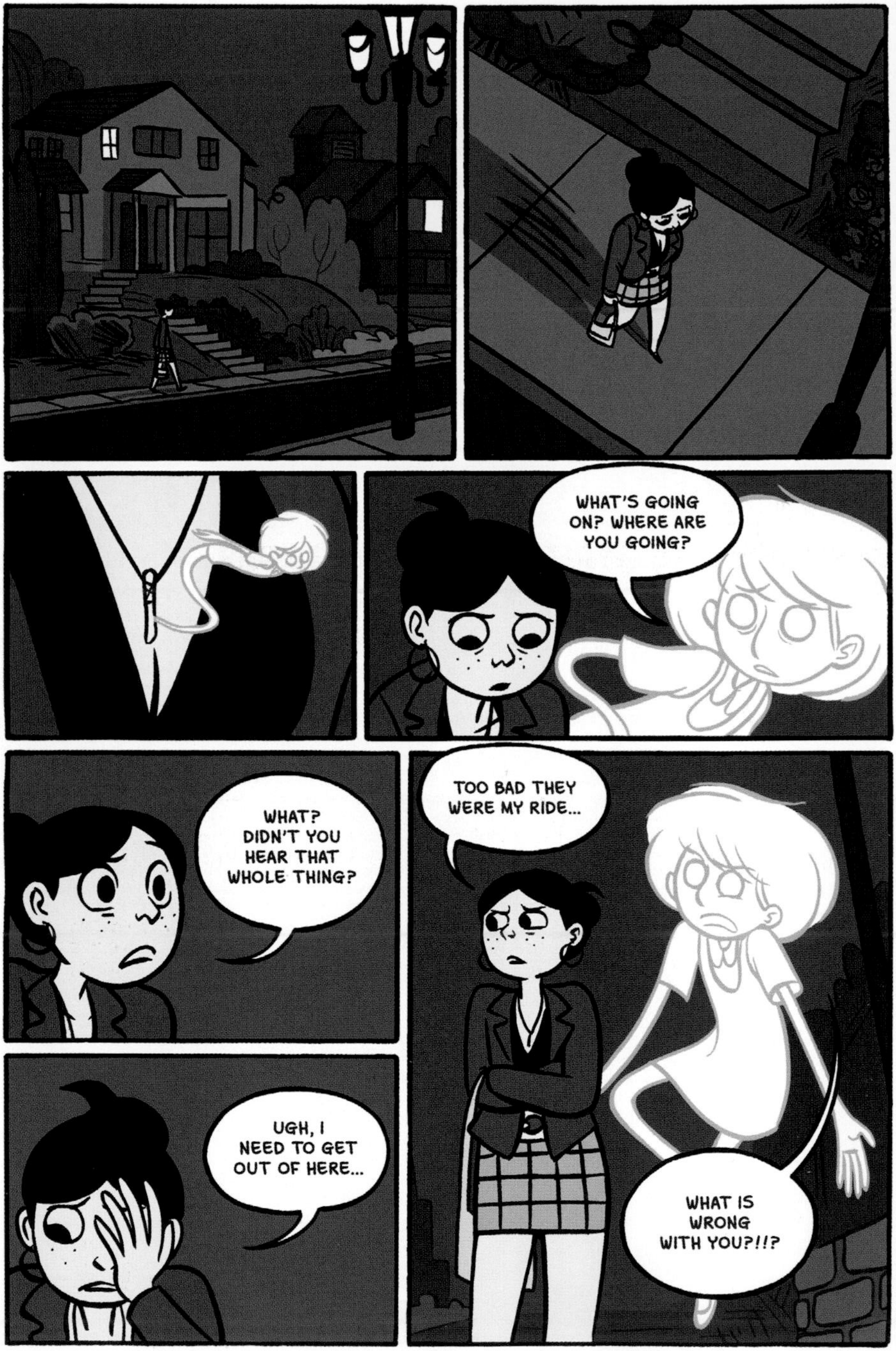
WHAT'S GOING ON? WHERE ARE YOU GOING?
WHAT? DIDN'T YOU HEAR THAT WHOLE THING?
TOO BAD THEY WERE MY RIDE...
UGH, I NEED TO GET OUT OF HERE...
WHAT IS WRONG WITH YOU?!!?

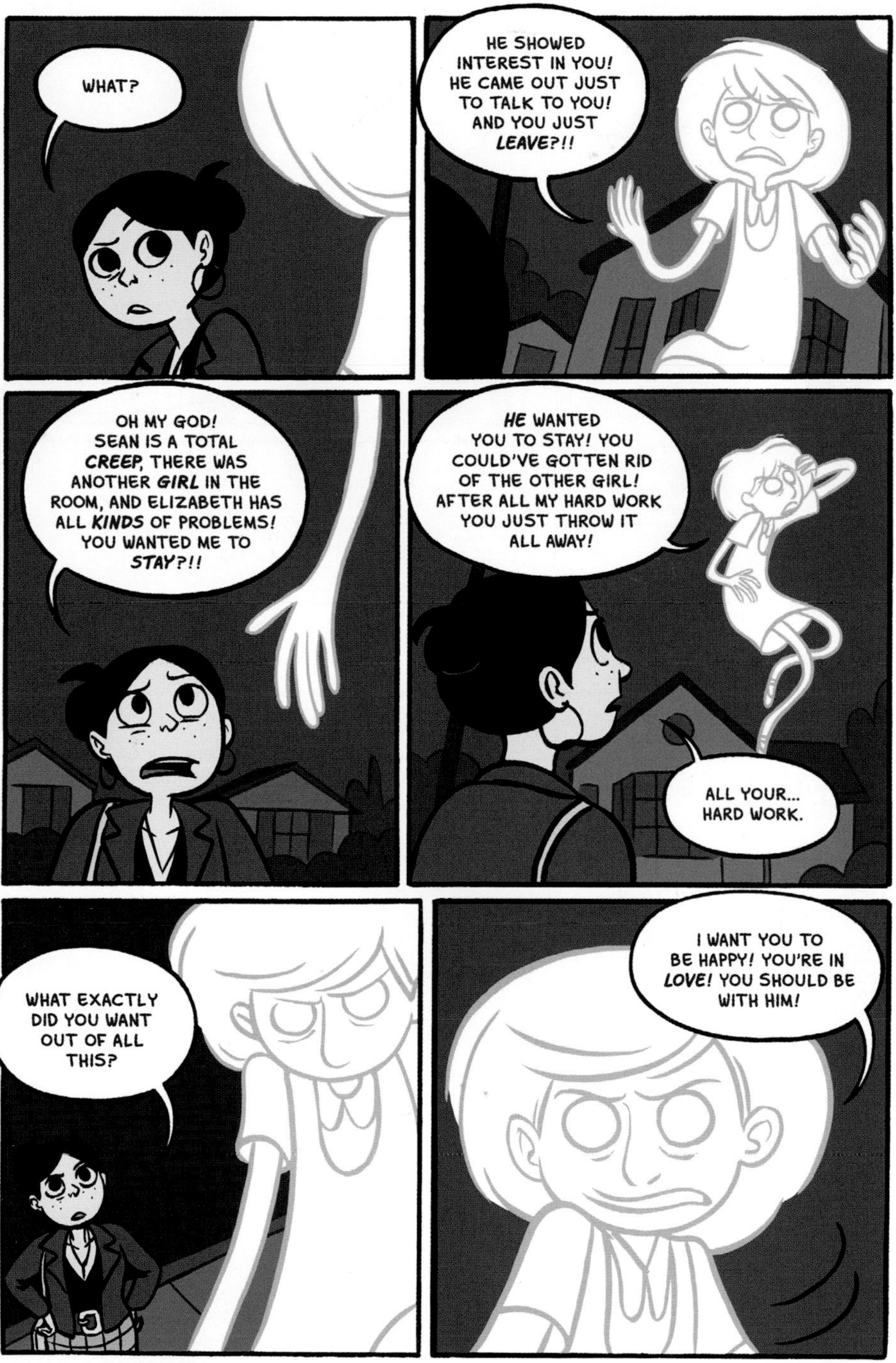
WHAT?
HE SHOWED INTEREST IN YOU! HE CAME OUT JUST TO TALK TO YOU! AND YOU JUST *LEAVE*?!!
OH MY GOD! SEAN IS A TOTAL *CREEP*, THERE WAS ANOTHER *GIRL* IN THE ROOM, AND ELIZABETH HAS ALL *KINDS* OF PROBLEMS! YOU WANTED ME TO *STAY*?!!
HE WANTED YOU TO STAY! YOU COULD'VE GOTTEN RID OF THE OTHER GIRL! AFTER ALL MY HARD WORK YOU JUST THROW IT ALL AWAY!
ALL YOUR... HARD WORK.
WHAT EXACTLY DID YOU WANT OUT OF ALL THIS?
I WANT YOU TO BE HAPPY! YOU'RE IN *LOVE*! YOU SHOULD BE WITH HIM!

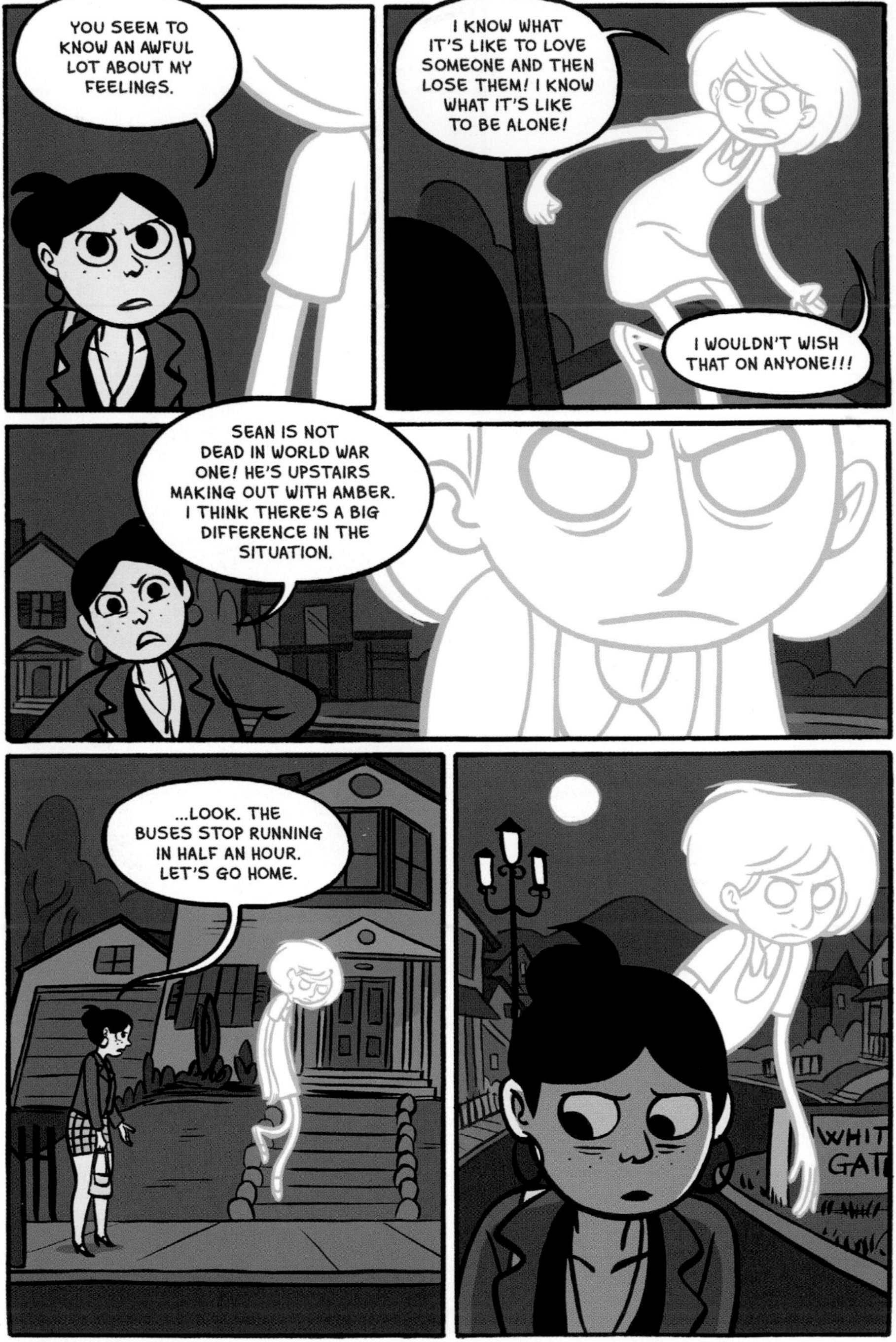
YOU SEEM TO KNOW AN AWFUL LOT ABOUT MY FEELINGS.
I KNOW WHAT IT'S LIKE TO LOVE SOMEONE AND THEN LOSE THEM! I KNOW WHAT IT'S LIKE TO BE ALONE!
I WOULDN'T WISH THAT ON ANYONE!!!
SEAN IS NOT DEAD IN WORLD WAR ONE! HE'S UPSTAIRS MAKING OUT WITH AMBER. I THINK THERE'S A BIG DIFFERENCE IN THE SITUATION.
...LOOK. THE BUSES STOP RUNNING IN HALF AN HOUR. LET'S GO HOME.
WHIT
GAT

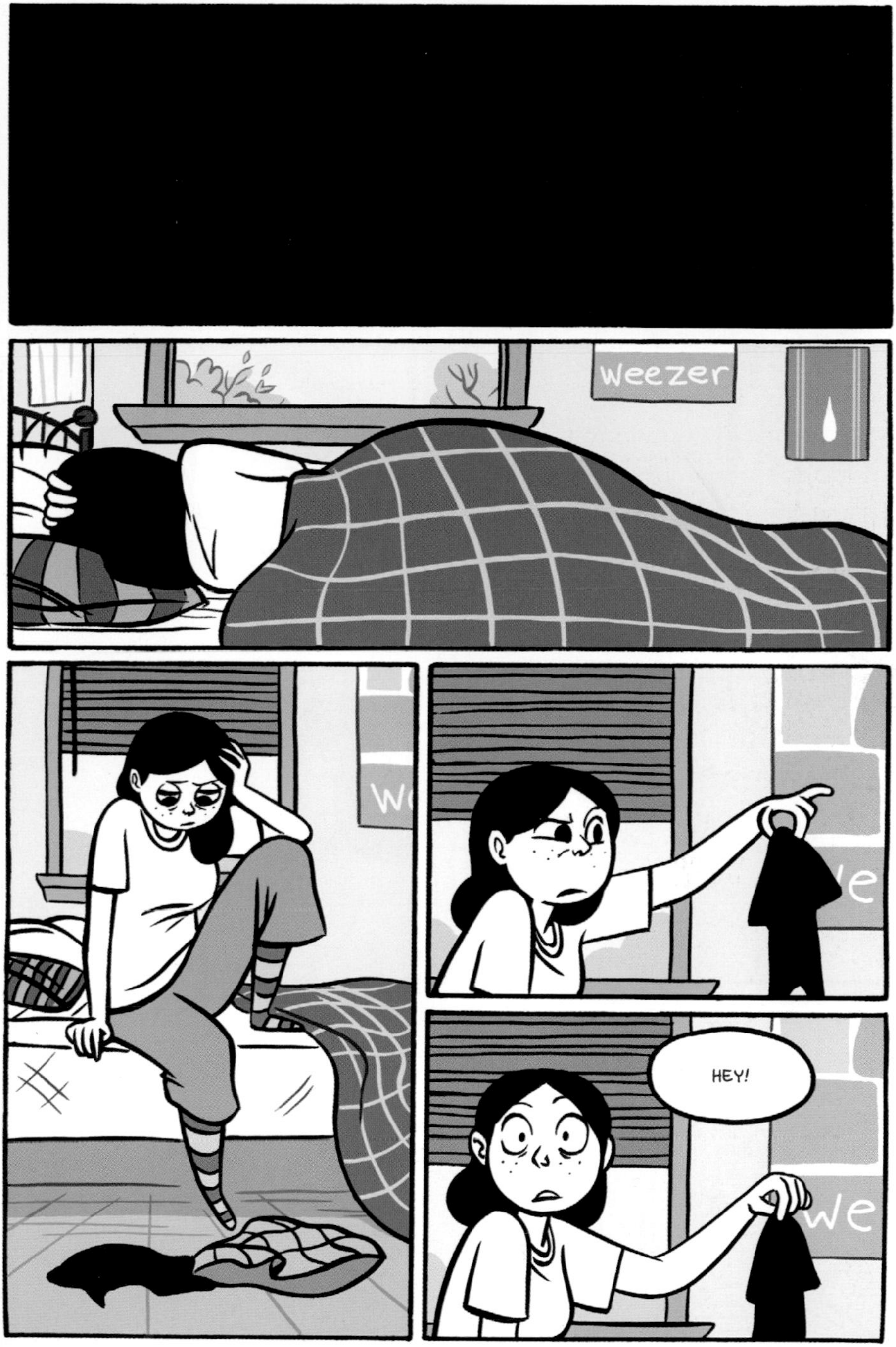
weezer
HEY!

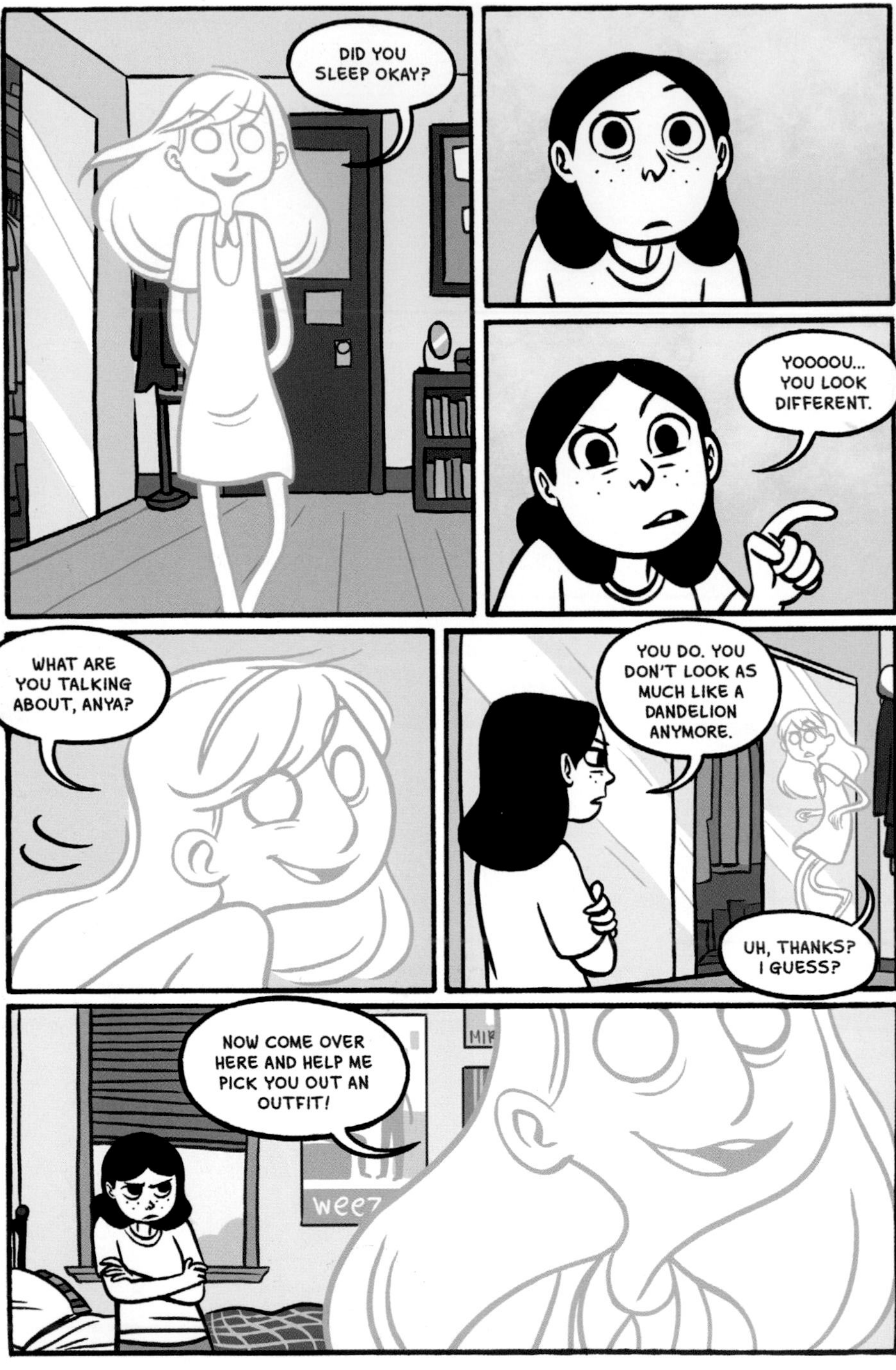
DID YOU SLEEP OKAY?
YOOOOU... YOU LOOK DIFFERENT.
WHAT ARE YOU TALKING ABOUT, ANYA?
YOU DO. YOU DON'T LOOK AS MUCH LIKE A DANDELION ANYMORE.
UH, THANKS? I GUESS?
NOW COME OVER HERE AND HELP ME PICK YOU OUT AN OUTFIT!

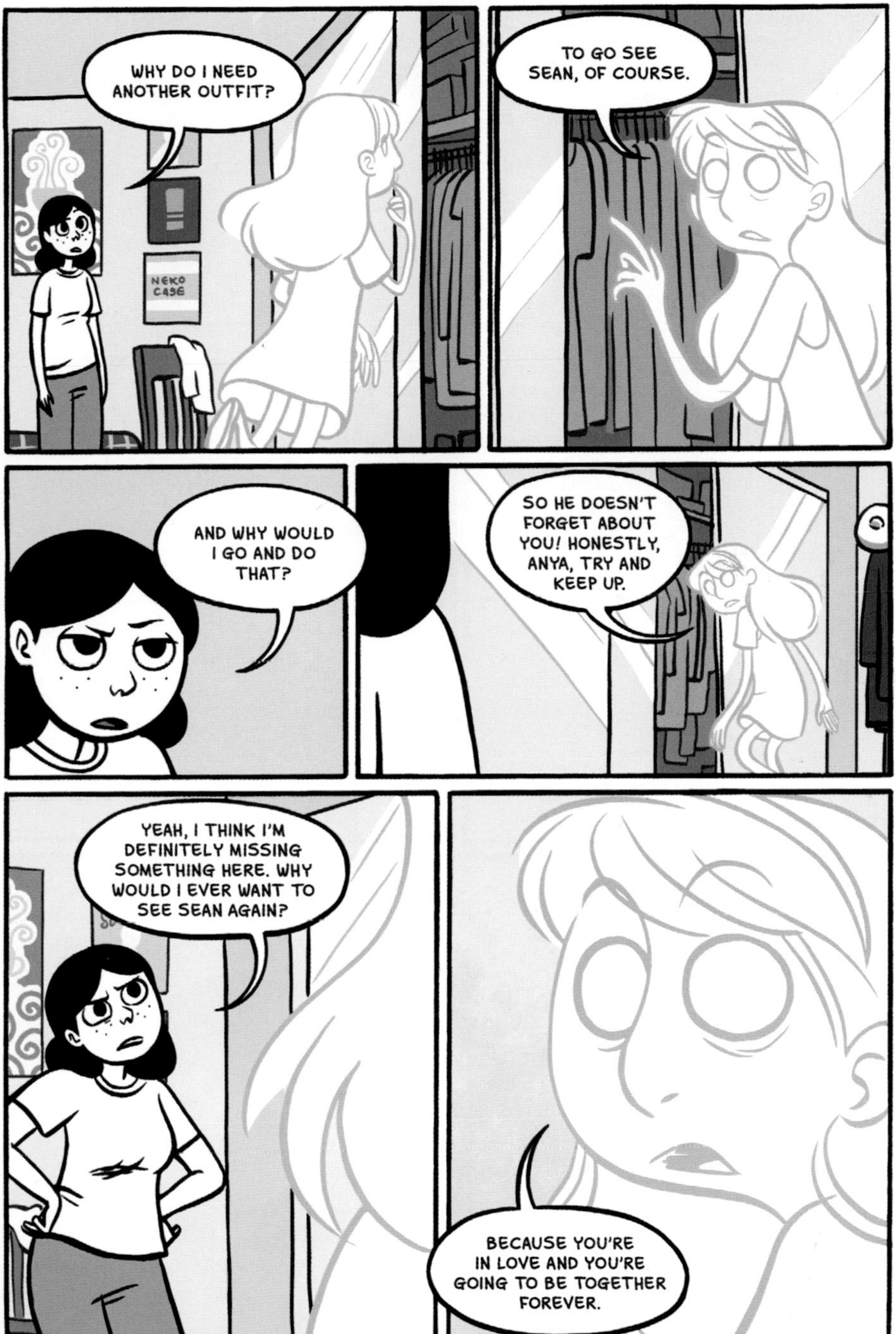
WHY DO I NEED ANOTHER OUTFIT?
NEKO CASE
TO GO SEE SEAN, OF COURSE.
AND WHY WOULD I GO AND DO THAT?
SO HE DOESN'T FORGET ABOUT YOU! HONESTLY, ANYA, TRY AND KEEP UP.
YEAH, I THINK I'M DEFINITELY MISSING SOMETHING HERE. WHY WOULD I EVER WANT TO SEE SEAN AGAIN?
BECAUSE YOU'RE IN LOVE AND YOU'RE GOING TO BE TOGETHER FOREVER.

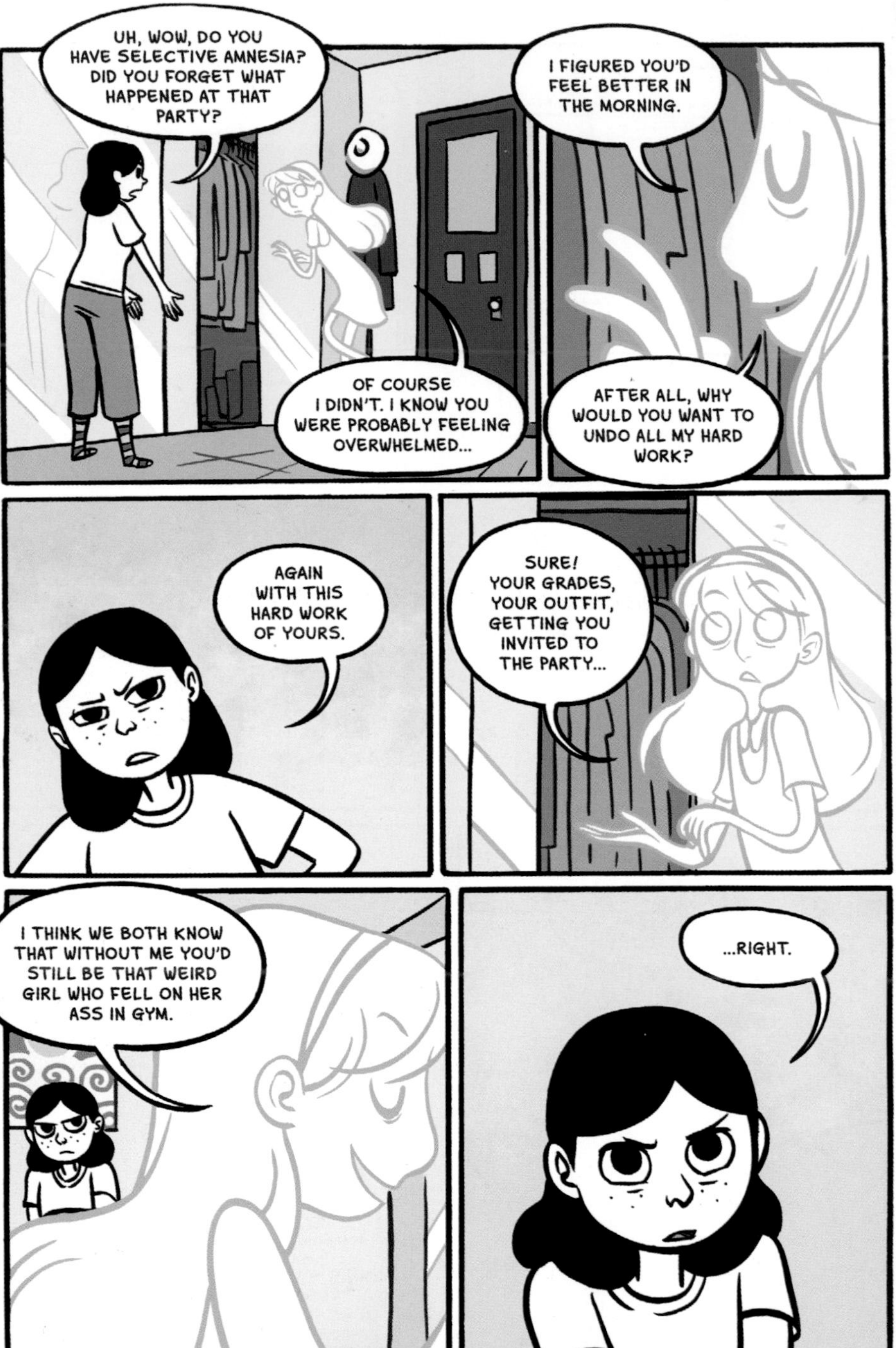
UH, WOW, DO YOU HAVE SELECTIVE AMNESIA? DID YOU FORGET WHAT HAPPENED AT THAT PARTY?
OF COURSE I DIDN'T. I KNOW YOU WERE PROBABLY FEELING OVERWHELMED...
I FIGURED YOU'D FEEL BETTER IN THE MORNING.
AFTER ALL, WHY WOULD YOU WANT TO UNDO ALL MY HARD WORK?
AGAIN WITH THIS HARD WORK OF YOURS.
SURE! YOUR GRADES, YOUR OUTFIT, GETTING YOU INVITED TO THE PARTY...
I THINK WE BOTH KNOW THAT WITHOUT ME YOU'D STILL BE THAT WEIRD GIRL WHO FELL ON HER ASS IN GYM.
...RIGHT.

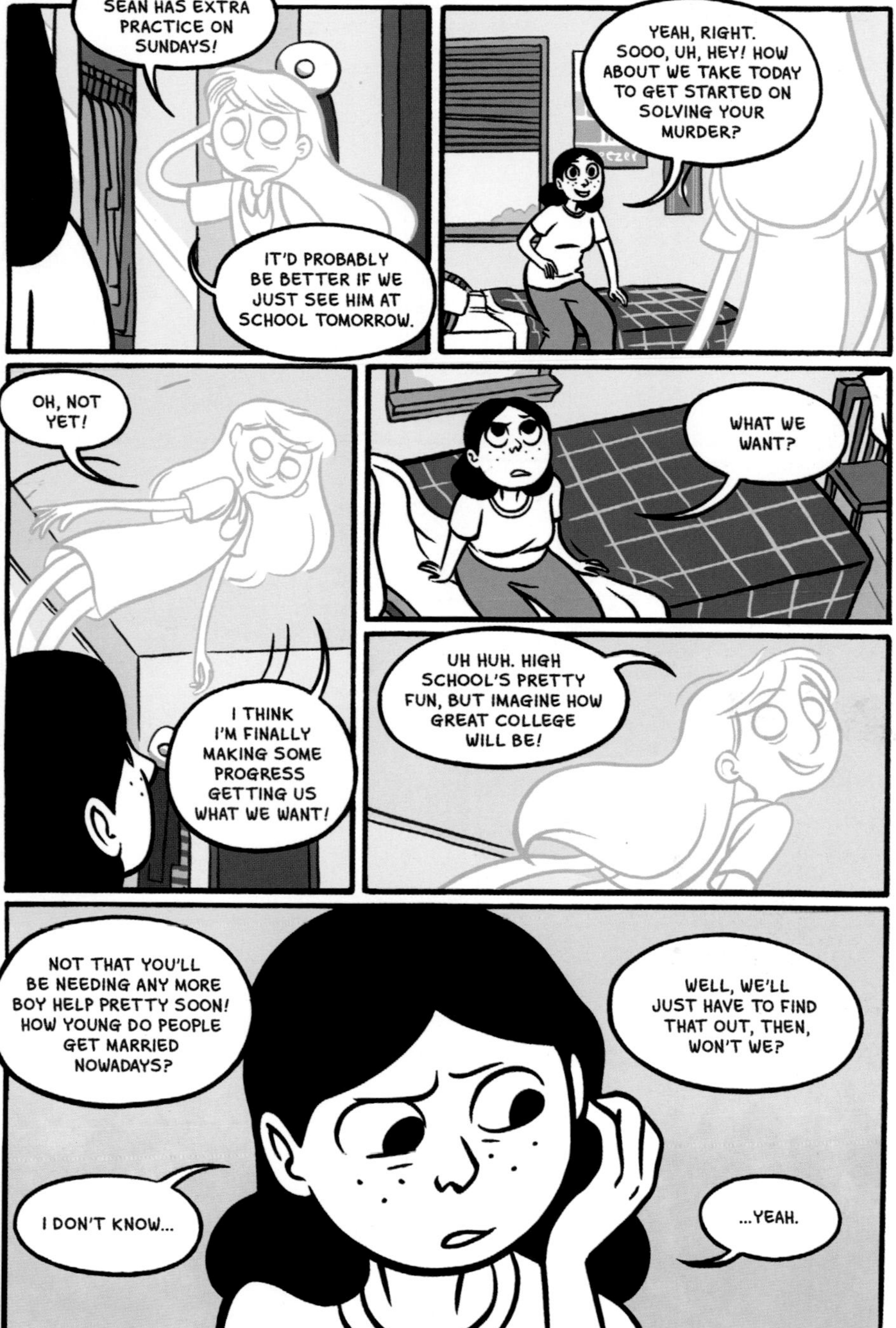
OH! I FORGOT. SEAN HAS EXTRA PRACTICE ON SUNDAYS!
IT'D PROBABLY BE BETTER IF WE JUST SEE HIM AT SCHOOL TOMORROW.
YEAH, RIGHT. SOOO, UH, HEY! HOW ABOUT WE TAKE TODAY TO GET STARTED ON SOLVING YOUR MURDER?
OH, NOT YET!
I THINK I'M FINALLY MAKING SOME PROGRESS GETTING US WHAT WE WANT!
WHAT WE WANT?
UH HUH. HIGH SCHOOL'S PRETTY FUN, BUT IMAGINE HOW GREAT COLLEGE WILL BE!
NOT THAT YOU'LL BE NEEDING ANY MORE BOY HELP PRETTY SOON! HOW YOUNG DO PEOPLE GET MARRIED NOWADAYS?
I DON'T KNOW...
WELL, WE'LL JUST HAVE TO FIND THAT OUT, THEN, WON'T WE?
...YEAH.

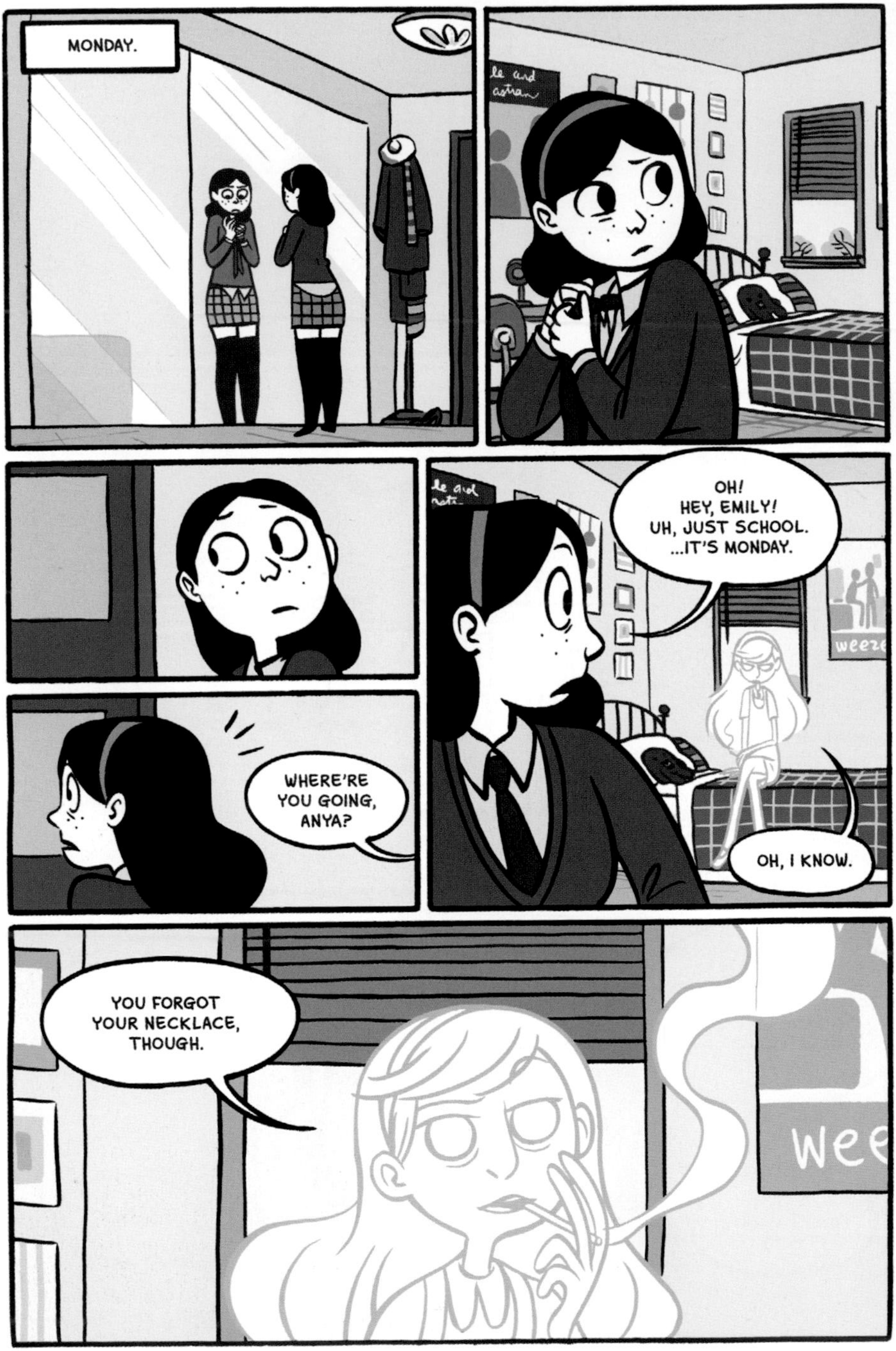
MONDAY.
le and astran
WHERE'RE YOU GOING, ANYA?
OH! HEY, EMILY! UH, JUST SCHOOL. ...IT'S MONDAY.
weeze
OH, I KNOW.
YOU FORGOT YOUR NECKLACE, THOUGH.
wee

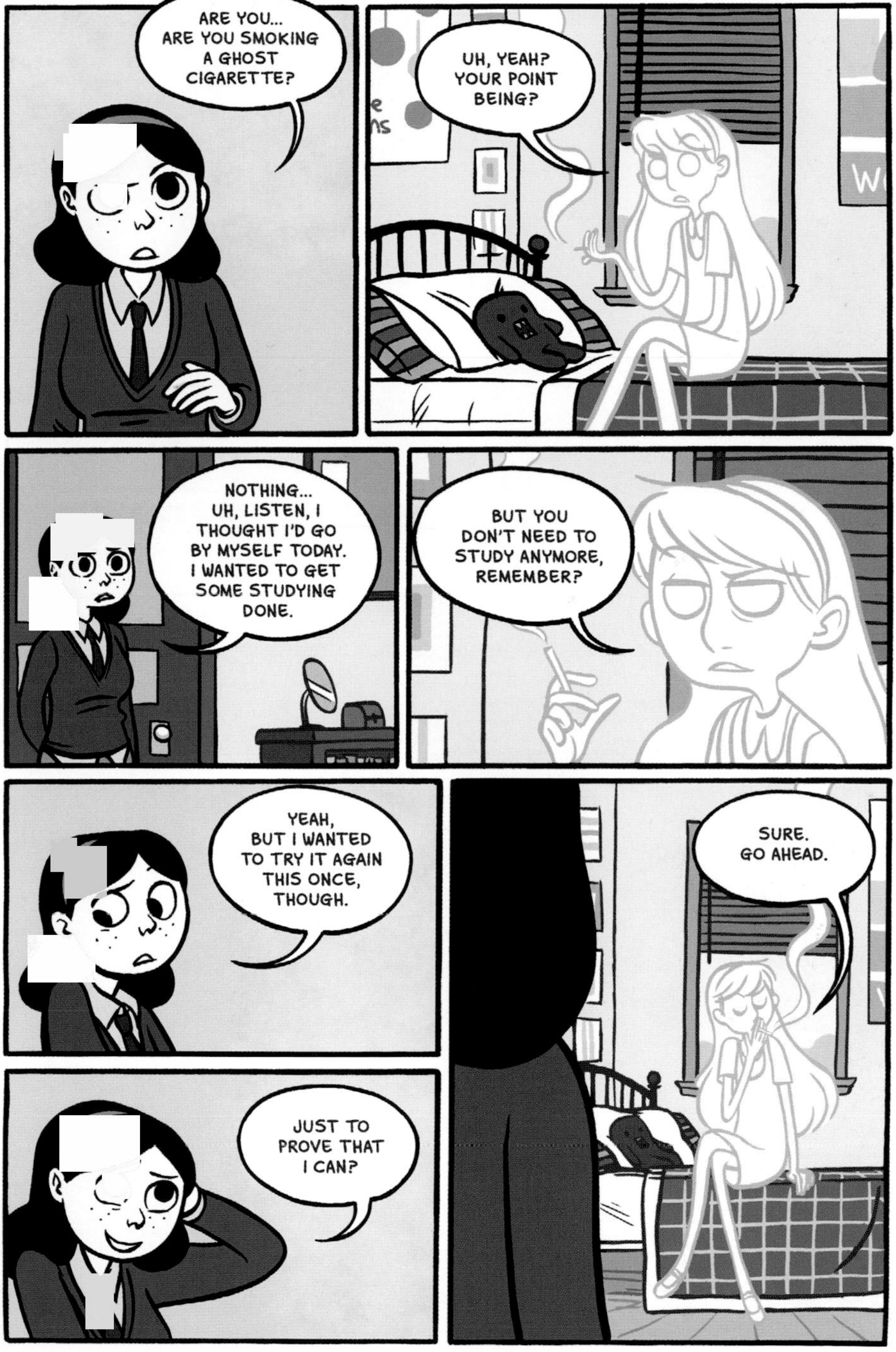
ARE YOU... ARE YOU SMOKING A GHOST CIGARETTE?
UH, YEAH? YOUR POINT BEING?
NOTHING... UH, LISTEN, I THOUGHT I'D GO BY MYSELF TODAY. I WANTED TO GET SOME STUDYING DONE.
BUT YOU DON'T NEED TO STUDY ANYMORE, REMEMBER?
YEAH, BUT I WANTED TO TRY IT AGAIN THIS ONCE, THOUGH.
JUST TO PROVE THAT I CAN?
SURE. GO AHEAD.

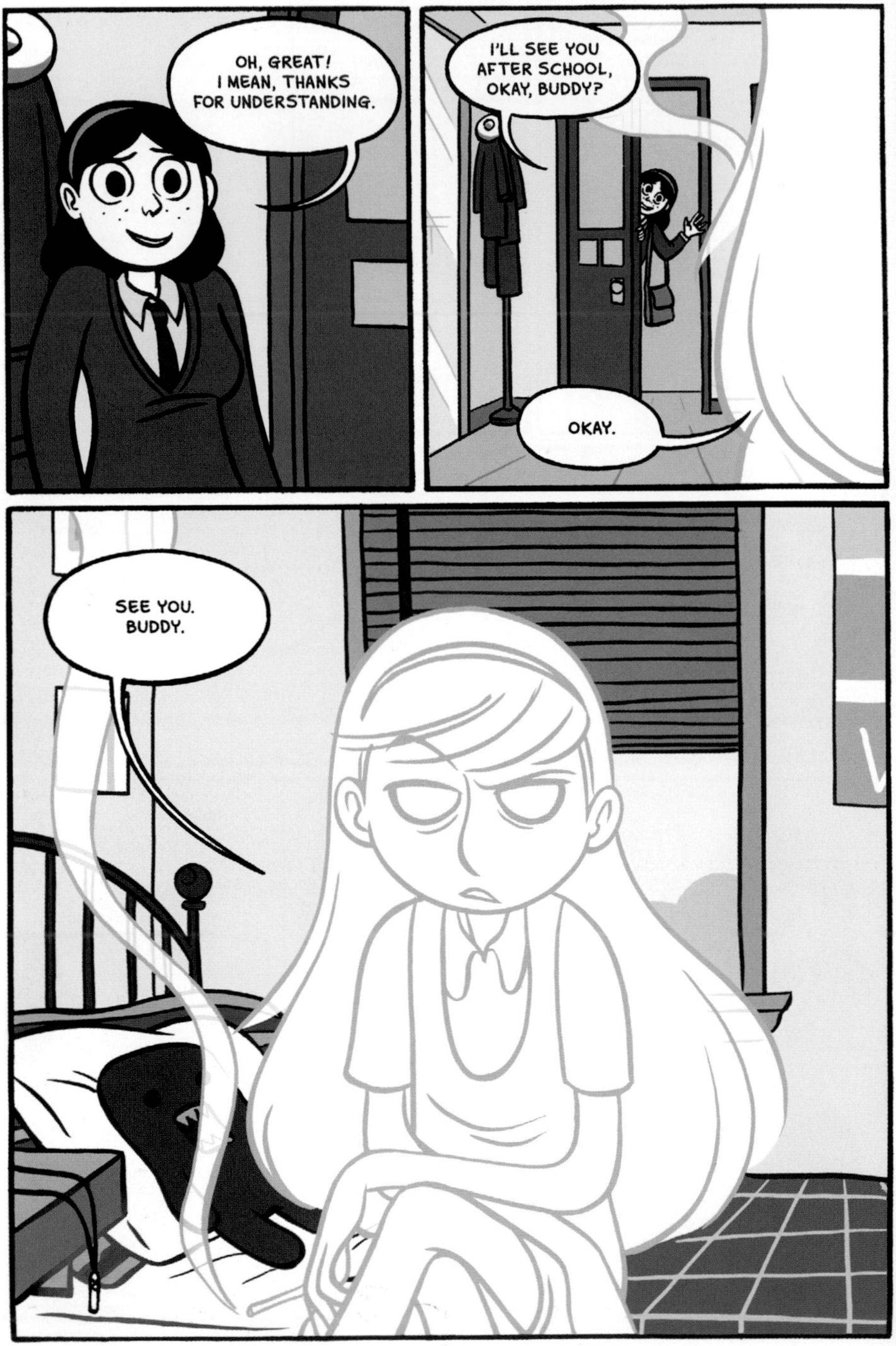
OH, GREAT!
I MEAN, THANKS
FOR UNDERSTANDING.
I'LL SEE YOU
AFTER SCHOOL,
OKAY, BUDDY?
OKAY.
SEE YOU.
BUDDY.

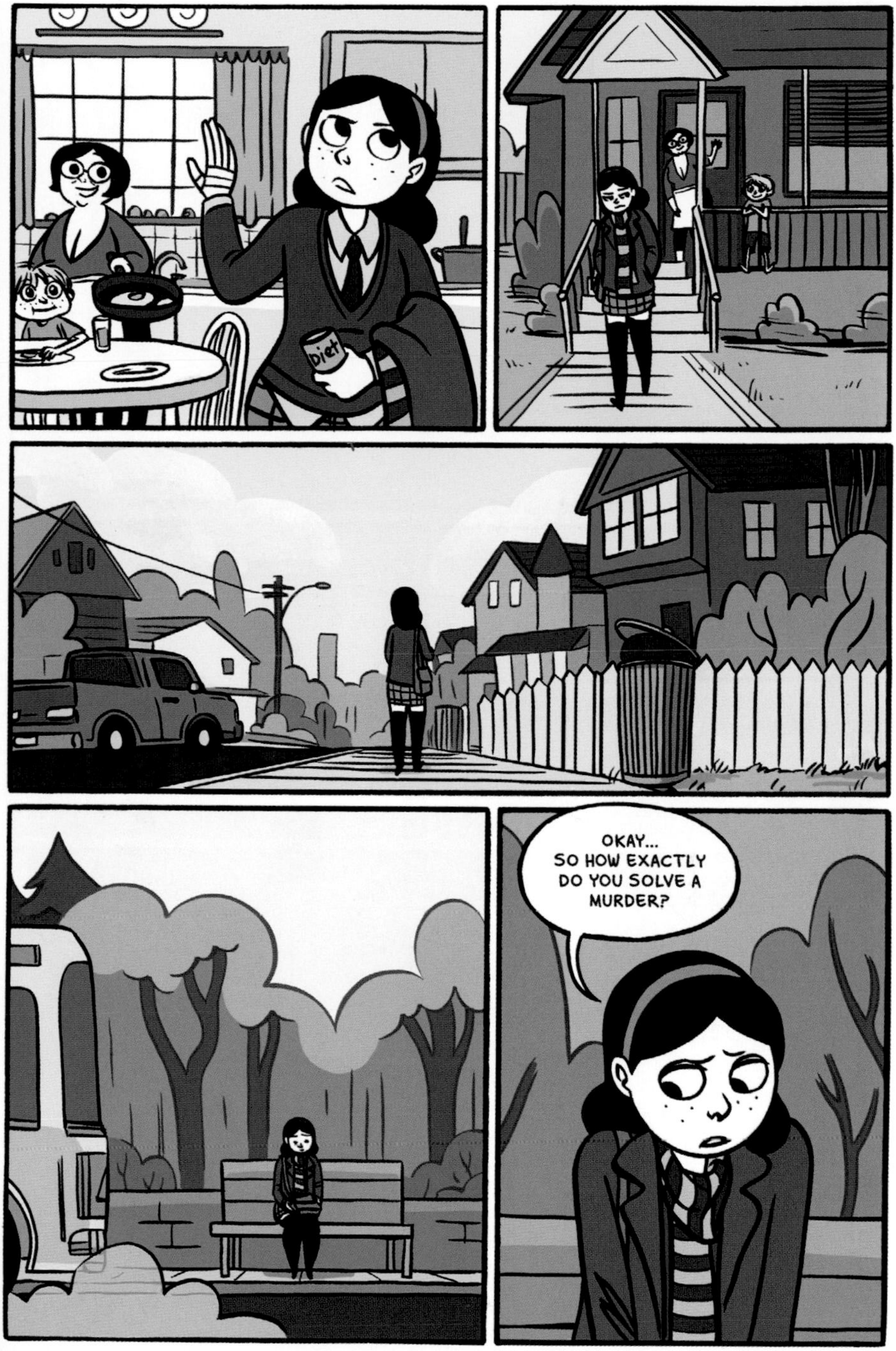
Diet
OKAY... SO HOW EXACTLY DO YOU SOLVE A MURDER?

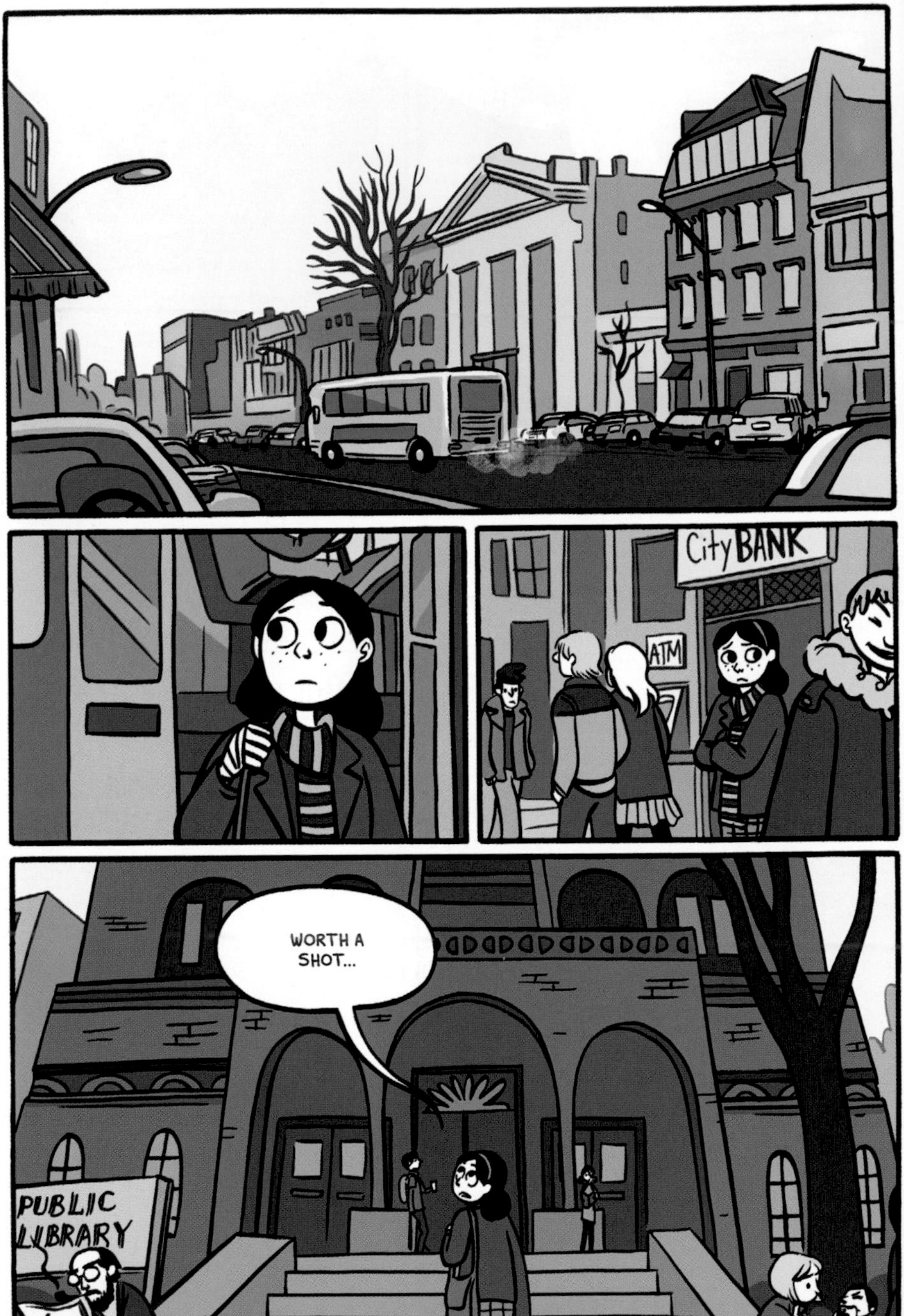
City BANK
ATM
WORTH A SHOT...
PUBLIC LIBRARY

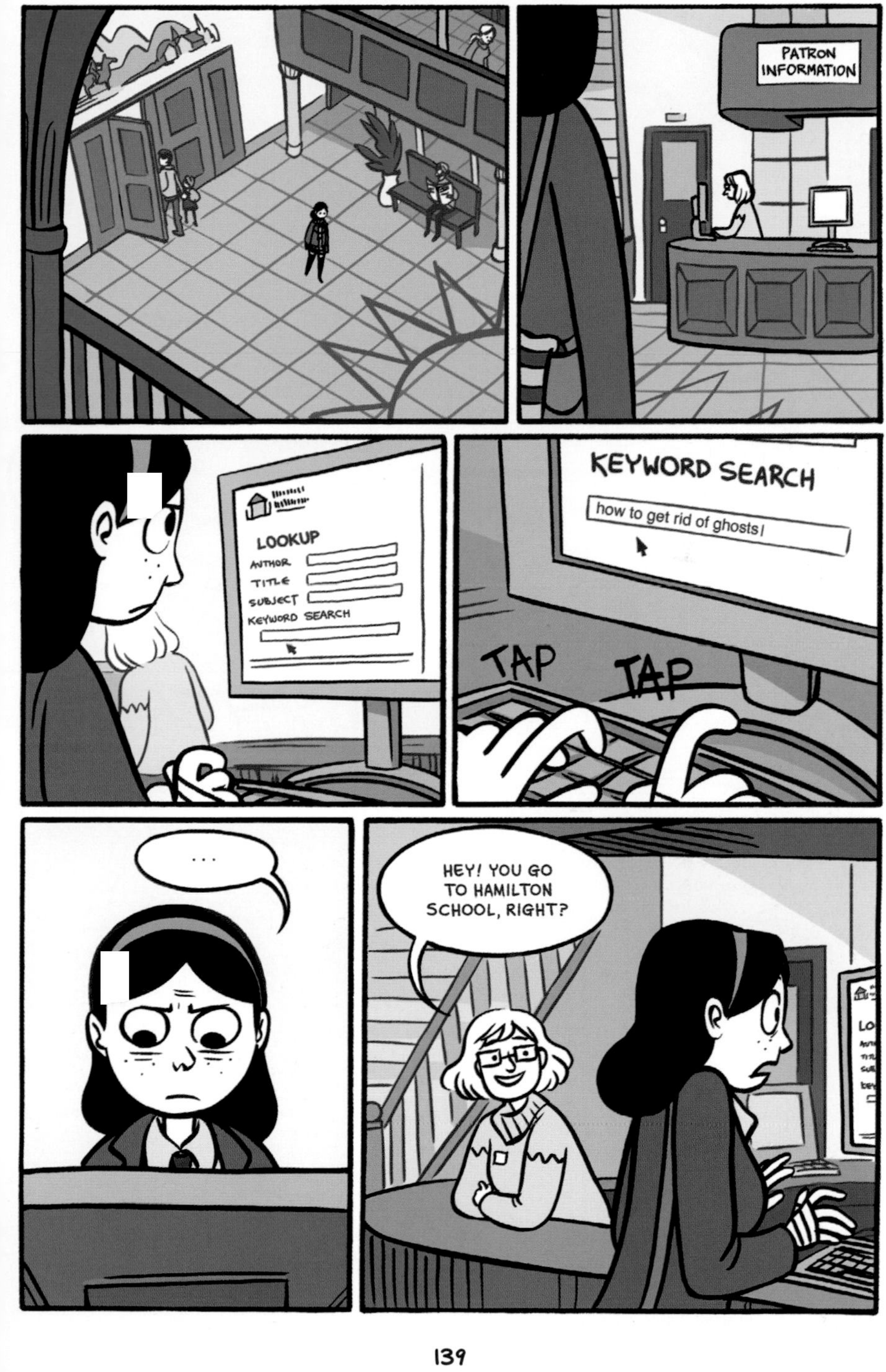
PATRON INFORMATION
LOOKUP
AUTHOR
TITLE
SUBJECT
KEYWORD SEARCH
KEYWORD SEARCH
how to get rid of ghosts!
TAP
TAP
...
HEY! YOU GO TO HAMILTON SCHOOL, RIGHT?

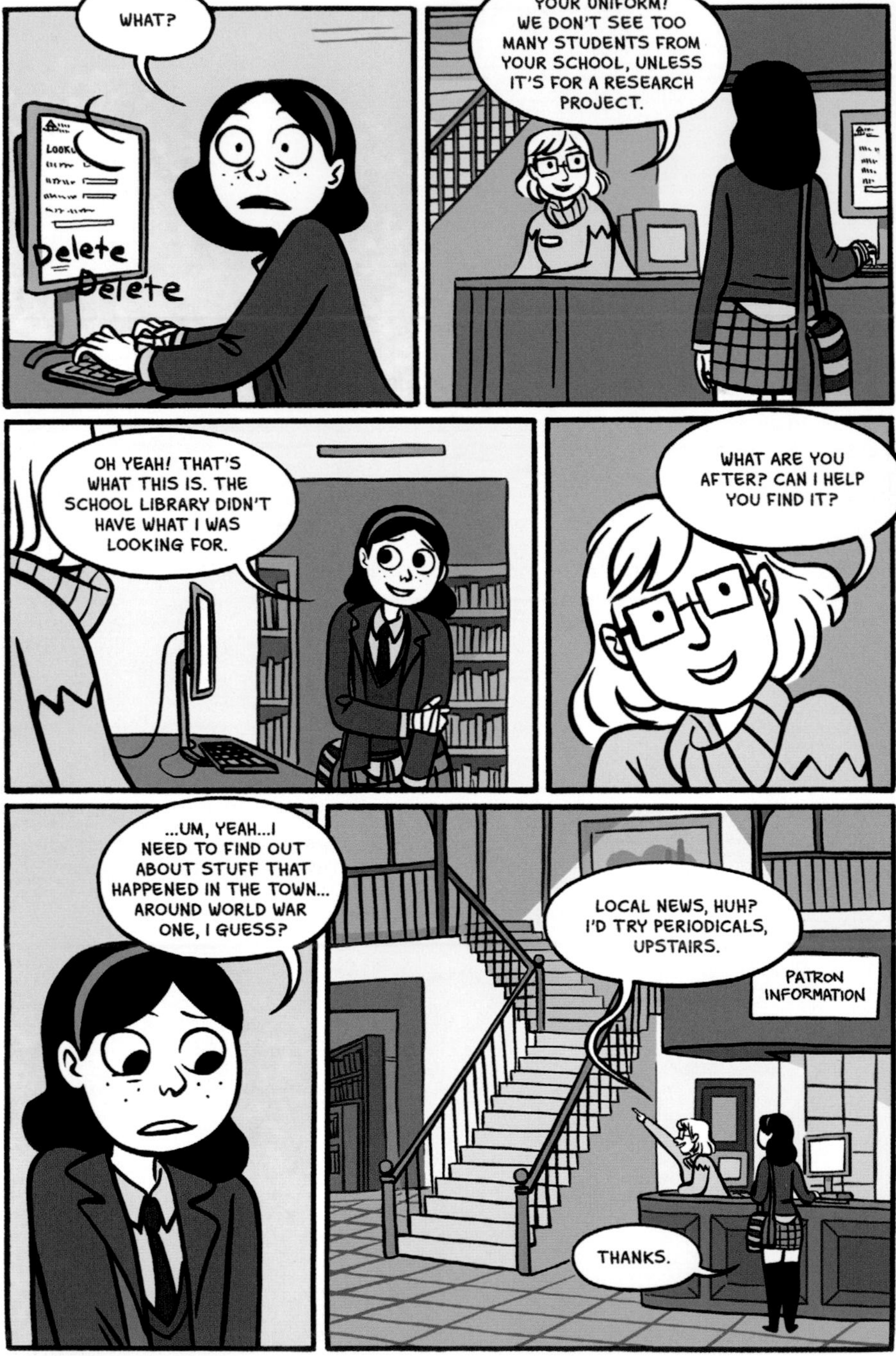
WHAT?
Delete
Delete
YOUR UNIFORM! WE DON'T SEE TOO MANY STUDENTS FROM YOUR SCHOOL, UNLESS IT'S FOR A RESEARCH PROJECT.
OH YEAH! THAT'S WHAT THIS IS. THE SCHOOL LIBRARY DIDN'T HAVE WHAT I WAS LOOKING FOR.
WHAT ARE YOU AFTER? CAN I HELP YOU FIND IT?
...UM, YEAH...I NEED TO FIND OUT ABOUT STUFF THAT HAPPENED IN THE TOWN... AROUND WORLD WAR ONE, I GUESS?
LOCAL NEWS, HUH? I'D TRY PERIODICALS, UPSTAIRS.
PATRON INFORMATION
THANKS.

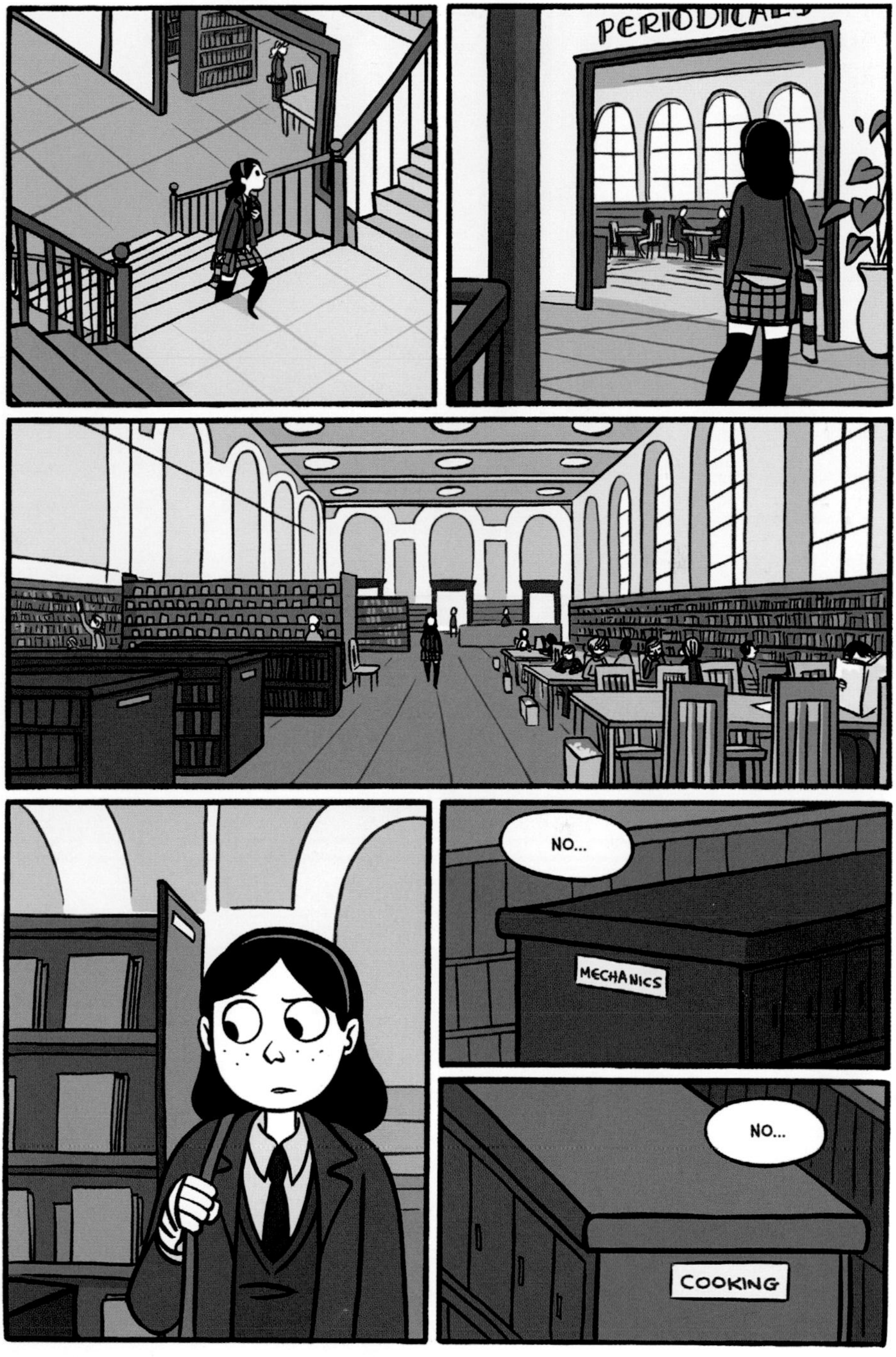
PERIODICALS
NO...
MECHANICS
NO...
COOKING

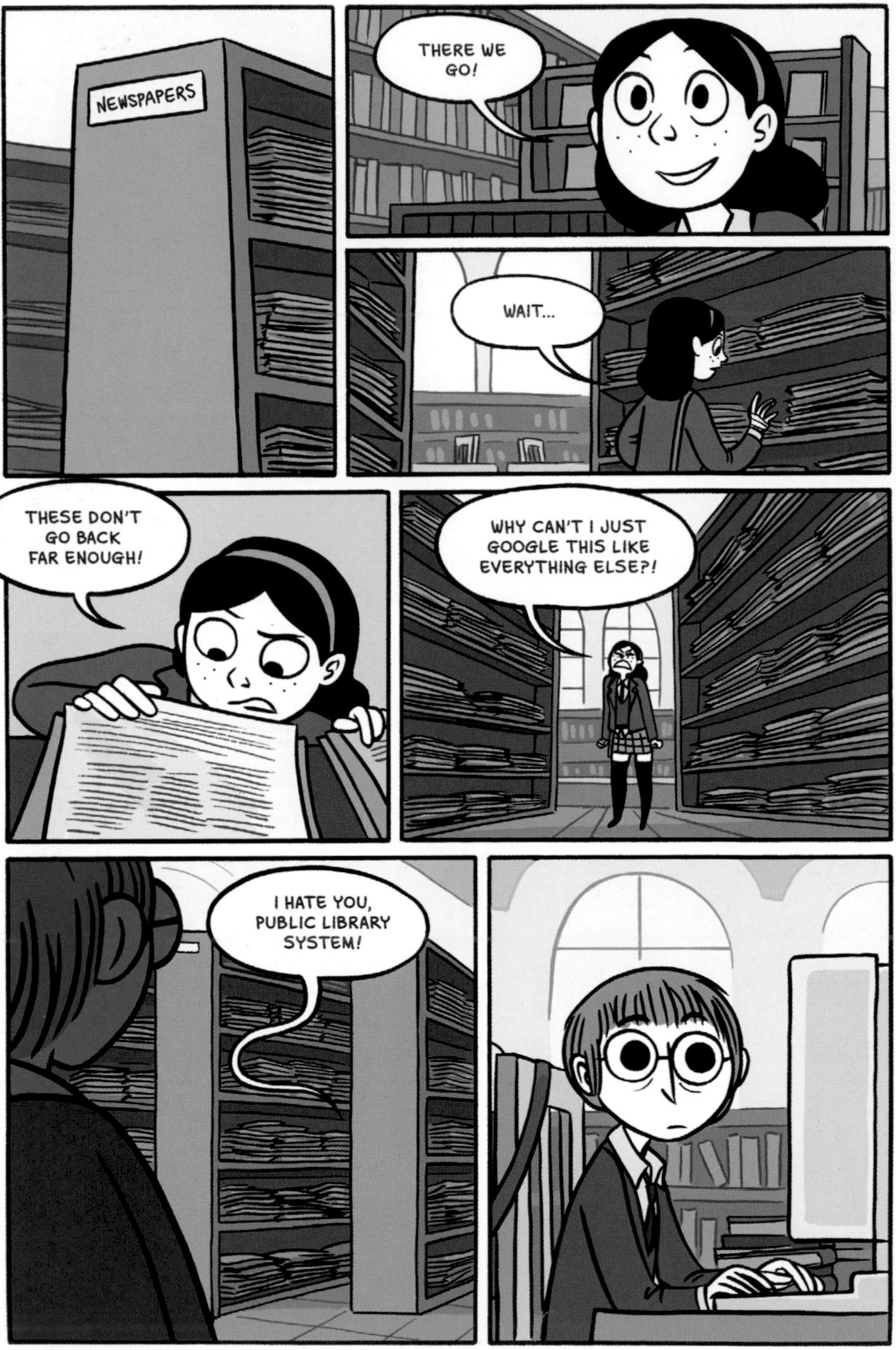
NEWSPAPERS
THERE WE GO!
WAIT...
THESE DON'T GO BACK FAR ENOUGH!
WHY CAN'T I JUST GOOGLE THIS LIKE EVERYTHING ELSE?!
I HATE YOU, PUBLIC LIBRARY SYSTEM!

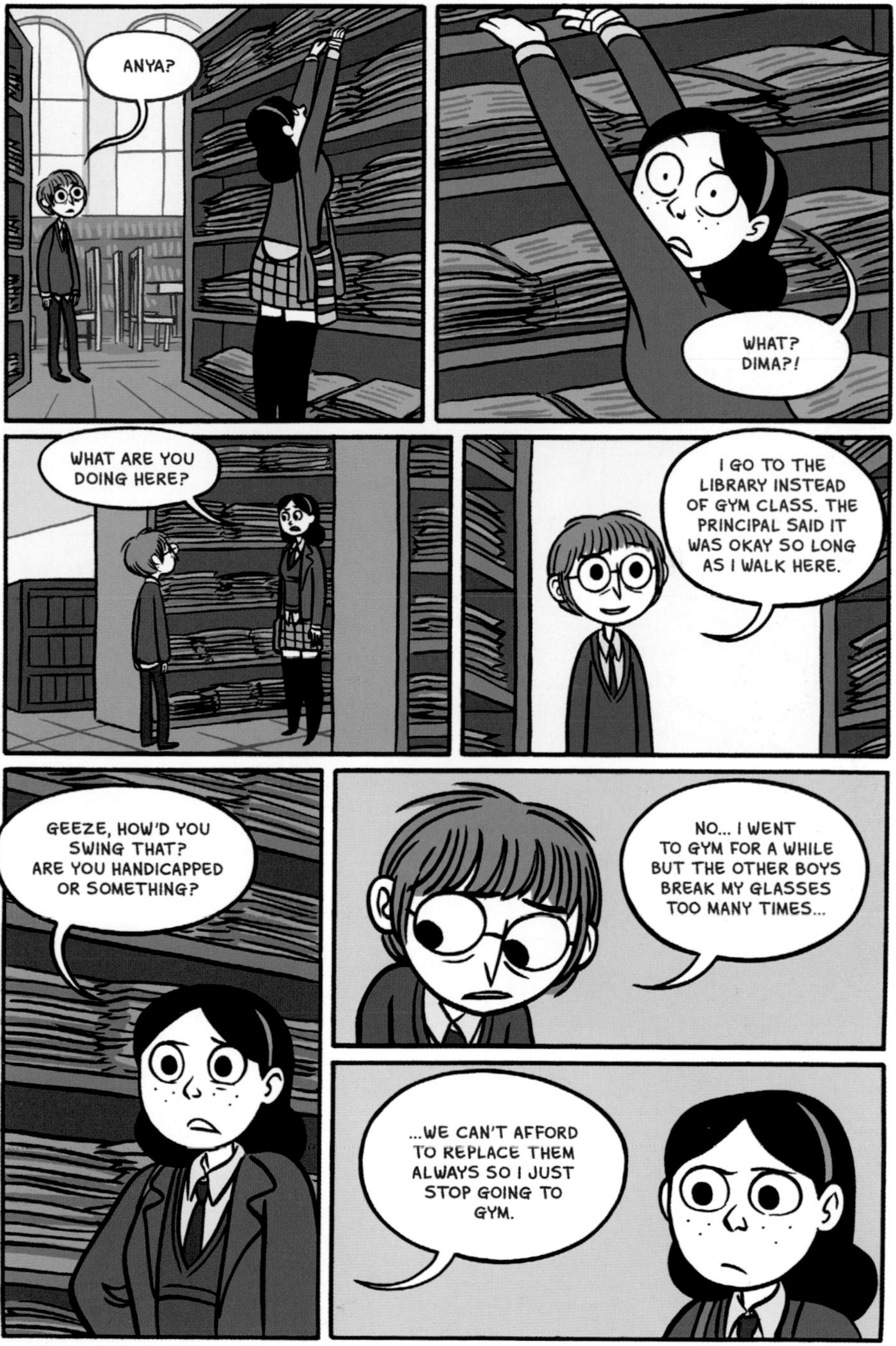
ANYA?
WHAT? DIMA?!
WHAT ARE YOU DOING HERE?
I GO TO THE LIBRARY INSTEAD OF GYM CLASS. THE PRINCIPAL SAID IT WAS OKAY SO LONG AS I WALK HERE.
GEEZE, HOW'D YOU SWING THAT? ARE YOU HANDICAPPED OR SOMETHING?
NO... I WENT TO GYM FOR A WHILE BUT THE OTHER BOYS BREAK MY GLASSES TOO MANY TIMES...
...WE CAN'T AFFORD TO REPLACE THEM ALWAYS SO I JUST STOP GOING TO GYM.

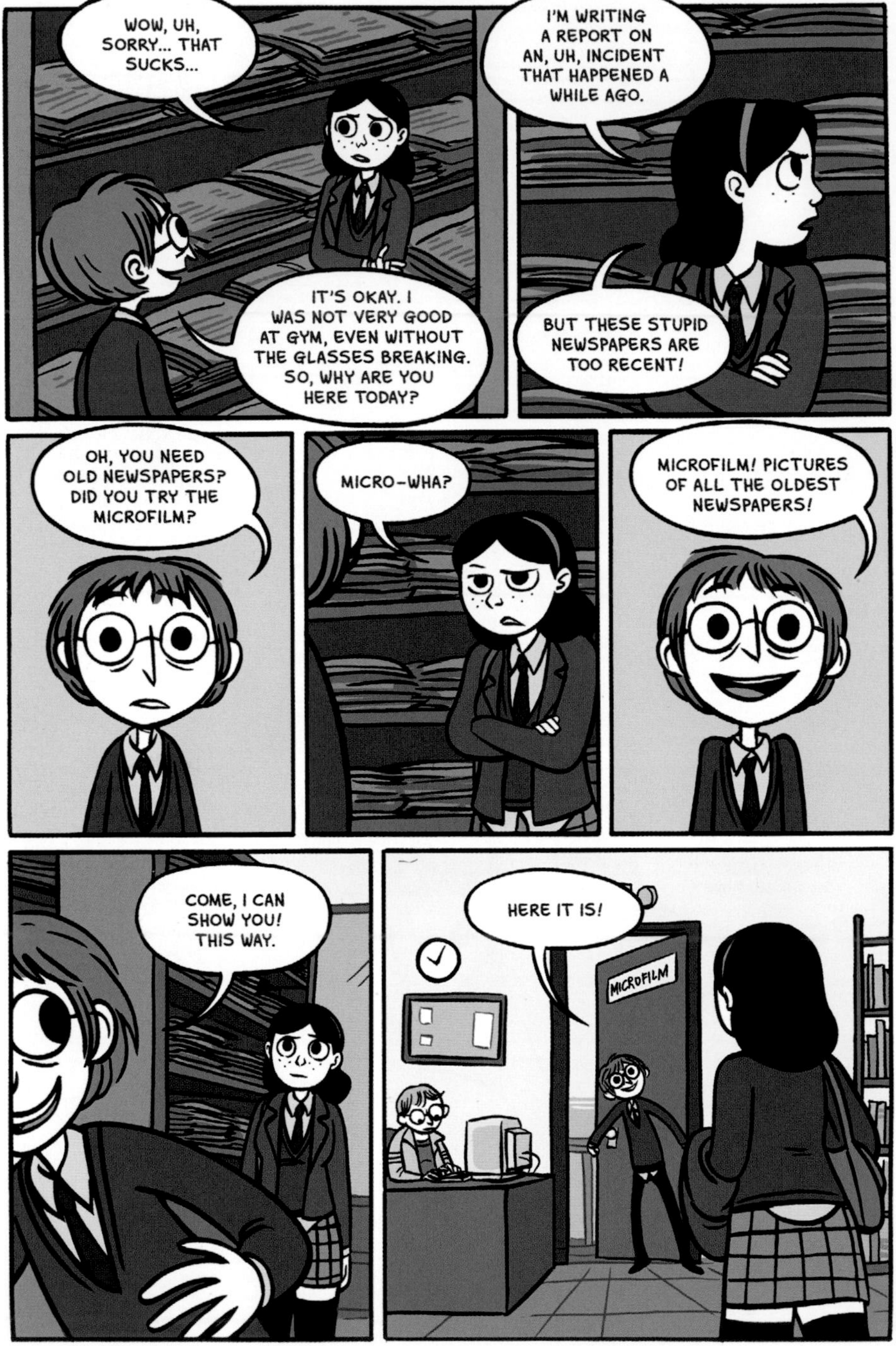
WOW, UH, SORRY... THAT SUCKS...
IT'S OKAY. I WAS NOT VERY GOOD AT GYM, EVEN WITHOUT THE GLASSES BREAKING. SO, WHY ARE YOU HERE TODAY?
I'M WRITING A REPORT ON AN, UH, INCIDENT THAT HAPPENED A WHILE AGO.
BUT THESE STUPID NEWSPAPERS ARE TOO RECENT!
OH, YOU NEED OLD NEWSPAPERS? DID YOU TRY THE MICROFILM?
MICRO-WHA?
MICROFILM! PICTURES OF ALL THE OLDEST NEWSPAPERS!
COME, I CAN SHOW YOU! THIS WAY.
HERE IT IS!
MICROFILM

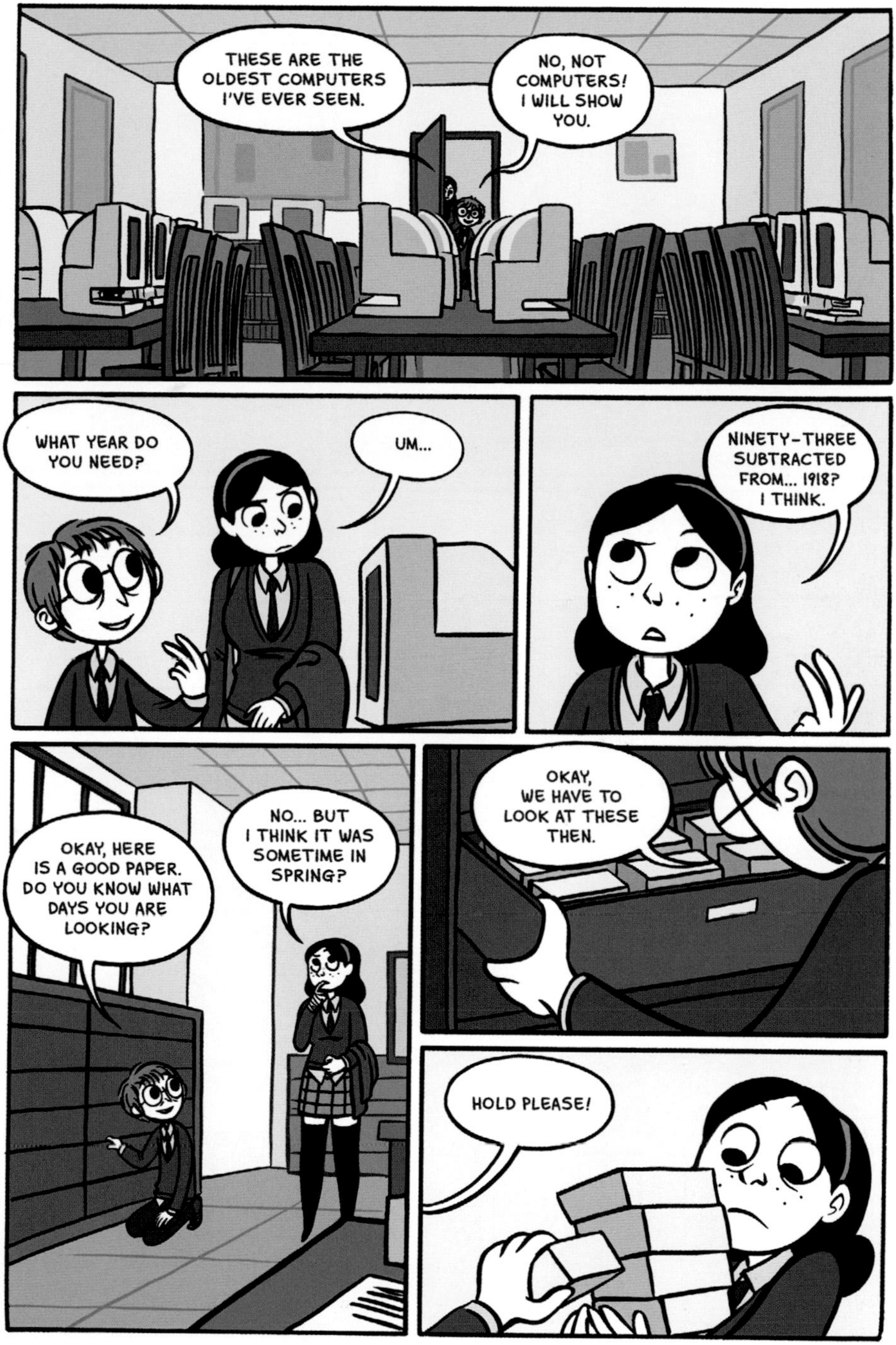
THESE ARE THE OLDEST COMPUTERS I'VE EVER SEEN.
NO, NOT COMPUTERS! I WILL SHOW YOU.
WHAT YEAR DO YOU NEED?
UM...
NINETY-THREE SUBTRACTED FROM... 1918? I THINK.
OKAY, HERE IS A GOOD PAPER. DO YOU KNOW WHAT DAYS YOU ARE LOOKING?
NO... BUT I THINK IT WAS SOMETIME IN SPRING?
OKAY, WE HAVE TO LOOK AT THESE THEN.
HOLD PLEASE!

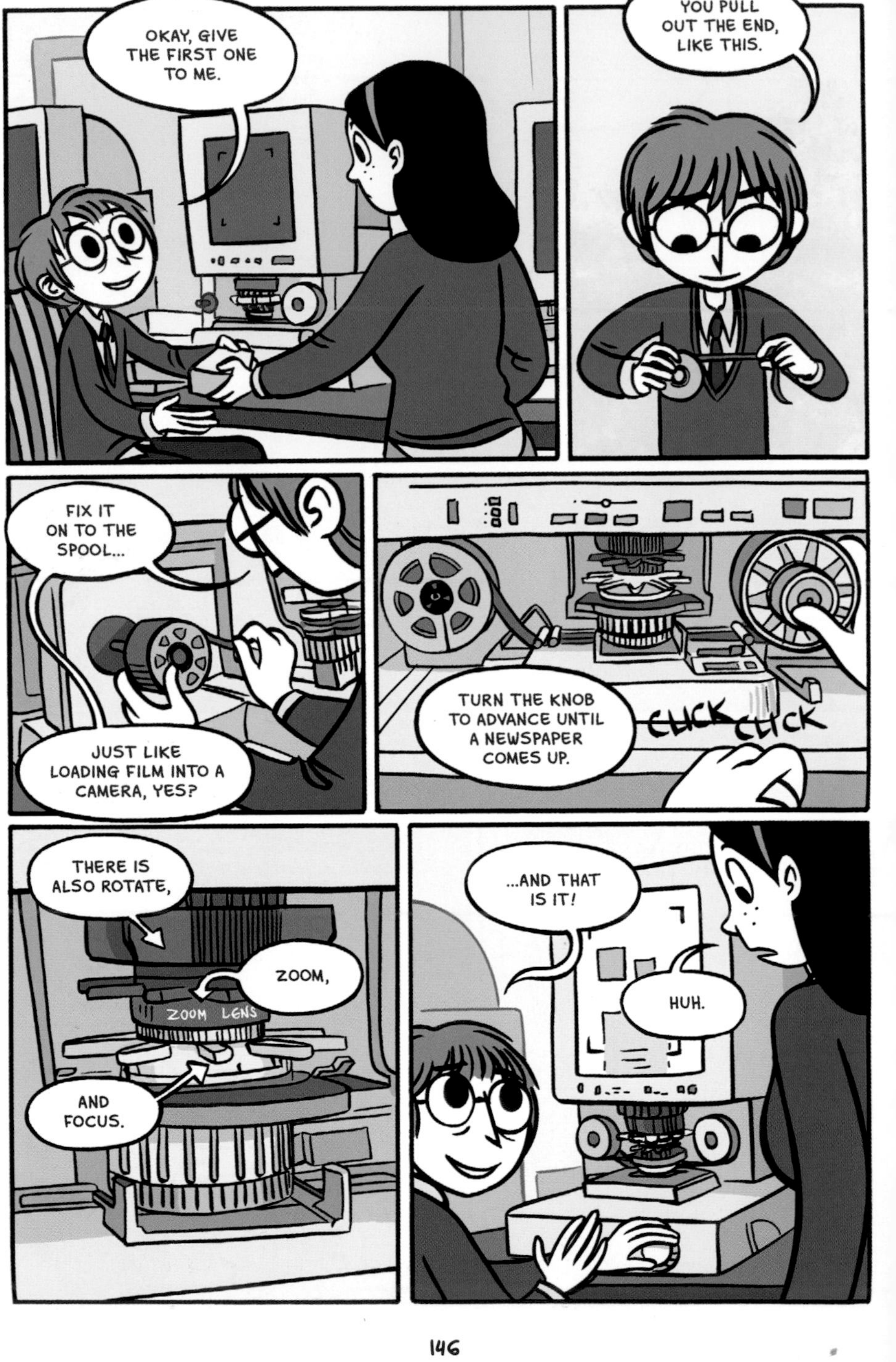
OKAY, GIVE THE FIRST ONE TO ME.
YOU PULL OUT THE END, LIKE THIS.
FIX IT ON TO THE SPOOL...
JUST LIKE LOADING FILM INTO A CAMERA, YES?
TURN THE KNOB TO ADVANCE UNTIL A NEWSPAPER COMES UP.
CLICK CLICK
THERE IS ALSO ROTATE,
ZOOM,
ZOOM LENS
AND FOCUS.
...AND THAT IS IT!
HUH.

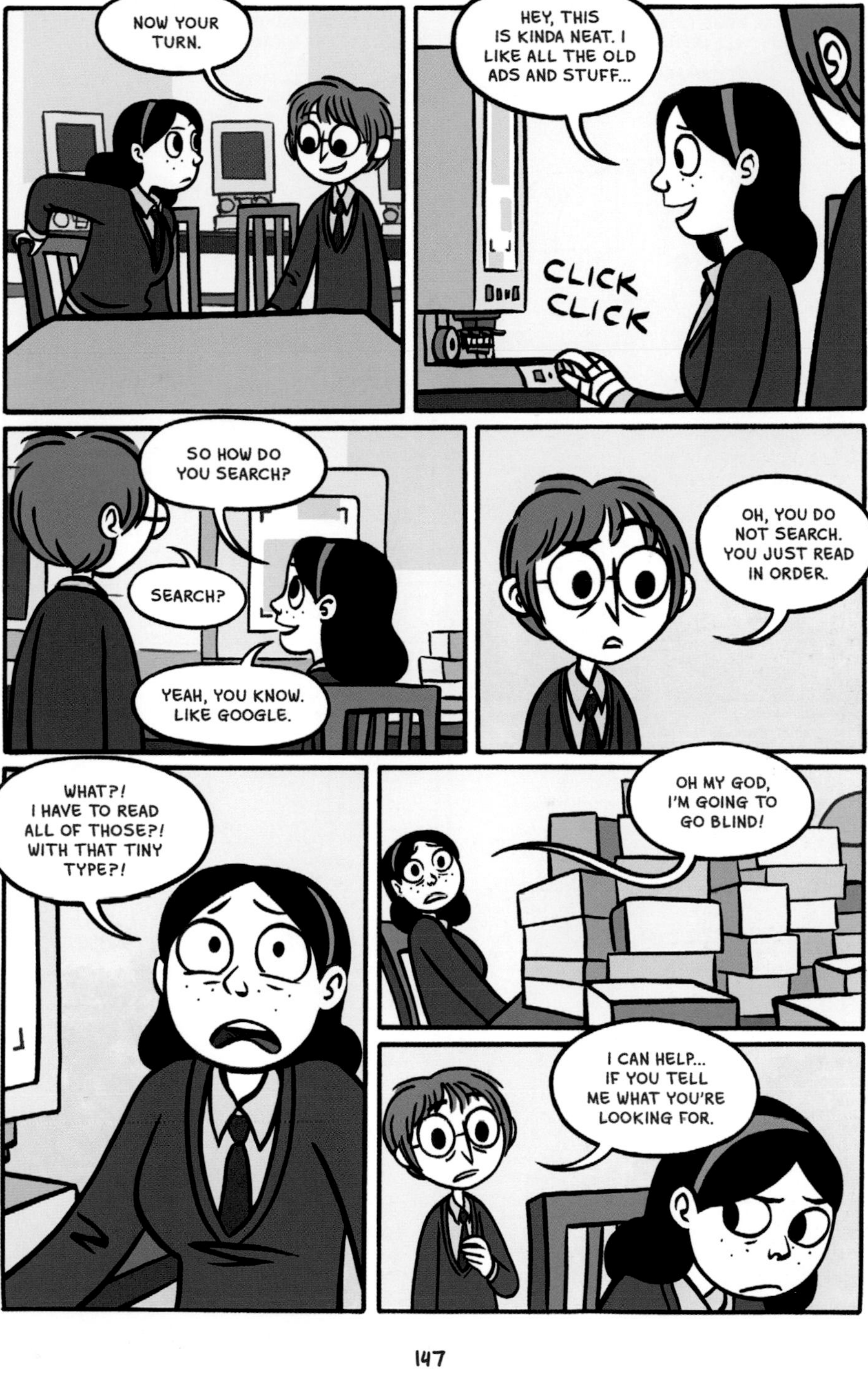
NOW YOUR TURN.
HEY, THIS IS KINDA NEAT. I LIKE ALL THE OLD ADS AND STUFF...
CLICK CLICK
SO HOW DO YOU SEARCH?
SEARCH?
YEAH, YOU KNOW. LIKE GOOGLE.
OH, YOU DO NOT SEARCH. YOU JUST READ IN ORDER.
WHAT?! I HAVE TO READ ALL OF THOSE?! WITH THAT TINY TYPE?!
OH MY GOD, I'M GOING TO GO BLIND!
I CAN HELP... IF YOU TELL ME WHAT YOU'RE LOOKING FOR.

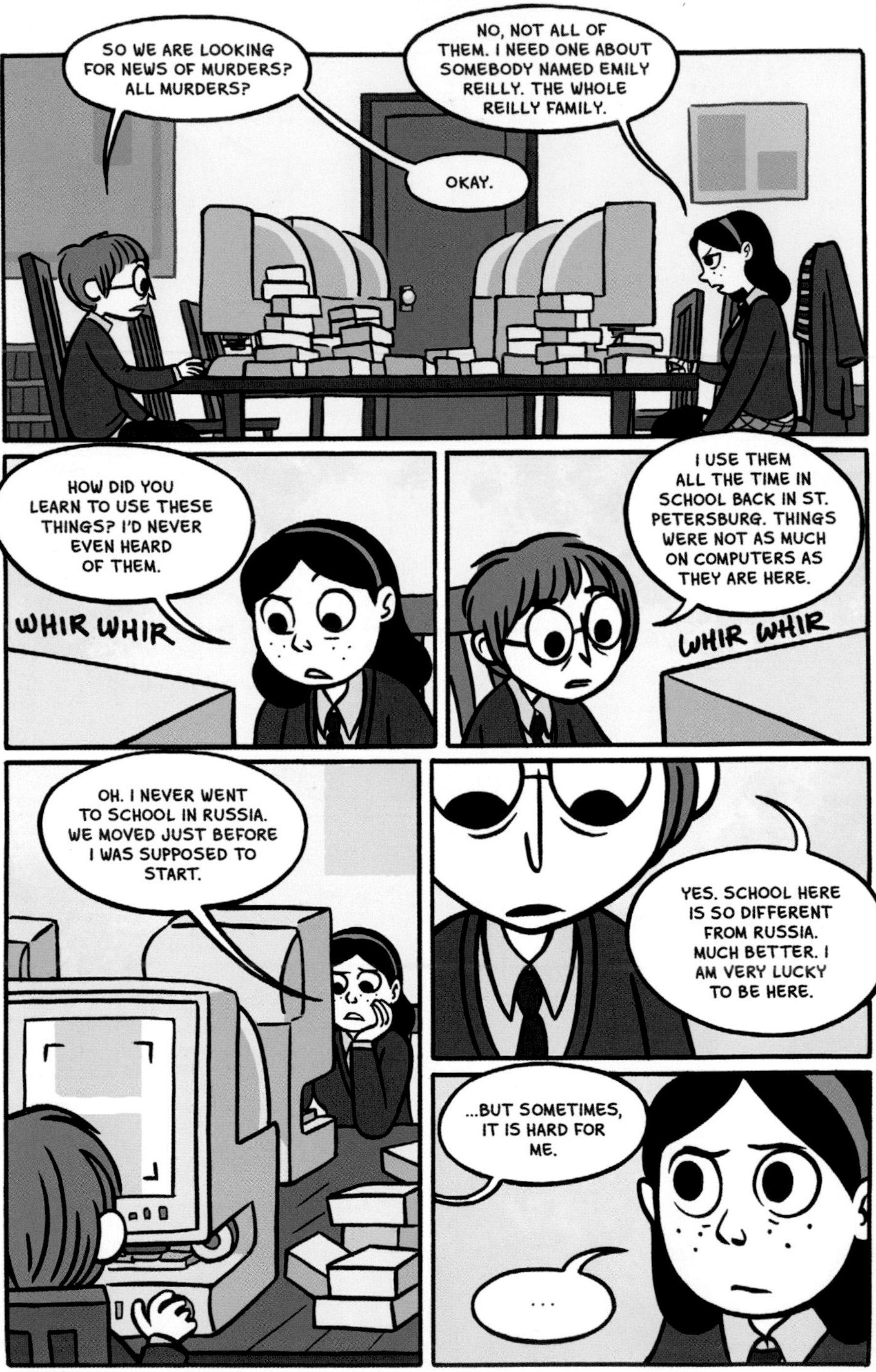
SO WE ARE LOOKING FOR NEWS OF MURDERS? ALL MURDERS?
NO, NOT ALL OF THEM. I NEED ONE ABOUT SOMEBODY NAMED EMILY REILLY. THE WHOLE REILLY FAMILY.
OKAY.
HOW DID YOU LEARN TO USE THESE THINGS? I'D NEVER EVEN HEARD OF THEM.
WHIR WHIR
I USE THEM ALL THE TIME IN SCHOOL BACK IN ST. PETERSBURG. THINGS WERE NOT AS MUCH ON COMPUTERS AS THEY ARE HERE.
WHIR WHIR
OH. I NEVER WENT TO SCHOOL IN RUSSIA. WE MOVED JUST BEFORE I WAS SUPPOSED TO START.
YES. SCHOOL HERE IS SO DIFFERENT FROM RUSSIA. MUCH BETTER. I AM VERY LUCKY TO BE HERE.
...BUT SOMETIMES, IT IS HARD FOR ME.
...

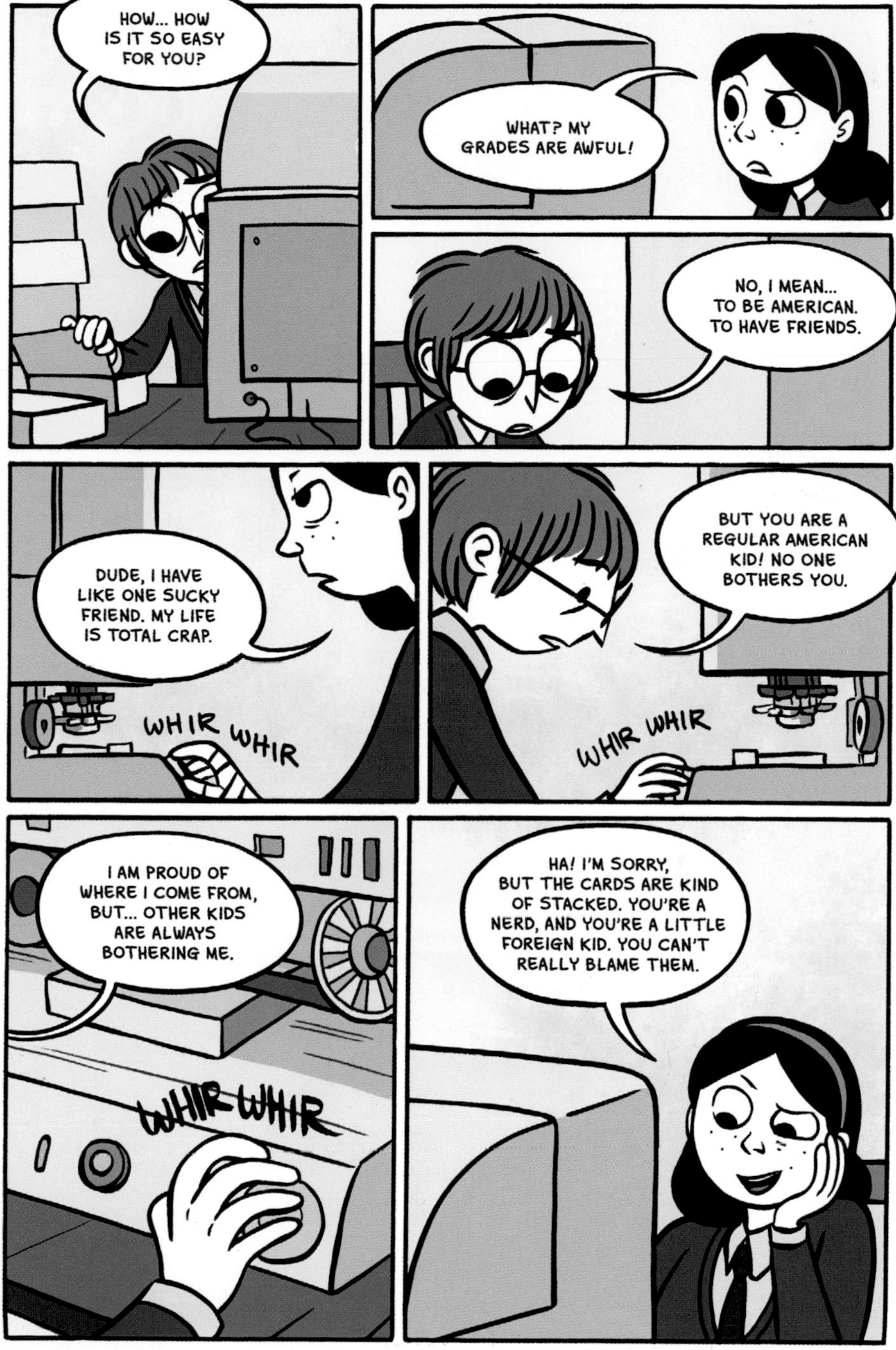
HOW... HOW IS IT SO EASY FOR YOU?
WHAT? MY GRADES ARE AWFUL!
NO, I MEAN... TO BE AMERICAN. TO HAVE FRIENDS.
DUDE, I HAVE LIKE ONE SUCKY FRIEND. MY LIFE IS TOTAL CRAP.
WHIR WHIR
BUT YOU ARE A REGULAR AMERICAN KID! NO ONE BOTHERS YOU.
WHIR WHIR
I AM PROUD OF WHERE I COME FROM, BUT... OTHER KIDS ARE ALWAYS BOTHERING ME.
WHIR WHIR
HA! I'M SORRY, BUT THE CARDS ARE KIND OF STACKED. YOU'RE A NERD, AND YOU'RE A LITTLE FOREIGN KID. YOU CAN'T REALLY BLAME THEM.

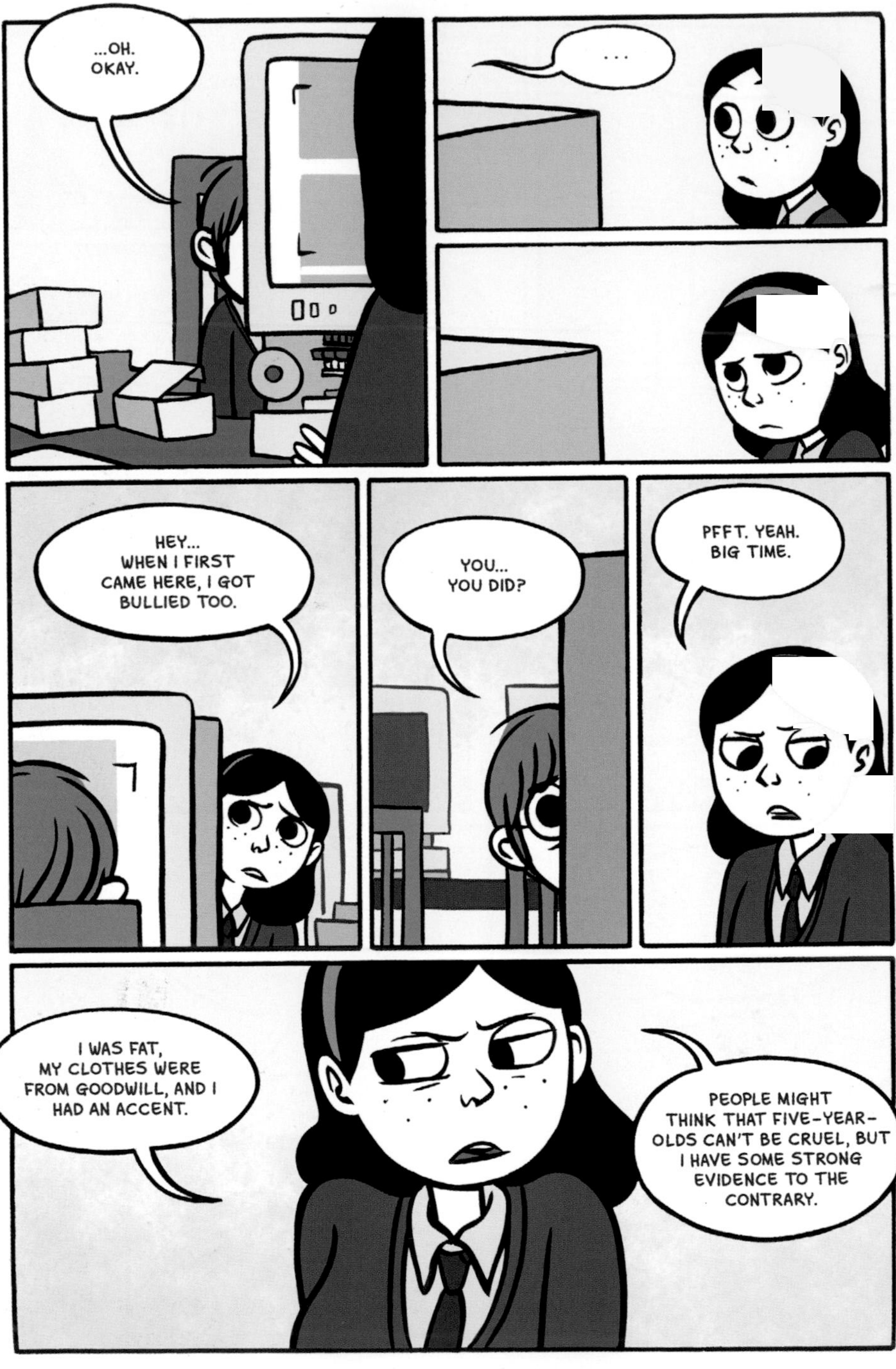
...OH.
OKAY.
...
HEY... WHEN I FIRST CAME HERE, I GOT BULLIED TOO.
YOU... YOU DID?
PFFT. YEAH. BIG TIME.
I WAS FAT, MY CLOTHES WERE FROM GOODWILL, AND I HAD AN ACCENT.
PEOPLE MIGHT THINK THAT FIVE-YEAR-OLDS CAN'T BE CRUEL, BUT I HAVE SOME STRONG EVIDENCE TO THE CONTRARY.

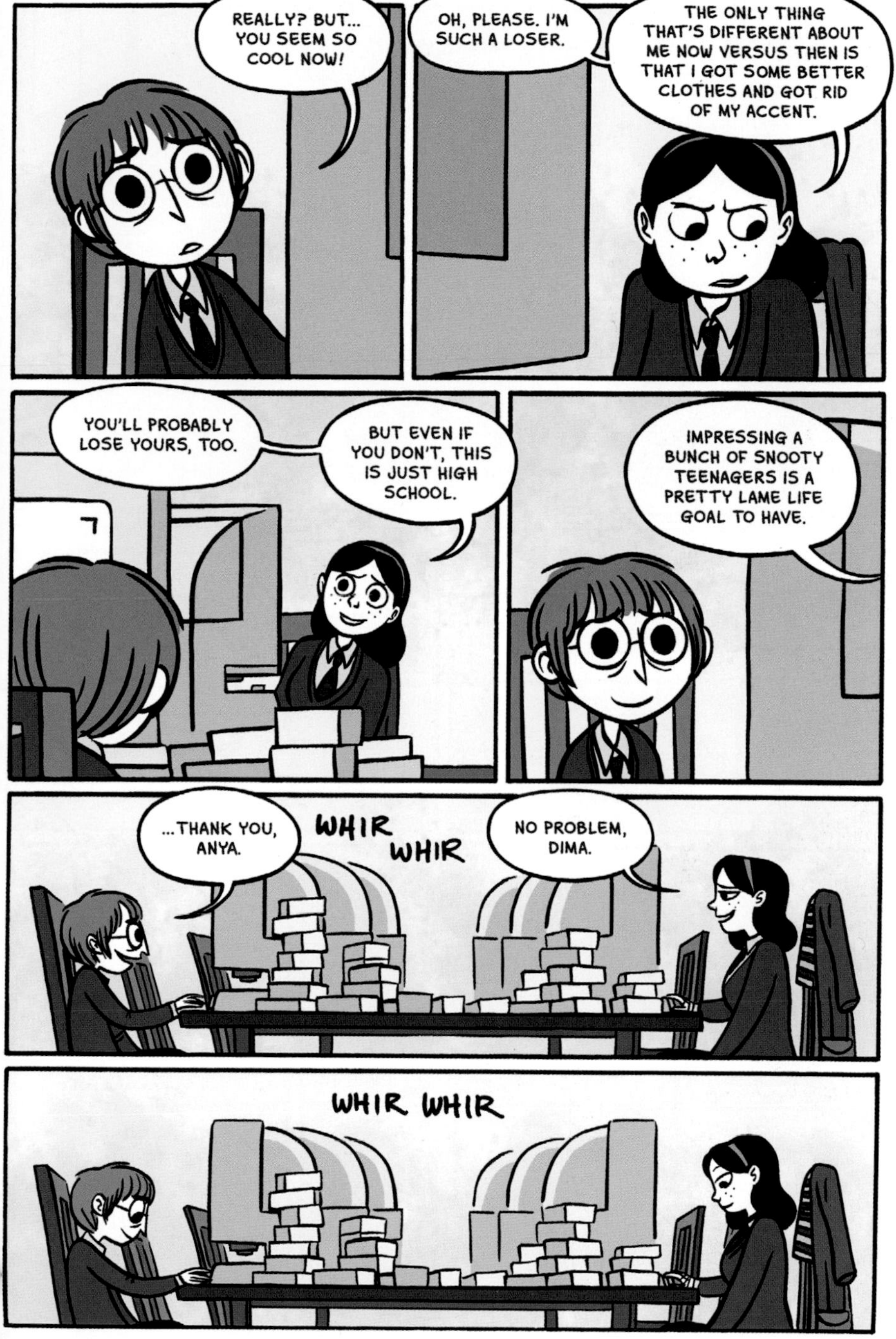
REALLY? BUT... YOU SEEM SO COOL NOW!
OH, PLEASE. I'M SUCH A LOSER.
THE ONLY THING THAT'S DIFFERENT ABOUT ME NOW VERSUS THEN IS THAT I GOT SOME BETTER CLOTHES AND GOT RID OF MY ACCENT.
YOU'LL PROBABLY LOSE YOURS, TOO.
BUT EVEN IF YOU DON'T, THIS IS JUST HIGH SCHOOL.
IMPRESSING A BUNCH OF SNOOTY TEENAGERS IS A PRETTY LAME LIFE GOAL TO HAVE.
...THANK YOU, ANYA.
WHIR
WHIR
NO PROBLEM, DIMA.
WHIR WHIR

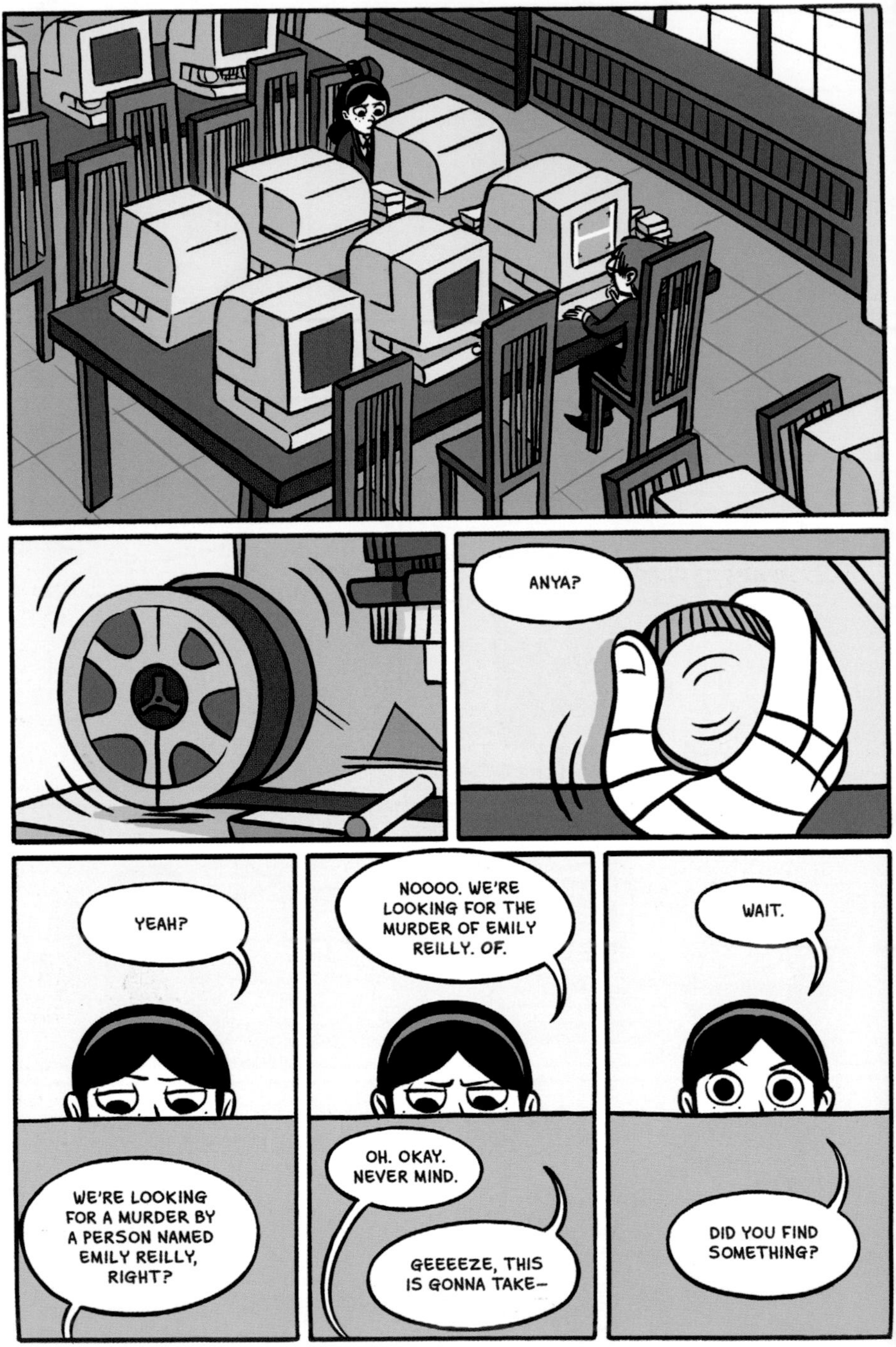
ANYA?
YEAH?
WE'RE LOOKING FOR A MURDER BY A PERSON NAMED EMILY REILLY, RIGHT?
NOOOO. WE'RE LOOKING FOR THE MURDER OF EMILY REILLY. OF.
OH. OKAY. NEVER MIND.
GEEEEZE, THIS IS GONNA TAKE—
WAIT.
DID YOU FIND SOMETHING?

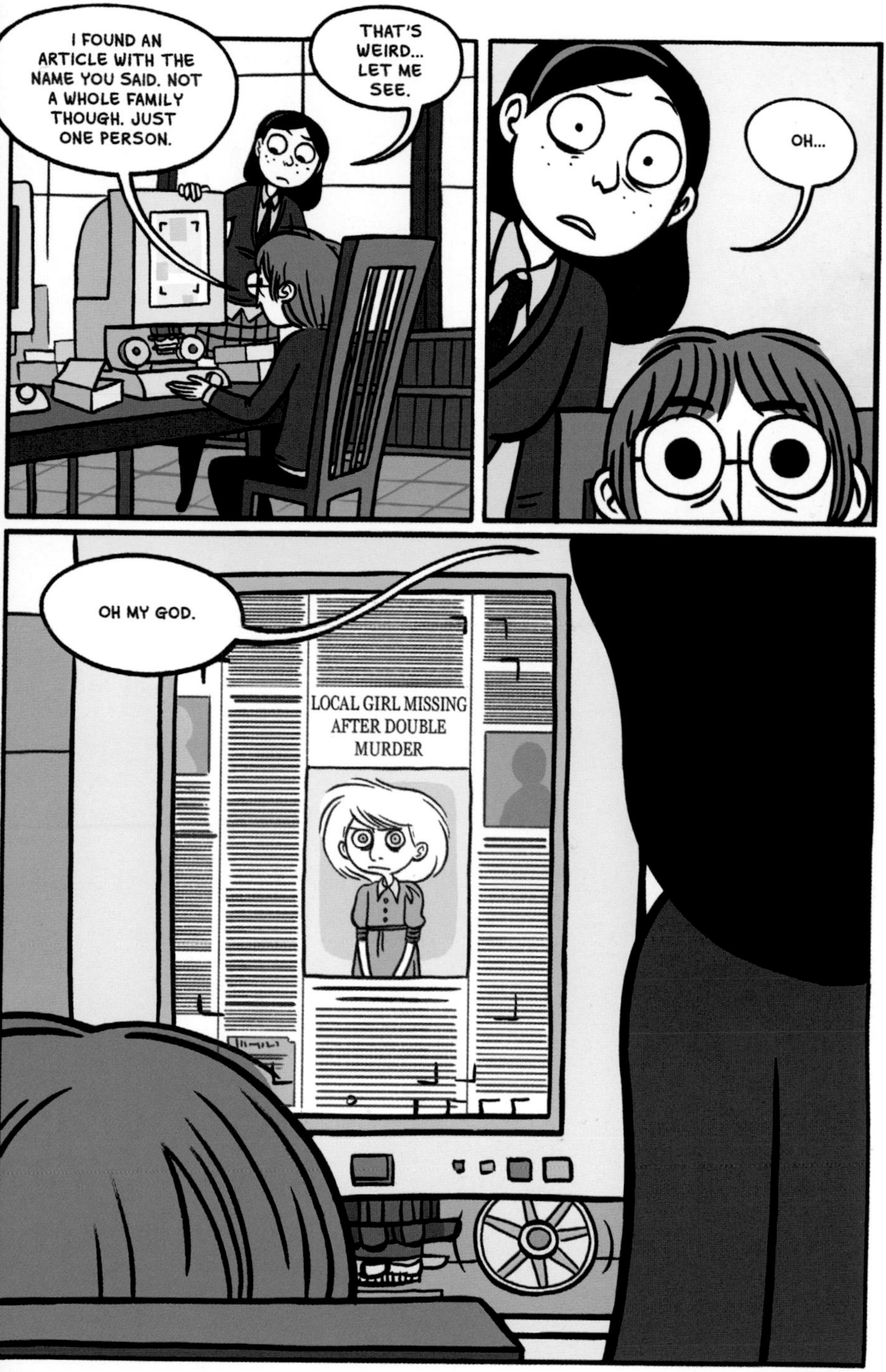
I FOUND AN ARTICLE WITH THE NAME YOU SAID. NOT A WHOLE FAMILY THOUGH. JUST ONE PERSON.
THAT'S WEIRD... LET ME SEE.
OH...
OH MY GOD.
LOCAL GIRL MISSING AFTER DOUBLE MURDER

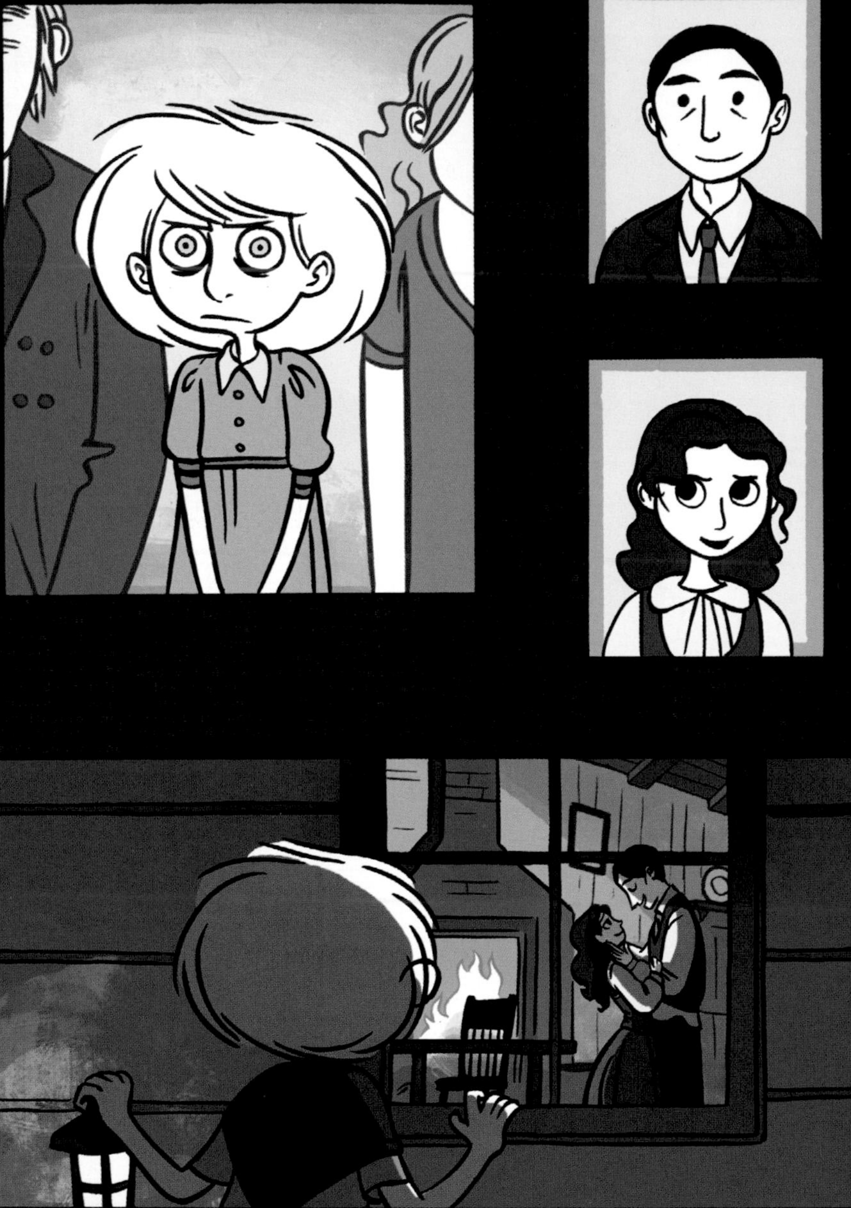

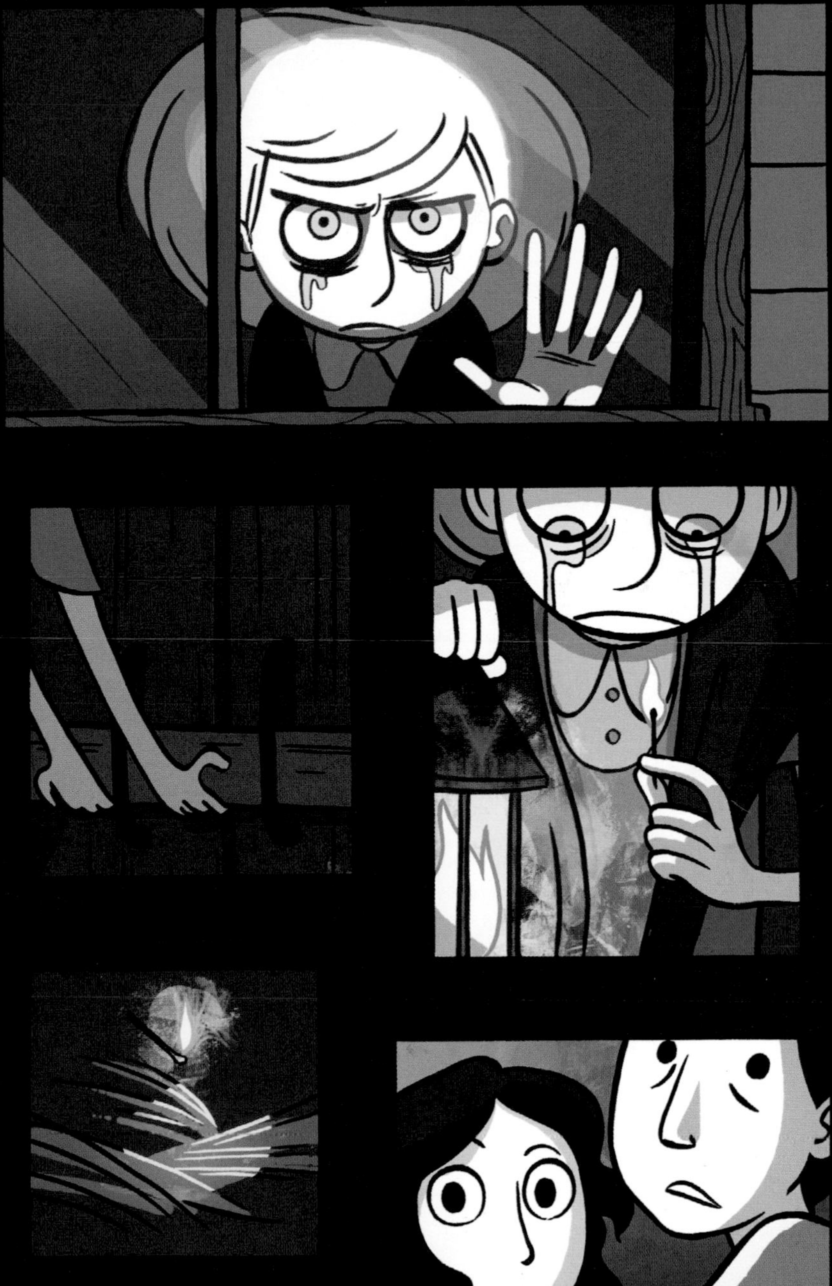

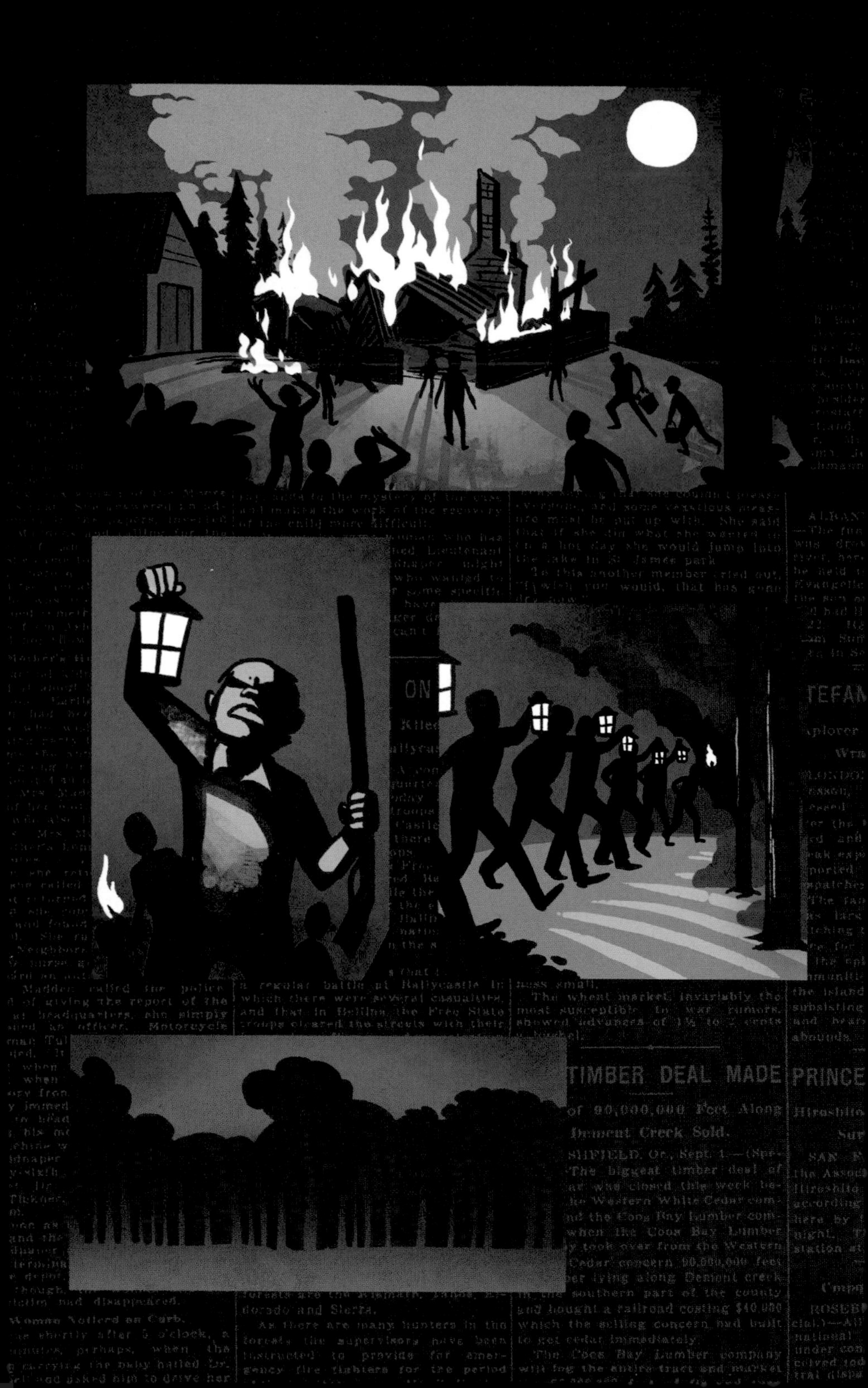

TIMBER DEAL MADE
of 90,000,000 Feet Along
Dement Creek Sold.
PRINCE

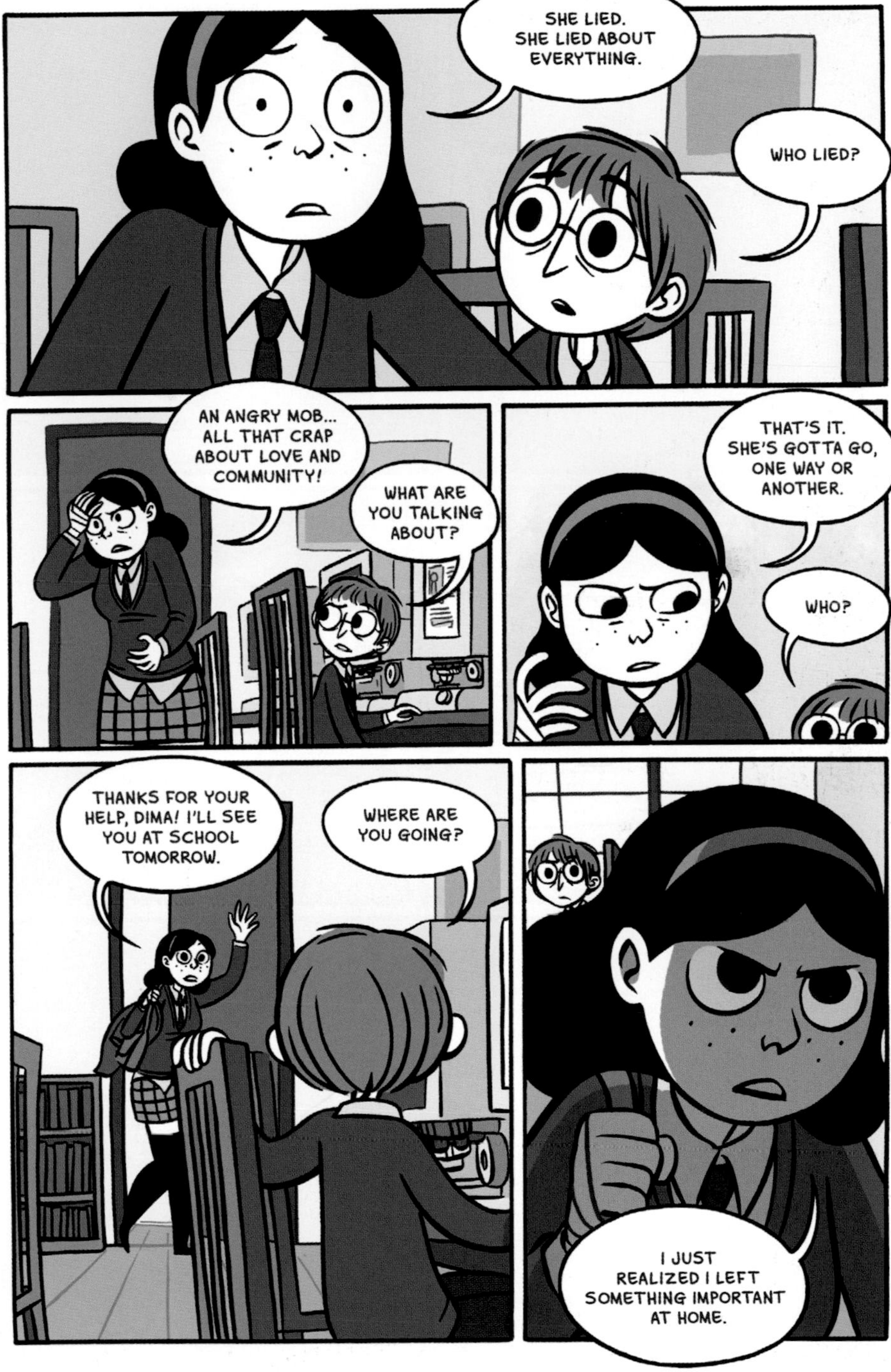
SHE LIED. SHE LIED ABOUT EVERYTHING.
WHO LIED?
AN ANGRY MOB... ALL THAT CRAP ABOUT LOVE AND COMMUNITY!
WHAT ARE YOU TALKING ABOUT?
THAT'S IT. SHE'S GOTTA GO, ONE WAY OR ANOTHER.
WHO?
THANKS FOR YOUR HELP, DIMA! I'LL SEE YOU AT SCHOOL TOMORROW.
WHERE ARE YOU GOING?
I JUST REALIZED I LEFT SOMETHING IMPORTANT AT HOME.

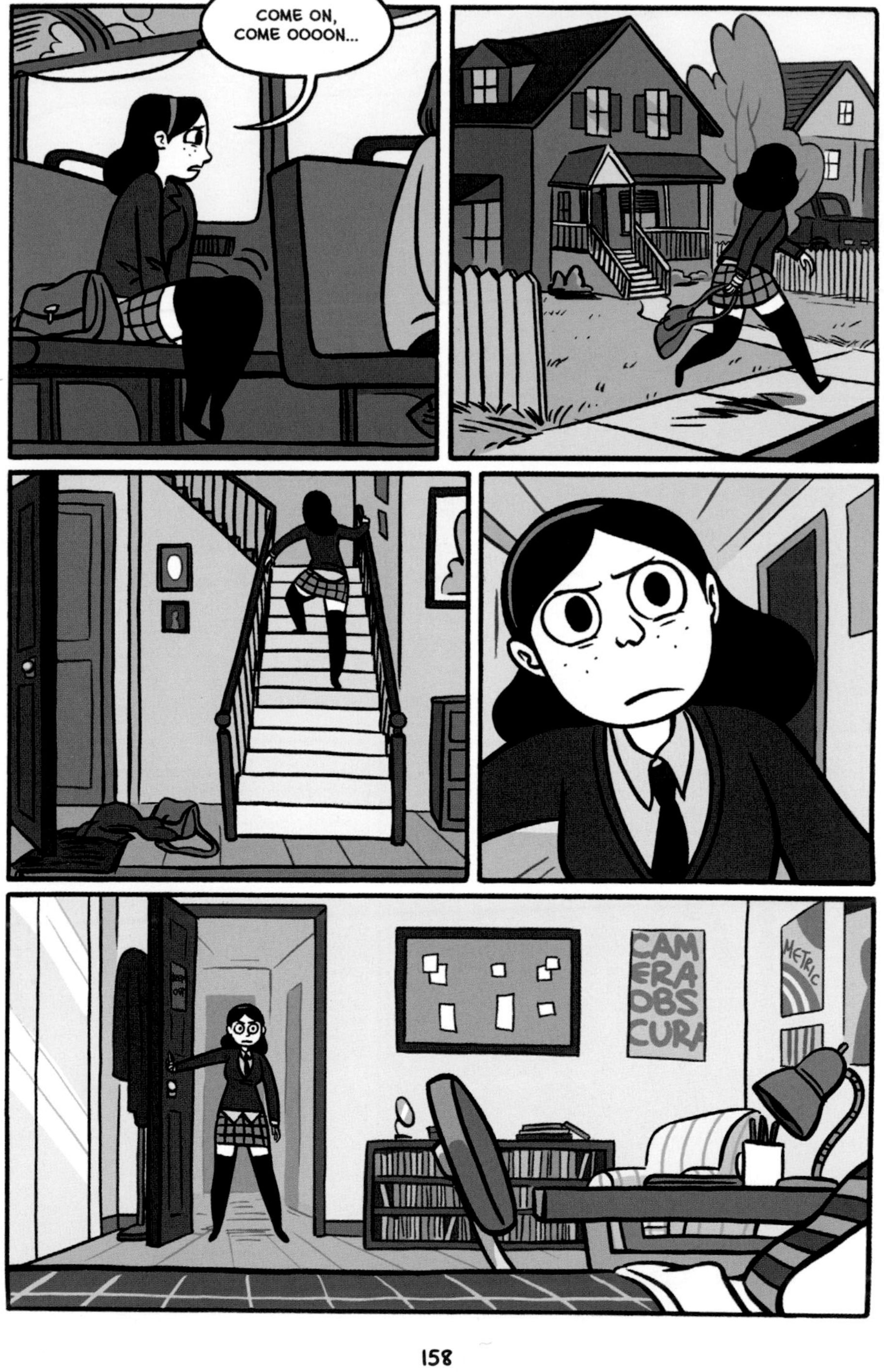
COME ON, COME OOOON...
CAM
ERA
OBS
CURA
METRIC

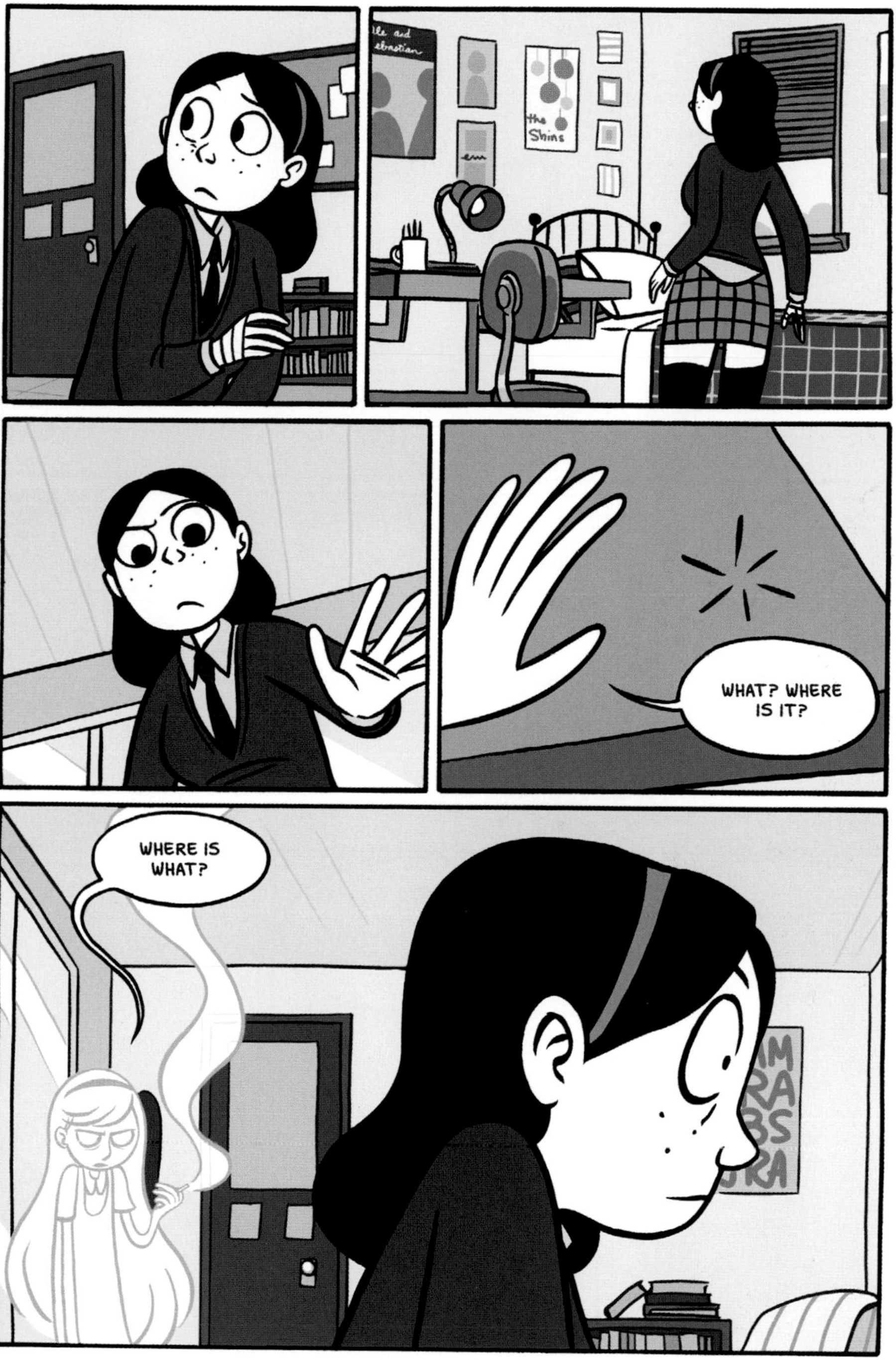
the Shins
WHAT? WHERE IS IT?
WHERE IS WHAT?

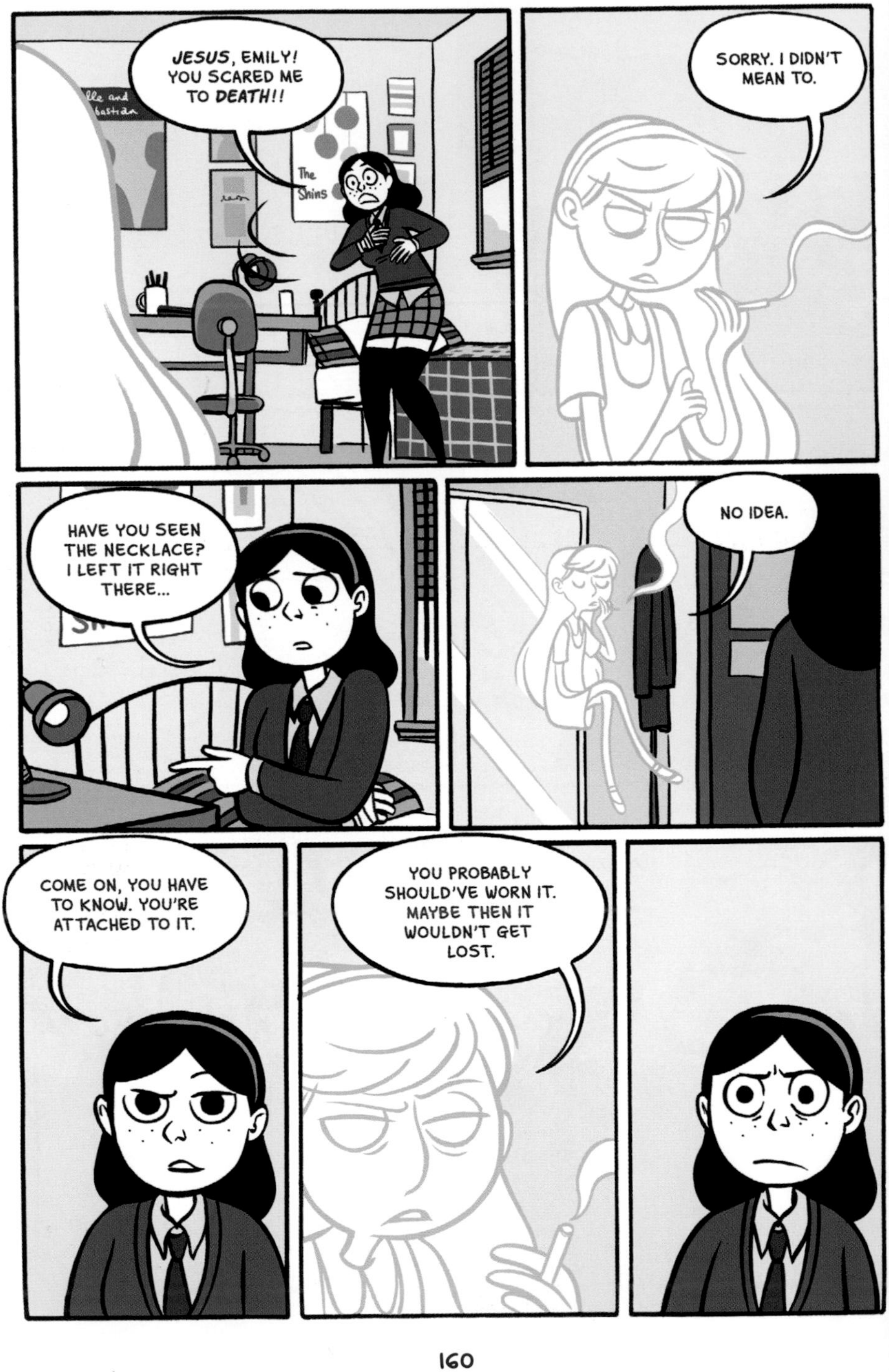
JESUS, EMILY! YOU SCARED ME TO *DEATH*!!
The Shins
SORRY. I DIDN'T MEAN TO.
HAVE YOU SEEN THE NECKLACE? I LEFT IT RIGHT THERE...
NO IDEA.
COME ON, YOU HAVE TO KNOW. YOU'RE ATTACHED TO IT.
YOU PROBABLY SHOULD'VE WORN IT. MAYBE THEN IT WOULDN'T GET LOST.

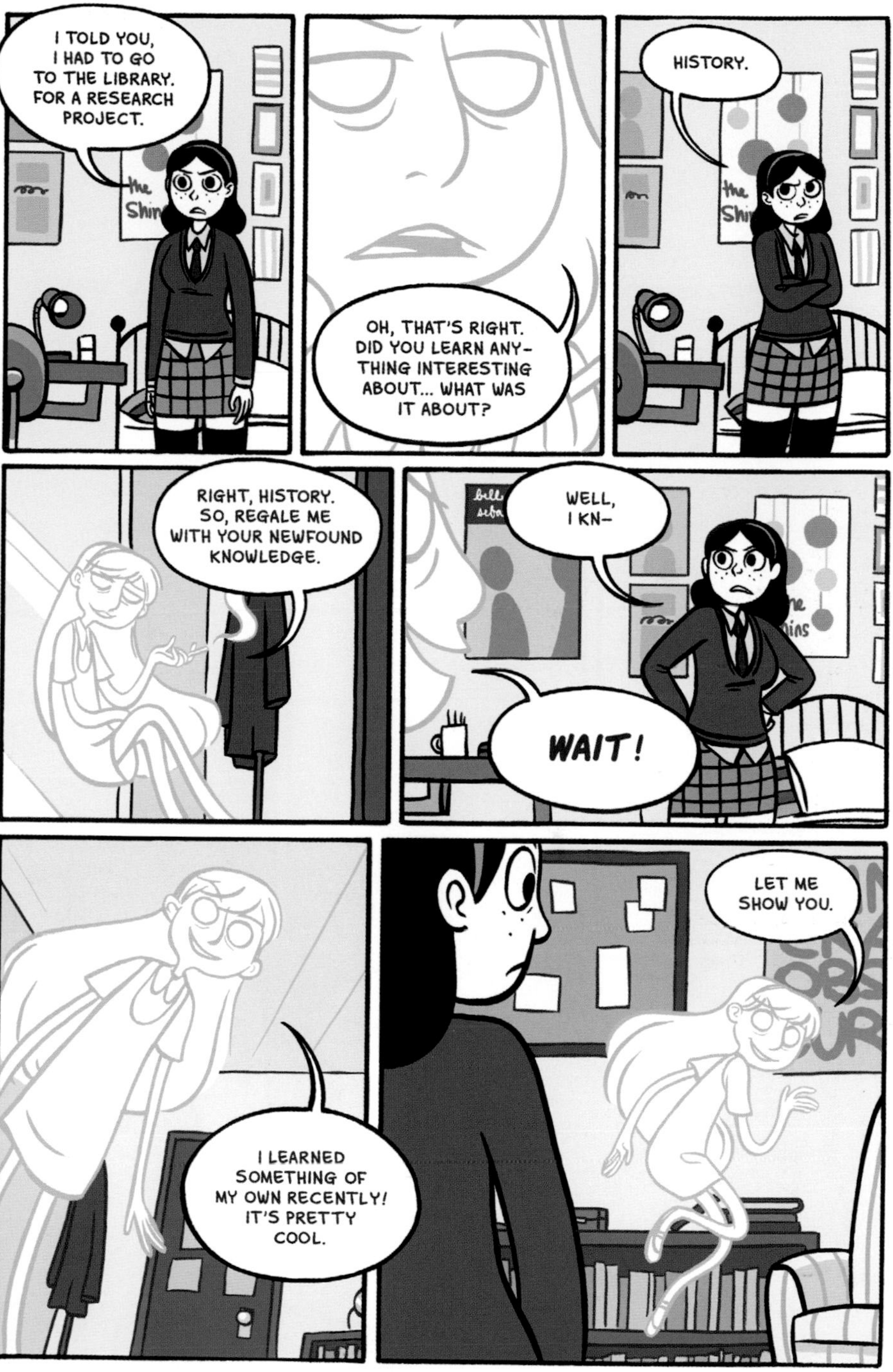
I TOLD YOU, I HAD TO GO TO THE LIBRARY. FOR A RESEARCH PROJECT.
OH, THAT'S RIGHT. DID YOU LEARN ANY-THING INTERESTING ABOUT... WHAT WAS IT ABOUT?
HISTORY.
RIGHT, HISTORY. SO, REGALE ME WITH YOUR NEWFOUND KNOWLEDGE.
WELL, I KN–
WAIT!
I LEARNED SOMETHING OF MY OWN RECENTLY! IT'S PRETTY COOL.
LET ME SHOW YOU.

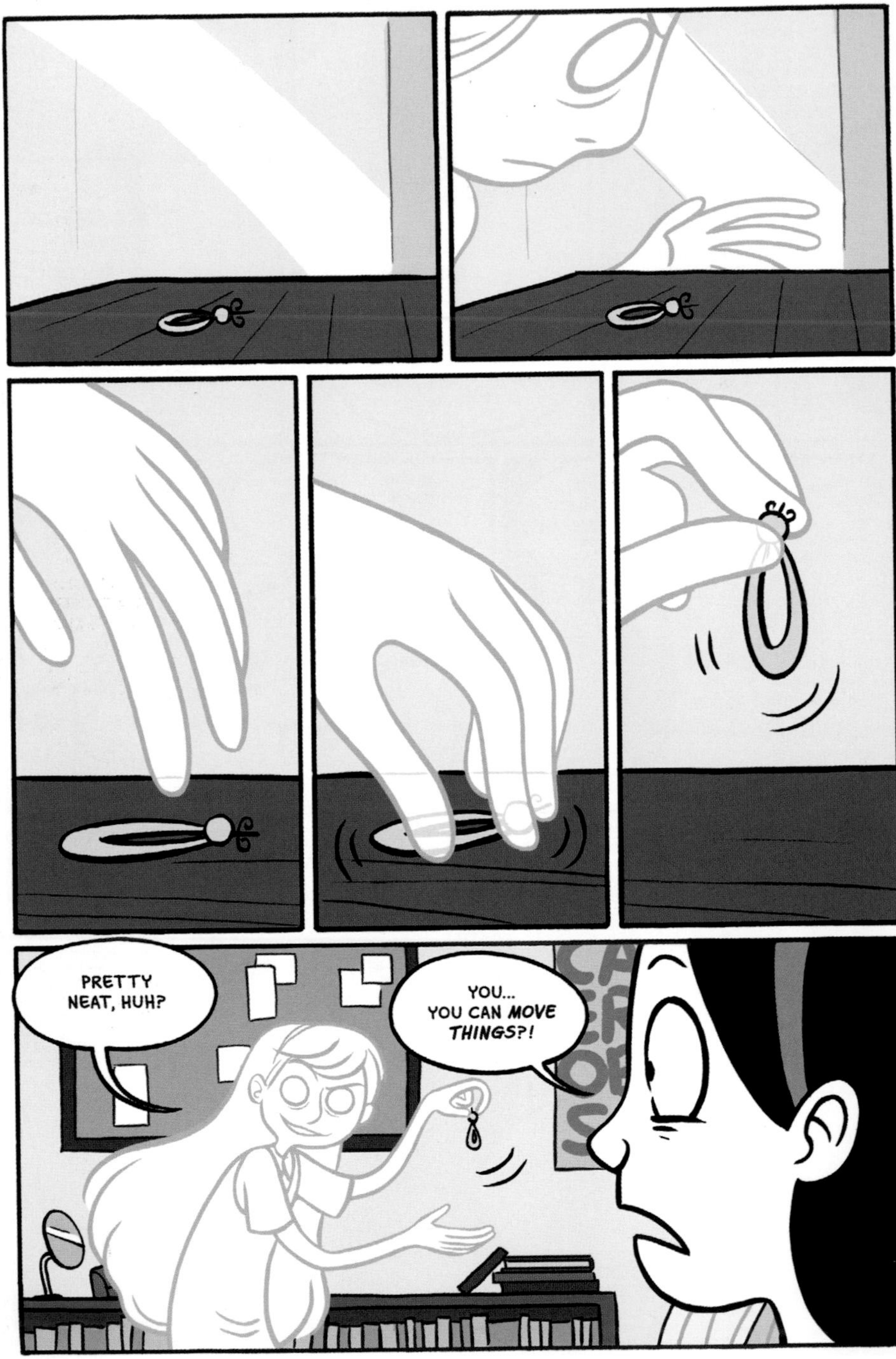
PRETTY NEAT, HUH?
YOU... YOU CAN MOVE THINGS?!

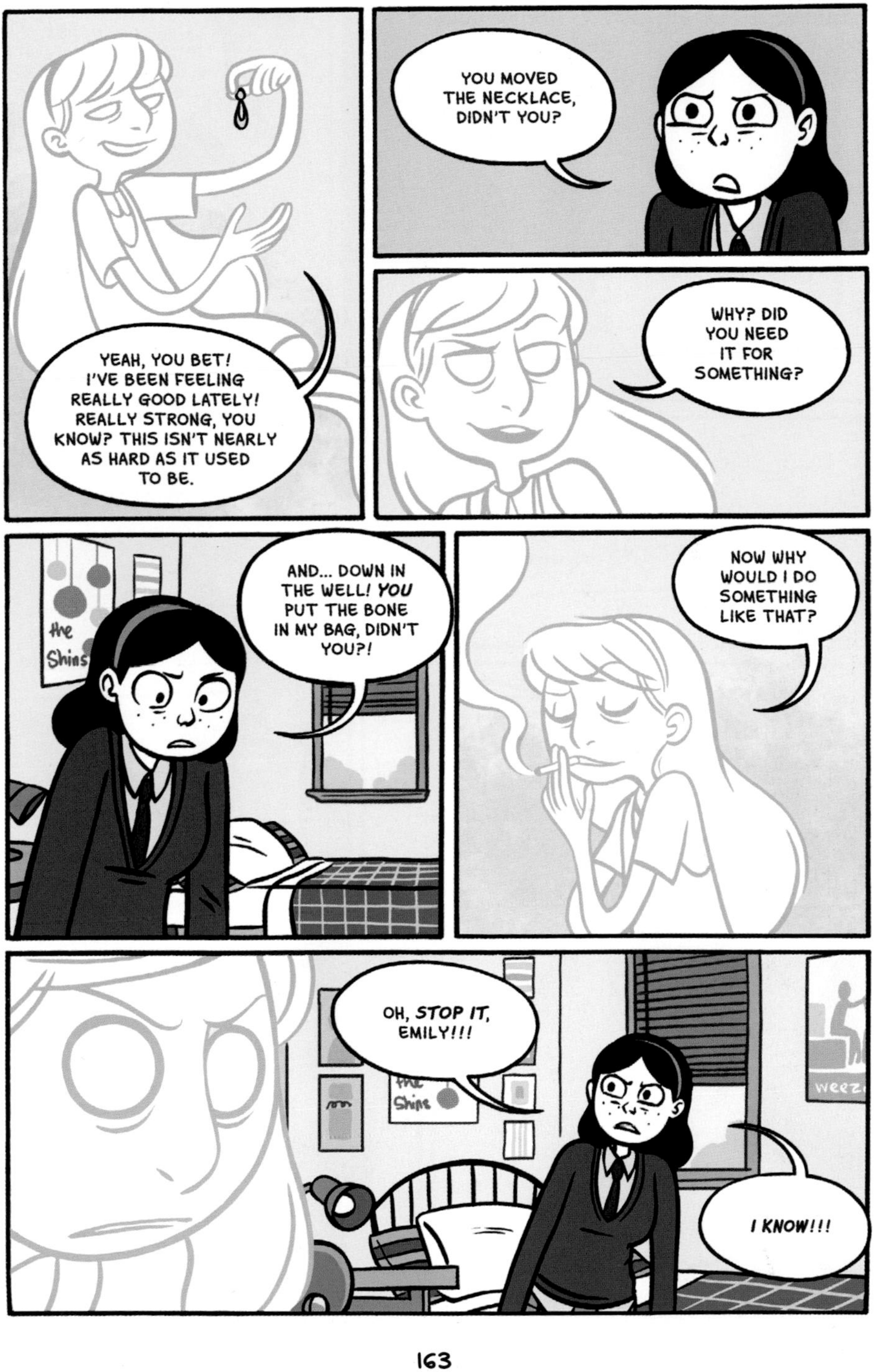
YOU MOVED THE NECKLACE, DIDN'T YOU?
YEAH, YOU BET! I'VE BEEN FEELING REALLY GOOD LATELY! REALLY STRONG, YOU KNOW? THIS ISN'T NEARLY AS HARD AS IT USED TO BE.
WHY? DID YOU NEED IT FOR SOMETHING?
the Shins
AND... DOWN IN THE WELL! *YOU* PUT THE BONE IN MY BAG, DIDN'T YOU?!
NOW WHY WOULD I DO SOMETHING LIKE THAT?
OH, *STOP IT*, EMILY!!!
the Shins
I KNOW!!!

AND WHAT, EXACTLY, DO YOU THINK YOU KNOW?

I KNOW YOU WERE LYING! ABOUT HOW YOU DIED, ABOUT HOW YOUR "BOYFRIEND" DIED... YOU KILLED THEM!!!

SIGH.

EMBELLISHED THE—YOU BURNED PEOPLE TO DEATH!!!!

OKAY... MAYBE I EMBELLISHED THE TRUTH A LITTLE.

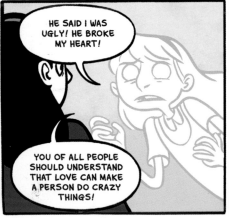

HE SAID I WAS UGLY! HE BROKE MY HEART!

YOU OF ALL PEOPLE SHOULD UNDERSTAND THAT LOVE CAN MAKE A PERSON DO CRAZY THINGS!

I DON'T THINK MURDER IS AN APPROPRIATE REACTION TO DISAPPOINTMENT.

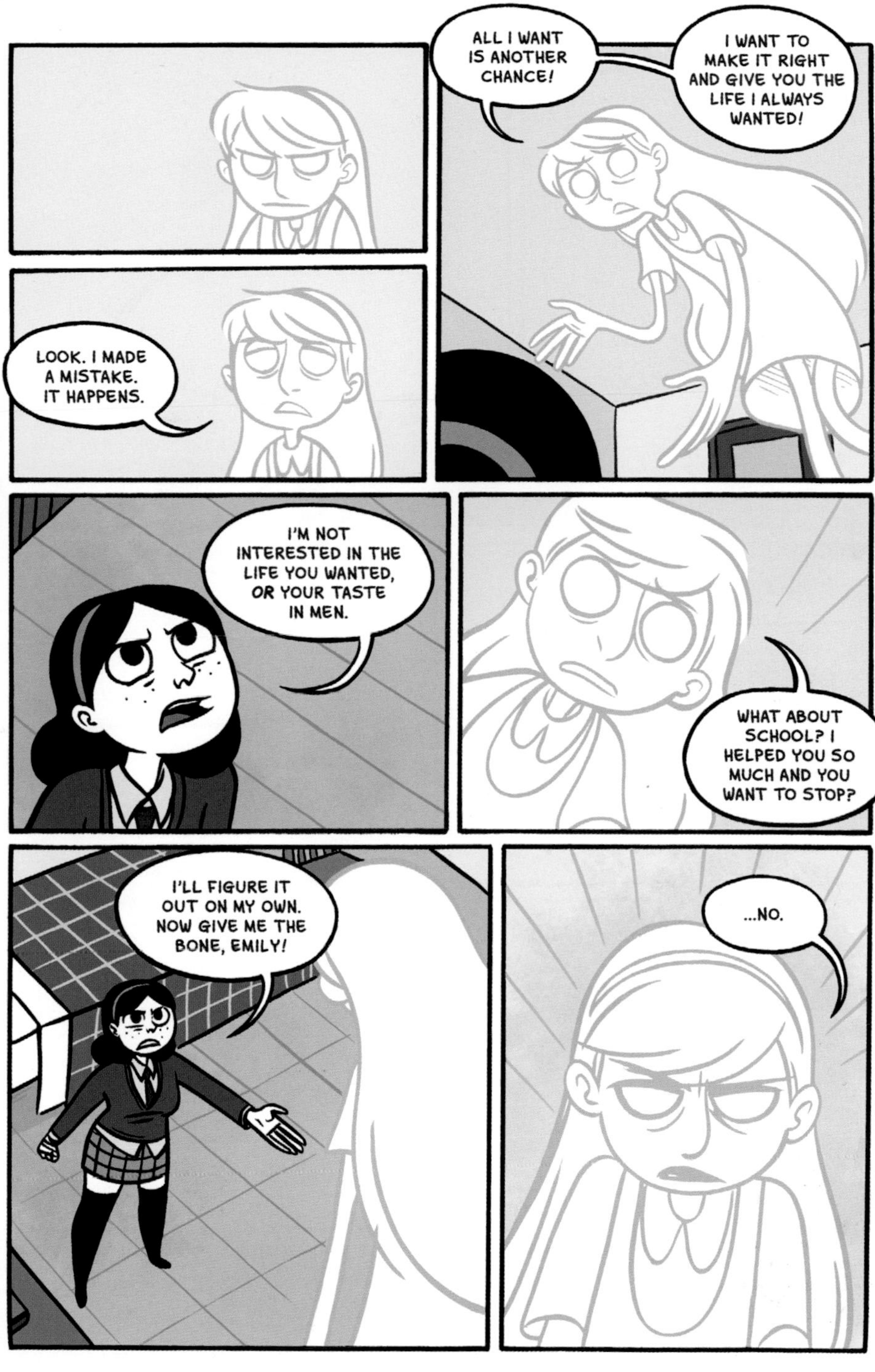
LOOK. I MADE A MISTAKE. IT HAPPENS.
ALL I WANT IS ANOTHER CHANCE!
I WANT TO MAKE IT RIGHT AND GIVE YOU THE LIFE I ALWAYS WANTED!
I'M NOT INTERESTED IN THE LIFE YOU WANTED, OR YOUR TASTE IN MEN.
WHAT ABOUT SCHOOL? I HELPED YOU SO MUCH AND YOU WANT TO STOP?
I'LL FIGURE IT OUT ON MY OWN. NOW GIVE ME THE BONE, EMILY!
...NO.

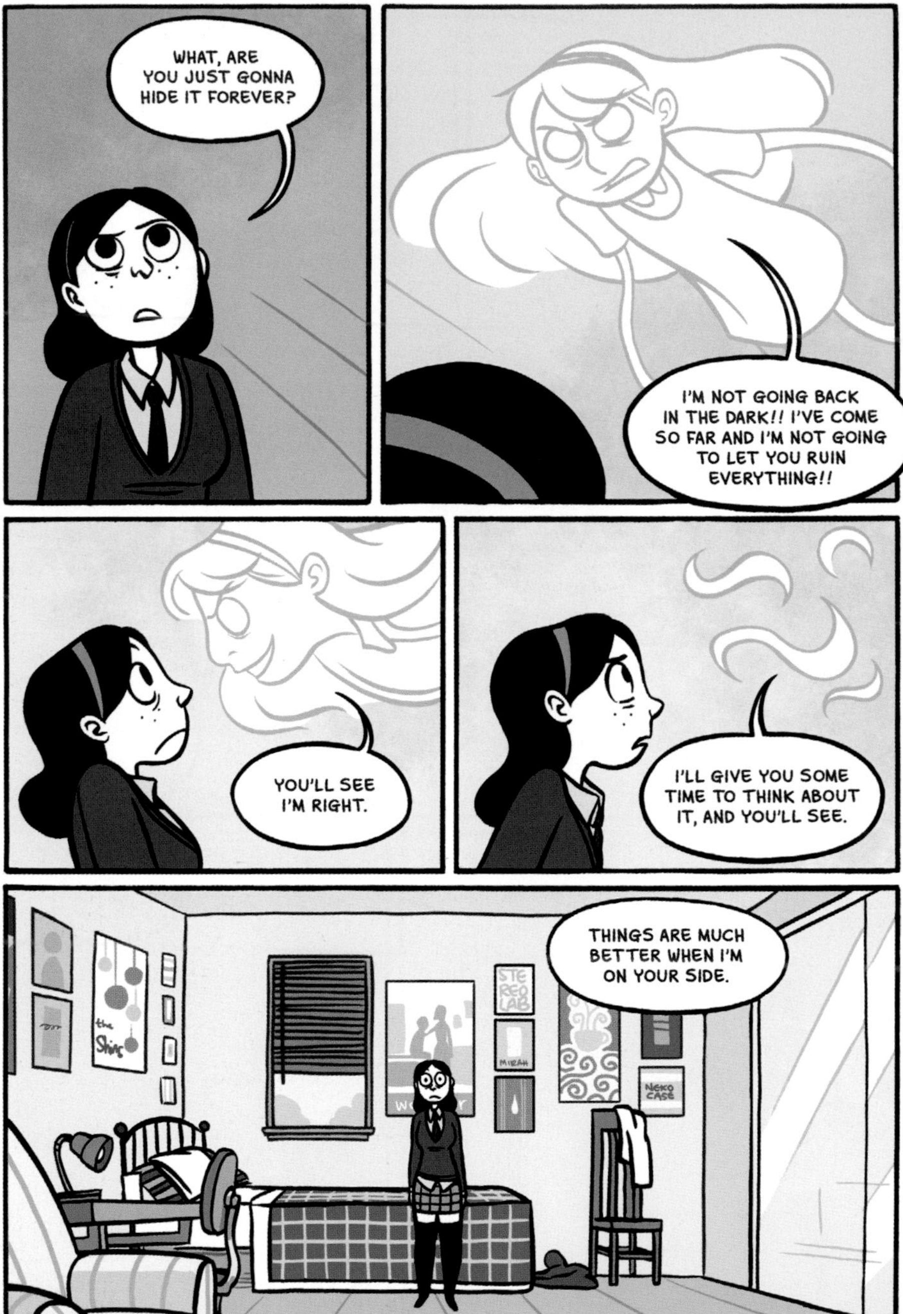
WHAT, ARE YOU JUST GONNA HIDE IT FOREVER?
I'M NOT GOING BACK IN THE DARK!! I'VE COME SO FAR AND I'M NOT GOING TO LET YOU RUIN EVERYTHING!!
YOU'LL SEE I'M RIGHT.
I'LL GIVE YOU SOME TIME TO THINK ABOUT IT, AND YOU'LL SEE.
THINGS ARE MUCH BETTER WHEN I'M ON YOUR SIDE.
STEREOLAB
MIRAH
NEKO CASE

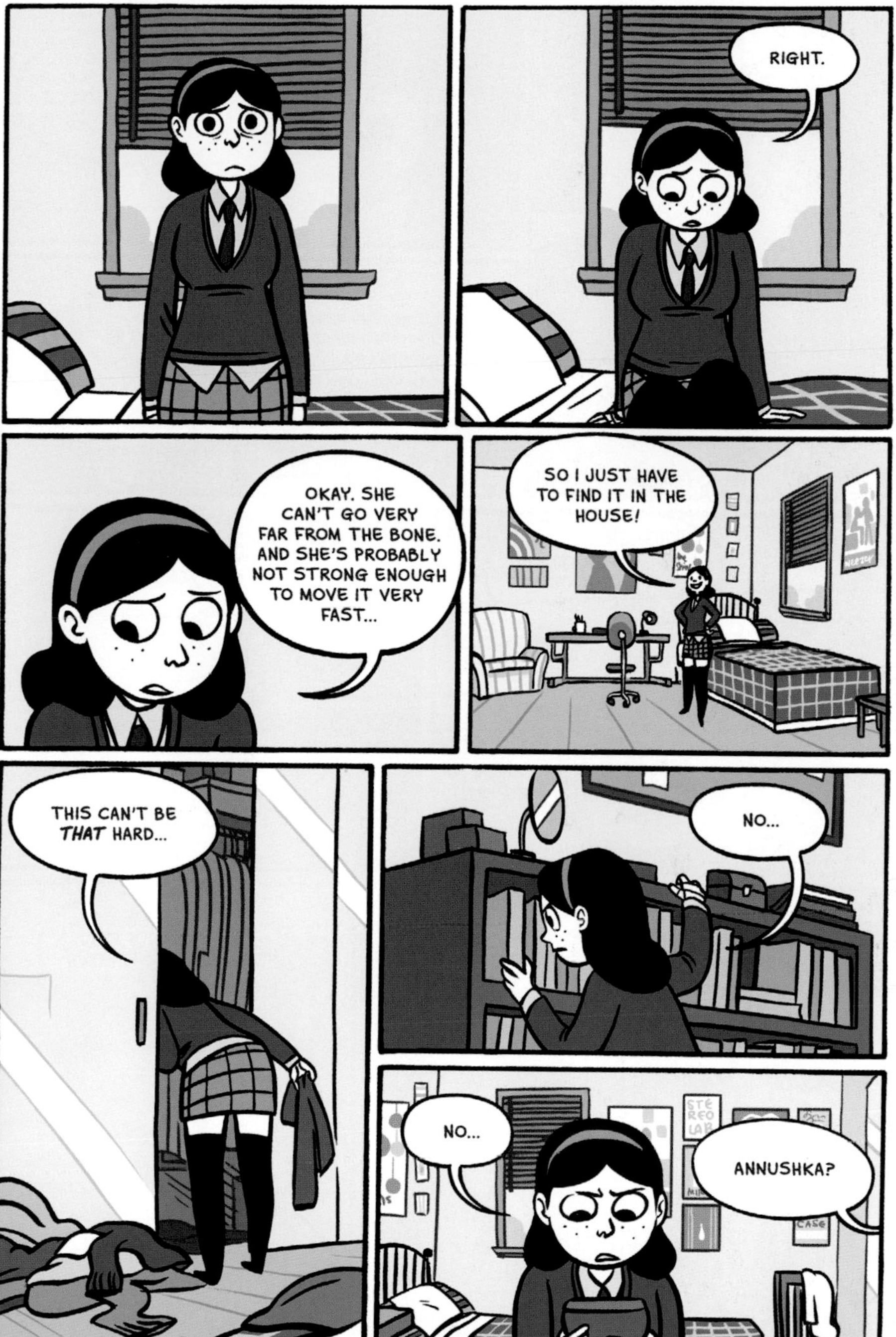
RIGHT.
OKAY. SHE CAN'T GO VERY FAR FROM THE BONE. AND SHE'S PROBABLY NOT STRONG ENOUGH TO MOVE IT VERY FAST...
SO I JUST HAVE TO FIND IT IN THE HOUSE!
THIS CAN'T BE *THAT* HARD...
NO...
NO...
ANNUSHKA?

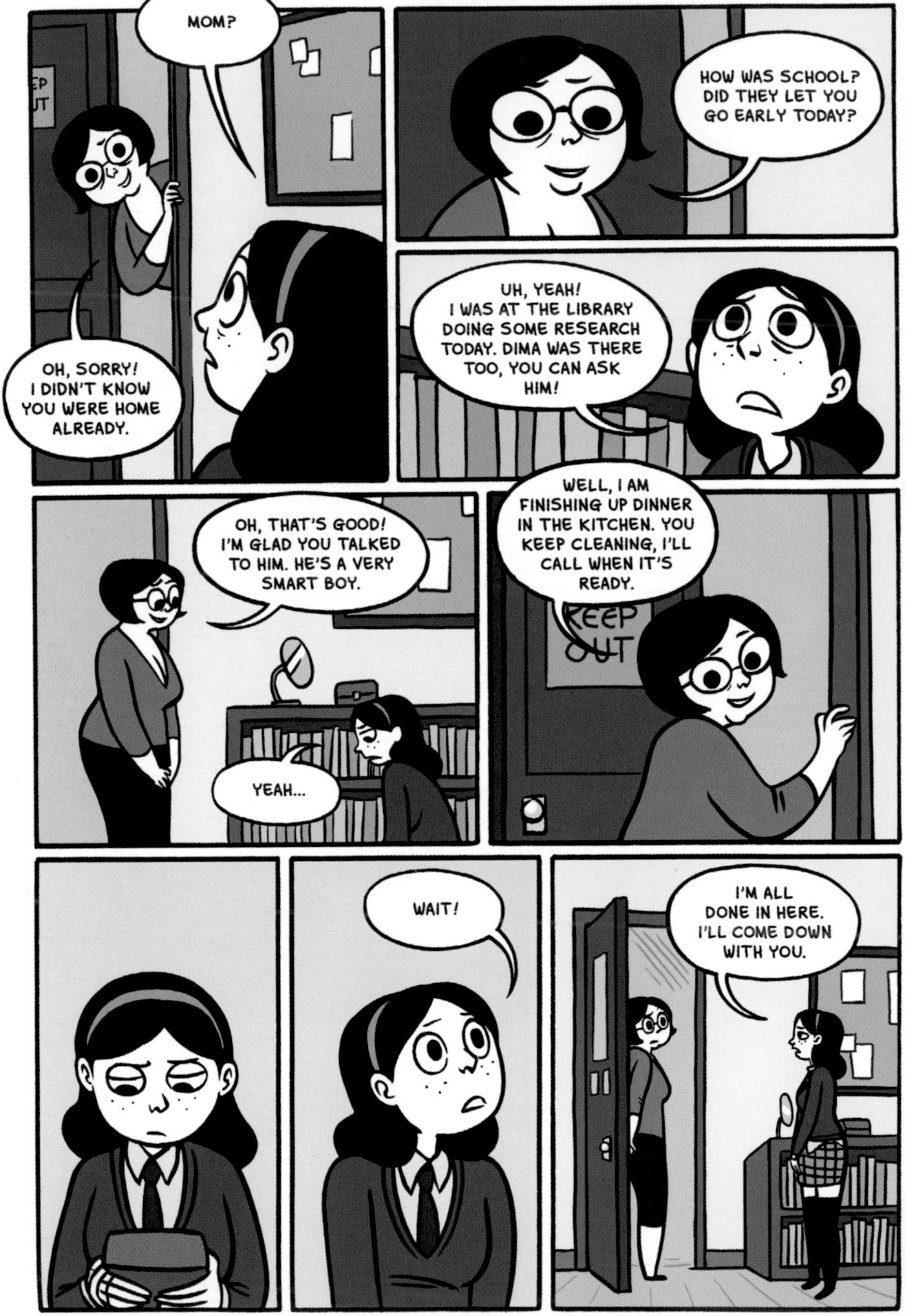

EP
UT
MOM?
OH, SORRY! I DIDN'T KNOW YOU WERE HOME ALREADY.
HOW WAS SCHOOL? DID THEY LET YOU GO EARLY TODAY?
UH, YEAH! I WAS AT THE LIBRARY DOING SOME RESEARCH TODAY. DIMA WAS THERE TOO, YOU CAN ASK HIM!
OH, THAT'S GOOD! I'M GLAD YOU TALKED TO HIM. HE'S A VERY SMART BOY.
YEAH...
WELL, I AM FINISHING UP DINNER IN THE KITCHEN. YOU KEEP CLEANING, I'LL CALL WHEN IT'S READY.
KEEP OUT
WAIT!
I'M ALL DONE IN HERE. I'LL COME DOWN WITH YOU.

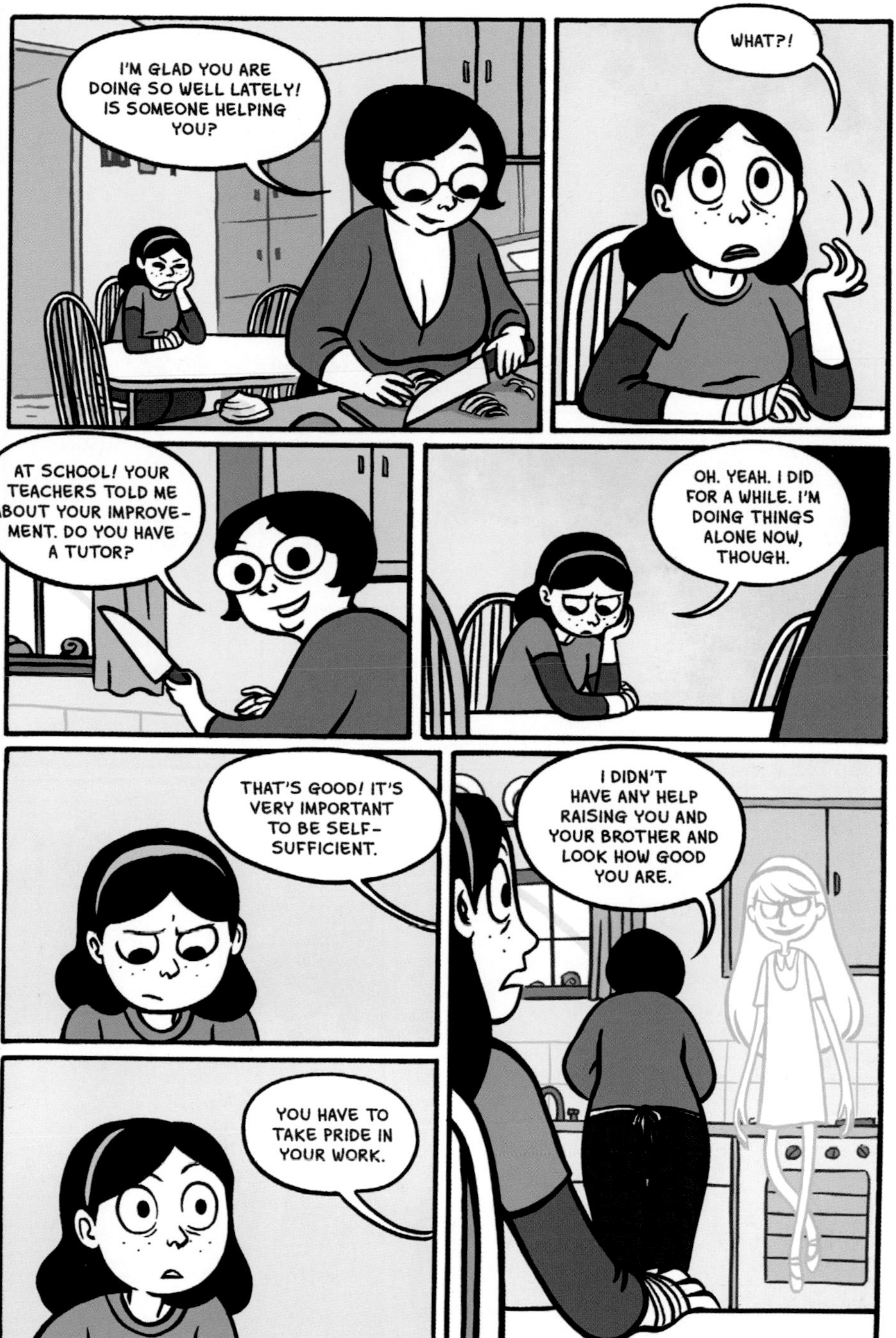
I'M GLAD YOU ARE DOING SO WELL LATELY! IS SOMEONE HELPING YOU?
WHAT?!
AT SCHOOL! YOUR TEACHERS TOLD ME ABOUT YOUR IMPROVEMENT. DO YOU HAVE A TUTOR?
OH. YEAH. I DID FOR A WHILE. I'M DOING THINGS ALONE NOW, THOUGH.
THAT'S GOOD! IT'S VERY IMPORTANT TO BE SELF-SUFFICIENT.
YOU HAVE TO TAKE PRIDE IN YOUR WORK.
I DIDN'T HAVE ANY HELP RAISING YOU AND YOUR BROTHER AND LOOK HOW GOOD YOU ARE.

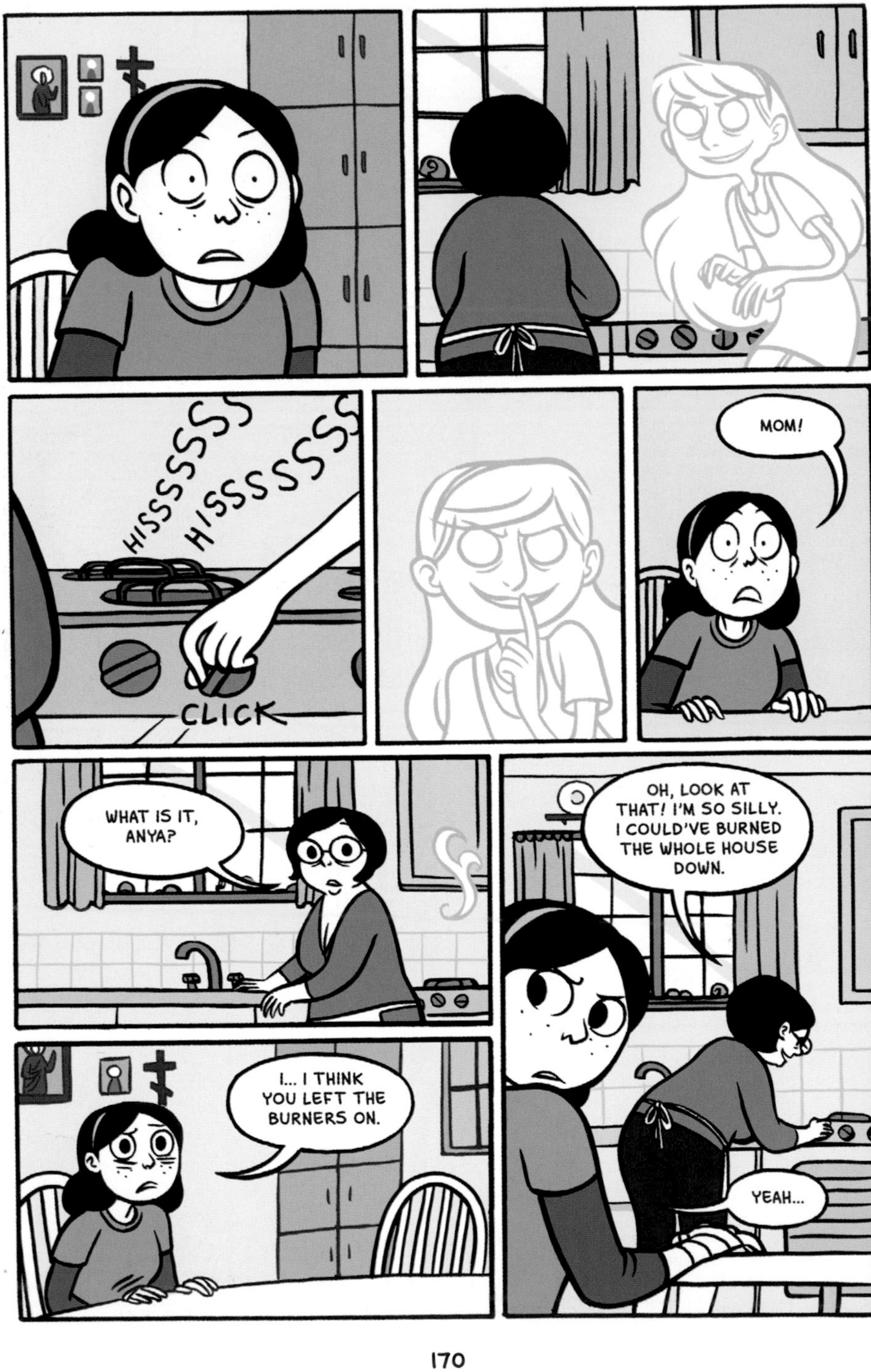
HISSSSSSS
HISSSSSSSS
CLICK
MOM!
WHAT IS IT, ANYA?
I... I THINK YOU LEFT THE BURNERS ON.
OH, LOOK AT THAT! I'M SO SILLY. I COULD'VE BURNED THE WHOLE HOUSE DOWN.
YEAH...

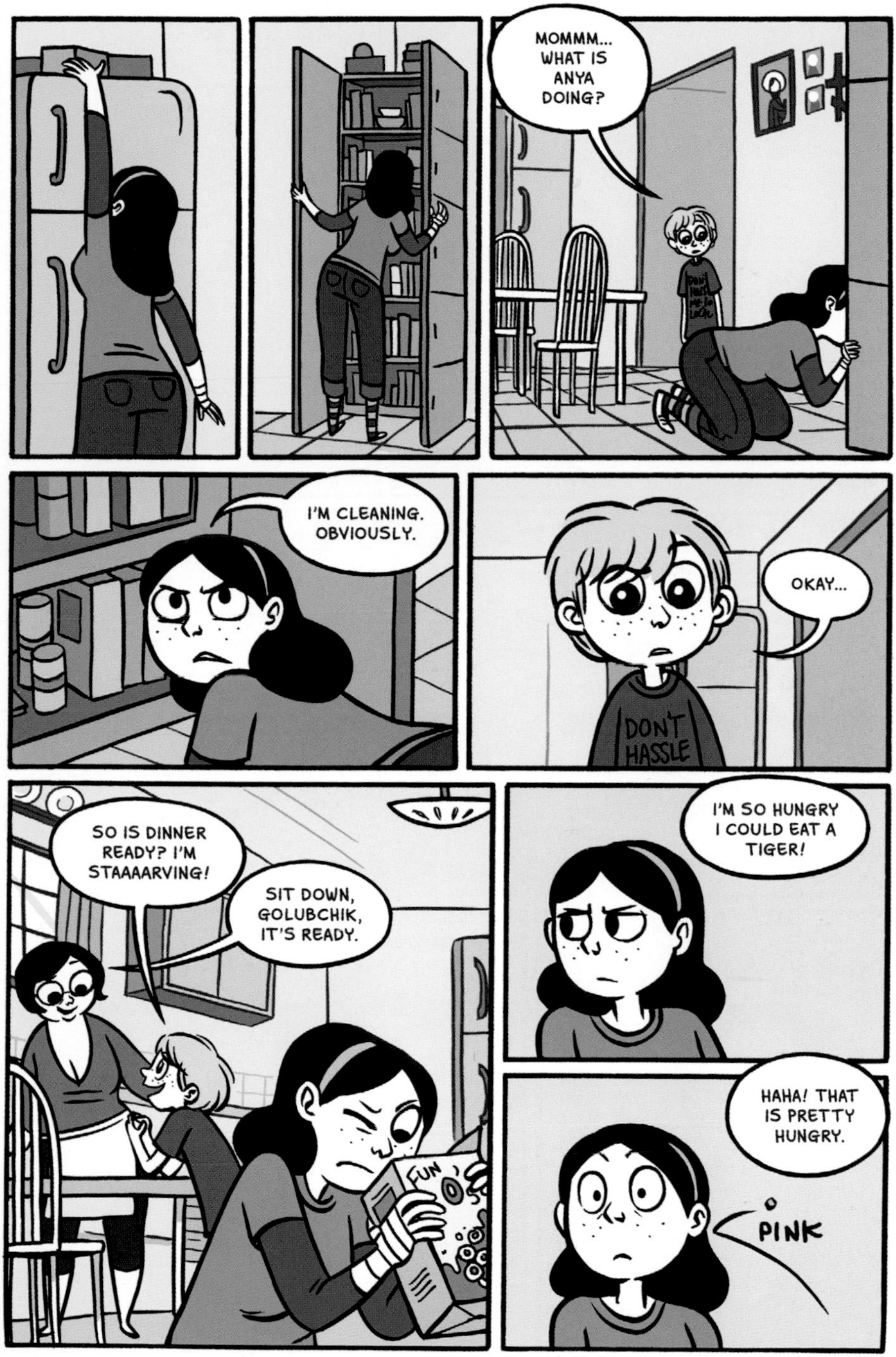
MOMMM... WHAT IS ANYA DOING?
I'M CLEANING. OBVIOUSLY.
OKAY...
DON'T HASSLE
SO IS DINNER READY? I'M STAAAARVING!
SIT DOWN, GOLUBCHIK, IT'S READY.
FUN
I'M SO HUNGRY I COULD EAT A TIGER!
HAHA! THAT IS PRETTY HUNGRY.
PINK

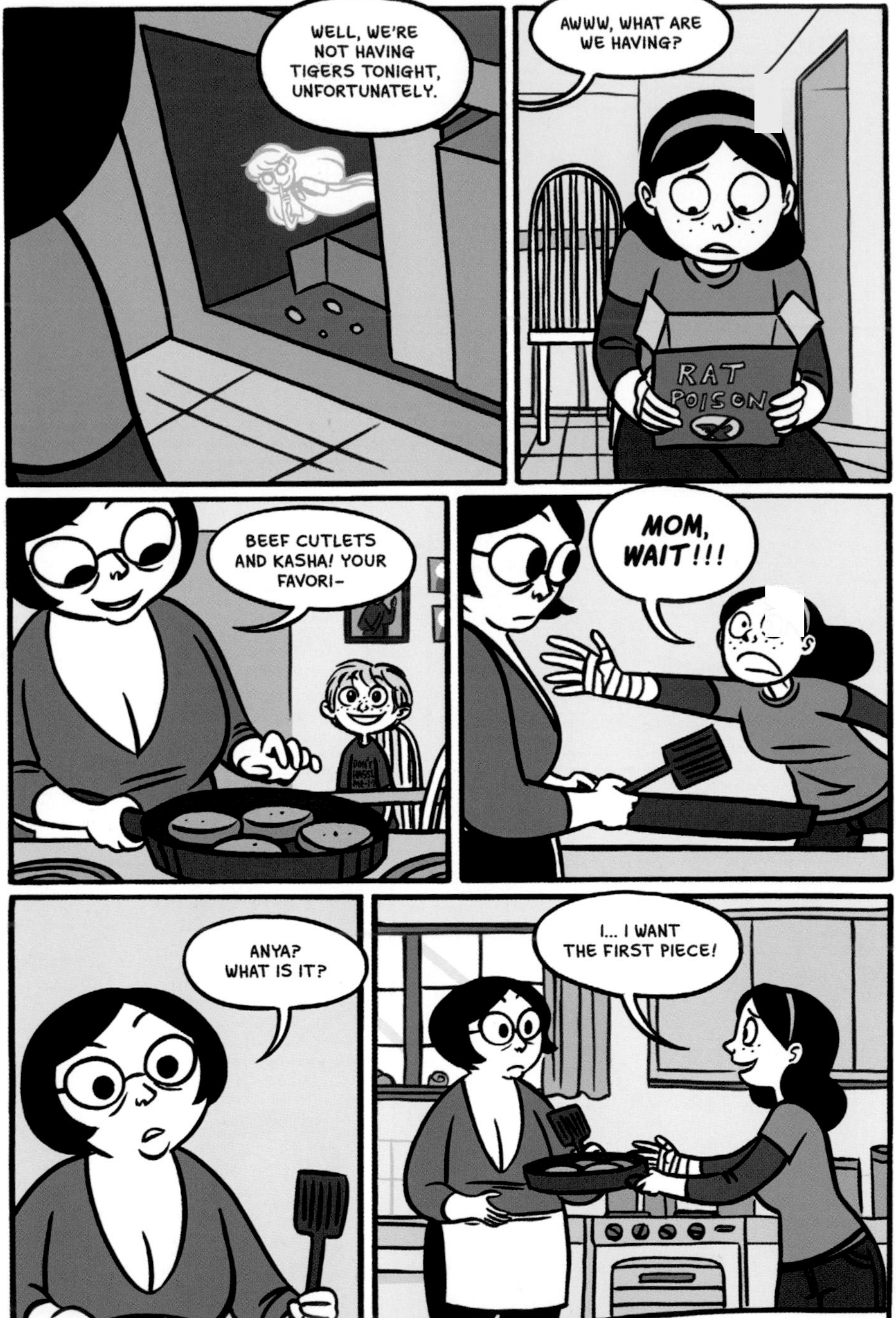
WELL, WE'RE NOT HAVING TIGERS TONIGHT, UNFORTUNATELY.
AWWW, WHAT ARE WE HAVING?
RAT POISON
BEEF CUTLETS AND KASHA! YOUR FAVORI-
MOM, WAIT!!!
ANYA? WHAT IS IT?
I... I WANT THE FIRST PIECE!

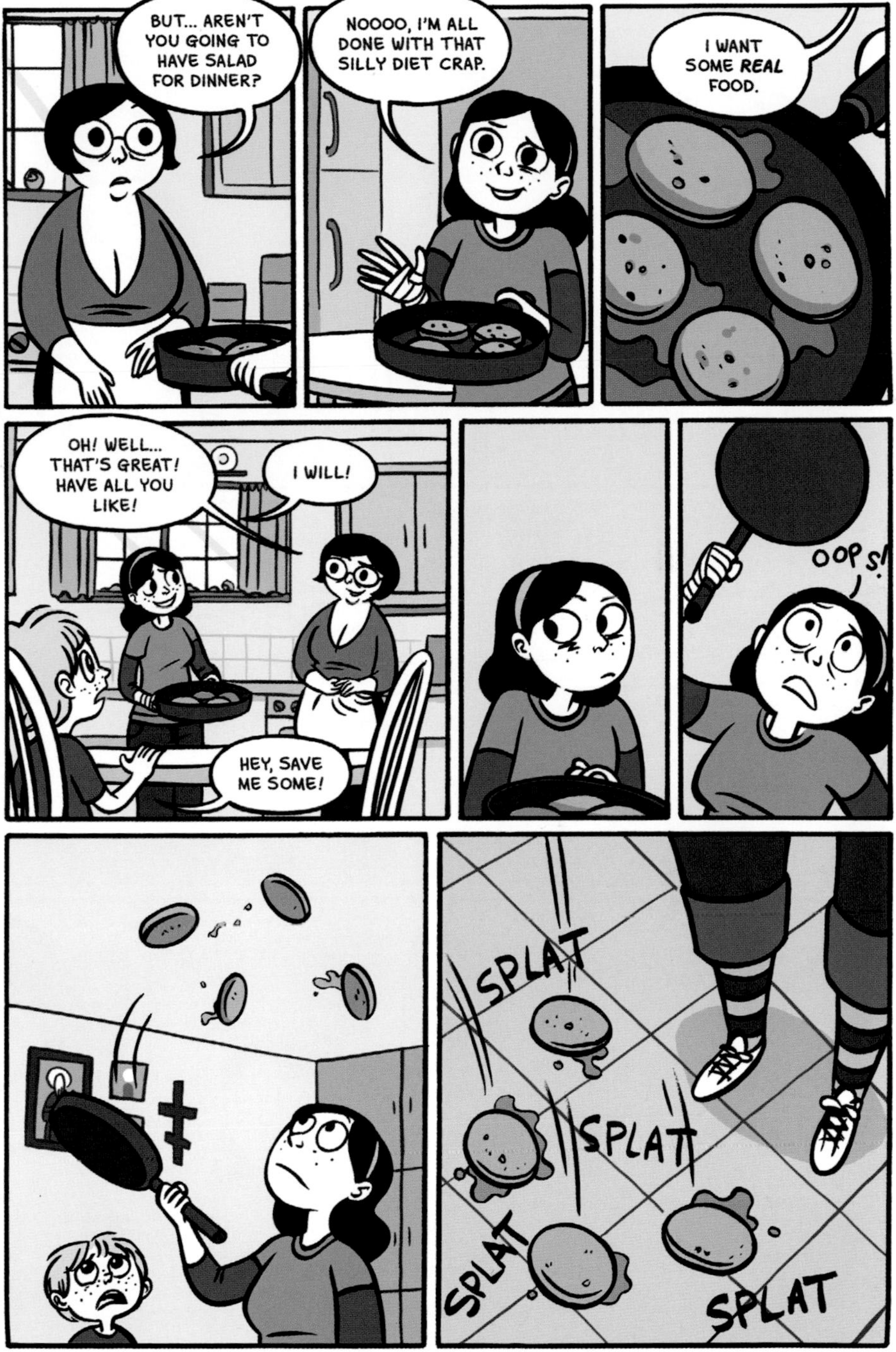
BUT... AREN'T YOU GOING TO HAVE SALAD FOR DINNER?
NOOOO, I'M ALL DONE WITH THAT SILLY DIET CRAP.
I WANT SOME REAL FOOD.
OH! WELL... THAT'S GREAT! HAVE ALL YOU LIKE!
I WILL!
HEY, SAVE ME SOME!
OOPS!
SPLAT
SPLAT
SPLAT
SPLAT

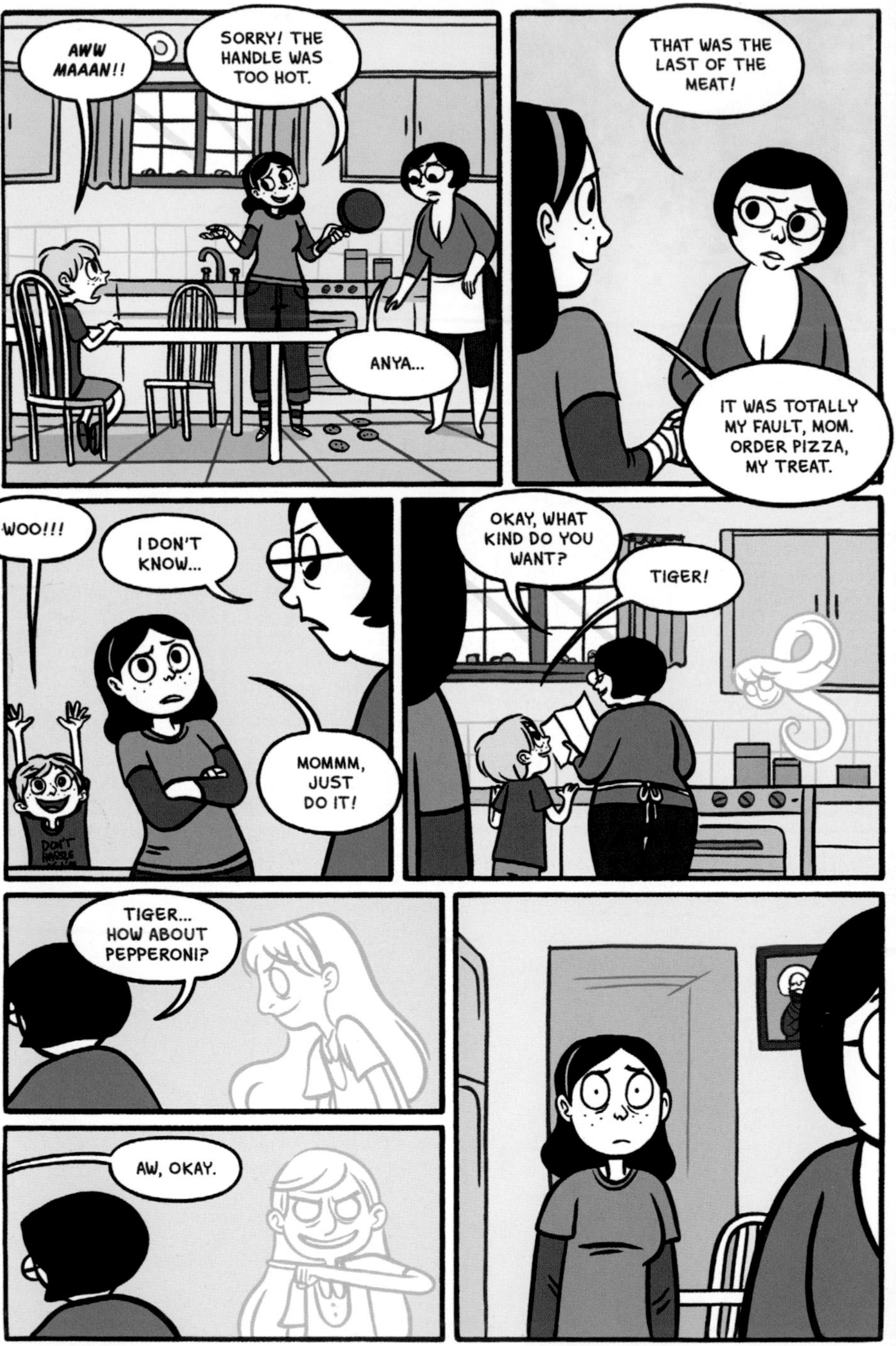
AWW MAAAN!!
SORRY! THE HANDLE WAS TOO HOT.
ANYA...
THAT WAS THE LAST OF THE MEAT!
IT WAS TOTALLY MY FAULT, MOM. ORDER PIZZA, MY TREAT.
WOO!!!
I DON'T KNOW...
MOMMM, JUST DO IT!
OKAY, WHAT KIND DO YOU WANT?
TIGER!
TIGER... HOW ABOUT PEPPERONI?
AW, OKAY.

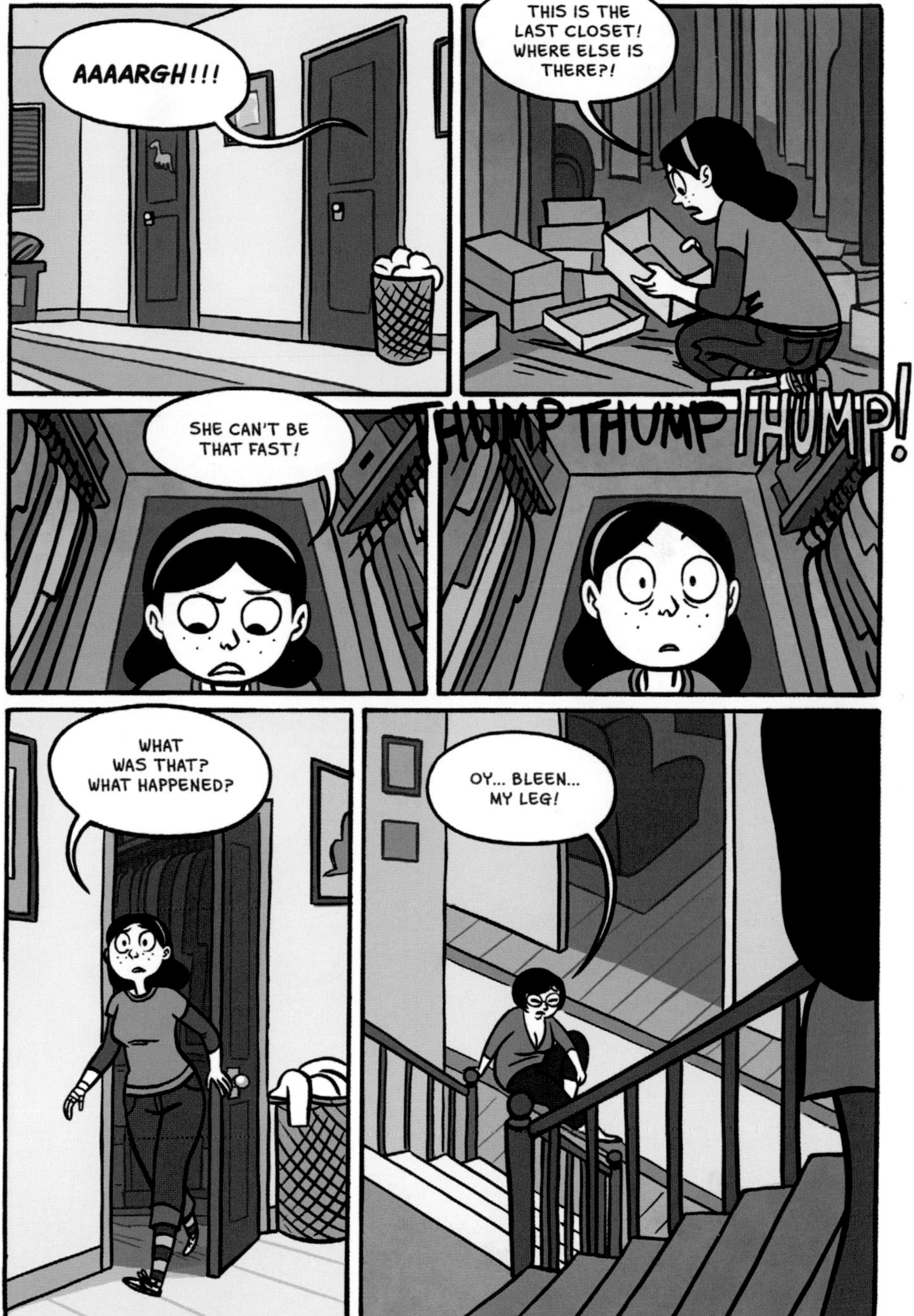
AAAARGH!!!
THIS IS THE LAST CLOSET! WHERE ELSE IS THERE?!
SHE CAN'T BE THAT FAST!
THUMP THUMP THUMP!
WHAT WAS THAT? WHAT HAPPENED?
OY... BLEEN... MY LEG!

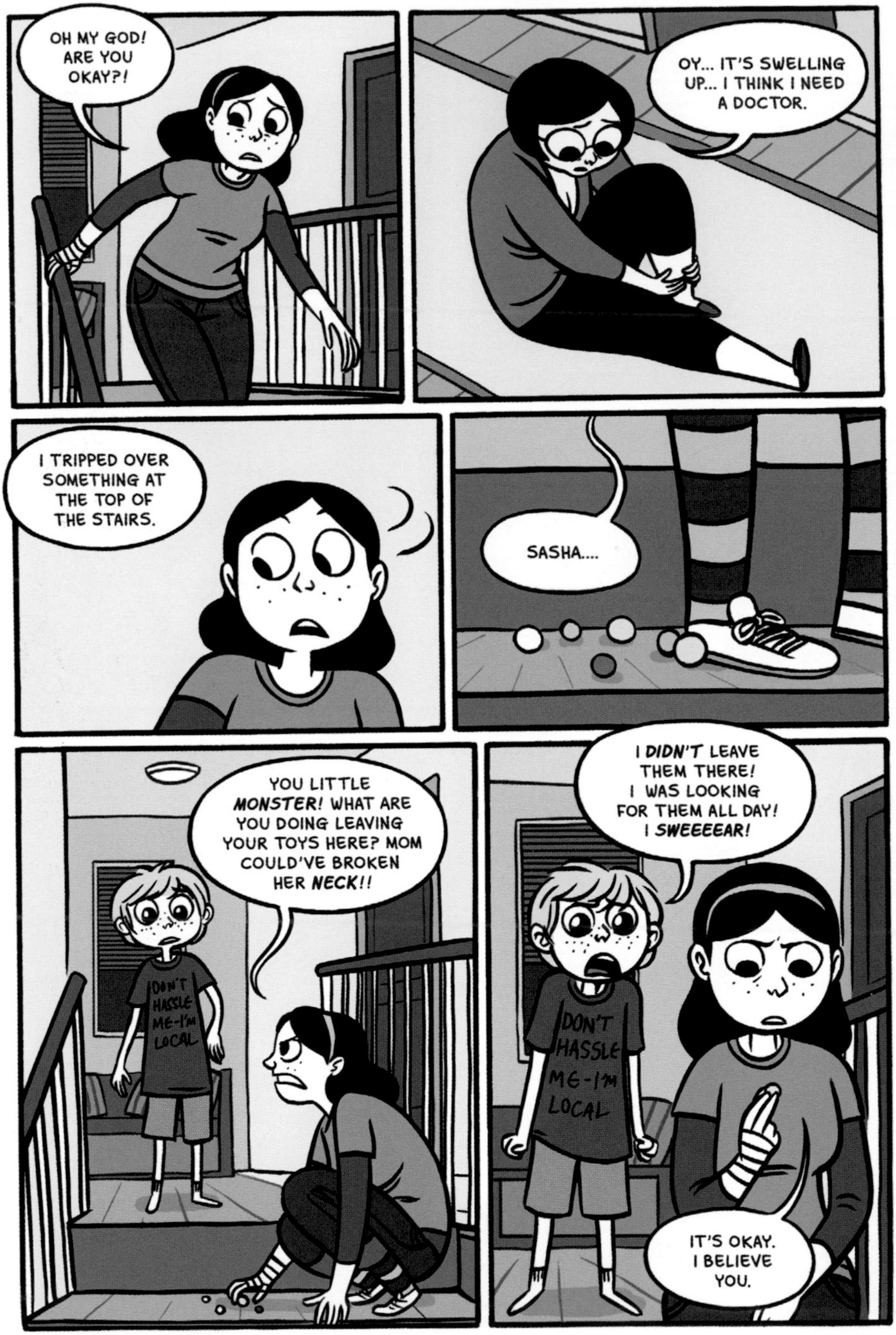
OH MY GOD! ARE YOU OKAY?!
OY... IT'S SWELLING UP... I THINK I NEED A DOCTOR.
I TRIPPED OVER SOMETHING AT THE TOP OF THE STAIRS.
SASHA....
YOU LITTLE MONSTER! WHAT ARE YOU DOING LEAVING YOUR TOYS HERE? MOM COULD'VE BROKEN HER NECK!!
DON'T HASSLE ME-I'M LOCAL
I DIDN'T LEAVE THEM THERE! I WAS LOOKING FOR THEM ALL DAY! I SWEEEEAR!
DON'T HASSLE ME-I'M LOCAL
IT'S OKAY. I BELIEVE YOU.

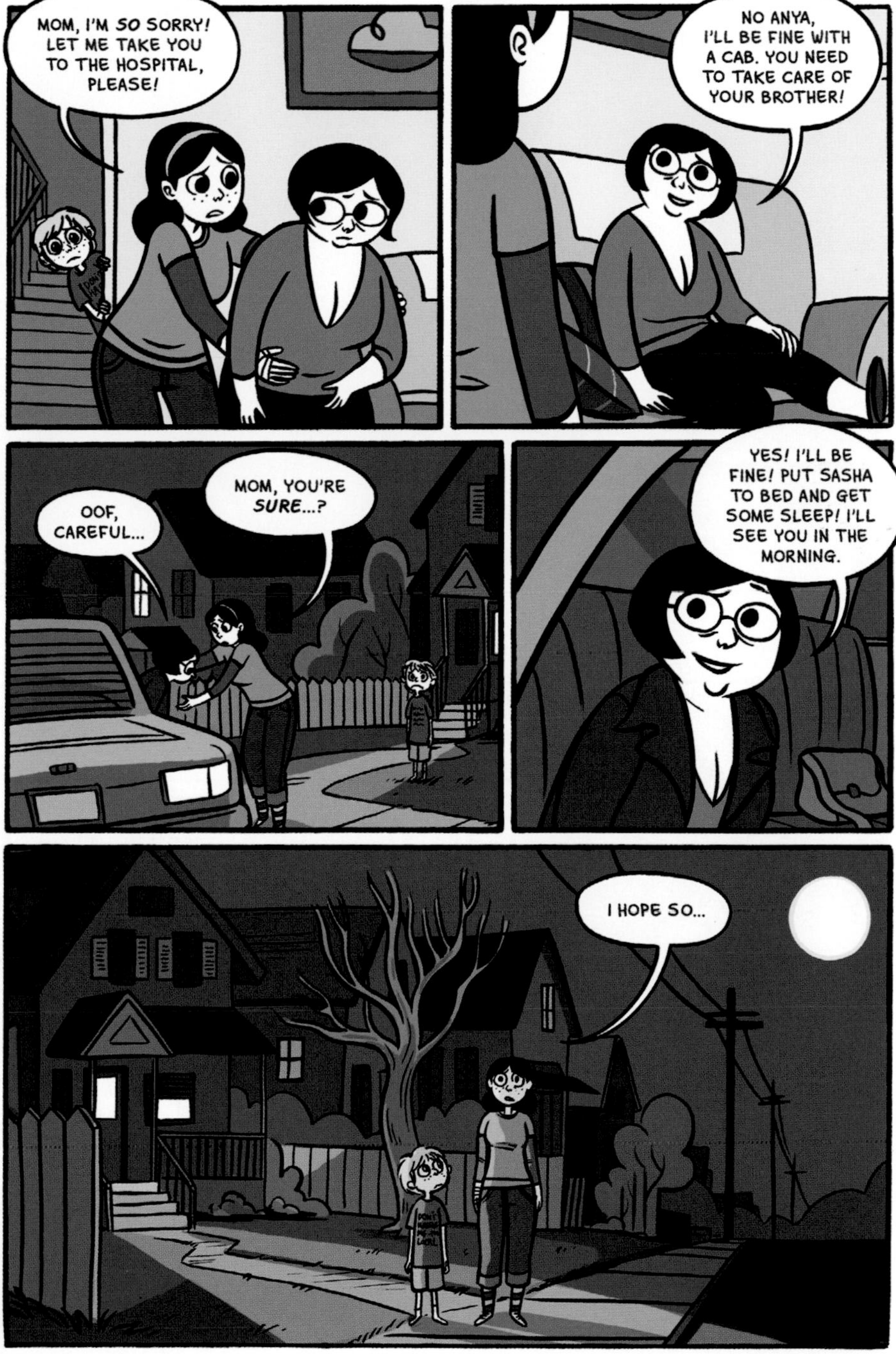
MOM, I'M SO SORRY! LET ME TAKE YOU TO THE HOSPITAL, PLEASE!
NO ANYA, I'LL BE FINE WITH A CAB. YOU NEED TO TAKE CARE OF YOUR BROTHER!
OOF, CAREFUL...
MOM, YOU'RE SURE...?
YES! I'LL BE FINE! PUT SASHA TO BED AND GET SOME SLEEP! I'LL SEE YOU IN THE MORNING.
I HOPE SO...

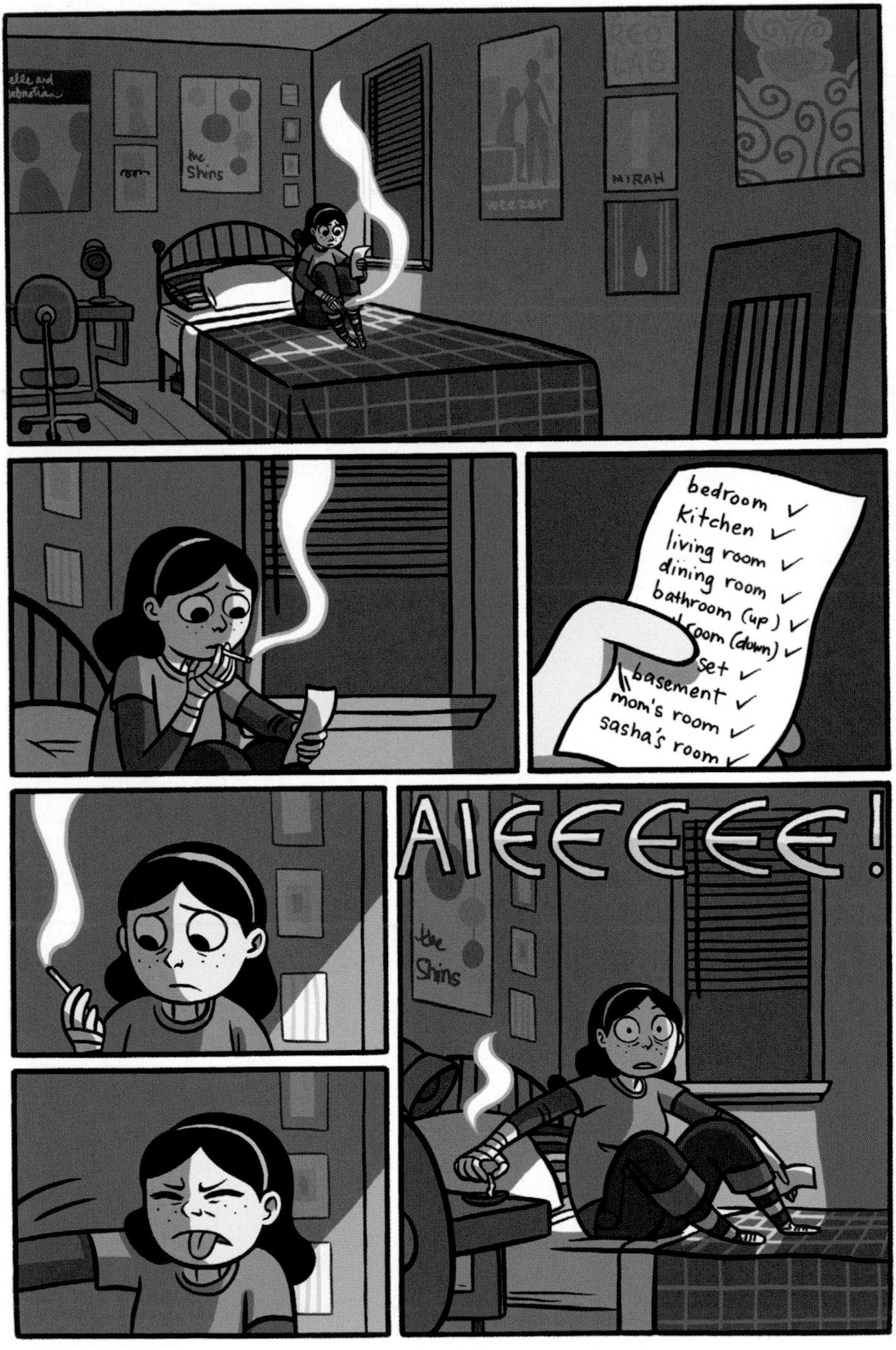

the Shins
MIRAH
bedroom ✓
Kitchen ✓
living room ✓
dining room ✓
bathroom (up) ✓
basement ✓
mom's room ✓
sasha's room ✓
AIEEEEE!
the Shins

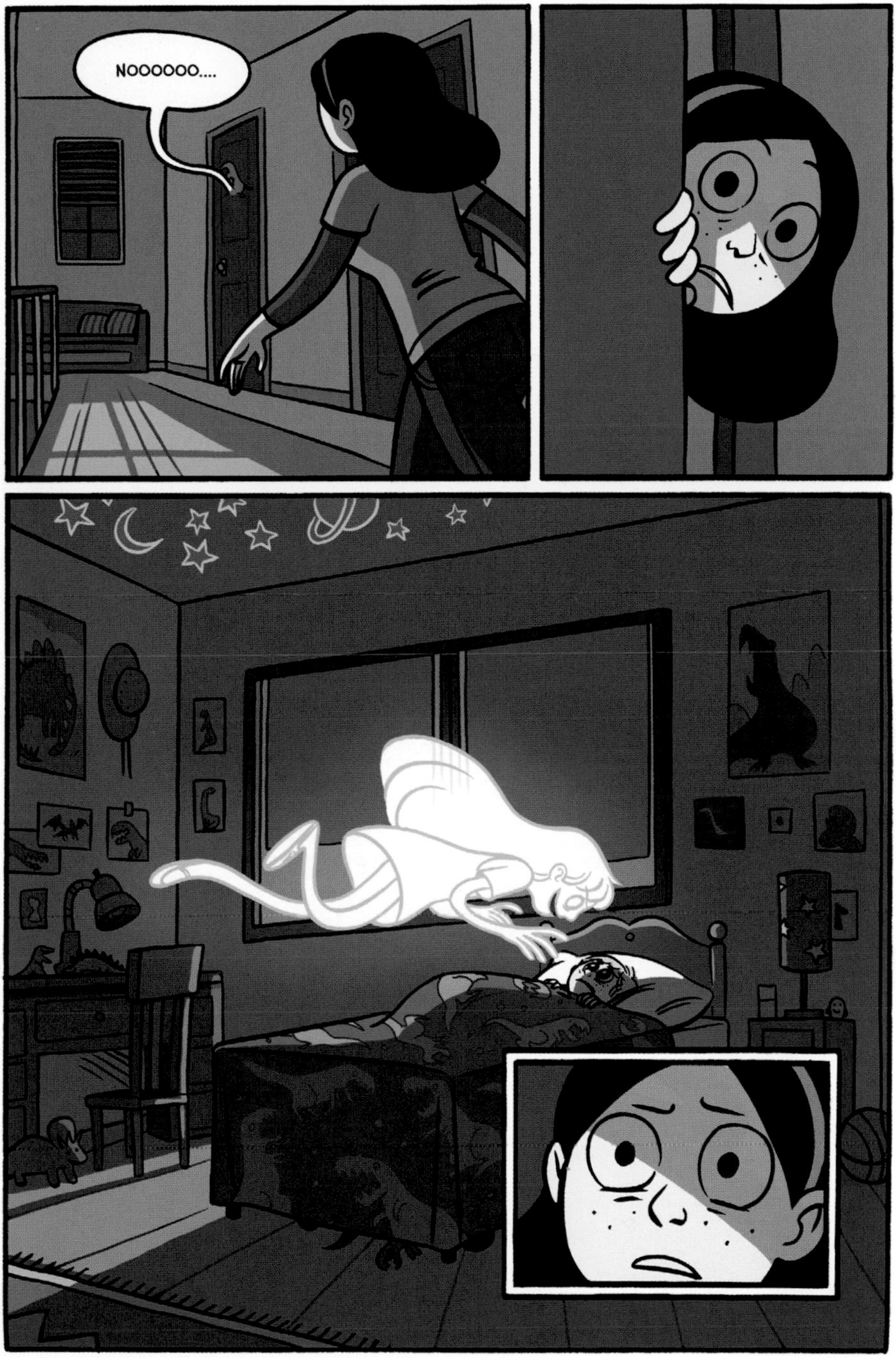
NOOOOOO....

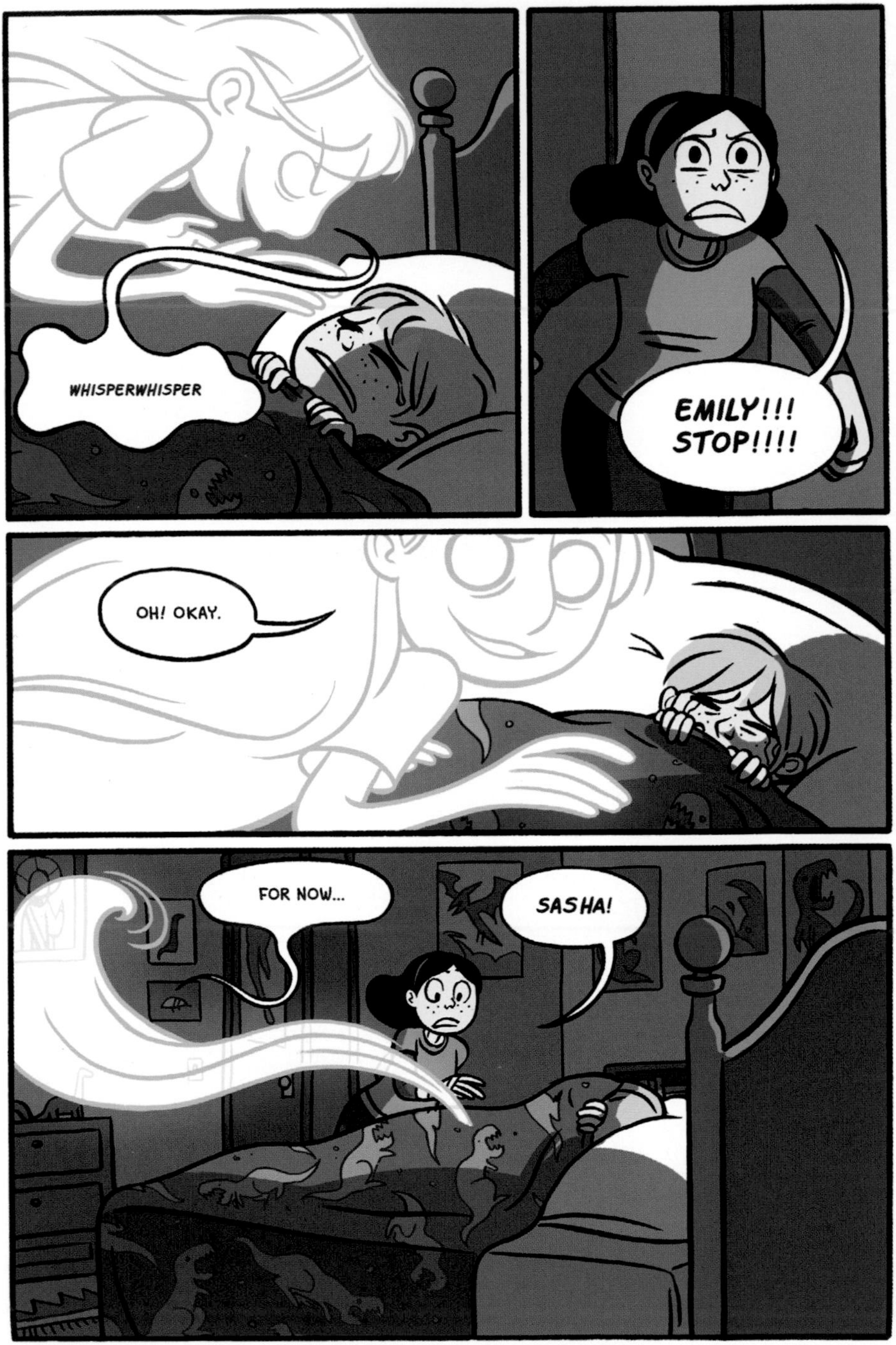
WHISPERWHISPER
EMILY!!! STOP!!!!
OH! OKAY.
FOR NOW...
SASHA!

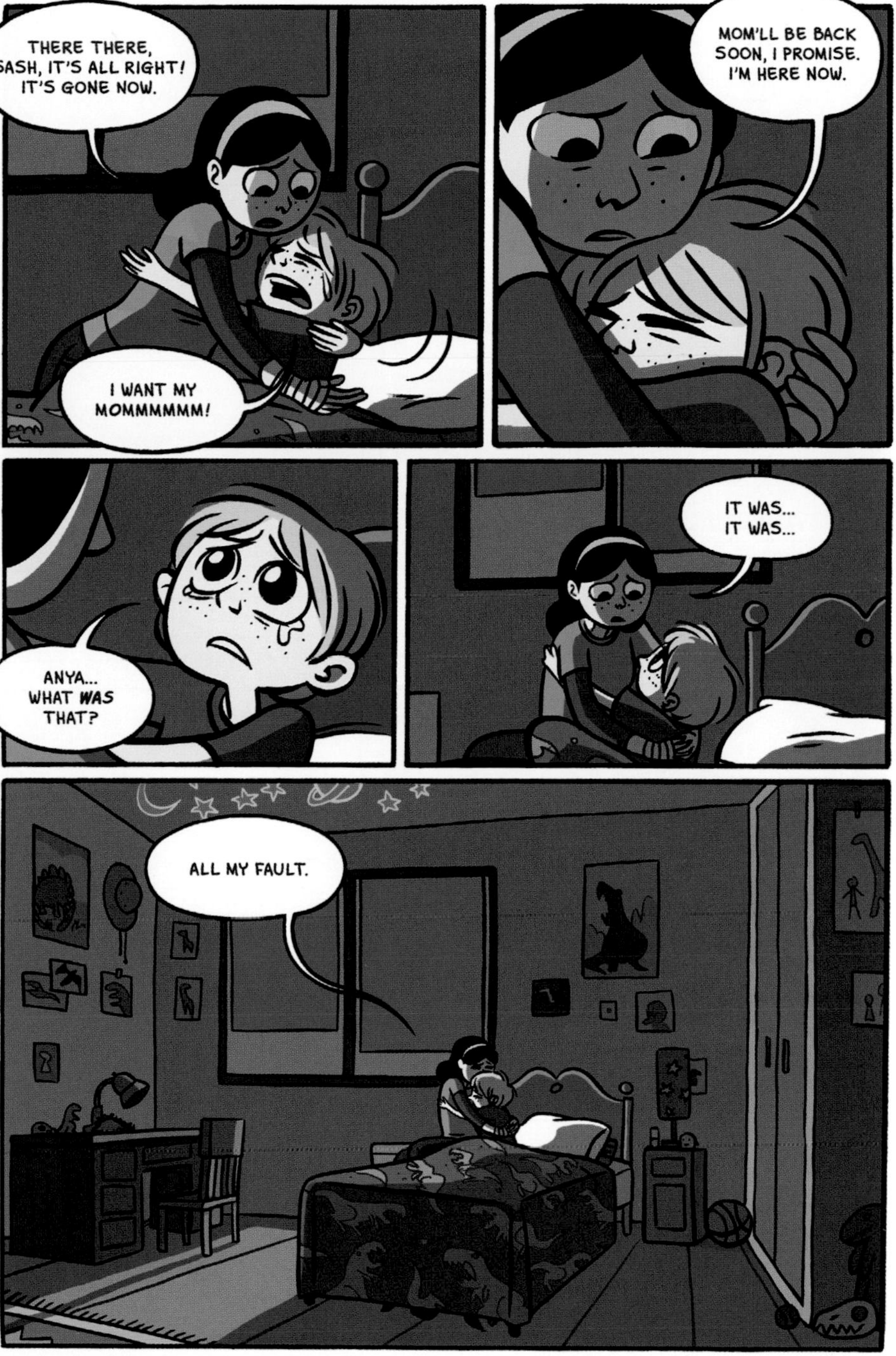
THERE THERE, SASH, IT'S ALL RIGHT! IT'S GONE NOW.
I WANT MY MOMMMMMM!
MOM'LL BE BACK SOON, I PROMISE. I'M HERE NOW.
ANYA... WHAT *WAS* THAT?
IT WAS... IT WAS...
ALL MY FAULT.

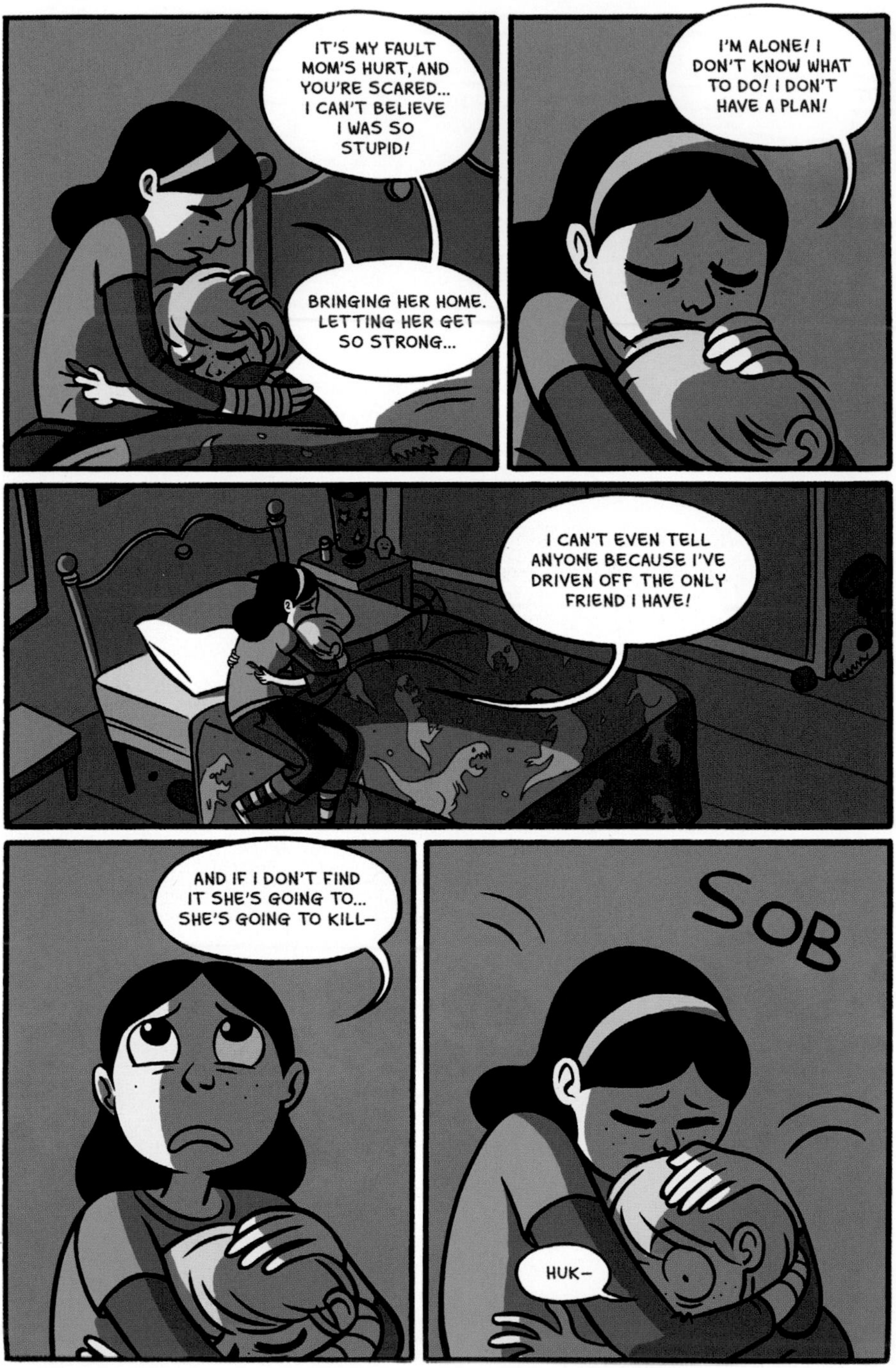
IT'S MY FAULT MOM'S HURT, AND YOU'RE SCARED... I CAN'T BELIEVE I WAS SO STUPID!
BRINGING HER HOME. LETTING HER GET SO STRONG...
I'M ALONE! I DON'T KNOW WHAT TO DO! I DON'T HAVE A PLAN!
I CAN'T EVEN TELL ANYONE BECAUSE I'VE DRIVEN OFF THE ONLY FRIEND I HAVE!
AND IF I DON'T FIND IT SHE'S GOING TO... SHE'S GOING TO KILL-
SOB
HUK-

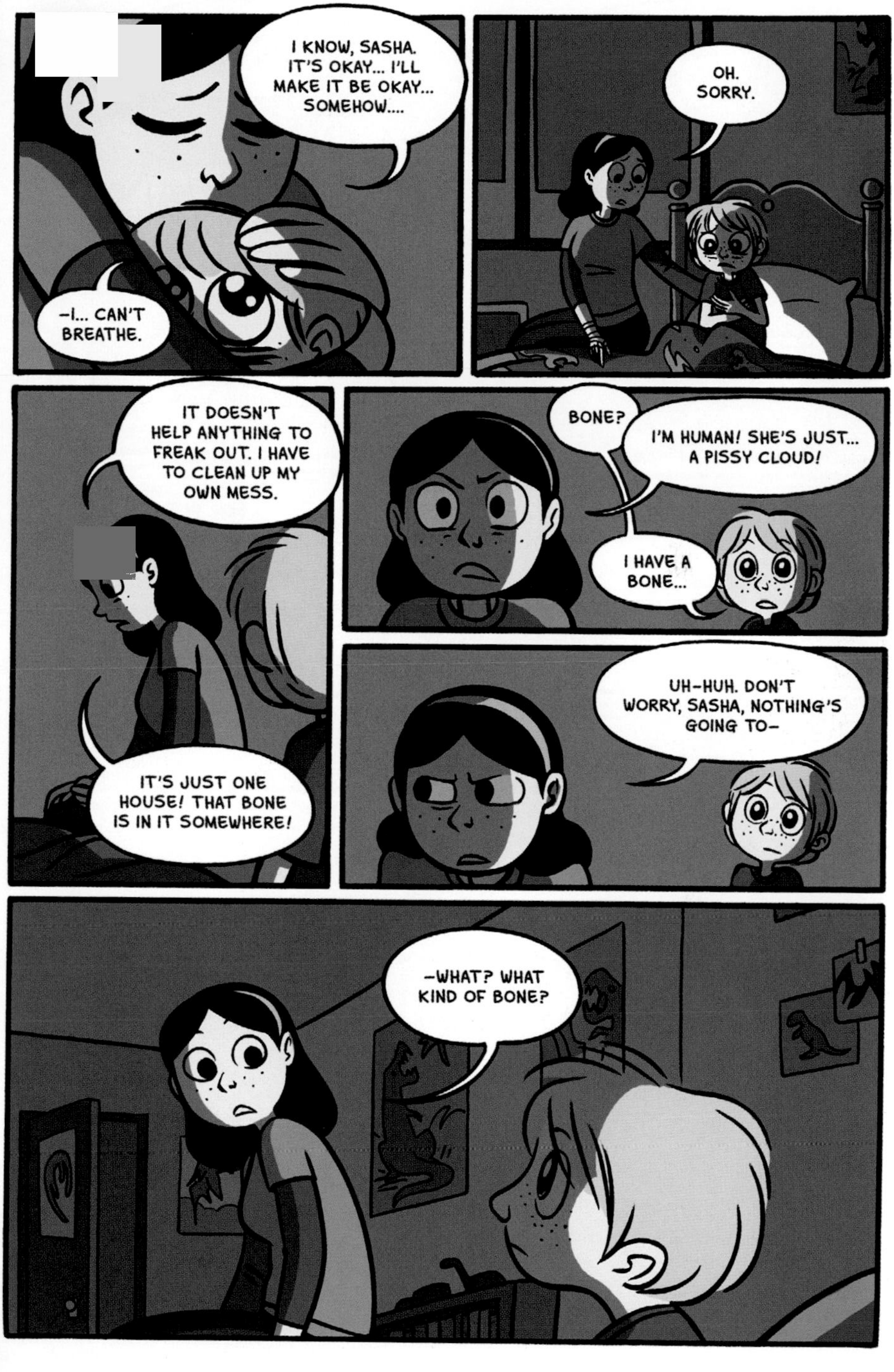
I KNOW, SASHA. IT'S OKAY... I'LL MAKE IT BE OKAY... SOMEHOW....
-I... CAN'T BREATHE.
OH. SORRY.
IT DOESN'T HELP ANYTHING TO FREAK OUT. I HAVE TO CLEAN UP MY OWN MESS.
IT'S JUST ONE HOUSE! THAT BONE IS IN IT SOMEWHERE!
I'M HUMAN! SHE'S JUST... A PISSY CLOUD!
I HAVE A BONE...
BONE?
UH-HUH. DON'T WORRY, SASHA, NOTHING'S GOING TO-
-WHAT? WHAT KIND OF BONE?

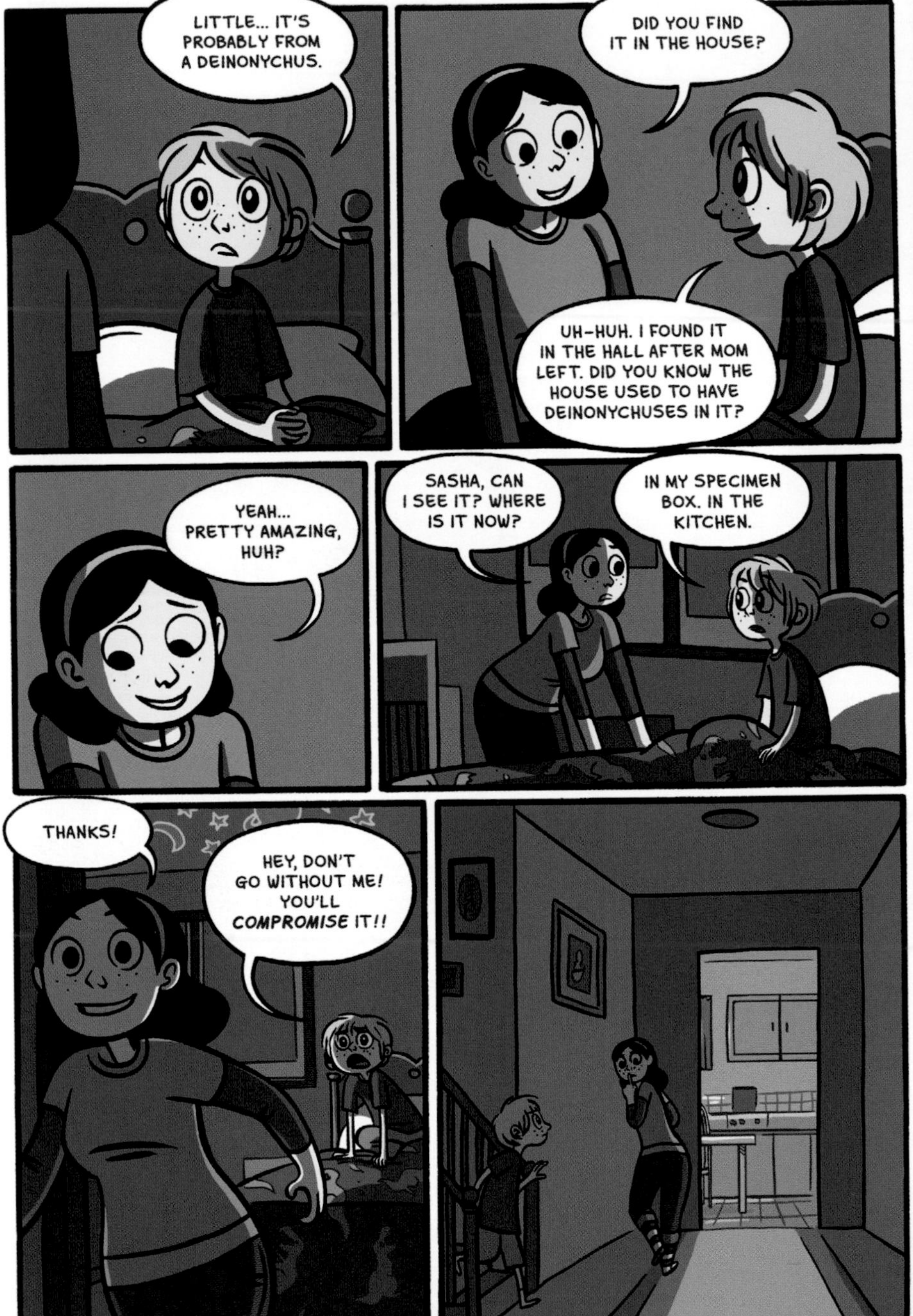
LITTLE... IT'S PROBABLY FROM A DEINONYCHUS.
DID YOU FIND IT IN THE HOUSE?
UH-HUH. I FOUND IT IN THE HALL AFTER MOM LEFT. DID YOU KNOW THE HOUSE USED TO HAVE DEINONYCHUSES IN IT?
YEAH... PRETTY AMAZING, HUH?
SASHA, CAN I SEE IT? WHERE IS IT NOW?
IN MY SPECIMEN BOX. IN THE KITCHEN.
THANKS!
HEY, DON'T GO WITHOUT ME! YOU'LL *COMPROMISE* IT!!

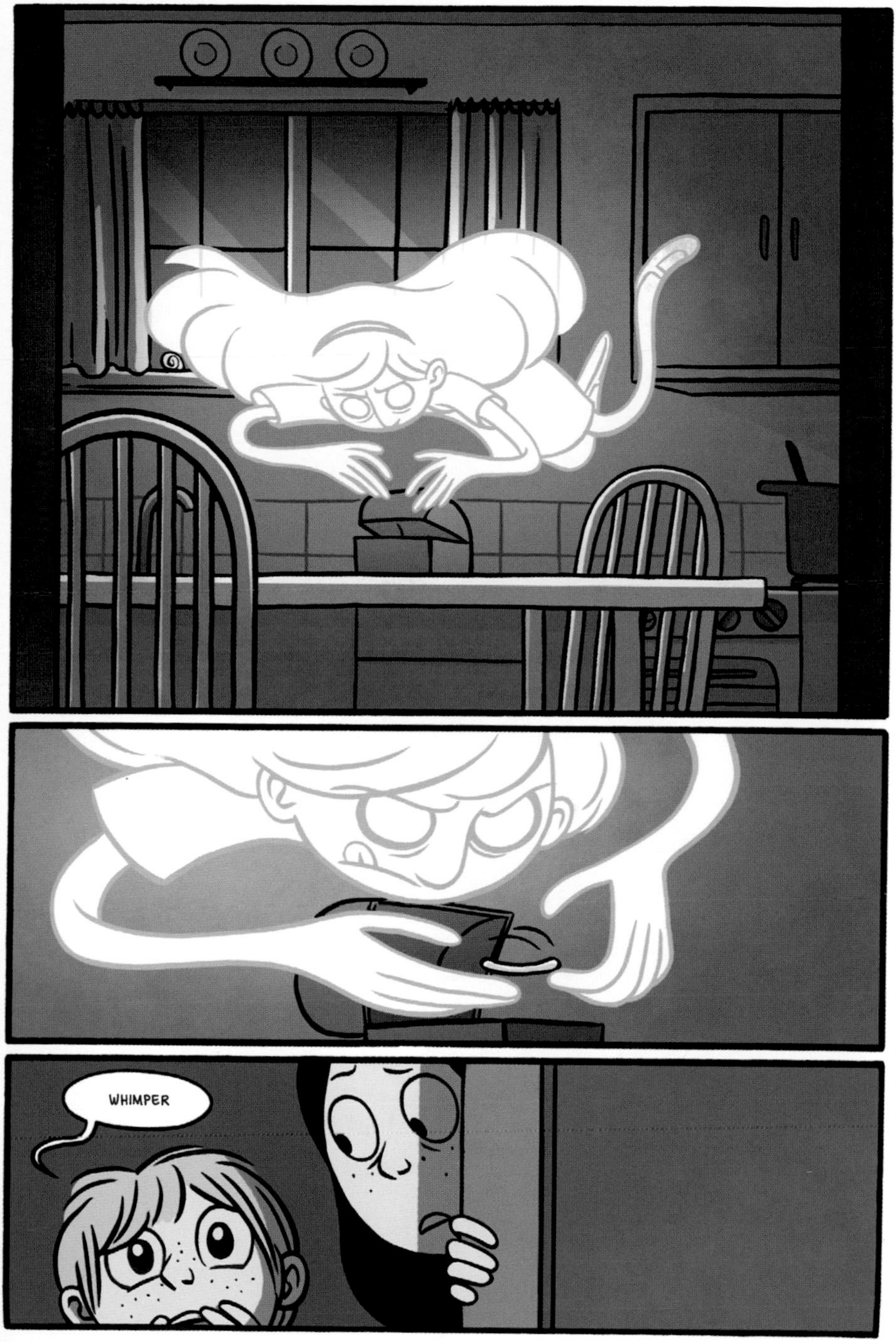
WHIMPER

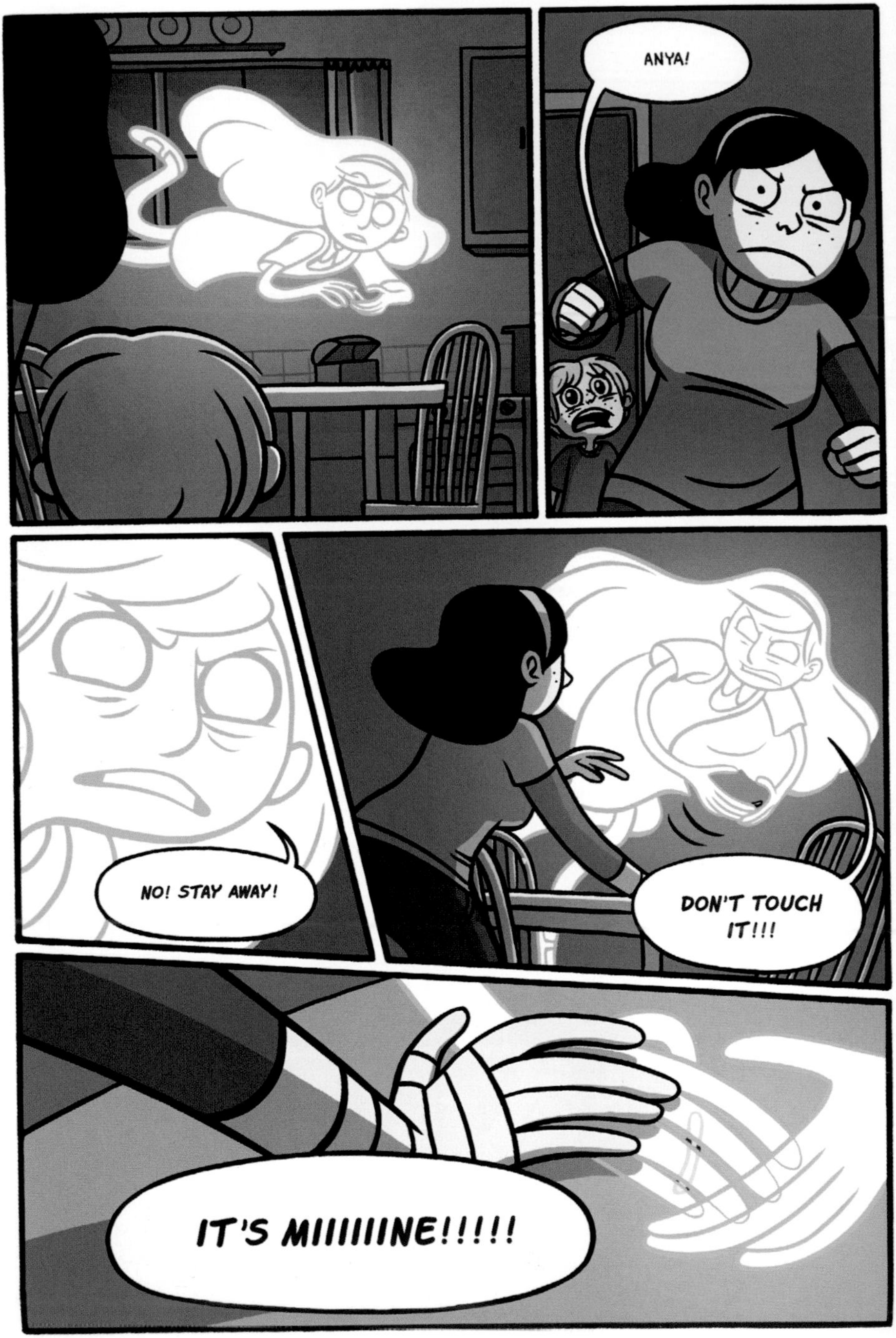
ANYA!
NO! STAY AWAY!
DON'T TOUCH IT!!!
IT'S MIIIIIINE!!!!!

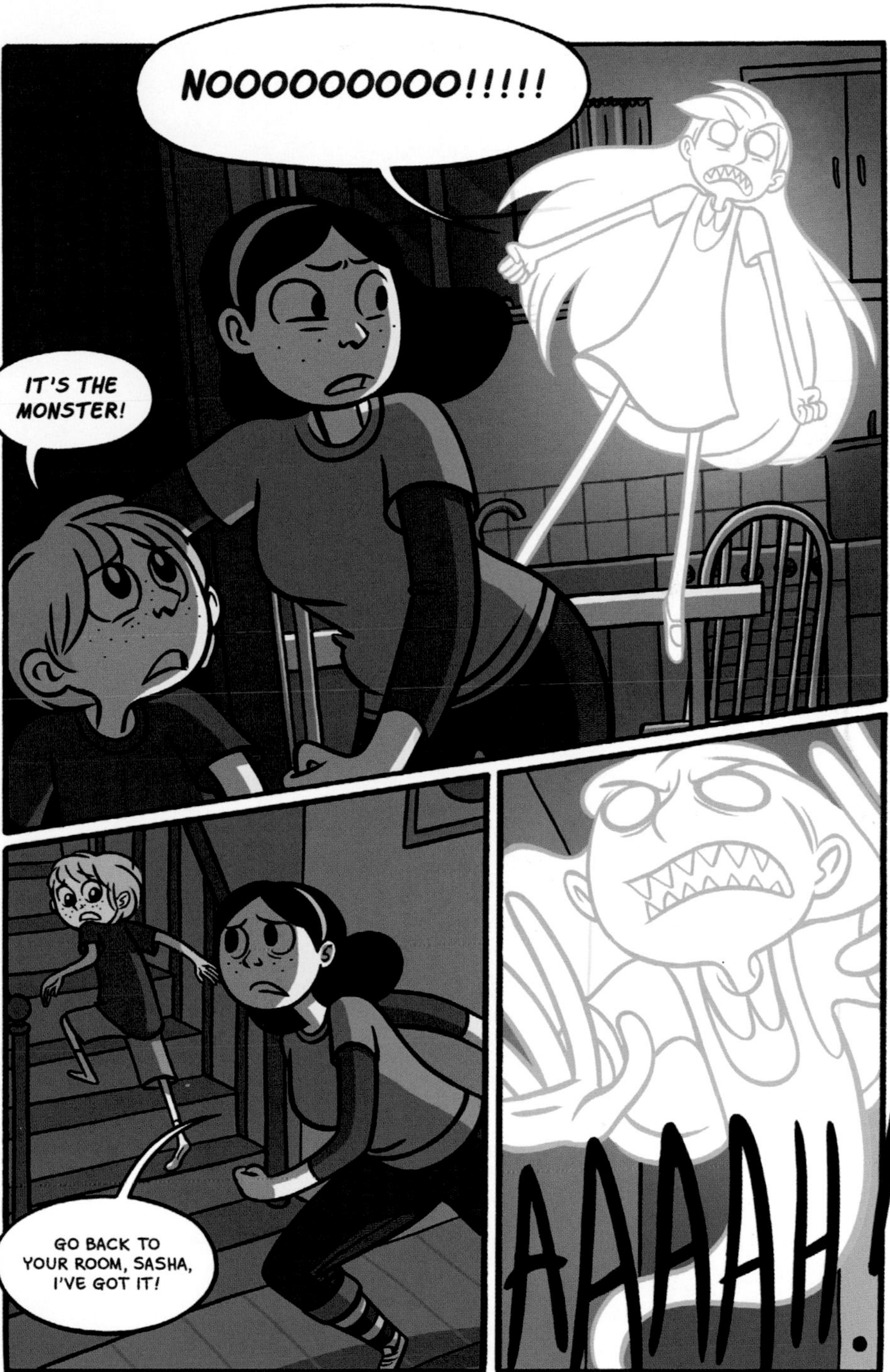
NOOOOOOOOO!!!!!
IT'S THE MONSTER!
GO BACK TO YOUR ROOM, SASHA, I'VE GOT IT!
AAAAH!

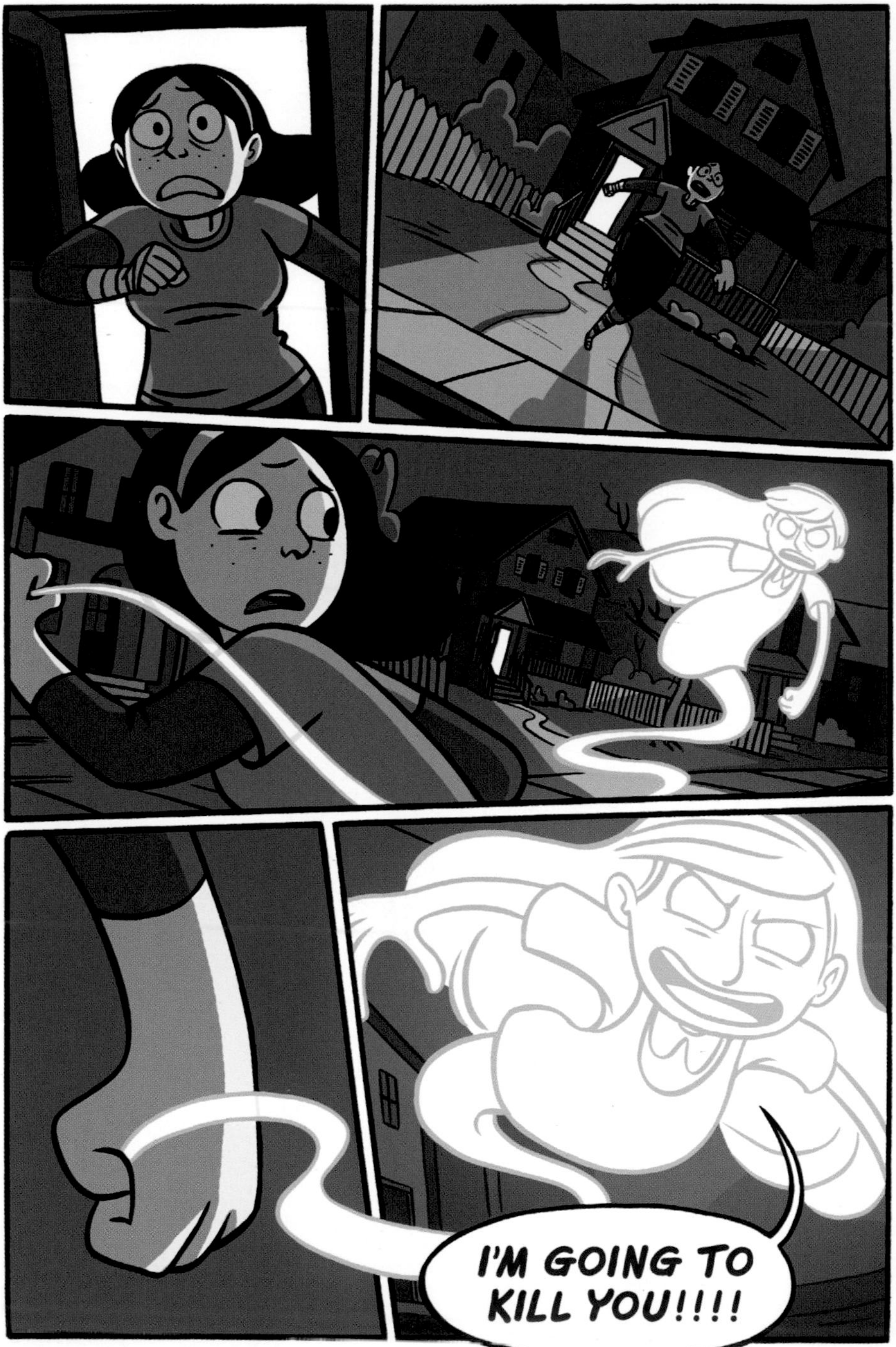
I'M GOING TO
KILL YOU!!!!

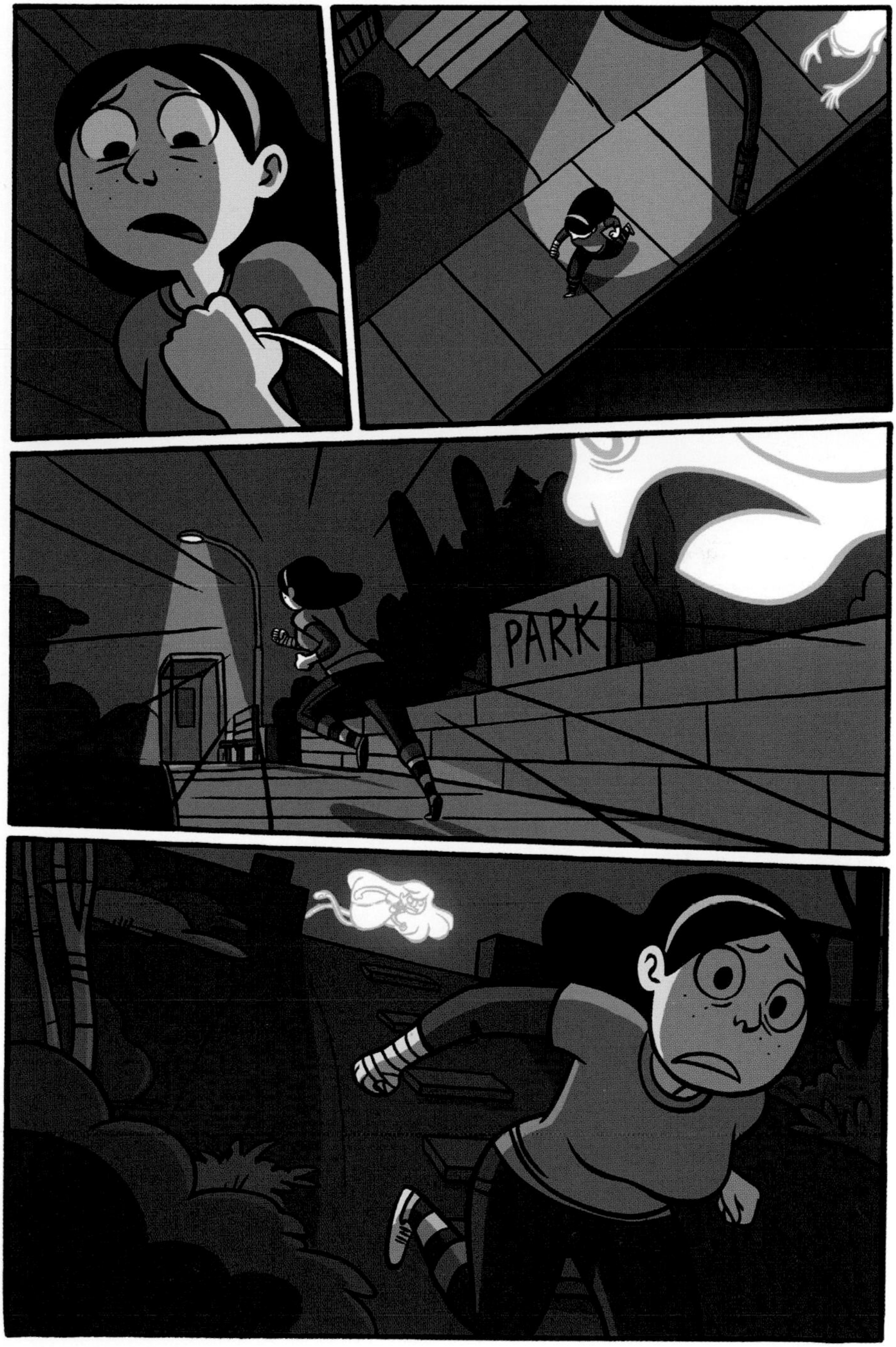
PARK

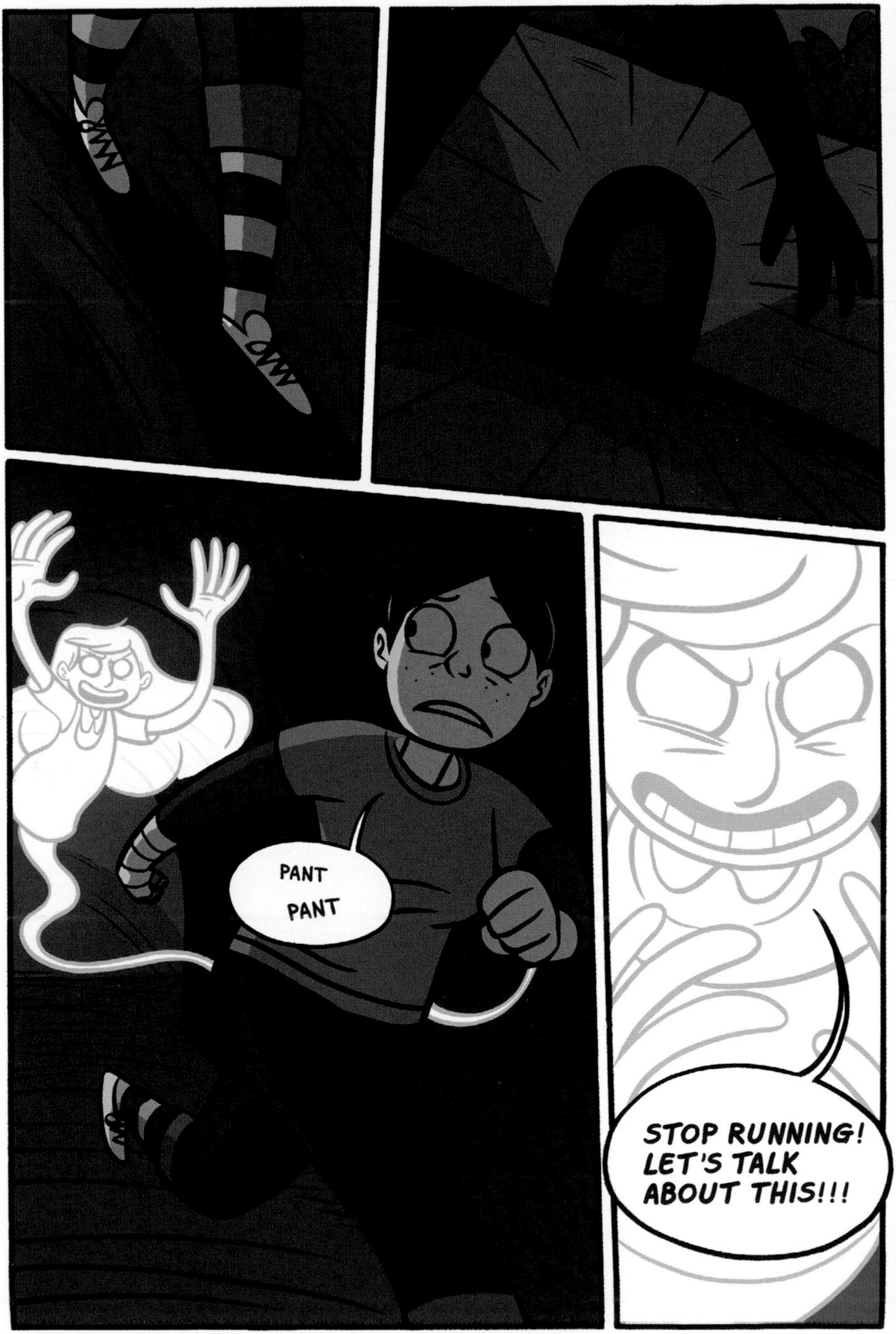
PANT
PANT
STOP RUNNING!
LET'S TALK
ABOUT THIS!!!

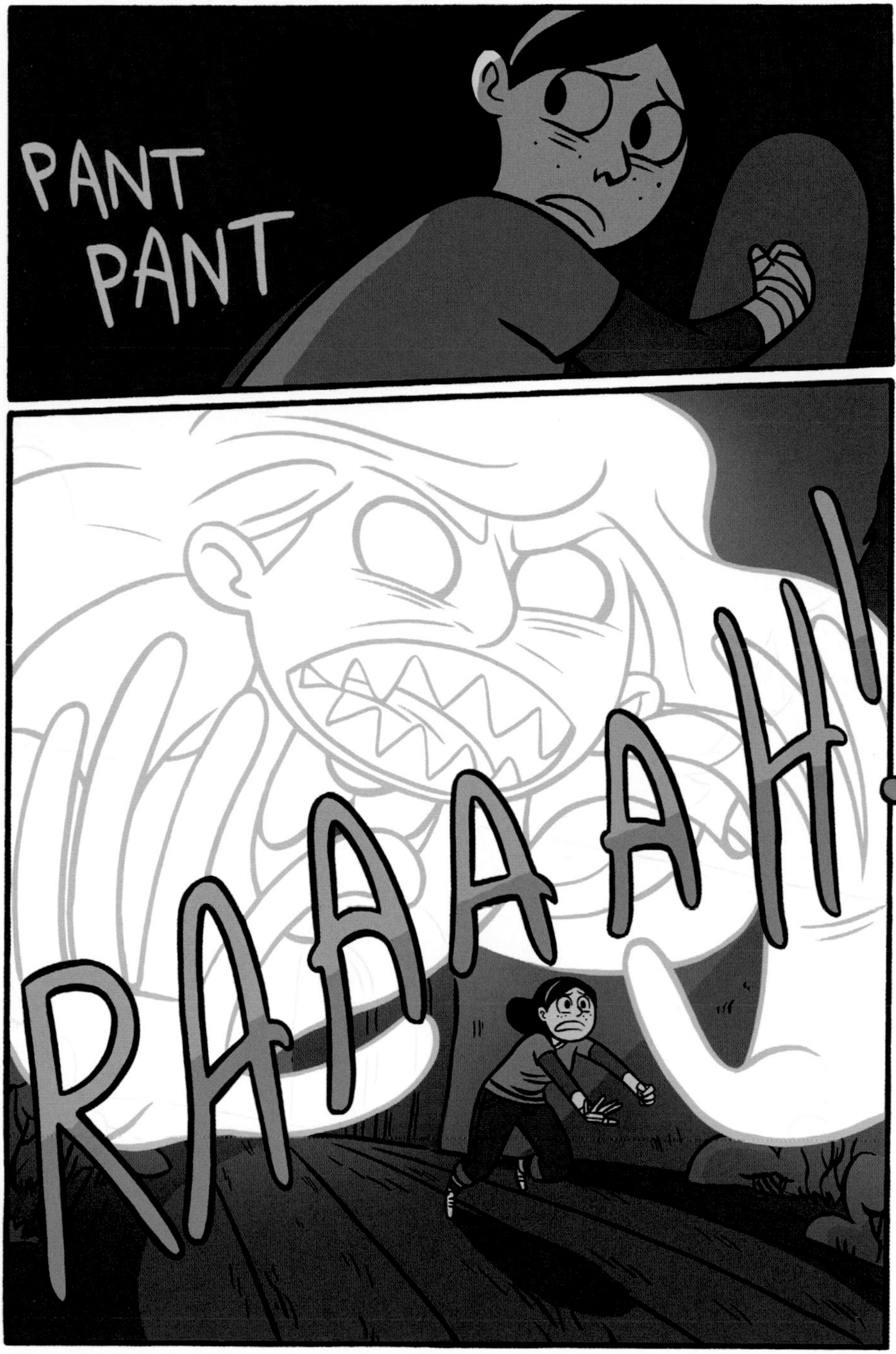
PANT
PANT
RAAAAH!

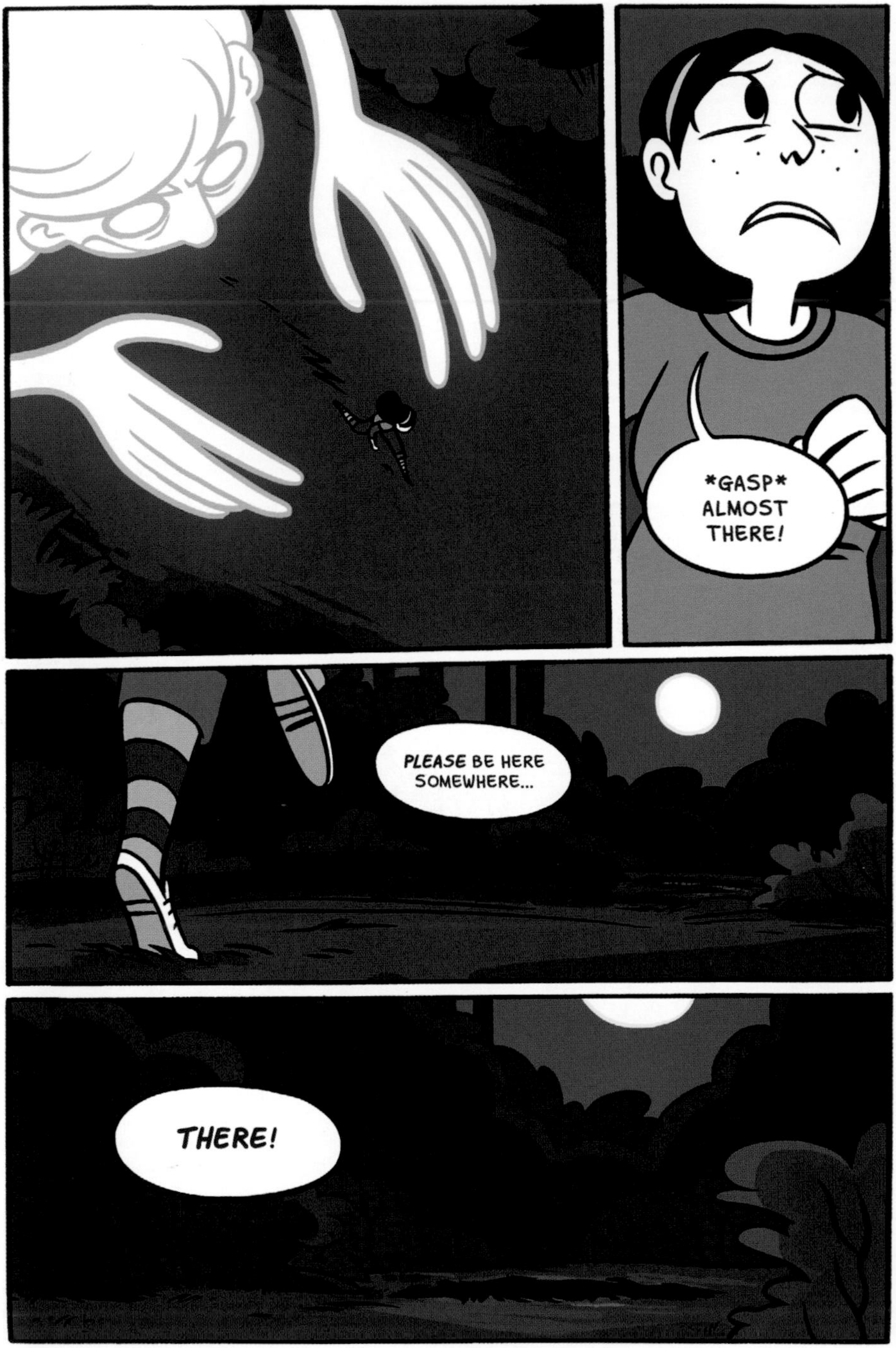
GASP ALMOST THERE!
PLEASE BE HERE SOMEWHERE...
THERE!

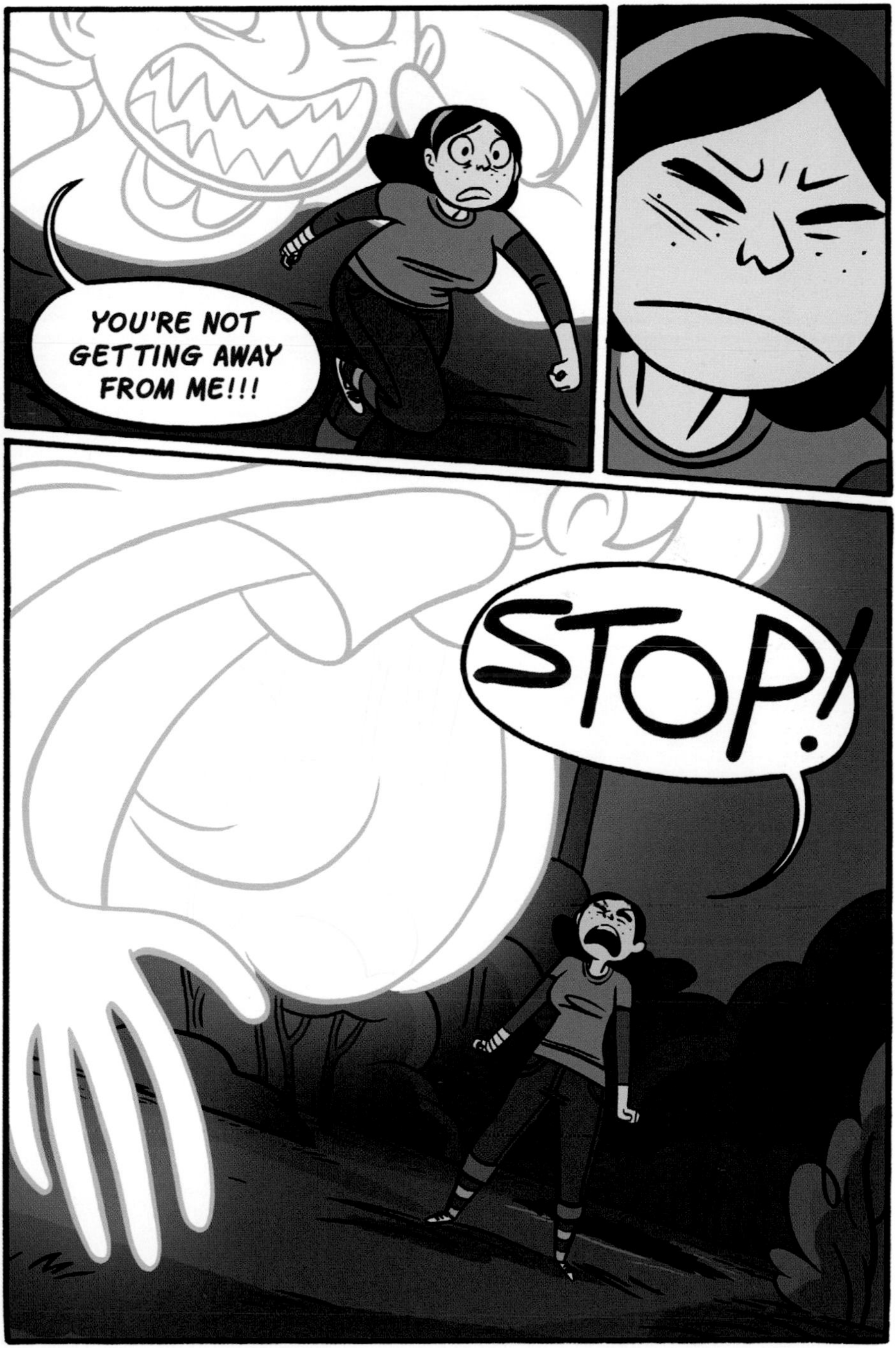
YOU'RE NOT GETTING AWAY FROM ME!!!
STOP!

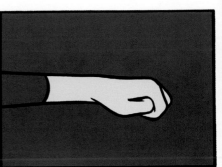

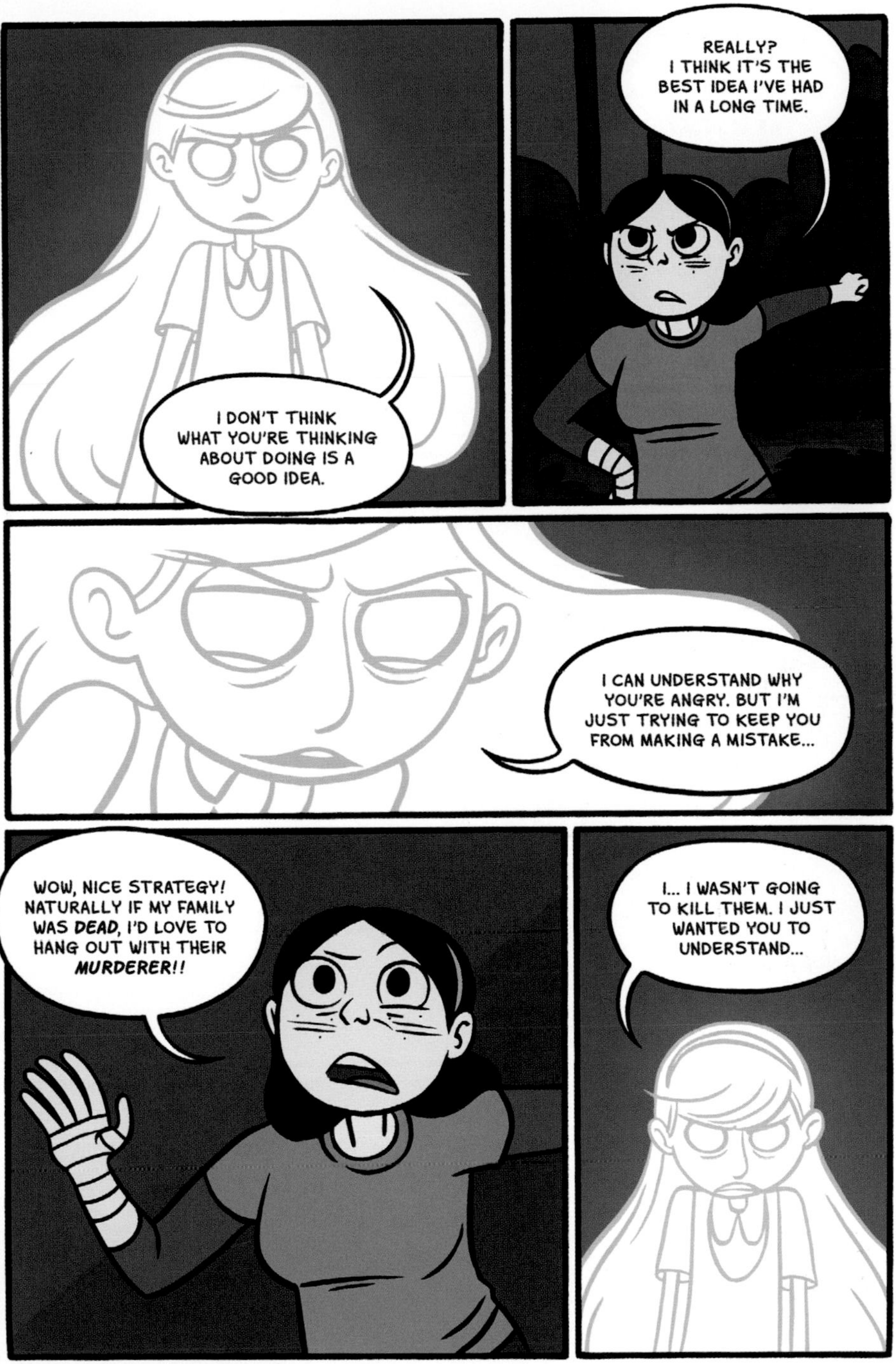
I DON'T THINK WHAT YOU'RE THINKING ABOUT DOING IS A GOOD IDEA.
REALLY? I THINK IT'S THE BEST IDEA I'VE HAD IN A LONG TIME.
I CAN UNDERSTAND WHY YOU'RE ANGRY. BUT I'M JUST TRYING TO KEEP YOU FROM MAKING A MISTAKE...
WOW, NICE STRATEGY! NATURALLY IF MY FAMILY WAS *DEAD*, I'D LOVE TO HANG OUT WITH THEIR *MURDERER*!!
I... I WASN'T GOING TO KILL THEM. I JUST WANTED YOU TO UNDERSTAND...

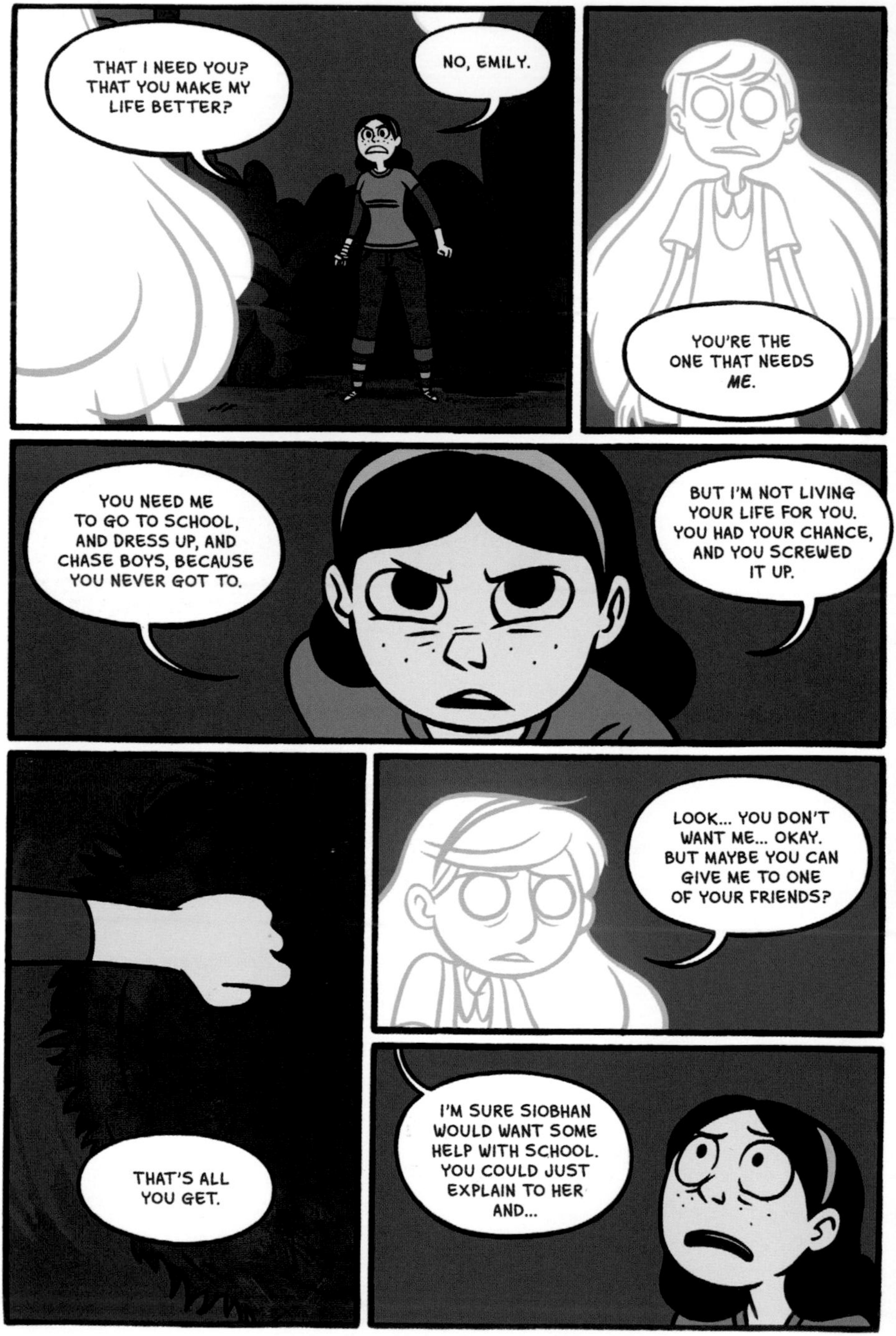
THAT I NEED YOU? THAT YOU MAKE MY LIFE BETTER?
NO, EMILY.
YOU'RE THE ONE THAT NEEDS *ME*.
YOU NEED ME TO GO TO SCHOOL, AND DRESS UP, AND CHASE BOYS, BECAUSE YOU NEVER GOT TO.
BUT I'M NOT LIVING YOUR LIFE FOR YOU. YOU HAD YOUR CHANCE, AND YOU SCREWED IT UP.
LOOK... YOU DON'T WANT ME... OKAY. BUT MAYBE YOU CAN GIVE ME TO ONE OF YOUR FRIENDS?
THAT'S ALL YOU GET.
I'M SURE SIOBHAN WOULD WANT SOME HELP WITH SCHOOL. YOU COULD JUST EXPLAIN TO HER AND...

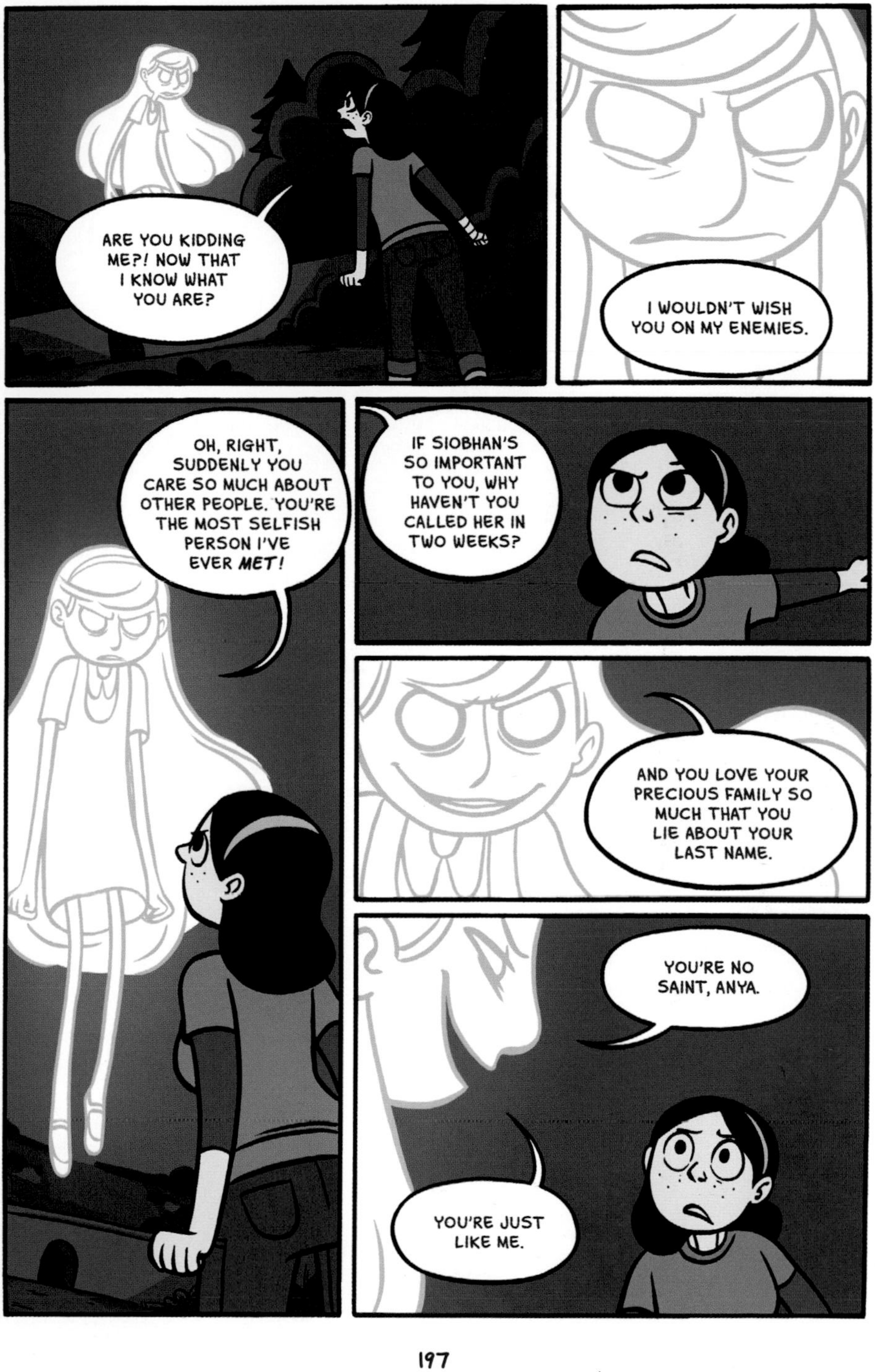
ARE YOU KIDDING ME?! NOW THAT I KNOW WHAT YOU ARE?
I WOULDN'T WISH YOU ON MY ENEMIES.
OH, RIGHT, SUDDENLY YOU CARE SO MUCH ABOUT OTHER PEOPLE. YOU'RE THE MOST SELFISH PERSON I'VE EVER *MET*!
IF SIOBHAN'S SO IMPORTANT TO YOU, WHY HAVEN'T YOU CALLED HER IN TWO WEEKS?
AND YOU LOVE YOUR PRECIOUS FAMILY SO MUCH THAT YOU LIE ABOUT YOUR LAST NAME.
YOU'RE NO SAINT, ANYA.
YOU'RE JUST LIKE ME.

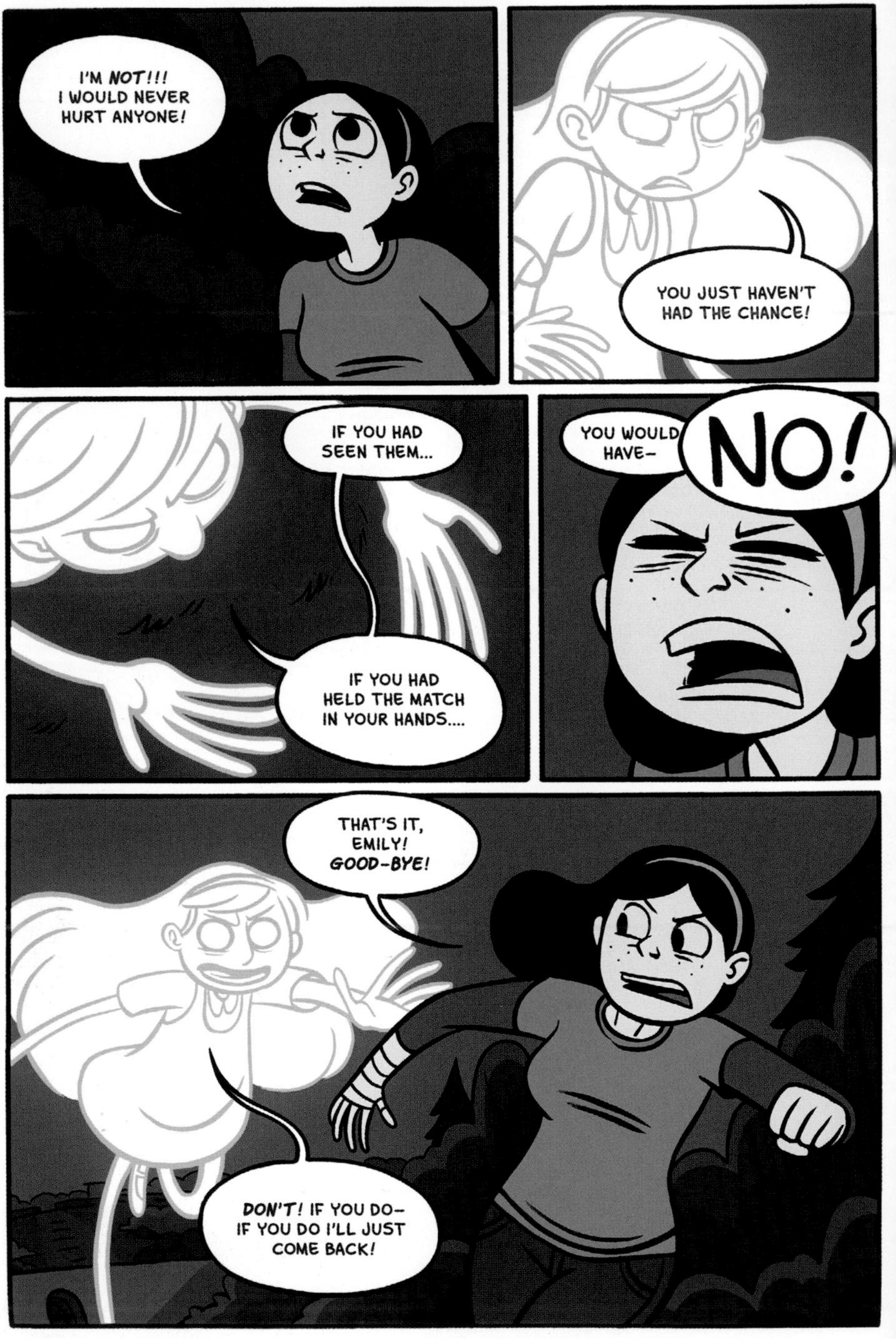
I'M NOT!!!
I WOULD NEVER
HURT ANYONE!
YOU JUST HAVEN'T
HAD THE CHANCE!
IF YOU HAD
SEEN THEM...
IF YOU HAD
HELD THE MATCH
IN YOUR HANDS....
YOU WOULD
HAVE-
NO!
THAT'S IT,
EMILY!
GOOD-BYE!
DON'T! IF YOU DO-
IF YOU DO I'LL JUST
COME BACK!

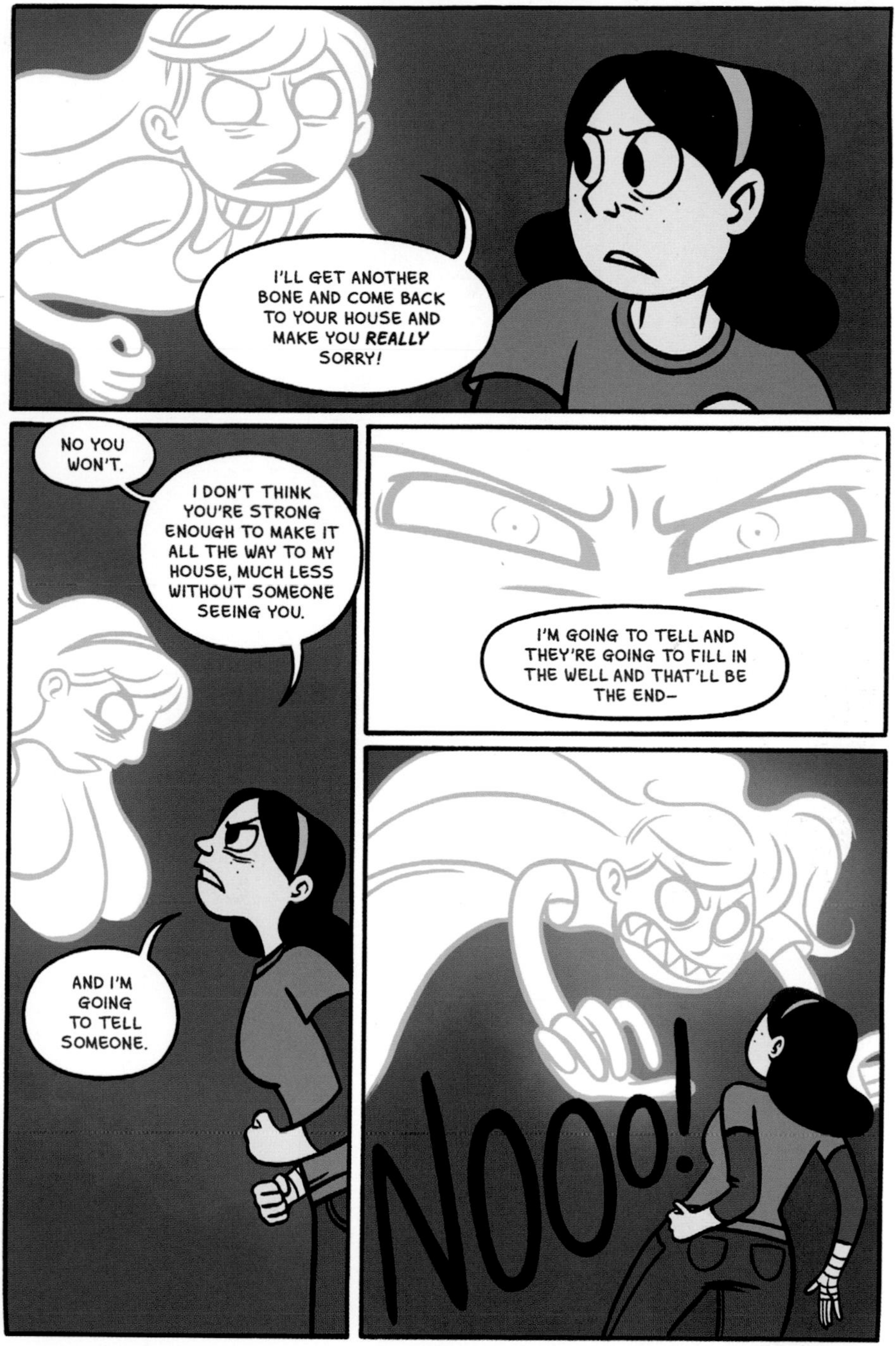
I'LL GET ANOTHER BONE AND COME BACK TO YOUR HOUSE AND MAKE YOU ***REALLY*** SORRY!
NO YOU WON'T.
I DON'T THINK YOU'RE STRONG ENOUGH TO MAKE IT ALL THE WAY TO MY HOUSE, MUCH LESS WITHOUT SOMEONE SEEING YOU.
AND I'M GOING TO TELL SOMEONE.
I'M GOING TO TELL AND THEY'RE GOING TO FILL IN THE WELL AND THAT'LL BE THE END–
NOOOO!

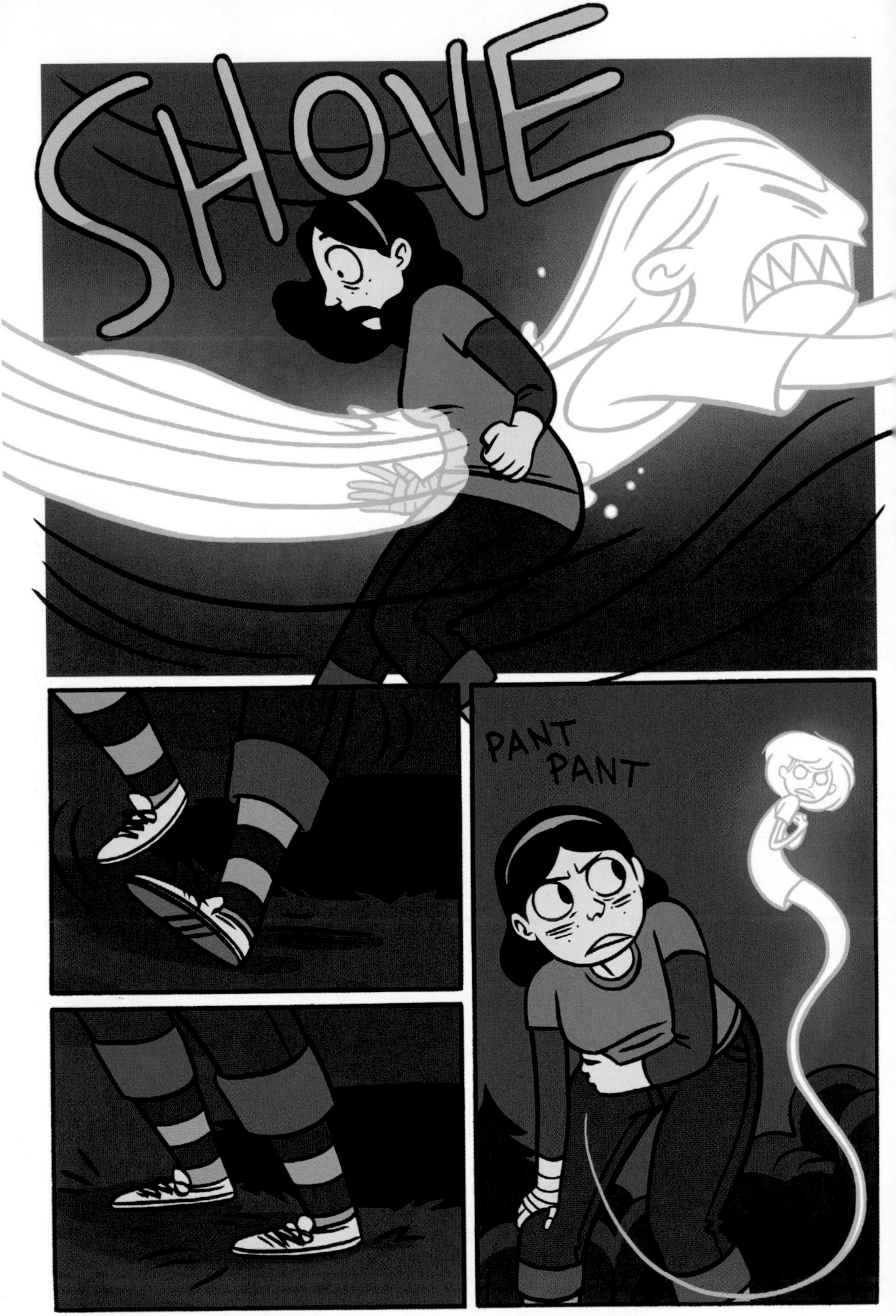
SHOVE
PANT
PANT

NO...
AAAAH!!!

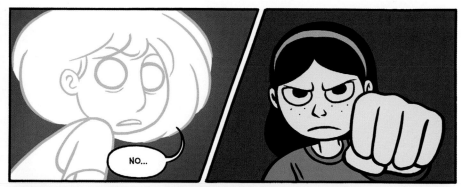

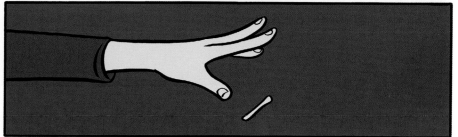

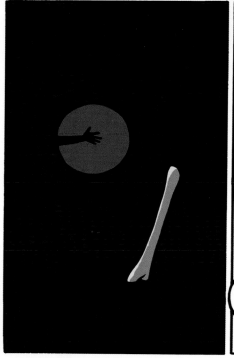

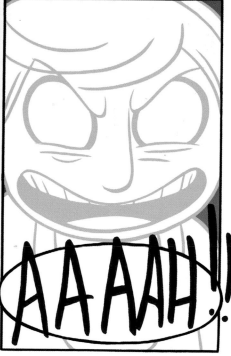

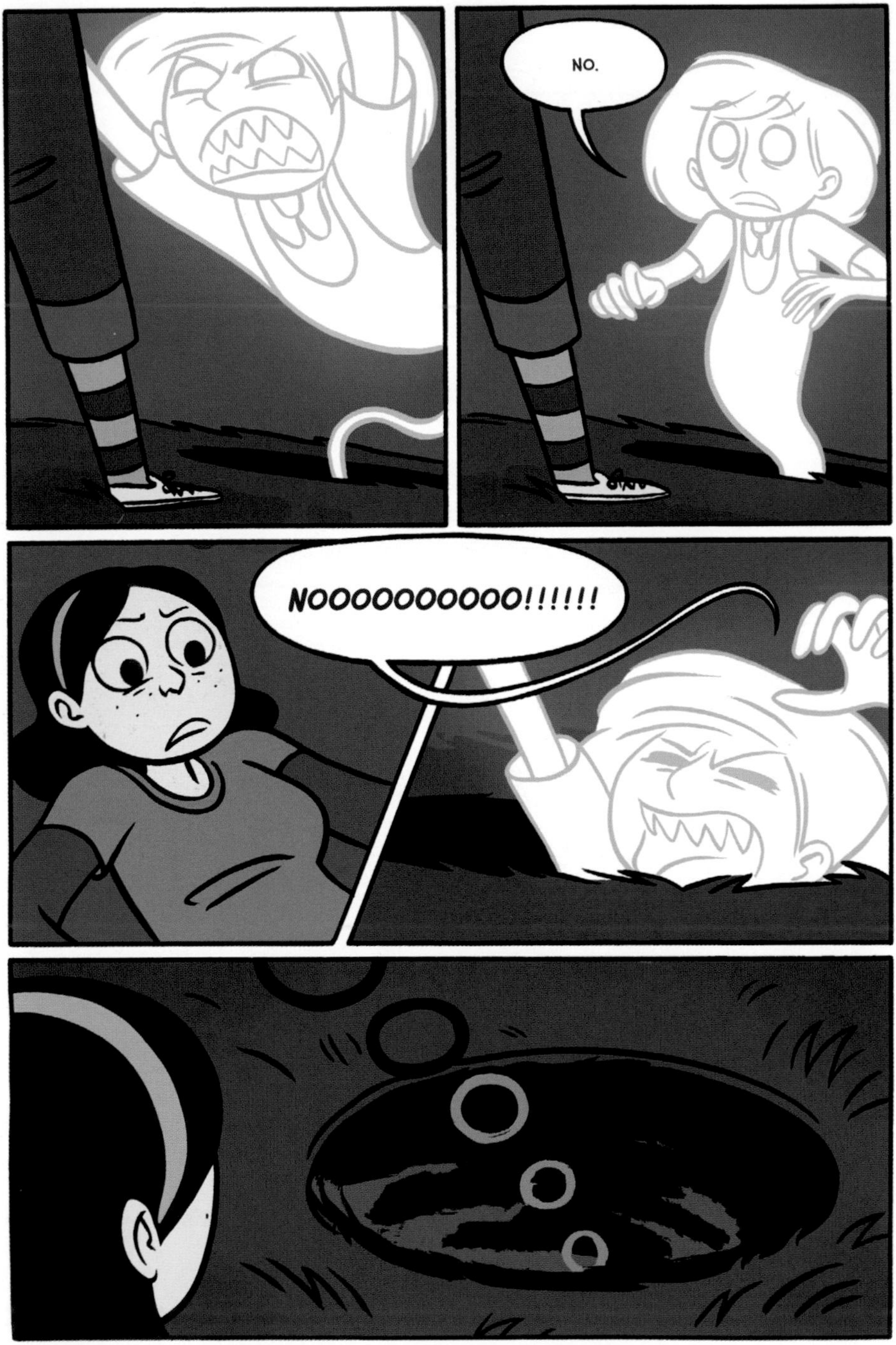
NO.
NOOOOOOOOOO!!!!!!

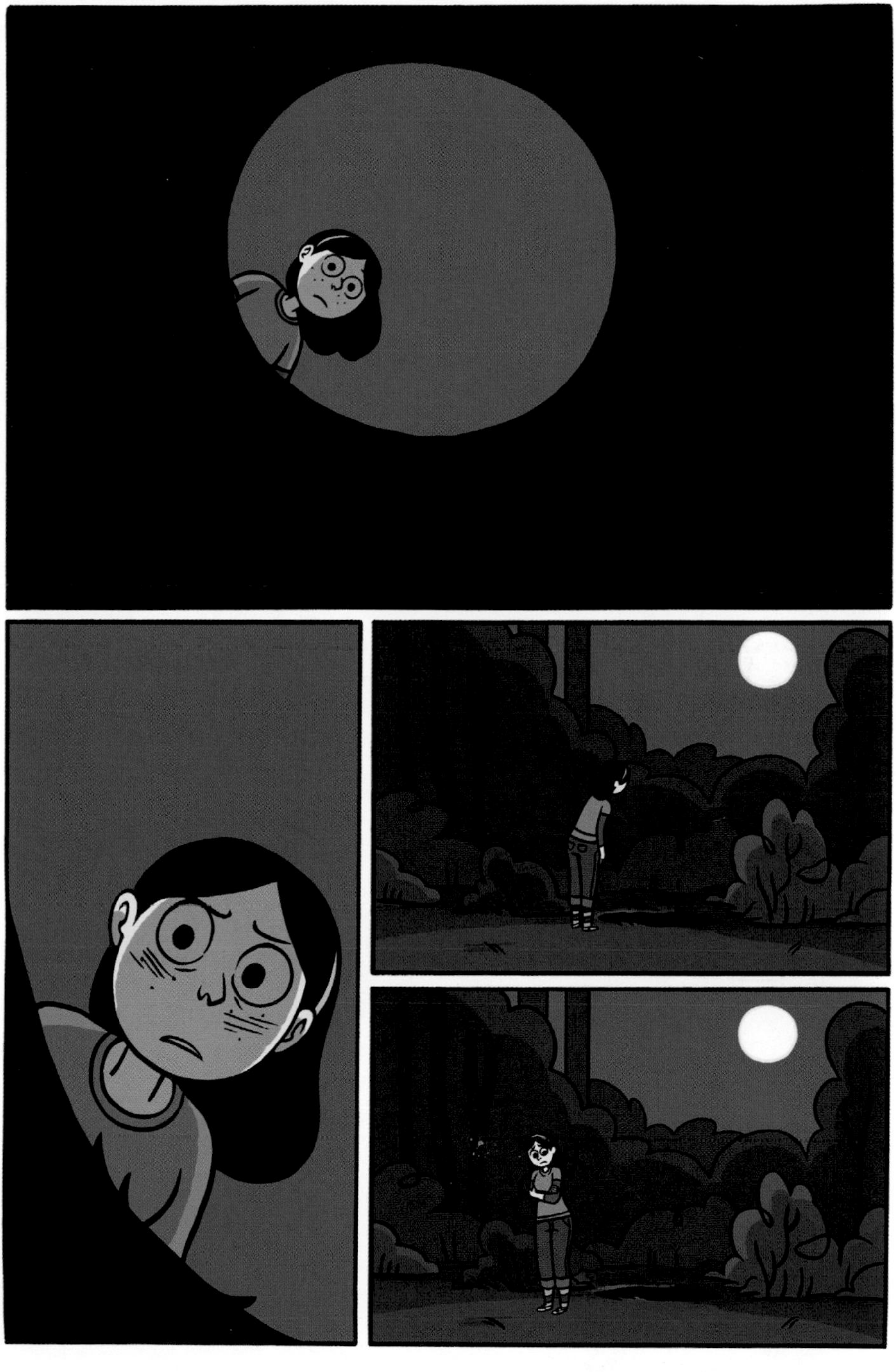

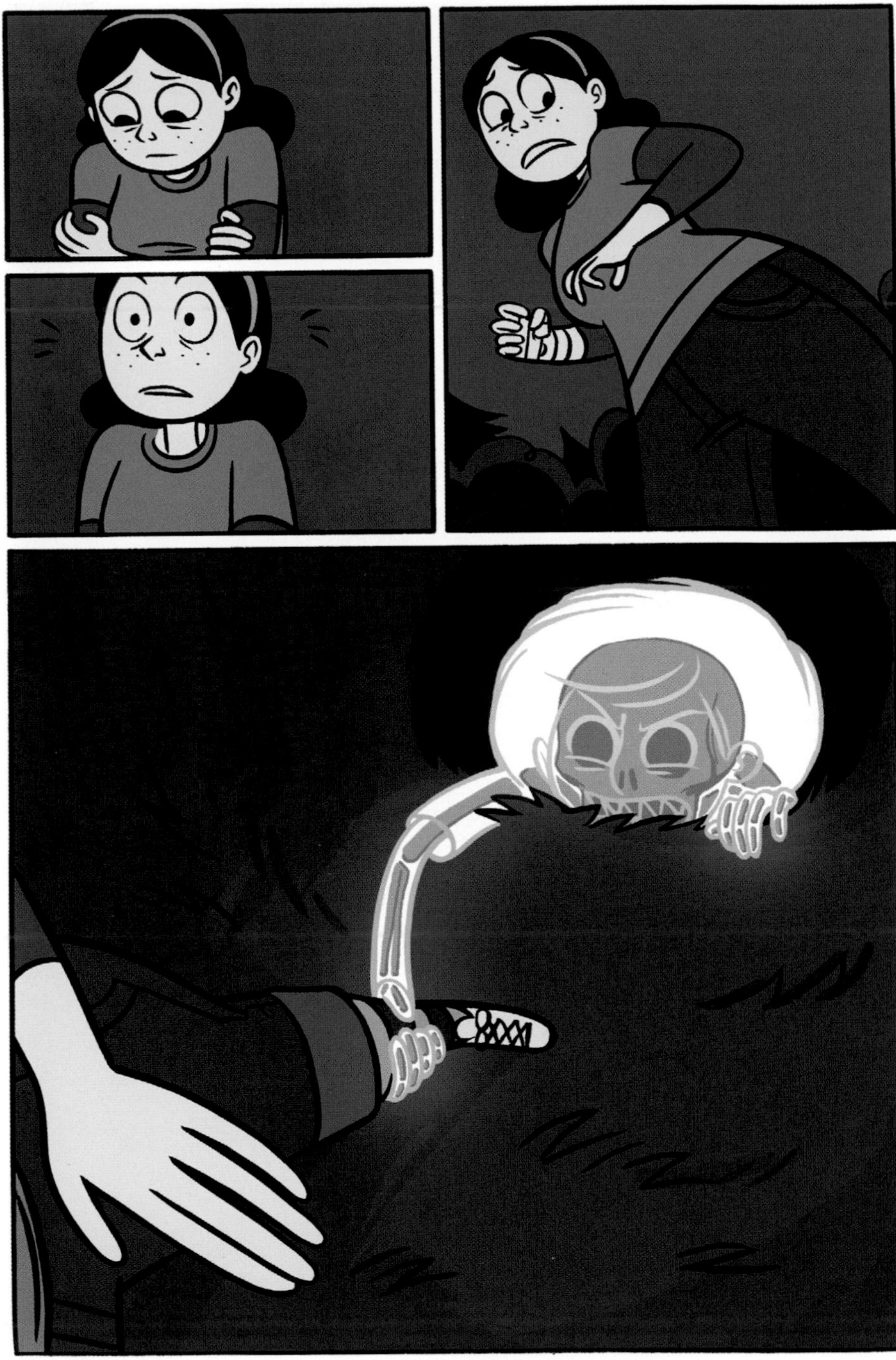

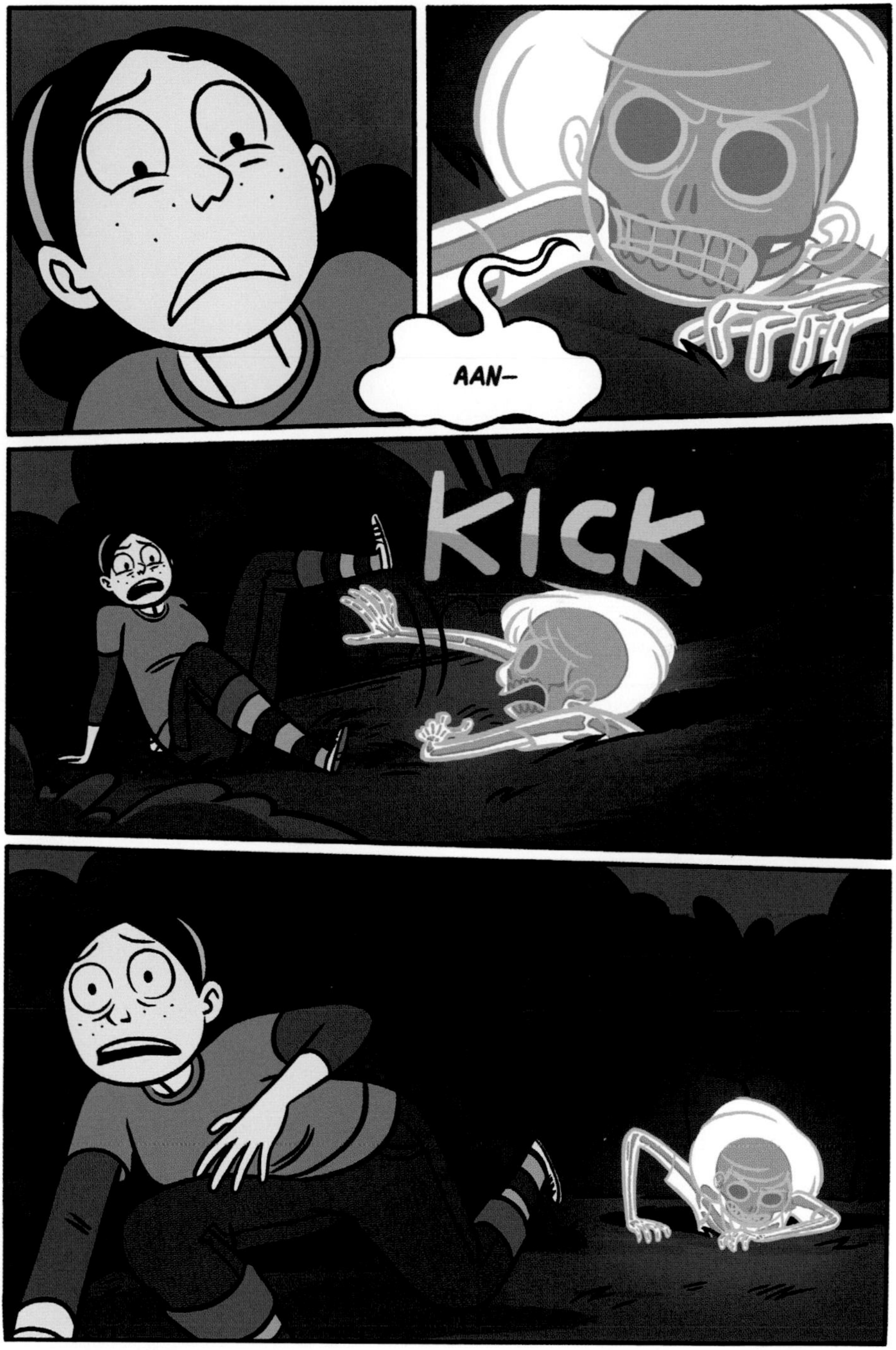
AAN-
KICK

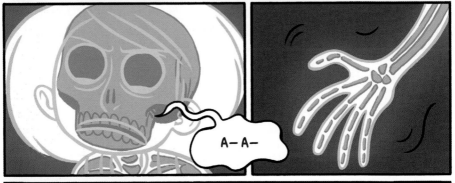

A—A—

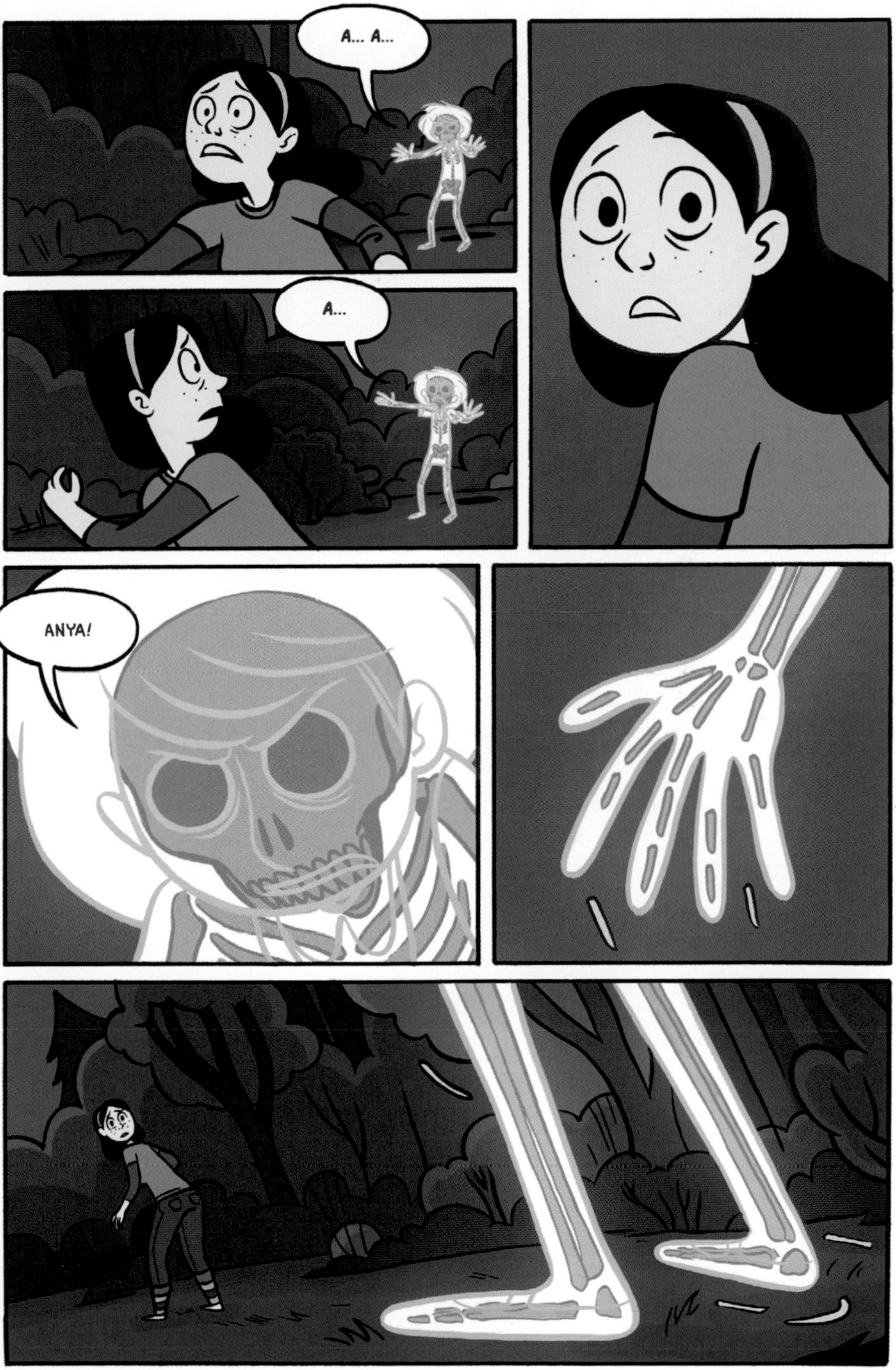
A... A...
A...
ANYA!

W—WAIT.

STOP.
I'M NOT RUNNING.

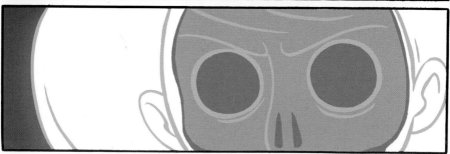

I KNOW—I KNOW I SAID BEFORE I WASN'T LIKE YOU... IT'S NOT TRUE.

I'M ENOUGH LIKE YOU TO KNOW HOW YOU FEEL.

WANTING HOW OTHERS LOOK, WHAT THEY HAVE, WHO THEY HAVE!

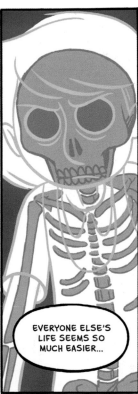

EVERYONE ELSE'S LIFE SEEMS SO MUCH EASIER...

BUT THAT'S ALL YOU KNOW! WHAT *YOU* WANT! YOU DON'T KNOW WHAT'S GOING ON INSIDE ANYONE ELSE'S HEAD.

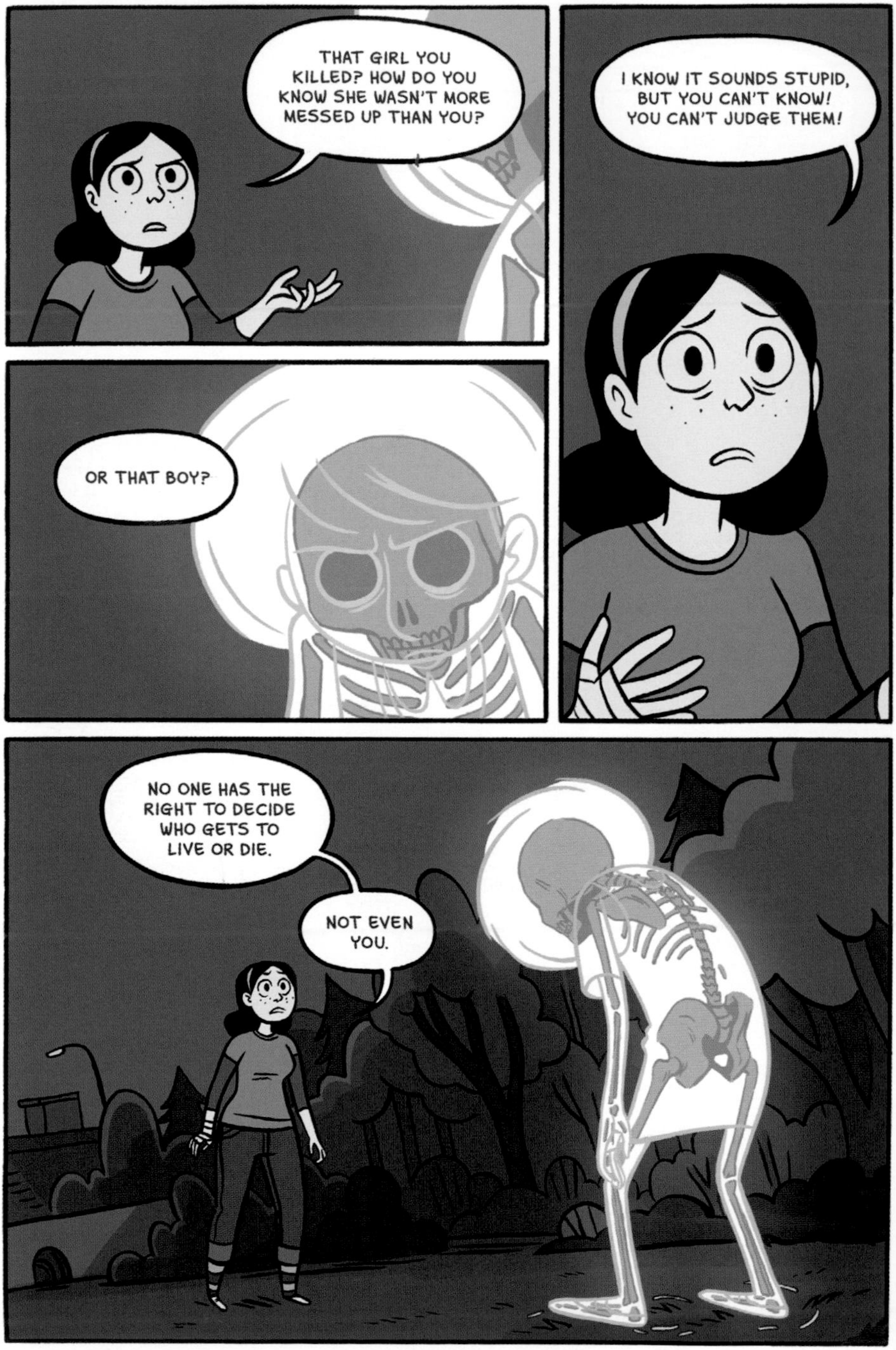
THAT GIRL YOU KILLED? HOW DO YOU KNOW SHE WASN'T MORE MESSED UP THAN YOU?
I KNOW IT SOUNDS STUPID, BUT YOU CAN'T KNOW! YOU CAN'T JUDGE THEM!
OR THAT BOY?
NO ONE HAS THE RIGHT TO DECIDE WHO GETS TO LIVE OR DIE.
NOT EVEN YOU.

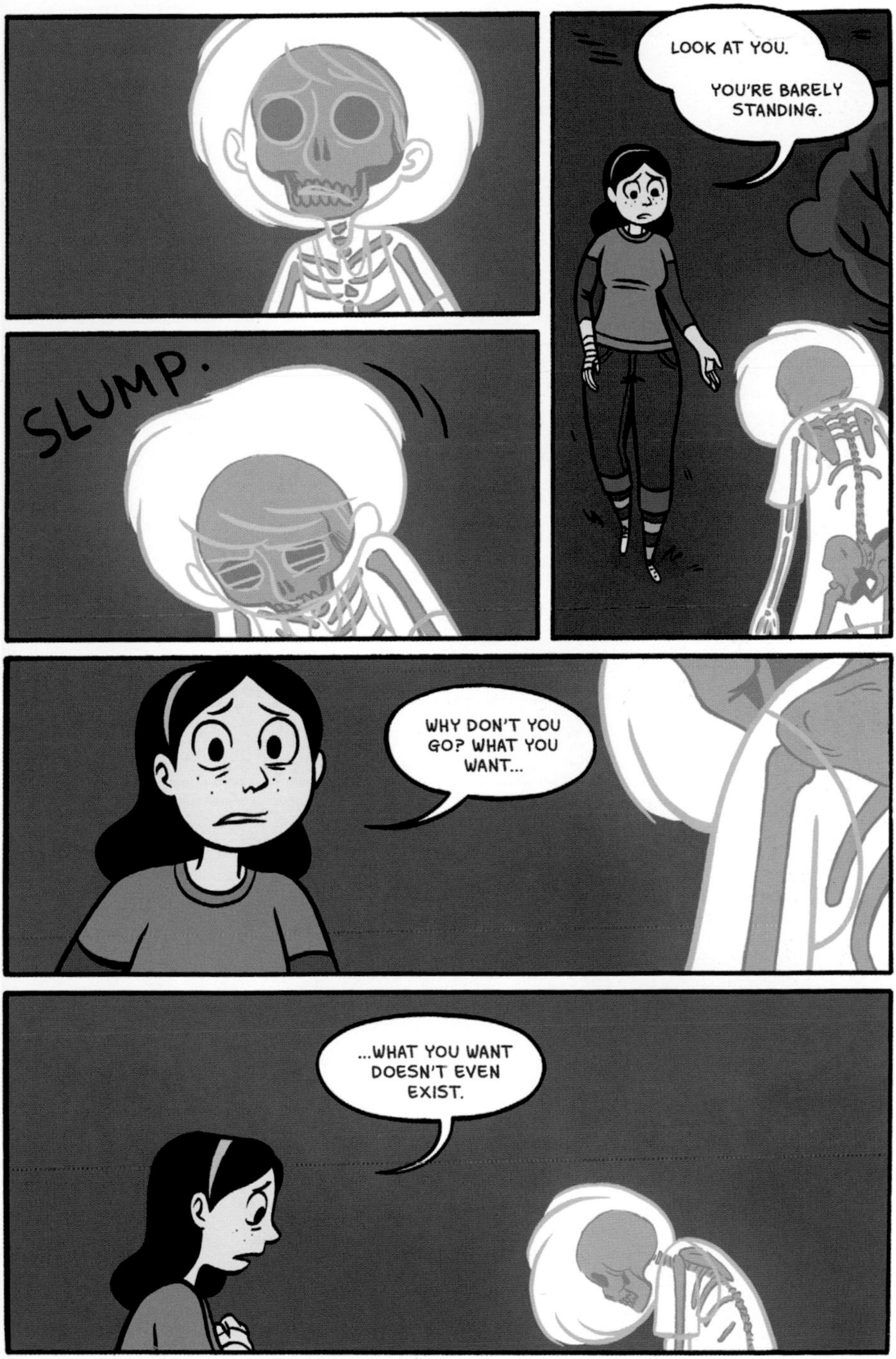
SLUMP.
LOOK AT YOU.
YOU'RE BARELY STANDING.
WHY DON'T YOU GO? WHAT YOU WANT...
...WHAT YOU WANT DOESN'T EVEN EXIST.

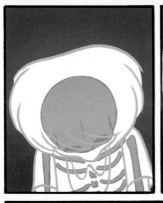  

SIGH...

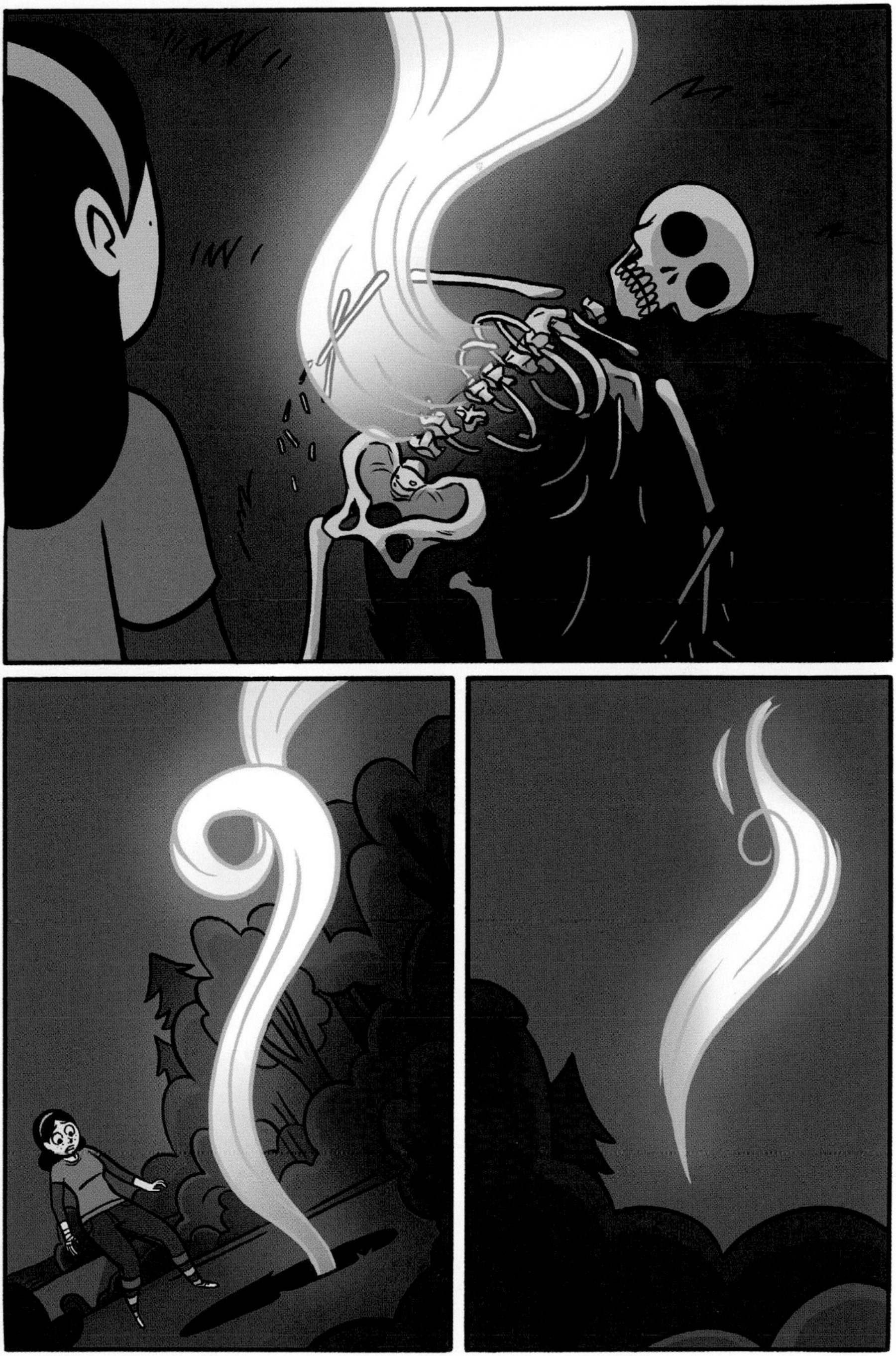

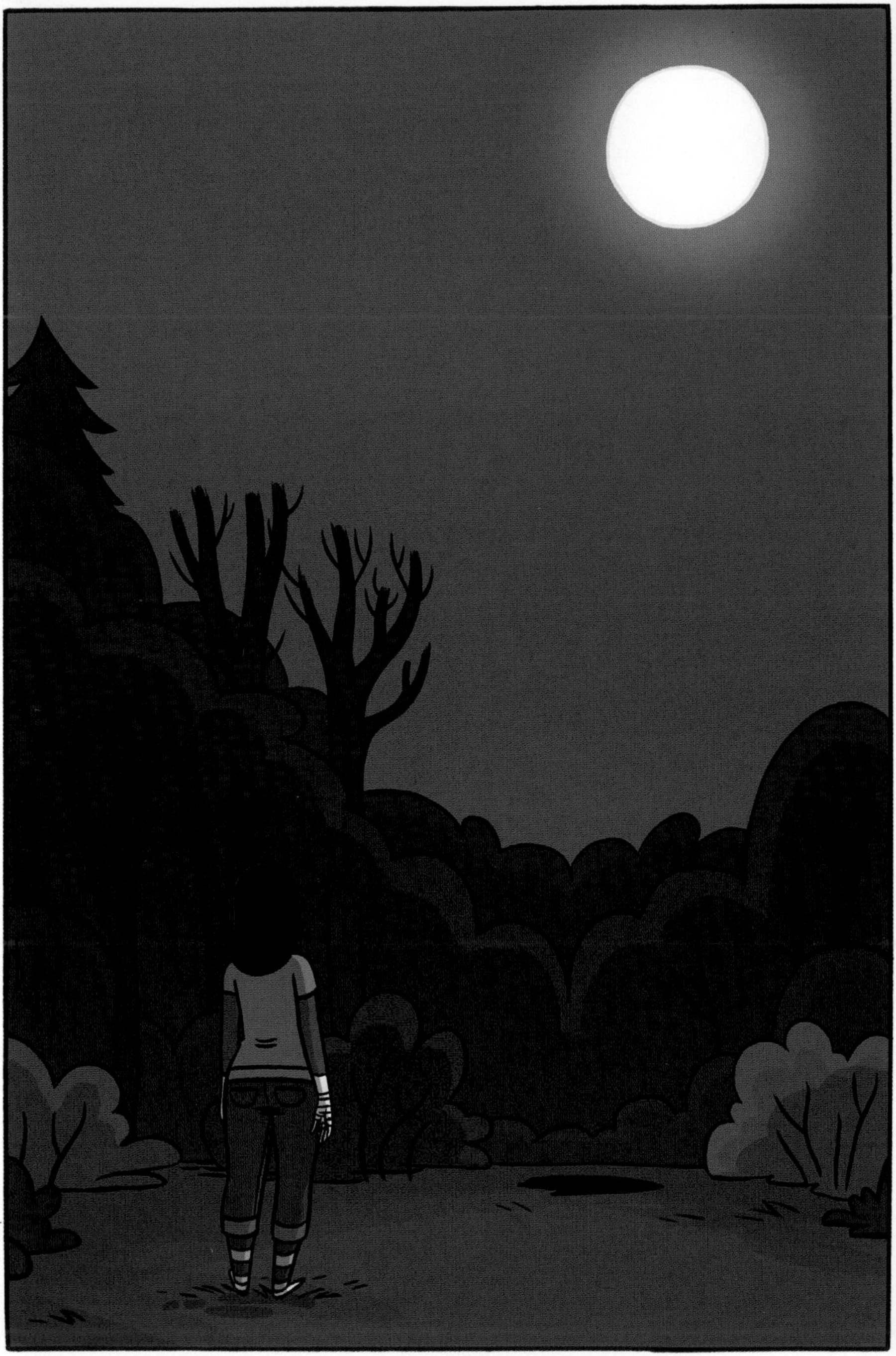

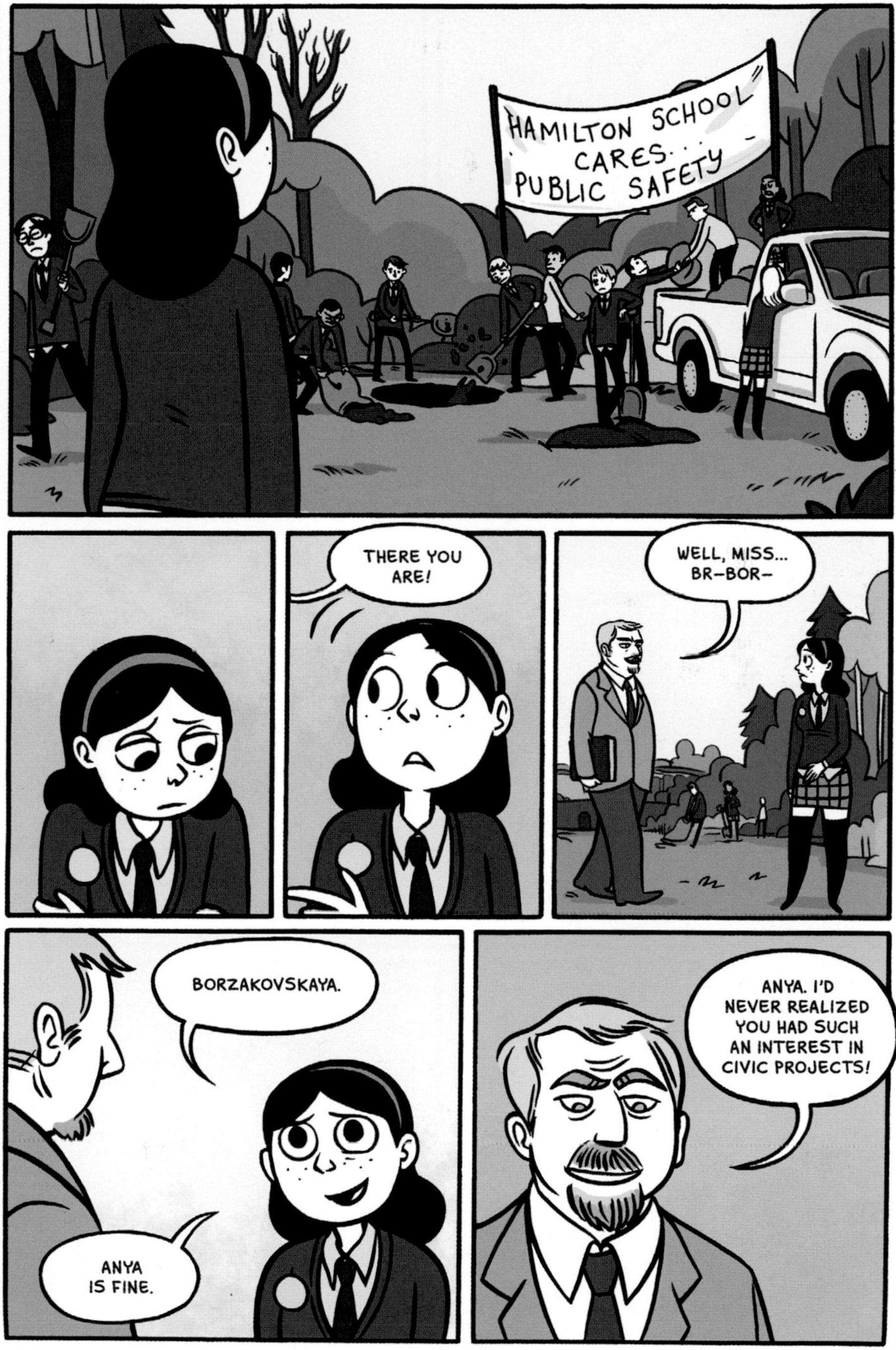
HAMILTON SCHOOL CARES... PUBLIC SAFETY
THERE YOU ARE!
WELL, MISS... BR-BOR-
BORZAKOVSKAYA.
ANYA IS FINE.
ANYA. I'D NEVER REALIZED YOU HAD SUCH AN INTEREST IN CIVIC PROJECTS!

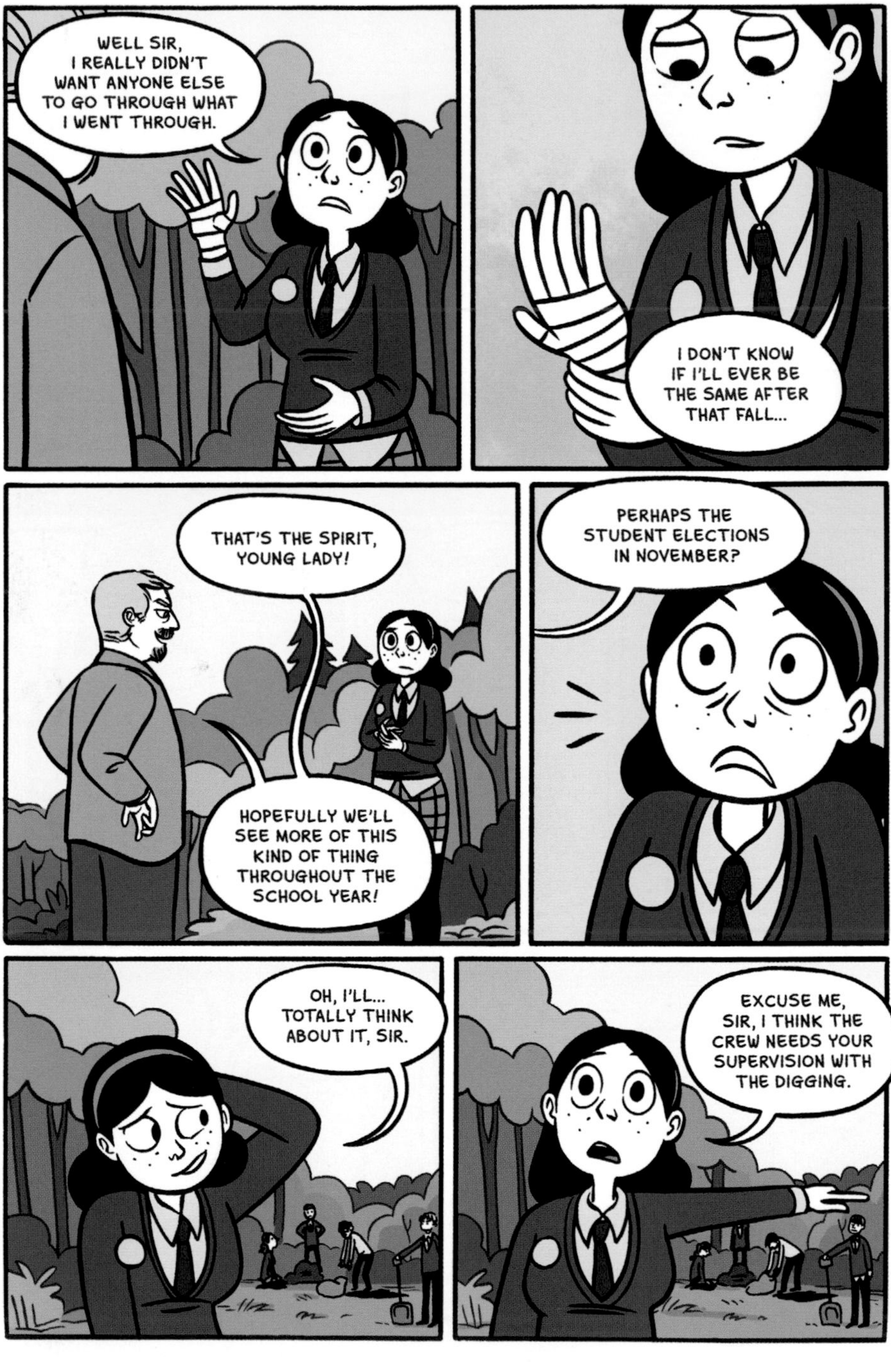
WELL SIR, I REALLY DIDN'T WANT ANYONE ELSE TO GO THROUGH WHAT I WENT THROUGH.
I DON'T KNOW IF I'LL EVER BE THE SAME AFTER THAT FALL...
THAT'S THE SPIRIT, YOUNG LADY!
HOPEFULLY WE'LL SEE MORE OF THIS KIND OF THING THROUGHOUT THE SCHOOL YEAR!
PERHAPS THE STUDENT ELECTIONS IN NOVEMBER?
OH, I'LL... TOTALLY THINK ABOUT IT, SIR.
EXCUSE ME, SIR, I THINK THE CREW NEEDS YOUR SUPERVISION WITH THE DIGGING.

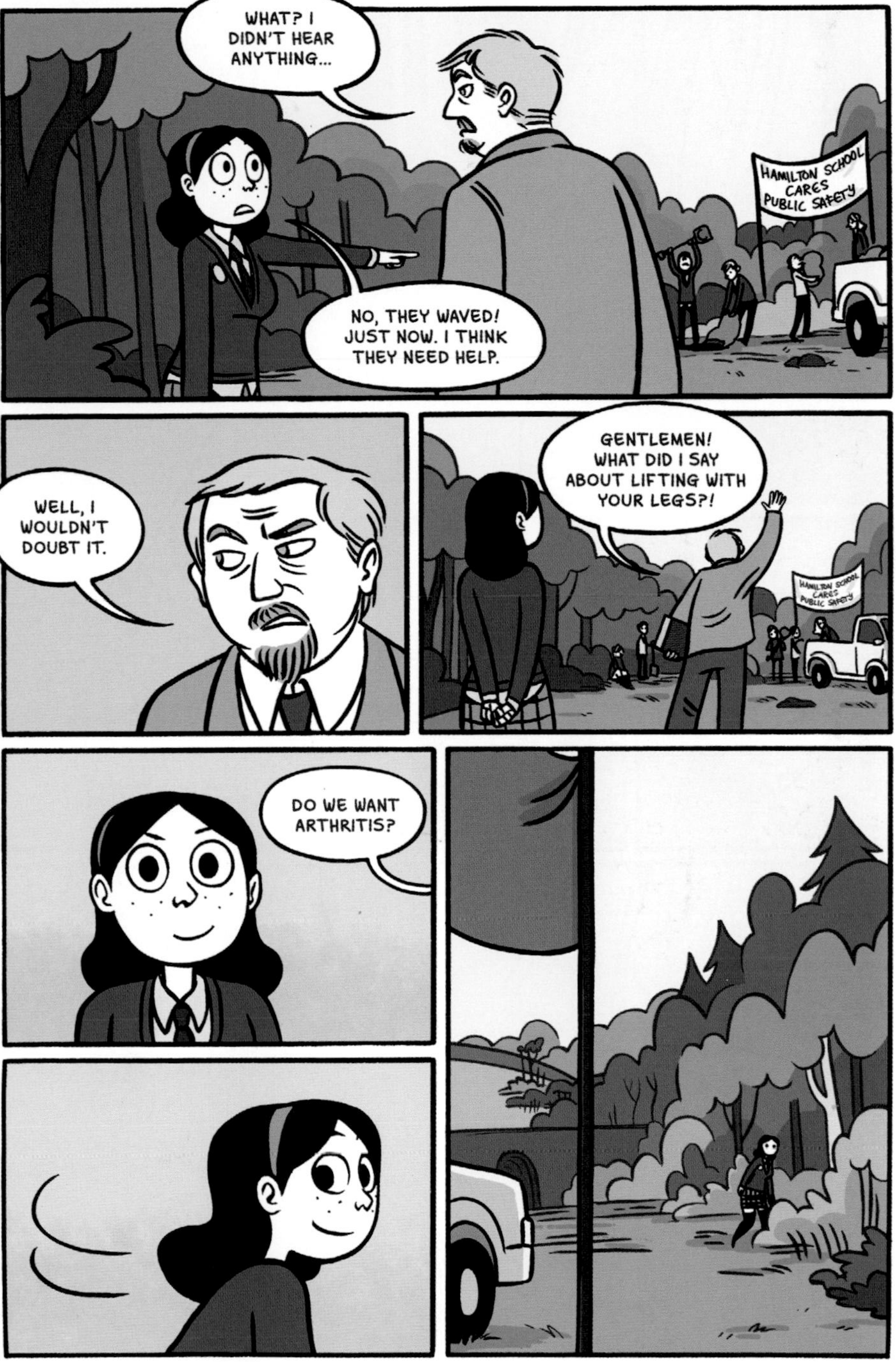
WHAT? I DIDN'T HEAR ANYTHING...
HAMILTON SCHOOL CARES PUBLIC SAFETY
NO, THEY WAVED! JUST NOW. I THINK THEY NEED HELP.
WELL, I WOULDN'T DOUBT IT.
GENTLEMEN! WHAT DID I SAY ABOUT LIFTING WITH YOUR LEGS?!
HAMILTON SCHOOL CARES PUBLIC SAFETY
DO WE WANT ARTHRITIS?

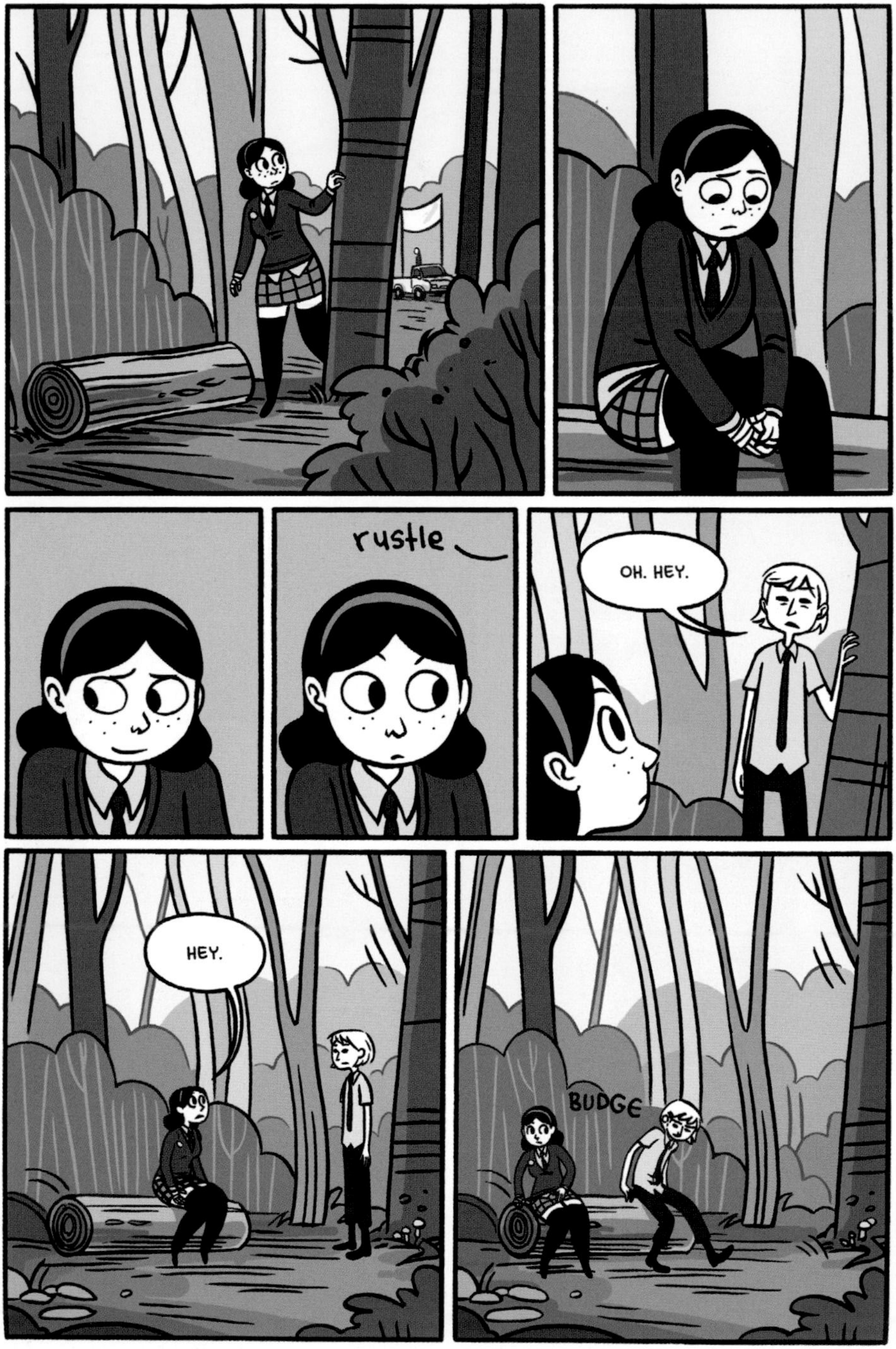
rustle
OH. HEY.
HEY.
BUDGE

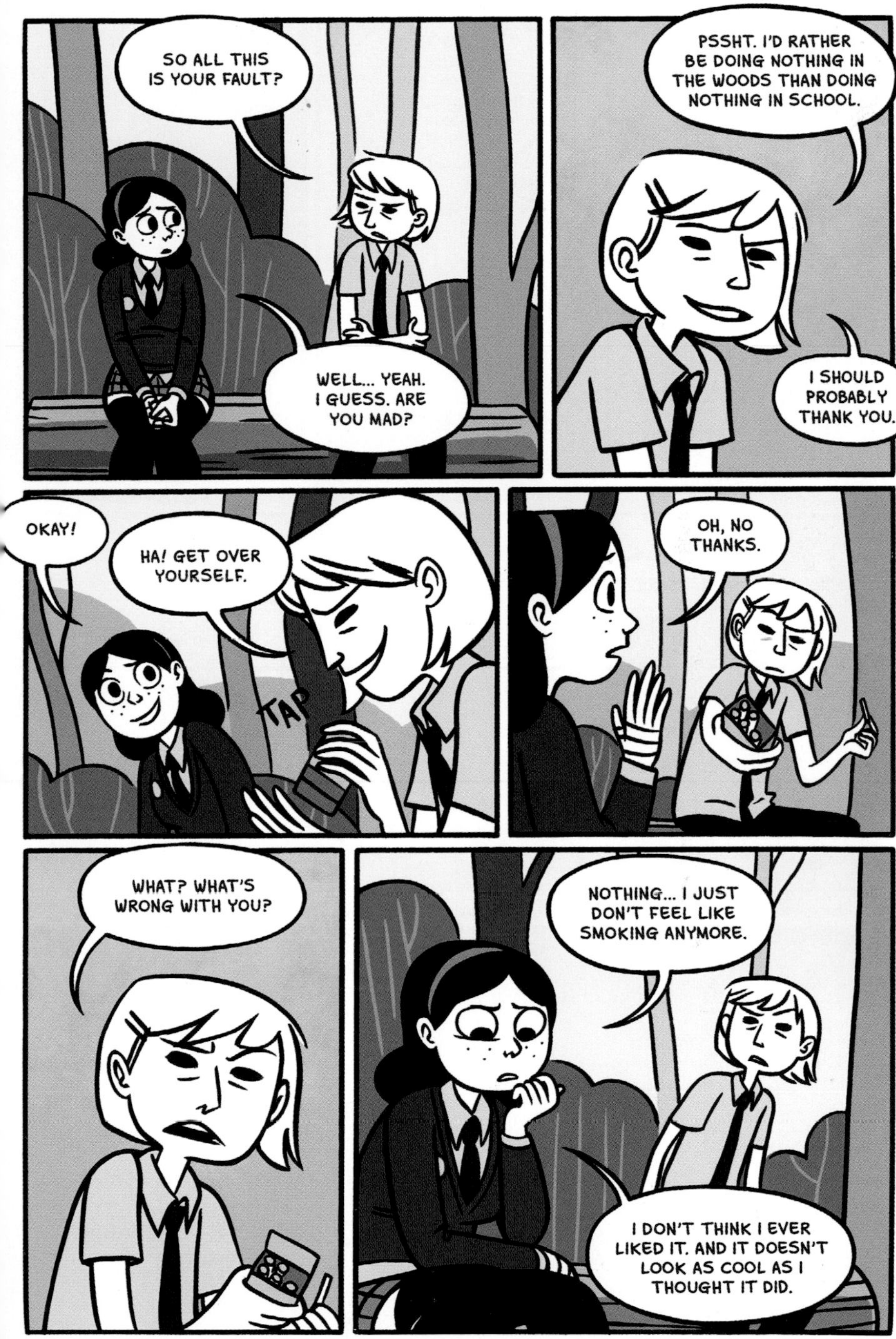
SO ALL THIS IS YOUR FAULT?
WELL... YEAH. I GUESS. ARE YOU MAD?
PSSHT. I'D RATHER BE DOING NOTHING IN THE WOODS THAN DOING NOTHING IN SCHOOL.
I SHOULD PROBABLY THANK YOU.
OKAY!
HA! GET OVER YOURSELF.
TAP
OH, NO THANKS.
WHAT? WHAT'S WRONG WITH YOU?
NOTHING... I JUST DON'T FEEL LIKE SMOKING ANYMORE.
I DON'T THINK I EVER LIKED IT. AND IT DOESN'T LOOK AS COOL AS I THOUGHT IT DID.

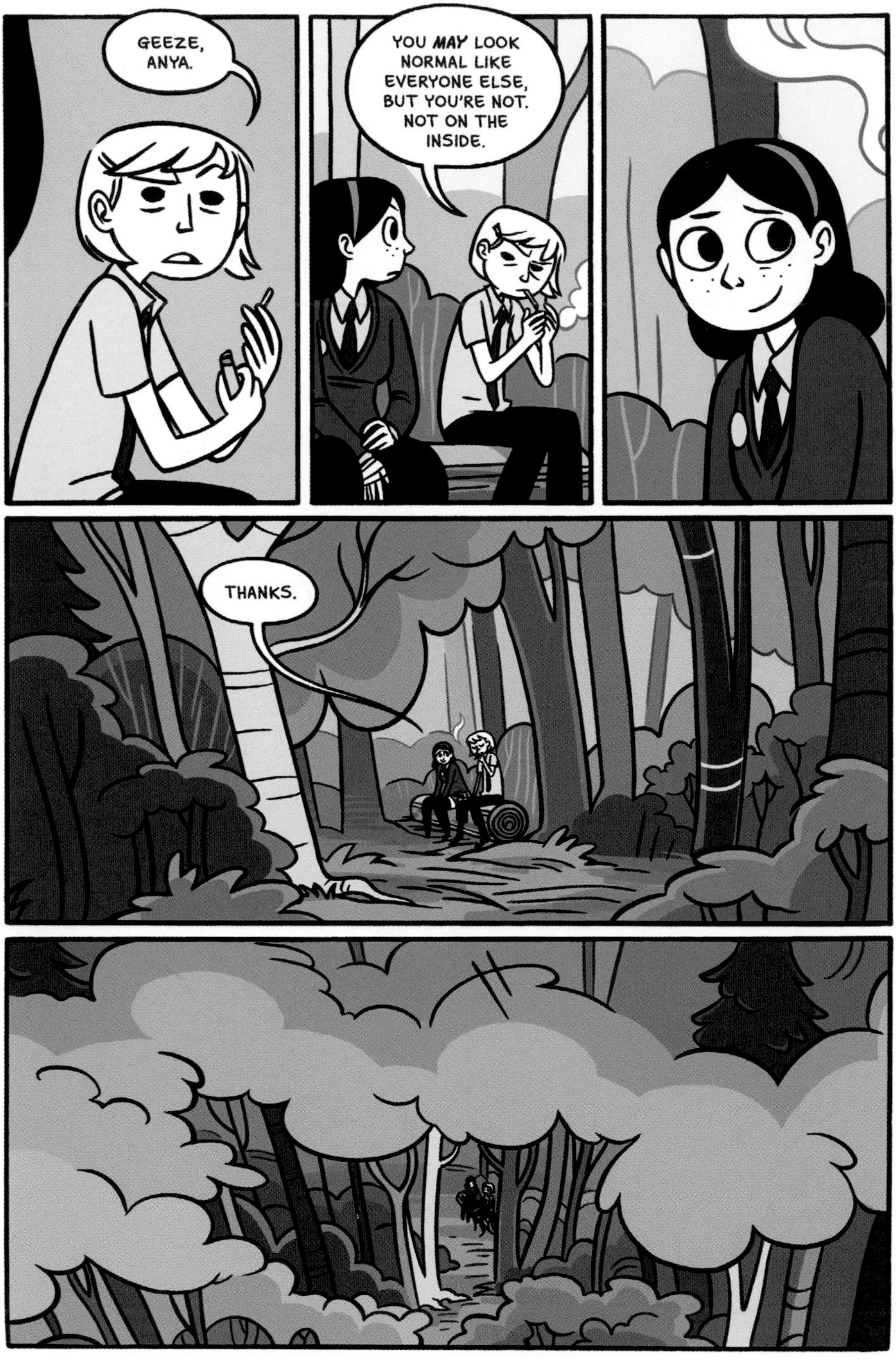
GEEZE, ANYA.
YOU MAY LOOK NORMAL LIKE EVERYONE ELSE, BUT YOU'RE NOT. NOT ON THE INSIDE.
THANKS.

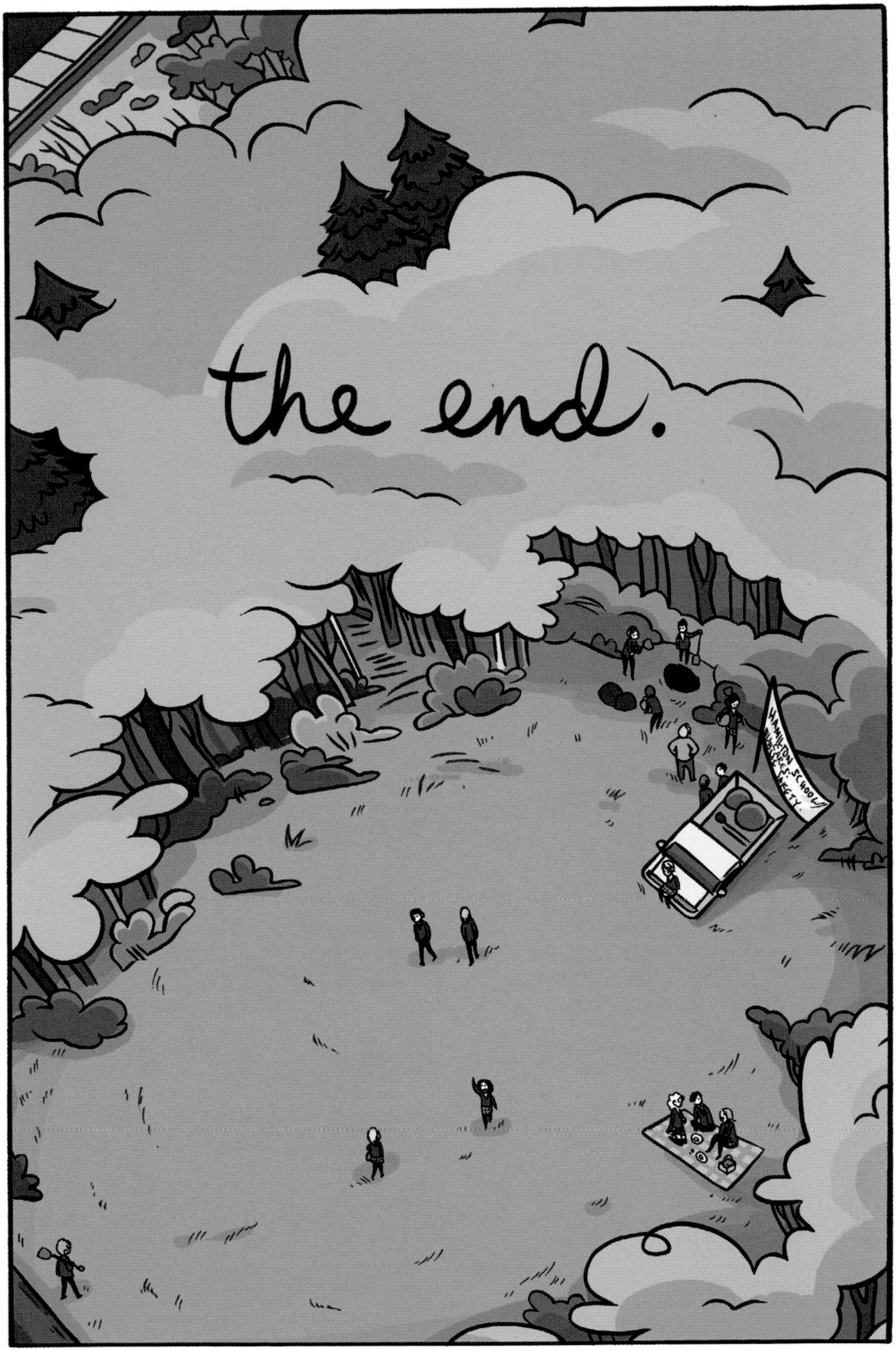
the end.
HAMILTON SCHOOL

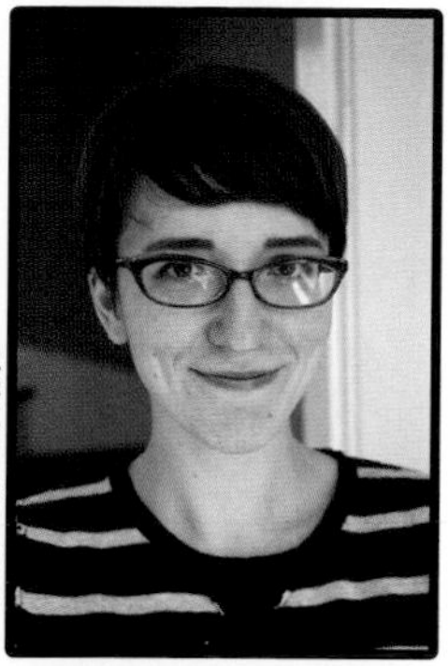

© JEREMY SPAKE

QUESTIONS FOR THE AUTHOR

VERA BROSGOL

What did you want to be when you grew up?

A FASHION DESIGNER.

When did you realize you wanted to be a writer?

WHEN I LEARNED ABOUT THE SEWING.

What was your favorite thing about school?

ART CLASS!

What were your hobbies as a kid? What are your hobbies now?

AS A KID, I DREW ALL THE TIME. NOW THAT I DRAW FOR A JOB, I LIKE TO DO ANYTHING BUT. I KNIT, BAKE,

GARDEN, AND DO OTHER GRANDMOTHERLY PURSUITS. I
AM LEARNING HOW TO SEW RIGHT NOW, ACTUALLY.

What was your first job?
MY FIRST JOB WAS COLORING BACKGROUNDS FOR
ANIMATION. I'M LUCKY THAT I'VE ALWAYS WORKED
SOMEWHERE IN THE ARTS.

What book is on your nightstand now?
THE SEWING BOOK BY ALISON SMITH FOR REFERENCE
AND *THE SILENCE OF THE LAMBS* BY THOMAS HARRIS
FOR FUN.

How did you celebrate publishing your first book?
I HAD A PARTY AT A LOCAL COMIC BOOK STORE. I MADE
SEA-SALT CARAMELS FOR EVERYBODY, IT WAS AWESOME.

Where do you write and draw your books?
I HAVE A STUDIO ROOM IN MY HOUSE WHERE I DO ALL
MY WRITING AND DRAWING. UNFORTUNATELY, IT'S ALSO
WHERE ALL MY YARN AND COMIC BOOKS LIVE, SO I GET
DISTRACTED SOMETIMES.

What sparked your imagination for *Anya's Ghost?*
I CAME UP WITH THE CHARACTER OF ANYA FIRST, AND WAS
TRYING TO THINK OF WHAT TO DO WITH HER. I THOUGHT
IT WOULD BE INTERESTING FOR A CHARACTER TO HAVE
WHAT INITIALLY SEEMED LIKE A PERFECTLY SUPPORTIVE
FRIEND, ONLY TO HAVE THAT FRIEND WIND UP MIRRORING
THEIR WORST TRAITS BACK AT THEM. I READ *THE WIND-*

UP BIRD CHRONICLE BY HARUKI MURAKAMI, IN WHICH ABANDONED WELLS PLAY A PROMINENT ROLE, AND THE REST FELL INTO PLACE FROM THERE.

In what ways are you similar or different to Anya?

WE'RE BOTH FIRST-GENERATION RUSSIAN IMMIGRANTS AND A LOT OF HER ANXIETIES ABOUT HER APPEARANCE AND HER BACKGROUND WERE ALSO MINE. BUT I WAS A MUCH BETTER STUDENT!

Do you have a favorite ghost story? If so, what is it?

GROWING UP, I LOVED SCARY STORIES TO TELL IN THE DARK BY ALVIN SCHWARTZ. I USED TO HIDE THE BOOKS UNDER THE BED BECAUSE I WAS TOO SCARED OF THE PICTURES ON THE COVER.

What challenges do you face in the writing process, and how do you overcome them?

FOR ME, THE HARDEST THING IS TO JUST SIT DOWN AND WRITE WHEN THERE ARE SO MANY EASIER THINGS TO DO. I GET A LOT OF THINKING DONE WHEN THERE ARE NO DISTRACTIONS AVAILABLE, LIKE WHEN I'M IN THE CAR ON A LONG DRIVE. HOPEFULLY BY THE TIME I'VE GOTTEN HOME, I KNOW EXACTLY WHAT TO WRITE, SO I RUN TO THE KEYBOARD BEFORE I FORGET IT.

What do you do on a rainy day?

COOK, KNIT, READ, WATCH MOVIES . . . I LOVE RAINY DAYS. FORTUNATELY I LIVE IN PORTLAND, OREGON, WHERE RAINY DAYS ARE PLENTIFUL.

What's your idea of fun?

THE PREVIOUSLY MENTIONED RAINY DAY, OR A NICE WALK IN THE WOODS.

Who is your favorite fictional character?

MATILDA FROM *MATILDA* BY ROALD DAHL.

What was your favorite book and/or comic book when you were a kid?

***CALVIN AND HOBBES!* I USED TO COLOR THEM IN.**

What's your favorite TV show or movie?

RIGHT NOW, I'M HOOKED ON *MAD MEN* AND JUST SAW *THE STRAIGHT STORY* FOR THE FIRST TIME. A PERFECT MOVIE.

If you could travel anywhere in the world, where would you go and what would you do?

I'D LOVE TO GO TO JAPAN AND SEE AS MUCH OF IT BY TRAIN AS POSSIBLE. I'VE ALSO BEEN OBSESSING OVER SCUBA DIVING, SO SOMEWHERE WARM AND FISH-BEARING WOULD BE GREAT.

If you could travel in time, where would you go and what would you do?

I'D GO FORWARD ABOUT FIFTY YEARS JUST TO MAKE SURE EVERYTHING'S STILL OKAY. THAT'D MAKE ME FEEL BETTER! ... OR WORSE.

What's the best advice you have ever received about writing?

NOT TO WORRY ABOUT THE FIRST DRAFT SO MUCH.

JUST GET SOMETHING, ANYTHING, DOWN. ALL IT IS IS A
STARTING POINT.

What advice do you wish someone had given you when you were
younger?
START WITH SHORTER STORIES! FINISHING SOMETHING
AND GETTING IT OUT THERE IS THE BEST WAY TO
IMPROVE AND STAY MOTIVATED.

Do you ever get writer's block? What do you do to get back on track?
SHOWING A FRIEND ALWAYS LENDS PERSPECTIVE AND
USUALLY A CONFIDENCE BOOST. DIPPING BACK INTO
RESEARCH OR WATCHING AND READING OTHER PEOPLE'S
STORIES IS A GOOD KICK START, TOO.

Who is your favorite artist?
ILYA REPIN.

What is your favorite medium to work in?
I REALLY LIKE WORKING IN WATERCOLOR, BUT I DO MOST
OF MY WORK DIGITALLY THESE DAYS.

What do you want readers to remember about your books?
THAT THEY WERE SAYING SOMETHING HONEST, IN THE
GUISE OF AESTHETICALLY PLEASING ENTERTAINMENT.

What would you do if you ever stopped writing?
I'VE GOT NO SHORTAGE OF HOBBIES, SO I'D PROBABLY
GET A LOT BETTER AT THOSE. I'D READ MORE, TOO.
RIGHT NOW, PRETTY MUCH THE ONLY TIME I HAVE FOR
READING IS AT THE GYM OR BEFORE BED.

If you were a superhero, what would your superpower be?

MICROSCOPIC VISION. I'M REALLY *REALLY* NEARSIGHTED, SO I FIGURE I'M HALFWAY THERE.

What do you consider to be your greatest accomplishment?

DRAWING A COMIC BOOK WHILE STORYBOARDING FULL-TIME ON *CORALINE*. I'M STILL TRYING TO FIGURE OUT EXACTLY HOW I PULLED THAT OFF.

What do you wish you could do better?

I WISH I WAS A BIT LESS SELF-CRITICAL AND A BIT MORE PRODUCTIVE.

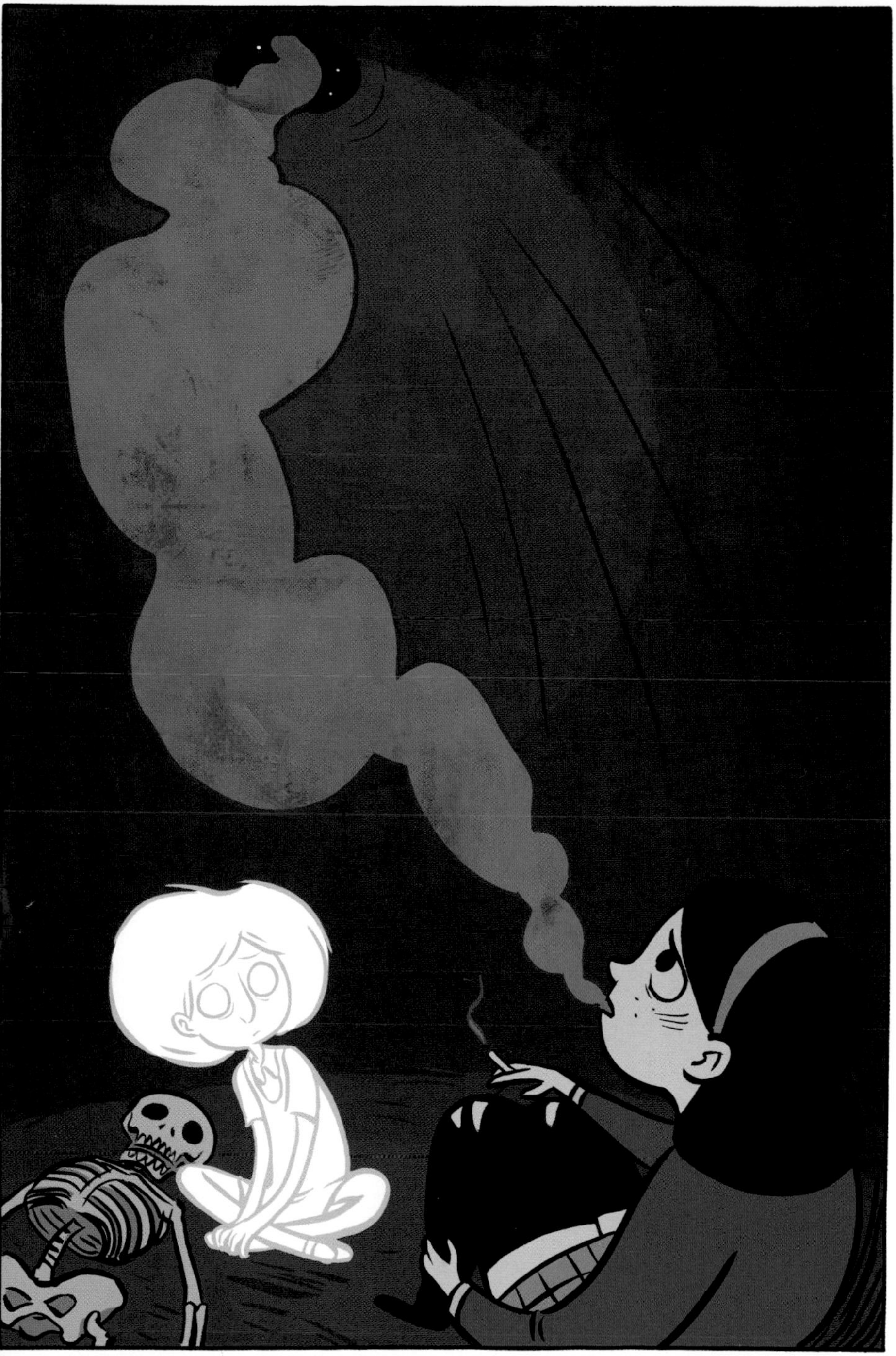